THE HIDDEN

SABOTEUR

Charles Besondy

This book is a work of fiction. Names, characters, and incidents are products of the author's imagination or are used fictitiously. Any resemblance to actual persons, living or dead, is coincidental. The town of Reef Bay, Washington is fictional.

Edited by Steve Statham
StrathamCommunications.com

Cover Design Concept by Charles Besondy and Sofia Besondy
Cover Design by James, GoOnWrite.com

Scripture quotations taken from The Holy Bible, New International Version® NIV®
Copyright © 1973 1978 1984 2011 by Biblica, Inc. TM
Used by permission. All rights reserved worldwide.

Published by Charles Besondy, 113 Firebird Street, Lakeway, TX, 78734 USA
Visit CharlesBesondy.com

For Sofy.

CONTENTS

PART ONE,
THE CALL.

Chapter 1

The noise inside the dark room was unlike anything Clay had ever experienced. It was a muffled shrieking. No, not a shriek, more of an amplified hiss with the occasional scream of some lost soul. He told himself the sound was just the gale-force wind and rain that lashed the tower. That knowledge was of little comfort because he was standing alone inside the dark tower and that darn noise sounded evil.

Clay had to admit; he was spooked. He shivered uncontrollably. The fear felt like a large spider under his shirt inching its way up his back. His first instinct was to run.

Yeah, why not get the heck out of here? Just turn around, open the steel door and leave this darn place. Go back to the house. Light a fire. Open a beer. Turn on the TV. But he knew he had a job to do. It was going to be a long night.

He had a job all right. He looked up. The beam from his flashlight caught the reflections of the metal stairs as they wound upward into the never-ending darkness, but could pierce the gloom only so far. After fifty feet the black overcame the white of the light. Didn't matter. Clay knew what was above. As the hissing sound of the wind rose another octave, he started the climb.

High above Clay, 117 feet from the ground floor, with a terrible storm raging outside, the unthinkable had happened—the lighthouse lantern had gone out.

Flashlight in one hand, canvas tool box in the other, he took the first step. One down, 186 steps to go.

Climbing the 187 steps to the top of the lighthouse was something Clay had done many times before. He knew (because he measured once) each step was seven inches higher than the previous step. Every sixteen steps there was a small landing. At every second landing, the lighthouse's architect had thoughtfully placed a small window to let some light into the tower's interior during the day. There wasn't even moonlight coming through the windows on this forbidding night.

Clay paused on the second landing. He was already a little short of breath. He looked up. There was only darkness, not even a hint of a shape or an object, just emptiness. He climbed upward, one seven-inch step at a time.

The climb was harder tonight. Sure, the darkness and devilish-sounding wind were tough on the nerves, but the climb was physically harder, too. Both of his hands were occupied. In the left, he held the heavy-duty flashlight. His right hand carried the tools he'd need later. No hands were available to grasp the metal railing and help pull his weight up the stairs. *Note to self, next time put the tools in a backpack*, he thought. Would there be a next time?

At the fourth landing, the perspiration on his forehead began to drip down his face. By the tenth landing Clay was breathing hard. His t-shirt and flannel shirt were soaked with sweat. His light caught the red number 10 stenciled on the wall. Halfway. "The point of no return," he whispered jokingly to himself. He was 59 feet off the ground and had another 59 feet to climb. It was a blessing that he couldn't see the floor far below in the darkness, even if he wanted to. He didn't want to think about falling.

For the next thirty minutes, he slowly climbed, resting at each landing to catch his breath, and moving on.

Finally, the stairs stopped at the larger landing. He had reached the top of the staircase. The diameter of the tower was at its narrowest here, just twenty feet across. Now he had to climb an eight-foot steel ladder and pull himself through a steel hatch into the lantern compartment.

This was going to be dicey. How was he going to climb a ladder in the pitch dark when both hands were occupied? *Two trips, that's it. I'll go up with just the flashlight first. Then a second trip with the tools,* he concluded.

He set the toolbox next to the base of the ladder so that he could find it easily in the dark. Then, grasping the flashlight in one hand, he slowly climbed the ladder. The right hand gripped the ladder, while the left hand held the light. For extra stability, he hooked his left elbow around the ladder's steps as he ascended. Up he went.

The hatch was another problem. It was heavy. Holding himself on the ladder with his hooked left elbow, he pressed his right shoulder and right hand against the hatch. It inched upward. By straightening his body a little, the hatch opened a few more inches. Carefully he moved his feet up one more rung on the ladder and with his shoulders was able to swing the hatch further open. Two more steps and Clay was able to crawl through the hatch. He laid exhausted on the floor, looking up. He was surrounded by thick panes of glass. The sound of the wind and rain was terrifying up here without the insulation of the thick masonry walls. Could he actually feel the tower swaying in the wind, or was that just the hard beating of his heart?

Whatever, he wanted nothing more than to do what had to be done and get out.

Now for the tools. Clay set the flashlight on the floor, so its beam shined across the open hatch. Then he eased himself down through the hatch and onto the ladder. Feeling his way down, his left foot finally met the floor. Even with the light beam above it was almost totally dark here. He felt around for the toolbox at the base of the ladder. *Got it.* Clay picked up the canvas tool bag and started to climb back up the ladder. But a large screwdriver in a side pocket caught on the ladder step and flipped out of the bag as if some invisible hand had grabbed it from the pocket and thrown it aside. Clay heard something clang against the metal floor twice, then silence. Feeling around the pockets of the tool carrier, everything was in order except—*no, not that!* He couldn't feel a long Phillips screwdriver. It was the first tool he had put into the carrier that night. It was his favorite tool because its length made it possible to reach a few of the screws on the lens cover. He needed that screwdriver.

Cursing his luck, he got onto his hands and knees in the inky darkness and searched the entire floor like a blind man looking for his shoe. It was unnerving crawling around on the floor knowing that in the darkness the only thing separating him from falling 116 feet straight down to his death, was two rows of chains protecting the edges of the final landing.

Back and forth he crawled around the landing feeling for the screwdriver. Several times his hands felt the edge of the landing just as his head touched the protective chain. Each time he recoiled as if he had touched a live wire and pulled back away from the edge.

His frustration was growing by the second. *I need that screwdriver, and I don't want to be up here all night! This is crazy*, he thought, *it has to be here. Where else could it be?* He tried to visualize the screwdriver's flight path after leaving the tool carrier. No good. Did it flip forward, backward or to the left? No way of knowing. While feeling around the dark, cold, metal floor, he replayed the event in his mind—the resistance he felt as the screwdriver caught on the ladder, the sudden release, then the sound—clank, clank. The screwdriver had hit the floor, bounced, and hit it again. Two clanks then silence. *It has to be here, where else could it go? Oh, no!* The answer hit him. Sitting on the floor at the base of the ladder in darkness, he realized what had happened. The twelve-inch Phillips screwdriver had flipped out of the carrier with a lot of force, bounced twice on the metal floor, and sailed over the edge to the floor 117 feet below.

He didn't know how he was going to repair the light without that screwdriver, but he had to try. And fast.

Clay, with the tool carrier, climbed up the ladder and back into the lantern room. He grabbed the flashlight and scanned the floor in the ladder room below just to be sure. Nothing. The floor was empty. Bye-bye screwdriver.

Standing up in the lantern room he paused to collect himself. He took a long drink from the bottle of water in the tool carrier, wiped the sweat from around his eyes and looked out into the night.

On a beautiful clear day, this was an exhilarating place to be, high above the rocks and waves with an unobstructed view all the way to the horizon. But tonight was a different story. The lighthouse was being assaulted. The wind and rain lashed the thick glass panes with evil fury. The noise was deafening. It reminded Clay of that summer he worked in a truck garage. Just about every day he was asked to steam clean truck parts before they were replaced on the trucks. The sound of that high-pressure water hitting the metal—that's the intensity of the noise he heard now all around him.

He noticed that his hands were shaking. He took another sip of water, replaced the bottle in the carrier, and glanced out the window one last time before getting to work.

Was that a light out there? He couldn't be sure. The rain was slamming against the windows and blurring everything. There it was again. A flicker, nothing, another flicker. Was it his spooked imagination or did he see a ship's light out at sea? He grabbed the flashlight and turned it off so there wouldn't be any reflection off the glass. He strained to see through the torrents of rain and dark.

There! No question. A light far off the point. He couldn't see the vessel. Just the white light, either a masthead light or stern light, he thought. Was the ship coming into the bay, or leaving? Who in their right mind would be leaving port on a night like this? Another light flickered. Red. The white and red lights were relatively close together. Clay knew the two lights had to be on the same vessel. And now he knew something else, too. The red light he saw was the port bow light. The boat, whatever it was, was trying to enter the bay and find safety in the snug harbor.

But the boat was on the wrong side of the bay. Clay knew treacherous reefs lined the southern entrance to the bay. The lighthouse had been built to guide ships into the bay using the deep channel on the north side. But tonight there was no light. Clay realized he was going to witness a terrible boat wreck unless he fixed this lantern. Lives depended on him.

He turned away from the glass windows, switched the flashlight back on and reached for the tool carrier.

This wasn't a difficult job. He'd done it once before, but lives weren't on the line then. His hands were shaking more noticeably now as he reached for the 1/4-inch socket wrench to unbolt the main electric panel.

Four bolts. That's all he had to unscrew to remove the plate. The harder he tried to control his hands, however, the more they shook. The wrench slipped off the bolt time after time.

Sweat poured down his brow and into his eyes, blurring his vision. Slowly and deliberately he used both hands to place the wrench on the bolt and turn to loosen. One at a time. It seemed like it was taking forever. All he could think about was the white and red lights of that boat on a dead course for the reef.

Finally, all four bolts had been removed. He lifted the plate and shined the flashlight into the box. He was shocked. It didn't look at all like he remembered. *This is crazy*, he thought. *I'm the only one who comes up here, and I certainly didn't change this control panel.*

He stood up and looked out the window. The white and red lights were still all he could see in the distance, that and the fact they were closer in the bay now and even closer to the reefs.

Back to the panel. He had to think and act fast. No time to figure out why the panel was different. He had to fix it. He studied each wire and connection. It reminded him of the plate of spaghetti he had for dinner tonight.

He traced one wire at a time with his fingers, searching for a loose connection. Why were there so many wires? He only remembered there being five. Now there must be dozens crammed into this tiny panel box.

He'd trace one wire, find it secure. Move to the next and so on only to lose track and have to start over. He remembered the wires had been different colors. These were all the same. All black.

He was beginning to panic now. Dark thoughts raced through his mind. He wasn't going to be able to fix this light, after all, was he? He wasn't smart enough to make it work, was he? Because of his incompetence, people were going to drown on that reef tonight.

The shrieking noise of the wind and rain never let up. Clay choked back a scream. He thought he was going to lose his mind.

Fingers traced one wire after the other. Time passed. Then he felt a loose wire. Finally! He pushed the other wires to the side the best he could. Yep, there was a loose wire all right. And deep into the control panel, he could see the screw connector from where the wire had come loose.

Who designed this piece of crap? he thought. All these wires, the connectors hidden behind the wires deep inside the panel. Made no sense. *I would have designed it better*, he thought. *Stop it, stupid! Fix the light. People are about to die.* With his left hand, he held the wires to the side. With his right hand he reached down to the tool carrier for the long screwdriver he needed to reach the connector deep inside the panel box.

No screwdriver. Then he remembered. The tool he desperately needed right now is at the bottom of the lighthouse. He frantically searched the carrier for another Phillips screwdriver. He found one and reached for the connector.

He couldn't reach it. This was insane. He had the full length of his arm plus the screwdriver inside the darn control box, and he was still several inches short of the connector. The connector was just out of reach. He screamed and slammed his body into the panel, thinking the extra effort would somehow close the gap. It didn't.

He shoveled through the tool carrier like a madman. He only had two screwdrivers. Neither long enough to reach the connector.

Vise Grips! *Ah, when in trouble reach for vise grips, that's what I say. And if vice grips don't work, use duct tape.* Clay laughed a tired, sick laugh. He had the solution. He'd clamp the short screwdriver into the vise grips. The extra length would be perfect.

He put the handle of the screwdriver into the jaws of the Vise Grip. It wasn't very secure. So he kept tightening the grips. Carefully he led the tool combination into the maze of wires toward the connector.

Wait, how was he going to get the darn wire onto the connector? He couldn't reach it with his hands.

Withdrawing the combination tool, he reached for the pliers in the tool carrier. With those he thought he could position the loose wire on the connector, but would it stay long enough to be secured?

His heart was beating fast, and his back ached from stooping over, but what really unnerved him was the slight sway of the lighthouse. He knew it had been built to withstand hurricane-strength winds and a little sway was to be expected. But that was of little comfort to him. The thought of the boat fighting the waves near the reef brought Clay back to his senses.

With pliers in his right hand, he held the loose wire and stretched it toward the connector. Slowly, he moved ever closer to the connector. When he was about an inch away, the wire wouldn't stretch any further. *What?* Clay yelled at the wire. *"You were on there once, you can be again."* But nothing Clay could do would move the wire close enough to the connector.

He withdrew from the panel. *Be cool, Clay. Think this through. You can do it.* He took another sip of water and dared to look out through the storm at the boat.

At first, he didn't see any lights, but that was because he had been looking in the wrong place. The vessel had advanced a lot farther into the bay during the time Clay had been working inside the wire panel. It was too late. Clay knew the bay like the back of his own hand. He knew there was no saving the boat now, even if the lighthouse should miraculously fire its beam across the darkness. The boat was doomed.

Clay watched the movement of the white and red lights as they were rocked in unison by the waves off in the distance. Clay screamed, *turn hard to port, turn hard to port!* The forward progress of the lights suddenly stopped. Clay wiped sweat from his eyes and peered intensely through the thick glass. No movement. The red and white lights were in the same position. In a few minutes, Clay could no longer see the red bow light. Only the white mast light remained. A few minutes later the light flickered and vanished into the darkness. The boat had sunk.

You stupid piece of crap! Clay screamed. *Because you couldn't fix the light, people are crab food now. You can't do anything right!* He picked up the tool carrier and threw it across the lantern room, scattering tools everywhere. He collapsed to his knees, totally defeated. Tears flowed like rivers down his face.

Chapter 2

"KIRO Radio Weather for Seattle today is rain showers this morning; partly cloudy in the afternoon. High of 52 and low of 39 tonight."

The annoyingly cheery weather girl was speaking to Clay from far off in the distance. For a few seconds, he was totally confused. Seattle weather? He wasn't in Seattle, he was . . . the lighthouse . . . where was he?

"And now the KIRO Copter Traffic Report, what's it like out there, Scott?" the over-caffeinated morning radio host asked.

"Not good. There's an injury wreck mid-span in the West-bound lanes of the Evergreen Point bridge. Traffic is backing up fast. If you can take an alternate route into town, take it now."

Clay opened his eyes. He scanned the room. He recognized the abstract paintings on the wall, saw the Bose clock radio. Six-fifteen a.m. It was his bedroom all right. No lighthouse. No cold metal floor. No lantern room. And more importantly, no shipwreck.

"Crap, another lighthouse dream!" Clay said out loud as we swung his legs out of bed and tried to stand.

He was exhausted as if he had never slept. He looked down at the bed, seriously considering returning to it. The bed was a total disaster. It looked like he had been wrestling alligators all night. Two pillows were on the floor, the comforter was nowhere to be seen, and the sheets where twisted into knots.

Well, no alligators, he corrected himself, but I'm sick and tired of having this same frustrating nightmare—fighting the same bolts, hearing the evil wind, and seeing the boat's lights sink from sight beneath the wind-whipped surf.

He'd had the same dream once a week for the past two months. It was getting to him. He was afraid to go to sleep some nights. He'd get into bed and just stare at the ceiling; afraid to close his eyes. So afraid that he started drinking a strong nightcap just before bed to help him sleep.

Maybe I need to talk to a shrink, he thought, as he walked toward the shower.

Chapter 3

lay swung his BMW M5 into the private stall of the parking garage and killed the engine. His ego loved this part of the day. The private parking space, the sign on the wall that said, "Reserved for Mr. Austin" next to the spiffy ADB logo for Austin Davis Behr. But the good feelings never lasted for more than a few seconds before the other voice inside Clay took over. That private parking space was costing his company $750 a month on top of the $21,000 a month lease payment for the offices exactly five floors up from here. He calculated how many hours the firm had to bill every month just to cover the rent *and* this parking space. *My parking space in* my *building. Why am I worrying?*

Walking to the parking garage elevator he had to remind himself that he *was* worth it. He had earned it. But, when he stepped inside the elevator, he wasn't so sure. That lighthouse nightmare flashed through his mind again. A shot of panic made his heart jump. Why couldn't he ever get the darn lantern to work? Why did the boat always have to sink?

Clay pushed the last button on the elevator's control panel inside the door. There wasn't a number on this button. Just a green ADB on a yellow background, the same colors as his alma mater, the University of Oregon. The button visually jumped off the elevator control panel. It was bright and vibrant compared to the gray and black of the other six buttons. He loved looking at the buttons every day. P1, P2, 1 ,2, 3, 4, ADB.

The polished metal doors slid closed, and the elevator carried its only passenger, now lost in thought, to the top floor.

The ADB building, as it was known to the locals, was located in the super-chic, super-trendy part of Seattle known to some as North Lake Union, or Fremont to others. The area had been redeveloped about ten years earlier and was now home to technology companies, high-priced condos, coffee shops, bicyclers, electric cars, and microbreweries.

The offices of ADB occupied the top floor of the building. The southern side of the office faced the tree-lined ship canal that connected Lake Union to Puget Sound via a series of locks, called the Ballard Locks. Yachts and tugboats pulling barges traveled up and down these waters around the clock.

The canal in this area was lined with parks, trees, and a jogging path called the Burke-Gilman Trail. It was all very nice, especially on the rare nice day when the sun decided to make an appearance.

Clay, with his business partner, George Davis and another investor, formed an LLC to buy the building in 2015. ADP was then and now the largest tenant in the building. The value of the building had skyrocketed since the purchase, but Clay felt little comfort in his paper wealth.

The economics had him worried: Eighty percent of Clay's net worth was tied up in this building; fifty percent of the lease income for the property was paid for by ADB, and ADB was bleeding money like a stuck pig.

The bleeding had to stop.

The elevator door opened, and Clay stepped into the main office lobby of ADB to start another work week.

"Good morning, Clay," the energetic and friendly voice of the receptionist immediately greeted him before he could take a second step out of the elevator.

"Good morning, Betsy. Go Ducks!"

"Go Ducks!" She responded enthusiastically. March Madness, the annual college basketball tournament, started this week and the Oregon Ducks were playing that night. Betsy was one of many employees who were graduates of the University of Oregon, but she was the most fanatical when it came to supporting Oregon sports.

Three steps past the reception counter and Clay's mind was racing through what he had to accomplish this week if ADB (along with his financial security) could be salvaged.

He looked down the corridor and directly into the glass-walled conference room at the far end. It was just 8:30 on a Monday morning, but the conference room was bustling. He knew the account team for Lazzr.com had an important presentation later this morning. They were getting prepared.

Closer now, Clay could see all the team members. He checked to make sure everyone was there. They had struggled lately to work as a team. The group consisted of strong personalities, but some hadn't been pulling their own weight, which surprised Clay. There was Ali, the SEO specialist. Jordan, the social media researcher. Larry, the WordPress expert. Donna, content manager extraordinaire. Suzette, account manager. Clay studied Suzette, his partner, and slowed his pace to give him more time to observe before he reached the room's door.

Suzette Behr was the only one standing. Everyone else was seated, heads buried in their notebook PCs. Even from here Clay could sense the tension in the room. Some pre-presentation tension was to be expected. Too much was not good. It meant something was bothering the team.

Clay studied Suzette's face. She looked tired, haggard. Geez, her hair even looked like it hadn't been washed in two days. He hoped she planned to jump into the office's showers down in the gym before the client arrived.

He reached for the door handle, opened it just enough to stick his head in. "Are we ready, guys?" Clay asked with an encouraging smile. Everyone but Suzette jumped. They hadn't seen him approach the room through the glass, so focused were they on their computers. All eyes glanced quickly to Suzette to Clay, and then back to their PCs.

Suzette spoke up, "We'll be ready. Got a curve ball thrown at us, though. Last night Jordan saw a press release that had just been distributed. Google has agreed to purchase one of Lazzr's competitors for $45 million. I called Loretta at home last night. She freaked. This changes everything. Now we're scrambling to adjust the plan before 11:30 when Loretta and her team arrive."

Clay was now standing in the room. He remained calm. Smiling. He scanned the room again.

"People, listen to me for a minute," urged Clay. All heads looked up. They were panicked and tired. Suzette looked irritated that Clay was going to say something to *her* team. "We knew that Lazzr was vulnerable to a stronger competitor. It just happened a little sooner than we thought." Clay was locking eyes with each person around the table now as he spoke. "But, let me tell you this. Lazzr is very, very fortunate to have the people in this room on their side because there isn't a better marketing team anywhere, and ADB is known for helping smaller companies beat the Goliaths of the world." He paused and started to leave, but turned to say, "Get your slingshots ready, people. You're going to have some fun!" The tension in the room subsided but could still be felt.

He nodded to Suzette, "Let me know if I can help, Suzette." She glared at him. That's the moment Clay knew they were in trouble. The look in her eyes was not fearful, or panicked like the others had been before his pep talk. Her eyes were filled with hatred.

Chapter 4

n his office, Clay removed the sleek notebook computer from its carrying case, set it on the desk, and plugged it into the docking station. He pressed on the button. Soon the computer's display filled the three 27-inch monitors on his desk. *Showtime.*

Tap, tap. Clay looked up. His assistant, Sheryl Landing, stood in the doorway. She had his coffee cup in her right hand, steam rising from the rim. Her cup was in the left hand. He knew it didn't contain coffee. Sheryl never touched the stuff. She was a tea girl; the more exotic the tea, the better.

"Good morning. I saw you in the conference room on the way to the kitchen and took the liberty of bringing you coffee." She handed him his cup.

"Thanks," Clay said, a little surprised by her kindness, and not sure what else to say.

"No problem. Just don't expect it . . ."

"I know. I know," Clay stopped her. "You don't pick up my laundry, and you don't do coffee."

They grinned at each other. What Clay said was not only a long-standing joke between them, it was symbolic of the close, respectful relationship they had.

Clay glanced at his open door and lowered his voice. "What are your tea leaves telling you about the presentation today?" He fully expected her to playfully look into her cup before replying. Instead, she looked right into his eyes.

"Something's wrong. The energy in the team is really negative," she observed.

"Well, they got hit with a big surprise at the last minute," Clay explained.

"I heard, but listen, that's not it." She quickly glanced at the door to make sure no one could overhear the conversation. "There have been rumblings for several days. You weren't here Friday to hear it."

Clay motioned for her to have a seat in one of the four ridiculously expensive contoured chairs that surrounded the equally expensive and stylish coffee table. He sat down in the chair next to her, facing the door so he could see if anyone walked in while they spoke. "Go on," he said.

"I work out with Jordan and believe me she's not a happy camper. She said that Suzette has been on the war path, been a real bitch."

"When did it start?"

"Jordan first started complaining to me after work last Monday," she answered.

Clay thought back to last Monday. The partner meeting. That explained everything.

"George, Suzette and I are under a lot of pressure right now. You saw my PowerPoint deck before the partner meeting, so you know what I'm talking about."

Yes, the three owners of ADB were feeling the heat right now, but Clay sensed there was more to Suzette's attitude than financial worries. He decided to keep the thought to himself until it became more fully baked. He didn't think Sheryl was completely convinced either, but there was a limit to what he should confide to his loyal assistant. It was times like this that he really missed having a wife with whom he could share this type of stuff.

"I know. George has been acting strange, too," she declared.

That news took Clay by surprise. He had had several meetings with George since the partner meeting—even one with a client. George had been George.

"How so?" Clay asked, trying not to appear as surprised as he really was.

"He has been tense. Not as friendly to everyone as usual. I think he started smoking again, too," she whispered the final words like she was revealing a secret code.

Clay was shaken. Not because George was rumored to have started smoking again, but because Clay had misread both of his partners during the past week. Both of them were acting strangely. Well, George was acting strangely. Suzette had always been a bit of a snake in the grass, but a snake that always came around to doing what was best for the firm. The look of hatred in her eyes earlier this morning told him a different story.

"Hey, it's nine o'clock. We're burning daylight, and I'm not paying you to sit here and gossip," Clay winked and stood up.

"Hey, look who's talking. You need to get off your butt and generate some billable hours," she winked back, stood and walked out of the office. She hadn't touched her tea.

Chapter 5

With all he had to do today, with all the crap hanging over his head, what was he doing this very minute? Staring out the window. Who could blame him, because a few hundred yards from where Clay stood, coffee in hand, an enormous yacht was passing from right to left, heading through the ship canal into Lake Union. *Yeah, and to a boatyard eager to sell several thousand gallons of diesel fuel.*

Yachts and boats of all shapes and sizes navigated these waters. Most of the time Clay didn't even notice, so calloused he was to the sight of a million dollars of fiberglass and teak gliding past his window at a snail's pace.

But this was no ordinary yacht. This was in the super-yacht category. Clay guessed it was about the length of a football field, stem to stern. Fenders the size of NFL linebackers hung along the yacht's side every twenty feet or so to protect the ship from scratches when it tied up.

A few of the crew with matching sweaters could be seen scurrying around the deck. Checking this, coiling that, talking into walkie-talkies. Clay wondered if the owner was aboard. Probably not. Why would an owner be on board when the vessel is heading in for fuel, provisions, and possible repairs? Heck, later in the week the owner and wife (or mistress) would probably fly into Seattle's Boeing Field on their private jet, where the yacht's helicopter will pick them up and bring them to the boat while the vessel is heading into the emerald green solitude of the San Juan Islands north of Seattle. *Wonder who the owner is?*

For the first time, it struck Clay as highly unusual that he never envied the owners of super yachts. He liked knowing who they were and how they made their millions (or billions), but he had never dreamed of standing on the deck thinking *this is mine; all mine!*

Why didn't he dream about owning a super-yacht? He loved boats. He had even owned a few sailboats in the years before ADB—before the demands of his firm stole away his spare time. Clay's sudden introspection surprised him. He had never asked himself that question before. He rationalized that he never dreamed about owning a super-yacht because he was too aware of how much it cost to buy and operate a vessel of that size. *I'll never make that kind of money.*

The sound of the yacht's horn brought him back from his deep thoughts. A group of kayakers was not moving out of the yacht's way fast enough for the ship's captain. A quick blast of the horn seemed to do the trick as the kayakers started paddling faster to one side of the canal.

This boat wasn't in his album.

Clay was getting pretty good at identifying who some of the super yachts belonged to. Just for kicks, he kept a photo album on his iPad to record the passage of impressive yachts. He researched the owners and tapped notes into his computer.

It was a fun hobby. Something to momentarily relieve the stress of running the leading marketing agency in the Pacific Northwest. He admired the beauty and power of the yachts at the same time.

He remembered a few years ago, when the 314-foot *Vava II* moved slowly past his office window. It was owned by Ernesto Bertarelli, the newspaper said the night it arrived. The *Serene*, owned by Yri Scheffler, a Russian vodka distributor, was over 500 feet long. It too plied the narrow waters of the canal past his office. Steve Balmer's Octopus, all 414 feet of it, had made the passage a few times. Its towering superstructure threw a shadow across Clay's office building that day as it inched past.

Clay picked up his iPad and snapped a few pictures of the gleaming blue hull as it slid by. He waited a bit longer until the stern was visible to take a picture of the vessel's name and home port.

El Faro, Cabo San Lucas, was written on the stern. *The Beacon*. Clay shuddered. The lighthouse nightmare roared through his brain like a wildfire destroying everything in its path.

He dropped the iPad on the credenza, then looked around to make certain no one noticed that he was shaking.

Pull yourself together, man!

A few deep breaths and a sip of lukewarm coffee did the trick. His shaking subsided, and heart rate fell back to normal.

In control now, he reached for his wireless mouse and clicked to enter the Contacts folder. He searched for Dr. Laura Shildstein, MD. Instantly the contact information for the doctor appeared on the screen. Clay glanced up at the open office door. He reached into his pocket, removed the cell phone and tapped the number. He didn't want this call to go through the office phone system.

Chapter 6

lay returned from lunch with his CPA, Brett Martin. They had lunch together every three months at one of the hip seafood restaurants overlooking Shilshole Marina. Sometimes they even talked about Clay's finances. Most of the time their conversation covered the usual stuff guys talk about. Oregon sports, the lousy weather, local politics, and could that waitress' skirt be any shorter?

Brett wasn't your stereotypical CPA. He was fun and had a wild streak—loved 25-year-old Scotch, scuba diving, and sky diving. But when it came to money and finance, he was rock solid. Brett's advice had saved Clay a lot of money over the years and made him even more. It was Brett that showed Clay how he could swing the purchase of the ADB building years earlier.

Brett honked as he roared off in the brilliant blue Audi R8 Spyder. Not boring at all.

As he opened the double door into the building's ground floor entry, the relaxation of the past ninety minutes evaporated. Clay remembered that upstairs, the Lazzr meeting would be over. Would they still have the account?

Part of Clay desperately wanted them to hold onto the account. The firm needed the revenue right now. But the other part of Clay wanted Lazzr to fire them. Well, not *them*. To Fire *Suzette*.

Forgoing the elevator, he walked up the stairs to the top floor. He paused to catch his breath after the climb and then reached for the polished door handle leading into Austin-Davis-Behr.

Walking toward his office, he scanned the private offices and open work areas looking for the telltale signs on faces indicating victory or defeat. Suzette's office was empty. George's office was empty. The energy level everywhere was low, too low, he thought for what was usually a rocking environment.

Sheryl looked up as he neared his office. One look and he knew. The Lazzr meeting hadn't gone well.

"Talk to me," he said, walking briskly past her desk and into his office.

She followed him in as he went to his desk and turned to face her. He wanted the information fast and short, so he kept standing. "Well ..."

Sheryl closed the office door before speaking. "Jordan confided to me that the meeting started great and ended terribly," her voice trembled a little. She knew what was at stake.

"And ..." Clay motioned with his hands for her to get on with the story.

"They presented the plan, which included a revised competitive strategy, of course."

"And ..." Clay was becoming annoyed at the preamble.

"Jordan said Lazzr was psyched about the plan, really liked it right up to the point when Suzette presented the campaign schedule," Sheryl explained.

"Huh?" Clay was taken aback by the answer. If client meetings go bad, it's because of disagreements with strategy, creative, or budget. Never schedule.

"Listen, Clay, Jordan said that Suzette presented a schedule *none* of them had seen before!"

"Okay, that doesn't sound right. Are you saying Suzette presented a schedule different from what they had worked on together?" Clay asked.

"Yep," Sheryl said with the same *I don't believe this really happened* look on her face that Clay was showing.

"What the heck was so weird about the stupid schedule?" Clay demanded.

"Suzette told them that work on the campaign should start in about two months," Sheryl knew what was coming next.

"Whiskey Tango Foxtrot! Lazzr needs action now, and we need the money now. Two months? B.S. Two weeks is the right schedule, not two months," he said. "Did Jordan say what Suzette's rationale was?"

"Something about now not being the ideal time and the big industry trade show coming up," Sheryl said.

She could see that Clay was seething. She didn't like seeing her boss upset. He was usually steady as a rock, with a quiet intensity that people admired. But, on the rare occasions when he got angry . . . well, objects can get broken, and holes can be punched in walls.

"Where the heck is Suzette now?" Clay asked, sounding a little too hostile.

"I saw her and George going out for lunch after Lazzr left about 12:45."

Clay glanced at the black iWatch on his wrist. The digital display read 1:52.

"Sheryl, please schedule a partner meeting for today. Topic: Lazzr Presentation." His assistant looked at him as if to say, *bad idea, amigo.* "Cancel that. Schedule a meeting just with Suzette for today. Not too late, I have a meeting out of the office at 4:30."

She nodded her approval and left Clay standing by the modern executive desk alone with his thoughts.

Chapter 7

ay-to-day meetings between partners followed a certain unwritten code or etiquette. Whereas formal partner meetings always occurred on neutral ground—one of the conference rooms, or even at an offsite location—less official meetings to discuss clients and staff occurred in a partner's office. Whose office the meeting occurred in could say a lot about the seriousness of the meeting and who was trying to impose their stature on the other. The dynamics of it all bored Clay, but he knew better than to ignore it. Sheryl was great at booking the "perfect room" for the occasion.

So, when Clay saw the accepted meeting show up on his computer calendar fifteen minutes later, it told him two things. Suzette had returned from lunch, and the meeting was going to be in her office.

Clay had to smile at Sheryl's brilliance. Having the meeting in Suzette's office, on her turf, wouldn't put Suzette on the defensive. Plus, it wouldn't reveal that Clay already knew a lot about what happened in the meeting. It was positioned as an informal, "hey, tell me how the Lazzr pitch went." A meeting in his office was more akin to calling someone on the carpet after a mistake. And while Clay was the managing partner with 50 percent ownership and Suzette a minor partner at just 17 percent ownership, it worked best for the partners to consider themselves as equals. This level of mutual respect had worked well at ADB. The idea of "unequal equality" carried the day, but had to end when business decisions were to be made. Then, the decisions and voting had to follow ownership percentages: Clay 50 percent, George 33 percent, and Suzette, 17 percent.

Clay didn't want to pretend with Suzette that he was completely ignorant of the Lazzr outcome. Suzette was very sharp. She would expect Clay to ask around and find out whether it went well or not. She also knew just how plugged in Sheryl was to everything at ADB. It was no secret that Suzette despised Sheryl for what she knew and who she knew. It didn't help that Sheryl was smart and one of the most attractive women in the building. Suzette was super-smart, too, but always looked unkempt and frumpy. It bothered Clay that her hair was seldom clean. It hung down from her head straight, stringy and greasy. He couldn't remember the last time her face was totally clear of a reddened pimple, or a cold sore. She was an awesome strategic marketer, however, and a tremendous asset to ADB—at least up until now.

Right on time at 3:15, Clay walked into his junior partner's office. It was one-third the size of Clay's office and didn't overlook the Ship Canal, but it was large enough for a desk, couch, coffee table, and a few large silk plants.

"So, is it true that the Lazzr folks aren't happy with your plan?" Clay decided to get right to the point and make it clear it was *her* plan, *her* team that evidently came up short. Clay sat down on the couch, crossed his legs, and sipped at a Coke while watching Suzette's every move.

The hatred in Suzette's eyes was gone. In its place was nothing. No, that wasn't quite right. He could read something in her eyes. It was a falsified look of *everything's under control*. But behind that, Clay thought he saw something else—a flash of *I'm beating you, and you don't even know it.*

She spoke calmly, "Don't know where you heard that. They loved the strategy."

Clay was immediately saddened and alarmed. His junior partner was concealing information from him. Why?

"Glad to hear it. What I saw last week was really impressive, but I know you had to make some changes at the last minute." Clay stopped and waited for more information to be shared.

"No problem. I handled it," Suzette said. She was playing this close to the vest, Clay thought. He didn't like the egotistical nature of *I handled it*. There was a team of four others who had busted their butts for two weeks on the plan.

"That's awesome," Clay tried to sound convinced while watching her very closely now. "When do we start?"

"The plan is anchored around eComm World, the big eCommerce trade show in May. Work will start in a month or so," her tone was matter-of-fact as if this timing was obvious to those smart enough to get it.

"How did Loretta react to the schedule?" Clay asked. "She's usually the most impatient one in the room," Clay continued, not wanting this to sound like a cross-examination in a TV court drama.

"She was taken aback by the schedule at first, but eventually came around the more I explained the rationale of the strategy and the wisdom of keeping our powder dry for a few months," Suzette explained.

"Cool. When do they sign the work order? You and I talked last Monday about Lazzr's billings. They've been declining for six months. The new plan is a great opportunity to boost billings at a time when we really need the money," Clay explained what should be obvious to his business partner.

The next question came at Clay like a sliced tennis serve with a lot of side spin on the ball. "Are you suggesting, Clay, that I put the interests of our firm ahead of the interests of Lazzr?"

Clay wasn't totally surprised by the sharp reply. What made him leery was the careful wording and pronunciation of her question. It sounded rehearsed, as if she had been setting up the conversation for this moment, and that question. *Is Suzette recording this conversation?*

Clay returned serve. "Not at all. You of all people know how I stand on that philosophy. Putting clients first is part of our mission statement. You know, the one we read to each other before every partner meeting." Clay loved that answer and hoped the conversation was being recorded just so it was on the record.

He continued, "I'm not being a Monday morning quarterback here, believe me. I do see three points. First, Lazzr is a company of action. It's in their DNA to act quickly. Second, being proactive when there's a shift in the competitive landscape is often the best course. Third, the earlier we start, the stronger Lazzr will be going into eComm World, *and* we'll be able to start billing them again, this month even."

Suzette snapped a backhand sharply across the net. "Let me remind you that I'm a partner here because of my strategic planning prowess." The word prowess sounded strange coming from her mouth. It was dripping with pride. "I'm a great marketer because I don't do the expected. I do what will shake up the market and move the needle. This is what Loretta understands now. She's on board."

Clay smiled. He liked her spunk. Really did. It was one of the reasons he and George invited her to buy into the firm five years ago. She had been Chief Marketing Officer at Zilbean. Took it public. Waited one year after the IPO to sell her stock and walked away with $5.8M. Not bad for three year's work. She immediately bought a larger house on Lake Washington and agreed to buy a 17 percent stake in Clay and George's firm, then Austin-Davis.

Clay's phone was vibrating in his pocket. It was time to end this. His forehand volley shot past her like a rocket and skipped inside the white lines in the back corner out of reach. "Okay, your call. Lazzr is your account. Just know, partner, that your projected billings are down this year by $800,000. Delaying the Lazzr campaign is only going to exacerbate the revenue shortfall." Suzette started to say something, but Clay cut her off and stood to leave. "By Friday, please let George and I know how you plan to make up the $800,000 this year. I'll have Sheryl set up a partner meeting."

Game. Set. Match.

The darn phone was still vibrating as he walked from Suzette's office to his own. He jerked it out of his pocket and stared at the display. The alarm for his 4:30 with Dr. Shildstein reminded him it was time to leave. He also had a phone message. Loretta from Lazzr had called.

Chapter 8

The meeting with Suzette was unsettling. Clay sensed something wasn't right, but couldn't put his finger on it. He acknowledged himself for how he handled the meeting, but his situation and the firm's wasn't any better off for his performance today.

Clay drove the silver M5 out of the parking garage and into a drizzling rain as winter darkness covered the city like an unwelcome blanket. He headed east toward the doctor's office, a smart little bungalow on the other side of the Ship Canal from the University of Washington campus.

Through voice commands, he instructed his phone to call Loretta at Lazzr. *This is going to be an interesting call.*

"Hello, this is Loretta," Clay's client answered her cell in her usual friendly, professional tone.

"Loretta, this is Clay Austin returning your call."

"Oh hi, Clay. Thanks for returning my call." Clay strained to hear through the car's speakers anything in her voice that could tip him off to what was coming next. It was useless. Too much noise. Rain was falling harder on the roof and window; the windshield wipers, sensing the rain, automatically started sweeping slowly back and forth.

"Clay, have you spoken with Suzette about the presentation today?" Loretta asked. *A perfectly normal question,* Clay thought to himself.

"Yes, she briefed me late this afternoon. She said there was a lot of debate about the schedule," Clay said, preferring not to reveal too much too early.

"I was very surprised, no, I was shocked actually that I'd ever hear from ADB a recommendation to do nothing in response to competition," there was irritation and stress in her voice now.

There it was. Clay had to decide to support his partner or his client. Usually, situations like this were easy. He always backed the firm except in cases of obvious error or misjudgment. But, in this case, he didn't agree with Suzette's timing.

He responded, "I admit the timing is a bit uncharacteristic, but I have confidence in Suzette's sense of strategy and market impact. We certainly aren't recommending 'doing nothing,' Loretta." Clay decided that sounded a little defensive and sharp. He wanted to soften it. He and Loretta were old friends after all. "Suzette has shown time and time again the wisdom of her plans," Clay stated, not wanting to believe it fully himself.

"I want to trust Suzette. I want to trust you and ADB, but delaying our campaign is so contrary to who we are as a company. We think fast and move fast. That characteristic plus our innovation has put us on the map" she said.

"That's correct. Responsiveness is in your DNA," he said while parking his car at the curb outside the doctor's office.

"It used to be in ADB's DNA, too," Loretta said with a lot of emphasis on the *used to be.*

Clay thought back to the original pitch that won the Lazzr account for ADB. They went out of their way to prove to Lazzr how fast and flexible they were. In the end, it was the agency's ability to think fast and work fast that swayed Lazzr's executives to go with ADB. The cultures were aligned.

"We still are, Loretta, but moving fast just for the sake of moving fast isn't a sound strategy. Suzette believes that the most impact and market disruption can be obtained by waiting a few weeks," Clay said, not liking that it sounded too much like a lecture.

"It's not a few week's delay, Clay. It's two months." Loretta was sounding exasperated and uncomfortable. "Look, I have dinner with Reggie and Charlotte tonight to review the recommendation with them. They will ask me if I support ADB's recommendation. I can't say that I do," she said.

Reggie and Charlotte were the co-founders of Lazzr. They had never been 100 percent in favor of ADB. Both had close relationships with other agencies, but they had wisely let Loretta make the marketing decisions.

Clay took a deep breath and slowly exhaled to calm himself before speaking, "Loretta, I know this is a tough situation, but please remember one thing. We are a team. Lazzr and ADB. Like a good marriage, we're going to have disagreements, but we work it out together. This isn't a client versus agency battle. It is two partners working together to find the right path to success." For the second time today, Clay was amazed at the wisdom of his words. *That was great stuff. Where did those words come from?*

"I hear you, Clay, and I want to believe it, too," she responded. "I'll call you Tuesday."

"Great. And don't forget who always invites you to the Oregon-Oregon State game every year," Clay said thinking some humor with his old friend would go over well right now.

Loretta chuckled, "Yes, and I've almost forgiven you for 2016. Such a terrible game and in the pouring rain, too."

"I promise to do better this year. Talk tomorrow," Clay said and touched the disconnect button on the steering wheel to end his call.

Opening the car door, he immediately felt the cold rain on his head. Scrambling up the walk to the door of the doctor's office, Clay couldn't help but think about his day. What a Monday! Ducking boomerangs all day long. *And tomorrow they'll be circling back at me again.*

Chapter 9

itting inside Dr. Shildstein's office for the first time, he scanned the room and compared it to the shrinks' offices he had seen in the movies.

This office was very comforting. No doubt a lot of effort went into designing and furnishing the space just for that effect. It was homey but definitely not cheap. The light brown leather sofa that Clay sat on looked like the one his interior designer had tried to sell him last year for $4,500. Clay opted for something almost as nice for $2,500. In front of where Clay sat was a low coffee table—a blue ceramic and mahogany combination that appealed to Clay.

Across from the sofa was the ubiquitous psychiatrist's chair. It was high-backed, sleek but not sharp. Rounded corners, but not over-stuffed like some chairs can be. It was upholstered in rich burgundy-toned leather. It looked very comfortable. Clay was tempted to run across the room and sit in the chair to try it out before the doctor entered the room to start the session. He decided the risk of being caught in her chair was too high. *Don't act like a child, Clay.*

On the gray walls were many photos, watercolors, and acrylics of the most incredible hot air balloons he had ever seen. Brilliantly colored balloons soared above all types of amazing terrain. A red and yellow balloon flew above the rolling wheat fields of eastern Washington's Palouse country. Drifting down the Columbia River Gorge was a black, orange, and silver beauty. Floating high above the sea cliffs with the ocean surf and a ... no way! Clay's eyes locked onto the painting. It was larger than the others, measuring about 36 by 54 inches. It dominated one entire wall next to a small desk. The perspective of the painting was dizzying. The viewpoint was from high above the balloon and to its right side, so one saw the balloon and everything far below it. There were the rugged tree-covered cliffs of the Washington coast. The crashing waves. But what caught Clay's attention and sent his heart racing was the other object in the painting below the balloon. A lighthouse.

Clay tried to brush it off as a coincidence. Here he was in a psychiatrist's office to talk about his recurring nightmare of a lighthouse, and what does the shrink have on the wall? A painting of a stupid lighthouse! *Whiskey Tango Foxtrot!*

He couldn't take his eyes off the painting, however. The balloon's design was simple—just brilliant white that made it stand out sharply from the background colors. There was an emblem of some type on the balloon. Only part of it was visible because of the angle. Clay squinted from his position on the sofa to make out what sort of logo was on the balloon. A sponsor of some sort, he figured. From what he could see, it looked like a simple stick figure. A vertical rectangle with a horizontal rectangle intersecting with it near the top. What was it? Clay's mind tried to match the partially exposed symbol to some logo pattern he could recognize. Just as he gave up, the answer came. It was a cross. A Christian cross.

Clay was so mesmerized by the painting he didn't hear Dr. Shildstein enter the room.

Dr. Shildstein stepped into the office and saw her new patient twisted on the sofa looking behind him at one of her paintings. She made a mental note of his interest.

"Mr. Austin, sorry to keep you waiting," she said calmly and quietly, not wanting to scare him.

Clay jumped anyway as his mind was torn loose from the painting. He swirled around as if he had been caught stealing cookies.

"Oh, uh, uh, hi, doctor," Clay stuttered, trying desperately to regain control and sound normal. "I was just admiring your art. Are you a hot air balloon pilot?"

Her eyes seemed to look right through him, but not in a hostile way. In an instant Clay felt that she had looked deep into him, like an MRI could, and saw everything. *She knew!* Her smile was warm and sincere.

Clay stood to shake hands. She was short, probably under five feet tall in heels, Clay estimated. She was slender and super-fit. Her handshake was strong. And while they shook hands, her eyes never left Clay's.

"No, I'm not a pilot, but I am a bit of an aficionado. Ever since my husband proposed to me on one twenty years ago, there has been a special place for them in my heart. We take a ride every chance we get. Plus the balloons are a great metaphor for how I help patients," she said, turning to sit in her chair and motioning for Clay to be re-seated on the couch.

Clay immediately thought of cracking a joke about hot air, but wisely thought against it. He sat down and poured a glass of water from the polished metal container on the coffee table.

"So, Mr. Austin, this is our first session together. I see that Brett Martin referred you," she stated after glancing to her notepad.

"That's correct. He spoke highly of you," Clay responded truthfully. According to Brett, Dr. Shildstein kept him from totally losing it after his messy divorce.

"Here's how this goes. First, we're on a first-name basis during our sessions. I'm Laura. You're Clay. If we happen to meet outside the office I am Dr. Shildstein; you are Mr. Austin. Understood?"

Clay nodded.

"Each session is fifty minutes. This being our first session it may run seventy-five minutes. Please be on time. If you miss a scheduled session, I'm still going to charge you anyway. As I said on the phone, each session is $225." She paused. "With me so far?"

Clay nodded. He liked her style.

"Of course, everything you say to me is completely confidential. The non-disclosure statement I had you sign before this session makes that fact very clear. It also makes it clear that this confidentiality does not cover situations where you mention illegal activity considered a felony. I am bound by law to report you to the authorities in those cases. Understood?" she said, her words were crisp and direct.

"Roger that," Clay answered. "I'll keep all planned murders to myself." His grin faded when he noticed she wasn't smiling.

She opened her notebook, removed a pen from the inside of her well-tailored suit jacket, and said, "Why did you come to see me today, Clay?"

Great question, he thought. Just why the heck was he here? He should be at the office going over the books figuring out how to make ends meet.

"This is going to sound silly, but I keep having the same nightmare," Clay said and waited for the next question. It didn't come. Instead, she kept looking at him. "I have this crazy dream maybe twice a week. It started two months ago, I believe." *This is where she's going to ask me what the dream is about*, Clay thought. She didn't. Her head was nodding up and down ever so slightly and slowly.

"You called this dream a nightmare. What makes it a nightmare rather than just a dream?" she asked.

"It's really frustrating," Clay answered right away.

"You consider the dream a nightmare because there's something about the dream that is frustrating?"

"Yes," he said.

"Are you in the nightmare? Is something happening to you?" she said.

"I'm in it all right. I'm the star of the show or villain. Not sure what I am."

The doctor made a notation in the notebook. "You don't know if you're a hero or a villain in the dream?" she asked.

"I start out being the reluctant hero. At the end, I'm a worthless idiot. People die because of me," Clay said, and felt the emotion of the nightmare well up inside him again.

Her pen was working furiously now. She looked up and locked her gaze onto Clay. "People died in the dream because of you?"

"Yep, I couldn't fix the light in time, so the boat crashed on a reef during a storm." Clay took another swallow of water and realized he had already consumed three-quarters of the water in the glass.

"What light is it that you're seeing in the dream?"

"It's a lighthouse, Laura. An old broken lighthouse. I have to fix it during a storm. A ship crashes on a reef because I can't fix the light in time."

"Do you recognize the lighthouse? Is it the same one in every dream?" s

"Same lighthouse every time. No, I don't recognize it," he said.

"Anyone else in the dream?" she asked.

"Just the poor unlucky folks in the boat. Never saw them. I just know there were people on the boat and it sank at night after hitting the reef."

"Just you, the lighthouse, the boat and the people on the boat. That's it?" she tried to summarize the elements of the dream as if writing a playbill.

"Yep, a small cast," Clay said trying to play along. But there was someone else, or something else, Clay remembered. He tried to think.

"What is it, Clay? You left me just now."

"Oh, uh, sorry, doctor, I mean Laura. I was back in the nightmare," Clay said taking another sip of water from the glass.

"And ...?" Laura asked with the ultimate open-ended question.

"I don't know. There were times during the dream when I thought there was a monster or something outside the lighthouse," Clay said, embarrassingly feeling like a little kid complaining about the monster under the bed.

"Did you see a monster?" she asked.

Grateful that the doctor wasn't laughing at him, Clay replied, "No, I never saw it. I felt its presence though. And it made a terrible sound somewhere between a hiss and a roar. I didn't know for sure if it was an evil presence or just the gale wind outside the walls," Clay explained.

"An evil presence. That's an interesting way to describe it," she remarked.

"Interesting when I'm awake, yes. Terrifying when I'm in the dream," Clay said.

"Indeed. Our dreams can be very terrifying and seem very real," she said. "You said the dream made you feel frustrated. Explain that feeling to me."

"Yeah, frustration, panic, hopelessness, fear. It was a real bummer."

"Go on."

"That's it. Those were my feelings."

"You had all those feelings because the boat was going to crash?"

"Yeah, the lighthouse lantern wasn't shining so the boat couldn't navigate the bay's entrance properly. I wanted to save the people."

"What stopped you from turning on the light?"

Clay felt as if an icy hand was squeezing his heart. He started breathing more quickly, fidgeting. Drinking water. *Get me out of here.*

The doctor noticed the change in Clay's mannerisms. She wrote in the notebook.

"Clay, what stopped you from turning on the light?"

"The light was broke, I guess. I tried to fix it."

"What happened when you tried to fix it?"

Clay exploded. He shot up from the sofa, spilling water from his glass on the table and floor.

"I couldn't fix the stupid light, okay." The words hurdled out of his mouth with a vengeance. "I couldn't reach the problem inside the control panel. My tools weren't the right length. I tried. I really tried!"

As if coming out of a trance, Clay suddenly realized he was standing, fists clenched, staring at the doctor still seated in her expensive leather chair with eyes locked on his. She wasn't even blinking, so intense was her focus on Clay.

"You're angry, Clay."

"Damn right, I'm angry!" He started pacing back and forth between the sofa and coffee table. "I come here to talk about a stupid dream, and you start blaming me for not fixing the broken light. I don't need this crap."

"I'm sorry. Please have a seat."

How could she stay so calm? Clay sat down, noticed the puddle of water on the table and floor. He pulled several tissues from the box on the table and soaked up the water.

"Sorry, doctor, er, Laura, I didn't mean to spill the water."

"That's okay. Not the first time, believe me." She paused, watching him, and Clay felt she was gauging his every movement. "Clay, it's interesting that you thought I was blaming you for not fixing the light in your dream. Are you aware that I never said anything about it?"

He thought back on the conversation for a few seconds. "You asked me why I couldn't fix the light."

"Actually, Clay, what I asked was 'what happened when you tried to fix the light.'"

"I thought you said 'why couldn't I fix it, or something like that."

"That's what you heard me say, but believe me, that isn't what I said."

Clay sat back into the sofa. He crossed his arms and legs, and stared at the table in front of him.

"When you thought I was criticizing you, you became very upset. Don't you think it's interesting that you thought I was criticizing you for not fixing the light, rather than criticizing you for not preventing the boat from crashing?"

"I guess. What's the difference?"

"Well, there is a difference, but we don't have to look at it right now. We still have time remaining in our session. I'd like to put the dream aside for now. Is that okay?"

"I guess that means you can't fix me in one session."

A warm, controlled, laughter rolled out of Laura. "I don't view this work as 'fixing you,' Clay. And, yes I'm afraid our work together has just begun."

"Whatever it takes. I want those dreams gone."

"Great attitude. Now then, tell me about your childhood, Clay."

Chapter 10

t seemed Clay had just found his rhythm telling the doctor about his childhood when she held up her hand signaling the session was over.

They set another appointment for Wednesday at 4:30. Clay wrote the ›ctor a check for $225 and slipped out the door. It was still raining as he dashed to his car.

Usually, when Clay pushed the Start button to bring his 560-horsepower coupe alive, it sent a pleasant rush of adrenalin through him. Not tonight. He was exhausted by the day's events. His hour with the psychiatrist didn't help any.

Deep in thought and drained of energy, he directed the sleek BMW south onto Montlake Boulevard toward its intersection with 520. Clay's two-story houseboat was not that far away, but getting there from this part of town wasn't simple. There wasn't a direct route. On any other night, he might take the more leisurely way, winding westward through neighborhoods until he reached Fairview Avenue that hugged the eastern shore of Lake Union. But tonight, he craved some energy. He had a need for speed.

Clay couldn't believe his luck when he realized that he was first in line at the intersection light waiting to enter the 520 freeway. The light turned green, and Clay's foot went down. The gleaming silver car fishtailed slightly on the wet pavement, straightened out and shot forward, pushing Clay's head back against the headrest. By the time he entered the freeway from the short ramp he was already doing 60 mph. There wasn't much traffic in this direction on the freeway, and he kept his foot on the accelerator.

He was doing 95 mph within a matter of seconds. This felt so good! He wanted to keep going, pushing faster, but his turnoff was just ahead. Turn signal on, he slashed between two cars in the right lane just in time to make the exit. He kept to the right for the Roanoke Exit. Now he had precious little distance to reduce the car's speed before the light at the intersection. His left hand flicked the paddle shifter, working the car down through the gears, while he gently increased pressure on the brake pedal. He roared up behind an SUV at the light and stopped without even a skid. *German engineering! Gotta love it.*

Clay's heart was beating fast. The entire speed warp had only lasted two or three minutes, but in those minutes he totally forgot all about Suzette, Lazzr, and Dr. Shildstein. It was just him, the road, and his magnificent machine.

A few minutes later he was on the narrow Fairview Avenue. He drove up to an electronic gate, swiped his security card across the sensor, and entered the private parking area reserved for owners of six exclusive houseboats.

Clay's houseboat was not a boat at all. It was a 3,000 square foot, award-winning home built on floats and secured to a dock together with five other homes. His home was the furthest away on the dock, which meant he had an unobstructed view of Lake Union beginning at his doorstep, and the Seattle skyline about a mile to the south. It also meant he had the farthest to walk from the car.

This was the small penalty one paid for living in a houseboat. One had to walk a distance in the wind and rain between your car and home. Carrying groceries was a real drag. Yet, the minute Clay stepped inside his home the cold, wet walk was quickly forgotten.

His architect had struck the perfect balance between modern and maritime. Wood accents and curved walls danced with polished steel. Every piece of furniture was selected to not only look fabulous but to be extremely comfortable. Clay lit a fire, poured himself a glass of Oregon Pinot Noir and settled into his favorite reclining chair facing the two-story window. The lights of downtown Seattle sparkled to his left. The dark ridge of Queen Anne Hill was just visible across the lake. A small tugboat plowed slowly up the lake.

It was calm now, but still raining. The lake bravely tried to reflect the city lights in a show of blurred color, but the persistent raindrops broke the reflections.

His mind raced through the day while he twirled the red wine in its glass.

Why did Suzette put the agency in such a precarious position when it wasn't necessary to do so? Why did she look so hateful in the conference room, and so coy talking about the meeting later in her office?

What was Loretta at Lazzr going to do as a result of the meeting?

And on top of it all, how was ADB going to survive if Lazzr walked?

Clay sipped the wine and thought back to last Monday's partner meeting, searching for clues. The meeting was as contentious a meeting as the three partners had ever experienced together.

Billings for the year were down, in no small part because Lazzr had been in a hold-pattern. Other clients had cut back their marketing budgets some, but the real pinch was because late last year the partners forecasted a twenty percent growth in billing and hired additional talent in anticipation of what appeared a sure thing.

How were they to know that in early January Wall Street would get the jitters over an interest rate hike? That action sent the market south, and ADB's clients got spooked and held back on marketing spending until they could see the road ahead more clearly.

So, here they stood, staffed to handle twenty percent more billing than they currently had. They either needed to cut back or add more billing fast. While the financial situation added stress, the argument that nearly turned into a brawl was over the other topic on the agenda.

In January Clay had received an overture from a top-20 agency in Dallas. They were interested in acquiring ADB. Phil Manicotti, the CEO of Pitt-Needham Group, had dinner with Clay the weekend before the partner meeting. Over a roasted king salmon dinner, he made his pitch.

ADB would become a subsidiary of Pitt-Needham Group. Clay would continue to run the shop, reporting directly to Phil. They would have access to the worldwide resources of the larger company. Pitt-Needham Group would have a blue-ribbon agency on the ground in the booming Pacific Northwest region.

The purchase price looked good. Clay told Phil he and his partners hadn't talked about being acquired. On the contrary, they were always on the hunt for talented boutique firms they could buy. Over coffee and Cognac, Clay told Phil he would discuss the offer with his partners in their next meeting.

There was a lot to like about the offer, but something deep inside Clay was screaming "*no!*"

He didn't know if he could trust Phil. Did he really mean to keep Clay, or would Clay get the axe within a few months of the deal closing so Phil could put one of his people in the top spot? The more Clay thought about it, the less certain he was that being acquired was the right move right now.

Being part of a larger firm, a public one at that, meant a lot more scrutiny on budgets and billings. Pitt-Needham Group was the big league all right. Was ADB up to it? Was Clay up to it, that was the real question?

Clay was comfortable being the managing partner of a well-respected, mid-sized agency. He really didn't have ambitions to climb any higher. Sure, he'd sell, but not until he was ready to retire.

That's where the argument started between Clay, George, and Suzette. Both of his partners were ecstatic when they heard about the intent to purchase ADB. They saw the chance to make some serious money on their shares and be part of a larger agency with offices and clients in five countries.

When he voiced concerns, they couldn't understand his hesitation. He stood to make the most money. He'd be a rich man. And, he'd be on the executive team of a worldwide agency. What's there not to like?

Clay tried to express his reservations. He wasn't convincing. Tempers flared, and Suzette accused Clay of playing small. She was a very ambitious woman, and when she was being held back, by a man no less, she could become ferocious.

George was also irritated with Clay. He was older than Clay by nearly 15 years. Cashing out now wasn't such a bad idea for him.

In the end, after heated debate, Clay tabled the discussion until the next partner meeting. In the meantime, he'd ask Phil for some more information about the structure of the proposed deal just to buy some time.

Clay tried to envision his name on a Pitt-Needham Group business card. He couldn't do it.

Clay stopped thinking about the partner meeting and realized he was still a little chilled after the walk from the car. He poked the fire and reached for another piece of wood from the rack by the fireplace. His hand gripped a piece of oak and tossed it into the flames.

The round log hit the embers, sending sparks into the protective screen of the fireplace. The log rolled off the flames and threatened to roll out of the fireplace until Clay stopped it with his poker.

Shouting, Clay yelled, "Get back in there you piece of crap. You're not coming out here." With his poker, he violently hurled the log back into the fire. Something inside him snapped.

A string of expletives rolled from Clay's mouth. He was actually swearing out loud at a log, of all things.

What the heck is going on? Twice in one day he had lost his cool.

He sat back in his chair, and took a long drink of wine to calm his nerves. His eyes went from the fireplace to the rack of wood next to it.

Then he heard a voice from somewhere in the darkness of the house.

"Stack it over again," was all the male voice said.

Chapter 11

ear shot through Clay like a flaming arrow. His heart raced as adrenaline pumped through his veins. It was all he could do to set the glass of wine down on the stand by his chair without spilling its contents all over his Persian rug.

Except for the glow from the fireplace the house was dark. Somebody was in the house. Somewhere. Or was it his imagination? His mind had certainly been working overtime lately. Anything was possible. But, he had heard the words clearly: "Stack it over again."

He gathered the courage to turn on the reading light by his chair and stand up in a single fluid motion. He faced the darkness ready for a ... ready for what? Fight or flight?

Familiar shapes in the house were now visible in the light from the single lamp. There was the outline of the dining room table and chairs with the overhanging chandelier. Farther back he could see the kitchen counter and stools. Small night lights on the stairs revealed nothing on the wood-and-steel stairs leading up to the master suite. *Way too many hiding places.*

A weapon. He needed a weapon. Hands trembling, he reached for the fireplace poker. Feeling its weight, seeing the pointed end, he was comforted. *That should work.* How many murder-mystery movies had he seen in which the fireplace poker always contained the critical clues to the whodunit. Sure, but whose blood would be on this poker at the end of the night? His?

Clay advanced slowly, silently, through the house with the poker ready to strike. Keeping his back close to an outside wall, he advanced on a path that would take him exactly opposite to a panel of light switches. His ears strained to hear any unusual noise in the house—any sound of footsteps. The winter rain had increased outside, its noise on the roof was all Clay could hear.

Clay was now standing, poker in hand, about twenty feet from the light switch panel. He would have to move across the open floor to reach the lights. He would be a sitting duck. *Heck, you're a sitting duck now! Just do it!*

Clay sprinted for the light switches, hitting them with his left hand repeatedly until every switch was in the on position. He whirled around so his back wouldn't be to the center of the room.

"*Who's there?*" Clay yelled, trying to sound tough and menacing. His eyes darted around the main room.

He raced into the dining room ready for battle. Nothing. He sprinted to the kitchen, certain someone was hiding behind the counter. Nothing there either.

Striding down the short hall, he started throwing open doors and looking inside. First the pantry door, then the restroom, guest bedroom, and the wet room, the special teak-paneled room for changing out of wet clothes after coming in from the lake. He checked its door that led to the private outside deck. It was securely locked.

The stranger must be upstairs. Had to be. Clay started up the stairs. The upstairs suite was dark, so he flipped all the lights on from the panel at the bottom of the stairs. With the second story fully lit, he advanced slowly up the stairs. No sense being quiet. It knew he was coming.

Clay checked the entire master suite. He even looked under the bed, recalling briefly his early childhood when he was absolutely certain that little-boy-eating monsters lived under his bed.

He checked and rechecked every room, every nook upstairs. Wasn't he supposed to yell "clear" or something? That's what the cops always did when they broke into a house, service weapons in hand, looking for a perpetrator of some crime.

A metal spiral staircase led up to a door that opened to the roof-top sitting area. He tested the door. It was solidly locked. The sliding glass doors across from the king-sized bed were also secure.

For the first time since picking up the poker, he held it loose at his side rather than in a striking positioning.

Feeling spooked and *very* foolish Clay walked back down the steps into the main living area. After checking that all doors and windows on the first floor were securely locked, he replaced the poker in its stand and sat down in his chair.

"Whiskey Tango Foxtrot," he muttered to himself.

He treated himself to several long drinks of the Pinot. It tasted different than before. Clay had read somewhere that fear can charge the chemistry in your mouth such that food doesn't taste right. Well this Pinot didn't taste right, and he had been scared. He drank it anyway and poured some more. Clay hadn't eaten dinner and soon the wine and warm fire worked together to soothe his raw nerves. He noticed he was hungry, so he shuffled into the kitchen and prepared a plate of fruit, cheese, and crackers.

Back in his chair, he began wolfing down the snack with more wine. His mind began to race again. What the heck had just happened anyway? He had heard the words clearly, "Stack the wood over again." Was he becoming schizophrenic, or another type of insanity? This morning he had been haunted by a lighthouse nightmare and now haunted by a hidden voice? What next? And why?

Staring now at the rack of neatly stacked wood next to the fireplace he thought back to that special relationship he had with wood and fireplaces. It was a minor miracle he had a fireplace at all, let alone a wood-burning one.

Any pile or stack of wood would call up memories of his childhood. And Vic.

Chapter 12

ray, gray, gray. Everything was gray. The heavy gray clouds filled the sky and hung so low they seemed to be glued to the rooftops and pine trees of the Salem, Oregon, neighborhood. It wasn't raining exactly, but it was damp and numbingly cold for early October.

Clay could see his breath vapor while he worked. The cheap cloth work gloves he wore were already soaked, making his hands ache in the chill of the darkening afternoon. He had been out here since noon in the vacant lot next to his parent's modest ranch style home. To his right were two piles of wood, just delivered that morning by dump trucks. One pile consisted of oak and laurel logs. The other pile was a messy mix of fir—waste pieces from a local sawmill—different shapes and thicknesses, each coated with damp sawdust.

In front of Clay was the beginning of a wood stack he was building from the pile of fir. The stack was about eight feet long and now about two feet high. He hated to stack fir. It was slow and agonizing work because the pieces were all so irregular. It was like building a vertical picture puzzle without a picture to follow. Just his luck he had no choice but to stack the fir first. It was the first to be delivered. The fir pile blocked his direct access to the oak pile.

And there he stood. He glanced over to the driveway and the basketball hoop above the garage door. That's what he wanted to do this afternoon. Shoot some hoops while imagining he was a star basketball player for his school. Imagining the girls who'd compete for his affections because he was such a basketball stud at fourteen.

He glanced at the neglected basketball on the lawn where it had been dropped when Clay heard the first of the dump trucks stop at the house, back up slowly into the vacant lot, tilt the dump body, and spill the messy fir pieces onto the ground. That meant Clay's plan to spend Saturday afternoon playing basketball and skateboarding had just gone up in smoke. Clay knew the rules. Wood piles were to be converted into wood stacks the same day. No, *and, if,* or *buts.*

The first truck roared off to ruin someone else's day. Unbelievably, a few moments later a second truck pulled up and repeated the same depressing show. When it, too, had left in a cloud of diesel, two loads of wood needed to be stacked. The weekend he had planned was not to be, it was officially going to be a forced labor camp for one.

Somehow, all the work associated with enjoying a wood-burning fireplace was Clay's responsibility and had been since he was ten years old. He was expected to: stack the wood neatly outside the house; bring a supply of wood into the house every day; chop kindling for starting the fire, and build a fire every evening before his mother and step-father came home from their respective jobs. It was even his job to remove the ashes from the fireplace every other week.

Every night sitting in the living room with Vic and his mom, watching TV, Clay could only fume in silence as Vic seemed to delight in setting new records for nightly wood consumption. The more he added to the fire, the more Clay had to carry into the house. The more Vic burnt up, the more wood they had to order, and of course, the more Clay had to stack.

With each log tossed into the flame, Vic seemed to be taunting Clay. *I dare you to say something, kid. Sure you had to stack it, but I had to pay for it!*

Never a thank you. Never a word of appreciation that because of Clay's labor he could sit in his chair by the fireplace and keep his stinking feet warm.

The fir wood pile looked as large as the minute it had arrived. Clay reached down and grabbed a piece in each hand. He took two steps to the left and looked for a place on the stack that could accept the size and shape of what he had in his hands. He didn't see any options and tossed the two into a third small pile. He'd deal with these uncooperative pieces later. He walked back to the pile, grabbed another two pieces and placed them onto the stack. Over and over again he repeated the process.

The gray October light was fading. It was late afternoon, and not much daylight was left. It was a race against the clock now. He had to get all the fir stacked today. Sunday he could attack the oak pile. Fortunately, that would go quickly. Oak logs were a lot easier and faster to stack than scrap fir.

To add insult to injury, drizzle had begun to fall from the leaden sky about a half hour ago. Clay's feet were cold and damp, his hands had been numb for hours, and he felt a chill come overtake his body as his sweatshirt soaked up the moisture. The dreaming of game-winning shots from the perimeter, and pretty cheerleaders rushing to embrace him in victory had faded several hours ago. He wasn't thinking of anything now. His mind slipped into a protective void absent of any thought. Well, not totally clear of thought. A hatred for Vic burned there.

Vic was due back from work today about 5:30. He was seldom in a good mood when he got home. Clay knew better than to not have the fir stacked by then. The stack would be inspected.

The problem with making the third pile of highly irregular pieces is that at some point Clay had to deal with them. Here he stood in the failing daylight, cold, tired, and challenged by the fifty or so pieces at his feet.

He briefly thought about hiding the pieces all over the vacant lot but thought better of it. There was too many pieces. So, one by one he added the pieces to his stack, forming the last two layers on the stack. He did it. He was done! He stepped back about ten feet from the stack and looked at it. Pretty good. Wasn't leaning.

The top didn't look very neat because of the irregular pieces, but what the heck. Those pieces would be the first to get chopped up into kindling anyway.

Car lights came up the street and turned into the driveway. Vic was home.

Clay was anxious but also proud of this accomplishment. He had stacked all the fir in time.

Vic stepped out of his car and walked directly toward Clay. It was still drizzling, and just enough light remained to be able to see the wood stack and remaining pile.

"When was the wood delivered?" he demanded without even preliminary greeting.

"About noon," Clay replied.

"What have you been doing all day?"

"Stacking wood." The flames of rage started to swell within him.

"It's after 5:30 and you just finished one pile?" "What did you do, go inside and watch TV for a while?"

Here came the rage like uncontrolled vomit. "No! I didn't watch TV. I've been stacking this stupid fir all afternoon!"

"Don't you talk to me in that tone of voice!" Vic threatened.

Clay stood there glaring at his step-father. He dared to clench his fists knowing Vic couldn't see them in the darkness.

Vic stepped forward and looked at the stack of fir.

Pointing at the stack and staring back at Clay he growled, "You call that a stack?"

"Yeah," Clay said a bit too defiantly.

"It's a mess. Probably going to fall over any minute."

"No, it's stable. The top looks funny because . . ." Vic cut him off in mid-sentence.

"Don't you talk back to me, boy!" He stepped angrily behind the stack and pushed. The top half of the stack fell forward onto the ground at Clay's feet.

"I thought you said it was stable! Does that look stable to you?" he asked, pointing to the pile in front of Clay.

Clay didn't answer.

"I asked you a question. Answer it," Vic demanded, his face distorted in rage.

As usual in these situations no explanation was allowed. No defense was permitted. There was only one answer that would get Vic off Clay's back and defuse the situation.

"No," was all he could say, and it took every last ounce of his strength to make the word sound sincere.

Vic stepped in front of Clay, glared down at him and pointed to the stack.

"Stack if over again. Do it right this time." Vic turned and walked back to the house, to his comfortable chair, a stinking pipe, and a roaring fireplace.

Chapter 13

The rich aroma of freshly ground coffee beans circled his head like a pungent, invisible cloud. Clay stood staring at the impressive espresso machine but not really seeing it. He was lost in thought. The events of the past two days and the difficult days ahead weighed heavily on his mind.

The whirring sound of the grinder suddenly stopped, and Clay snapped to as if some hypnotist had just commanded "wake up" to end his spell on Clay.

Now fully aware that he was standing in the kitchen of ADB while employees wandered in and out, he took a deep breath and brought his full attention back to the present.

The expensive Swiss-made espresso machine was automatically brewing Clay's first cappuccino of the day. The beans had finished grinding, and now the double shot of espresso was pouring into his mug with the perfect crema. Soon an equal amount of steamed milk would pour from the machine, followed by the same volume of foamed milk to top it off.

The espresso machine was a real luxury, and a huge hit with clients and employees. Clay calculated that the device cost approximately three times as much as the car he drove in college. Yep, he'd come a long way since then. So why didn't he feel better about it?

With a polite beep, the machine signaled it had completed its task. Clay grabbed his mug, smiled at the perfectness of the drink he was about to enjoy, and walked briskly to his office.

It was just 8:30 as he sat down at his desk. Looking out the door at the office he knew only about half the employees were here. The other half would arrive over the next hour. He picked up his phone and touched the extension for Sheryl. She picked up immediately.

"Good morning, boss, didn't see you come in," she said in her warm, friendly voice.

"Good morning, Sheryl. I'm ready when you are." Clay signaled to Sheryl that he was ready to review his schedule for the day and set priorities. Once set, Sheryl would keep him to the schedule and prevent anything, or anyone, from disrupting it. He liked to joke that she was his Calendar Cop.

She walked in carrying her notebook computer and sat in front of his desk.

"You look like you've seen a ghost," she said with real concern in her voice. "Do you feel okay?"

Clay didn't think his shaky state of mind was visible on the outside. What was he going to say? Couldn't tell the truth that he had searched for some boogey man in his house all night.

"It's cool. Just haven't slept well the past two nights. And speaking of tossing and turning, any messages from Lazzr this morning?"

"Nothing. Suzette hasn't come in yet either, in case you wondered."

"Let me know when she does. No need to set up a meeting. I just want to know when she's in the office."

"Right."

"Here's what I have going on today. Oh, before I forget, on Wednesday I have a 4:30 meeting outside the office and I won't be returning. I haven't put it on my shared calendar yet, so you don't see it yet."

Sheryl made a note. He could see the wheels turning in that attractive head of hers. He knew she was curious about the offsite meetings in his calendar that didn't have a place or person listed. Two mysterious meetings at the same time in the same week. Must be driving her crazy trying to figure them out. He vowed to himself to tell her—someday.

"Today, my priorities are Lazzr and setting up a Partner meeting for Thursday. I also want to see Gerald to go over the books." Gerald was ADB's controller.

"Okay. I have a request from the Yukon Air team to review their campaign proposal with you. Can you work that in?"

"Absolutely!" Clay was extremely proud of the work his shop did for the regional airline. In the past two years, the fledging airline had grown its market share by 24 percent because of the agency's brilliant strategy and creative execution.

"I'll give you until 10:30 to deal with Lazzr. As for the Partner meeting . . ." she tapped the keyboard on her notebook to display the schedules of George, Suzette, and Clay. "You're in luck. Three to five is open."

"Perfect. End of the day is good. Book it and send the meeting notifications. Subject is: 'Partner meeting continuation'". Sheryl stopped typing and looked up at Clay.

Somewhere between hurt and angry, she said, "You know, I could help you better if I knew what the heck was going on! You have mysterious meetings offsite; you call a Partner meeting without a specific topic. What's up? Don't you trust me?"

Clay stared back at her. He wanted to tell her everything, but couldn't. Not yet.

"Sorry, and you're right. Please trust me that I will reveal what is prudent to reveal at the right time." That answer didn't appease her, so Clay continued. "The offsite meetings are personal. That's all you need to know for now. As for the partner meeting, I deliberately don't want a descriptive subject that everyone with access to our calendars can see. You know the nature of the financial discussions we've been having. You already know more than anyone else here except George's admin. No sense worrying the troops."

Sheryl had helped him prepare his slides for the last partner meeting, so she knew the tough financial situation. The topic of being acquired by Pitt Needham Group was not in the slides then, nor would it be on Thursday. That topic had to remain top secret.

"All right, I just scheduled the Partner meeting for 3 p.m. on Thursday. As for today, you're working on Lazzr until 10:30. I'll book the Yukon team for 10:30 in the Ogilvy conference room. I'll book a working lunch with you and Gerald until 1 p.m. You'll have all afternoon to work on preparing for the Partner meeting." The Calendar Cop had spoken.

"That's perfect, Sheryl. Thanks."

She left his office, leaving Clay alone to think about what he had to do next— call Loretta at Lazzr.

Three short blasts from an air horn in the distance split the morning silence. Clay turned to the window in time to see a beautiful sloop, easily sixty feet in length, slowly power its way eastward up the canal toward the Freemont bridge, its horn requesting that the bridge open. The three short blasts from the yacht were answered by one long and one short blast from the bridge tender acknowledging the request. Soon, Clay knew, the steel drawbridge would slowly open to permit the sailboat to pass while dozens of angry drivers sat in their cars on both sides of the bridge impatiently waiting for the bridge to close again.

Clay ran his eyes over the sleek yacht. He briefly pictured himself behind the wheel of the gleaming vessel but the pleasant vision ended abruptly. He heard a voice in the back of his mind say, "don't kid yourself."

Chapter 14

Clay busied himself by organizing his desk, scanning his news feed and checking email. He started to click on ESPN.com to check the latest college football news. *Stop it! You are procrastinating. Stupid dork!*

Guilty on all accounts. He had been finding things to do just to avoid calling Loretta. An internal battle was already raging inside Clay. The optimist was presenting a case for why Lazzr would hold the course and remain with ADB. In the agency's favor was a record of consistent results and the friendship between Clay and Loretta. The pessimist side of Clay had a case, too. Once trust is shattered, as Clay believed it had been with Suzette's odd time table, the game is over. Desperate companies (and Lazzr was desperate) start reaching for miracle cures. They decide "a change is required that is more aligned to their future market challenges . . . A fresh approach with new ideas . . ."

Get a grip and make the call.

Clay reached for his desk phone and punched speed dial for Loretta's office at Lazzr.

After four rings an automated voice greeting said, "Thanks for calling Lazzr. If you know your party's extension you many dial it now." Clay was surprised. The number he had dialed went directly to Loretta's office. If Loretta didn't pick up, her admin did. This time the call went to the automated receptionist.

He hung up and checked the number for Loretta against the main office number for Lazzr to confirm the numbers were different. He punched the autodial again. Four rings, "Thanks for calling Lazzr . . ."

She must have changed her number, he reasoned. Thinking back, he realized that most of his conversations with her were by cell, not to her office phone. Clay interrupted the annoying automated voice by punching "0" on his phone to get to a human being.

"Lazzr Corporation, this is Anna, how can I help you?"

"Hi, Anna, sorry to bother you, but I was trying to place a direct call to Loretta, and the phone number I have for her must not be valid anymore. Please connect me."

A brief pause, then Anna said, "Oh, Loretta is no longer with Lazzr. Today was her last day. Is there anyone else I can connect you with?"

Clay couldn't speak. He wasn't prepared for this scenario. It hadn't been even a possibility in his mind. All he could mutter before hanging up was, "No."

Whiskey Tango Foxtrot. What the heck is going on around here?

He picked up his cell phone off the desk and dialed Loretta's cell.

"Hi, Clay, I wondered when I was going to hear from you. Actually I was about to give you a call."

"What the heck happened?"

"I was fired. Well, technically I was asked to resign. Effective immediately."

"Are they crazy? You're a rock star."

"Not in their eyes. Not after the campaign proposal ADB gave us," the edge of bitterness in her voice was unmistakable.

"They fired you because of Suzette's time strategy?"

"It's more complicated than that, but yeah."

Clay walked over to his office door and shut it. This conversation required privacy.

"Who else knows this outside of Lazzr?" Clay asked, his mind now getting into gear after the initial shock.

"I haven't told anyone except my husband. I wanted to speak with you first."

"I appreciate the courtesy. I'll break the news here. Were you and Suzette scheduled for a call today?"

"Yeah, I was to call her at 10:30 with feedback from Reggie and Charlotte."

Clay glanced at his watch. It was 10:05. "Okay, don't call. Let me talk to her. Tell me what happened at dinner with Reggie and Charlotte."

"It started out great, as usual. I briefed them on the campaign strategy. They weren't blown away by it but didn't hate it either. I thought their reaction was unusually reserved."

"Unusually reserved? What do you mean?"

"You've been around Reggie and Charlotte, so you know that they get excited about new ideas. Last night the usual level of energy just wasn't there. I think they were disappointed. They told me that they were expecting a really big idea and the didn't get it Then they took turns ranting about how marketing has been letting the company down. This took me by total surprise."

"Let the company down? No way. Did you point out the market share gains, the cover articles on Wired and Inc. magazines, the . . ." Loretta cut him off.

"Of course I did, but the more proof I presented, the more entrenched they became in their warped view of the situation. Charlotte even looked me in the eyes and said, 'all that is yesterday's news, Loretta. We need leadership and a plan to take us to the next level. This strategy doesn't do that.'"

"I couldn't disagree more, Loretta. We presented a sound and bold plan."

"I agree with you. It was the right strategy except for the timing."

"What did they say about the schedule?"

"Nothing. The plan was being rejected. Heck, everyone in marketing was being rejected at this point, so I wasn't going to add gasoline to the fire by talking about the schedule. Unfortunately, Reggie asked me point blank how soon the campaign could start. So I laid out for them Suzette's strategy of waiting several months. That's really when the excrement hit the fan!"

Clay had been pacing back and forth in his office during the conversation, but he suddenly felt very tired. He collapsed into one of the chairs and put his feet on the coffee table. "And then . . ." Clay asked, knowing that a lot more was coming.

"Reggie and Charlotte looked at each other and then at me. It was as if some encrypted signal had just passed between them. Then Reggie gives me the 'it's time for fresh leadership speech.' Charlotte acknowledged my past contribution, but said firmly that they had decided a change of leadership and agency was necessary to take the company to the next level."

"A clean sweep," said Clay gloomily.

"Yep. It's funny though. Now that I've gone over the conversation several times it's clear to me that they were set on making a change before we had dinner. I think they were prepared to pull the plug on the marketing department and ADB no matter what."

"Sounds that way. I'm really surprised I haven't received a call from Reggie by now."

"Me too. And you haven't heard anything from Suzette either have you?"

"No. She wasn't in the office when I got here. I'll talk to her as soon as we hang up. Two questions before I let you go, Loretta."

"Shoot."

"I know it's early and you're still in shock, but any ideas about you want to do next?"

"None. I'm still processing all of this, honestly. They gave me a good severance package, so I'm going to take some time off and figure out next steps."

"Recruiters will be burning up your phone within 48 hours, Loretta. Heck, if I could right now I'd bring you into ADB."

"I appreciate the kind thoughts, Clay. Let me cool my jets for a while though. Grant and I haven't had a real vacation in over two years. I think we're going to disappear and refocus. What was the second question?"

"Who's the lucky agency?"

"They dodged the question when I asked. Charlotte said an announcement would be made when the time was right. Reggie said it wasn't a local shop. That's all I know. This has been in the works for some time I think. You know how plugged in I am to industry gossip. There hasn't been any hint of a change. Frankly, I am more than a little pissed and hurt that they've been working behind my back."

"Loretta, looks like both of our lives have changed today. Do me a favor and when you're back from vacation let me know how I can help you."

"Definitely. Take care and good luck."

"Bye, my friend." Clay tapped the phone to disconnect the call. He tapped his Contacts app, searched for Loretta, and edited the record to remove the company name, company address, company phone, and company email. She wasn't a client anymore. Just a friend. He hoped.

It was 10:20. If he missed the 10:30 with the Yukon Air team they would be devastated. Yet, he had to talk to Suzette before she tried to call Loretta at 10:30.

He opened his office door. Sheryl was at her desk and turned to him when she heard the door open.

A short nod of his head invited her into his office.

"Okay, here's the skinny. Confidential for now. Loretta is gone from Lazzr, and we're going to be fired at any minute. I am the only one at ADB that has this information right now. At least I think so. Please contact the Yukon team and ask for a 15-minute delay until 10:45."

"Consider it done."

"And get Suzette in here right now."

Sheryl nodded her head and briskly walked out the door on a mission.

Clay felt terrible and didn't know why. He wasn't ill but felt deflated. His office seemed to grow around him as if he was getting smaller. One of his prized accounts had rejected his firm and was going to hire another agency. Some unknown agency that in some way was better than ADB. Some distant agency who had a president that was better than Clay.

His company, his very heart, and soul, was in danger of sinking and he felt powerless to stop it.

Chapter 15

A tapping on the door brought Clay out of his trance.

"You wanted to see me, Clay?" asked Suzette.

"Yes, good morning. What do you hear from Lazzr?" Clay decided to play his cards close to the vest. Behind his smiling face and warm eyes, he was intently studying every word, every blink, every mannerism of his junior partner.

"Nothing, but I'm scheduled to call Loretta in a few minutes to set up the next steps."

Clay couldn't see anything unusual. There wasn't any sign of nervousness. On the contrary, there was an outward confidence.

"Suzette, you know that Loretta and I go way back."

"Yeah, you went to college."

"We did. We became friends there. Stayed in touch after graduation. It was because of that friendship and trust that she reached out to me when she was brought on board at Lazzr to be their CMO. She wanted us. Didn't want to do an agency search."

"Right, I'm aware of the story." Suzette's attitude shifted suddenly. A look of impatience flooded her face, and she even glanced nervously at her watch. "It's 10:30. I need to call her. What was it you wanted to talk about? Is this supposed to be a reminder about how attached you are to Lazzr and Loretta? I mean, I get it, okay? But don't forget that you brought me into the agency specifically to lead the Lazzr account. It was me that sealed the deal."

Suzette's impatience transformed quickly into bitterness and defensiveness. The reaction surprised Clay. This was the third time in as many meetings that Suzette had spoken sharply to him.

"It was definitely a team effort that won the account. No doubt about it." Clay took the high road to avoid further distractions. It was time to get to the point. "You don't need to call Loretta."

Suzette's head flinched. "Huh, why?"

"Because when you call her number no one will answer."

"I don't understand."

"Loretta was fired last night." He delivered the news and studied her face.

"What? How is that possible? What for?" Suzette was visibly shaken. Clay couldn't tell if the reaction was real or really good acting.

"She had dinner with Reggie and Charlotte Monday night to brief them on the campaign strategy. They didn't like the plan. Told her that her services weren't required anymore." Clay didn't continue. He wanted to hear Suzette's next questions. He hoped he could unlock some of the mystery around here based on the questions she asked.

He noticed that she had regained her composure after the initial shock. Her look of confidence that bordered on arrogance had returned.

"But it was a brilliant plan. She must not have sold it well. I should have been there," she reasoned.

Interesting response, he thought. All about her plan. How she could have sold it. Nothing about a concern for Loretta. And why didn't she ask the most obvious question about ADB's status as agency of record?

"According to Loretta, the founders didn't think the plan represented a big enough idea to take the company to the next level."

There. He saw something in her eyes. The same flash of hatred he saw on Monday in the conference room. The angry spark vanished, replaced by her usual cold brown eyes. "Well, the idiots are wrong. They wouldn't know a great plan it if hit them in the face."

Clay was fascinated, yet also alarmed. Right now Suzette wasn't talking with Clay about getting a meeting with Lazzr, ironing out the differences, revising the plan and moving forward. That was the type of thinking one had when trying to salvage an account. Instead, all she could do was act offended that the client hadn't seen the brilliance of her plan. Instantly he knew what needed to be done, but he needed a little time and a private conversation with George first. For the moment though, he needed to drop the other shoe and tell Suzette that ADB was going to be fired.

Clay's desk phone buzzed. He knew that Sheryl wouldn't bother him unless it was important.

"Excuse me, Suzette. This call must be important. Please wait." Suzette looked a little bored and sat down in one of the chairs. She immediately started viewing email on her tablet.

Clay picked up the phone, "What's up?" he asked his assistant through the handset.

"Reggie from Lazzr is on line two for you."

"Okay." Clay punched line two on his phone. "Good morning, Reggie. Feels like a day of transition, doesn't it?" Clay wanted Reggie to know that he was on top of the situation, but he didn't want to sound defensive. After all, Loretta was gone, but the axe hadn't fallen yet on ADB. Clay made himself comfortable in his desk chair and faced forward so he could watch Suzette.

"Indeed, it is a time of transition, Clay. That's the reason for my call. You know of course that Loretta has resigned."

"Yes, I spoke with her this morning. I didn't see it coming."

"We think it's all for the best. The entire Lazzr team thanks her for her contribution and wishes her well," Reggie said, sounding like the news release they had undoubtedly been writing this morning.

Clay decided to take the offensive and charge the machine gun.

"Reggie, you can rest assured that ADB is in gear and ready to implement the new plan. In fact, Suzette is in my office right now. We were discussing the situation. In the interim, we can interface directly with you or Charlotte. I assume you'll be looking for a new CMO, but that'll take some time." Clay noticed that Suzette was staring at her tablet, but her fingers weren't moving as they would if she was actively reviewing emails and text messages. She hadn't even looked up when Clay mentioned her name.

"Clay, that won't be necessary. You see, Charlotte and I believe that what Lazzr needs right now are fresh ideas; a different perspective on the market. We're beginning to compete with some very established and well-financed companies. We believe, and the Board agrees, that a complete change of marketing direction is required."

"Sounds like you're firing us, Reggie."

Suzette looked up from her tablet. Her expression was oddly blank.

"I don't like to use that term, Clay, but just to be clear we are terminating our agreement with ADB effective in sixty days. You'll have the official termination notice from our attorney before the end of the day."

"Is there anything I can say or do to change your mind? ADB has done some amazingly effective work for Lazzr."

"The decision has been made, and we're moving on. I know that sounds cold. I want you to know that the Board greatly appreciates your contribution."

Clay swallowed hard. This guy was beginning to piss him off. Right now he had to be professional and play nice, but what he wanted to do was call Reggie a two-faced lying bag of crap.

"We've greatly valued and enjoyed the association with Lazzr. We'll work to make the transition smooth, of course." It was time for *the* question. "Who is the new agency?" Clay was looking down at his desk pretending to take notes. In his peripheral vision, he continued to watch Suzette.

"No decision yet. We're reviewing shops. The right chemistry is really important to us."

"Of course, it is," Clay said in a facetious tone meant to let Reggie know that Clay had heard enough of his B.S. "I'll look for the termination letter this afternoon. If you're planning on issuing a news release that refers to ADB in any way, I'll need to review it in advance. And I'll make sure your accounting department receives our invoices in a timely fashion over the next sixty days so we can make the transition cleanly. Agreed?"

"Oh, sure. That's fine. Thanks for your contribution. Let me know if there's anything I can do for you or ADB. Bye." Reggie hung up without waiting for Clay to say another word.

Clay wrote a few notes about the conversation then looked up.

Suzette was looking directly at him. Her face showed no sign of emotion whatsoever. No concern. No anger. No worry. For someone who had just lost her largest account, she was oddly cool, calm and collected.

"Well, you heard. We've been fired. Sixty days from now we remove Lazzr from our client list."

"I better tell the team," Suzette volunteered.

"Absolutely not!" Clay fired back. "You'll say nothing to anyone until the end of the day. I'll tell George later this morning. Is that understood?"

"Sure, but I'm going to be asked. The team knows I was to talk with Loretta this morning."

"Tell them the truth. You couldn't reach her." Clay looked at his watch. He had one minute to get to the Ogilvy conference room and his meeting with the Yukon team.

Chapter 16

S omehow Clay had been able to put Lazzr, Suzette, Loretta, and Reggie out of his mind while he walked to the Ogilvy conference room on the other side of the office. When he stepped into the room at precisely 10:45 everyone was already seated. Easels at the front of the room were covered. The video projector was running. It was showtime.

For the next forty minutes, the team presented their research, strategy and creative concepts for the next Yukon Air campaign. The airline wasn't ADB's largest account, but it was its most visible account. The agency's creative had not only raised the airline's market share over the past three years but had attracted at least three other pieces of new business to the agency. It was a gem of an account.

At 11:25 the presentation was over. Clay stood and walked to the front of the room. He looked around the table and said nothing. Eager faces looked back. Clay raised his hands and clapped. While he clapped, his head nodded up and down as if to say, "You guys nailed it."

"Awesome work, everyone. Truly awesome. Looks like you're ready for the presentation on Thursday. Call me as soon as you can." The team was flying to Anchorage on Wednesday night and presenting to Yukon on Thursday.

Clay left the meeting room in high spirits once again. He loved it when a plan came together. The strategy, the creative, the media. He thought about the team members on Yukon. He had to find a way to keep them. Two of them also worked on Lazzr, however. Everyone on the Lazzr account was at risk of losing their job.

That brought him to the topic of the next meeting with Gerald, his Controller. Clay walked by the kitchen and was tempted to make a cappuccino, except he remembered that lunch was being brought in for Gerald and himself.

When Clay entered his office, Gerald was already there, seated at the work table in the far end of the office. Two bags with their lunch were also on the table.

He closed his office door and greeted Gerald.

"Good morning, Gerald. Are the numbers adding up today?" Clay almost always greeted Gerald this way. He knew it slightly annoyed his too-serious accountant.

"Hi, Clay. No, they don't add up. Seems one column is bigger than the other column."

Clay laughed. "Good one, Gerald, you've been practicing your humor. Hey, one minute before we get started." Clay picked up his office phone and dialed Sheryl's extension.

"Sheryl, thanks for the lunch. Please hunt down George and get him on the phone right away. You might have to call his cell. I think he had contractors at his house this morning."

Clay hung up, and sat down across from Gerald at the table.

For Clay, a working lunch meant eating then working. So, he and Gerald made short talk while they finished their gyro sandwiches.

Clay had just swallowed his late bite when the phone rang. He stood and answered it.

"Hey, George. Thanks for calling. I have some bad news. Lazzr just fired us and Loretta. They said she resigned, but I talked with her first thing this morning, and she was forced to walk the plank. Leaving wasn't her idea."

Gerald stopped chewing and immediately opened his notebook to study a spreadsheet. *Smart man*, Clay thought. *He's calculating the damage while I'm on the phone.*

George angrily said, "That's the last thing we need right now. I'm shocked. Who knows?"

"At ADB, just you, me, Suzette, Sheryl. I ordered Suzette in no uncertain terms to not tell anyone. We have some tough decisions to make, partner. I'm here with Gerald right now to crunch the numbers."

"Good," replied George. "I'll be in the office in a couple of hours. Let's connect then. We need to make the announcement before it leaks."

"Agreed. Talk to you later. Bye." Clay hung up the phone and walked back to the table. Gerald's fingers were flying across the keyboard as data flowed into the spreadsheet.

"I guess you know now why I wanted to meet with you this morning, Gerald. Let me remind you that what you just heard cannot be shared with anyone before George and I can make the announcement."

"Of course. Uh, Clay, we were on shaky financial ground before losing Lazzr. Now the ground is turning to mud. The situation isn't sustainable."

"I know. Give me the details, in executive-speak, not accountant-speak please."

Gerald frowned while his eyes scanned the reports on his computer.

As you know, we've been burning through cash reserves this year as expenses have exceeded billings by roughly $20,000 a month. We're down to $50,000 in the bank. Not much to fall back on considering we need $500,000 a month to keep the lights on."

"What's our receivables?" Clay asked.

"This month $480,00. Next month and the month after it will fall to about $390,000 because of Lazzr."

"Don't make me do the math, Gerald."

"We're looking at a loss of $240,000 over the next three months."

The immensity of the number made Clay's head spin.

"Ok, you already know my next question. Tell me."

"Twelve people. And all can't be junior level. The savings won't be enough."

"We cut twelve people, and we're back in the black in four months?" Clay asked.

Gerald looked back at the computer screen. "No, but we're breaking even with some reserves remaining."

Clay stood and paced around the office, thinking. He looked out the window as a rusty barge and its slightly less rusty tug worked their way down the canal.

"Work a few scenarios for me, Gerald. In the first scenario, we let go everyone we've hired since December. I think that was around ten people. In the second scenario, everyone on the Lazzr account goes. The third isn't really a full scenario. More of an option. What if the partners didn't take a salary for the next three months? Got that?"

"Sure, one question about the second scenario. You said everyone on the Lazzr account. There's only five total people on the account. That won't get us to the number we need."

"Gerald, I said everyone on Lazzr. There are six."

Gerald looked up from the computer and right at Clay.

"You want me to include Suzette? She's a partner."

"Gerald, I have to consider all our options, don't you agree?"

"Yes, of course." He looked back down at the computer screen.

"After you work up the scenarios, if another one comes to mind please present it, too. But, Gerald, I need your magic in two hours, and you have to be completely discreet."

"You can count on me," Gerald said while snapping closed his notebook.

Gerald opened the office door to leave. Clay said, "We'll be all right. Don't worry."

Clay stood alone in his office. He was suddenly very tired. Fatigue crashed down on him like a wet mattress. He needed a break. Needed some air. He grabbed his coat.

"Sheryl, I'm going to take a walk. Won't be long. I have my cell. Call me when George comes in."

"Ok," she said as her boss walked down the hall toward the exit.

Outside it was a typical winter day in Seattle. Damp and cold. No sun was visible as dark gray clouds scudded overhead. Clay walked from the office toward the trail that paralleled the canal. In a park, just before the trail, he stopped at a concrete step to retie the laces on his left shoe. He sat briefly on the chilly concrete. The urban park was a very attractive and functional combination of wide concrete steps and terraces of well-manicured grass.

He studied the recently mowed lawn on each terrace. Every section of grass had perfectly trimmed edges. The wheel indentations from the mower were still visible in the grass. Clay couldn't help but notice that each set of wheel marks was perfectly straight.

Shoe retied, Clay stood to continue his walk. But the second he stood he felt light-headed. Blood seemed to have drained from his brain. He paused, waiting for the discomfort to pass. Out of nowhere, the weight of two gigantic hands on his shoulders pushed him back down to the cold concrete step.

It was a sparkling clear day. The clouds and rain from the past week had vanished to reveal a marvelous spring morning. Perfect weather for eight-year-old Clay to ride his bike through the neighborhood, inventing the type of imaginary adventures only a young boy could create.

Clay brushed his teeth after breakfast, put on his sneakers, and raced out the door to get his red Schwinn in the garage.

Entering the garage through the side door, he noticed right away that the main garage door was open. He wasn't alone. Standing there by the immense, cluttered work bench was Vic.

Clay reached for his bike and started to lift the kickstand with his foot.

Vic looked up from the project on his bench and glared at his stepson through squinting eyes fighting a losing battle against the stinging smoke of a cigarette dangling from the corner of his mouth. "Where do you think you're going?" Vice demanded.

"Ride my bike," replied Clay.

"I didn't give you permission to ride your bike."

"I asked Mommy. She said it was okay."

Vic's glare suddenly transformed into a look of anger.

"I don't care what your Mommy said. You didn't ask me if you could play."

Clay felt like a ping-pong ball between two paddles. He couldn't think. All he could do was look down at the garage floor. He noticed to his relief that the garage floor was clean that day.

"Well, did you?"

"No."

"No, what?"

"No, sir, I didn't ask you if I could play. I asked Mommy if . . ."

"Don't talk back to me!" Vic said strongly. His eyes were beginning to bulge slightly in his growing anger. He was breathing faster, too.

Clay desperately wanted away from here. Couldn't he just become invisible and walk right out the door? If only he could shrink to the size of a mouse and hide under some shelves. Anything to avoid the verbal lashings he was taking.

"Well, you're not going to ride your bike today. It's time you started to help more around the house. Do you think it's right that you should play all day while your mother and I work? Answer me!"

There was only one acceptable answer. "No, sir."

"We work hard all week to put clothes on your back and food in your belly. Then we work on weekends to take care of the house, so you have a roof over your head at night. All you care about is playing with your little friends. Don't you think that's being selfish?"

There was only one right answer in this line of interrogation. "Yes, sir."

Vic smothered his cigarette in an old tuna can on the bench and lit another, all the while never taking eyes off Clay, who stood there looking down at the garage floor, one hand still on the bike's handlebars. One hand still grasping a dream of escape.

"I have news for you. Today you're helping me in the yard. And if you don't work hard today, you can forget about riding that bike for a full week. Understand?"

Clay felt like he was in some terrible whirlpool that was pulling him down, down, down.

"Answer me, boy!" Vic demanded.

"I understand," Clay said weakly.

"Good. Now take your hands off that darn bike and come over here. You're going to mow the lawn."

Clay's house was in a lower-middle-class neighborhood of Medford, a small sawmill town in southern Oregon. The neighborhood consisted of small, single-story homes. Most of the homes were well-maintained by their owners who may not have had much money but were proud of their little part of the American dream. Houses were freshly painted, lawns green and manicured. Nearly every house had a flower bed or two in the front yard, and everyone, except the divorced man down the street, had a hanging basket of petunias by the front door.

Clay's house was different. It sat on a corner lot. The house was larger, and the yard was easily twice the size of other lots. That meant more lawn to mow, more flower beds to trim and weed.

And today was the day that eight-year-old Clay was going to be taught how to mow that lawn. His disappointment in not being able to ride his bike partially faded away. He was going to mow the lawn! He was going to use a power mower just like the older kids did!

Vic muscled the heavy Briggs & Stratton reel lawn mower out of its storage area in the corner of the garage next to the work bench. "Come over here and watch. How do you expect to learn anything?"

Clay walked closer to the mower, not knowing what to expect, or what to do.

With the lit cigarette still dangling from his mouth, Vic flipped the choke lever on the carburetor. He fiddled with the clutch to make certain it was disengaged. Placing a foot on top of the mower's tire, he reached down for the starter cord and pulled upward violently. The 2.5 horsepower engine sputtered and stopped. Vic pulled the starter cord again. And again. It wouldn't start.

Breathing harder now, Vic closed the choke and pulled the wooden handle connected to the starter cord one more time. The engine roared to life like an angry monster awakened from sleep. Clay pulled back in response to the volume. The sound was amplified inside the garage walls. Vic pivoted the mower around, so it faced outside. Before Clay knew what was happening, Vice had engaged the drive of the mower and was steering it out of the garage toward the front yard.

Clay walked behind not knowing what else to do.

Vic positioned the mower at a corner where the dirt driveway, dirt street, and green grass intersected. He impatiently signaled that Clay should step closer. Over the growling sound of the mower, now in neutral, Vic started the lesson.

"Pay attention. This lever controls your speed. Pull it back to go faster. Push it forward to slow down. This lever makes the blades turn or stop. Pull back to make the blades turn. Push forward to make them stop. Now, walk with me and watch."

Vic pulled back on the throttle with his right hand; with his left hand, he pulled back on the clutch. The mower moved forward with blades spinning and cut grass spitting out behind the machine. Clay walked alongside, watching. Looked simple enough. Just walk behind the mower. At the end of the lawn where a sidewalk marked the other boundary of the property, Vic spun the mower clockwise in a smooth pivot around the right tire. Before Clay knew it, Vic and mower were headed in the opposite direction cutting a new row.

When they reached the driveway, Vic executed another flawless pivot of the machine, this time around the left tire. He pushed the clutch forward, stopping the blades, and reduced the speed by pushing the lever forward to idle.

Over the noise of the idling engine, Vic gave his last instruction. "Just follow the tire mark," he said while pointing to the long straight indentation in the grass made by the mower's left wheel in the second cut row.

Vic stepped aside and pulled Clay behind the mower. Clay reached up to grasp the handle bar. It was at an awkward height for little Clay, just below his chin. He studied the control levers to his left and right. His eyes followed the handle down to the exhaust-belching machine that growled and vibrated in front of him. He was too excited to notice the ironic fact that the handle of the mower was like the handlebar on his bike, right down to the black rubber grips.

Vic reached down and pulled the throttle back. The engine roared. Clay's heart raced.

"Pull the clutch," Vic yelled over the noise of the gas engine. "Pull the clutch."

Clay paused for a few seconds trying to remember all the instructions. He reached with his left hand and pulled the clutch cable's lever.

Instantly the roaring machine lurched forward and to the right. Clay desperately tried to gain control as the machine rolled—no, veered widely, across the lawn. The power of the mower totally surprised Clay. It looked so tame when Vic was operating it. Now it was all Clay could do to hang on and try to steer this demonic thing. Vic appeared from nowhere, grabbed the mower's handle and released the clutch. The machine stopped in its tracks. Clay's momentum continued forward and he hit his chin hard against the handle.

"What are you doing?" Vic screamed. "Hold onto the handle and steer it."

He pushed Clay aside and directed the mower back into a line parallel to his last row. Clay rubbed his sore chin.

"Keep the tire just inside the wheel mark. Overlap it a bit. Keep it straight!" he barked.

Clay was afraid of the mower now. He wasn't strong enough. Wasn't tall enough. It was too powerful, but he didn't have a choice. Vic increased the throttle and motioned to Clay to engage the clutch. Again, the mower leaped forward. Clay was ready this time though. He wrestled with the mower. It took all his strength and concentration to keep the mower moving forward rather than left or right. He kept his eye on the left tire's relationship to the previous tire mark in the grass. The beast of a mower had a mind of its own and kept twisting away from the line.

The sidewalk boundary of the lawn was getting closer. Clay panicked. He'd have to turn the machine around somehow. Could he do it? What was it Vic had done? Clay couldn't remember. The turning motion had been so fast and smooth. Did he reduce the speed? Did he disengage the clutch?

At the end of the row, all Clay could think to do was disengage the clutch to stop the machine. From behind him, he heard Vic screaming. "What are you doing? This is terrible. What's wrong with you?"

Clay reduced the throttle and turned around to see Vic standing in the newly cut path—his very first row of cut lawn, his first step from child to a big boy. The row was anything but straight. Gaps of uncut lawn stood between his row and Vic's last row.

Vic was furious and stormed up to Clay and the idling beast. "For crying out loud, steer the mower. Didn't you listen to a word I said?"

Vic pushed Clay aside, jerked the throttle and clutch. He spun the mower, so it was straddling the same row Clay had just cut. The right tire rested about six inches inside the tire mark from Vic's last row.

"Go over it again. Make it straight," Vic demanded, sweat dripping from his forehead.

Clay looked down the row. It wasn't straight. Not at all. He engaged the clutch and directed the mower the best he could. He locked his eyes on to the right tire. Had to keep that tire inside the other tire mark. As before, the mower had other ideas and fought him every foot. Above the roar of the engine, Clay could hear Vic screaming at him. "Keep it straight. What's the matter with you? Can't you do anything?"

The end of the row was approaching. Clay was determined to make the turn this time. Doing a good turn would make up for his crooked lines, he reckoned. At the end of the row, Clay tried to pivot the mower around the left tire as he had seen Vic do. But, instead of a complete 180-degree turn, Clay lost control of the mower, and it headed off at an angle toward the center of the lawn. Clay helplessly tried to steer the mower back to the line.

Vic raced to the mower taking over control after pushing Clay roughly aside. "Where in the heck are you going?" Vic was exploding with anger now. He left the mower idling in the middle of the lawn and grabbed Clay by the shirt sleeve. He pulled him over to the row Clay had finished cutting before the failed turn.

"Look at that row. Does that look straight to you?"

"No," Clay said, his voice breaking into a sob.

"Quit crying, you little crybaby. Watch me one more time. I'm losing my patience with you."

Vic stepped back to the mower and directed it to Clay's misaligned row. He set the left tire inside the previous row by half the width of the mower, a distance necessary to make up for the previous errors. He directed the mower across the lawn all the way to the sidewalk, spun it around, lined up the next cut with the same overlap and steered the mower back to Clay, standing defeated in the driveway.

"Look, it's even now. Try it again, and I'd better not have to redo your work."

And so went the remainder of the morning. Row after row, Clay tried his best to mow a straight line with the powerful mower. Though he improved, none of the rows were good enough for Vic, who'd yell and scream, then go back over each of Clay's row to straighten them out.

The last row of the lawn had been mowed and re-mowed when Clay's mother appeared wearing her apron calling them into the house for lunch.

Vic drove the mower back into the garage while eight-year-old Clay slowly ambled toward the back door of the house. He had tried this morning. Really tried.

But he had come up short. His best efforts hadn't been enough for Vic. His valiant attempt to control the mower row after row had only resulted in accusations of laziness and not paying attention. With head hung low in exhaustion and defeat, he studied his grass-stained sneakers shuffling through the straight rows of the freshly cut lawn. He found no satisfaction in the finished job. There was no level of excitement or sense of accomplishment from mowing his first lawn. Every tire line in the grass made by the heavy mower was a reminder that he wasn't good enough to make those lines straight.

Chapter 17

aughter and the sound of roller blades on concrete brought Clay out his . . . out of his what? Trance? He looked around to see who behind him was responsible for rudely pushing him down to the step. No one was there. He studied the few people mingling in the park around him. Nobody was paying any attention to him. Nothing out of the ordinary. A young couple on roller blades glided past on the trail; a few Asian nerds were huddled around a notebook studying its screen intently. Others were either strolling down to the trail or coming up from it.

Clay glanced at his watch. Amazingly, only ten minutes had passed since he had left the office. He stood and started to walk. This time nothing stopped him. With the flashback still fresh in his mind, he walked over the grass terrace, hoping the dampness wouldn't hurt the leather soles of his Ferragamo Oxfords.

No wonder I live in a houseboat now, Clay thought. *No lawn to mow. Vic was a real jerk all right.*

Clay stepped off the lawn and onto the concrete. He headed west down the multi-purpose path called the Burke Gillman Trail.

When he left the office moments ago, he was confident that upon his return he'd know how to handle the situation back at the office. Now he wasn't so sure. He had to convince George that major and immediate layoffs were unavoidable. Some of those who had to be let go played important roles in account teams that George led. But, George was a good businessman and would see the necessity of the layoffs, even if there would be a heated debate about who would get pink slipped.

The bigger question in Clay's mind was how George would react to the recommendation that Suzette, their junior partner, also be shown the door. George liked Suzette. *Why* Clay didn't know. Clay had watched with some amusement how Suzette had played up to George the past few months. The brown-nosing was obvious, but not to George.

Then there was the two of them taking sides against Clay on the Needham acquisition proposal. George wasn't going to easily agree to a move that weakened his voting power on such an important decision.

Clay's confidence had faded. He didn't know why. He just wasn't sure he could navigate through all the crap that lay ahead.

More troubled now than when he had left the office for his walk, Clay did an about-face and headed back to ADB.

The canal to his right was clear of any ship traffic at the moment. He could have used the pleasant distraction of nice super yacht right now. He needed something to erase the weird flashback from his mind. He needed something to take his mind off the painful decisions waiting back at the office. Instead of a pleasant distraction, he got an empty canal, and the rain started to fall again.

Clay's phone buzzed. The caller ID told him it was Sheryl. He kept walking briskly back to the office to get out of the rain.

"Hey, Sheryl. I'm on my way back," Clay said.

"Good, because George just got here. He'll see you in your office at 1:30."

"Perfect. Thanks. Uh, is Suzette in?"

"Yes. Last I saw she was eating a salad in her office," the ever-observant assistant responded.

"Ask her to join George and I at 3:00. And be sure that Gerald is my office at 1:30, too."

"Right. Gerald at 1:30. Suzette at 3:00," Sheryl repeated and hung up.

At the last intersection before the ADB office, Clay hesitated briefly as the crosswalk light said *Wait* in red letters. The rain intensified. Clay looked up and down the street. He dashed across against the light and didn't slow down until he was inside the building lobby. *Stupid not to have taken an umbrella.*

Clay decided to take the elevator rather than the stairs but didn't know why exactly. Something about the solitude of the gleaming elevator promised comfort to him. He realized that he was thinking more about the lawn mowing flashback than the decision he and George had to make to lay off twelve people. The memory of being yelled at for not being able to mow a straight line continued to haunt him as he rode the elevator up to the top floor.

Clay acknowledged the receptionist with a nod as he stepped from the elevator and walked directly to the men's room to dry off and pull himself together. He was relieved to see that he was the only one in the room to see him like this.

Clay's hair was a wet and tangled mess. That was to be expected. A few paper towels and a comb would fix the hair. But, what shocked him were his eyes. The eyes that stared back at him from the mirror were not the eyes of a confident, talented founder of the best marketing agency in the Northwest. These were the blue eyes of a hurt little boy.

He shook his head and blinked hard as if that would reset his eyes back to normal. His hands started to shake, and he felt a little dizzy. He turned on the cold-water faucet and splashed water on his face, a face already damp from the rain. Again and again, his hands carried the cold water to his face. He looked in the mirror. *That's more like it.* The little boy eyes were gone.

He jerked several paper towels from the dispenser and dried his hair and face. He guided a comb carefully through the tangled hair wishing there was a hair dryer in this restroom like in the men's locker room downstairs. No problem. It was Seattle. Nothing unusual about seeing someone with wet hair. His wool sports coat was very wet, so he took it off and shook it to remove some of the water that hadn't soaked in yet.

Hair combed, jacket on, Clay took one last look in the mirror. Clay looked back at him. *Showtime!*

Chapter 18

O n the way to his office, Clay stopped in the kitchen to make a cappuccino for himself and an Earl Grey tea for Sheryl. He had no idea whether she wanted the tea or not, but he felt compelled to do something nice for his invaluable assistant.

Sheryl wasn't at her desk, so Clay placed the mug of tea next to her phone. He strode into his office and shut the door behind him. Both George and Gerald were waiting for him. It was 1:31.

His partner and controller were seated at the work table. Both wore serious expressions.

"Did we disturb your shower?" George asked sarcastically after looking over Clay's appearance.

"Nope. Just doing my imitation of Gene Kelly outside," Clay responded. The banter from the two agency partners made Gerald look up from the columns of numbers on his computer screen. There was serious business to attend to, and these guys were joking around.

"Who's Gene Kelly?" Gerald asked.

Clay smiled, winked at his older partner and said, "Gene Kelly was an actor and dancer back in the old days when our George was growing up. One of his most famous movies was called *Singin' in the Rain*. It featured a very creative dance scene on a sidewalk in pouring rain. Google it some time."

"Hey," protested George, "I'm not that old. All of his movies were released years before I was even born."

"If you say so, George," Clay said teasingly while sitting down at the table. Turning serious, Clay started the meeting. "So, let me set the stage again. Not that it's necessary, but I think it will help us focus. Then, Gerald, talk us through the financial options we have. I want decision and plan before 3:00 p.m."

George asked, "Shouldn't Suzette be here for this?"

Gerald was suddenly very occupied with the spreadsheet on the computer.

"I asked her to join us at 3:00 p.m., George. I didn't want her team to get spooked by her being in a closed-door meeting you us." It was a lie, but Clay had to admit that keeping her visible in the office would help ease the nerves of her team for a little while longer.

Clay continued.

"Lazzr fired Loretta last night. They fired us this morning. The official termination letter should arrive from their attorney at any time. No chance of reversing their decision. I think the founders have been working on this for some time. Another agency has been retained already. I expect the announcement will be made as soon as we sign the termination agreement."

"Any guess to who the new shop is?" George asked.

"No. This was a total shock to Loretta, too. And, it doesn't matter right now. What matters today is our financial situation. It is precarious. Gerald, walk us through the numbers for the first two scenarios only."

Gerald concisely laid it out for the two partners. The money they were losing. The depleted cash reserves, and the solution—an immediate firing of 12 people.

George studied the numbers in front of him while sipping bottled water. "The numbers don't lie. We have to cut back on staff. Which brings the next question. Who gets the axe?"

Gerald handed out another printout with rows of names of all employees and partners including their average billable hours for past three months, the accounts they are assigned to, and their salary. Shaded in gray at the top of the list were twelve names.

"George, this morning I asked Gerald to prepare some alternatives for our consideration this afternoon," Clay explained.

"I see," George said while reviewing the names. "This can't be right. The list has two of my best creative directors for the LowG and Port Authority accounts. Axing them puts those two accounts in jeopardy."

"They are on the list for two reasons, George. First, their average billable hours are 15 percent below other creative directors. They aren't being utilized as much. And second, the list must include at least six high-salary people, or else we're not cutting enough overhead," Gerald explained.

George continued the debate with Gerald. Clay was unusually quiet.

"Their utilization is down temporarily. If you look at the past year, you'll see a different picture. I tell you if we cut Karla and Sammy there's a real chance we'll lose LowG and Port Authority within six months. No way can our finances and reputation withstand losing three accounts in one year. Who else can we cut?" George demanded.

And so the discussion went back and forth over the next forty-five minutes. Clay joined in from time to time. Who was invaluable? Who wasn't? Who did the client love? Who was expendable? Around and around the three debated. After mostly constructive, but often heated, discussion they had reached a stalemate. The numbers didn't work without including George's two creative directors. Clay agreed with George that cutting this creative duo would hurt the shop sooner or later.

It was time. Clay said, "Gerald, hand me the other scenario I asked you to work up. And, you can go now. Great work today. Please don't leave the office, we may need you to crunch some more numbers."

Gerald handed Clay two identical reports, snapped close his notebook, and walked out the door.

Clay looked at George and said, "Well, partner, we're in a fine fix aren't we?"

"Indeed, we are, Clay. I really regret voting to staff up in anticipation of higher billings."

"No sense having regrets for past decisions," Clay said. "There is one more scenario for us to consider."

"How could there be, we looked at Gerald's list every way possible."

"George, I'm going to show you a list of people we can let go that doesn't include Karla and Sammy, but gets us to the $240,000 reduction we need." Clay handed George a copy of the report and watched his partner and friend's face closely.

George Davis was a legend in the agency business. He had started and sold three different graphic design and advertising companies in California and Washington by the time his path crossed Clay's at a marketing conference in San Francisco.

In the mirror-lined bar at the Sir Francis Drake hotel, Clay was standing at the bar waiting for his single malt to be served. George elbowed his way through the crowd until he was next to Clay and able to get the bartender's attention. The bartender served Clay his glass of Aberlour neat with a second glass of water. George caught the eye of the bartender and ordered "Aberlour neat with water on the side please."

Clay lifted his glass in salute to George after hearing his drink order.

"Good choice, my man. That's what I'm drinking, too. My name is Clay Austin."

The story varies from there depending on who is telling it and how much alcohol had been consumed before the storytelling began. But every version of the story ends the same way. By the end of that night, the two men had become friends with a plan to "create the best agency in the world" together.

And now, ten years later, Clay was studying the face of his partner as they wrestled to keep their dream, their reputation, their livelihood intact.

George's face was lined with deep crevasses around the eyes and mouth that gave him character. People saw him as the elder statesman of the agency, which he was. His bushy red hair was fighting a losing battle against the advance of gray, but that too added to his respectability in the eyes of clients and staff.

He had a relatively slender body only recently falling victim to an expanding waistline. After suffering a mild heart attack three years ago, George stopped smoking, started exercising regularly, and eating more wisely. He owned 33 percent of ADB. He had confided to Clay early last year that he was planning on retiring in a few years as soon as Clay could buy him out.

Now, Clay thought while watching his partner, George was likely very scared that the very comfortable retirement he had worked so hard to secure was in serious risk.

George spoke at last. Slowly and calmly he asked, "Are you serious, Clay? This list includes Suzette."

"George, I wanted to consider all the options. As you can see, Suzette's comp is equal to Tammy and Karla's combined. Her billings have been declining, and her hard-headedness with Lazzr's campaign schedule was the tipping point to our being fired."

George took off his glasses and set them on the table. Everyone knew this was a sign that George was thinking deeply about something.

"Suzette brings a lot to ADB. I don't have to tell you that, Clay," George said.

"Not as much as she used to, I'm afraid," responded Clay. "She has taken her eyes off billings. She hasn't brought in any new business since Lazzr, and let's face it; it was my relationship with Loretta that got us in the door there."

"You're right, but letting a partner go can get messy. Think about how it'll look on the street, Clay."

Clay looked directly at his partner. "How will it look if the Port Authority and LowG dump us because we fired the creative whizzes that these clients adore? We won't survive more client losses, George. No more ADB."

George looked back at Clay, then to the report in his hand, then to Clay.

"I like Suzette. She has a lot of spunk," George said thoughtfully.

"I know you like Suzette, but she's no longer carrying her weight. She's no longer contributing at a level that justifies her stature as junior partner," Clay argued.

He looked at his watch. Time was running out. Suzette would be here in ten minutes. Clay realized his heart was racing. His mind was fluctuating between certainty and doubt like a strobe light in a techno dance club.

George placed the glasses back onto his head and sat up erect. "Let's do this thing in two stages. Today we'll let everyone go on the list except Tammy and Karla. Tomorrow, in our scheduled partner meeting, we'll tell Suzette. This will give our attorneys time to draft the termination agreement."

Clay was beaming inside but managed to hold it back.

"Wise move. Great suggestion. I'll have Gerald prepare another list of ten to show to Suzette. Let's announce the layoffs at 4:00 p.m. Everyone on the list will be escorted out of the building by 4:15. Why don't you schedule an all-hands meeting for 4:30?"

"Right," replied George.

"Oh, one other request," Clay said. "I think you're the perfect guy to lead the company meeting."

This was a last-minute idea of Clay's. As majority shareholder and managing partner, it was typical for Clay to lead company meetings. But most of the employees had never experienced a layoff at ADB. It would be a huge shock to hear about the loss of an account and the loss of ten colleagues. George was more of a father figure and had been the majority owner of ADB until Clay purchased 19 percent of the company shares from George four years ago. Besides, it would fall on Clay's shoulders to make another announcement on Thursday that Suzette's name would be removed from the agency's door.

Clay's desk phone buzzed. He walked to the phone.

"Yes? Okay. Give me five minutes and send her in."

Clay hung up. And immediately pushed the extension number for Gerald. He answered it on the first ring.

"Gerald speaking."

"Gerald, this is Clay. Revise the first list. Remove Tammy and Karla. Suzette will not be on the list. Bring it to me immediately. Got it?"

"Yes, sir, Gerald replied and hung up.

Clay walked to the door and opened it.

"Hey, Suzette, thanks for being on time. Come on in. The three of us have some big decisions to make."

She walked by him into the office. Clay glanced out at Sheryl. She looked back and held up her mug of tea as if to say, *thanks*.

Clay nodded. Showing a little kindness with the tea had made him feel a little better, considering he had to fire ten people today.

He closed the office door.

Chapter 19

Since George was already seated at the work table in Clay's office, Suzette took a chair across the table from him.

Clay took his usual seat at the head of the table. The chair was completely different from the other five chairs. In fact, it was different in style from everything in the office. It didn't fit the clean, modern décor at all. It was heavy and looked sturdy rather than sleek. The ornate arms were hand-carved mahogany. On the front of each arm was a carved lion's head. The back of the chair rose a full foot higher than Clay's head when he sat down. It too was ornately carved. The seat cushion was regally upholstered in gold and red fabric. A matching pillow was in the chair providing lumbar support for an otherwise rigid and uncomfortable chair. Clay often thought it would be more at home in one of the old mansions in Seattle's Queen Anne Hill neighborhood than in a modern and hip agency like his.

But the chair kept its place at the head of the table anyway. It had been a birthday gift from George and Sheryl—their way of reminding him he was the king of the agency. That was something he tended to forget from time to time. Even today, as the weight of the moment and his unsettling episode in the park pressed down on him, he felt undeserving of the chair's stature.

Clay started, hoping his direct tone didn't reveal the inner battle that was raging inside him, "I'll get right to it. By the end of this meeting, we will have an agreement on how to cut expenses to be in line with billings." His two partners both nodded their heads ever so slightly in recognition of the severity of the moment.

"In our last partner meeting, we saw the P&L statement and cash flow forecast that Gerald had prepared. It was gloomy, but not without a glimmer of hope." Clay looked to George, wanting him to say something supportive. George got that hint. He cleared his throat as he often did when nervous, and spoke.

"I recall we decided to not take any actions at that point because we believed Lazzr was just a week or so away from ramping up their launch activity. The expected increase would have gotten us to the break-even point," said George.

Suzette added, "That's what we *all* believed based on the situation." She emphasized *all* to make it clear she wasn't guilty of misreading the situation. Clay and George shared the same belief.

Clay was not eager to get into a blame game. At least not in this meeting. Thursday's meeting would be different. "Yeah, we were thrown a major league curveball with the count 3 and 2. We swung and missed. So, let's get on with the reason we're here—saving the agency."

There was a knock on the office door. Expecting Gerald with the financial reports, Clay shouted, "Come on in." Then to his partners, "Here are the numbers for us to consider."

Gerald walked directly to the table holding four sheets of paper. He handed one sheet to each partner and kept the fourth for himself. Still standing, Gerald waited until George motioned that he should sit.

Clay explained, "You can see in the table at the top our projected revenue and expenses for the next six months. We're staring at a $240,000 loss. Without cutting expenses immediately, we will have no other option than covering the expenses out of our own pockets. Something I'm sure none of us are prepared to do for this long." Clay was watching Suzette who was seated at this right. She was seeing the numbers for the first time.

"How were the ten names on the list selected?" Suzette zeroed in on the list of personnel being considered for pink slips.

Clay responded, "This morning I asked Gerald to work up a cost-cutting plan. What was the criteria you used, Gerald?"

Like the accountant he was, Gerald revealed in a matter-of-fact tone his formula involving gross salary, utilization factor, and involvement with the Lazzr account.

Suzette studied the list. Her Lazzr team was going to be decimated. Only a few had substantial roles on other accounts and were completely vulnerable. Completely expendable.

George spoke up, "Each of us is losing talent we don't want to lose." He hoped the statement would prevent Suzette from becoming combative.

"I don't understand why we're letting go so many senior people. There must be another way," Suzette complained.

Clay nodded at Gerald giving him permission to explain.

"It was the only way to reach the $240K number," Gerald said.

"Well, where are those other scenarios? I'd like to see them," demanded Suzette looking defiantly at Gerald.

Clay was prepared for this response, and before Gerald could speak, he interrupted. "Suzette, you don't need to see all the other options. George and I have looked at them and believe us; this is the only one that works."

"That's right. In the end, only one option got us to where we can be on solid financial ground within a few weeks," George said.

Suzette paused and studied her two partners. She couldn't have liked losing so many of her people, Clay knew, but that's the agency biz. When an account walks, staff get the boot. Clay could see by the expression on her face that she wanted to put up more of a fight, to show a level of loyal support for her team. But in the end, she didn't, her own self-interest winning the day. "Okay, I don't like losing these people, especially to our competitors who are going to grab them. You must have considered the impact of this talent going to another shop."

"Oh, we have, Suzette. We've considered all the ramifications. Keeping ADB financially sound and able to service our clients exceptionally well has to be our number one goal," George stated.

"Gerald, thank you for the excellent work today. You're excused but stay in your office for a while. We'll need you again," Clay said. "Oh, and ask Sheryl to come in with her laptop."

Gerald left, and Sheryl entered the room.

"Sheryl, please make a record for the official Partner Notes," Clay instructed.

Sheryl sat at the table and typed while Clay and George recapped the decision to lay off ten people. Each of the names were read from the list, and Sheryl entered them into the record. She had friends on the list, Clay knew, but she showed no emotion.

It was agreed that right after the meeting George would convene with Gerald and Ravenna, their outsourced HR Manager to implement the layoff at 4:00 p.m. today. The connection to the company's computer network for those on the list would be cut at exactly 4:00. Each would be called into Ravenna's office to be given their termination letter. They would be given fifteen minutes to clean out their desks and then politely escorted out of the building. Each employee would be given two weeks of severance pay.

George had already announced a company meeting for 4:30 for the remaining employees.

With everyone gone from his office, Clay stood up wearily from the king's chair. He reached for the comfort of his half-consumed cappuccino and sipped it while staring out the window into the dreary light of a winter afternoon. Had he really considered all of the possibilities?

His desk phone buzzed. Sheryl announced that the company attorney was on line one.

"Hey, Reuben, am I keeping life interesting enough for you?" Clay light-heartedly said, trying desperately to rid himself of the dread that filled his head.

"Yes, you are. I don't hear from you for months and then bang-bang," said Reuben. "First, I want you to know that I received Lazzr's termination agreement from their attorney. It is completely in line with the terms of our original agency-client agreement. No surprises or special requests."

"That's a relief," sighed Clay.

"Second, I've drafted the termination letter for Suzette as you requested. It is in your email. It is completely in line with her employment agreement," said Reuben.

"Can it be contested?" asked Clay.

"Anything can be contested, but you and George are being fair. She'd be stupid to fight you in court on this. Besides, she is a minor partner. You and George call the shots."

"We sure do. Speaking of shots. We're firing ten people today. Gotta cut expenses fast because of losing Lazzr. Ravenna is handling the terminations, so I expect everything to be done by the book."

"I expected a layoff was imminent. Thanks for letting me know though," Reuben said.

"Thanks for the quick turnaround on all this. Our meeting with Suzette is in the morning. Will you be reachable in case we need you?"

"Absolutely, I'm in my office all day. Just call."

"Thank you and goodbye," Clay said and hung up.

Clay collapsed into his chair and punched his keyboard to wake up the computer. The display on one monitor opened first to reveal his calendar.

"Oh, crap!"

Clay grabbed his cell and hit the speed dial for Dr. Shildstein.

"Hello, you've reached Dr. Shildstein. I'm in session right now and can't answer the phone. Please leave a message so I can return your call. Have a blessed day."

"Hi, doctor, this is Clay Austin. I screwed up. We have a 4:30 appointment today, but I have an urgent company-wide meeting to attend. I won't be able to leave until 4:45. I'll be at your office around 5:00. Please text me to confirm that this is okay, or if we need to reschedule. Sorry, doctor. Kinda crazy around here."

Kinda crazy? That's a huge understatement Clay thought. He sipped his coffee and noticed that his hand was shaking ever so slightly.

Chapter 20

The ten employees deemed expendable were summarily given their walking papers and a box for their personal effects. The building's guard escorted the ten out of the building and watched each load their cars and drive away from the parking garage. There would be no mischief. No keying of the partners' cars by disgruntled ex-employees. More importantly, the guard had the photo of each employee on his computer and in his brain. He'd be on alert if they returned to the office.

Between 4:10 and 4:30 you could hear a pin drop at ADB. Employees were in shock. For good reason. This was the first layoff any of them had experienced at the agency. For several, it was their first layoff ever.

Suzette was in her office with door closed. George was in his office making notes for the company meeting. His door was open. Clay, too was in his office on the phone talking with the Yukon Air team who were in Anchorage presenting the new campaign to the client. They told him that the client was very excited about the campaign concepts and was going to boost the media budget as soon as the initial market tests were known.

"Great job, guys, and gals!" Clay said. For a minute, he forgot all about the miserable day. This is what he lived for—happy clients. After letting them tell him all about the presentation, he had to give them the bad news about the layoff. He hated to add bad news on top of such great news, but he wanted them to hear it from him. He reassured them that their jobs were secure, but there would be shifting of account responsibility necessary. "Hey, I'm going to patch you through to Sheryl who can figure out a way for you to hear the company meeting at 4:30. I won't want you to miss it, okay?"

Clay put the call on hold. Walked out to Sheryl's desk and asked her to make it possible for the team in Anchorage to hear the meeting. Whatever it took.

Back inside his office Clay felt strangely uplifted. The light outside looked a little brighter, too, which was impossible he knew, but still, it wasn't as dreary as before.

He loved good news. And there was no better news for an agency than news followed by "the client loved it". Whether it was a successful pitch for a new client or a new campaign presentation to an existing client, those were magic words of affirmation. Seeing the client get excited about the work really meant a lot to Clay. Heck, it meant a lot to everyone in the agency. But to Clay, it was like life or death. Like breath or suffocation. *Wait a minute!* He couldn't believe where his mind was going now. Rather than think about the company meeting in a few minutes, here he sat like some amateur shrink analyzing his emotions.

But he couldn't stop. *Winning is everything*, he thought. *Losing is like death.* He shook his head. Why did he take it so seriously? Why did he light up so much when a client said, "Great job, Clay."

The answer was out there but came in and out of sight like white lines on the road in a thick fog.

"Clay, it's time for the company meeting," Sheryl announced while standing in the doorway. She glanced twice at Clay. He didn't look totally present. He looked miles away. Then snapping too, he looked up at her, placed his cell into his pocket and followed Sheryl out of the office.

This floor of the agency was rimmed by private offices, several small rooms configured for meetings of two or three people, and two large conference rooms suitable for meetings of up to twelve people. The interior consisted of a centralized kitchen, office cubes, and randomly placed easy chairs, sofas, and bean bags. In the end of the office nearest the reception area was the most open space, and it was there where the thirty-two remaining employees of ADB and its three partners congregated for the company meeting.

Everyone who could stand did. The two employees in wheelchairs positioned themselves in front of those standing. Clay noticed with a small smile that nearly everyone had a beverage of some sort in their hands, including Clay. Coffee mugs were outnumbered by cans of highly caffeinated energy drinks.

George positioned himself to face the employees. This placed him in front of the elevator. Suzette was standing close to the crowd to George's right. Clay stood to George's left, about ten paces. Just far enough away to make it clear George was the leader of the meeting, but Clay was there in front to be observed and to observe. Clay knew that his body language was going to be studied by the employees.

At 4:30 sharp, Clay reached behind him and flicked the light switch off and on to signal the start of the meeting. The crowd's voices immediately fell silent.

George cleared his throat twice and spoke. "Thank you, everyone, for gathering on such short notice. I promise that this will be short," he began.

"You've probably noticed that I have a mic." He glanced down toward the lavalier mic clamped to his sports coat lapel. "That's because the Yukon Air account team is listening from their hotel room in Anchorage. Say hi." With that George unclipped the mic, held it at arm's length toward the crowd. The crowd in front of him yelled hello in a dozen different ways, including more than one good-natured jab about staying clear of the moose crossings. George was good at this, Clay thought.

George re-clipped the tiny mic onto his lapel. "We're going to hear more about Yukon Air, but first I want to speak to you about the state of ADB and the layoffs this afternoon."

He cleared his throat again, giving away his nervousness that was otherwise well concealed.

"Late last year Clay, Suzette and I made a decision to increase the size of ADB in expectation of higher billings. Some of you were hired as a result of that decision. We felt we lacked some talent in certain areas, and we also believed we needed additional bandwidth to handle the business that was forecast to come. Well, it didn't. The economy unexpectedly stalled, and our clients cut back. You know the story of how it's been this year." George swept his right hand, palm up, in front of him. Heads nodded up and down in the crowd.

"The truth is, the agency has been losing money every month this year. Our expenses were out of line with revenue. We hoped that Lazzr's new campaign would provide the additional short-term revenue we needed to at least break even." Eyes slowly turned toward Suzette who pretended not to notice.

George continued. "Then, this morning we received word from Lazzr they were terminating our relationship." As if a bomb had just gone off in the room, heads that had been studying the floor while George spoke, suddenly snapped to attention. Clay watched as eyes nervously scanned the three partners while George spoke. He felt uncomfortable but kept a look of somber confidence on his face. Suzette reacted differently. Her face was reddening slightly as she stared forward at George, not daring to look at the employees. She stepped forward, and half raised her hand as if to say, *I want to say something now.*

George noticed Suzette's movement to the front. He held his hand out signaling to her to stop. "Please wait a few minutes, Suzette, let me finish." She stopped. Now clearly embarrassed and angry she retreated to her place.

"Yes, the news about Lazzr was totally unexpected. Unfortunately, with no boost in revenue from Lazzr our financial picture was looking grim. We had no choice but to cut staff. But what I'm going to say next is really important for you to hear." He paused. "With the adjustments to overhead that we've made today, the agency is on solid financial ground once again." George paused for a second. "We don't anticipate any further reduction of staff will be required." Clay sensed a collective sigh of relief from the employees.

George said a few more words about the importance of staying focused on servicing our clients. He mentioned that there were some prospective new clients on the horizon. He was concise and to the point. Better yet, he was believable. Some of the employees were asking questions now. George and Suzette fielded the questions.

Clay sipped his coffee and continued to study the faces of his employees. Some still had concerns, he could tell. Others were ready to get back to work. So why did Clay feel he was being watched? Not just watched; he felt examined. No, worse than examined. He felt accused. He stood there feeling like everyone in the room right this very minute was accusing him of causing the whole fiasco leading to the layoff of ten friends and colleagues. He agreed to the staff build-up. He was friends with Lazzr's CMO but couldn't prevent them being fired. The sensation was terrible. He had failed the people who trusted him. *If only I was better, all this could have been prevented.*

Clay's phone buzzed in his pocket. The vibrating calendar alert told him he had to leave for his appointment with Dr. Shildstein. The agency meeting was breaking up. As employees headed to their desks, Clay slipped back to his office, grabbed his notebook and coat, and slipped out of the office unnoticed.

Chapter 21

t was 5:02 when Dr. Shildstein heard the doorbell of her bungalow office. She opened the door almost immediately.

"Clay, so glad you made it; please come in," said the doctor.

"Thank you for being flexible, doctor. I apologize about having to reschedule. I don't like doing that," said Clay.

"The important thing is you're here. Have a seat and let's get started."

Clay removed his overcoat and hung it on the rack by the door. He sat on the couch facing her chair.

Dr. Shildstein studied her patient. On the outside, he seemed calm, in control. But she was well-trained to see below the surface of her patients. With Clay, she didn't have to see very deep to know that he was troubled. Clay's eyes were the first to betray him. They weren't calm at all. They flickered about nervously as if trying to watch a hundred TV screens in the room at the same time.

There were circles under his eyes, a sign of restless nights. He didn't sit straight up on the coach but slumped into the cushions like a despondent, pouting teenager. That was a sign of tremendous stress and the onset of depression. Clay's smile tried to be warm, but she knew the smile was a brave attempt to hold back a primal scream.

"Tell me about your week. How have you been since we last talked?"

"It's been interesting."

"How so?" She noticed his emphasis on the word *interesting*.

"I had to lay off ten people today. We lost an account. No choice but to cut back." Clay answered in a matter-of-fact tone.

"How did that make you feel?"

"I didn't like it, but we had to cut overhead, or else the entire shop would have gone under within a few months."

"What didn't you like about it?"

"Have you ever had to fire a lot of people, doctor?" Clay was beginning to show irritation.

"Fortunately, I haven't. What's it like?"

"It sucks. It really sucks," said Clay despondently.

The psychiatrist sensed Clay was feeling a lot worse even than his short statements and slumped body language revealed. She needed him to open up, so she changed tactics.

"I can see that you are sad about having to fire people. Help me understand the situation better. You said that your company lost an account. Staff reductions were necessary as a result. Can you tell me a little about the situation with the client you lost?" She wanted Clay to open up, and the best way was to have him talk about what he knows—his business. And I don't need a lot of details, Clay, just the facts so I can really understand what you're going through."

Clay poured a glass of water from the carafe on the coffee table in front of him and took several sips. He set the glass down and started to talk. In just five minutes Clay summarized the Lazzr situation.

Dr. Shildstein was amazed at how concisely her distraught patient was able to describe the situation to her. He failed to convey his emotions with clarity, but ask him to describe a business situation, and his response was incredibly vivid.

"That must be very disheartening," the doctor responded, "to lose an account you've had for years."

"Worse than disheartening. It is frustrating, very frustrating." Clay took another sip from his glass. The slight shaking of his hand while holding the glass did not go unnoticed by the doctor.

"Clay, can you describe the frustration for me?"

Clay set the glass down on the coffee table. He was sitting ramrod straight on the edge of the couch now. He glared at the doctor. Again, there was irritation in his eyes.

"If you must know, I felt really frustrated because we had been very effective for Lazzr over the years." Clay began to speak louder. "Made them a lot of money, to be honest. Then, we get fired for no good reason. Those ungrateful SOBs!" Clay stopped suddenly as if his own anger had just slapped him in the face. He slouched back into the sofa. "No matter what I do it's not good enough," he muttered under his breath.

Dr. Shildstein had been taking notes while watching and listening intently to Clay. After years of practice, she was able to write notes in her journal without ever looking at the paper. This way she never lost eye contact with her patients even while recording critical observations. So, she saw Clay slouch into the sofa in an expression of emotional surrender after a display of anger and indignation. She saw his lips move. She barely heard him whisper. *"No matter what I do, it's not good enough."*

Her writing hand immediately made a star in her notes to indicate a key observation.

"Clay, I don't think I heard the thing you said. It was very softly stated. Can you repeat it."

"Sure, I said 'those ungrateful SOBs'," Clay responded.

"Yes, I heard that. What did you say after you sat back on the sofa?"

Clay thought. He didn't recall saying a word.

"I didn't say anything," he said

"Yes, you muttered something to yourself. You don't recall?"

"No."

"It sounded to me that you said, 'no matter what I do it's not good enough'," the doctor said.

Clay gazed at the doctor. His eyes didn't blink. The doctor noticed a vacancy in Clay's eyes that were looking directly at her. No, not really looking at her, he was looking right through her, she thought. She could tell that at this very moment Clay was not present to her or this room. Clay was somewhere else.

"Clay, I'm relatively certain I heard you say those words. I even wrote them in my notes. Let me ask you something. You said the Lazzr account was the responsibility of Suzette, your partner. So, why do you feel that what you did wasn't good enough?"

"I just feel that way sometimes," Clay said, still collapsed into the deep cushion of the sofa's back. At this very moment, he didn't feel like a successful business executive. Not at all.

"When else do you feel that way, or say that to yourself?"

"I don't know."

"Can you remember the first time you thought that way? Perhaps as a kid growing up?"

Clay shrugged, frowned, and tried to think back to when he first had this sense that he wasn't good enough.

Dr. Shildstein saw that Clay was struggling to answer the question, but not resisting. That was progress. She decided to probe.

"Did anything ever happen to you in school? Kids laughing at you for not knowing the answer to a teacher's question?"

"No."

"Did you play sports? Any feeling of not being good enough for the team?"

Clay laughed, "Sure, but I really wasn't good enough for first string most years. I was comfortable with my physical limitations on the field and on the court." Clay was actually smiling.

"I recall from our last session that you and your mother were very close. Did she ever do or say anything that made you feel not good enough, perhaps not good enough for her love?" The doctor watched Clay carefully.

"Not once," Clay said without hesitation.

"What about your father?"

"Which one?" Clay asked.

"Oh, well, let's see." The doctor quickly flipped through her session notes. "Ah, you said your biological father left you and your mother when you were four."

"That's what they tell me, yeah,"

"And you don't remember anything about the day he left?"

"Nope."

The doctor was writing furiously in her session journal. She could talk and write at the same time too.

"Your mother remarried, when? You were nine?"

"No, seven," Clay corrected.

"That was to Vic, correct?"

"Yes."

Clay reached for his water glass. It was still three-quarters full, but he poured in more water from the carafe anyway. Dr. Shildstein never stopped writing. She noted his every movement.

"What about Vic? Did he ever say or do anything to make you feel not good enough?"

Clay smiled, but it was a sad smile. The sadness was so pronounced on Clay's face, Dr. Shildstein was reminded of a circus clown she had seen as a child. She had wanted so desperately to make the clown happy—to give him a happy smile. Little wonder she became a psychiatrist. And now sitting in front of her was one of her patients looking just like that circus clown. But, Clay wasn't wearing any makeup.

"Sure he did. Like every day," Clay said, still wearing the sad smile.

"I see. Can you tell me the first time you remember?"

"Doctor, I can tell you the first, second, third, and 103rd time."

"Please tell me the about the first event you remember."

Clay told her about the lawn mowing episode with Vic and the monster Briggs & Stratton mower. It took him less than three minutes to recount the story. It helped a lot that he had just relived the entire episode that every afternoon on the park steps by the canal.

"That was very traumatic. Can you remember when Vic complemented you on a good job of mowing the lawn after you got better at it?"

"Never got a compliment about the lawn," Clay said without hesitating.

The doctor started to ask another question about the lawn mowing event, but Clay stopped her. He had a score to settle with Vic.

"Wait, there's more. Wait until you hear about the wood."

Clay proceeded to tell the wood stacking story. Once again, his perfect recall enabled him to tell the story powerfully in about three minutes.

While Clay spoke, the doctor watched him intently as her fingers guided the pen back and forth across the page. Never did a sentence stray from between the ruled lines of the page.

When the wood-stacking story ended, Clay drank more water from his glass. He stood up nervously and walked slowly around the room looking at the items on shelves and the wonderful photo and art collection of hot air balloons.

Dr. Shildstein stopped writing and started talking. "Thank you for sharing those events with me, Clay. You were a boy looking for the love and acceptance of a father. Vic didn't know how to give that kind of love and patience. He just knew discipline—that's probably how he was raised."

"Would it have hurt him to give me some encouragement?" Clay said bitterly.

"No, but based on how he treated you I bet he was raised as harshly by his parents, if not more so."

"Well, having a normal father would have been really nice." Clay said.

He continued to study the photos, water colors, and acrylics on the office walls. The doctor noticed that one in particular seemed to captivate him. It was a balloon soaring over a beautiful lighthouse. Three-quarters of a purple cross was visible on the white balloon. No other insignia was present.

I need to take a ride in one of these things. Yep, as soon as life settles down at the agency, I'm going for a ride in a balloon.

Clay sat back down on the sofa. The doctor watched and waited for him to say something.

"So, Dr. Shildstein, you should know that I've had a very disturbing week that actually started Tuesday night after leaving here."

"Oh? Tell me about it. We still have a little time left." They were making great progress. She didn't want to stop, but rules were rules, and besides, it was nearly six o'clock, and she had tickets to the theater.

Clay proceeded to tell her everything in concise, vivid detail as if he was writing descriptive ad copy. He told her about The Stranger in his house saying, 'stack it again.' The strong reminiscence of the wood stacking episode triggered by a wood rack next to the fireplace, the haunting memory of the lawn mowing hallucination triggered by nothing more than straight lines in freshly mowed grass at the park.

"Doctor, am I going crazy?" Clay asked. He was dead serious.

Dr. Shildstein put down her pen and smiled. "No, Clay, you're not going crazy. The pressure you're feeling at the office is forcing to the surface this perception of not being good enough. The office challenge is inflaming this fear that no matter what you do you won't be good enough to be accepted; to be loved."

Clay drank more water, wishing for something much stronger.

"I've had business challenges before and never had nightmares, mysterious voices in my house, or upsetting flashes from the past."

"Have you ever faced losing your company?"

"No, this is the worst financial situation we've been in."

"Your successful company is a daily reminder to yourself that you are good enough, Clay. But, a client rejected you. Your company is under attack, in a financial sense. Therefore, you feel under attack. Your entire sense of worth—of being good enough in your mind—is under attack, too."

"Attack? Who's attacking me?"

Dr. Shildstein looked at her watch. "We'll have to get into that in our next session when we have more time. Let me say this to you now," she said.

In the last sentence, the doctor's tone changed from clinical to a motherly softness that surprised Clay.

She continued in the same soft tone, her eyes locked on his. "The attack is very real. And it will be defeated.

She stood and escorted her troubled patient to the door. "See you next week, Clay."

As he drove home from the doctor's office, her words kept echoing through his head. "The attack is very real. And it will be defeated."

What the heck was he supposed to do with that idea? Clay thought the doctor missed her calling. She should have been a mystery novel writer the way she left him hanging.

The rain had stopped, and a full moon was low in the sky. Clay opened the sunroof and turned up the heat so he wouldn't get chilled in the cold winter air. He took the long way home, wanting a few more minutes to clear his head.

At home, he poured a single malt scotch, grabbed the last cigar from his humidor and took both up to his roof-top deck. It was an amazing sight. It was utterly calm on Lake Union, so all of the city's lights were vividly reflected. It was as if he was seeing two heavens. One above in the sky with stars, and the other below in the lake with reflected lights.

He pulled his coat collar up against the chill and sat down in his favorite deck chair. Alternating between puffs on the Macanudo cigar and sips of his Aberlour 16-year-old scotch he managed to put the week behind him. *Attack or no attack I have a very big meeting tomorrow. Suzette must go, and she won't go lightly.*

Clay pulled out his cell. He punched the number in his Contacts for Northlake Pizza and ordered a Logger Special for takeout. By the time he had finished his cigar and scotch, the wonderful pizza would be ready for him.

Then he quickly checked his business email. Yes, the termination papers for Suzette had been sent to him and George. He'd read them later.

For now, though, he puffed and sipped, taking in the tastes as completely as he took in the moonlit night.

Chapter 22

"Clay, both George, and Suzette are in the McCann room waiting for you," Sheryl announced.

Showtime!

Clay was eager to get the partner meeting done and over with. He and George had compared notes via phone before either had reached the office. They were in agreement on the terms of firing Suzette. The issue of how to divide her shares between them after her termination would be settled in a subsequent meeting.

Clay grabbed his tablet, coffee mug, and a folder containing the termination letter the agency's attorney had drafted. The attorney was standing by at his office downtown in case he was needed.

George and Clay had also agreed to make this meeting short, firm and business-like.

Clay strode into the agency's second conference room two minutes late. He sat at the head of the long table. George was seated to his right and Suzette to his left.

"Good morning. If there are no objections, I want to call this meeting of ADB partners to order." As the words came out of Clay's mouth, he realized it would probably be the last time he would refer to his firm as ADB. After today it would be AD, or Austin Davis, just like the old days.

"No objections here," said George.

"Likewise," said Suzette.

"Yesterday was a tough day for all of us," Clay said referring to the layoff. "Is there anything anyone wants to say about it?"

George spoke up, "I've already had six calls from other shops wanting to know what happened. The sneaky SOBs were extending their condolences, but I could tell they were fishing for information."

"That was expected. Can't blame them. I've done it myself," Clay admitted.

"Well, I didn't give them anything they could use against us. And I encouraged them to hire the folks we let go," said George.

"Several of the people you laid off called me at home last night," said Suzette.

You laid off. Clay caught her language. Not *we laid off*, but *you laid off*. As if she had no part in the agency's dire financial situation or the mandatory decision to cut ten people from the payroll. He wanted to reach across the table and strangle her. He took a sip of coffee and caught George looking at him. Both men were seething.

"What did they want? What did you tell them? You know, it's not a good idea to talk to terminated employees," George said.

"They just wanted to understand what happened and why they were chosen," replied Suzette.

"They were given that information personally by Ravenna. Anything more was unnecessary and unwise. Very unwise, Suzette," George cleared his throat in agitation.

"I didn't see any harm in it," said Suzette defensively.

"Suzette, let's hope that last night you didn't make us vulnerable to a lawsuit," Clay said, barely able to contain his anger.

"I know what to say and what not to say. I . . ."

Clay cut her off. "Look that's water under the bridge now. I want us to address the agenda, which includes two topics. Our financial situation and the acquisition offer by Pitt-Needham," Clay asserted.

"Fine. We already know the financials, Clay. That issue has been resolved by cutting staff," Suzette said. "I want to vote on the Pitt-Needham offer." She was glowering at Clay. Her voice challenging.

Clay felt his anger and impatience begin to race to the surface. She was forgetting her place. She was a junior partner with just seventeen percent of the shares. George saw that look in Clay's eyes and wisely took control of the conversation. He knew what Clay was like when he lost control of his temper.

"Actually Suzette, the financial issues are not resolved," said George sternly. "If you had cared to study the financials as carefully as Clay and me, you would have noticed that terminating ten people wasn't enough. It didn't add up to the $240,000 reduction target."

Suzette looked puzzled. Clay let his partner control the conversation, not trusting himself to take the next steps professionally.

George cleared his throat twice and continued, "Which is why we find it necessary to terminate your partnership effective immediately." George slide the folder containing the termination letter toward Suzette.

"What!" Suzette screamed. "You can't fire me like this. I'm a partner."

Clay reentered the conversation. "Yes, we can. Yes, we have. You're a junior partner. According to your contract and partnership agreement, you can be terminated by a vote of the majority of the shareholders."

Suzette fumed while reading the termination letter.

George tried to soften Clay's hardline statement and provide some justification. "Listen, Suzette, Lazzr was your account. You lost it. Your billings are below your goals for the year, and there is no sign that they can turn around, especially with Lazzr gone."

"I didn't lose Lazzr, Clay did," Suzette claimed. "He didn't do enough to sell my plan with Loretta."

Clay shot up out of his chair like an angry rocket. The sudden and violent motion shocked George and Suzette completely. While standing, Clay placed both fisted hands on the table top and leaned forward over the table. He was practically leaning into Suzette's face. He could see blackheads in the crease where her nose met her cheek. Her breath smelled of sour milk or fear.

"You are fired! I want you out of the building in fifteen minutes," Clay said through clenched teeth.

"You can't just fire me. You have to buy my shares," Suzette said while drawing back away from Clay.

"Suzette, in the folder with your termination letter and a copy of your contract is a check and an accounting of the worth of your shares as of today," George said in a calm, businesslike voice.

Suzette fingered through the papers, picked up the check and just stared. "Where's the rest? Certainly, you're not telling me my shares are only worth this much." Suzette's face looked like she had seen a ghost.

It was Clay's turn to speak, "Welcome to the world of business finance, Suzette. The agency is teetering on bankruptcy no thanks to you. The value of your shares has been carefully calculated based on the formula in your contract. What you see is what you deserve per the agreement."

"I'm going to contest this. I'll have my accountant look at this. And where's my severance?" demanded Suzette, no longer holding back any anger.

"A partner's severance package is completely optional. Read your partnership contract. Due to the dire financial conditions of the agency, George and I simply couldn't justify any severance for you. I'm sure you understand," Clay said, now back in his chair.

George looked up and motioned to Larry, the guard, who was standing outside the glass door to the conference room. The guard opened the door and stepped into the room.

"Suzette, Larry here will escort you to your office and then to your car. Ravenna is in your office now and will help you pack your personal belongings. You can expect a call later today from Reuben, the firm's attorney, who can answer any of your legal questions and review with you the conditions of your non-compete agreement," explained George. He stood and motioned to Suzette to follow the guard.

She pushed the papers back roughly into the folder. She stood up defiantly and stormed out of the conference room.

Clay and George sat there both staring down at the table.

"Had to be done, George," said Clay.

"Yes, unfortunately. Necessary or not, that wasn't much fun. Do you think she'll make waves? Talk to the press?"

"Reuben will put the fear of God in her," said Clay. "In fact, let me call him right now."

Clay called their attorney to advise him the meeting with Suzette was over and remind him to discuss the conditions of her termination with his former partner. After the short call, Clay placed his cell back in his pocket. "I guess that leaves the topic of Pitt-Needham's offer for us to discuss."

"Yes, but I want to ask you something first," said George.

"Shoot."

"What made you so angry when Suzette said Lazzr was your fault? I thought you were going to leap across the table and strangle her."

Clay looked at his partner and then down at the table as if the answer was written there. "I did get angry, didn't I? I just lost it when she blamed me for Lazzr. It was her arrogant approach to her sacred plan that caused the Lazzr folks to doubt us."

"True," agreed George.

"Besides, being unhappy with the plan was just an excuse. Lazzr management had been planning to clean house in Marketing for some time. How else do you explain their firing Loretta, too?"

"I suppose if there's a lesson here, it is to keep closer to the top management and Board members of our clients, not just the head marketing person. I know every time I forget this rule, I get bit in the butt," said George.

"Excellent reminder, George. I'm making a note for us to put a plan together for doing just that." Clay retrieved his phone and typed a note to himself.

"But, my friend, you scared me for a moment with your anger. Are you all right?"

If you had lighthouse nightmares, heard voices in your house and had flashbacks from childhood all in one week, you'd crack a little, too. "Sure. I'm okay. Just the pressure of our finances got to me," Clay didn't think he sounded very convincing.

George studied him. "I understand, heck I even yelled at the cat last night." George chuckled. Then Clay started to laugh. The vision of his partner yelling at a harmless cat was hilarious right then for some reason. Soon both men were laughing uncontrollably. The tension had been broken thanks to the cat.

"Back to business," Clay said feeling better, but a little guilty for laughing only moments after firing a partner.

"Back to business," George replied. "I can't help but think that Pitt-Needham is going to revise their offer downward. I'm sure they know about Lazzr and the layoff by now."

"It wouldn't surprise me at all. In fact, I'm shocked I haven't received a call by now from Phil Manicotti asking me what's going on. But, George, we're getting the cart before the horse. Do we really want to be acquired by these guys, or anybody for that matter?"

"I've been giving it a lot of thought since our last meeting, Clay. Frankly, selling now makes sense to me. I get a big check now, less stress for the next couple years before I retire."

Clay could see his partner's point. Selling now made sense for George, if the money was right.

"I don't know that we can count on the same purchase price, George. Our situation is different now. The 'big' check you spoke of might not be so large."

"True enough, but the books will show that we're returning to profitability. Besides they are buying the future with us, not the past. But I haven't heard your thoughts yet. Have they changed any in past couple of weeks?"

"I have mixed views. On one hand, I love the idea of being part of a bigger agency. Just think of what we can do for our clients with Pitt-Needham's resources. I like the idea of the type and size of accounts we'll be able to pitch with their support, too."

"Indeed, we can take our services to the next level," George said.

"On the other hand, can we really trust these guys, George? What prevents them from showing us the door a few months after we sign the papers? Heck, we could end up being escorted out of our own building by Larry, just like Suzette was today."

The image of being walked out of their offices by the security guard was sobering to both men. The terrible train of thought was interrupted by a short knock at the door. Sheryl stepped inside.

"Suzette has left the building. You wanted to know."

"Oh, thank you, Sheryl. Has Ravenna finished the news release?"

"Yes, it is in your email," Sheryl responded.

"Please print two copies so we can review it in here."

Sheryl nodded and left the room.

"To your point about getting fired after the acquisition, there are some safeguards we can request in the agreement, but mostly we'll be expendable employees just like everyone else," said George.

"And, honestly, I don't know if I can go back to taking orders from someone. I like being the boss." Clay was looking at his partner. George looked back. They both nodded in agreement. Being told what to do and operating within a bureaucracy wasn't appealing to either man.

"The letter of intent was clear. You'd retain control here. Heck, they're even giving you a seat on their Board. That's sweet," George reminded Clay.

"But for how long? Sure, I'll be in control, doing things my way until Phil decides to pull in the reins. I don't even know if I can work for the man."

George studied his partner. "I don't hear much self-confidence in you, Clay. That's unusual."

"I'm just being cautious; trying to see all the possibilities here. Some of the scenarios aren't very appealing you have to agree," Clay said.

"I propose that we meet with Phil within a few days. Heck, he might even want to rescind the letter of intent because of our situation. If he wants to proceed, the two of you need to spend some time together so you know what to expect from him. Let me be clear, though; I'm in favor of the acquisition."

"Good proposal, George. I second it. All in favor raise your hand."

And with that formality, the partner meeting concluded.

Sheryl appeared with the news release. Both men studied it and made a few revisions with pen. It announced the departure of Suzette Behr who was leaving to pursue other interests. The release stated the agency's name would be Austin-Davis, effective immediately.

"Sheryl, please ask Ravenna to make these revisions, ask Reuben to approve it, and then distribute the release before end of the day. I want it on the News page of our website, too."

"Sure, and speaking of the website . . ." Sheryl knew she didn't have to finish the sentence before her two bosses would react.

"The logo has to change, the website has to change, our invoices, our letterhead. Wouldn't it be easier just to find another partner with a last name beginning with B?"

Both men laughed. They had saved their company. The pressure was off for now.

George returned to his office. Clay walked toward his on the opposite side of the building. He sensed something wasn't the same, but couldn't put his finger on what. A hiss filled his ears. He strode by Suzette's old office. The door was closed. Lights off. Her name tag had been removed from its holder mounted on the outside wall. Clay checked the door. It was locked. As it should be, even without him requesting it. He wondered briefly if it was Ravenna or Sheryl who made sure the door was locked. Didn't matter, he was very glad to have such competent staff.

Striding past Suzette's office, Clay noticed the strange feeling and hiss grew in intensity. He looked across the area of cubes and to the door of the central kitchen. What was different? Everything was where it was usually. Nothing out of place. The LED lighting in the ceiling was illuminating properly for this time of day. But, as he looked up, he noticed something. At first, it was subtle, but once he noticed, it was very apparent. The ceiling seemed higher. That was preposterous of course, but he couldn't deny that the ceiling *looked* to be several feet higher than he recalled. He slowed his pace to look at his surroundings more closely. The cubicle walls seemed taller, too. In fact, as he studied his surroundings, everything seemed larger than he remembered it being only an hour or so ago on his way to the McCann conference room.

Alice, one of the copywriters, walked by, looked at him curiously and said good morning to Clay. She looked tall. *Not possible,* Alice was only about five feet tall. Clay stood 14 inches taller than Alice, but today he felt like he had to look up to her.

So, the room wasn't larger. Somehow he was smaller. Definitely smaller.

Clay was glad that Sheryl wasn't at her desk. He didn't want her to see him this way. She could read him like a book. And right now, he had Stephen King written all over him.

Once he stepped into his office, the hiss suddenly stopped. The room and his contents appeared to be the proper size, too. Clay sighed in relief. The hallucination, or whatever it was, had stopped. *Just stress. Back to work.*

Clay saw many phone messages on his desk and decided to return the calls before he got busy. He picked up the phone to dial, but there was noise outside that irritated him. How was he supposed to make calls with all that noise? He stepped to the window and looked down. The maintenance crew was mowing the small strip of lawn that bordered this side of the building.

Weakness swept over Clay like a wave. He sat down. Suddenly he didn't want to return calls. He didn't want to do anything. He felt deflated. His mind kept going over the conversation with George about Phil Manicotti. Could he do it? Could he work for Phil? Was he ready for the big time? Or, after a few weeks, would Phil decide he wasn't good enough for the job and fire him?

Clay's eyes grew heavy, and he fell asleep in his chair.

Chapter 23

When Clay opened his eyes, he saw Sheryl standing in front of him. She was looking at him with concern and curiosity. Her gaze, while tender, bore into Clay like a laser seeking a cancerous cell. A large mug with a fresh macchiato was in her hand.

"You don't drink coffee," Clay mumbled, his mind desperately trying to get into gear after the surprise nap.

"And you don't fall asleep in your office chair," responded Sheryl, handing him the mug.

"No. I don't know what happened. I just felt really tired and fell asleep."

"Stress will do that, boss. The invitation to join me in Yoga class still stands." Sheryl had been urging Clay to do Yoga for years.

"I'll pass."

"If not Yoga, come to church with me Sunday. She stood there looking at Clay. He looked back. Awkward silence filled the room until Sheryl spoke again. "I, uh, mean I think you'll find peace there."

Clay was caught off-guard by the invitation. Nobody had invited him to church before. The only times he had been in a church was for weddings. And then, he never felt comfortable there. Never felt like he belonged there. Churches were for other people. Certainly not for him.

Clay sipped his coffee and dared to look directly at his assistant. While her facial expression said "embarrassed," her eyes held a depth of affection and compassion that he had never seen in her before. Heck, he had never seen that look in anyone's eyes before. Though she was now struggling to be coherent with her words, Clay marveled at the authentic affection that beamed from her eyes. It was as though her eyes were communicating separately from the rest of her body.

"Is church easier than Yoga?" Clay winked. He hoped the humor would buy him some time to think. Her invitation had made him uncomfortable, but at the same time, her eyes relaxed him. He felt like a human yo-yo suddenly.

"Doing church is easy. Having faith can take work," said Sheryl.

"I've never been big on Bible-thumpers," said Clay.

"Neither have I," she responded with a sincere grin. "We have a saying at my church. 'No perfect people allowed.'"

"Great line, who is your copywriter?"

"I think the Spirt had something to do with it, Clay."

"Spirit, eh? Is that the first name or last?" Clay continued to reach for humor to avoid answering her invitation. Sheryl wasn't buying it.

"Look, Clay, you haven't been yourself the past week or so. I can tell that you're deeply troubled by something. You'd be surprised what God can do if you simply give Him a chance."

Clay's resolve was weakening. He couldn't believe he was beginning to think that going to church with Sheryl wasn't such a bad idea after all. Why not, he was seeing a psychiatrist for the first time, wasn't he? Why not double down and go to church, too?

"How early would I have to get up on Sunday?" Clay asked with a frown, deliberately trying to show Sheryl how much of a sacrifice he was considering.

"We can attend the 11:30 service, and I'll even treat you to brunch afterward," she said cheerfully.

Clay only heard the first few words out of Sheryl's mouth before her voice was drowned out by the noise from the lawn mowing crew outside. The decibel level increased until it started to hurt Clay's head. He couldn't believe that a mower could be so loud. It was as if the darn machine was right in his office running full throttle without a muffler.

He looked at Sheryl, who was studying him with a fresh look of concern. She didn't seem to be bothered by the noise. Her lips were moving, but he couldn't hear anything but the beast of a lawnmower. He covered his ears, grimaced against the noise that wouldn't stop. He glanced past Sheryl to the corner of his office. There, next to the expensive leather seats, was a 1958 Briggs & Stratton lawn mower belching exhaust. Rusty metal showed in patches where the red paint was chipped. A sticky mess of dirt, lawn clippings, and oil covered the horizontal surfaces on both sides of the engine. But the blades glistened. They looked new and razor-sharp as they rotated ever so slowly in the front of the machine. The beast of a mower rocked back and forth like a mad rodeo bull in its shoot. *Why didn't Sheryl see it?*

Suddenly the spasmodic rocking of the mower stopped, Clay watched in horror as the throttle lever moved all the way forward. The engine screamed in response. Then, unbelievably, the clutch lever began to move, too. The mower lurched forward right at Clay where he sat. Knife-sharp blades spinning at full speed were headed at Clay's feet.

Clay screamed. In one desperate motion, he pushed his chair back and raised his legs to escape being torn to pieces. Hot coffee from his mug flew in all directions. The mug shot from his hands like a missile only to shatter against the wall by the table.

Chapter 24

heryl was petrified. Right before her eyes, her boss appeared to have lost his mind and experienced a violent fit. One minute he was fine, sipping his mug of coffee, the next he was screaming in terror and acting as if some terrible monster in the room was trying to consume him. Now he slumped unconscious in his chair.

People began to rush into Clay's office after hearing his primal scream.

"Someone run down to Dr. Hennessey's office and bring him up here," Sheryl ordered. The doctor had a walk-in emergency clinic on the ground floor of the building. Sheryl calculated that the doctor or his RN could be here a lot faster than an aid car from the neighborhood fire station five blocks away.

Sheryl turned her attention back to Clay. She was by his side now checking vital signs. Yes, he was breathing. Her fingers touched the carotid artery in his neck. She could feel a pulse but wasn't trained to know if the pulse was weak or strong. Clay was alive, that's all she knew.

It was then she realized that her blouse was stained with coffee and both arms stung from minor burns the hot coffee had inflicted on her skin. Clay's clothes were stained, as well. Sheryl began wiping coffee from Clay's face. Her fingers tenderly ran across his smooth forehead and down his cheeks, rough with beard stubble. In all these years as his assistant, this was the first time she had actually touched him. While always deeply fond of her boss, never had she entertained romantic notions about him. Yet, right now, her heart was sending a different signal.

Dr. Hennessey burst into the room carrying a satchel. Sheryl told him what she had witnessed. Then she ordered everyone out of the office and closed the door.

No sooner had the doctor arrived next to Clay when Clay's eyes began to flutter. For the second time in less than an hour, he awoke in his chair with a confused look on his face. Except this time, he was looking into the face of Dr. Hennessey, not Sheryl.

"Clay, I'm Dr. Hennessey from the clinic downstairs. You passed out a few minutes ago. I'm going to check your heart and breathing."

Sheryl saw Clay nod at the doctor all the while looking at her. His eyes asked, *what the heck is going on here?*

The doctor quickly checked Clay's vital signs, including listening to his heart and lungs with a stethoscope. He took a pen light from his pocket and shined it into Clay's eyes.

While responding to the doctor's questions, Clay shot nervous glances around the room. He seemed to be looking for something or someone.

"Clay, you're physically fine. No sign of stroke. You may have had a severe anxiety attack. I can't rule out epilepsy either. I want you to see a specialist so they can do further tests to rule out epilepsy. I also want you to see a psychiatrist about the anxiety." The doctor was writing names of the specialists on a pad of paper when George burst into the room without knocking.

"What happened? How is he?" asked George who had just returned to the office from his weekly barber appointment.

"They say you're making me work too hard," joked Clay.

Sheryl and the doctor briefed George on Clay's condition.

Sheryl took the paper with the specialist names from Dr. Hennessey as he walked toward the door.

The doctor turned and said, "Oh, one more thing. No driving today. Consider yourself grounded until you've seen the neurologist. Mention my name when you call for an appointment. His scheduler will get you in faster."

Sheryl escorted the doctor out of Clay's office and to the elevator.

"You're not going to get sick and make me run this ship by myself are you?" George asked. His light tone betrayed the worried look on his face.

"Nah, I just reacted to some bad coffee," said Clay noticing for the first time the coffee that covered his desk and clothes.

George looked around the room. He couldn't miss the large coffee stain still dripping down the wall by the work table. "You're definitely taking the remainder of the day off. We can't afford any more broken coffee mugs," said George.

"I hear you." Clay knew what George was really saying. He was in no state of mind to be making decisions or talking with clients. He needed to back away before he screwed up something much bigger than a coffee mug.

"Have Sheryl drive you home. She can take a cab back. I'd drive you except I need to smooth the edgy nerves around here and assure everyone that all is well."

"How are you going to explain my outburst? Sheryl said some people heard it."

"I'll say you've been working long hours, spilled your coffee, yelled in pain and then fainted."

"Sounds about right."

"I suggest you leave by the back stairs," said George.

CHAPTER 25

S heryl drove Clay to his house boat. The ride felt weird. Clay was certain this was the first time he'd ever ridden in his car while seated on the passenger side. The strangeness of the feeling in the car only multiplied the sense of unease in his head.

He sat in silence as Sheryl worked the car through traffic, clearly enjoying her opportunity to drive a high-performance car—even if only for a few miles on city streets.

At the private lot, she backed Clay's car into its stall as if she did it every day. How did she know Clay preferred to back the car in? He made a mental note to ask her someday.

"Come in for a drink, Sheryl. You deserve it for what I've put you through today."

"If you insist," she said with a wink.

Clay unlocked the front door and let Sheryl in. She had only been to his house twice before. Each time for holiday parties Clay held during the week when the yacht clubs would parade dozens of colorfully lit boats around Lake Union at night.

"Red wine, right? Clay asked.

"Please."

Clay opened a bottle of Texas Tempranillo that he'd been wanting to try. He poured two full glasses.

"Should you be drinking?" Sheryl wondered out loud.

"Probably not," said Clay while taking a long sip. "But I'm too much of a gentleman to let you drink alone."

She laughed and sipped her wine.

They sat on the couch facing the windows and the lake.

"Clay?"

"Yep"

"What scared you so much today in the office? You looked like you saw a ghost."

There it was. The question he didn't want to answer. How could this woman respect him if he told the truth? *Oh, nothing much, just an antique Briggs & Stratton lawn mower with sharp, hungry blades. That's all. Perfectly normal.*

He didn't want to lie. He didn't want to tell the truth. In fact he had a few questions of his own—*didn't you see it? Didn't you hear the darn thing?*

All Clay could do was stare out the window and take long sips from this wine glass.

"You know you can trust me, right? All I want to do is understand so I can help you."

He turned to face her. "I do trust you. I know you want to help. But it's complicated."

"Of course, it's complicated. Clay, you passed out twice this morning. That's not a normal morning for you," she said with a touch of sarcasm.

"I've been seeing a shrink. That's what my unmarked appointments away from the office have been lately."

Clay's cell phone rang. He frowned and dug it out of his coffee-stained sports coat. A number he didn't recognize was displayed on the screen.

"Clay Austin speaking," he answered.

Sheryl stood up and stepped across the room to stand by the windows, looking out at the lake. She did this to give Clay some privacy for the call, but also to help her think about the feelings for Clay that had bubbled to the surface today so unexpectedly.

Whoever was on the phone was doing all the talking and Clay was listening.

"Okay, thanks for the call," Clay said somberly, and placed the phone into his coat pocket.

He stood up and walked over to the window next to Sheryl. Without looking at her he said, "That was some attorney in Reef Bay letting me know that my Uncle Charley has died. The service is next Wednesday. He said I'm mentioned in Uncle Charley's Will and should come to his office on Thursday."

Clay sipped his wine thoughtfully, his mind now lost in thought.

Sheryl was lost in her own thoughts. She was dumbfounded. Her boss was seeing a psychiatrist! Until today she thought he was the most well-balanced person she knew. But what really surprised her was the other feeling she was experiencing. She was actually happy he was seeing a psychiatrist. She had to admit to herself that she was relieved he was seeing a doctor and not having a date. *Oh-oh. What's happening here?*

Chapter 26

ot, dry air poured through the open car windows as the blue Comet bounced along the dirt road. Mile after mile of desolate sand and sagebrush spread out from the little car in all directions. An occasional saguaro cactus pierced the otherwise featureless horizon of the Sonoran Desert outside Phoenix, Arizona.

Eleven-year-old Clay and his Great Uncle Charley were going rock hunting. This meant driving deep into the desert where it had been reported that agates and jasper could be found. Little Clay was excited. Maybe he'd get lucky and find some petrified wood, or a thunder egg, the informal name for a geode.

It was only 9:30 in the morning, but already they had been driving for nearly two hours. The temperature on this June day was already over 90 degrees on its way to 109 degrees according to the forecast.

"Thirsty?" asked Uncle Charley.

Clay nodded.

"Pour us a drink from the Thermos and let's have one of Lillian's cookies, too."

Clay took two plastic cups from the bag on the floor, unscrewed the top of the thermos and tried to pour the ice-cold Coke into the two cups. The bouncing and jerking of the car on the rough road made the task difficult, but Clay managed to pour the Coke and replace the Thermos cap without spilling a drop. He handed one cup to his uncle and set the bag of cookies on the seat where Charley could easily reach them while driving. Clay took a sip from his cup. The carbonated bubbles tickled his nose. The cold, sweet liquid flowed across his tongue and down his parched throat. It was beyond a doubt the best drink he had ever had! Of course, he had drunk Coke and other soft drinks before, but this was different somehow.

Back home in Medford, he wasn't allowed to drink soft drinks. If he wanted a treat, there was Kool-Aid. He could drink all the water or milk he wanted, but not soda pop. In fact, for Christmas, one year Clay put soda pop on his gift list. He was thrilled to see a wrapped six-pack of pop bottles under the tree come Christmas morning but had to hide his disappointment when the wrapping came off to reveal cheap, discount brands and unusual flavors. Was a six-pack of Coke or Pepsi too much to ask for? Guess he wasn't good enough for the good stuff.

So, far from the rigid rules of his home, bouncing along a desert road with his Uncle Charley, Clay relished his ice-cold Coke. Here he was good enough for the good stuff.

About twenty minutes after finishing his Coke with two oat and chocolate chip cookies, Uncle Charley turned left off the rough county road onto an even rougher road that led them up a slight elevation to a knoll. Uncle Charley checked his notes and announced they had arrived. He pulled the Comet, now covered in dust, to the side of the road, turned off the ignition and got out of the car.

Clay followed him to the trunk to retrieve their shovels, hammers, and canvas buckets. It was hot. Not a cloud in the sky. What Clay noticed the most was silence. Every step he took in the gravel and sand was pronounced, almost magnified by the utter stillness of the desert.

They walked away from the car and up a small rise. Along the way, Clay saw holes in the ground where other rock hounds before them had dug in search of the wondrous agates and jasper. The closer to the top they got, the more numerous the holes. This was the place all right.

Uncle Charley stopped and looked around. Then he pointed to their right and said, "Let's dig here."

And so they dug. The dirt and sand were easy to dig, but the intense sun and heat made the job uncomfortable. Still, the thrill of unearthing a beautiful stone was worth it.

Clay dug one hole. Uncle Charley dug another about ten feet away. After about fifteen minutes of digging, Clay noticed that Uncle Charley was beginning to pick up some rocks from his hole, examine each, and either drop it into the canvas bucket or toss it aside to the desert floor.

Clay saw nothing in his hole except more sand. He walked over to Uncle Charley.

"Look in the bag, Clay. What do you think?"

Clay saw six stones of different sizes. He picked up each and looked closely. They were agates all right. Clay brushed the sand off of one that looked particularly promising. He put saliva on his thumb and wiped it across the surface of the stone, just like he'd seen Uncle Charley do hundreds of times. The wetness of the spit on the stone made the colors dance in the mid-day light.

"Uncle Charley, look at this one!" Clay held up the moist rock for his uncle to see.

Uncle Charley looked up from his digging and said, "Yep, we're going to find some good stuff today."

"But I haven't found anything yet," Clay declared disappointedly.

Uncle Charley stopped digging and walked over to Clay's hole. "Let's both dig here some more to make the hole deeper. If nothing turns up, we'll start you digging somewhere else."

Man and boy dug side by side in the hot Arizona sun.

After a few minutes with nothing but sand and worthless rocks to show for the effort, Uncle Charley declared that the hole should be abandoned.

"Tell you what. Let's have another drink. Then you take my hole, and I'll start another just up the hill."

After another hour of digging, Clay and Uncle Charley had filled their buckets with agates.

"I'm pooped. Let's leave the rest of the rocks for other guys. I'm ready to go back if you are?" asked his uncle.

Clay had to admit he was ready to leave. His bucket was so heavy he couldn't carry it, so Uncle Charley carried the two buckets of rocks back to the car, while Clay carried the shovels, rock hammers, and Thermos.

The heat and exhaustion from digging put Clay sound asleep in the front seat only minutes after Uncle Charley had turned the Comet around and headed back to Phoenix.

He woke up when they were about a half mile from Charley and Lillian's mobile home in a fashionable mobile home park.

"When can we cut some of the rocks, Uncle Charley?" Clay was eager to open a few of his newly discovered rocks with a rock saw to see what was inside. This was the real thrill of rock hunting. Cutting open the rock to see the treasure inside. Sometimes when an agate was cut open, it revealed an ordinary smoky clear stone. But other times, the saw revealed a multi-colored design that took your breath away. This is the stuff that made the best jewelry—rings, pendants, brooches, earrings and belt buckles.

"This afternoon. Let's have lunch and rest first." Uncle Charley liked his afternoon naps.

After their afternoon siesta, the two ventured outside the comfort of the air-conditioned mobile home into the suffocating heat of a summer afternoon. The covered workshop next to the mobile home, contained a rock saw, two grinders, a polisher, tumbler and a long workbench where Uncle Charley created his sterling silver jewelry.

The two rock hounds decided together on the best rocks to cut first. Uncle Charley watched while Clay placed the rock securely in the vice inside the covered rock saw. Clay checked the depth of the lubricant in the base of the saw to make sure the 18-inch diamond tipped saw blade was reaching the lubricant. He glanced up at his uncle. Uncle Charley nodded his head, giving approval that Clay had prepared the stone for cutting properly, as he had been taught. Clay shut the lid of the slab saw and pushed the Start button. The saw went into action. Within about thirty seconds he could hear the sound of the blade engaging with the rock as the agate was automatically fed into the blade by the saw's screw drive.

While the saw did its job Clay and Uncle Charley reviewed the day's bounty. Out of the 48 stones they brought back from the desert, six looked very promising and were placed into the pile on the floor for cutting next.

Forty minutes later the sound of the saw changed suddenly. The first cut through the six-inch diameter stone had been completed. The saw turned itself off. Clay and Uncle Charley waited impatiently for the blade to stop turning so they could lift the hood and see what it had exposed in the rock.

After what seemed like eternity, the saw was quiet and safe to open. Clay lifted the hood. Lubricant dripped from inside the hood. He reached for the part of the rock that had been cut away and brought it out to the daylight. After anxiously removing the oily lubricant from the stone he held it up for both to see.

What they saw made them smile. Clay's eyes grew big.

Inside, the agate was creamy pale blue with plumes of black and burnt orange that looked like moss.

"You found yourself a pretty nice moss agate," Uncle Charley said, with a smile on his face.

Clay was speechless. "Let's make another cut. I want a slab," said Clay referring to a quarter-inch thick slice they'd cut, like a steak from a roast, as the first step in preparing a stone to make jewelry from it.

"Tell you what. Why don't you take the rock out of the vice so we can look at it closely? I wonder if cutting it in the same direction is a good idea," advised Uncle Charley.

Clay removed the rock and handed it to his uncle, who looked at it carefully. "I think we're okay with this direction. See how big the plumes look? Cutting in another direction probably won't give you as good a result."

Clay returned the rock to the saw and adjusted the next cut to generate a quarter-inch slab. He double-checked the tightness of the vice and the depth of the lubricant before shutting the cover of the saw and turning it on.

After ninety minutes the two had cut several of their rocks and cleaned lubricant from each of ten agate slabs. At the workbench, they worked together with a template to draw oblong shapes of different sizes on the slabs. Inside each pencil-drawn shape was captured an attractive aspect of the agate—a particular arrangement of the moss plume, or a striking display of indigo and carnelian bands, or simply an unusual shape made by a rainbow of colors.

At 4:00 they stopped for the day. Both rock hounds were tired and ready for the dinner that they could begin to smell coming from Aunt Lillian's kitchen.

That night, before falling to sleep on the guest bed, Clay realized how good he felt, but didn't know why exactly. It had been a perfect day. Tomorrow would be a good day, too. He'd get to cut, grind and polish the agates into glorious cabochons that his uncle would mount into silver.

Sleepily he recalled that one of the inch-long oblong shapes that he had drawn on the first agate slab, encircled a single perfect black moss plume surrounded by a milky-clear agate. It was elegant and beautiful. It was going to make a fabulous dinner ring. Clay knew his mother would love it

Chapter 27

riday morning Clay was shaving when his cell began ringing next to the sink. The display told him the caller was George.

"Good morning, George. Checking in on me?"

"As a matter of fact, I am," George responded. "How are you feeling?"

"I'm okay considering I've only had one cup of coffee so far. I slept pretty good though."

"Good to hear. Have you made an appointment with the Neurologist yet?"

"I believe Sheryl is handling that for me. I'll ask her when I get into the office this morning."

There was a brief pause. George cleared his throat once before speaking. "Clay, as your friend and partner I'm suggesting you take the day off. Rest, see the doctor."

"You afraid I'll have another episode or something in the office?" Clay managed a nervous laugh.

"I want you to take care of yourself and get well. I can't run this place by myself; you know that."

"George, I can't run it without you, so I guess we're stuck with each other."

"That's right. So, as the Hallmark card says, 'Get well soon'".

"Okay, partner. I hear you, but since we're talking about taking time off, I have to be gone a few days next week. My uncle died, and I have to go to Reef Bay for the funeral."

"Oh, gosh. When it rains, it pours. I'm sorry to hear that. You never mentioned an Uncle. Were you close?"

"Sort of. Only saw him once a year when I was growing up. Then we lost touch. Geez, he must have been in his nineties. Anyway, I'll drive to Reef Bay for the service on Wednesday and stay the night. Should be back late Thursday," Clay said.

"Listen, you take care of Clay today and rest over the weekend. When you talk with Sheryl this morning ask her to schedule time on Monday for us to talk about the Needham offer. We need a resolution."

"Indeed we do, partner. I'll give the deal serious consideration over the weekend. Oh, and, George?"

"Yep."

"Thanks for the call. Means a lot," Clay said.

"Don't mention it. Somebody must look out for you. You refuse to find a wife for yourself." George hung up.

George was right. Clay hadn't put much effort into a serious relationship. Too busy building the agency. Too afraid of being hurt again.

He pushed thoughts of love and romance out of his mind. He finished dressing and went downstairs to make breakfast.

At 8:30 he was about to call Sheryl when his phone began to buzz. It was Sheryl.

"Good morning, Sheryl, I was just reaching for the phone to call you. You beat me to the punch."

"As usual," Sheryl said warmly.

"Hey, I'm sorry about spacing out on you last night. The news about my uncle, on top of everything else, just made my circuits overload. I must have been a lousy host."

"That's okay, Clay. You needed to cry."

"I what!" Clay exclaimed.

"You cried. After the call about your uncle, you just stood looking out the window, and the tears flowed down your face. It was sweet actually."

"Must have been an allergic reaction to the sulfides in the wine." Clay had no recollection of crying last night.

"Right, tough guy, so if you don't want to talk about crying let's talk about your schedule," Sheryl directed the conversation to a safe place for Clay. "The Neurologist can see you late this afternoon. I couldn't believe it. A doctor who was in the office on a Friday afternoon."

"That's fine. Anytime today is good. I'm taking the day off, per George's orders. Uh, could you make another appointment for me today? I better see my shrink, too. If you have the power to get me into a neurologist on short notice, getting an appointment with a psychiatrist should be a piece of cake."

"I don't have the name or number, Clay, remember?"

"Oh, right. Top secret. I'll text it to you. I don't mind if the appointments are back to back. Another thing, please schedule a meeting with George, Reuben, and me for Monday to discuss the Needham offer. The topic is very hush-hush, of course. Just text me the final schedules for all of this as soon as you know."

"I will."

"And I expect you to skip out early today," Clay said.

"I was planning on it," she replied.

Clay set the phone on the granite counter top and went to work on making his breakfast—a cheese and mushroom omelet, English muffin with blueberry jam, and fresh squeezed orange juice.

After eating, Clay was putting dirty dishes into the dishwasher when the phone buzzed. The text from Sheryl gave him the schedule in four lines.

Fri 3 pm Dr. Reddi
Fri 4 pm Dr. Shildstein
Sun 11:30 church with Sheryl
Mon 10 am meeting with George and Reuben

Clay almost didn't see the Sunday appointment in the list. It was so cleverly sandwiched between Friday and Monday. Ordinarily, Clay would have politely declined the Sunday offer. But, this was the second time this week she had asked him. She could be relentless. Had she no mercy? Couldn't she see everything that he has been going through? The pressure. Did she honestly think that sitting on a hard bench in some drafty church with organ music was going to be beneficial to him?

He could visualize Sheryl staring anxiously at her phone waiting for his reply about church; wondering what he would choose. Wondering if she had over-stepped their relationship.

Right then, for some reason, he recalled how he felt when she drove him home in his car yesterday. Sitting in the passenger seat was weird all right, but having her drive his car in traffic like a NASCAR driver wasn't bad at all. In fact, he felt perfectly at ease. He trusted her with his expensive automobile. The flashback didn't stop there either. Suddenly he remembered the unusual sensation he had experienced letting Sheryl into his home. He had unlocked the door and swung it open for her to walk in. Her shoulder had brushed his arm as he held the door open. An electric shock had shot up his arm. Funny, he didn't pay any attention to it then, but now those sensations were racing through his brain.

Her eyes were different that day, too. They had a depth of wisdom and compassion he hadn't noticed before. Come to think of it, her entire persona was different—warmer, more feminine if that was even possible.

Clay shook his head as if that would help him think more clearly. He trusted Sheryl, didn't he? Of course. So, would she recommend something that wouldn't be good for him? Not likely, he reasoned. What was the worst thing that could happen to him in church? He might be embarrassed. Might do the wrong thing. Might stand when everyone else is sitting down, or sit when the congregation stands up.

Trust, Clay. Trust, said the little voice in his head.

Clay typed a response using both thumbs.

Got it. Good job on appts. Church. What time r u picking me up?

He paused before tapping Send. Doubt and fear swept over him. Was he really going to church? What sort of a hypocrite was he? He didn't want to go to church. Was he just agreeing to get Sheryl off his back? Wouldn't it be better to stay true to himself and decline her offer? She'd understand.

His thumb, shaking slightly, hovered over the Send button.

Chapter 28

lay was in and out of the Neurologist's office within forty-five minutes. Certainly, a record for a visit to a new physician considering all the paperwork and such. Dr. Reddi asked a lot of questions while examining Clay. It always bothered him that the questions a doctor asked on the first visit were almost always the same as those he answered in the medical history paperwork while sitting in the waiting room. Dr. Reddi told him to come back in a week for results of the tests they were going to give him next. The nurse drew blood and led him to another room for an EEG.

Pocketing the reminder card for his follow up appointment, Clay walked briskly out the door and to his parked car. If traffic cooperated, he had just enough time to get to Dr. Shildstein by 4:00.

There wasn't a parking space close to Dr. Shildstein's office, and Clay had to park nearly three blocks away along a tree-lined street. He walked quickly toward her bungalow office. The daylight from the winter day was all but gone. The day had been sparkling clear, breezy and cold. Now that the sun had vanished over the Olympic Range of mountains to the west the temperature was dropping fast. *Going to freeze tonight* Clay thought to himself while walking even faster.

Once inside, the doctor offered Clay hot tea, which he eagerly accepted. Clay sat down in his usual spot on the couch and noticed that the artwork had been moved around. What used to be on the walls behind him were now hanging on the walls within his range of sight. The piece that drew his attention every time he was here—the painting of the purple hot air balloon with a partially visible cross soaring high above a coastal lighthouse, was now hanging on the wall behind the doctor.

"You moved the art," Clay said.

"Yes, I do that periodically. Whenever I get a little bored with the room, I just change the art around. Much less expensive than redecorating," she said with a smile. "But you didn't request a last-minute session today to discuss my office decor."

"No, I didn't. Thank you for seeing me. I've had a rough week. Been hallucinating. Passed out."

That information got her attention. The doctor shifted in her chair and opened the journal to take notes. Her eyes never left Clay. "Tell me about it, Clay."

And so he did. The meeting with Suzette. The wood stacking memories. The lawn mower episode in the park. The lawn mower episode in his office. The news about his Uncle Charley. He felt like some reporter laying down the facts about another person's life.

"You really should see a Neurologist. Sounds like you had a couple of seizures in your office yesterday."

"Just came from one. A Dr. Reddi. I'll know results of the tests next week," Clay said.

"Good. We can't overlook the possibility of a physiological disorder. Have you ever passed out before?"

"Nope."

"Learning to mow the lawn was a very traumatic experience for you, wasn't it?"

"I guess."

"For some reason, that memory was disturbing you a lot this week. Why this week and not in other weeks?"

"Good question, doctor. I suppose that's why I'm here to find out."

"Any theories?"

"The stress at work must have triggered it," Clay reasoned.

"I understand it was a particularly stressful week, but you've had many stressful weeks in your life up to know, haven't you?"

"Sure, like everybody."

"But this is the week an imaginary lawn mower attacked you in your office." Ordinarily, that statement would have made Clay erupt in laughter. The statement was absurd, but Dr. Shildstein wasn't joking. Neither was she patronizing Clay. She was dead-serious as if she had experienced the shining blades of death too.

Clay was getting uneasy. His attention kept being attracted to the hot air balloon painting that hung on the wall behind and to the left of the doctor.

"Clay, let's go back to the lawn mowing lesson. It doesn't sound like Vic was very understanding of your physical limitations at that age."

"That's an understatement," Clay said tersely.

"Do you remember how you felt?"

"I was really frustrated. I wanted to learn how to mow the lawn like the big kids did. It was really hard to control the lawnmower. I just wasn't strong enough."

"That would be frustrating. What else were you feeling?"

"I was confused. I didn't understand why Vic was angry with me and yelling."

"Had any adult ever yelled at you like that before?"

"No. Not like that. I had been scolded and even spanked before, but always because I had done something wrong."

"And so here you were trying your best and still getting yelled at."

"Exactly." Emotion began to rise from deep in Clay's heart. "I couldn't make sense of it."

"Go on; you're doing great, Clay."

"I wanted to mow the lawn. I wanted to help."

"Clay, what else were you wanting?"

Clay shook his head. He didn't know. It was so long ago. All he could remember was the terrible hurt and shame from not being able to control the lawn mower. He searched his memory. His eyes scanned the room as if the answer to her question could be found on a book shelf, or behind a lamp. The purple balloon painting was there. He couldn't avoid seeing it. All at once the emotion he had been holding back during the session overtook him.

Tears poured from his eyes. He tried to talk, but his ability to speak was overpowered by deep, uncontrollable sobs of sorrow. Through his tears he saw the psychiatrist watching him, her fingers writing furiously in the journal.

"Clay, you were a very young boy who never knew his real father. What do you think you wanted more than anything?"

Clay was struggling to gain control so he could speak. He grabbed a tissue from the dispenser on the coffee table, wiped the tears from his eyes and blew his nose. Breathing hard, he took a sip of tea. It was only lukewarm now, but it soothed him. Her question burned in his heart and echoed through his mind. "What do you think you wanted more than anything?"

"I just wanted him to love me," he said through another eruption of tears and sobs.

"Of course, that's what you wanted. Every child seeks love from a parent. You were no different. You had a loving mother, but your real father left you when you were four. In your heart, you desperately wanted the love of a father. Vic was the father figure. He wasn't up to the task, unfortunately for both of you."

"I just wanted him to love and accept me" Clay nearly choked on the words, so hard were they to say.

"And you didn't receive love and acceptance that day, did you?"

"No!" Clay responded bitterly.

"Think, Clay, what did you tell yourself that day after the lawn mowing was finished?"

"Huh, I don't understand what you mean."

"You had just spent several hours trying to learn how to mow a lawn. How to control a very powerful lawn mower. All you got in response from Vic was impatience and yelling. When the day was over, and you walked back to the house, what do you think you were telling yourself about the experience of that day?"

Clay searched his memories for any clue. He pictured himself back in time. A tired little boy with grass stained sneakers, head hanging low, walking slowly, dejectedly, across the lawn to the back door.

"I was telling myself I couldn't do it."

"Right. What else, Clay?"

"I . . . I . . ." The answer was there. Lurking just under the surface. Clay wanted it out. The idea, the words, the thought, the emotion, whatever it was had to be pushed from him like warm pus from a festering wound. Clay realized he was in a battle. He wanted to identify this thought and spit it out, but the idea was hanging on, hiding in the darkness, wrapping its tentacles around Clay's soul.

Clay's mind kept digging. He was thinking harder than he had ever thought before. His eyes shut tight for added focus. And then it was there. He opened his eyes and said in a voice shaking with emotion, "I wasn't good enough."

The doctor's lips turned upwards ever so slightly at the corner. She spoke slowly and deliberately so Clay would follow her after his emotional ordeal.

"Vic yelled and screamed at you for hours. You tried your best, but couldn't control the mower well. His reaction to you made you feel that you weren't good enough. But Clay, there's more here. On the surface, you believed you weren't good enough to mow the lawn correctly, but subconsciously you were telling yourself that you weren't good enough for Vic's love. That was your justification for why he was yelling at you."

Clay was drained from the emotional release. He slumped back into the couch. He stared at the coffee table in front of him.

After a long pause, Clay regrouped slightly and responded, "I guess this not-good-enough stuff needed to come out, but you still haven't told me why I'm hallucinating and passing out."

"Clay, at age nine you told yourself you weren't good enough for the acceptance and love of a father figure. That inner belief of 'not good enough' has defined your life ever since."

The doctor continued. "You had a very challenging week. Don't you think those challenges pushed the 'not good enough' button a few times? You were caught between having to make tough decisions with major consequences and the inner belief that you weren't good enough to make the right decisions. Your mind protected itself by passing out. It reacted like a circuit breaker."

"That makes sense, I suppose."

The psychiatrist closed her journal, signaling the session was wrapping up. As she had in previous sessions, she looked deep into Clay's eyes. "Do you remember what I told you after our last session?"

"Yeah, something about me being under attack, but I'll be okay."

"That's correct. Clay, are you religious?"

The question, coming from a shrink, surprised him.

"No. Never."

"What I'm going to say may not make a lot of sense, but I'll say it anyway," the doctor said. "Clay, you weren't born 'not good enough,' were you?"

"I guess not."

"No, you were born without limitations. Before Vic, you probably thought you could do just about anything with a little learning and practice."

"Pretty much."

"Listen carefully. Vic didn't make you not good enough. Your brain told you, you weren't good enough because it had to rationalize why you were being yelled at rather than being loved and nurtured. That's the psychological explanation for it. But, why did your brain do that to you? It's hurtful, isn't it? It has certainly hurt you."

Clay nodded in agreement.

"Does God want you to hurt? Does God want you to put limitations on what you think is possible?"

"Never really thought about it."

"I don't expect that you have pondered the question, but I'd like you to do so now and over the weekend. Our God is a loving God. He loves us unconditionally. He isn't telling you you're not good enough. So, who is telling you that, Clay?"

Clay frowned in confusion. "I don't know."

"The Deceiver. Satan uses lies to weaken us and turn us away from God. Satan is encouraging you to believe that you're not good enough. And he's so adept at this deception you don't even know that it is running your life. So, that's why I said you're under attack, but you will prevail. I believe it. I see it in you."

"I guess it's a good thing I'm going to church Sunday," said Clay.

"I thought you said you weren't religious."

"My admin invited me, and she has great judgment about things and people. Can't hurt, right?"

Dr. Shildstein laughed, "No, it can't hurt." She was grinning from ear to ear. She glanced at her watch. "When do you get the neurology test results?"

"Next Friday, a week from today."

"Okay, let's have our next session on Friday, same time, at four."

"Sounds good."

"Don't hesitate to call me if you have other episodes. Just remember, the 'not good enough' is a lie."

Clay paid the doctor and walked out into the cold, dry night. A full moon was just visible on the horizon and gave him some welcome light for the walk up the tree-line street to his car.

Back in her office, Dr. Shildstein checked the lock on the front door. She picked up the dishes from the table and took them to the sink in the bungalow's small kitchen. Coming back into the main room she turned off all lamps except the one by her chair. She sat down and bowed her head in prayer. After a few minutes, she stood and walked directly to the painting of the white hot air balloon that hung on the wall behind her chair. She removed it from the wall and set it aside in a corner by her desk. She loved that painting and was going to miss it.

Chapter 29

Clay woke up on Sunday to brilliant sunlight pouring in though the large sliding glass doors of his bedroom. He put on his robe and walked downstairs for coffee. He had slept well and was feeling better than he had in a long time.

He had an idea. *This is a perfect day to take the kayak out on the lake.* Sunny, no wind, briskly invigorating temperature. Besides, sunny days like this in early March were rare. Another front was certainly on its way bringing clouds and rain. One thing Seattleites learned was to get outside and play when the sun shined. Screw work. Screw house chores. Those things could wait for cloudy days.

He could be on the lake in less than an hour, just needed to dress and slip outside to where his kayak was stored in a sling above the deck walkway that ran along the side of his house. Heck, he'd make a day of it. He could leave his house, paddle to the north end of the lake, then west, then south along the opposite shore. He'd time the circumnavigation of Lake Union so he'd be at the guest dock of Chandler's Crab House in time for brunch. After a few Bloody Mary's and a Dungeness crab omelet, he'd paddle north back along the east shore of the lake to his house. He'd end the day relaxing with a good cigar in his hot tub on the downstairs deck. A pitch-perfect Sunday.

He started to head upstairs to change when his phone rang. It was Sheryl.

"Good morning, Clay. Hey, I'm running about ten minutes late. I'll be there to pick you up a little after eleven."

For a split-second Clay was confused. Pick him up for what? Then he remembered. Church. He had agreed to attend church with Sheryl today. It had completely slipped his mind even though he had mentioned it to Dr. Shildstein as recently as Friday.

"Oh, uh, no problem. I'll meet you at the guest gate to save us time. Umm, what should I wear? I'm new to all this, you know."

"No worries. There isn't a dress code at my church," Sheryl said with a chuckle. "I'm wearing one step up from my usual office clothes if that helps."

That helped somewhat. At the office, Sheryl portrayed a look of casual sophistication. She fit the typical ad agency vibe of jeans, flannel shirts and expensive shoes, but she looked better put together than the others. Everyone else, other than the partners, looked like they had just pulled on some clothes out of the dryer and rushed to work. Sheryl, looked classy, but never enough to stand out from the others. Clay knew, because they had talked about it once before, that she believed that as the administrator for a partner she was a reflection of him. How she looked, how she talked, how she worked, were all an extension of Clay and his office as managing partner and co-founder of one of the Northwest's best marketing agencies.

"Ok, I'll wear slacks, sweater and sports coat."

"And remember to comb your hair," Sheryl said with another chuckle. She was enjoying this moment.

"Yes, ma'am. And I'll wash behind my ears." Clay had to admit he loved the rapport he and Sheryl had developed over the years.

"Okay. See you at the gate, don't be late," Sheryl ended with a rhyme to end the call.

Church! Instead of a fantastic day on the lake, alone with his thoughts, he was going to be trapped in a stuffy old church. Why on a sunny day? Why not on a rainy day? He wouldn't feel so bad about the wasted time if the weather was bad.

He glanced back at the clock on his phone. Yikes! Not much time left. He headed for the bathroom.

Clay had been standing only a few minutes outside the guest gate to his neighborhood dock when Sheryl pulled up in her white Miata with the top down.

Clay stepped into the roadster and smiled. "Gotta love the sunshine."

"Of course," she said as she spun the car around and headed back up the lane.

The Pathway Church was located northwest of the University of Washington. Its campus of multiple buildings and parking lot covered many acres. This wasn't the typical small church with a white steeple that Clay had been expecting. He figured the parking lot could hold a thousand cars, easily.

Apprehension rose inside Clay as he followed Sheryl toward the main building. In a courtyard, he was astonished to see several tables serving coffee and tea. Sheryl walked directly to one table and, without asking Clay, poured two cups of coffee complete with lids. She handed a cup of the hot coffee to Clay and smiled.

"Hey, we don't have time to drink this, Sheryl, it's almost 11:30."

"Relax, we can drink it inside," she replied.

"Oh, cool," was all Clay could say.

From the courtyard, they walked into the main building. Inside the lobby, Clay's apprehension level increased. He really felt out of place. He had this terrible feeling that everyone in the lobby was looking at him; that everyone knew this was his first time; that everyone didn't think he belonged. He wanted to turn and run back out the door. Instead, he followed Sheryl to a set of large doors. A cheerful and sincere girl in her twenties with tattoos covering her left arm greeted them with a smile and a program pamphlet. They both took one and walked into the sanctuary.

No, this wasn't like any other church building Clay had been in. This was an auditorium. In front where he expected to see a pulpit and maybe some bleachers for a choir, there was a stage the spanned the full width of the building. On the stage was a drum set, electric piano, and three guitars in their stands. No choir today, he figured. Good so far. He disliked choir music. There wasn't a pulpit either. Odd. From where was the pastor or priest or whatever he was called going to talk? Behind the stage was an enormous screen with video messages and announcements being displayed silently. Two other large video screens framed the stage above like bookends. He felt like he was in reserved seating for a concert.

Sheryl led them to seats in the third row, and they sat down. The seats weren't hardwood pews either. They were seats like one would find in a movie theater. The seats even sported cup holders.

At exactly 11:30 the band and a young man walked onto the stage. The band members silently took their positions with their instruments while the man welcomed everyone in the audience. After a few announcements that made no sense to Clay, the lead singer for the band asked everyone to stand. A guitar started to play a familiar riff. Scenes of desolate streets and roads began appearing on the video screens. The music volume grew louder.

The riff, Clay knew it. It couldn't be. Not in church. A drum beat began under the repeating guitar riff. People in the audience started clapping.

The beam from a spotlight hit the lead singer the instant he started to sing.

Incredible. The band was playing. "Where the Streets Have No Names", a song from U2. It was one of Clay's favorite songs, but he had never considered it to be spiritual. But now as he watched the lyrics appear on the large screens above the stage, he heard the song as if for the first time. Before he knew it, he was clapping in time with the audience.

The song ended. He looked at Sheryl who was looking at him.

"Good band," Clay said. He might have said more about the impact of hearing the song in church, but the band transitioned into another song. This one he didn't recognize. It wasn't by U2. The lyrics were something about Jesus' love. Others in the audience knew the song because they were singing along, even Sheryl.

The band finished that song, played a third and then left the stage to an enthusiastic applause. The audience sat down as another man walked onto the stage carrying a music stand for a lectern. It looked like the sermon was about to begin. Clay settled into his seat and sipped his coffee.

Clay's mind was racing to compute all the inputs from this morning. So far, absolutely nothing had been what he had expected. While struggling to make the adjustment, he realized he was tuning in and tuning out of the sermon.

The pastor was talking about paths narrow and wide, opportunities obvious and concealed. He spoke about trust and God's love. Clay snapped to attention when the pastor began to speak about the forces that work against us, that deceive us. A passage of scripture appeared on the screen.

For our struggle is not against flesh and blood, but against the rulers, against the authorities, against the powers of this dark world and against the spiritual forces of evil in the heavenly realms."

-Ephesians 6:12

Clay didn't have a clue who or what Ephesians was, but it was eerie that Dr. Shildstein had talked to him on Friday about the battle with evil, and here he was getting a similar message on Sunday.

Was he really under attack by Satan? If so, why? Why him? Why now?

The pastor continued to talk about the devil and temptation. He recounted a story in the Bible about Jesus being tempted by Satan in the desert. That was news to Clay. He didn't know that Jesus and Satan had actually met. Of course, Clay didn't know anything in the Bible. He didn't know anything about Jesus either except He was born to a virgin, made a lot of people mad, got crucified, and somehow came to life again. That was it for Clay's understanding of the Bible and Jesus.

Clay watched as the pastor walked back and forth across the stage energetically telling the story of how Jesus, after being Baptized, went into the desert to commune with God. He fasted for forty days. During this period Satan appeared before Jesus three times and tempted him to sin and forsake God.

Clay was trying to imagine what condition Jesus must have been in after no food or water for forty days. He must have been very weak physically and certainly very hungry.

The pastor explained that Satan makes his move on us when we are weak, just like he did with Jesus in the desert. Despite being hungry and thirsty, Jesus rebuked the clever offers and suggestions of the devil. He relied on the strength of his connection with God to withstand the tempting arguments of the devil.

So, had Clay been weak? Was the devil responsible for the lighthouse nightmares, the strangers in the house, the mid-day hallucinations about his childhood, and the screaming Briggs & Stratton in his office? Or, was Clay simply losing his mind?

The more he thought about his situation and the words of the pastor the more confused he became. Nothing made sense. He had been strong as a bull before the nightmares and hallucinations took over. Now he felt like a calf on wobbling legs trying to take its first steps. He had been confident. Now we was second-guessing himself.

He had thought he was good enough, but now . . .

Sheryl nudged his right arm. He had been deep in thought and hadn't even noticed that the service was over. People were standing to leave. He picked up his coffee cup from the cup holder and stood in the aisle to leave.

"Well, what do you think?" Shery asked as they walked through the outer doors to the courtyard.

"Don't people come to church to find answers for their life?" Clay asked.

"Yes, that's the general idea," replied Sheryl.

"Then I flunked the test because all I have now are more questions."

Chapter 30

George and Reuben were chatting while munching hot scones with jam when Clay walked into the Ogilvy conference room for the scheduled Monday meeting about the Pitt-Needham acquisition offer.

"There's one left, but better grab it before Reuben does," George said, pushing the paper sack with a sole scone toward Clay.

"Thanks."

Reuben wiped a drop of blueberry jam from his chin and said, "I've reviewed the letter of intent. It's solid from a legal perspective. Regardless, I have two burning questions."

"What are they?" asked Clay.

"Do you really want to sell, and is the price fair? I mean, do you even know what the agency is worth?" The attorney asked.

George looked at Clay. Clay looked at George. Neither spoke.

"Nobody talk all at once," said Reuben.

"George and I have talked at length about this ever since I was approached by Phil Manicotti. We think the number is about right, maybe even generous considering our current financial situation."

"They haven't rescinded or revised the letter of intent following the loss of Lazzr, so I suppose the number is still good for them, too," added George.

"The number can be adjusted following an audit. You should be prepared for some tough negotiations after the audit, but what about my other question? Do you really want to sell?"

George looked at Clay. Clay looked at George.

"I do," said George. "It's a good way for me to cash out, relieve some stress, and retire in a couple of years."

Both men looked at Clay.

"The cash is tempting, but we could demand more in another year or so. I'm not ready to hang up my spurs like George. I like the idea of being part of a bigger agency, but frankly, I have concerns," said Clay.

"Like what?" said Reuben.

"Like what prevents them from axing me two months into the deal?"

"We can work on a management contract that protects you to a degree, Clay, but I have to advise you that once you sell they can do whatever they please with you, even if you are on the Board, as they've suggested. You'll be bound by a non-compete agreement, too, I expect. Both of you will. Your options for starting a new shop, or working for another agency will be limited for one or two years."

"Yeah, I could be out on the street with nowhere to go," said Clay.

"Out on the street with $10 million in the bank," George said facetiously. "And don't forget we still own this building. It's separate from the agency. If they kick you out, you won't starve anytime soon, Clay."

"Clay, I've known you for many years. I've seen you grow as a manager and leader. This is a great opportunity for you to take another step up the ladder; to play on a bigger field," said Reuben.

"I couldn't agree with Reuben more," said George with a fatherly smile.

Clay's mind began to swirl. He respected both men immensely. Their words were complimentary and encouraging, but instead of making Clay feel good, the words just bounced off him as if blocked by some invisible force shield.

Could he do it? Could he be successful in a larger agency? Wouldn't there be people better and smarter than him? People who'll not respect him. People who'll criticize him. Clay's stomach was getting queasy.

"Guys, excuse me for a minute. Nature calls. I'll be right back," Clay stood and walked quickly toward the nearest restroom.

In the restroom, he splashed cold water on his face, trying hard not to throw up. He looked in the mirror. Scared and confused eyes stared back. This was crazy. Why the emotional turmoil here?

Clay remembered what Dr. Shildstein said and the words from yesterday's sermon. So, what was this? Was he being attacked now? Was he being tempted? Tempted by what? By the money? Was he weak, or was this attack making him weak? The questions swirled around in his head. All questions, no answers.

"To sell or not to sell, that is the question," Clay said to himself in the mirror doing his best Hamlet imitation.

He finished drying his face and hands. On the way out of the restroom on the inside of the door, someone had taped a flyer announcing a Yukon Happy Hour on Friday. The client was in town for a series of meetings with the account team, so the agency was throwing a small party Friday afternoon. He was glad that he'd be back from Reef Bay by then. He needed to be in the Friday meetings. Heck, he needed to host a dinner for them on Friday. Better tell Sheryl to arrange something at Canlis restaurant.

Friday. Something about Friday stuck in his head. He had an overwhelming feeling that he had forgotten something important for Friday. Better check with Sheryl.

Just then the restroom door opened and almost hit Clay in the face while he was studying the flyer. Standing there. An awkward exchange of apologies followed as Burt from the art department stepped by, and Clay headed back to the Ogilvy conference room. *Friday? Whiskey Tango Foxtrot!*

Clay stepped back into the conference room. George and Reuben were laughing hard. *They are laughing, and I'm sweating blood.*

"Remind me to tell you Reuben's college school story about the deer and his Triumph sports car," George said, trying desperately to bring his laughter under control.

Clay grinned. He liked that about George. He wasn't going to waste time re-telling the story right then, and we wouldn't be rude by not explaining to Clay what the laughter was all about. George was always considerate. He had a quiet power that could take control of a room full of people without the people even knowing they were being controlled. The laughter and cheerful face couldn't hide the dark circles under George's eyes, however. Clay knew that George was tired. The agency business had taken its toll on him, especially this year. But, the real drain on George's energy had nothing to do with the agency. His wife of twenty-five years, Melissa, was receiving treatment for cancer. She had her good days and her bad days. And so did George.

Selling Austin-Davis was a way for George to cash in and slowly withdraw from day-to-day operation of the firm. His time and energy needed to be at home with Melissa, not wet-nursing some junior copywriter who is throwing a fit because his headline wasn't used in an ad.

If the agency wasn't sold now, Clay should do the right thing and buy out his partner to set him free. Problem is, Clay couldn't afford it.

Friday. There was the day again ringing through his head.

"All right, if we're done with the funny stories, maybe we can get back to the topic," Clay said sarcastically but with a warm smile.

Clay had no idea what he was going to say next. He just knew that it was decision time. Slowly the words started to form in his head and work their way downstream to his mouth.

"First of all, Reuben, no matter what we decide, the ownership split has to be made formal. I haven't seen anything from you on that since Suzette left."

"It's nearly complete. You'll have the paperwork this week to sign. The split is 51-49, as both of you directed, with Clay retaining his title and George retaining his."

"Great," said George.

"We can't have the official vote until that paperwork is signed, but let me say now that I approve of the Pitt-Needham acquisition with a few conditions." There he said it. His stomach churned. His hands were beginning to shake, so he held them in his lap out of sight of the other two men.

George was visibly relieved and happy. It seemed to Clay like the dark circles under George's eyes were beginning to fade. He appeared to sit straighter in his chair, too.

"What are the conditions?" asked Reuben.

"Do some research and draft for me the world's best management agreement. I expect they'll push back on some things, but I want to start from a point of strength. George should have one, too, but it'll be different because his goals are different."

"What conditions are you most interested in?" asked the attorney, already taking notes on his iPad.

"What are my responsibilities? What are the grounds for termination? What is the severance package for termination or layoff? Who do I report to? What is my position on the Board? And compensation, of course."

"Typically, Clay, the management agreement is written by the employer. In this case, Pitt-Needham will present the agreement for you to sign."

"I know, but I want to be proactive," replied Clay.

"Okay, makes sense to me to be prepared. Another point. We need to respond to Pitt-Needham's letter. The sooner, the better. Want me to call them?" asked Reuben.

"George, what do you think? Should Reuben call today and say we agree in principle and will reply formally by the end of this week?" Clay asked his partner.

"I agree. One other thing. No word of this decision to anyone. Not even our Admins. And, Reuben, demand secrecy from the Pitt-Needham people. Let's don't say anything until the letter of intent has been signed. Probably on Friday, right, Clay?"

"Yeah, Friday," said Clay. Friday was shaping up to be one heck of a day.

Chapter 31

Wednesday morning, Clay had just finished packing his overnight bag for the trip to Reef Bay to attend Uncle Charley's funeral service when Sheryl called.

"Good morning, Sheryl."

"Good morning, Clay. You are confirmed at the La Quinta in Reef Bay. I forwarded the confirmation to your email. The address is on it."

"Thanks."

"Reef Bay is pretty small, and the La Quinta is the best hotel in town. You can rough it for one night, can't you?" Sheryl liked to kid Clay about his expensive tastes in wine, cars, and hotels.

"Yes, as long as no one I know sees me checking in," Clay said, jokingly. "How do you know what size Reef Bay is? Do some research on it?"

"As a kid, I spent several summers there with relatives. I know the place well. I go back every now and then to visit. Listen, you must eat dinner at the Surf View Bistro. You'll like it."

Clay had no idea Sheryl had spent time in Reef Bay. He realized that there was a lot he didn't know about Sheryl. Lately, he was becoming more curious about her. He didn't know why.

"Good to know. Hey, speaking of dinner, were you able to reserve a room at Canlis on short notice for Friday night?"

"Sure was. I reserved your favorite room. Seats 10. That'll be sufficient, won't it?"

Clay quickly did the math in his mind. "Yep. Perfect. Make sure everyone on the Yukon team is invited. Even the intern. Hmm, let's arrange a limo for the Yukon folks to take them to the restaurant and back to their hotel."

"Will do."

"Friday is going to be a very busy day. I need your help to finesse the schedule so I can squeeze everything in. George, Reuben and I must meet Friday morning. Reuben has papers for us to sign. I want to be in as many of the Yukon meetings as possible. I have afternoon appointments with Dr. Reddi and Dr. Shildstein. I'll have to miss the Yukon happy hour, but will join everyone at Canlis at 6:30."

"Roger that," said Sheryl. "Watch your calendar. I'll update it as things solidify."

Another thought came to Clay. It was interesting how lately unusual thoughts suddenly exploded in his head. Like the day *Friday* first popping into his head while standing in the men's room at work. Another idea just swooped into his brain from far away.

"Sheryl, what are you doing Friday night?"

"I planned to do laundry and wash my hair. No, actually I have a blind date with a billionaire from Bellevue who is picking me up in his helicopter and taking me to dinner at his cabin on Whidbey Island."

Classic Sheryl.

"You could have just said that you don't have any plans," Clay said.

"What fun is that?"

"It occurred to me that no one will be at the dinner to make sure everything flows smoothly. You know you can't depend on me in these situations, besides, my brain is going to be fried by dinner time considering the funeral, and all the stuff happening on Friday."

"You want me to be there?"

"Your presence will improve the odds of an enjoyable evening. Besides, you deserve a great dinner, too."

"That's for sure, boss."

"Is that a yes?" asked Clay.

"I'll wash my hair another day, and tell the billionaire that I get air sick."

"Wonderful. Okay, I'm leaving in about an hour. Call me if anything urgent arises."

"Drive safely. I'll pray for you," Sheryl said.

"Oh, um, thanks." Clay tapped the phone to disconnect the call. He carried the suitcase downstairs and set it by the door. Then he checked the locks on all the doors, poured the remaining coffee into an insulated traveler cup and turned on the dishwasher. From the closet, he fetched a dark blue wool Burberry coat and an insulated Eddie Bauer down jacket. He slipped on the down jacket. Then after studying the remaining items he needed to carry to the car, he decided how best to carry the dress coat, coffee mug, computer case and suit case in one trip. He set the alarm, opened the door and stepped into the rain for the dash up the dock to the car.

Chapter 32

t had been many months since Clay had taken a road trip. He was actually looking forward to spending a few hours in the M5, experiencing the handling and smooth power of the German sedan. Trips like this gave him a chance to think. Well, not think, really. Whenever he looked back on a road trip, he had a difficult time remembering anything concrete that he had thought about or decided. Clay had to admit that he often spent hours not thinking about much of anything. Someone once said that men liked to retreat into their "nothing box." And it was the nothing box that Clay found himself in now as his favorite classic rock music pulsed from the auto's ten stereo speakers.

Clay headed south. The car took the rain and wind in stride as he moved from lane to lane through the ever-present traffic on I-5.

After an hour Clay took an exit westward toward the Pacific Ocean and Reef Bay. The metropolitan areas of Puget Sound gave way to fields and forests. Clay stepped on the accelerator and turned on the radar detector. He was driving thirty miles per hour above the speed limit. A ticket would be expensive.

In two hours he reduced speed as the city limits of Reef Bay came into view. The funeral service wasn't until three o'clock. He had time to check into the hotel and eat lunch.

The BMW's navigation system directed him to the La Quinta hotel located on the west side of the main highway leading through town. He parked near the front door, collected his belongings from the trunk, and walked inside.

After checking in and going to his room, he immediately unpacked his suit and dress shirt so they could hang in the closet to release their few wrinkles in the hours before the service.

Clay walked to the window. A white sheer curtain covered the window and let some of the gloomy light from outside into the room. His room looked out at an indoor courtyard with swimming pool. Deck chairs were stacked in a corner. Nobody was dumb enough to lounge by a cold pool in the middle of winter on the Washington coast.

He sat at the small desk and checked his phone for email and messages. Nothing important. Sheryl had already completed his schedule for Friday.

Not wanting to spend any more time in the room than absolutely necessary, Clay headed out the door to find something to eat. He asked the desk clerk for a recommendation. The man looked up from the magazine he was reading. "The Beach Comber is up the street one block. It's good."

"I'll try it. Thanks," Clay said.

Clay walked across the wet parking lot and up the sidewalk in the direction of the restaurant. The air was cold, damp and salty. He pulled the collar of his jacket up closer around his neck. *How could anyone live here? Seattle is cold and damp enough, but somehow this is worse.* Clay walked a little faster, realizing that the drizzle was now a light rain falling on his bare head.

The sign for the Beach Comber Café came into view right where the clerk said it'd be. Clay walked in the door and brushed the beads of water from the shoulders of his waterproof jacket.

A waitress directed him to a small table for two by the window. He ordered a bowl of clam chowder, the house salad, and hot tea. While waiting for his food to be prepared he checked messages again on his phone. Reuben had just sent an update about Pitt-Needham. According to Reuben, they were pleased with the decision and eagerly waiting the signed paperwork on Friday from George and Clay.

Clay's stomach churned. Was he really going through with this? He should be excited about the big check coming his way, but all he could think about was the fear of not measuring up in the big leagues of marketing agencies.

The waitress brought his food. Clay sampled the chowder. *Hmm, not bad.* He added a little salt. Tasted again. Then he added pepper and tasted again. *Ah, perfect.*

He ate the chowder, a package of crackers, and the salad. The hot soup and tea warmed him. He wasn't looking forward to the cold walk back. The wind had started to blow too, he could see out the window.

Clay glanced at his watch, left a 20 percent tip on the table and walked out of the café.

Back in his hotel room, Clay dried his wet hair from the walk and changed into a gray wool suit, light blue shirt with cuffs, and a silk Hermes tie. The look was sharp and slightly understated—appropriate for a funeral, he hoped.

He checked the address of the church where the service was going to be held. Then, he slipped on this long Burberry coat and walked out the door one more time.

In the car, Clay was relieved that the navigation system found the church's address and immediately plotted a course. The church was 2.5 miles south of town on Rhododendron Drive.

While driving, Clay looked at the buildings and shops that lined the main highway. He supposed they looked more festive and alive in the summer tourist season, but now the town simply looked wet and dreary. On the way through town, he counted three gas stations, one pawn shop, four gift shops, one antique store and a number of real estate offices. Just outside of the main downtown area a large sign pointed to the right saying, "Surf View Bistro. Where the Locals Eat." Clay remembered Sheryl's advice and decided to eat there tonight.

The GPS system directed him into the parking lot of Reef Bay Bible Church. *Second church in a single week, I'm really setting a record.*

The parking lot was nearly full. People were dashing through the rain into the church. *It appears Uncle Charley was well known.* As Clay turned off the ignition, the reality hit him. He was here to say goodbye to his Uncle Charley. One of the most beloved people in his life. Granted, he hadn't seen or heard from his uncle in many years, but the man was dead now. Clay would never see him again. His throat tightened as grief and guilt slowly slithered up from deep inside him like a snake awakened after a long hibernation.

Good grief, man, pull yourself together and get into the church.

Clay stepped out of the car and sprinted to the church, stepping carefully to avoid the puddles that threatened his expensive Italian loafers.

He stopped just inside the church door to brush the water off his coat and remove it. Others were doing the same. He walked into the sanctuary and managed to find a seat toward the back of the room. He sat next to a little girl and her mother. He reckoned the girl was about six or seven years old. Both looked at him curiously as he sat.

"Is this seat taken?" Clay asked in a whisper.

The mother shook her head and said, "No."

"Good." Clay settled in and began to notice his surroundings. This place looked like a church, all right. Wooden pews with Bibles and Hymnals in pockets attached to the seat backs. Up front was a pulpit, a large organ, and a small set of bleachers for a choir, now empty. Stained glass windows were on three of the four walls.

The sanctuary was full. Clay estimated about 300 people were in attendance. Some were whispering to each other. Most just stared ahead to the front of the room where an elderly harpist wearing a long gray dress was playing. *Nice touch. Harps. Heaven. Sets the right mood.*

Next to the harpist stood a single table covered in white linen. On the table was a large framed picture of Uncle Charley. The photo must have been taken recently because Clay had a difficult time recognizing his uncle, so long it had been since he had actually seen him in the flesh. The snake of guilt crawled a little further up Clay's throat.

Next to the picture was a plain-looking ceramic urn and a large bouquet of pastel flowers. What seemed out of place, however, was not on the table. In a floor stand at the end of the table opposite the harp stood a banjo.

Tears began to pool in Clay's eyes. His throat tightened. He had forgotten all about Uncle Charley's banjo. His uncle could play the banjo and the organ. Though the organ mostly played hymns and hits from the 1920s, the banjo was reserved for bluegrass—music from Uncle Charley's childhood growing up in the dirt-poor hills of Kentucky.

Clay had the eerie sensation that he was being watched. He nonchalantly dabbed his wet eyes with the sleeve of his suit coat. Out of the corner of his eye, he saw her. The little girl next to him was looking up, studying him intensely.

"It's okay. Don't be sad. Charley is in heaven now," whispered the little girl to Clay.

The girl's voice was heard by her mother who immediately turned and leaned closer to both of them.

"I'm so sorry if my daughter is disturbing you," she said to Clay and without waiting for a response said to her daughter, "Trisha, mind your manners. This nice gentleman might not wish to be bothered."

"He looked sad, mommy. I just wanted him to know that Charley was okay in heaven."

Clay responded to both. "It's perfectly okay. Your daughter is absolutely correct. Uncle Charley is in heaven."

"You said 'Uncle Charley.' Are you, uh, were you his nephew?" The mother asked with a look that had a lot more questions than her words.

"Great Uncle, actually. I'm Clay. Clay Austin from Seattle."

"Oh, I'm so sorry for your loss, Clay. We loved him. As you can see he was well liked here in Reef Bay," the woman said, sweeping her hand in the air to point out the capacity crowd. "I'm Molly. We live down the road from Charley's place."

Just then the harpist stopped playing, and the pastor stepped up to the pulpit. Clay, Trisha, and Molly stopped their conversation and turned their attention to the man standing at the pulpit.

Based on the pastor's words, Clay concluded that Uncle Charley had been a long-time member of this church. The pastor spoke warmly of his uncle's volunteer work, even to his repair of one of the priceless stained glass windows that had broken in a gale. The pastor said that Charley was a regular, but could seldom find his way to church on time. Apparently, it was accepted that Charley would always come through the door during the second of three worship songs. Being late, he'd have to sit in the back on the aisle.

"Third row from the back was where we could always find Charley, but never during the first song," the pastor said and pointed to the back. Soft laughter rippled through the audience. Many heads turned to where the pastor was pointing. Clay turned just enough in his seat, so he could spot the place in the third row where his uncle always sat. There was the row furthest back. That was number one. Next was two. The second row from the back was immediately behind

Clay's row. No way! In a second he counted again. One, two, three. No mistake. He was sitting in the third row from the back. He was sitting in Uncle Charley's seat!

His hands began to shake, the snake inside him was really on the move now. It didn't help that about half the congregation was staring at him. He felt a tug on his right sleeve and looked over to Trisha.

"It's okay, mister. You can sit here," said the little girl.

Those were the kindest words Clay had ever heard. But the comfort was soon over. Now he was completely lost in his emotions. He never heard the remaining eulogy. Nor did the words of the next two speakers have any meaning to him. He felt like he was in a bubble. Everything in view was foggy. He could hear words, but they were just gibberish. Most people in the room, even some of the men, were wiping their eyes now.

People were remembering. They were remembering what they had just lost.

The second speaker stepped away from the pulpit, and a boy in his teens walked up to the side of the table, picked up the banjo, and slipped the strap over his shoulder.

"Hello, everyone. Most of you know me. For those who don't, I'm Billy Morris. Charley taught me how to play the banjo and encouraged me to stick with it when other kids made fun of me. I sing a little, too, so I want to do a song for you in honor of Charley. It's an old bluegrass tune called *Wayfaring Stranger*." His voice cracked at the end from emotion.

Billy started picking the banjo strings, and it became immediately obvious that Billy had talent. He started to sing. *Yep, the boy had talent all right.*

I'm just a poor wayfaring stranger
Traveling through this world below
There is no sickness, no toil, nor danger
In that bright land to which I go

Clay recognized the tune as one that Johnny Cash made famous.

By the third verse, nearly everyone in the congregation was wiping tears from their eyes.

I know dark clouds will gather 'round me
I know my way is hard and steep
But beauteous fields arise before me
Where God's redeemed, their vigils keep
I'm going there to see my Mother
She said she'd meet me when I come

Clay watched Billy play that song from deep in his heart. Tears were streaming down his face, but the words and music poured from him and then everyone, including Clay, was drinking it in like fine wine.

The song ended. Billy gently and with great respect replaced the banjo in its stand. With his back to the audience, Billy picked up the urn.

"God bless you, Charley. Thank you for being so kind to me." Billy set the urn back on the table and left the stage sobbing.

The pastor stepped back to the pulpit to let the mourners know that refreshments were being served in the fellowship hall next door to the sanctuary. People stood to leave. Clay did the same and immediately felt another tug on his sleeve. It was Trisha again.

"Are you going to have some cookies with us?"

"Trisha, stop bothering the poor man," Molly said, clearly embarrassed by her gregarious daughter.

What Clay really wanted to do was get into his car and drive as fast and as far away from Reef Bay as he could. He wanted to escape the thought that haunted him right now. He had failed to keep in touch with a man who was the closest thing to a father Clay had known. A man who loved him and patiently taught him many things. How could Clay lose touch? How could Clay not know that his uncle lived for years less than 200 miles from his houseboat in Seattle? Right now, Clay despised himself and felt about two feet tall.

"If you're up to it, I think you'll enjoy speaking with the town folk who knew your uncle. The cookies will be good, too," Molly said with a smile.

Before Clay could answer, Trisha took his hand and started to pull him toward the hallway that led to the fellowship hall. Escape wasn't possible now. He had been kidnapped by a little angel and her mother.

Chapter 33

The cookies were exceptional. There wasn't an espresso machine in sight, but the hot spiced tea did the trick to warm Clay and ease his troubled mind. Trisha and Molly apparently felt it was their duty to introduce Clay to everyone.

These were God-fearing, small-town folks. Clay liked everyone he met. They were warm, welcoming, compassionate—down to earth people scratching out a simple life in a small coastal town. Amazingly, each one had a great story to tell about Charley. His uncle had touched many people.

Molly introduced Clay to Roger Bildgewood, the mayor of Reef Bay. Bildgewood's handshake had the grip of a politician—strong but insincere. The grip matched the man's smile perfectly. Of the dozen or so people he had conversed with already in the fellowship hall, the Mayor was the first with whom he did not feel comfortable.

"Real sorry for your loss, Mr. Austin. Real sorry. Your uncle was a stalwart supporter of this community. Folks even voted him the Grand Marshal of this year's Fourth of July parade," the mayor said in a way that did little to hide the official's jealousy. He leaned in closer to Clay for his next sentence. "Can't say the old man was much of a public speaker though. Nearly put us all to sleep, but bless his heart he tried. My goodness, he tried," Bildgewood chortled.

Clay just smiled, sizing up the snake talking in front of him.

"One thing's for sure. Ol' Charley loved this town and loved his property out there on the point."

Clay wanted away from this guy but had a natural curiosity about where his uncle had lived. Clay just assumed he had lived in a trailer court, considering that was the man's chosen style of residence for as long as Clay could remember.

"What property?" asked Clay.

"You didn't know? I thought you were his nephew. You never been to his place?"

"No, I haven't been. In fact, it has been at least ten years since we've been in touch."

"Well, then you ought to take a drive out there. The place is on Deception Point. Charley never did get it fixed up right. Too much work and expense I guess. If he had been smart, he just would have demolished everything and built a nice B&B or something. But, Charley liked to tinker, and there was plenty of tinkering to do there. That's for sure." The mayor took another bite from his cookie. Crumbs fell to his shirt and joined the crumbs already there from the previous cookie. Clay wanted to leave the disgusting man, but he kept on talking, not leaving an opening for Clay to cut and run.

"Yes, sir. Lots of tinkering. In fact, it was the tinkering that killed him, you know."

Clay was getting annoyed, "What do you mean?"

"Oh, I guess you don't know because you were way up in Seattle when it happened."

"What happened?" asked Clay.

"The poor man was up a ladder re-caulking a window when he fell and hit his head. Why someone his age was twenty feet up a ladder in the first place is beyond me."

"Twenty feet up. So, it's a two-story house?" Clay asked.

"No, sir. The house is just a single story. It should be demolished, too, if you ask me."

"Mayor, if the house is one story, what on earth was my uncle repairing that had a window twenty feet off the ground?"

"Mr. Austin, you're not listening. Your uncle didn't fall off the residence. He fell off the lighthouse."

Chapter 34

Clay's head, which had begun to clear in the fellowship hall, was now a swirling mess of confusion and emotion. Somehow Clay managed to disengage from the talkative Mayor Bildgewood and work his way to one corner of the room to say goodbye to Molly and Trisha.

"But you're coming to church Sunday, aren't you? You can sit in Charley's seat. It's okay." Little Trisha never gave up.

Clay kneeled down, so his face was on the same level as the little girl's. "Maybe someday, sweetheart. I live in Seattle, and I'll be driving back tomorrow."

The look of disappointment on her face was heart-breaking. It was obvious to Clay there wasn't a father in this little girl's life.

"But, thank you for inviting me to have the yummy cookies. I bet you helped bake them, didn't you?" Clay played his hunch. He was right. The little girl's face lit up, and a big grin spread ear to ear.

"Yes, I did. Mommy helped."

"Well, I'm going to take one in a napkin, so I can eat it later." He didn't think her smile could grow any wider, but it did. Clay stood and said goodbye to Molly. She wore a sad smile on her face. He could see she was missing a father for Trisha, too.

Clay ambled over to the cookie table, wrapped two of the chocolate chip wonders in a napkin, and headed back to the hallway to claim his overcoat. He slipped the cookies into a coat pocket and walked out into the gloom of late afternoon.

Sitting in the car with the engine idling, he had to make a decision. One part of him wanted to drive out to inspect his uncle's property on Deception Point, wherever that was. The other part of Clay wanted a stiff drink and a hot shower to remove the chill he felt from the funeral service, the chill of the damp day and the lingering chill from the knowledge that a lighthouse had somehow played a part in his uncle's death. *A lighthouse! Whiskey Tango Foxtrot.*

Clay checked the time. Only about an hour of daylight remained. He opted for a drink and a shower before dinner.

Back at the La Quinta Inn, Clay ventured into the lounge for a drink. The bar was practically deserted, so he ordered a scotch on the rocks at the bar and carried it over to a small table next to a gas fireplace. The fire didn't put out much heat, but the ambience was better there than elsewhere in this sad, threadbare corner of the hotel.

Clay placed his overcoat in the unused chair at his table, loosened his tie, and sipped at the scotch. Soon he was checking email and messages on his phone. All was well back at the office. That was a relief.

He checked the home security app on his phone. It showed no alarms had been tripped. He cycled through the different security camera views that showed live feeds from six locations in and outside the house. All quiet on the home front, too.

Clay finished his drink, signed for it at the bar and headed to his room. There, he flipped on the TV news channel, got undressed and into the shower. The hot water immediately soothed him. He felt the chill leave his body only to be replaced with hunger. He dried off, brushed his hair and changed into fresh casual clothes consisting of dark blue cords, a heavy gray wool sweater, and tan Eddie Bauer work boots. He wasn't going to be afraid of any puddles tonight. No sir.

After flipping off the TV, he grabbed his down-filled jacket from the closet and headed back outside to the car.

He drove south down the main street through Reef Bay to where he had remembered seeing the Surf View Bistro sign. He turned right as the sign instructed and followed a winding road lined on both sides by small homes without garages. The bright beams that streamed from the custom LED headlamps of the M5 reflected off the sides of the muddy vehicles parked in the driveways. Clay couldn't help but notice that every home had at least one, often two, pickups parked in front. Quite a contrast to his own neighborhood, where the large vehicle of choice was a land yacht SUV tucked neatly into a three-car garage.

No sooner were doubts about the Surf View Bistro entering Clay's head—after all, would a nice restaurant be in a buffalo wings and pizza neighborhood like this—when the neighborhood changed. The homes on the right side of the street were much larger and tucked back from the road into the trees. Instead of muddy pickups in front, there were manicured lawns. Instead of gravel driveways, paved driveways lined with landscape lighting led to large garages with varnished doors. The road became narrower. Clay shifted down to reduce speed.

Clay drove on for another five minutes. Up ahead in the headlights Clay saw two signs. On the right side of the street, the sign read, "Dead End. No Exit". On the left side of the street, a friendlier sign announced, "Surf View Bistro, Just Ahead."

Clay dropped the M5 down one more gear and was soon entering the small, dimly lit parking lot of the restaurant. Only a few cars were in the lot.

A young hostess led him to a small table by a large picture window. Clay had just sat down when the waiter approached his table and expertly poured ice water into a glass.

"Welcome to Surf View Bistro. My name is Billy, and I'll be assisting you this evening. May I bring you a cocktail or wine?"

Clay looked around and noticed a door leading into the bar at the end of the restaurant. He thought about ordering a scotch and then decided against it. The selection probably wouldn't be that good here. He quickly scanned the wine list. *Well, maybe there is hope after all.* The wine list was extensive and very well selected.

"I'm going to have fish tonight, so please bring me a bottle of the Sixto Moxee Chardonnay," asked Clay.

"Yes, sir. Excellent choice. I'll be right back."

Something about the Billy, the waiter, was familiar. Clay couldn't put his finger on it. Clay looked around the restaurant. If he was to describe it in one word, the word would be "cozy." The room was slightly upscale, but not pretentious, like restaurants can be. The little restaurant contained about 20 tables. At one end was a wide door leading into the bar. Next to the door was a gigantic stone fireplace with a mantle made from rough-hewn cedar. A real fire blazed inside. Its warm light spilled out into the dining area and added to the cozy atmosphere.

Billy returned with the wine and wine bucket. He presented the label for inspection. Clay nodded in approval and Billy expertly opened the bottle while explaining the day's specials.

Billy left Clay to give him time to decide. Clay tasted the wine and smiled. There were elements of almond butter and citrus that made the wine very interesting and very delicious.

For the first time since sitting down, Clay looked out the window next to him. Outside was pitch black except for several floodlights that had been mounted on the cliff below the restaurant. The lights shone down, revealing the churning surf far below. If it wasn't for the floodlights, Clay couldn't have known the little restaurant was perched on top of a cliff above the crashing waves of the Pacific.

The sound of a woman's laughter reached Clay from a nearby table. He thought of Sheryl. He had an idea. He retrieved the smartphone from his pocket and carefully took a picture of the menu. He then sent the pictures in a text message to Sheryl asking, "What do you recommend?"

Clay smiled at his cleverness. Sipped his wine and looked down at the foaming white waves far below in the darkness.

Within a few minutes, his phone vibrated. Sheryl's text replied, "Start with a crab cocktail. For entrée, the grilled halibut with lemon dill sauce. Must eat the sourdough rolls." She ended the text with a smiley face.

Clay typed back, "Thnx. Impressed with the place so far."

"How was funeral?" Sheryl inquired.

The question hit Clay surprisingly hard. Just a few hours ago he had been at Uncle Charley's funeral with tears in his eyes. Here he sat now only thinking about what he was going to eat. He hadn't thought of Uncle Charley since he left the funeral. What kind of unfeeling monster was he? Why wasn't he sitting here honoring his uncle by recalling all the great moments? No, instead he was preoccupied with the hedonist pleasures of food and wine.

The thing was, Clay didn't know how to respond. How was he going to answer Sheryl's question? *How was the funeral, anyway, huh, Clay? How was it? What was it like to say goodbye to Uncle Charley who loved you very much but hadn't seen you in ten years because you were too busy? How was the funeral, little buddy? Let's hear it. How convenient that the minute you got in your fancy car to leave the church you had pretty much put Charley out of your mind.*

"You still there?" Sheryl texted again.

"Still here. Got distracted. Funeral good. He was very popular here. Nice people. Except the mayor." Clay tapped Send.

Billy returned to take Clay's order. Clay ordered exactly what Sheryl suggested. The waiter repeated the order, added some wine to Clay's glass, and left.

"Mayor Bildgewood?" Sheryl texted back.

"Yep, the Honorable Mayor Bildgewood."

"He is piece of work. Hope you checked your wallet after you left him."

"No, but I took a hot shower after." Clay included a smiley face and tapped Send.

"LOL"

"How are things at office?" Before sending Clay decided to edit his text. "How are things with you?" He tapped Send.

"It's been quiet. Catching up on stuff. I re-arranged your office."

"You what?!!!" Clay was not happy that Sheryl would reorganize his office without talking to him first.

"LOL. Just kidding."

"That's a relief."

"Oh, I ran into Suzette at lunch today. She gave me the cold shoulder."

"Interesting. Who was she eating with?" Clay asked.

"Don't know. A sloppy middle-aged guy who could use a diet."

"Sounds like Dub Garcia from Kole Partners." Clay made a mental note to mention to his attorney that Suzette may be trying to violate her non-compete agreement.

Billy brought Clay's dinner to the table.

"Appetizer is here. Gotta go. Talk later." Send.

"Bon appétit."

Clay almost typed, "wish you were here," but quickly changed his mind. Evidently the wine on an empty stomach was impacting his judgment.

The crab cocktail was delicious. Plenty of fresh, chilled crab meat with a tangy sauce. The warm just-out-of-the-oven sourdough rolls were a perfect match with the crab cocktail. Soon the main entrée was served, and Clay was lost in the succulent flavors of the halibut and dill sauce.

Rain began to spray hard against the windows of the bistro. Occasionally the large window next to Clay would vibrate in response to the gusts slamming into it. While enjoying an after-dinner coffee, Clay checked the weather forecast for Reef Bay. A storm warning had been posted tonight for winds of 40 mph with gusts of 50 mph.

Clay finished his coffee and placed a credit card in the leather folder for Billy. Another blast of wind-driven rain hit his window. Then he saw a flashing light through the window. Just a brief flash. Nothing more. A few seconds later it flashed again from outside somewhere in the distance. The rain on the outside of the windows together with dining room lights reflecting off the inside of the window made it nearly impossible to see anything outside in the darkness. Still, every few seconds a short beam of light would appear and then disappear. It dawned on Clay that he must be looking at the beam from a distant lighthouse.

Lighthouse? Clay wondered if it could be coming from Uncle Charley's lighthouse. He was curious. When Billy returned with the credit card receipt to sign, Clay asked him, "I see a light from a lighthouse off in the distance. What lighthouse is it?"

"That's the Point Jeopardy light," Billy responded.

"Do you know if that is the lighthouse owned by Charley Gragg?"

"Charley? No. His light doesn't work anymore. Charley passed, too. His funeral was today." A sudden sadness swept over Bill's face.

Funeral! That's where Clay had seen his waiter's face before. Billy. Bill Morris, the banjo player.

"You're the banjo player from the funeral," said Clay.

Billy looked surprised for a few seconds and replied, "Yes, sir, I am. I guess you were at the service."

"I sure was. I'm the guy who was sitting in Charley's usual seat," Clay said with a smile.

Billy smiled back, "Right. You were wearing a suit then. Sorry I didn't recognize you here."

"No problem. I loved what you said and how you played," said Clay.

Emotion was beginning to overtake Billy, "Yes, he was kind to me."

"Charley was my uncle," Clay said.

Billy looked at Clay without speaking, as if his mind was reassembling facts and dates. "Is your name, Clay?" asked Billy.

"Yes, Clay Austin from Seattle. Uncle Charley may have mentioned me."

"Mentioned you? My gosh, Mr. Austin, he talked about you nearly every day. He was very fond of you, sir."

A wave of nausea swept over Clay. For a minute he thought he was going to lose his dinner. He took a drink of water to settle his stomach and his nerves.

"Sorry, I have to take care of my other customers. Nice to meet you, Mr. Austin."

"Likewise, Billy. Likewise."

Clay put on his jacket and walked into the blustery night.

The wind and rain seemed to be swirling from all directions at the same time. It accosted Clay like a family of angry animals. First from the front, then the sides and back. The gravel parking lot was littered with small branches, pine cones, and pine needles dislodged from the surrounding trees by the gale.

Clay unlocked the BMW and jumped inside out of the maelstrom. He fretted about the wetness of his coat on the expensive leather seats and made a mental note to dry the seats with a towel as soon as he got back to the La Quinta

He pushed the Start button next to the steering wheel. The engine, which usually roared into life instantly, only made a slow whirring sound.

"Crap, are you kidding me?" Clay pushed Start again. All he heard was the same slow whirring sound. Of all the places, of all the times, to have a dead battery, his car chose tonight.

Now what? Clay thought to himself. Should he call a tow truck for a battery jump? Good luck finding one anytime soon in this small town. He looked around the parking lot. It was vacant except for one car, probably belonging to the last diners in the restaurant. Maybe they could jump his battery. The car was a new Escalade SUV. *It's doubtful they even carry jumper cables, but it's worth a try.*

Clay opened his car door and sprinted back to the restaurant in the howling wind and driving rain. *This running back and forth in the rain is getting old.*

Inside the Bistro he stood in the foyer dripping wet looking around for someone to notice him, not certain what his next step should be. The last customers were paying their check to Billy, who had his back to the front door. Hearing the door open and close, Billy turned to see Clay standing there like a lost puppy dog.

Billy walked over to Clay. "Did you forget something, Mr. Austin?"

"No, my battery is dead. I was hoping someone here could give me a jump."

Billy didn't hesitate. "No problem. I'll do it. My shift is over. Just give me a few minutes to clear the table and punch out."

"Great, Billy. Do you have jumper cables?"

"Sure do. I'll drive around to the main lot in about ten minutes. Which car is yours?"

"There are only two cars left in the lot. I'm the BMW."

Clay could swear he saw a slight smirk on Billy's face when he said "BMW." He didn't care. He just wanted to leave.

Again, Clay dashed through the storm back to his car. He got it, tried the Start button one last time. He heard the same weak whirring sound and leaned back in his seat to wait.

Seeing all the debris in the parking lot from the wind increased his anxiety. The parking lot was surrounded by towering pine and cedar trees that were being whipped about by the wind. He feared a falling branch or sharp pine cone might hit his car. All he could do was wait for Billy.

After a few minutes, Clay felt a deep vibration through the driver's seat and steering wheel. For a second he thought maybe his car had miraculously started without him. Then an intense light filled the car as Billy's diesel Dodge truck pulled up next to the BMW.

Clay looked over to his right. He saw a pickup with mammoth tires. The truck body had been raised so the bottom of the driver's door was at Clay's eye level. The loud, rough idling of a diesel engine was all he could hear. The driver's door opened, and Billy jumped out.

Clay popped the trunk of the M5 and stepped out of the car.

With jumper cables in hand, Billy walked to the front of the BMW. At the same time, Clay was walking to his trunk on the left side. Billy stood near the car's front end waiting for Clay. Clay stood in the rain waiting for Billy at the rear of the car. It would have been comical if the weather wasn't so miserable.

Clay realized the problem and shouted above the truck and wind, "Battery is back here, Billy."

Billy shook his head in disbelief and walked to the rear of Clay's car. Clay had the trunk lid open. The trunk light was weak but just bright enough to enable Clay to find the floor cover revealing the trunk compartment that held the battery.

"What's the battery doing back here?" Billy asked.

"Weight balance," said Clay.

"Whatever. Hey, hold these cables. I gotta back up the truck to get closer."

Billy backed up the huge truck, so its engine compartment was closer to the BMW's battery. He opened its hood, and while standing on the truck bumper attached the cables to the truck's battery. He stepped down from the bumper, walked to the BMW, and placed the terminal clamps on the dead battery in the trunk.

Clay got back into his car and pushed the Start button. The M5 roared to life. Billy disconnected the cables from the BMW's battery and from his Dodge.

Clay reached a wet hand inside his pocket to pull out a twenty to give Billy.

Still having to raise his voice to be heard above the growling truck and wind, Clay said, "I really appreciate your help, Billy. Please take this." He handed the twenty-dollar bill to Billy.

Billy looked at it and said, "That's not necessary, Mr. Austin. I'm glad I could help you out tonight."

"You sure?"

"Absolutely. It wouldn't be right me accepting money for this. Especially from Charley's nephew." Billy extended his hand and Clay shook it.

"Okay. You're a good man, Billy."

"Thank you. Have a good evening, Mr. Austin." Billy climbed up into his truck and roared off into the night.

Before getting back into his car, he quickly took off his coat, shook it hard to remove as much of the water as possible and jumped inside. He placed the coat on the floor of the passenger side before backing out of his parking space and leaving the Surf View Bistro.

Driving back on the narrow road from the bistro, Clay had to turn the fan on high to help remove the condensation that was forming on the inside of the windows, making it hard to see.

The black road ahead was littered with small branches and pine cones. The windshield wipers were on high speed, trying to keep up with the rain that fell in wild sheets on the car.

Clay wanted more visibility ahead; he reached to flip on the fog lights when suddenly out of the darkness a deer appeared, just standing there in the middle of the road, frozen by the BMW's headlights.

Clay's right foot slammed hard against the brake pedal. The M5's oversized brakes and anti-skid electronics took over, bringing the sedan to a quick stop, its bumper just inches from the deer.

For a few seconds, the deer looked up the car's hood at Clay. Its brown, fear-filled eyes revealing that it didn't completely comprehend what had just happened. The animal came to its senses and bolted off the road and into the darkness.

Clay's hands were shaking. His knees, too. That was a close call. First a dead battery and now a near collision with a stupid deer. *This place must not like me. Let's get back to the hotel, get some sleep, see the attorney in the morning and then get the heck out of Reef Bay.*

Attorney! That's right. Thursday he had an appointment with Uncle Charley's executor. Clay's mind went back to the funeral service earlier today; back to the kind words that the town's people had for his uncle. He felt a lump of sadness form in his throat. It was sadness mixed with guilt. How could he be so self-centered as to not keep in touch with his uncle? How must Uncle Charley have felt about it? Billy said that Charley talked about Clay all the time. So, he must have been terribly hurt that Clay didn't care enough to stay in touch. The thought of Clay's selfishness hurting his uncle brought real tears to his eyes. The lump in his throat turned to gasping sobs. With the tears in his eyes and the rain on the windshield, Clay could barely see to drive. He was thinking of stopping on the deserted road just long enough to pull himself together when bright headlights appeared in his rearview mirror. Now Clay had to proceed.

He wiped the tears away and drove on, but the headlights in the mirror were getting larger and brighter. Gauging from the height of the lights, it looked like a truck was approaching. It was coming fast, too. Too fast for this night, Clay thought.

The narrow road was barely wide enough for two small lanes. Clay figured if the guy wanted to pass, he could squeeze by.

Within thirty seconds the truck, or whatever it was, was right on his tail. The headlights filled the inside of his car with harsh light. The reflection from the rearview mirror was so intense and distracting that Clay turned the mirror down so it couldn't reflect the light into his eyes. Clay sped up to put space between himself and the truck. The truck stayed on his bumper. Next Clay tried tapping his brakes and slowing down gradually. The truck slowed, too. *Whiskey Tango Foxtrot. Go around. Pass me. There's room on the left.*

The truck didn't pass. Passing didn't appear to be what the driver was wanting to do. If not passing, what then?

A shriek like that of a furious animal cut through the night. Clay was beginning to panic. He couldn't explain that noise or the truck stuck on his tail. He decided enough was enough. His foot went down on the accelerator. The M5 shot forward like a rocket as its 500-horsepower engine propelled the car down the street away from the truck.

The truck was still there but falling back now. Another shriek filled the night and sent chills down Clay's spine. *What is going on?* His car shot down the road through the fashionable neighborhood at 100 miles per hour. When he reached the other neighborhood of small house without garages, he backed off the accelerator. The truck lights were nowhere to be seen in his rearview mirror, but he expected the behemoths parked in every driveway to come after him in a pack.

None of the parked trucks left to follow Clay. Another day perhaps. He reached the highway, turned left and headed north back to the La Quinta.

Chapter 35

After a restless sleep and a mediocre breakfast, Clay checked out of the motel. Before leaving the parking lot, he entered the attorney's address into his GPS system. The car's navigation system directed him southward, back through town. As the Surf View Bistro sign came into sight, Clay was grateful that his GPS was telling him to continue south on the highway, not turn right. Clay didn't want to venture down the road to the bistro ever again. All that road had to offer was crazy deer and crazy truckers. Never mind the unexplainable shrieks that made Clay's skin crawl.

About five miles from the Surf View sign Clay turned into a small strip mall on the right side of the highway. Clay read the signs on the five stores there. Seven-Eleven, Hilda's Nails, Wilson Insurance, Reef Liquor, and at the end, Law Office. That was it. Clay parked in a space in front of the Law Offices.

Walking in, he was greeted by a middle-aged woman that would look more at home in a kitchen with toddlers on the floor than in a law office.

"Hello, can I help you?" she asked.

"Good morning. Yes, I have an appointment with Glenn Bartlett. I am Clay Austin."

"Yes, Mr. Austin. He is expecting you. Please have a seat. Can I get you some coffee? It's fresh."

Clay thought about the lousy cup of coffee he had back at the motel. "Yes, that would be wonderful."

Clay sat down in the small reception area. This was a far cry from the attorney's offices he was accustomed to in Seattle. The reception area looked like it belonged in a barbershop. Even the magazines on the ancient coffee table in front of him seemed out of place in a law office. *Modern Mechanics. Field & Stream. People. Home & Garden.* Clay had to remind himself that he was in a small town and this was a small-town lawyer, not a big-city corporate attorney billing at $600 per hour.

The receptionist handed Clay his coffee. "Did you need cream or sugar, Mr. Austin?"

"No thank you. Black is great." He sipped the hot coffee. It was excellent. Really excellent. "The coffee is very good, just what I needed this morning."

"I'm glad you like it. Mr. Bartlett and I are very particular about our coffee. Some say we're coffee snobs. Why would they call us snobs just because we only buy beans from Ethiopia?" She laughed.

Clay was trying to recalibrate his opinion of the attorney. The office wasn't much, but he had good taste in coffee. That counted for something.

"Mr. Austin, sorry to keep you waiting, I'm Glenn Bartlett." The attorney stood next to the coffee table with his hand extended to shake.

Clay stood and reached for Glenn's hand. "Nice to meet you. I was just complimenting your assistant on the excellent coffee."

"Yes, Betty and I often kid ourselves that if we ever get tired of the law, we can always open a coffee shop. Please come into my office," said Glenn.

Glenn took his place behind a massive polished wood desk. It was made from a tree trunk, cut length-wise, polished to a brilliant shine and mounted on sturdy legs.

Clay thought that the attorney was either very organized, or business was very slow. The top of his desk only held a notebook computer and a single file folder. The bookshelf and side table in the office were neat and orderly, too. He studied the man seating across from him. He guessed the man was in his early fifties. Thick gray hair made him look older than he probably was. The man had a rugged appearance and a weathered face. More akin to a mechanic or lumberjack, thought Clay, than an attorney.

The man's hazel eyes were sharp and warm. Lines were etched on his face as if he spent the day squinting and smiling. Based on the photos on the office walls, Clay could see the man spent time in the outdoors. There were pictures of him holding large salmon, kneeling next to dead deer and elk, huddled in a duck blind, and standing on the sidelines of a football field.

Glenn opened the file folder in front of him and looked at Clay. "Mr. Austin, before we get down to business I want to express my condolences for the loss of your uncle. He was a fine man. Much loved here in Reef Bay."

Clay nodded.

"I saw you at the service. Ironic isn't it that you sat in his seat?"

Clay nodded again and felt his eyes moisten.

"I wanted to introduce myself after the service, but unfortunately I had to return to the office for an appointment," Glenn said. "Anyway, we are going to miss Charley Gragg around here. I've known Charley for years, and have helped him with legal affairs."

"That's kind of you, Mr. Bartlett. Everyone I've met here has only had wonderful things to say about my uncle," said Clay.

"That brings us to the business at hand, Mr. Austin. Your uncle has a will, and I am the executor of his estate. You are named in the Will, but before we continue, I must ask you for some photo ID."

"Oh, sure, of course." Clay retrieved his driver's license from his wallet and handed it to Glenn, who studied it carefully. "All right. If you don't mind, I need to ask Betty to make a copy for the records and court filing."

Glenn picked up the phone and asked his assistance to come in and take a photocopy of Clay's driver's license. After she returned with the copy and original, she shut the door behind her and left the two men to talk.

"Mr. Austin, your uncle didn't have many heirs. He left what little cash and investments he owned to relatives in Kentucky." He opened the file folder in front of him and flipped to a page bookmarked with an adhesive note. Clay sipped his Ethiopian coffee and made a mental note to buy some as soon as he returned to Seattle. "To you, your uncle bequeathed his Ford pickup truck, his tools, and his residence."

Clay had started wondering what on earth he was going to do with a pickup and tools. He almost missed the last part. "Residence? He left me his residence?"

"Ah, yes, your uncle owned his residence and about five acres of land debt-free. He left the property to you, Mr. Austin. I know you, and your uncle were close, you've probably been to his house on the point."

Clay felt his face redden slightly in embarrassment. "No, unfortunately, I haven't been to his home. I'm very sorry to say I didn't keep in touch with my uncle." Clay's voice dropped off in sadness.

"Oh, well then you are in for a very pleasant surprise, Mr. Austin. Your uncle owned a very nice piece of property. I can share that its tax appraised value is exactly $2,250,000."

Clay's eyes opened wide. "Did you say two and a quarter million? No loan?"

"That's correct, sir. Your uncle was very good with his money. He had no debts when he passed. I've already paid what few outstanding bills he had—for utilities, taxes, and such."

Glenn referred to the will again. "Yes, he left it all to you—the land, the house, a tool shed, and the lighthouse, of course."

Clay had been fighting back tears of guilt. A man he hadn't expressed his love to enough had died and given him property worth over two million dollars. He was trying to make sense of it and barely heard the attorney itemize the property.

"I'm sorry, could you repeat the list of property again," Clay sniffed.

Glenn reached behind him for a box of tissue and pushed the box across the polished desk to Clay.

While Clay dabbed his eyes with a tissue, the attorney repeated the list of property items.

"Mr. Austin, in addition to the Ford pickup and tools, your uncle has bequeathed to you his land holdings at 3100 Deception Point Drive, plus everything on it. This consists of a residence, a tool shed, and lighthouse." The attorney looked up from the Will and with a slight smile asked, "Mr. Austin, I bet you never thought in your wildest dreams that you'd own a lighthouse."

Chapter 36

After signing what seemed like an endless stream of legal forms, Clay left the attorney's office carrying a thick folder of documents and a set of keys to the property.

He sat in the car for several moments. Numb. Not sure what to do next. It was noon already. A quick text exchange with Sheryl revealed that all was well at the agency. Everything was arranged on his Friday schedule. He let his loyal assistant know that he might not make it into the office today.

He entered the address into the Bimmer's navigation system. It directed him farther south down the highway.

After a mile and a half, the GPS alerted him that Deception Point Drive was 500 feet ahead. He shifted down in preparation for the turn. There were no buildings or signs at the intersection, just a small hard-to-read street sign. Clay made the turn. Deception Point Drive was one of the curviest roads Clay had driven in a long time. He allowed himself to have a little fun taking the turns a lot faster than the posted speed limit of 25 mph.

The narrow road wound westward through tall trees, gaining in elevation. After about a half mile the road leveled off, and the tall trees gave way to short wind-swept cedars, bent in contorted shapes by the constant wind blowing in from the ocean.

Through the trees, Clay could catch glimpses of the gray Pacific Ocean to his right. He slowed down as the road narrowed to a single lane and approached a gate. He stopped in front of the gate and parked. In an envelope, the attorney had given Clay a large number of keys, each labeled with its lock location. Front door. Tool shed. Back door. Pickup. Lighthouse. Safe deposit box. Gate.

He selected the gate key, stepped out of the car and unlocked the metal gate. It swung easily to the side. The sculpted cedars were thick here and crowded the gate as if keeping guard. He couldn't see the ocean from the gate and noticed that standing by the gate the cedars provided an excellent wind break.

Clay smiled. That's no coincidence. Uncle Charley let those cedars grow thick right here so he'd have some protection from the cold, salty winds every time he got out of his truck to open the gate. Classic Uncle Charley.

Clay got back into the car and drove through the gate. Inside the property, the road took a sharp bend to the right and exited the protection of the gate cedars.

What Clay saw next made him gasp.

He was looking directly westward across the expansive Pacific Ocean. The mostly gray panorama was only broken by the silhouette of a white lighthouse situated at the end of the road.

He drove down the final 100 yards of gravel road to the residence and lighthouse. Wind gusts buffeted his car as if to say, "you don't belong here."

Clay parked in the car port next to the Ford pickup. He got out and walked around the house, preferring to explore outside first, not eager to venture inside his uncle's former home yet. No, he wasn't ready for that. The wind was strong and cold in his face as he walked through the grass beside the house and toward the lighthouse.

The lighthouse and residence were perched on a promontory jutting out from the hill. A rusty metal fence lined the cliff edge. Clay walked toward the fence. He looked down. Five hundred feet below, waves crashed against the rocky cliffs, sending spray in all directions. Clay never liked heights that much. The strong wind and the proximity to the cliff made him very uneasy. He backed away from the decaying fence.

He scanned the horizon to his right. All he could see were rugged cliffs and a distant shoreline far off to the north. He squinted against the wind and looked to his left. Below, he could see the entrance to a bay, Reef Bay he figured. A stone breakwater partially guarded the bay from the incessant waves.

To the south, on the opposite side of the bay, a cliff rose, a twin to where Clay stood. He could barely see in the mist the outline of a lighthouse. Must be the Point Jeopardy lighthouse that Billy told him about at the bistro last night.

He looked up at his uncle's lighthouse. *Correction, Clay. Your lighthouse.* He noticed that the structure was much in need of repair and painting. There were many visible gaps in the mortar between the bricks on the west side of the lighthouse that was exposed to the worst of the elements. The paint had long ago been worn away.

Clay shivered in the cold wind and walked quickly back to the house. It was time to go inside.

He reached into his pocket for the key marked Front Door. He unlocked it and stepped inside.

Clay felt like he was breaking into someone else's house, and at any moment he'd be discovered and turned over to the cops. After being accosted by the wind outside, it was eerily calm and quiet inside the house. He stepped further into the main living area. It was simply furnished with couch, small painted dinette set, several book shelves filled with books, a well-used easy chair next to a reading lamp, and a wood burning stove. The floor was linoleum tiles. A round threadbare rug covered a portion of the floor in front of the chair and couch.

He walked through the main room. Off to one side was a door leading to a bathroom and another door leading to a bedroom. Clay continued straight through the main room into the kitchen, which was surprisingly large and well lit by windows on each side. He opened a door thinking it was the back door to the outside. The door opened instead into a narrow corridor lit only by a small window on the right wall. To the left, half way down the twenty-foot corridor, was a sturdy-looking door leading to the outside. Straight ahead was the outline of another door in the side of the lighthouse.

Clay flipped on the light switch for the corridor. It didn't work. He slowly walked down the darkened corridor until he reached the lighthouse door. He extended his hand in the dim light to touch it. The wood was cool and rough, reminding Clay of the side of a barn. This door was twice as wide as the others in the house and a foot or two higher. It was constructed of rough-hewn wood planks that hung from over-sized metal hinges secured to the masonry of the lighthouse with large bolts. The door looked out of place. *Was it built to keep something in? Or keep someone out?*

He ran his hand down the wood to where the handle would be. It was secured with a large padlock. He shook the padlock just in case it might not be latched. It was locked tight. He reached into his pocket for the keys. In the darkness, he couldn't read the small tags on the keys. He couldn't tell if he was holding a key to the lighthouse, or to the Ford pickup parked outside. A sudden strong gust of wind slammed into the side of corridor, startling Clay. The keys in his hands tumbled to the floor. *Oh, great!* He knelt down and felt around on the floor in the darkness. He reasoned that the keys should be right at his feet, but he couldn't find them. The wind assaulted the outside of the corridor again as if trying to tear down the walls and get at Clay. He didn't feel secure here, kneeling in the darkness expecting the walls to crash in on him at any minute. Clay tried to reason that it was only the wind, but he had to admit he was spooked. He wanted out of that corridor. His left hand finally brushed against the metal of the dropped keys. He snatched them into his hands and stood up.

He walked back to the light of the kitchen to sort out his keys. There, in his hands along with others he had dropped, was a large key with a neatly printed tag, "Lighthouse." He pocketed the other keys and stood in the doorway looking at the key in his hand. Reality hit him like a blow from a prizefighter. He held the key to a lighthouse. He owned a lighthouse! A lighthouse! Scenes from his nightmare flashed through his mind like lightning bolts. The endless, cold metal stairs, the frantic search for the dropped tool, the feeling of utter failure and helplessness as he watched the green and red bow lights of the little vessel, disappear beneath the waves of the storm-churned bay.

No, he couldn't open that door today. His inspection of the lighthouse would have to wait. In fact, if he never opened that darn lighthouse door, it would be just fine with him. That was one place he just didn't need to go right now; maybe never.

He placed the lighthouse key back into his pocket, and quickly closed the kitchen door. Turning around, he began to inspect the kitchen. It was spotless. He opened the refrigerator door expecting to be overtaken by the smell of rotting food and spoiled milk. Instead, the refrigerator and freezer compartments were completely empty.

Uncle Charley had been dead about two weeks. Somebody with a key to the house had been here and cleaned house during that time. Did Uncle Charley have a friend? Of course he did. Nearly everyone in town, according to what Clay witnessed at the funeral service yesterday. Did Uncle Charley have a "special" friend? A lady friend with a key? That was a possibility, certainly.

Clay walked back into the living room. His uncle's easy chair sat between the wood-burning stove in the corner of the room and a floor lamp. It faced at a slight angle toward the two windows on the opposite side of the room that looked out across the shaggy lawn and contorted cedars.

The chair looked welcoming. Clay sat down and pushed back to slightly recline the La-Z-Boy. It was without question the most comfortable chair Clay had ever sat in. He sat still for a very long time letting his eyes scan the room, viewing the few pieces of art and framed photos covering the walls.

There were several photos of his uncle and aunt on the walls. A wedding photo, long-faded by time, was surrounded by numerous photos of the married couple at different stages of their lives. It was very touching. Clay wondered if he'd ever have his own wedding photo to look at when he got old.

Clay continued to sweep the room and its contents with his eyes. On top of a book shelf, five photos were positioned with their faces turned toward the chair, rather than straight out into the center of the room. Whoever cleaned the place after his uncle's death knew to adjust the position of those photos, Clay thought.

Then he saw it. There on the bookshelf in an 8x10 frame was a picture of his uncle and a little boy about eleven years old standing in front of the frame of a house under construction. His uncle was resting his hand on the boy's shoulder. The boy, in t-shirt and jeans, stood there squinting into the sun, holding a hammer by his side. It was Clay.

He didn't remember posing for the photo but immediately recognized the place. One summer Clay had spent two weeks with his aunt and uncle at their cabin in the mountains of Arizona. His uncle was building a large cabin to sell, and Clay went with him each day to help. At his age, there wasn't much he could do, but his uncle was very patient and showed him how to place the tongue and groove boards together and nail them into place. He remembered the feeling of accomplishment when at the end of a day he could look back to the rows of lumber neatly nailed into place.

Memories of those days in the White Mountains of Arizona were reborn and flowed over Clay like warm air from a furnace.

He saw himself walking through a forest with his aunt and uncle. In his hand was a wooden-shafted golf club. In his pocket were several golf balls. The three were winding their way through the woods from their cabin to the golf course of their resort community.

They stepped out of the woods and snuck onto a fairway of the local golf course. Clay had never been on a golf course before, had never hit a golf ball except at a putt-putt course.

But there he was standing on the greenest, most perfect grass he had ever seen. It was well after dinner time. The sun was below the horizon; nothing to cause a shadow. All the trees, bushes, and homes were bathed in the same warm light that accentuated the richness of their colors unburdened by shadows.

Being late in the day, less than thirty minutes from dusk, no golfers were on the course where the three walked now. Uncle Charley stopped. Took a golf ball out of his pocket and with Clay's club gave him a quick lesson on how to hit a golf ball. He explained the basics to Clay, took a few practice swings and then struck the ball.

"Now you try. Have fun with it," encouraged his uncle.

Clay's first attempts missed the ball completely. After each swoosh of the club past the white ball in the grass, Clay would look up at his Uncle expecting a harsh word about not trying hard enough.

Instead, he only received encouragement and tips in between welcome humor.

"That ball is afraid of you Clay. It keeps moving so you can't hit it. Try holding your head steady next time."

Clay did as he was told. He brought the club back and swung again. Crack. The club hit the ball and sent it flying down the fairway. The ball didn't fly far, but little Clay let out a cheer.

"Good shot. Don't just stand there, go to the ball and hit it again." Clay raced up to the ball while his aunt and uncle walked behind. He swung the club again. Crack. The ball flew another thirty yards up the fairway.

And so, the three progressed slowly up the fairway. At the green, his aunt showed him how to use the putter she had been carrying. After four putts the ball dropped into the cup. The sound of the hard ball bouncing inside the cup was magical.

The threesome turned around and headed back up the fairway with Clay hitting the ball sometimes two feet, sometimes thirty yards. Sometimes straight.

Oftentimes sharply to the left or right. It didn't matter. After every shot, he'd get encouragement, empathetic chuckles and helpful tips from his aunt and uncle.

They reached the path leading back to their cabin. It was almost too dark to see now. A sudden cold wind started to blow hard through the tall trees, making Clay shiver. Clay looked around. It was getting dark fast. He couldn't see his uncle. He couldn't see his aunt. He couldn't see the trail. He began to panic. Where did they go? How was he going to get back to the warmth of the cabin?

He called out, "Uncle Charley!"

Clay woke with a start. He was shivering in a reclined position in his uncle's chair. He could hear the wind gusts slam into the house with renewed energy. He checked his watch. It was two o'clock. He couldn't have been asleep for more than ten minutes. He had to drive back to Seattle.

Clay checked the lock on the kitchen door. He took one more look around the living room, grabbed the photo of he and his uncle off the book shelf, and left.

After locking the gate to the property, Clay headed his BMW down Deception Point Drive. He looked in the rearview mirror at the closed gate.

What he was going to do with this place he hadn't a clue.

Chapter 37

As Clay drove north on the highway, he passed the attorney's office. Glancing down at the thick envelope of documents on the passenger seat he made a mental note to review those documents carefully and consider hiring Bartlett to handle the property for him.

Meaning what? What on earth was he going to do with a piece of windswept property and a crumbling lighthouse? *Uncle Charley, of all the people you could have left this property to, you chose me. What were you thinking?*

It was raining again as Clay drove toward town past the turn to Rhododendron Drive. He thought of the church and all the townspeople who showed up for his uncle's funeral service. Clay made another mental note to find out where his uncle had been buried. Another pang of guilt hit him deep inside. Why hadn't he thought about the burial spot before? What kind of an insensitive nephew was he anyway?

He shot past the Surf View Bistro sign, daring to take a quick glance down the road he had been on just the night before. The road was empty. No regiment of muddy trucks waiting to give chase. Clay laughed at his ridiculous thought but stopped laughing when he realized that he really couldn't explain the ghostly encounter with the monster truck, or the primal screams in the night. *Some things just can't be explained*, he concluded and pushed the memory out of his consciousness.

Clay left the city limits of Reef Bay in his rearview mirror. Accelerating to highway speed, he realized the irony that just this morning he had been grateful that he'd never have to come to this miserable little town again. Now he wasn't so sure. He looked down at the envelope of documents and keys. No, he'd have to come back at least once. In the meantime, he couldn't just let the property sit there.

Clay picked up the envelope. Sure enough, the attorney's label included his phone number. Clay took out his cell from a coat pocket and dialed.

"Law Offices."

"Hi, this is Clay Austin. I was in your office this morning about the Gragg estate. Is Mr. Bartlett available?" Clay asked.

"Yes, Mr. Austin. I'll put you through."

After a brief wait, the attorney picked up. "Hello, Mr. Austin. What can I do for you?"

"Well, I'm not sure really. I just left the property about thirty minutes ago. I have to get back to Seattle for important meetings. The thing is, I don't know when I'll be able to get back here. I think the place needs somebody to check on it, at least until I figure out what to do with the property," Clay explained.

"Of course. I can take care of that for you. I have a small property management business. A lot of people own vacation rental property around here, and my company takes care of things. We make sure utilities and taxes are paid, arrange for any repairs, we even do a monthly walkthrough of each property to make sure everything is in order."

"That's perfect. Where do I sign?"

"I'll email the property management agreement to you. Just check the services you want me to handle, sign and return. I'll need a set of keys, of course. I gave you all I had."

"Great. I feel better already," said Clay. His uncle's kitchen flashed through his mind. "Oh, one other thing before I let you go. Did my uncle have a girlfriend?"

Bartlett chuckled. "No, there were numerous casserole widows at church who tried to catch his attention. Nothing serious though. Why do you ask?"

"The house was spotless. Even the refrigerator had been cleaned."

"Oh, we took care of that, Mr. Austin. I hope you don't mind. As executor, I wasn't sure how long the house was going to be vacant. We thought we'd tidy it up a bit."

"That was very thoughtful, Mr. Bartlett. Thank you. I don't think I could have handled a mess this morning. I'll look for the agreement in my email and send it back this weekend. Bye."

"Good bye, Mr. Austin."

The call elevated Clay's mood considerably. Having Bartlett watch over the lighthouse property bought Clay some time to think about what to do. Sell it? Develop it? Who knows?

Clay was glad to be out of Reef Bay, but as his mind cycled through his brief visit, he realized how many wonderful, down-to-earth people he had encountered. Bartlett and his assistant, Billy, everyone he met at the funeral service, especially little Trisha and her mother, Molly.

There's something to be said about small-town folk, thought Clay, as he drove on through the drizzle toward the metropolis of Seattle.

Chapter 38

lay's time of departure from Reef Bay put him into rush hour traffic as he neared Seattle on I-5. The solid ribbon of taillights stretched northbound and southbound for twenty miles. Nothing he could do about it but listen to some light jazz on the radio and prepare himself mentally for tomorrow.

He walked into his house a few minutes after seven o'clock and deactivated the alarm system. It felt really good to be home even though he had been gone less than forty-eight hours. He hung his two coats in the closet, set his suitcase by the foot of the stairs and walked directly to the kitchen for a glass of wine.

Next, he ignited the gas lighter in the fireplace and positioned a few small logs, so they'd begin to burn. He wanted the warmth and ambiance of a fire tonight. Sitting down in his chair by the fire, he couldn't help but compare this one with his uncle's chair back in Reef Bay. This was a $2,400 item from Bradington-Young, covered in supple dark tan leather. It had a sleek, almost Scandinavian look to it. His uncle's chair in comparison was an ancient recliner-rocker from La-Z-Boy upholstered in a velour-type fabric. Clay doubted the chair cost more than $750.

The Bradington-Young chair had been a favorite of Clay's up until now. It always comforted him while providing the perfect amount of lumbar support. But, after sitting (and falling asleep) in his uncle's chair early today, he had to admit that the expensive leather chair was now his *second* most favorite chair.

Refocusing his mind, he flipped open the protective cover to his tablet. Quickly scanning email, he read first the messages from Sheryl, George, and Reuben.

Clay carefully read the letter of intent from Needham that Reuben had attached to a message a few hours earlier. Was he really going to sell Austin-Davis tomorrow morning? Was he really going to walk into a conference room on Friday to sign a document that will start the acquisition process, a process that will remove him as the top gun; a process that will culminate with Clay having a boss for the first time in fifteen years? He looked at the letter of intent again. Needham was offering $19.6 million for Austin-Davis. Clay's take, as the majority shareholder was going to be a hair under $10 million. That was quite a payday, but for some reason, it didn't excite Clay.

He found himself staring into the fire, lost in thought. He stood up and gently tossed another log onto the flames from the neat rack of wood. Clay was troubled as he sat back down in the recliner. Something didn't feel right. He wasn't sure if it was the deal, or if it was himself.

He opened the other attachment from Reuben. It was the management agreement that Reuben had been negotiating with Phil Manicotti at Pitt-Needham. Clay read it carefully. The details of Clay's employment were clearly described. He was being given a lot of responsibility. Not only did he retain management control over the Seattle office, he'd oversee offices in Portland, Boise, and San Francisco. Boise? Clay wasn't aware that Pitt-Needham had an office in Boise. He made a mental note to research it. In addition, Clay was to have a seat on Pitt-Needham's Board of Directors.

His new salary represented a nice bump from what he was currently paying himself, and he was given stock options for 50,000 shares. His title would be Senior Vice President and Regional Director.

Clay re-read the responsibilities part of the letter. He was expected to grow the billings at least fifteen percent per year while achieving "creative excellence," whatever that was.

Everything was pretty much in line with what he and Reuben and discussed. He looked at the paragraphs under the "Termination" sub-heading.

As Reuben had forewarned, Clay could be fired at any time for cause. His golden parachute wasn't very golden, however. He would receive three months' salary. Period. He pictured Reuben arguing for twelve months' severance and getting shot down. Manicotti probably countered that anyone who had received ten million dollars doesn't require much of a severance package. Clay's need for financial stability had nothing to do with why he wanted a larger severance package. He had asked Reuben to push for twelve months so that the decision to fire him couldn't be taken lightly. He saw what his attorney was able to wrestle out of Manicotti in the indented sections of text that followed. If he was terminated within one year, he'd receive eight months' severance. Not surprisingly, if Clay resigned at any time, he'd receive nothing in the way of severance. The negotiations must have been tough, because of what he saw next in the neat lines of 10-point type. If Clay resigned for any reason within the first year, he'd forfeit one million dollars from his second and final payout that was scheduled for thirteen months after the acquisition was concluded.

A million bucks. Was that Clay's value to Pitt-Needham? He could take this provision of the agreement two ways. Pitt-Needham had annual billings just over $2 billion. Did the one-million dollar penalty for walking away mean that Manicotti valued Clay's potential contribution to the company a lot, or a little? Was he being complimented, or insulted? Did they want him to stick around, or hope he'd leave prematurely so they could save an extra million on the purchase price? Clay couldn't decide which it was.

He reached for his wine glass and took a drink of the red wine. The way the wine hit his stomach he realized that he was hungry. No wonder, he hadn't eaten anything since breakfast, but eating didn't appeal to him now. His mind was racing in a dozen directions at once. Nothing was clear. He drank some more of the Tempranillo.

The fire made a hissing sound like fires when the wood is a little damp. A sudden loud pop made Clay flinch as a pocket of heated vapor inside one of the logs exploded, shooting small embers into the protective screen in front of the fire. He studied the position of the logs in the fire. They looked securely in place. He didn't want one of them to roll off the grate. The warmth of the fire was very comforting right now. He thought about putting another log onto the flames but changed his mind. He didn't want to use too much wood. The more he used, the more he had to bring in to the stack inside the house from the small supply outside on the deck under an eave. Even though last Fall he had paid a couple of college kids to transport half a cord of wood from the gate to the deck of his boat house, he had stacked it himself. He didn't trust the kids to do it right.

From his tablet, Clay opened the website for Pitt-Needham. He scanned the profiles of the men and women on the Management Team page. These were heavyweights, all right—people who had made a mark in the worldwide advertising industry even before they joined Needham. Clay read the bios of the other Senior VPs. He tried to imagine his picture next to them. Each one of them looked directly at him from the web page as if to say; *you don't belong here; you're not good enough to be one of us.*

He reviewed the Board of Directors. Twelve mature faces stared back at Clay. They were top executives from multi-national financial institutions, oil companies, media conglomerates, internet companies and non-profits. One person was a former U.S. Ambassador. Another a former U.S. Attorney General.

Clay pictured himself walking into a Board meeting for the first time with these titans of business. He could feel each one of them sizing him up, checking him out, all the while thinking, *What's this punk doing in here? He's not fit to shine my shoes.*

Clay stood and turned his back to the fire, feeling the heat remove the chill that had suddenly crawled up and down his body like an icy spider. He was still conflicted about selling. No backing out now, but the second thoughts he was having were strong. His gut was telling him it was a bad idea, but could he trust his gut right now?

Well, right now he wasn't thinking all that clearly; he was hungry and getting a little buzzed from the wine. He stepped into the kitchen to fix a snack of sliced apple, cheese, and crackers. With the snack neatly arranged on a plate, Clay returned to his chair to think.

The laptop sitting on the table still displayed the Pitt-Needham Board members. He closed the browser to remove the judgmental faces looking back at him. Without the distraction of the computer, Clay gazed out the large windows to the darkness outside. Whether in his home or office he had a habit of staring out windows while thinking as if the right answer would float by written on a balloon.

No balloons tonight. Just the lines of sparkling lights across the lake. Clay finished wolfing down his snack and realized he was utterly exhausted. He checked the fire to make sure no logs would roll off the grate in the middle of the night. He placed the plate and glass in the dishwasher and went upstairs to bed.

Chapter 39

After a fitful night of troubling dreams, Clay got out of bed, shaved and showered and stood in his closet for the longest time deciding what to wear. It was casual Friday, but this wasn't an ordinary Friday. He had client meetings, a client dinner at Canlis tonight, and, oh yeah, he was selling his company today.

Clay opted for a gray Armani suit, white shirt with French cuffs, and a pure silk Jacquard tie. For his feet, he slipped on a new pair of Italian-made lace-ups. He inspected himself in the mirror. He was wearing over $2,500 worth of clothing, not including his watch. The expertly tailored wardrobe boosted his confidence. He liked the way he looked and made a note to wear the same suit to his first Pitt-Needham board meeting. Maybe the suit will buy you some respect, a little voice said to Clay from the back of his mind.

He walked downstairs, grabbed his long wool dress coat from the closet and headed out the door. He was ready for business.

Clay exited the elevator at Austin-Davis and was greeted by the receptionist.

"Good morning, Clay. Welcome back. I'm sorry for your loss."

"Good morning, Betsy. It's good to be back, believe me!" Clay looked around the reception area and smiled. The area was like an art gallery and flight museum rolled into one. As was the agency's practice, they had made a special effort to personalize the reception area for a visiting client. Since Yukon Air was visiting, the reception area contained breathtaking photos of the airline's destination points, its colorful fleet of jets and props jets, and smiling crew members. Samples of the award-winning ads Clay's team had produced were displayed on easels and flat screen monitors. It was very well done. Clay felt a little tightness in his throat. He didn't know if it was sadness or pride.

He decided to walk a different route to his office. It was just 8 o'clock, and most of the staff hadn't arrived yet. He walked by the cubes, offices and open-work spaces on the right side of the building. He hardly ever walked down this side of the office even though his office was on this side, but at the far end. It felt like a different office over here. Clay made a mental note to spend more time in all parts of the office. That is, if he had more time between visits to the offices in Portland, Boise, and San Francisco.

He looked ahead and could see Sheryl at her desk outside his office. He knew everything was under control because Sheryl was there.

After a quick stop in the kitchen for coffee and a bagel, he headed to his office.

"Good morning, Commander Sheryl. How are the troops this morning?" Clay asked with a grin.

Sheryl had been concentrating on her computer and hadn't noticed Clay's approach. She jumped slightly. "Oh, you're here early. I didn't see you. Glad you're back."

"I'm glad to be back. Do you have a few minutes to bring me up to speed?"

"Sure do. I'll be right there. Did you really just call me 'Commander Sheryl'? I kinda like that."

Clay was about to step into his office but stopped to answer, "Yes, I said it, but don't get used to it." He winked and continued into the office. He set his computer, coffee, and bagel on the desk, then hung his coat on the hanger behind his door.

Clay changed his mind about sitting at the desk and moved his coffee and bagel to the coffee table in the sitting area where they could be more comfortable, less formal. He sat down in one of the chairs while Sheryl sat in the other. There was a brief, unusual pause. Neither spoke. They both just looked at each other, as if waiting for the other to start. Clay was momentarily speechless not because he was waiting for her to say something, but because he was overtaken by how peaceful he felt in Sheryl's presence. It was good to be back. The feeling was so noticeable it took him by surprise. If that wasn't disruptive enough, for a few seconds, he felt completely lost in her eyes. He wanted nothing more than to gaze longer into her incredible blue eyes. *What's going on here?*

Both snapped out of their brief trance at the same time. Sheryl spoke first. If Clay had been more aware, he would have noticed that Sheryl's cheeks were slightly blushed with embarrassment.

"Sorry, I was waiting for you to start. Nice choice of wardrobe, by the way. Did you pick that out all by yourself this morning?" Sheryl said teasingly. She knew Clay had excellent taste in clothes and frequently complimented him on his choices. She also knew that there wasn't anyone else in Clay's life to select clothes for him each morning.

"Thank you, big day ahead." Her mention of his suit made him look twice at what Sheryl was wearing. "Speaking of wardrobe, you're looking pretty sharp today yourself." Sheryl was wearing a red tweed fringe jacket over a white silk blouse. A black and gray pleated skirt fell just below the knees.

"It's not every day that a girl gets to dine at Canlis, or have you forgotten that you invited me to attend the Yukon Air dinner party?"

Clay smiled, "I certainly did not forget." And he *hadn't* forgotten his invitation, which was made for practical reasons—so the dinner would be a success without Clay having to worry about all the details—and for a personal reason that Clay had to admit to himself.

Charles Besondy

"Well, if we're done admiring each other's clothes now, perhaps we can get to work," Sheryl said. Not waiting for a reply, she referred to her tablet computer and read Clay his schedule. When she mentioned his afternoon appointment with the neurologist, she glanced up from the tablet at Clay, then back down to the tablet. Clay saw concern in her eyes. Sheryl finished recapping his schedule then looked at him again.

"How was Reef Bay?" she asked.

"You were right about Surf View Bistro. Great dinner." Should he tell her about the ghost truck nearly running him off the road? *Don't think so.*

"And..." Sheryl tried coaxing more information from him.

"My uncle was very much loved. Nice service." Clay responded, desperately wanting to get to work and avoid revealing more details. He knew Sheryl wouldn't stop until he had told her everything. She had a way of getting him to talk.

"That's all? Just 'nice service'"?

"One other thing, you've spent time in Reef Bay, right?"

Sheryl nodded.

"Did you ever go out to the Deception Point Lighthouse?"

"Of course. We used to go up to the point all the time when the Coast Guard operated the light, and the grounds were open for picnics. Did you see it?"

"Yep. I own it now."

156

Chapter 40

At a few minutes before 9:00, Clay left his office and strode over to the McCann conference room. He was the first one there. He sat facing the door, so he could see George and Reuben as soon as they walked in. Through the glass door, he could see the agency come to life as his employees arrived for work. Most of the younger people in the company were night owls and arrived at work between 9:00 and 9:30, walking in like zombies with cups of takeout coffee in their hands. The older employees, in their late 30s, 40s and 50s, tended to arrive by 8:30. With a big client in the office today, everyone associated with the account would arrive earlier than usual.

At first, Clay was proud that for Yukon the campaign development and meeting preparations had required so little of his time. It was the sign of a strong account team that he and George had carefully built for Yukon over the past eighteen months. Clay's momentary glow of pride in his stewardship evaporated when he began to feel unnecessary. He remembered how he and George and a few others worked for weeks on the speculative pitch that wowed Yukon. They successfully competed against the best agencies on the West Coast. Winning Yukon gave the fledging agency their first consumer brand client with a large broadcast media budget. The agency's creative product, the spots they created for TV, radio, and social media, would be visible to mass audiences along Yukon's routes in major markets. The campaign on which Clay contributed was hugely successful. It not only brought thousands of new customers to Yukon Air, it brought confidential calls to Clay and George from executives of other companies who were "considering their advertising options." The first campaign for Yukon increased the airline's market share by fifteen percent in one year. It garnered numerous awards in regional and national advertising contests and was directly responsible for attracting three new clients to the agency collectively billing in the neighborhood of $10 million a year. In short, the campaign Clay worked so hard on, put his company on the map. And today, the account team was flying high without him. And today, he was selling out. Or was he selling *up*?

George and Reuben walked into the conference room together. George was smiling broadly. He looked very dapper in a navy blue double-breasted blazer and gray slacks. He wore an expensive-looking tie that Clay hadn't seen him wear before. In the blazer's breast pocket a silk pocket square, perfectly matched to his tie.

Clay looked George up and down in an exaggerated manner. "Been reading *GQ Magazine* I see."

George responded with a green, "Sure have." He gestured at Clay. "I didn't know Walmart was having a suit sale this week."

That line brought a huge laugh to all three men. They settled into seats at one end of the table. Reuben handed George and Clay each a folder containing several documents.

"If you two are done comparing suit labels, perhaps we can take care of a little business here that will make you rich."

He smiled at each of them, paused, and when he heard no further bantering, he continued. "The first document is the Letter of Intent. It is a duplicate of what I've shared with you via email during the week. Pitt-Needham intends to purchase Austin-Davis for $19.6 million cash; sixty percent paid when purchase agreement signed, forty percent paid exactly thirteen months after the agreement is executed. They are extending to both of you management contracts, which are included in your respective folders. Of course, the final purchase price is pending an audit, which will begin within one week of your signature. The audit and definitive purchase agreement are to be finalized within sixty days of today. If Austin-Davis backs out of the agreement for any reason after today, there is recourse. You agree to pay a penalty of $100,000. If Pitt-Needham declines to move forward with the purchase agreement, they will pay a penalty of $100,000."

Reuben studied his two clients closely. "Any questions?"

Both George and Clay were studying the documents in front of them.

Clay spoke, "Any possibility that Suzette will make trouble once this becomes public? She's going to be angry as a hornet that she isn't getting a piece of this deal."

"Her terms of severance were very clear. When she accepted the severance payment, she waived all claims to her shares. That's no guarantee she won't sue. And you can count on the auditors reviewing her contract and termination very carefully. But, I have a card up my sleeve if things get nasty," Reuben said with a wink.

"What's that?" asked George.

"I have proof that she violated her agreement by initiating conversations with three different competitors, and even receiving an employment offer from one. An offer she didn't accept, but regardless, if she causes waves I'll hit her with a suit so fast it'll make her head spin."

"Good work. And that is why I've never complained too loudly about your fees, Reuben," George said with a grin.

"Any other questions about the Letter of Intent?"

"I see it's stipulated that the office building is not part of the acquisition and we retain ownership. That's what I wanted. Thanks for getting that in the terms. The agency's lease runs for another three years, so George and I can count on having a fully leased building for at least that long." Clay paused and then looked at George. "Well partner, you ready to do this thing?"

"Ready as I'll ever be," George said, with a touch of sadness in his voice.

"Okay, sign the documents where they've been tagged. You'll be signing a copy for yourselves, for me and two for Pitt-Needham. I also need you to sign my Notary book."

After the Letter of Intent documents were signed and Notarized, Reuben gathered the copies and placed them into his brief case. George and Clay were already engrossed reviewing the management agreements in their respective folders.

Clay was having difficulty concentrating. Somehow he had been able to sign the Letter of Intent despite the nervous trembling in his hand, and now as he tried to read his management agreement, the words kept going in and out of focus. He sat back and sipped his coffee to calm his nerves.

"Are you okay, Clay?" asked Reuben.

Clay didn't know how to answer. Was he okay, or not? He was about to reply to Reuben when outside, the high-pitched growl of a gas-powered weed trimmer tore through the morning air like a rusty knife. RerrrrrrrreeeeRerrreeeeeeeeRerrrrrrreeeeee.

Clay swore as he shot up from his chair. He looked out the window down to where the lawn maintenance crew was working. "It's the middle of winter for crying out loud, does the grass really need to be cut this week?" he shouted angrily.

George and Reuben glanced at each other and then to Clay who was clearly irritated, pacing around the conference room, speaking with a snarl, gesturing with his arms, speaking to no one in particular.

"How can we concentrate with that noise? Someone should have told the service to come on a different day. We have big meetings today. The noise will disturb the Yukon meetings. How am I supposed to think with all that noise?"

Ever the father-like statesman, George stepped in. "Tell you what, let's take a break to refresh our coffees. The noise should stop by then. There's not that much grass to cut out there, after all."

Reuben said, "Good idea. We still have thirty minutes before our video call with Manicotti. You okay with taking a break, Clay?"

Clay stood at the far end of the conference room looking at the other two men. His felt like he had seen a ghost.

The three men walked from the conference room toward the kitchen to replenish their coffees. Clay felt like he was walking through thick mud. Every step was an effort.

Sheryl was at her desk when George walked up, his expression all business. He leaned in and spoke quietly.

"Sheryl, I need a favor, quick." He motioned for her to step into Clay's office where they could speak privately. "Clay is acting, uh, unusual again. I'm afraid he's having another fit or something. Would you find a reason to go into the kitchen right now and speak with him? If you think something's wrong give me a signal. He has to be 100 percent Clay for our video call, or I'll have to cancel it."

Sheryl nodded, concerned, but not letting it show. She headed to the kitchen.

When she walked in, Clay was fumbling around with the espresso machine, muttering to himself.

"Good thing I'm here to help you with this big bad espresso machine," Sheryl said with a teasing sarcasm that she hoped didn't sound forced.

"For some reason, the machine is fighting me today," Clay said.

"Machines will do that. Let me help." She touched his arm, but rather than guide him away from the espresso machine she let her hand rest on his arm while looking calmly into his eyes.

Clay looked back at Sheryl.

"Let's try again, shall we," Sheryl said with a smile, removing her hand from his arm.

Clay rested his cup under the spout and pressed the touch screen, requesting an Espresso Macchiato. The automatic bean grinder whirred, starting the process.

Sheryl pulled a clean cup from the cupboard and moved to the hot water dispenser to prepare a cup of tea. She didn't really want the tea but needed to pretend she had a reason for walking into the kitchen.

While Sheryl prepared the tea, her phone buzzed. It was a text message from George. "How is he?"

Sheryl turned to see Clay remove his coffee cup from the espresso machine, and clear the grounds from the portafilter, making the machine ready for the next user. His eyes looked clear and alive. She texted back to George, "A-OK."

"Thanks, Sheryl," Clay said. "I wasn't able to concentrate there for a minute. I've gotta get back to the meeting now."

Sheryl just smiled and said, "No problem." Walking back to her desk she whispered quietly, "Thank you, God."

∆∆∆

Clay walked back to the McCann conference room feeling better than he had all day. His irritation began to fade, the fog in his mind began to clear, too. He couldn't explain why, but he felt more settled, more grounded. Felt more like himself, in fact.

George and Reuben looked up anxiously when he walked in. The room was wonderfully quiet. The lawn maintenance crew had finished work on this side of the building.

"A quiet room and a Macchiato, life is good," Clay declared as if nothing had happened. He sat down and began to study the management agreement in his folder.

Reuben spoke, "Each of your agreements are different, of course. George, yours is structured so you have the option of a part-time role after twelve months. You can hang up your spurs after twelve months if you want without penalty. If you resign from the company for any reason, except medical, within the first twelve months, you will forfeit $500,000 from the final payout. Your title will be Vice President and Managing Director of the Seattle office for the next twelve months. The usual perks and such are itemized on page three."

He continued, "Clay, you'll be Senior Vice President and Regional Director with responsibilities for revenue, profit and creative excellence of four offices— Boise, Portland, San Francisco, and of course, Seattle. You're also being offered a position on the Board of Directors, subject to Board approval." Reuben looked up at Clay, "A Board seat is a big deal, Clay. They must have plans for you."

Clay didn't hear a word Reuben said. He was re-reading the terms of early resignation— the million-dollar penalty. Was that a compliment, or an insult?

"Your respective salaries, bonus structure, and stock options are noted on the first page," Reuben said. "I must say, gentleman, Pitt-Needham wants this company badly, and they value both of you a lot. It was easier to get these terms than I thought it would."

George reached into his pocket for a pen, turned the document to page three and signed it with a flourish. He handed the signed agreement to Reuben.

Clay stared blankly at the papers in front of him. The moment of truth. No, the moment of truth was earlier this morning when he signed the letter of intent to sell his company. Now was the time to secure his future, to step into the big leagues of adverting. Now he has being handed responsibility for four marketing agencies with combined annual billings approaching $100 million. Could he really do it? Maybe this was a sick trap. Maybe, just maybe, Pitt-Needham had figured out a way to screw him out of his company and leave him with nothing. Maybe they'd recognize the mistake of their trust and fire him within the first year.

"Clay, Clay," a voice in the distance brought him back to reality. George was trying to get his attention. "I can see you're troubled, my friend. This is a great opportunity. I'm going to enjoy watching you take command of the region. I hope you remember me years from now while you're sitting in that big Board room at Pitt-Needham," George kidded warmly.

Clay looked hard at George, his friend and trusted partner. He looked at Reuben, also a friend and advisor. Neither of them had given him an ounce of bad advice in all the years he'd known them. Why on earth was he reluctant to sign the management agreement? One half of him wanted to reach for his pen. The other half wanted to run out the door, never to return.

Time stood still. Both George and Reuben had the good sense to stay quiet; to let Clay process the momentous decision.

George looked nervously at his watch. The video conference with Manicotti was scheduled to start in five minutes.

Clay slowly withdrew his Montblanc pen from an inside coat pocket. He turned to page three of the management agreement. Time seemed to stand still. The pen was suddenly so heavy he had trouble controlling it. He dashed his signature in the space provided. It wasn't his best signature, but it'd have to do. It was done.

Reuben and George applauded, and Clay forced a smile to his face. He replaced the fine writing instrument into his coat pocket and was shocked by how much his hand was shaking.

George immediately prepared the video conference system for the meeting. They were right on time.

Chapter 41

The meeting with Manicotti was short and businesslike. Importantly, it had a positive energy to it. Both parties were excited. Manicotti explained that his auditors would arrive on Monday. The men also discussed the news announcement that was necessary because Pitt-Needham was a public company and had to disclose material events such as a major acquisition. Manicotti agreed to forward the announcement to Clay and George immediately, so they could announce it to staff before the news hit the web news feeds.

The video conference ended. Reuben gathered up the signed documents and headed back to his office. He had done a great job for Clay and George. And it would probably be his last for them, Clay knew. Now that Austin-Davis has been acquired, Pitt-Needham attorneys would take care of legal matters.

Clay went into George's office where they retrieved the news announcement that Manicotti had just emailed to them. It presented a very concise and positive view of how the acquisition would strengthen Pitt-Needham's footprint in the booming Northwest region. It also gave glowing remarks about the addition of George and Clay to the management team. It was written so clients and shareholders alike would be pleased by the strategic move of the international agency. George immediately sent a reply email stating the announcement was approved.

He and George made a quick plan for how to personally call every client today with the news, and how to inform the employees.

It was 10:20. Time for Clay to stop being a business tycoon, and start being an ad guy. There were Yukon meetings to attend to, but first, he had to talk with Sheryl.

He walked from one side of the agency to the other side where his office was located. The workspace was now a buzz of activity with employees huddling in meetings and tapping on keyboards. When it came right down to it, that's what they did here—they had meetings and entered ideas, shapes, words, and commands into computers. Somewhere in the process marketing got done, the client's products and services got sold, and money was made. Clay never ceased to be amazed at the process, this combination of business strategy and communications creativity. The process wasn't always pretty or comfortable, but the result—a campaign—was always amazing. It was a birthing process for sure. A process not of two people but of a dozen individuals working as a team. He couldn't imagine any better business to be in, or any better agency. He loved this place, these people. He sure hoped he hadn't just screwed it all up.

Clay reached his office and asked Sheryl to step inside for a few minutes.

He walked to his desk, opened his tablet and retrieved Manicotti's email containing the news announcement. Sheryl entered and walked to the front of his desk.

Clay carried his tablet to the sitting area, but before taking a seat, he shut his office door. Sheryl sat down, and Clay could see she was suddenly very alert. He rarely shut his door.

"Sheryl, I have some big news. Great news, actually. At least I think it's great news. I want you to be the first to know outside of George and me." He looked at her. She looked back. The apprehension on her face partially transformed into a look of expectation. Clay wasn't sure how to say it, how to spin the news in the right direction. *Better get the words right, Clay.* "You're being promoted." He wasn't sure where this approach came from exactly, but the creativeness (and playfulness) of it pleased him.

"What? What do you mean?" Sheryl said, apprehension flooded her face.

"What you do for me in this office is irreplaceable and invaluable. You're capable of broader responsibilities." Clay was looking directly at her while speaking. Sheryl was one of the reasons he loved this place. "And so, I want to offer you a promotion to Operations Assistant for the Senior Vice President and Regional Director of Pitt-Needham."

Sheryl looked back at Clay with a blank look on her face.

"It's the perfect job for you, but the downside is you'll still report to me."

Sheryl continued to look back. Sternly, she said, "Clay, stop it, what's going on?"

"Okay, relax." Clay was beginning to think that this approach with Sheryl was about to backfire. "Austin-Davis is being acquired by Pitt-Needham, the 12th largest agency in the world. They want me to be their regional director over four offices, and I will need all the help I can get, so I want you with me."

Sheryl said nothing, just continued staring at Clay. He handed her his tablet with the news announcement. She took the tablet but didn't look at it right away. Instead, she continued to study Clay. He felt like she was looking right through him and it made him uncomfortable.

"Go ahead, read the announcement," Clay said, hoping to interrupt her stare.

Sheryl looked at the computer screen. The words of the short announcement were clear enough. She handed the tablet back to Clay and returned to reading Clay.

"Why?" was all Sheryl could say.

"Because you really know how to make an office work. You have great people skills, you . . ."

Sheryl interrupted Clay. "No! That's not my question." She was very serious now. "Why are you selling *your* company?"

Clay proceeded to explain how Manicotti approached him, George's situation, the money being offered, the chance for everyone to have the resources and opportunities provided by a much larger company.

"No wonder you've been acting weird lately," Sheryl said. She jumped out of her seat and paced around Clay's office, staring out the window. Clay hadn't seen her do that before.

"It has been the toughest decision I've ever made, Sheryl. Even today, signing the letter of intent and my management contract made me jump the rails for a while."

Sheryl looked at her watch, ever the vigilant assistant. "I'll consider your offer later. No time now. You have some meetings to attend. Besides, you haven't even mentioned what my new salary will be."

"Right. Just think about it. The deal won't close for another three to four weeks. Pitt-Needham's auditors will be here Monday. Check with George's new assistant, Alicia, to see if she needs help setting up office space for them. Perhaps Suzette's old office. And, please work with her and George on the announcement to employees today," Clay instructed.

Sheryl was making notes in her tablet. "What about the Yukon folks? When are you going to tell them?"

"George and I will call every client today. That's another thing to coordinate with Alicia. I figured I'd call Yukon's CEO just before telling her people that are here today. Please schedule it out for me."

"I'll take care of it. Hey, boss, are you going to be rich?"

"The offer is very fair. I won't be hurting for cash anytime soon," Clay responded.

"That's good because you're going to need money to fix up your lighthouse," she gave him one of her special Sheryl winks, opened the door and left.

Chapter 42

lay removed his suit coat and hung it on a hanger behind his door. He also unbuttoned the collar of his shirt and loosened his tie slightly. He didn't want to appear too "slick" for the working meetings with Yukon. He sat down at his desk, slipped Reuben's folder into a lockable drawer, and proceeded to review, again, the presentations his team had prepared for the Yukon meetings today.

After a few minutes, he felt "in gear," picked up his tablet and headed to the Ogilvy conference room. This was going to be fun.

Indeed, the meetings with Yukon were fun. Everyone was in good spirits. The campaign strategies and creative concepts were very well received. The agency team and client team really "clicked" as a working partnership. Achieving this level of chemistry between client and agency wasn't easy. It was a lot harder for some of their clients than others, but as Clay observed the interrelationships during the meetings, he realized that this chemistry was one of the things Austin-Davis did very well.

He and George had somehow instilled the philosophy and attitude that made this mutually respectful teamwork possible. The formula broke down with Lazzr because of Suzette's power play. Actually, if Clay was to be honest with himself, Lazzr failed because he failed to properly oversee Suzette. That could happen again if he wasn't careful.

Could Austin-Davis maintain this successful formula after the acquisition? Would Pitt-Needham impose procedures and bureaucracy that could snuff out their "secret sauce"? The biggest question of all was this, would Clay be strong enough to instill that "secret sauce" in the three other offices?

Close to noon, the meeting was winding down in preparation for lunch. Clay's phone buzzed. It was a text from Sheryl. "Announcement ready. See me ASAP." He tapped back, "K."

Just then George stepped into the conference room to say hi and shake hands with the Yukon people. His timing was perfect and not by accident did he arrive when he wouldn't interrupt anything important.

At Austin-Davis every account received partner-level supervision by either George or Clay. The level of involvement of the two partners in their respective accounts varied depending on the requirements, personality, and budgets of the accounts. But, it was Austin-Davis policy that every client receives some exposure to both partners. Today it was George's turn to be seen. Clay knew that George would join them for lunch. He also knew that his trusted partner had studied the presentation materials and could converse about the campaigns almost as well as Clay. Clay did the same when one of George's clients was in the office.

The meeting broke for lunch. People headed to the restroom, to the lobby to make calls on their cell phones, and others drifted to the kitchen. Clay headed straight to his office.

Sheryl and Alicia greeted him. They showed him the announcement timeline. It was a masterful job of coordination. On the first page, Clay saw the list of client CEOs that he was to call. Sheryl had already contacted their assistants and scheduled a ten-minute call that day with each for "an important announcement." George had a similar list. Next on the timeline was the announcement to the Yukon team immediately after the last meeting of the afternoon. Finally, there was the employee meeting and company-wide email announcement at 3:00.

On a second page was the Pitt-Needham announcement. On the third page was the internal announcement that George had prepared.

"You accomplished all of this in under two hours! Great work, you two," said Clay.

"Thanks." Sheryl looked at her watch. "I'll grab some lunch for you and bring it in. You need to be on the phone now."

And so, for the next hour, Clay spoke with the CEOs of each of his clients, starting with the brilliant and charming, Deborah Wright, the only female CEO of an airline in North America. His calls concluded with Otto Debrief, the crusty, hard-nosed CEO of TenState Trucking Company.

Each CEO appreciated being informed. Each and every one expressed concern that their account teams would be kept intact. Each one, in their own way, also expressed an interest in hearing "real soon" what the larger agency was going to do for them that Austin-Davis could not on their own. The calls went well, Clay thought, but something didn't feel right. He couldn't put his finger on it, but something about the calls was eating him like an annoying squirrel nibbling an acorn.

Clay took a few minutes to finish his lunch and make a few notes to himself on the internal announcement page. In the meantime, George had finished his lunch with the Yukon folks and politely excused himself. He left the kitchen, returning to his office where he settled in behind a closed door to make calls to his list of client CEOs per Sheryl and Alicia's schedule.

Clay returned to the Ogilvy conference room a few minutes after one. In the next two hours, the tricky part of the announcement schedule was to be orchestrated. He saw Sheryl's ingenuity in the plan. The afternoon Yukon meeting had been scheduled to conclude at 3:00 or so. The Yukon people would be shuttled back to their hotel and picked up again for dinner at six. Sheryl had arranged with the Austin-Davis team to wrap up the meeting fifteen minutes early to be ready for a brief company-wide meeting after Yukon left the building. She said that Clay wanted a few minutes alone with Yukon before they left.

The meeting reconvened, and soon positive energy was pulsing through the room again as further details of the proposed campaign were presented, discussed, amended and agreed to.

Around 2:00 George texted Clay that he had completed his assigned calls. All went well with the CEOs on his list, too.

Clay's meeting wrapped up right on time. The Austin-Davis people filed out of the room, each one giving Clay a subtle, questioning glance on their way out. Clay stood at the head of the room, took a few seconds to make eye contact with each of the Yukon people dispersed around the table, and began to speak.

"I hope you guys had as much fun today as I did. Something magical happens when talented people focus on a challenge or opportunity and pull a campaign together. I felt magic happening in this room today." Five heads around the table were nodding enthusiastically.

"Yukon Air is aggressively expanding with new routes that will bring its Wolf logo to Texas for the first time. After Texas, in the years ahead, Deborah plans to expand to other U.S. cities. This expansion is not a surprise for you. What may be a surprise is what I learned from Deborah during lunch in a phone call. She is working on a 24-month plan to begin service to Japan, Singapore, and Taiwan." The eyes around the room got big with excitement then turned to concern. Nobody in the room had worked for an international carrier.

He continued, "I don't have to tell you that launching a new route in the U.S. is one thing, bringing the proud Wolf to foreign markets is another matter entirely. Let's be brutally honest. No one in this room has international marketing experience. Deborah admits she lacks it, too. If Yukon hopes to succeed, it has to get international expertise fast." He paused, but not long enough to invite comments from those around the table. He had to keep this short.

"Which brings me to why I wanted to have this time alone with you today. In a few minutes, George and I will announce to our people that we've signed a letter of intent to be acquired by Pitt-Needham, the 12th largest agency in the world. You may not know that Pitt has extensive international airline experience. Their German and Brazilian offices are each handling an airline. They don't have U.S. or Asian carriers. No conflict, but there is a depth of international transportation experience in the agency. After the deal is finalized in a month or so, we can talk about how to make Pitt-Needham resources available to Yukon, as needed."

The questions poured in. "Will they retain the agency's name?" "Are you staying?" "Why are you selling?" "Will our account team change?" "Will you still be on our account?"

Clay did his best to answer some questions and dodge others but was mindful of the time. Through the glass wall of the conference room, he could see the employees gathering in the open area for the company-wide meeting.

"I want to address all of your questions, but they'll have to wait until dinner. I'm really excited about the future that our two companies are creating together." Clay's phone buzzed. It was a text from Sheryl about the shuttle service. "Oh, I'm told your shuttle is waiting downstairs. Just take the elevator down to the lobby, and you'll see the limo parked outside. That same limo will pick you up at the Westin at 6:15 and take you to Canlis where I'm hosting you for dinner tonight. Bring your appetites."

The five Yukon people finished packing up their belongings and headed for the elevator.

Clay walked briskly back to his office. He only had a few minutes before the meeting with the employees. He noticed that the employees were studying him as he walked by. Each would look at him and then quickly look away, avoiding eye contact. The atmosphere in the office was tense. Besides the shuffling of feet on the floor, it was eerily quiet. Clay put a confident smile on his face to help put people at ease. After all, the last company-wide meeting like this announced bad news and a layoff. The people were scared. He didn't blame them. And he definitely didn't want them to see how scared he really was.

George, Sheryl, and Alicia were waiting for him in his office.

George spoke, "How did the Yukon people take the news?"

"I don't know what shocked them more. Our deal with Pitt-Needham or the news about Yukon entering the Asian market that I just learned from Deborah in my call with her at lunch. That news was fortunate because it opened the door for me to point to the resources and expertise that would soon be available to them. Consider the Asian information very confidential, by the way. Our Yukon team doesn't even know yet." Clay said.

Sheryl brought the conversation back on point, "It's three o'clock. You two ready? Who is saying what? Who speaks first?"

George looked at Clay and winked then said in his most serious voice, "What do you mean? Clay and I aren't saying anything. We thought you were making the announcement. You and Alicia have done everything else today." Clay played along. The two men stood there looking at Sheryl with stern expressions on their faces.

It worked. For the first time that Clay could remember, Sheryl got flustered.

She tried to speak, but couldn't get a full sentence out of her mouth. "Me! What? I'm not . . . I don't have. . . you're supposed to . . ."

Clay broke down first. He laughed, a huge smile on his face. Sheryl's face turned red immediately, almost matching her red jacket. "Oh, you two!" She playfully struck out and hit each man in the chest with her first. All four stood laughing in Clay's office. Before Clay knew what he was doing, he had instinctively placed his arm around Sheryl to comfort her. Feeling his arm, she moved in a little closer.

It was Alicia's turn to take control. "If you two jokesters are done messing with this poor girl, I suggest you get your act together and prepare for those nervous employees outside."

"Right you are, Alicia. You guys go ahead. I'll be right there," said Clay.

The three left his office. His watch read 2:59. The laughter with George, Sheryl, and Alicia felt good and left Clay with a sense of family. This was good. This deal better not screw it up. He decided to put his Armani suit coat back on for the employee meeting, but he left his collar and tie loosened.

While slipping on his suit coat, motion outside his window caught his attention. The radar mast of a super yacht slowly moved westward. He stepped to the window for a closer look. Crew members were scurrying around the deck securing fenders and coiling lines, preparing for the locks ahead in the canal.

Clay grabbed his phone and took a picture of the stern of the vessel for his collection. "Invisibilia—Los Angeles" was painted on the light blue stern of the yacht. "Invisible," Clay whispered to himself, recalling some of his high school Latin. Odd name for a yacht. Maybe the owner had a sense of humor. A multi-million-dollar boat that was over a 100-feet long was anything but invisible.

The word, "Invisible" clung to Clay's mind like a soup stain on an expensive tie. His previously buoyant mood was replaced by a deeply troubled sensation, which he couldn't explain. He replaced the phone in his pocket and walked toward the waiting crowd of employees. He'd sort out the feeling later.

By previous agreement, George was to make a statement first, followed by Clay. As soon as Clay took his place, George gave the signal to Sheryl to flick the lights in the room on and off to signal the start of the meeting. The room instantly became as quiet as a library.

"Good afternoon. Seeing all of you here again reminds me that it was only last week when Clay and I had to tell you about the necessity for a layoff. I'm very happy and relieved to say that we have very good news to share with you today," George said, wearing his biggest and warmest smile.

The tension in the room immediately and noticeably receded. People were relieved, but their curiosity was now inflamed.

"I realize that many of you are relatively new with Austin-Davis. About twenty-five percent of our team has been added in the past twelve months. Another twenty-five percent in the past eighteen months. Permit me to share with you the highlights of the Austin-Davis journey." George then proceeded to tell the story of how the agency was founded and grew.

While George captivated the audience with his story, Clay's mind went back to the yacht; back to Invisibilia. He should be organizing his thoughts for what he was going to say to the employees, but he couldn't shake the word, invisible, or why it stuck like a thorn in his brain.

George was mentioning how the agency won account after account, each victory a milestone of some sort. As he said the names of the clients, Clay realized that earlier in the day he had spoken on the phone with the CEOs of at least half of the companies. That got him to recall the conversations. Invisible. Invisible. A thought from deep inside hit Clay like an electric shock. None of the CEOs had inquired if Clay was staying on at the agency, or on their account, after the acquisition. Didn't they care? Didn't they see him as valuable to their businesses? The answer seemed clear. No, they didn't see Clay as having a meaningful contribution to their business at all. He could stay or leave. Didn't matter. That was how Clay was taking it. That seemed the obvious conclusion. He felt totally deflated.

Here he stood, just moments before making the speech of his life, and all he could think about was how worthless he was in the eyes of his clients. Never mind that the Yukon team had asked if he was going to stay on the account. The point was, the CEOs didn't care enough to ask.

The applause brought Clay out of his stupor. Everyone in the room was looking at him. It was time for him to speak. As he stepped forward, the room began to swell in size, and he shrank in comparison. It was the same sensation he had experienced last week in the same area of the office. He was getting smaller in relation to the room and other people. A hint of panic raced through his gut. A droplet of sweat trickled down his right temple. He scanned the audience. Giants looked back, but to a person, they were looking at him with admiration and expectation. He saw Sheryl study him warmly from her position next to the wall just a few feet away. Before he knew it, she was next to him, towering above his head by two feet or more, offering a bottle of water. Their eyes met for a brief second as he reached for the water. In that instant, the unnerving sensation faded. The room slowly returned to normal. He felt himself again and started to speak to the group.

"The journey that George just highlighted was made possible by all of us in this room. Through our dedication to strategic and creative excellence, we have built a very effective agency. Our culture of respect and partnership, when freely expressed, binds us together with our clients in a mutually rewarding relationship. In the past couple of weeks, I've been reminded of how good we are when we follow those principles, and how fast we can fall when we don't." Clay was off script now but didn't care. This needed to be said. "The meetings today with

Yukon were a perfect example of a beautiful partnership. Good work team Yukon."
He clapped, and everyone joined in the enthusiastic applause.

He loosened the cap on the water bottle, took a sip and continued, "We saw
last week, what can happen when we don't stay true to our principles. It was
painful. We lost a valuable account. People lost their jobs. The loss of Lazrr was a
wakeup call. It showed what happens if we aren't constantly improving our ability
to serve our clients. We lost Lazzr for several reasons. First, I didn't do my job of
creating the partnership at the highest levels at Lazzr. Second, we became
arrogant in our attitude with the client. We forgot our t-shirt slogan from last
year's annual meeting, 'Our way or the freeway is a dead-end street.' But, the
third and most significant reason for the loss of Lazzr is that the client lost
confidence in our ability to meet their growing requirements." He paused to let
the thought sink in.

He was feeling comfortable and more in control now. He had gone off script
with the Lazzr discussion but was about to masterfully use it to segue into the
announcement. "No matter how great we are at this moment in time, if we stop
improving as an agency we will slowly die.

"Here's the cruel truth of our business. We bust our butts to help our clients
grow. As they grow, their requirements for marketing services expands. If we fail
to add skills and capabilities that the clients require, they'll leave us for a larger
agency," he said.

"The same holds true for each of you. As you grow into your profession, you
look for bigger challenges, more responsibility, more money. If Austin-Davis can't
provide a path for your growth, you'll leave us for another, larger shop." Clay
knew that statement would strike a chord. The majority of employees looking at
him right now had left smaller firms or freelance jobs for the chance to "step up"
to Austin-Davis.

"A little over a month ago I received a call from Phil Manicotti. If you read *Ad
Age*, you'll recognize the name. He's CEO of Pitt-Needham. He flew in from Dallas
to have dinner with me. He couldn't say enough great things about the work we do
and how well we'd fit within their organization. He offered to acquire Austin-
Davis." Gasps of surprise could be heard in the audience.

Clay continued, "For the past month George and I have agonized over the
decision to sell. Today, we signed a letter of intent agreeing to the terms. If all
goes according to plan, Austin-Davis will become a part of Pitt-Needham in a few
weeks." Hands shot up from the shocked employees.

"We'll answer all your questions the best we can. Let me get a few of the
obvious questions out of the way first. Neither George nor I are going anywhere.
George will be taking a larger role in managing this office. I'm being given
responsibilities for Needham's offices in Boise, Portland, San Francisco, and

Seattle. Our office will continue to be in this building, at least for the next three years. It's unclear at this time if we will retain our name or become Pitt-Needham. A group of auditors will be here beginning Monday going over our books and contracts; that's normal procedure. As I said, the deal should be finalized in a few weeks' time."

He was eager to hand the meeting back to George, so he touched upon the other points in rapid-fire fashion. "All of our clients have been given the news already. George and I spoke with each CEO today. In your email, you have the official announcement. Manicotti's people are releasing the news right now on the business wire and Web. I think it would be very smart if each account supervisor called their counterparts this afternoon and gave them the news. George will help you with the calls."

He paused and scanned the room to make eye contact with as many as he could. Hands shot up wanting to ask more questions. He ignored them. Instead, he finished, "Congratulations people. You've made it to the big time. You'll be working for the 12th largest agency in the world soon." With that remark, Clay turned to return to his office, and George took over. As he walked away, he could hear the excited questions from the employees. Clay felt a lot of positive energy in the room. If only he was feeling that great himself.

Chapter 43

After sending a quick email to Manicotti letting him know that the company meeting was a success, Clay retrieved Reuben's file from the locked desk drawer and placed it in his leather computer bag together with a few other files he wanted to review over the weekend. He grabbed his overcoat from the hanger, shut off the light and left his office for the day.

During the short drive to the neurologist's office, Clay did a quick inventory of his feelings and state of mind. This was something he'd started doing in the past few weeks after his life got crazy. It was his way of trying to make sense of all the weirdness—the lighthouse dreams, the ghost in his house, memories of Vic, the beastly lawnmower, fainting, monster trucks in the night, the sensation of smallness in his office—yep; there was a lot of weirdness going on all right.

He arrived at Dr. Reddi's office building and parked. He was early, so he sat in the BMW completing his mental inventory. How did he feel right now? A little tired from a stressful day, that's for sure. Actually, the past two weeks had been unusually stressful for him. Being tired was normal, he justified.

Instead of continuing to focus on how he was dealing with life, Clay's mind escaped to safer, more pragmatic areas. Like his car battery. He took a note pad from the console and wrote a reminder to go to the auto garage Saturday to buy a new battery. He had been very lucky the battery had lasted since dying at the Surf View Bistro parking lot. The car's sensors hadn't flashed a "low battery" warning light; the car had started strong every time Thursday and today. He was indeed fortunate that he hadn't been stranded somewhere again. He placed the note on the digital display, so he would see it.

His mind looped back to the question of the moment, *how was he feeling?* He'd better have some good answers ready because both Dr. Reddi and Dr. Shildstein, his next two appointments, were most certainly going to ask him that question. Before he could seriously contemplate the question, his thoughts shot off in another direction, back to the Pitt-Needham announcement.

He reached for his phone and tapped the Google News icon for his news feed. He scrolled through the business news releases. There it was. The headline link read, "Pitt-Needham to Acquire Austin-Davis in Move to Become Northwest Powerhouse." He scanned through the release. It was essentially the same as what Manicotti had sent them this morning. He looked at the time stamp of the release. It had been released fifteen minutes ago. He opened his email. Forty-two new messages in the Inbox in the past ten minutes. His social media accounts were lighting up. Twitter showed 102 new Tweets, LinkedIn had twenty-eight notifications of messages. It was going to be an interesting weekend because of the announcement.

Clay noticed the time on the phone. He switched his phone to silent mode, replaced it in his pocket and headed for the doctor's office.

Inside the elevator, he pushed "4" to take him to Dr. Reddi's office on the fourth floor. The elevator door closed. Clay was alone. *One last time, how are you feeling, Clay? Be honest. You've been avoiding something, haven't you? Thinking about car batteries, and news releases when you should be focusing on what's going on inside you right now. What's there, Clay?*

The elevator jerked to a stop. Clay glanced up at the digital display. The glowing "4" glared back at him in ugly orange letters. It seemed like the door took forever before it shook and finally opened. Clay stepped into the hallway, turned left and walked unsteadily toward the doctor's office suite.

It was a typical hallway in a typical medical office building. No sense of style whatsoever. The mundane earth tones made Clay want to jerk open any of the doors in a desperate search for color. Light tan walls met a carpet consisting of darker shades of tan. The doors leading off the hallway were a shade of flat green with frosted glass. A small sign by each door identified the specialist. Doctor Reddi's office was at the end of the hall, but the hall seemed to Clay to be much longer than when he was here for his first appointment.

How are you feeling, Clay?

Because every foot of the monotonous hallway looked like every other foot, he had the eeriest sensation that he wasn't making any progress walking down the hallway. It was like the carpeted floor suddenly became a slow-moving treadmill—he'd walk and walk but go nowhere. The sensation was unsettling, made worse by the old fluorescent lighting that violated the light waves.

How are you feeling, Clay? Why aren't you answering?

Time was running out. The end of the hallway and the door to Dr. Reddi's office was only twenty feet ahead.

Clay was breathing faster now. His palms felt damp. His legs and feet were heavy.

He stood outside the doctor's door. He didn't want to open it. He didn't want to walk inside. He certainly didn't want to hear the annoying Patient Channel on the TV in the reception area as some washed-out movie star prepared her healthy recipe of shrimp with Brussels sprouts.

What was worse? The surreal, endless hallway, or the doctor's office? He reached for the door knob, turned it and walked inside.

"Hi, I'm Clay Austin. I have an appointment with Dr. Reddi," Clay said to the nurse-receptionist.

"Please sign in. He'll be with you in a few minutes," was the emotionless reply; the same she'd given to dozens of other patients that day.

Clay sat down, thankful he was the only one in reception and very thankful the TV volume was off. He could think. Information pamphlets were stacked neatly in a rack mounted to one wall. "Life with Epilepsy," "Care for Cerebral Palsy," "Choices for Brain Tumors."

Would Dr. Reddit give one of these pamphlets to him? Would a nurse prepare a neat folder containing brochures and instructions for his treatment? Now Clay knew how he felt. Now he could answer the question.

He was scared! More scared than he had ever been. He was scared of failing at work, sure, but what he was most scared of is test results the neurologist was going to give him in a few minutes. Did he have a medical condition that would prevent him from working? Would it blow up the Pitt-Needham deal? Was he going to die? Sure, he could answer the question now. He was scared to death!

With everything going on at the agency and in Reef Bay he had been able to conveniently forget the potential seriousness of this doctor's appointment. His life, as he had been living it, could be over. Was he ready to accept that possibility?

His phone vibrated in his pocket. Probably a reporter wanting a comment. He looked at his phone. It was a text from Sheryl. "Praying for you," was all the message said.

"Mr. Austin?" A nurse was trying to get his attention from the doorway leading to the examination room area of the office suite.

Clay replaced the phone in his pocket, stood, and followed the nurse.

She directed him to the first examination room on the right. "Dr. Reddi will be with you in a minute." She left Clay alone and closed the door behind her.

Not knowing how long he'd have to wait, Clay retrieved his phone and started to check his messages. He had just started to open email when he heard a brief knock on the door before the doctor entered. Clay put the phone back into his pocket. He was nervous.

"Mr. Austin, you're here for your test results, correct?" Dr. Reddi was looking at the tablet computer in his hands, not at Clay.

"That's what they tell me," Clay said with a smile, hoping his humor would make him less nervous. Didn't work.

"Have you had any more episodes of fainting?" the doctor inquired, now looking at Clay.

"No fainting." Clay wondered if he should tell the doctor about the mysterious monster truck of Reef Bay, and the amazing shrinking sensation in his office. He decided against revealing anything more.

"That's good. All of your tests reveal perfectly normal brain and nervous activity, Mr. Austin. From a physiological perspective, you're healthy. Nothing to worry about," the doctor said.

"That's a relief." Clay felt a weight lift off his shoulders.

The doctor studied the medical records in his notebook. "In your previous appointment, you mentioned that you had been experiencing unusual stress at work recently. Has the situation changed?"

"Actually, the situation has improved. I just sold my company today. Well, to be accurate I just signed the letter of intent. Deciding to sell or not was weighing heavy on my mind, definitely," Clay responded.

"I see. Well, stress causes a lot of physiological and psychological issues. Your tests rule out that the fainting and hallucinations were physiological. My advice is to see a psychiatrist. I can refer you."

"That won't be necessary. I've had a few appointments with Dr. Shildstein. In fact, I'm heading there after I leave here," Clay said.

"Excellent choice, I know her. I'll make your test results available to Dr. Shildstein if she wants them. You can go. No need for a follow-up appointment unless the fainting and blackouts start again." He stood, reached out his hand to shake Clay's.

"Thanks, doctor. Have a great weekend."

The doctor left the examination room and turned right. Clay turned left, walked through the reception area, and back to the dreary hallway.

He reached the elevator quickly. Too quickly. The elevator he was standing in front of was only about 15 feet from Dr. Reddi's office. There must be another further down the hall he thought. He remembered how long it took him to walk from the elevator to the doctor's office. He must have walked fifty feet or more. Were there two elevators? He ventured further down the hallway. No other elevator.

His mind was contorting his perception of space. Hallways were longer than they really were. Offices expanded beyond their actual size. Both sensations made Clay feel small. It was partially comforting to know that physically his mind and nervous system were okay. He sure hoped Dr. Shildstein had a cure for the mental part.

Chapter 44

D r. Shildstein welcomed Clay into her office at 5:00 sharp and offered him coffee, which he accepted.

Clay settled into the couch across from the psychiatrist's usual chair. Something was different about the room. Oh, right, the artwork had been rotated again. He took a brief moment to glance at each of the four walls. Most of the pieces he remembered even though they were in different places in the room now. Directly behind the doctor was a painting he hadn't seen before. It was magnificent! A silky purple hot-air balloon soared above the desert as the rising sun shot brilliant beams of golden light between two red and orange tabletop bluffs. He recognized the area as Sedona, Arizona. One of his favorite places.

The doctor opened her journal and prepared to take notes. "How have you been, Clay?"

As usual, with Dr. Shildstein, he didn't know where to begin. So much had transpired since his last visit.

"I've been good, I guess. So much has happened. It's kind of a blur."

The doctor smiled and waited patiently for Clay to say more.

"Most important news is my neurological tests were perfectly normal, according to Dr. Reddi. I just left his office. He gave me a clean bill of health but suggested I talk with a psychiatrist. I said I was talking with you. You can see the test results if you wish."

"That's really good news, Clay. How do you feel about the test results?" she asked.

"Relieved, but still concerned about what's going on with me."

"Have you had any more hallucinations? The lawnmower?"

"No. Lawnmowers haven't chased me, but monster trucks might have."

The doctor made a note in her journal. "Monster truck?" she asked with calm interest.

Clay proceeded to tell her about the episode of the wild truck and animal screams in the night on the way back from the Surf View Bistro. He didn't say why he was in Surf View. He could mention his Uncle Charley later.

"It was probably just some redneck having fun with me, although I can't explain the animal scream sounds," Clay said, trying to sound rational.

"No other episodes with mechanical objects?" the doctor asked as if there was a special category of weirdness involving mechanical objects.

"Kind of. I got furious and very flustered this morning when the noise from a lawn crew disrupted an important meeting at my office."

"Where was the crew?"

"Oh, they were outside cutting the lawn and trimming. I was in the office with my partner and attorney signing important papers. I just lost it. Got furious. Then we took a break so I could calm down, but I couldn't even make myself a macchiato," Clay said, shaking his head slightly back and forth in disbelief.

"What papers were you signing, Clay?"

"A letter of intent to sell my business and a new management agreement with the company that is buying us."

Dr. Shildstein was writing furiously while Clay spoke.

"I suppose you want to know how I feel about selling my business and working for someone else?" Clay knew she was going to ask.

"I certainly want to know how you feel. That's a very large decision for any business owner. I know you are very proud of your agency and its reputation."

"I justified the decision. It was the right thing to do for my partner, who wants to retire soon. It was the right decision for our clients, many of whom need expertise we don't have. It was the right decision for the employees, who now have resources and career paths of a much, much larger agency."

"I see," she said, "Sounds like you thought it through." She paused and spoke again. "I didn't hear you say why selling was good for you." She looked at him with her usual warm intensity.

"I didn't? Well, it puts a lot of money in my bank account. I have a job supervising four offices now and a seat on their Board of Directors."

"How do you feel about all of that, Clay?"

Clay sipped his coffee. Thoughts raced through his head followed by nothing, then more random thoughts. He couldn't focus on an answer. He couldn't speak.

If Clay had been watching the doctor instead of studying the coffee in his cup, he would have noticed a slight frown. She studied her notes, turning pages back.

"You said you were signing the legal papers when the sound of the machinery outside upset you."

"That's right."

"You said you were signing two documents in the meeting this morning, correct?"

"Yes."

"When did the noise disturb you? During the signing of the first document or the second?" she asked.

Clay thought back to the morning meeting. "My partner and I signed the letter of intent first. While I was studying the management contract, the darn weed trimmer started outside."

"You were reviewing the management contact when the noise started?" she asked.

"Yes. I was trying to concentrate on the terms of the agreement, but the irritating sound made me furious."

"Clay, were the terms of the agreement what you had expected? Or did they surprise you?"

"They were what I had expected. They were pretty much in line with what I asked my attorney to negotiate. Actually, the responsibilities and compensation are more than I had expected."

"No concerns at all?"

Clay didn't answer.

"There is something about this deal that is bothering you, Clay. Based on what you've said you should be very excited right now, but look at you, you're not. You're reserved; withdrawn even. So, what's bothering you? What's the worst thing that can happen?"

Clay took a few seconds to think about the question. "The worst thing that could happen is that I get fired shortly after the deal is finalized."

"You're afraid of being fired," she restated without judgment.

"Yes, in the back of my mind I'm afraid they'll fire me after I've been in the new job for a few months."

"Why would they do that?" she asked.

"Any number of reasons. Because if I'm fired, they get to cut the final payout by a million bucks. Because after they see me in action, they might think I'm not up to their management standards." Clay was becoming fidgety. His left foot started tapping rapidly on the carpet. His eyes were looking down at clenched hands in his lap.

"Right now, right this minute, you're feeling very uncomfortable, aren't you?" she asked.

"I guess so, sure. I think my concerns are perfectly justified. I don't see anything wrong with being a little worried."

"Consider this, Clay. You're a lot more than a little worried. You are very confronted right now. I bet you'd like to leave, wouldn't you?"

Leaving was a great idea. That would stop this stupid line of questioning. He could leave and get ready for dinner with the Yukon team. Just walk out the door and put all this crap about feelings behind him. What good is this doing anyway? He felt worse now than when he arrived!

"Yes, I should leave. You're making it appear that I'm committing a crime simply for being a little worried about what might happen. It's no big deal!" Clay voice was elevated, sharp, agitated.

"Do you feel I'm judging you?"

"Heck, yes! You sit in your cushy chair and tell me not to be worried about my business. What do you know about business anyway? You're a shrink." He lashed out, putting a derogatory snap on the last word like the crack of a whip.

"You're free to leave anytime you wish, but I'd like you to stay." Her voice was calming, almost loving.

Clay sat still on the couch, brooding, staring at the floor between them, avoiding eye contact. He was angry and not completely sure why. He knew this much; the anger felt good somehow.

"Let me know if I understand or not. You believe that I'm making you wrong for being concerned about the possibility of your being fired."

"That's right, you are," Clay said with bitterness still in his voice.

"Can you see that all I did was notice how upset you were being? I said nothing about it being right or wrong," she said.

"Well, not in so many words, but your tone implied that I was over-reacting. That I was flipping out for no good reason. First, I wasn't flipping out. I'm just a little worried about being fired and losing a lot of money. In my situation, that's perfectly normal behavior," Clay said defensively. "What's flipping me out right now is your attitude and all these stupid questions!"

"What's 'flipping you out,' as you say, right now isn't me, or my questions, Clay." She firmly and calmly made the statement and let it hang out there waiting for a response.

"Oh, really! Why don't you tell me what it is then? That's what I'm paying you for isn't it?" Clay said.

"Actually, you're paying me to help you find the answers yourself, which is what I've been doing. Shall we get back to it? Blaming me for being judgmental is just a way to avoid having to look deep into why you are so worried about the outcome of a wonderful business deal," the doctor stated.

Clay said nothing. He frowned and took another sip of coffee, which was getting cold.

"What you're expressing and feeling right now is really good, Clay. It needs to come out. And what I want is for you to look very hard at two things. What's behind your worry about being fired? Why do you think I'm making you wrong? Something is there, Clay. Something just below the surface is making you respond to your situation with a lot of fear and anger," she explained.

"There's nothing unusual about how I'm feeling. I'm not crazy," he said, still defending his actions.

"That's correct. You're not crazy, but Clay, you're not happy either." Her words hit home. Clay looked at her directly for the first time since his angry outburst had begun.

She continued, "What would it be like for you if this worry was gone?"

Clay thought. It was hard to imagine. The worry about selling Austin-Davis, and lately the worry about being fired, had consumed him. The worry and doubt had wrapped itself around him, so completely he wasn't sure how he'd feel if it was gone.

"It would feel good," was all he could think to say.

"What else? Think, Clay," she said, encouraging him to go deeper.

"I don't know. I'd feel lighter I guess, I mean, no weight on my shoulders."

"You'll feel good and lighter. What else?"

Clay frowned. He didn't like this much at all. "I don't know," he said with frustration in his voice.

The doctor referred to her journal. "You said a few moments ago that you were afraid the company would decide 'you didn't measure up to their management standards'." She emphasized Clay's quote by using both hands to form quotation marks in the air. "Isn't that what you said?"

"Yes."

"Would they have bought your company and offered you a very big position, plus a seat on the Board if they didn't think you'd measure up?" she asked.

"No, but they could be wrong. I don't know if I can handle it," Clay said.

"You're afraid you can't handle the new responsibilities," she repeated.

"That's what I've been saying to you over and over," Clay said irritatingly.

"Yes, you have been clear. Work with me on this. You're very close. Think back to this morning in the conference room. You were reviewing the management agreement, then what happened?"

"I was reading the agreement, trying to focus on it, when the noise of the weed trimmer interrupted my concentration," Clay recalled.

"And then?"

"I got irritated and angry."

"Was your anger unusual at that point?"

"Yea, I don't get angry, at least not visibly angry."

"The sound of lawn equipment made you furious."

"Right."

"Wasn't it a lawn mower that you saw inside your office last week that made you faint?"

"Yes, an old Briggs & Stratton reel lawn mower."

"Why that type of lawn mower, do you think?"

"That was the first lawn mower I ever tried to use."

"Right. That was the lawn mower Vic wanted you to use. The lawn mower that was too hard for you to control because you were too small. The lawn mower that caused Vic to yell at you all day."

"Right."

"And remember, how did you feel after that day cutting the grass?"

"I felt bad."

"Yes, you felt bad, but why? Remember we've discussed this."

"I felt unloved. Not good enough," Clay said, suddenly beginning to choke up.

"Exactly. Vic's yelling and impatience that day made you feel that you weren't good enough to earn his love, the love of a father-figure."

"I guess so."

"Clay, listen this is important. Ever since that day when little Clay was on the lawn with Vic and the mower, you've believed you weren't good enough to be loved, especially by people of authority. Your lawn mower hallucination, the outrage at the noise of the weed trimmer—all came at times when you were contemplating important decisions, didn't they?"

Clay nodded.

"Inside you, Clay the strong businessman was battling Clay, the hurt little boy. The good enough side of you was fighting the not good enough side. It has been an epic battle all your life, Clay. You just didn't know about the internal warfare until the past few weeks when the intensity of the battle grew so strong it began to affect your behavior in very noticeable ways. Think about this: Even when very successful and authoritative people were willing to pay you a lot of money, and entrust you with a lot of responsibility, you struggled to accept their trust. Part of you wanted to believe it, but the other part couldn't accept it because of this perception of not being good enough."

Clay sat stunned on the couch. The doctor's words made sense one moment and didn't the next. He realized he was debating with himself whether to believe her or not. "I see what you're saying, but I'm having a hard time accepting it."

"That's understandable. You'll need to process it. I want to give you some homework before our next session. Think about how this perception of self as not being good enough has molded your life over the years. Write down what you've discovered. Will you do that?" she asked.

"Ok, but I can't think of anything right now."

"Of course not. This realization is all very new to you. Over the next few days think about your past relationships, personal decisions, and business decisions. The not good enough perception, or your compensation to it, can show up in many ways, even in your choice of clothes." She gestured at Clay's impeccable Armani suit.

He instantly remembered that this morning he had carefully selected his best suit to wear today, but more importantly, he had made a mental note to wear the same Armani suit to his first Pitt-Needham Board meeting. He could see how he was relying on the quality of the suit to tell others he was acceptable, that he was good enough. He was a scared little boy hiding inside an expensive suit.

"Clay, shall we meet same time next week? Bring your homework journal so we can discuss what you discovered, or what you didn't discover."

"I hope I won't disappoint you with what I uncover," said Clay.

"You won't. In fact, what you just said can be the first entry in the journal."

"Huh?"

"You're already thinking that your homework notes won't be acceptable to me; that they won't be good enough."

She was right. Clay was stunned again. Maybe this homework will be insightful after all. He stood and walked to the door to leave. The doctor stood up from her chair and walked towards the door, too.

"One minute, Clay. I have something for you." Next to the door, on the floor leaning against the wall was a large flat package wrapped in dark purple paper with a simple pattern. She picked it up and handed it to him. "Don't open it until you get home, please. This is a tradition of mine. I give one of these to each of my patients when they reach a certain point in their treatment. Open it when you get home. We can talk next Friday about it."

Clay took the package from her, slightly embarrassed. "Thank you; I don't know what to say. This is unexpected."

"You don't need to say anything now. You'll have lots to tell me next week." She reached out her hand. Clay shook it with his available hand. Her warm grip was firm and caring. "Good work today, Clay. Have a wonderful weekend."

Chapter 45

lay carefully placed the doctor's gift in the trunk of his car before starting his drive to Canlis restaurant for the Yukon dinner. It was six o'clock. He wasn't that far from the restaurant, but in Friday night traffic it would take him at least fifteen minutes to get there. Before leaving his parking spot on the tree-lined street, Clay texted Sheryl with his phone. "On my way. Be there soon."

Immediately, she replied, "What did doctor say?"

"Which one?" he replied.

"Reddi."

"Fit as a fiddle," he texted using a phrase his grandmother had often used.

"Yeah! But fiddle out of tune," she texted back and included a smiley emoji.

"That's what shrink said," his fingers typed. He sent the message and typed another. "Talk later. Gotta start driving." He placed the phone in the car's console.

He could partially relax now, knowing that he'd arrive on time. In this traffic the client's limo would probably be late to the restaurant, so Clay figured he'd still arrive first and be there to greet them. After the deep session with Dr. Shildstein, rather than think more about what had been uncovered, he wanted his mind to go blank; to think about nothing. He told himself he wanted to relax before the Yukon dinner, but actually he was avoiding further thought about the idea that his whole life up to now had been shaped by that one day with Vic and the smoke-belching Briggs & Stratton mower. The idea seemed pretty far-fetched. The idea seemed highly possible, too.

As he drove down Aurora Avenue, he knew the restaurant was just ahead. He was amazed that the GPS system got him there on time, considering the route it had selected. It had twisted and turned through neighborhoods, down back streets; touching main boulevards only occasionally. More than once on the way Clay thought the GPS was crazy and considered turning it off in favor of making his own decisions about how best to get to his destination. Each time he had opted to trust the GPS. It would get him there eventually, he reasoned. And it did. At 6:28 Clay flipped the turn signal indicator, down-shifted, and entered the parking area of Canlis Restaurant. There were four cars waiting for valet service. He didn't want to wait. Clay impatiently drove through the small parking lot and found an open space at the far end.

It seems in Seattle whenever valet parking isn't available; rain is sure to fall. Clay could see large drops of rain begin to splash on the windshield just as he was about to leave the car. He grabbed his wool overcoat from the backseat, retrieved the travel umbrella from the map pocket in the door and headed for the restaurant door.

Upon entering the upscale restaurant, he first checked his damp overcoat and umbrella with the coat check attendant. Next, he headed to the men's room to freshen up. Inside the marble-walled restroom, Clay looked at himself in the mirror. *You're looking a bit frazzled, my boy.* He washed his hands in warm water, then splashed repeated handfuls of cold water on his face, taking care not to throw any water on his clothes. Washing his face always revigorated him for some reason, as if the water was removing the stress and worry of the day, giving him a fresh start.

He reached for a cloth towel from the neat stack in an ornate basket sitting on the countertop. After drying his hands and face, Clay buttoned the shirt collar and straightened his silk tie. After smoothing hair that had been blown this way and that by the swirling wind outside, he stood in front of the mirror for final inspection. The psychiatrist's comment less than an hour ago about his attire came to mind. Was he really compensating for his insecurity by wearing an expensive suit, or did he just have good taste in clothes and could afford a large wardrobe of brand names? He decided not to care about the answer right now. He pushed out of his mind the doctor's comment and the revelations that had been uncovered in his session with her. Right now, he had to be good enough. He had to be Clay, the famous and talented marketing executive. He had to be Clay, the gracious dinner host. And he better be ready for whatever questions the Yukon people will ask. Who knows what questions he'd receive after everyone had several glasses of wine. He winked at himself in the mirror and left. *Showtime.*

He entered one of the restaurant's private dining rooms to find Sheryl there locked in conversation with the manager. The Yukon people hadn't arrived. His team was there—some sitting, others standing with drinks in hand. Sheryl looked away from her conversation just long enough to give Clay a quick smile. The smile vanished as she turned her attention back to the manager and whatever seriousness was being discussed.

Clay made the rounds, shaking hands with each of his people, congratulating them again on their work. He wanted a drink badly but decided to wait until Yukon arrived, and everyone was seated. He wanted his hands free. He noticed that the waitress had left the room, Sheryl looked at her phone, and then left the room, too. Clay was really glad Sheryl was here. When she was involved in something, he didn't have to worry about it. Like the announcement and company meeting today. She pulled that off beautifully. Considering Clay's state of mind for most of the day, he doubted he could have done it alone. Heck, he couldn't even prepare a cup of coffee without her assistance today. She was priceless.

Sheryl returned like the pied piper leading the Yukon people to the room. So that's why she left the room after looking at her phone. He surmised that she had left instructions with the limo driver to text her the minute they arrived at the restaurant, so she could go to the front door and escort them here. Nice touch of class.

For the next twenty minutes, everyone mingled about in the room, while two waitresses took drink orders. Sheryl had been mingling, too, and now was beside Clay for the first time. "It's time to be seated and start dinner," she told him. Clay nodded in approval. She proceeded to tap a water glass with a spoon to get everyone's attention. The conversation slowly subsided. "Please have a seat. They are ready to serve us now," she announced.

For the first time since arriving, Clay noticed the table. A neatly printed name tag had been placed on each plate. Clay scanned the names and saw his at the head of the table; other people were walking around looking for their assigned seat. Soon, it became apparent why Sheryl had taken this step. The seating was strategically arranged, so agency and client people were mixed around the table. This avoided the embarrassing situation where client personnel sit on one side of the table and agency personnel sit on the other. To Clay's right was Yukon's VP of Marketing, Barry Weitzel. To Clay's left was Sheryl. It seemed perfectly appropriate and smart that she be next to him. Down the table media specialists sat with their client counterparts, creatives with creatives, planners, sat with planners. This ensured productive conversations and further bonding.

When everyone was seated, including Sheryl, a waiter and waitress entered. They strode around the table handing menus to each person, then left the room.

Sheryl touched Clay's arm to get his attention. He leaned to his left to hear her over the noise of the conversion in the room. She said in his ear, "I ordered Champagne before dinner, so you better get a toast ready." He looked at her. With anyone else, he'd be furious for being put on the spot like this. But with Sheryl, he knew the Champagne and toast was absolutely the right thing to do, whether he was ready for it or not. Besides, he had given her responsibility for planning this dinner, and plan it she did. So, he'd better get with the program.

"Okay, good idea, thanks for the warning," he said with a touch of sarcasm. Just then, the waiters re-entered with three bottles of Champagne in ice buckets. They proceeded to pour glasses of the bubbly for each person.

Clay had to assemble his thoughts quickly. He didn't know if he could improvise a toast or not. The truth is, he was exhausted. It had been a long, tense day. What he really wanted to do was have a quiet meal, a good glass of wine, and go home to bed. Instead, he had to say something wise and witty in a toast.

Might as well get this over with. He stood at the head of the table and picked up his glass of Champagne. He was always fascinated by the effervescence of

Champagne—all those tiny bubbles racing to the surface to be free after years of captivity.

The conversation in the room died completely as everyone turned to look at Clay.

"It has been a very special day. A perfect day. Together we have shown that close teamwork can produce amazing marketing. Cutting edge marketing. Breakthrough marketing that will put 50,000 Texans onto Yukon flights this year for the first time. Those 50,000 people will experience the service of the Proud Bear. A toast to teamwork." Clay raised his glass as if offering it to those seated in front of him, then took a sip as everyone clinked the glasses of those nearest them, and sipped the wine.

He remained standing and continued to speak. "And I can't imagine a more perfect client to have in our office on the day we announce that Austin-Davis would be joining Pitt-Needham. A move that will open a world of resources and opportunity for our two companies and for everyone in this room." As he spoke, he made eye contact with each person sitting around the table. Once again, he extended his arm holding the glass. "To the bright and shinning future." More glasses clinked together. Clay sipped his Champagne and sat down.

Immediately, Barry Weitzel stood up, glass in hand. "On behalf of Yukon Air, I thank all of you at Austin-Davis for your hard work, dedication, and friendship. We work in an incredibly competitive industry, but you guys always find ways for us to gain an edge. We are also excited about the Pitt-Needham deal. I have to tell you that when I got my hotel room this afternoon, Deborah called me. We had a very frank discussion about your announcement. She and I both agree that the deal has the potential to be very good for Yukon Air. So, Clay, we share your excitement. Look out world, here comes, Yukon Air!" He drained his glass and sat down.

Clay leaned over and offered his hand to shake Barry's. "Thanks, Barry."

Barry leaned closer to Clay without releasing a firm grip on Clay's hand. While still smiling he whispered to Clay in a dead-serious tone. "Deborah asked me to tell you that she better not hear that Pitt-Needham is courting a larger U.S. carrier."

"I understand," was all Clay could think to say.

"I hope you do," Barry said firmly, finally releasing his grip on Clay's hand.

Client conflict, as it was called in the agency business, was a situation in which an agency went after, or was approached by, a company viewed as a competitor by one of their clients. The nature of the agency business precludes it from working for two competitive companies simultaneously. But, frequently the quality of work for a client attracted the attention of the client's competitor who would begin a confidential dialogue with the agency or send an invitation to pitch the business in an upcoming agency review. The decision to dump an existing client in order to chase a new client was never easy. Relationships had been formed. Often the client and agency had grown and prospered together. There was an implied loyalty and an explicit non-compete clause in their working agreement.

But, business is business. If the annual billings from Company A are $12 million a year and Company B's budget is $30 million, there are strong motivations for agency management to resign the smaller account in favor of the larger.

Clay and George had only faced this situation once in the young history of Austin-Davis. However, with large international agencies, the potential for client conflicts was much more frequent.

All of this roared through Clay's mind like a runaway freight train. It troubled him that somehow neither he nor George had thought much about the client conflicts that would surely arise now that Austin-Davis was part of an organization that had hundreds of clients.

Sure, Clay had made a point to check out Pitt-Needham's airline experience before alerting Yukon's CEO about the acquisition, but he was looking for information that would make the news more acceptable to Deborah. There weren't any conflicts, fortunately, but what shook Clay right now was that he hadn't thought about the impact of client conflicts. It dawned on him that as Regional Director for Pitt-Needham, he'd be in the hot seat. It would be his responsibility to decide if and when to resign existing accounts to take on others. That wasn't going to be fun. Could he do it even? Could he tell Yukon someday to take a hike because the Chicago office of Pitt-Needham was pitching the much larger Laker Air?

He looked down the table as the two teams talked and laughed together like one big family sitting around the table at Thanksgiving. Someday he might have to decide to break up the family. Could he do it? Was he going to be able to handle this new position at Pitt-Needham? Clay drained the remaining Champagne from his glass. He felt oddly removed from the others at the table. Everyone was deeply engaged in conversation. Even Sheryl. She was talking cheerfully with a young advertising coordinator, fresh out of school, that Yukon had brought to the meetings.

Clay's sense of separation from the others strengthened. He felt detached. Their voices were just white noise in the distance. A waiter finished taking Barry's order and stepped a little closer to Clay, leaned over slightly and spoke to him.

Clay didn't hear a word. He looked up . . . and up. The waiter was towering above him. Inexplicably, the waiter had to be at least fifteen feet tall; looking down at Clay from far above. Clay felt icy shocks of panic race up his back. He felt himself shrinking in his chair. The table and people were growing larger in comparison. It was happening again! *Not now! Not here!* He felt an urge to run, to escape this room that had become like the House of Horror at some cheap carnival.

Then, just like that, the hallucination stopped. Sheryl was tapping her foot against his shin under the table to get his attention. He looked at her, glad to have been brought out of the nightmarish sensation.

"They told me the Miyazaki Strip is especially good tonight, Clay," she said.

"Huh. . . what . . . oh, good to know." His mind was rapidly clearing. Clay's size was coming back to normal, too. The waiter was no longer a fifteen-foot giant looming over him; rather he was a diminutive young man standing several inches under six-feet tall. Clay opened the menu and made his selection for each of the four courses. Canlis salad, rutabaga with crab, the Miyazaki strip loin, and a port glazed pear for dessert.

The waiter made a note on his writing pad and turned to leave the room. The other waiter topped off the Champagne glasses before leaving with her serving partner to place the orders at the kitchen.

Watching as both waiters left the room together, Clay turned to Sheryl, "How did you swing two waiters for the dinner? A room this size is always served by a single waiter," Clay asked, recalling his frequent dinners here.

"I didn't think anyone was going to be in the mood for a long drawn-out meal tonight. Our team is tired. Yukon has an early flight back to Anchorage tomorrow. Two waiters are a lot faster than one. The restaurant argued with me about it when I got here, but after I reminded them of how frequently Austin-Davis entertained here, they agreed to my humble request," she said with her power smile.

△ △ △

While Clay could easily appreciate Sheryl's wisdom and event-planning prowess, what he didn't know was her consideration for the tired team seated around the table was secondary to a much more dominate concern. She was watching out for Clay—not so much to make sure he looked great as a host to their guests tonight. No, her mission was much bigger than that.

Tonight, before coming into the restaurant, Sheryl had felt a need to pray even though she was anxious to check on the room preparations. So, pray she did, sitting in her car. Praying was usually a very peaceful time for Sheryl. Not tonight. She saw a disturbing vision of Clay's frightened and anguished face. His face was nearly transparent, so she could see deep into his skull. The folds of his frontal lobe were squirming like wound snakes in a bucket. Flashes of brilliant white shot out from the writhing mass like heat lightning across a hot summer night sky. The flashes were quickly blanketed by black shadows only to be reappear again elsewhere in the brain. Over and over the white flashes and darkness seemingly took turns dominating Clay's brain while his face contorted like a rubber Halloween mask.

The vision terrified her, but as so often happened to her during prayer, insight and peace soon followed as the Holy Spirit revealed meaning to her. She started to make sense of the nightmarish vision. Forces inside Clay were at war. She was seeing a battle take place between light and dark—between good and evil—between God and Satan.

The voice she heard next was strong and clear, as if someone in the car with her had spoken.

"Protect him. Bring him to me."

The vision ended. The voice became silent.

"Amen," she said and opened her eyes. Sheryl looked at her face in the sun visor's mirror. Her makeup was a mess. She had been crying during her prayers and didn't realize it. As she repaired the damage to her mascara and eye liner, she resolved to be on guard tonight for anything that might threaten Clay. And though she felt that, as his executive assistant, protection was part of her job description anyway, this was different. Sheryl didn't have a job description anymore. She had an order from God. God had a plan for Clay.

After a final inspection of makeup, she left her car and headed to the restaurant. While walking through the parking lot, she realized that the tough part of her mission was to protect Clay without him knowing it. Clay was not one to accept the idea he needed to be guarded. So, she'd work in the background, pulling strings, orchestrating events, ever on guard for anything that might hurt him.

For the next hour, the two waiters served the four-course meal to the happy and hungry people around the table. Many bottles of the best Washington State wines were also served as part of the feast and celebration.

At close to 9 o'clock, Sheryl nudged Clay, who was deep in conversation with Barry.

"You should wrap this up, the limo will be here in a few minutes to take them back to the Westin," she advised.

"Got it," he replied. Clay took a last sip from his coffee cup and stood. The conversation subsided when Sheryl clicked her spoon repeatedly against a water glass. Clink, clink, clink, clink.

"I've been informed that your limo will arrive shortly. This has been a lot of fun. Good food, good wine, good friends, and a little business mixed in." Lighthearted chuckles came from the dinner participants. "But, before we all disappear into the night I want to thank Sheryl, who made this evening such a joy for all of us." He looked down at her and started clapping. The others applauded, and one by one stood. Within seconds Sheryl was receiving a standing ovation.

Deeply moved and embarrassed by the outpouring of affection, Sheryl still had the presence of mind to stand and accept the gratitude directed at her.

People said their good-byes and sauntered out of the room. The Yukon team got into the waiting limo. The Austin-Davis people headed for their cars. Clay and Sheryl stayed in the private dinning room. A waiter brought the check. Sheryl took it, examined it carefully and handed it to Clay.

"Hope this doesn't exceed the spending limit on your Amex card," she joked, knowing full well that Clay's business credit card status could handle dozens of dinners like this. Clay gave his card to the waiter and sat back down to finish his coffee. Sheryl sat down, too.

"I hope the Bellevue billionaire wasn't too disappointed that you canceled your date," Clay said.

Sheryl grinned. "He'll get over it."

"The evening was perfect, Sheryl. You did a fabulous job. Thanks again."

"No problem. I enjoyed it. Thanks for inviting me to participate."

"I wouldn't have it any other way, which reminds me, you and I need to talk about the future," Clay said.

At first, Sheryl was taken aback by the statement. Was this an intimate suggestion coming from Clay? *Don't be silly.* Clay was only talking about her role after the acquisition. The reaction surprised her, but she couldn't deny that her feelings for this man were evolving.

"I haven't had much time to think about it. Today was pretty busy," she responded.

"That's for sure. No rush. We should sit down and talk within the week though," he said.

"How about brunch on Sunday?" Sheryl surprised herself with the boldness of the suggestion.

Clay thought about his schedule for a few seconds. "That will work if you want to do it that soon."

"Let's have brunch . . . right after church." She tried to say it with a matter-of-fact tone that didn't entirely succeed.

"You are determined to make a churchgoer out of me, aren't you?" Clay said, a touch of irritation noticeable in his voice.

"Not really. Not a 'church-goer' as you said, but I believe you'd really enjoy and benefit from a relationship with God, the Heavenly Father."

△ △ △

Clay stared into his coffee cup. He wanted to put an end to this. Was she going to pull him into church every Sunday just because he was kind enough to go once with her? Irritation began to swell inside him. She was being too invasive, too pushy. This needed to stop. She was going too far. She was taking their relationship for granted. She was his employee, that's all. She had no business trying to trick him into attending church with her.

He looked up at her with every intention of telling her no. His eyes locked onto hers as if by some magnetic force. The care and compassion he saw in her eyes made him melt. It wasn't quite the look of a loving mother, but close. There was something else there in her eyes; something more than just caring. He didn't know what he was seeing and sensing, but it touched him deeply. His irritation vanished.

"Okay, I'll go. It wasn't so bad the last time," he said.

"I knew you'd say yes," she said grinning ear to ear.

"I'll go to church with you on one condition," he said seriously.

"What's that?"

"That we have brunch at my house afterward. There's a yacht race Sunday afternoon on the lake. It's fun to watch," he said.

The smile on Sheryl's face remained. "Do you cook? I won't accept just cereal and toast, you know."

"Yes, I cook. You won't have to eat cereal."

Restaurant staff entered the room and began to noisily clear the table. It was time for Clay and Sheryl to leave.

They retrieved their coats and umbrellas from the coat check. Clay tipped the attendant. Then they walked outside into the night.

"Where'd you park?" Clay asked.

Sheryl pointed off to the right. They headed toward her car together. At the car, Sheryl retrieved keys from her purse and opened the door of the roadster. They both stood there looking at each other in the dim light of the parking lot lamps. It was an awkward moment.

"Drive safely, Sheryl. What time are you picking me up Sunday?"

"I will keep all four tires on the road at all times. Eleven," she said and turned from Clay to get into her car.

"Wait a second," Clay said. Sheryl turned back around to face him.

He opened his arms, "Could I give you a good night hug?"

She looked into his face, and Clay thought he could detect the same nervousness he felt in her. "I think a hug would be appropriate," she said, moving into his arms, clutching him closely to her.

Even through their heavy coats, Clay felt something magical with the embrace. It was like no other hug in his life. He instantly had the feeling that this woman belonged in his arms. She fit perfectly. Holding her felt so natural as if she was a part of him. So good. Too good, perhaps. *Stop it.*

With a little extra squeeze of his arms, he released Sheryl, said good night again and walked down the sloped parking lot to his car. His mind was swirling. Holding Sheryl had disoriented him.

As he approached his car, he felt in his coat pocket for the car key. His left hand reached into the left pocket. He felt a strange object. It wasn't a key. He withdrew it from the pocket. A napkin was wrapped around two chocolate chip cookies.

Cookies. The little girl. Reception. Funeral. Uncle Charley. The lighthouse. Images shot through his brain like muzzle flashes from a machine gun.

He had forgotten about the lighthouse—his lighthouse.

Chapter 46

lay returned home, parked in his reserved space, and headed for the dock leading to his houseboat. Ten steps from the car he remembered Dr. Shildstein's gift in the trunk. He walked quickly back to retrieve the package. It was starting to rain again.

Package in hand, Clay walked down the dock to his front door. He let himself in, turned off the alarm, and walked into the kitchen. He removed the cookies from his coat pocket and set them on the granite counter with the wrapped present. He hung up his coat in the entry closet and moved wearily up the stairs to his bedroom suite. Next, he disrobed, carefully rehanging his suit on its hanger. He changed into stylish workout clothes, but exercising was the last thing on his mind tonight.

He went back downstairs, lit a fire, poured a glass of Aberlour scotch and settled into his favorite chair—second-favorite, actually, after Uncle Charley's—to reflect on this amazing day. It made Clay's mind buzz just to recall all that had transpired during the past twelve hours or so.

Had he really agreed to sell his company today? Did he really get a good report from the Neurologist? Did he really get angry at his shrink for suggesting he had been damaging himself most of his life because of some inferiority complex, or whatever it was? At least she hadn't suggested Clay had some perverted fantasy about his mother. Don't shrinks attempt to explain all behavior with the Oedipus complex?

Still, she had made a very interesting point about the impact Vic had on him. That made him remember his homework assignment to write in a journal every day. He made a note in his phone to buy a journal tomorrow for that purpose.

He sipped at the golden fluid in his glass and continued to recall the day's events. Interesting, today he got angry twice. Once in the conference room. Once in Dr. Shildstein's office. A public expression of anger was unusual for him; twice in one day was unheard of for level-headed Clay. Of course, thinking he was being attacked in his office by a Briggs & Stratton lawn mower with a serious attitude problem, certainly qualified for unusual, too.

What else happened today? Clay asked himself while staring out into the rainy night. He had gotten flustered making coffee this morning in the office kitchen. Oh, and let's not forget the giant waiter in the Canlis dining room. That was special. He drained his glass and stood to pour a refill.

As he walked by the kitchen counter on the way back from the liquor cabinet, he spotted the two cookies. Cookies and Scotch. Why not? He sat down in his chair and munched a cookie then chased the bite with a sip of scotch. The chocolate and scotch were an enjoyable pairing, but not as good as chocolate and Cabernet, or cookies and cold milk, for that matter. Did he have any milk in the house?

The glowing logs in the fireplace popped loudly like a tiny firecracker. Clay checked to make sure the fire was secure in the grates and brought his focus back to recalling the day's events. Funny how his mind took him to cookies just when he was recalling the weirdness from the day, especially his hallucinations or whatever they were. He decided he was avoiding looking inward. Let's see, he could think about how screwed up he was, or he could escape into cookies and Scotch. With one cookie remaining, he decided to complete his inventory of the day.

The Yukon dinner had been a big success, in spite of Clay's momentary anxiety triggered by fears of client conflicts. He was very glad that Sheryl had been by his side at the dinner. Her presence had comforted him and stopped the towering waiter hallucination. Then it dawned on him. Today in the office kitchen, he was struggling with the espresso machine. Poof, Sheryl was there and made everything right again—the coffee and Clay. In the employee meeting, he was hallucinating again until she stepped forward with a bottle of water and instantly he was okay. Three times today, Clay had been drowning, and Sheryl was there at the perfect time to save him with just a touch and a smile.

But, of all the strangeness in his day, one event stood out. The event surpassed the hallucinations in its inexplicable nature. The event even ranked above his anger in terms of rare emotional expression.

What took the prize today? He had hugged Sheryl in the parking lot.

He reached for his phone and sent a text to Sheryl, "Did you get home okay?"

A few minutes passed before his phone buzzed. "Safe and sound. Thanks for asking," her text replied.

Now, what should he say? Should he ask another question? Should he play it safe and just say good night? Should he say what was really on his mind now? His heart was speaking to him, he thought, but then again it could be just the Scotch and cookies. For crying out loud, he was thinking like a teenager. *Get a grip!*

"You still there?" Sheryl texted after more time had gone by.

"Yep. Sorry. Lost in thought," his thumbs typed the response and tapped Send. Oh, oh, why did he say that? He wanted to recall the text but couldn't. The "lost in thought" left it wide open for her to ask him what he was thinking about. No way was he ready to share that he had been thinking about her. He wanted to crawl under a blanket and hide.

"Thinking about what?" Sheryl asked.

There it was. Now he had to think quickly. Seconds of digital silence passed before he had an idea.

"Thinking about church Sunday. What time?" It was plausible that he had been thinking about going to church again with Sheryl on Sunday. It could have happened.

"I'll pick you up at 11. Did you also forget what we're going to do after?" Sheryl texted back.

For a few seconds, he panicked. Indeed, he had forgotten. He was thankful this wasn't a phone conversation. The texting gave him time to think. After church . . . after church . . . what were they going to do . . . Ah-ha! He had it.

"Certainly not. I'm fixing you brunch," he texted finally.

Her response was a smiley face emoji.

He needed to end this exchange before he got himself into trouble.

"Good night. See you Sunday," he texted.

"Nite," she replied.

Clay got up from his chair and walked down the hallway to use the restroom. On his return, he stood in the kitchen and thought about pouring another scotch, but changed his mind. He had consumed enough alcohol for the night, and tomorrow was going to be busy. He checked the to-do list on his phone: car battery, journal. He added "brunch shopping" and "property management" so he'd remember to look in his email for the property management agreement that Bartlett was supposed to send him.

A wave of exhaustion washed over him. The day's tension and the night's alcohol consumption combined to suck the remaining energy from Clay. He poked the logs in the fire, pushing them far back onto the grate. The logs spit defiant sparks, but otherwise submitted to being moved. He replaced the metal poker in its stand, reset the house alarm, and headed upstairs to bed.

Chapter 47

The view from the top of the lighthouse was breathtaking. Clay could see for miles out to sea; all the way to the horizon—that misty line where ocean met sky far off in the west. It was a fabulous day. Bright, warm sunshine flooded into the lantern room through the thick panes of glass all around him. Clay felt free and joyful as his eyes scanned the sparkling ocean.

Three seagulls soared around and around outside of where Clay stood. Each one seemed to be looking with their piercing eyes inside the lighthouse at Clay. "What are you doing up here?" their accusing eyes seemed to say. He tried to ignore the obnoxious birds and just enjoy the view, but around and around they glided in the sea breeze, hovering just outside the glass as if suspended from the sky with invisible wires.

In Clay's hand was a canvas tool carrier filled with tools he didn't recognize. In fact, he wasn't sure why he had the tools in the first place. Was there something he needed to fix up here? He began to feel guilty that there was something in need of repair, but he didn't have a clue what it was. Guilt and frustration soon replaced his sense of joy. Something wasn't right. He was supposed to do something up here, but couldn't remember. He walked around and around the small lantern room trying to remember.

A noise caught his attention. It seemed out of place on this day when the only sounds up here were the wind and occasional harsh cries of the seagulls. The noise wasn't coming from inside the lighthouse, but from outside, from down below. Clay stepped to one of the window panes and looked down.

Below him in the grass field that surrounded the lighthouse was a lawn mower cutting a jagged path through the grass. Smoke belched from the machine, giving it an angry, hostile appearance. No one was operating the mower. It appeared to have a mind of its own, cutting madly in one direction then the next, making a mess of the grass.

This made no sense. Who put the lawn mower there, and why didn't it just run in a straight line right off the cliff into the ocean far below? To Clay's fascination, the mower could jerk this way and that, but would always turn at the right time when it got to the boundary of the grass. The noise level increased. From behind the caretaker's house, another mower appeared and soon joined the first one on the lawn, cutting uneven paths in the grass.

Clay's fascination quickly turned into fear. What was going on down there? Who was releasing these mowers? What was steering them?

The noise decibel increased again as a third and fourth mower lurched from behind the house and joined the other two on the lawn.

Clay turned away from the window. He had to think. What was he going to do? Obviously, the mowers had to be stopped. Could he just walk out there and turn them off one by one? Of course, he could. That's what he'd do. Go down there, turn off the runaway Briggs & Stratton mowers, and then start looking for the jokester who turned them loose on his property.

Probably a promotional stunt by a lawn service, reasoned Clay. Clearly, the guy needs some help with his promotional tactics. Clay resolved to walk down the long winding stairs, walk outside and turn off the four mowers. He looked down at the lawn again. To his horror, the four mowers were now a dozen growling machines tearing around the yard, cutting to pieces anything that got in the way. More mowers were joining them from behind the house; a steady stream of machines marched to the lawn like an invading army.

Clay was truly frightened now. He couldn't stay in the lighthouse forever. He had to go down there. He had to put an end to all this. To make matters worse, the sun was setting. It was getting dark. He couldn't turn off all those mowers in the dark. They'd cut him to pieces.

He cautiously walked down the spiraling stairs. Down and down; around and around. With each step closer to the ground the raucous noise became louder. Each step took more and more effort as fear gripped him. He paused on the final landing before reaching the ground level. Only a few steps remained. The noise was hurting his ears; he could even smell the rancid exhaust from the mowers outside. He wondered how many were out there now. He started to hear other sounds. The sound of steel against stone. The sound of sharp metal blades chipping at rock. In horror he realized what the sound was—the mowers were running into the lighthouse now. The portal window at the stairway landing gave him a limited view outside. He glanced out and screamed.

Hundreds of mowers surrounded the lighthouse. Line after line of them were charging the lighthouse, crashing their spinning blades against the old brick and mortar. Sparks flew into the growing darkness as bits of stone were slowly being eaten away by the constant siege of angry machines.

His only chance now was to leave the lighthouse, walk through the corridor to the house, through the house and make a dash for his car. That was the only plan that made sense. He had to escape the property and these sinister machines.

He took another step down into the darkness; just seven steps remained. A high-pitched grinding sound sent his heart into his throat. The noise level rose and rose. Clay set down the canvas tool carrier, so he could cover his ears, trying to protect them from them painful din. An explosion of wood and metal sent debris flying into the ground floor of the lighthouse. Pieces of chewed wood were hurled at Clay's feet, making him jump. The doorway to the corridor crashed down and six smoke-belching Briggs & Stratton mowers jerked into the room like a pack of wild dogs in search of meat.

He was trapped. Even if he could somehow avoid the six fiendish machines in front of him and race to the corridor, how many of the evil things were waiting for him there? He couldn't escape.

The pack of mowers jerked and raced in zig-zag patterns around the stone floor of the lighthouse. They were behaving like blind wolves insane with hunger, frantically searching for food. The machines bumped into walls with their tires and spinning steel blades, reversed, turned slightly and moved forward again. Four of the mowers were repeatedly crashing into the interior wall of the lighthouse sending chips of stone flying into the air. Two other machines bumped into the staircase. Metal striking metal, sparks lit up the darkness like a sparkler on the Fourth of July. Both machines smashed into the stairs again and again. Clay was petrified. With trembling legs, he managed to move up another two steps to put distance between himself and the sharp spinning blades. He never took his eyes off the mowers as they repeatedly crashed into the staircase, their tires spinning wildly trying to gain traction on the cold steps. To his horror, Clay realized what they were doing. They were trying to climb the stairs! They were coming after him.

This was insane. Crazy. Lawnmowers don't climb stairs, but now below him, all six mowers were taking turns attempting to scale that first step like angry crabs trying to claw their way out of a bucket. The fumes from exhaust and burnt tire rubber were making Clay lightheaded. He had to get away before he passed out. There was only one way to go. Coughing and gasping for air, he grabbed a flashlight from his tool carrier and began climbing back up the long dark stairway. He needed fresh air; he needed time to think.

Badly out of breath, he made it to the top, to the lantern room. He was utterly exhausted. He could still hear the screeching pack far below. The deadly fumes had risen to the top, as well, but not as suffocating as on the ground floor. He needed air. Of the numerous panes of thick glass that surrounded him now only one was designed to actually open. He twisted the heavy bronze latch, releasing the window on his hinges. Cool air poured into the room. The window was just large enough for Clay to stick his head out and gulp deep breaths of the fresh salt-laced air. With his head still sticking out the window he looked down.

Outside in the growing darkness, hundreds of mowers surrounded the lighthouse and the house. In neat rows they faced the white tower, idling as if resting for the final assault.

Clay pulled his head back inside. He couldn't go back down stairs. He might be able to outrun a few of the hungry mowers, but not all of them. He sat down on the floor beneath the open window. Fatigue and hopelessness overtook him. Deep sobs erupted from inside him. He was trapped. He didn't know how he was going to save himself, or if he was going to. He was either going to die down there torn to pieces by the evil machines or die up here of carbon monoxide poisoning.

He was safe up here. At least until the fumes made him pass out, alone, never to wake again. He needed a plan. He needed hope. He had neither. He rested his head on his knees and wept.

Chapter 48

Clay's body jerked violently, and he woke drenched in sweat. The nightmare faded away. His mind began to clear. Reality slowly refilled his head. He was in his own bed. In his bedroom. Outside the large windows, he could see a dark Lake Union, not a field filled with crazy mowers wanting to slice and dice him. No sounds of screeching metal blades against steel and stone. Just peaceful quiet. But what was he smelling? Smoke!

He leaped from bed and raced downstairs. The odor of smoke was stronger down here, though not visible in the air. He checked the fireplace first. A chunk of log had broken off and fallen off the grate just enough that some of its smoke was entering the room rather than up the chimney. He grabbed the fireplace poker and pushed the smoldering chunk back. Next, he selected the small fireplace brush and swept the remaining debris of ash and embers back into the fireplace. Didn't he push the logs back before going to bed? How did this one jump out? He had no answers.

Satisfied that the source of smoke had been found and corrected, he replaced the fireplace tools into their holder. He looked into the kitchen to see what time was displayed on the microwave oven's clock. It was 3:16. Clay groaned. He had only been asleep about four hours. Now that the adrenalin was subsiding after the smoke scare he was aware of just how exhausted he was. What did they say in the country, "run hard and put up wet." That's how he felt right now but going back to bed was not an option; not if there was a chance of re-entering that terrible nightmare. Though awake, the fear from his dream lingered. He wasn't going back to bed. Maybe he'd read.

The aroma of smoke still hung in the air, so Clay opened the large glass sliding door facing the lake. A light rain was falling outside, and the breeze was cold. Clay shivered in his bathrobe but left the door open to air out the room.

He had a strong desire for hot chocolate, so he used his home espresso machine to heat frothy milk into which he stirred spoonfuls of Mexican chocolate powder. Hot chocolate was comfort food for Clay, and he needed a lot of comforting right now. He sipped the smooth hot brew. Its intense chocolate and cinnamon flavor invaded his mouth. He remembered when his mother would make him hot cocoa with marshmallows on cold winter days. Warm memories of his mother made him smile. Vic may have been a SOB, but he certainly had had a very loving mother.

Still chilled, he turned the furnace on to combat the cold air pouring into the room from the opened door. The room needed to air out a little longer. Standing in the kitchen, Clay was pondering what to do next when the wrapped present on the countertop caught his eye. *Might as well open it now.*

The last of the little girl's cookies sat on the counter next to the wrapped rectangle gift. He took a large bite of the cookie and began to unwrap the gift.

Every time Clay opened a wrapped gift he had to stop himself from simply ripping open the paper. As a small child, his mother encouraged him to not rip the paper, but instead carefully lift the taped edges in order to retain the wrapping paper for another use on some future gift-giving occasion. It wasn't unusual for the same paper to be used for two or three Christmases. Though these days Clay didn't bother with re-using wrapping paper, he still carefully and respectfully removed the wrapping from every gift.

The gift in his hands at this moment was roughly 24 inches by 24 inches. He could tell holding its irregular edges that the contents were not in a box. It weighed a few pounds. He gently shook it. No rattle. The gift had been meticulously wrapped in a deep purple paper with a subtle light purple pattern. The paper was gorgeous. *Maybe I'll save this one. Too nice to just toss away.*

With his fingers, he released the tape along one edge, being careful not to tear the beautiful paper. Next, he undid the tape from the opposite end. Then he very gently and slowly peeled back the taped seam running the full length of the package.

When he pulled the paper away, all he could see was a wooden frame, and a wire strung from one side to the other. It was art of some sort. He removed the paper completely and turned the object around to view the front.

The shock nearly made him drop the gift. The painting was from Dr. Shildstein's collection of hot air balloon scenes that Clay had admired every time he was in her office. Clay looked down at the gorgeous white balloon with a purple cross on one side soaring above a rocky coastline. It was flying above a lighthouse, but not just any lighthouse. It was his lighthouse!

No, it couldn't be *his* lighthouse. The coincidence would be too great. *Many lighthouses look alike,* he thought. He studied the painting more closely. Though he had only been to the Deception Point property once, he could recognize many things in the painting—the lighthouse itself looked very similar, there was a structure between the house and lighthouse tower, the house itself, even the roof of a carport was visible in the painting. The coastline certainly resembled the cliff below the property. If this painting wasn't of the Deception Point lighthouse, it was of another property exactly like it.

Clay thought back to the first time he saw the painting on the doctor's office wall, many days before he knew anything about Uncle Charley's lighthouse. He remembered being attracted to it but couldn't recall any of the details of the lighthouse and other buildings. The painting was unique in her collection in that it was the only balloon scene at a coastal location. Clay knew very little about the sport but figured the onshore-offshore winds of a coastal region weren't conducive to safe, reliable soaring.

Clearly, the artist had experienced a balloon ride above this lighthouse or else had simply used his or her imagination to paint one at this location. One fact was certain, the artist either knew the property well or used a photograph for reference. Clay looked more closely in the lower right corner of the painting to see the artist's signature. There, written to blend well with the rocks and grass was a single letter, "G."

He stood there staring at the painting. It drew him in; it mesmerized him somehow. The generosity of the doctor's gift moved Clay nearly to tears. Yet, there was the question of why she had selected this particular painting out of the dozen or so in her collection to give to Clay. Had she noticed him looking at this one more than the others? Was it because he had told her about the lighthouse inheritance? No, it couldn't be. He hadn't told her anything about Uncle Charley and the Point Deception lighthouse yet. He made a note to ask her in his appointment next week.

Clay shivered and remembered the open door to the deck. He closed it, satisfied the house had aired out enough. He couldn't smell any more smoke. He left the painting on the counter and brought the remaining cookie and cup of hot chocolate to his chair. He sat deep in thought. What was going on with him? The last couple of weeks had been very unsettling, to say the least. Maybe things would begin to settle down some now. He let his head rest against the back of the chair. He closed his eyes and drifted off into a deep, peaceful sleep.

Chapter 49

When he woke, daylight was streaming into the living room. As his eyes adjusted to the light, he could see two kayakers paddling slowly by his front deck. He recognized them as neighbors from the next dock. Every Saturday, rain or shine, the couple would take their sleek sea kayaks out for a spin.

Clay lifted his phone and saw the time, eight o'clock. Noticing the cup of now cold chocolate and a partially eaten cookie on the stand next to his chair, he began to recall the early morning events—the smoke, unwrapping the painting. He stood, returned the dishes to the kitchen sink, took another look at the balloon painting, and made his way upstairs. The wall along the staircase was one place he could hang the painting, he thought, while climbing the polished wood stairs.

In the master bathroom, he took a long, hot shower that invigorated him. He put on jeans, sports shoes, a light-yellow shirt, and a dark-green Oregon sweatshirt. Downstairs he hurriedly consumed a macchiato and toasted bagel before slipping on a parka and heading out the door to run his errands—car battery, journal, and groceries for Sunday brunch.

Returning home in the afternoon, he sat at the kitchen counter to wolf down sushi he had purchased at the grocery store. While eating he studied the painting. Clay had to admit, it was stunning. The rich colors, the detail, the hypnotic perspective of looking down on the balloon as it sailed above the lighthouse. He simply loved it.

Clay retrieved the journal he had purchased earlier in the day, opened it to page one and started writing.

After a few minutes, he remembered why he didn't like to journal. He hated having to recall things that made him uncomfortable. Much better, he believed, to put issues behind him, forget they ever happened. There was one problem with that philosophy now—the frequency of hallucinations during the day and nightmares at night made it impossible to turn his back on the upsetting weirdness that had invaded him the past few weeks. So, he wrote. After thirty minutes he had chronicled the dream well enough to spook himself all over again. One thing he knew for certain—nobody but Dr. Shildstein could ever read this. He set his writing pen down on the counter. He wanted to stop but realized he hadn't done his homework properly. His assignment was to write down whenever he felt not good enough. Okay then, he took his thoughts back to the dream. With eyes closed he pictured the scenes of the dream and re-lived his emotions. Fright, frustration, futility. Check. Not good enough? Not really, unless believing that he couldn't win against hundreds of flesh-starved lawn mowers qualified him as being not good enough. He decided to categorize his behavior in the dream as exhibiting good survival instincts and solid common sense. He shut the journal's cover and reached for his notebook computer instead.

His email Inbox contained 153 new messages, well above the normal level after spending less than twenty-four hours away. He decided to answer emails from his office first. Several employees had sent him messages with questions or comments. He answered each the best he could, making certain he cc'd George on every reply. Next, he replied to friends and business acquaintances. Most were congratulating him on the sale. Others expressed shock. What he wasn't prepared for was the eleven messages from other agency executives around the Northwest. Most were congratulatory in nature. Others were disappointed that Clay would let a big international agency like Pitt-Needham get a foothold in the Northwest market. As if they wouldn't have made the exact same decision if Manicotti had approached them.

An email with an attachment from Bartlett in Reef Bay caught his attention. It was the property management agreement the attorney had promised him. Clay reviewed the online documents and applied an electronic signature. Done. Now he could relax knowing that the lighthouse property would be looked after until Clay could figure out what on earth to do with it. He stared at the painting still laying on the kitchen counter. Great question. What *am* I going to do with the property? A simpler question presented itself. Where should Clay hang this magnificent painting?

There was space available on the wall next to the stairs, but the light wasn't very good. He took the art upstairs. Standing in the middle of his bedroom he looked around inspecting the walls. Above the bed was a possibility. The wall contained a large painting of a magnificent old sailing vessel working hard against a gale while rounding the Cape of Magellan. Clay next studied the master bathroom. He didn't have any art in this room for some reason. A skylight let plenty of light into the room during the day. From the shower, he could see the bare wall. The wall needed something. Should the lighthouse be hung there, or the old sailing frigate? He considered the earth tone colors of the tile in the bathroom and decided the sepia tones of the frigate painting and its frame would fit nicely there.

Ten minutes later the painting of the white balloon soaring above the Deception Point lighthouse hung above his headboard. The sailing vessel, with spray-covered decks, now adorned the wall in his bathroom. He was very pleased.

Maybe, just maybe, the new painting above his head would keep the nightmares away. Clay laughed out loud. Maybe that was why Dr. Shildstein had given it to him.

The rest of the afternoon was spent running errands and making preparations for his brunch with Sheryl. His housekeeping service had cleaned on Friday, so there nothing to do but think about food preparation and set out the dishes. One question kept invading his mind. Was tomorrow's brunch just brunch, or something more?

Chapter 50

lay slept soundly and woke refreshed Sunday morning. Before showering, he spent forty-five minutes on the elliptical machine in the exercise room next to his bedroom. He had been neglecting his workouts and resolved to get back into a routine of cardio and weight resistance exercise. The small exercise room was crowded with the elliptical machine, a Bowflex home gym, and a rowing machine. One wall of the mini-gym was a sliding glass door overlooking Lake Union. A TV monitor was hung from the ceiling, so he could watch a movie or the news while working out, if the sweeping view across the lake wasn't enough to take his mind off the monotony of the workout.

Today, Clay decided to watch the Sunday news shows to catch up on political events. After his forty-five minutes on the elliptical device, he headed for the shower. Standing in the glass-enclosed shower while the hot water beat on his back Clay studied the frigate painting on the opposite wall. He admitted that placing the impressive piece of art where he could see it from the shower had been a great idea. He might add other pieces to the wall for a complete maritime theme.

After shaving, he stepped into his wardrobe closet to dress. He recalled from his last visit to Sheryl's church the people were casually dressed. It really didn't matter what he wore to church, but Clay was nervous about being around all those religious strangers. He felt out of his element at church.

He opted for a brown and tan patterned sports coat over a black silk turtle neck sweater and jeans. After slipping on a pair of driving loafers, he evaluated the look in the mirror. It was casual but respectful. Successful and slightly understated. Maybe too understated. He was Clay Austin, successful businessman and entrepreneur, after all. Besides, he wanted to look good for Sheryl, being her guest. He needed something more for the wardrobe today. He reached into a drawer and pulled out a deep green and gold silk pocket handkerchief and placed it into the chest pocket of the sports coat. Satisfied with his appearance, he walked downstairs for a light breakfast and cup of coffee.

At 10:45 he double-checked his preparations for brunch. He had staged everything in containers in the refrigerator to minimize the preparation time when he and Sheryl returned from church. Two place settings were laid out on the dining room table. Satisfied that all was well, he slipped on a leather coat, armed the house alarm and headed for the dock gate to meet Sheryl.

Half way up the dock in the cold morning air he got nervous. How should he greet her? He had everything so well prepared and thought out, but in a few minutes, he'd be facing her. How was he supposed to act? What was he going to say?

Stupid him, why did he have to go and hug her after dinner Friday night? That hug could have changed everything. Or did it? What's wrong with an innocent hug? *Innocent? Who are you kidding, Clay? There was more to your hug than a casual expression of gratitude for a job well done. Your hug was more than some sort of slap-on-the-back, that-a-girl sort of thing, wasn't it, Clay? Okay, okay it was more than a friendly hug, but maybe she didn't see it that way. Maybe she took the hug as a simple 'thank you' from a grateful and slightly intoxicated boss.*

The closer Clay got to the gate the more nervous he became. He didn't have a clue what to do or how to be with Sheryl now. He took his eyes off the wet dock in front of his feet and looked ahead. Sheryl's white Miata was waiting on the other side of the gate.

"Good morning," Clay said as he squeezed his six-foot-two frame into the Miata's passenger seat. With the top up it was a lot harder to get in than the first time he rode with her when the convertible top was down. Once seated he turned to look at her, hoping his eyes didn't reveal his nervousness.

"Good morning," Sheryl responded. Much to Clay's discomfort she didn't immediately put the roadster into gear and drive off. Oh no, she looked into Clay's face and smiled with the warmest, most welcoming smile Clay had ever seen. If she was nervous too, it didn't show. Sheryl's relaxed demeanor took the edge off Clay's nervousness. "Are you ready for church, mister?"

"Let's do it," Clay replied, forcing a grin to his face.

Chapter 51

heryl and Clay walked from the parking lot toward the church buildings arranged around a large central courtyard. While Sheryl fixed two coffees, Clay studied the surroundings. They were unchanged from his previous visit, except a large banner on the side of one of the buildings appeared to be advertising what the sermon was about.

"Gifts" was the only word on the huge banner.

Sheryl handed him a coffee in a disposable cup with lid. She noticed him staring at the banner. "Should be a really good service today," she said in a tone that sounded to Clay like she had some inside knowledge about the subject matter.

"If you say so," he replied.

With her free hand, she gently gripped Clay's arm and directed him toward the front door. While they walked, she kept her hand lightly hooked on his arm.

She guided him to the same two seats from his last visit. He wondered if everyone had assigned seating. He helped Sheryl remove her coat; he did the same, and they settled into their seats just as a young woman walked onto the stage, welcomed everyone, and made a few announcements. While she spoke the band quietly took their positions on the stage behind her. The announcer, or whatever she was, walked off the stage and the music started. Everyone in the audience stood, clapping to the beat; many were singing along with the band as the lyrics appeared on the huge overhead video screens.

Clay looked at Sheryl out of the corner of his eye. She was lost in song, smiling broadly. Clay had never heard the song before but managed to clap to the beat. The band was really good, he thought.

With the three worship songs over, the band ambled off the stage, the audience sat down, and the pastor walked to the front carrying an adjustable floor stand to hold his tablet computer.

This was a different pastor from before, so Clay surmised the church must have several people that took turns giving sermons. This person was about Clay's age. He wore jeans, hiking boots, and a colored tee shirt under an unbuttoned plaid wool shirt. He looked more like a lead singer in a garage band than a pastor of a large church.

After a few light opening remarks, the pastor skillfully transitioned into the topic.

"Today we start our series on Gifts. Relax, don't run out of the door, I'm not going to talk about tithing this morning." He waited for the audience's laughter to subside. "That sermon will be next month." More laughter from the audience. "In this series, over the next three weeks, we'll explore together what the Bible says about gifts."

Gifts? It was all new to Clay. He sipped his coffee and listened, expecting to receive some insight about the gifts that the wise men gave baby Jesus. That was the only thing he knew about gifts in the Bible.

"Did you know there are eighty-nine verses in the Bible that discuss gifts? Gifts include words of wisdom, words of knowledge, faith, healing, miracles, prophecy, distinguishing between spirits, speaking in tongues, understanding of tongues. Throughout the series I'll discuss these types of gifts—the role they played in the Bible and most importantly, what these gifts mean in our daily lives.

"For most Biblical scholars, the definitive passage about gifts is in 1 Corinthians, chapter 12. This book in the New Testament consists of a letter Paul wrote to the church in Corinth because he had received word that the followers in that Greek town were bickering among themselves. There were arguments about 'who's got the best gifts,' or 'who's got the most gifts.'

"Paul skillfully, and at times with a touch of humor tells the Corinthians (and us) the various ways God's Spirt gets worked into our daily lives. I'll summarize for you the points Paul makes."

Verses from the Bible filled the large screens while the pastor spoke. Clay had difficulty understanding the verses on the big screens and was grateful the pastor was explaining them.

"In verses 4-11, Paul emphasizes that everybody gets something in the way of spiritual gifts. First, God's gifts are handed out everywhere, but originate in God's spirit; second, there is a wonderful variety of gifts; and third, the gifts are handed out one by one. The Lord decides who gets what and when.

"Pretty cool, isn't it? When we let the Spirit into our hearts, we are awakened to a gift. And the gift is a whole lot better than a discount coupon. It could be the gift of healing or the gift of wise counsel."

"I know that as of last night over 840 of you had participated in the spiritual gifts survey we offer online. The survey helps us identify our gifts. If you haven't already taken the survey, I encourage you to do so."

Clay whispered into Sheryl's ear, "What are your gifts?"

"Tell you later," she whispered back.

The pastor continued, "In verses 12 and 13, Paul helps the Corinthians understand by using the human body for an example. He draws the parallel between the church—all believers—and the human body. Each is made whole by many parts. The body has many different parts. The church has many different parts—you and I.

"This passage goes further to explain that once we have the Spirit, we're not calling our own shots anymore. God is orchestrating our life, integrating it with everyone else. At the end of this passage, Paul makes it clear that we're all equal in God's eyes. The old labels, like Jew or Greek, slave or free, are no longer useful.

"Now remember, there was turmoil in the Corinthian church at this time because some were claiming superiority over others based on their spiritual gift. But Paul was very wise. He knew that some people would think that their role was not important. In verses 14-24 Paul puts to rest any idea that one person is better or worse than the other. He states, 'I want you to think about how all this makes you more significant, not less. A body isn't just a single part blown up into something huge. It's all the different-but-similar parts arranged and functioning together.' Today we'd probably call this teamwork and wear a t-shirt saying, 'There is no I in Team.'" The audience laughed as a picture of a t-shirt with the slogan appear on the giant screens.

"Paul doesn't stop there. Even though he just told the church of Corinth that everyone was important, everyone had an important gift, he warned them about becoming proud or arrogant. Look at what he says in verses 19-24. He warns them against taking their significance and blowing it up into self-importance.

"I love what he is saying here, 'For no matter how significant you are, it is only because of what you are a part of.'

"In the final six verses of the chapter, Paul summarizes by telling the Corinthians that Christ's church is a complete Body and not a gigantic, unidimensional part. It's not all Apostle, not all Prophet, not all Miracle Worker, not all Healer, not all Prayer in Tongues, not all Interpreter of Tongues. Everyone has a part, equally valuable to the body of Christ. In a way, as Christians, we're living a beautiful co-dependence with each other."

Members of the band were quietly taking their places behind the pastor as he concluded his sermon.

Clay wasn't paying any more attention to the pastor. He was stuck on something he had said. What on earth was speaking in tongues?

The band started playing. The audience stood. Many slowly made their way to the exits, but others remained standing while clapping and singing. He noticed a handful of people walked down the aisles to talk with individuals who seemed to be stationed there.

"What are they doing?" Clay asked Sheryl, pointing to the individuals conversing in front of the stage.

"They are asking to be prayed for. We call the volunteers there, Prayer Warriors," Sheryl replied. "Have anything you'd like to ask God about?"

That question took Clay by surprise. "No, just wondering what was going on down there, that's all." Besides, Clay thought, prayer was for religious people. Not for him. He wasn't good enough to pray to God.

They walked up the aisle, out the church door and to Sheryl's Miata.

"I'm sure hungry," said Sheryl squeezing Clay's arm playfully. "You better be. I make a mean bowl of cornflakes."

Chapter 52

n the car, Sheryl said, "You asked about my gifts. Do you want to know what the survey told me?"

"Sure, I'm curious."

"My top three are Discernment, Administration, and Artistry in that order," she said while weaving the roadster in and out of Sunday afternoon traffic.

"I totally see your Administration gifts every day at the office. That makes sense. You always seem to have great judgment, too, is that discernment?"

"Discernment, as defined in the survey, is the ability to see words and behavior as being of God, human, or satanic." She glanced at him to see his reaction while shifting down to take the next turn.

"Okay. So, you see the difference between good and evil."

"Yep."

"So, what do you see when you look at me?"

She glanced at him again, feigning a look of serious contemplation. "You are human." She knew it was a short statement, and it looked like Clay was expecting more, but she left it at that for now.

Sheryl returned her focus to driving. Clay was too busy watching the cars, buildings and leafless trees fly by the swift roadster to notice the slight upturn at each corner of her mouth.

After another ten minutes, Sheryl pulled the Miata into the guest parking space by the gate to Clay's dock. As she turned off the ignition, the sense of calm and confidence she had felt all morning vanished together with the dying engine. While Clay removed his tall frame from the tight passenger seat and walked around to open Sheryl's door, she checked her makeup quickly in the rearview mirror. What on earth was she doing here? Going to church with your boss was one thing. Having brunch at his house was another. By agreeing to his invitation, she had crossed a line. "Thou shall not date your boss." Oh, sure, she told herself it wasn't really a date. Just two colleagues enjoying each other's company. They'd probably spend the afternoon talking about business anyway. She replayed the justification in her mind. It rang just as hollow.

Her door opened, and Clay extended his hand to help her step out of the car. She took his hand and felt herself being lifted up effortlessly. His hand was soft but strong. Touching his hand pleased her, just like receiving his warm embrace Friday night pleased her. All day Saturday that moment in the parking lot had been replayed through her mind. Had the hug been a genuine expression of affection by Clay, or simply an intoxicated thank you? But, what if the embrace been more than just affection? She didn't know for sure. What she did know was in Friday's parking-lot hug, and now holding his hand, it felt like the most natural thing in the world—like her purpose was to be next to him.

Skating on thin ice, girl, don't you think?

△ △ △

They walked silently down the dock toward Clay's houseboat, each lost in their own stew of mixed emotions.

Clay took Sheryl's coat and hung it in the entry closet.

"Could I interest you in a mimosa?" he asked, walking to the kitchen.

"Yes, you could."

He retrieved a bottle of sparkling wine from the refrigerator. As Sheryl watched in amazement, he proceeded to remove and slice six fresh oranges from a bowl on the counter, slice each in half, place the halves one by one in a manual juicer, and squeeze juice into crystal glasses. Into each glass half full of orange juice he then poured the sparkling wine. After a quick stir with a long spoon, he handed a glass to Sheryl.

"Orange juice out of a carton isn't good enough?" she asked.

"Nah, we're celebrating."

"We are?"

"Yep. We can celebrate a lot of things, but most of all we're celebrating that we made it through last week in one piece." He clinked his glass lightly against hers and took a long drink of the fruity effervescence.

"You're right, we have a lot to be grateful for—you have a lot to be grateful for, and I think we should talk about it, but first I have a very important question to ask you."

He saw a *this is serious* look on her face, as she gazed deep into his eyes, and he looked back, wondering what was so seriously important. Deep down he was afraid she'd ask him about where this day was headed for them—what this brunch meant for their relationship. *Oh, please don't ask that. I don't have a clue.*

Sheryl turned her head to the fireplace. "Does that fireplace work?" she asked.

"Yes, of course it does."

"Well, this lady requests a fire. I'm a little chilled. Besides, I love sitting by the fire."

"Your wish is my command, princess." He bowed playfully and set about to prepare a fire.

The voice was faint but unmistakably clear from the dark depths of his mind. "The more you burn, the more you have to stack." Instead of building the fire with his usual four-log arrangement, he used three. He triggered the gas lighter, closed the spark screen and turned back to Sheryl.

She was standing close to the wall of sliding glass doors looking out to the gray lake and sky. Clay thought that she looked really good standing there—like she belonged in the house. That was a very different sensation from what he experienced when other women had been here. He didn't date much, but over the years he had probably invited six different women to his home. In every case, he felt like the women were invading his privacy when they stepped into the house. Not Sheryl.

"Your fire awaits," he said.

$$\triangle \triangle \triangle$$

She turned around and walked directly to where he was standing. She was smiling broadly and never took her eyes off his as she walked. She stopped when they were toe to toe. "You called me princess."

"Yes, I did."

"Why?"

"Do I have to have a reason? I mean . . . you requested fire . . . you seem . . . like a royal princess to me sometimes . . . I, uh, didn't mean to offend."

With two fingers of her left hand, she gently reached up and touched his lips. "Shhh. It's okay. I love that you called me princess. No one has called me that before. Deep down every girl wants to be a princess, not a queen, but a princess. And every girl wants to be a princess for her knight in shining armor."

Sheryl felt a jolt, as if she'd touched an electric fence.

"But I bet you call all your dates, princess." The words snapped from her mouth. She stepped away from him coolly and sat down on the couch.

She had gone too far. Revealed too much. *Stupid girl!* What on earth was she doing flirting like that with her boss? Being vulnerable. Hoping he was different from the other men in her life. She felt miserable. She wanted to leave. She shouldn't be here. This was a bad idea.

$$\triangle \triangle \triangle$$

Clay stood in front of the fireplace looking like a confused, abandoned puppy. The change had come over Sheryl so quickly it surprised him. "Actually, Sheryl, I've never used the word before with anyone. I don't know where it came from today." He felt awkward just standing there, so he sat down next to her on the couch. "I think it's very interesting and kinda cool that I see you as a beautiful, talented princess when we're together outside of the office."

She looked at him, her eyes softening, but the smile hadn't returned. "But you don't see me as a princess in the office?" she asked.

"No. Definitely not. In the office, you are the . . . the . . . queen . . . no not the queen. What are you? Ah, you're the drill sergeant."

"Drill sergeant!" Sheryl laughed and playfully pushed his shoulder hard. "You see me as a tough drill sergeant?"

"Yep. People march to your orders. Even me."

"I'm not mean though."

"No, you don't have a mean bone in your body. But you have grit."

"Oh, great, now I'm John Wayne!" Sheryl exclaimed, draining the last of her mimosa.

"An eye patch would be a nice touch. I think you should wear one in your new job."

"I will not wear an eye patch, mister," she giggled. "Besides, this princess needs another mimosa and her brunch." She handed Clay her empty glass.

"My pleasure." Clay took their glasses into the kitchen.

"Do you need any help?" she asked.

"No, but you can put on some music if you'd like."

Clay began preparing brunch while Sheryl selected a playlist from the digital display of the sound system. He was relieved that whatever had come over Sheryl was gone, at least for now.

"I don't believe you have an old country playlist! My gosh, Merle Haggard, Waylon Jennings, Willie Nelson, Patsy Cline."

"What's not to believe? There's something so true, simple and beautiful about country lyrics. I like to remind myself about the roots of America. Wholesome and good."

"Like getting drunk, smoking too much, and cheating on your wife?"

"No, like pickup trucks and hunting dogs," he laughed, and she laughed with him.

Soon the gravel voices of Haggard and Nelson filled the houseboat with melancholy ballads and toe-tapping tunes. The music seemed so out of place there in the expensive house floating on a lake in the middle of a major metropolitan city. But Clay sang along while fixing their brunch, and Sheryl twirled around the living room without a care in the world.

Clay soon had the meal prepared and served on plates in the dining room where he had previously staged two place settings.

"Brunch is served," he announced while replacing his kitchen apron with the sports coat.

He seated Sheryl on the side of the table that looked out into the living area and the lake beyond. He sat facing her. The feast was displayed nicely in serving dishes. Water and mimosa glasses were filled.

"Dig in," he said while gesturing that Sheryl should help herself to the food.

"Let's pray first," she said. "Take my hands." She extended both of her hands across the table palms up.

He took her hands, happy to have the opportunity to touch her, but was unsure of what to do next. He had never prayed, or "said Grace" before. "What am I supposed to say?"

"Just listen to me." She then closed her eyes, bowed her head and prayed. "Heavenly Father, we are so grateful for the fabulous day you have created for us. Thank you, Lord, for Clay's health and for giving him strength to endure the past week. We ask that you forgive us when we don't trust you 100 percent. Both Clay and I ask for wisdom we'll need in the days and weeks to come. We are especially grateful, Father, for the gifts you have given each of us. Our hearts' desire is to use those gifts in ways that please you. Thank you for the food that Clay has prepared for us. May it nourish our bodies. Amen." She gave Clay's hands a slight squeeze and released them.

With the prayer over, Sheryl proceeded to help herself to one of the omelets sitting in the warming dish. She also selected several pieces of the smoked salmon on rye. After choosing a muffin from a cloth-lined basket, she began to sample each item.

"Oh, my, this is wonderful, Clay. I like your cornflakes."

"Thanks. First time I've fixed this. It really is tasty, isn't it?"

"Uh-huh," Sheryl agreed with her mouth full and a look of pleasure sweeping across her face.

"You know, I've never heard anyone pray like you did. Not that I've heard many prayers before. The ones I recall are more flowery and structured, almost like poetry being read. Yours was different. You were just having a conversation with God," he said.

"That's very observant of you," she said with a smile. "Prayer should be the most personal thing you do. God doesn't care what form it takes as long as it is from the heart. I prefer a simple, humble, no-BS conversation."

"I thought there were specific prayers you had to memorize for different occasions," he said.

"Well, there are many prayer books that offer suggestions for what to say at different times or for different occasions. Many are very beautiful, but I don't want to have to remember someone else's words when I talk with God. I just want to talk with Him and hear what He wants to tell me. I really value His love for me. I value a relationship with Him above all else." She placed another forkful of omelet into her mouth and watched Clay as he processed what she had just said.

"That makes a lot of sense to me."

"The disciples once asked Jesus how they should pray. He told them. What he said is now referred to as 'The Lord's Prayer,' but Jesus wasn't telling his followers that they had to use his words every time they prayed. The Lord's Prayer was an example to follow, a prayer that had the right parts. Are you interested in learning more?" she asked.

Clay thought for a few seconds. "Some other time, sure. I'm more intrigued about the sermon today. I want to know more gifts."

Sheryl proceeded to explain about the personal surveys that exist to help shed light on a person's gifts. She recalled for Clay how taking on of the surveys two years ago revealed that her strongest gifts were Discernment, Artistry, and Administration.

"I had been aware of Administration. Organizing and leading always came easy to me. Artistry was somewhat of a surprise. I have a knack for home decoration, but I've never painted or written. I am attracted to good art though, so maybe one day I'll try it."

Clay made a mental note to show Sheryl his newest painting before she left.

"The most interesting revelation was the gift of Discernment. This one hadn't been on my radar at all, but after I thought about it, I could see how Discernment has been present in my life for some time." She paused to take the last bite of her muffin and wash it down with the last swallow of mimosa.

"Yeah, you always seem to make the right decisions at work," Clay said.

"I do, don't I," she replied with a large grin. "Discernment goes deeper than that, however. God gives us Discernment so we can recognize the difference between good and evil; between the spiritual and the worldly."

"So, do you see little devils and angels running around?" Clay asked. His tone was light-hearted, but he meant the question.

After a short laugh, she said, "That's one way to put it. Actually, I don't *see* good and bad. I *sense* it. I can sense when a person is filled with the Spirit. There's a warm, loving energy that they emit."

"What about bad, what about evil? Have you been near that? What is that sensation like?" Clay's tone was serious. His nightmares and hallucinations came to mind.

"Just the opposite of good. I feel a cold, dark energy coming from the person. They can be smiling and laughing, but if evil is present in them, I'll know it. "

Sheryl stood to clear the table. "What does a princess have to do to get a cup of tea around here?"

Clay thought it odd that Sheryl chose that particular moment to break the conversation. It was almost as though she suddenly became uncomfortable with the topic and wanted to divert them to something else.

"Is Earl Grey okay?" He asked.

"Perfect. Does this floating castle of yours include a lady's room?"

"Just down the hall."

Sheryl rinsed and stacked the dishes in the sink before heading to the restroom. Clay selected two large mugs from the cupboard and began to heat water. He stepped to the fireplace and carefully placed another log onto the fire. Outside on the lake, a few sails were visible. The Sunday Duck Dodge race was underway.

Sheryl returned from the restroom and took a seat on the couch. "Has the race started?"

"Apparently so," he said while bringing their steaming mugs from the kitchen. He sat down next to her. They watched the maneuvering sailboats in silence.

After several moments, Sheryl removed her boots, tucked her legs underneath her on the couch, and rotated to face Clay.

"You haven't said much about your uncle since the funeral. Did you really inherit the Point Deception Lighthouse from him?"

"Yep. He left the lighthouse property and a pickup to me."

"I can't believe that I used to have picnics up there and now I'm sitting on the couch with the man who owns it."

Sheryl was quiet in thought. She turned her head to look out the glass doors at the sails that now filled the lake in front of them. She turned back to face him. "It's not a coincidence, you know."

"What, that you're sitting here?"

"Yes, partially. I mean it's not a coincidence that you, your uncle, and I are connected by that lighthouse."

"Are you cooking up some conspiracy theory?" Clay said jokingly.

"Not a conspiracy, as you put it. But, there is a plan behind it."

"You've lost me. What plan?"

"Things like this—the people we meet and have relationships with—they happen for a reason. Do you believe that?"

"Never really thought about it much."

"Clay, God has a plan for you, for me, your uncle, for everyone. Do you know that?"

"No."

"It's true. It's written in the Bible. I'll show you some time. What many people call coincidence, people of faith see as the handiwork of God. Oh sure, there are coincidences in life, but the power and implication of some things are just too important to be a simple coincidence."

"I see your point. Like how I ran into George at the hotel bar in San Francisco."

"Exactly!" Sheryl said excitedly, seeing that Clay was beginning to understand. "Any of us can point to chance meetings that resulted in a new opportunity, or a fortuitous change of direction. That's God putting people into each other's path. What we do with the opportunity is up to us, because God gave us free will."

"So, I could have blown the opportunity with George if I hadn't been friendly and started a conversation?"

"Right, or if the idea of starting an agency had come up in your conversation, but one of you nixed the idea. Free will."

"So, you're saying the lighthouse is part of God's plan for me."

"Yes, but not just you. It was part of God's plan for your uncle, too. I have a hunch the more you learn about your uncle's life in Reef Bay the more you'll understand about the role of the lighthouse."

Clay looked at Sheryl. "I think I'm ready to upgrade my coffee for something stronger. Would you like a Bloody Mary?"

△ △ △

"Perfect." She handed him her empty tea mug. He took the mugs to the kitchen. While mixing the drinks, he said above the music in the room, "Hey, you never said what God's plan for you was."

She stood and walked to the kitchen. "I don't know, Clay. It's not clear to me, but I'm excited about it." Sheryl knew more than she was willing or able to reveal. If she tried to explain what the Spirit had been telling her the past few weeks, she was afraid it would totally spook Clay.

"How can you be excited about something you don't know?"

"I trust God. It's that simple. Whatever his plan is for me, it's going to be great."

"How spicy do you like your Blood, Mary?"

"Medium spicy."

△ △ △

Clay added the right measure of Tabasco sauce, stirred the mixture and added a celery stick garnish before handing the glass to Sheryl. She took a sip. "Oh, that's good. You're a great bartender."

He sipped his drink and nodded approvingly. "Yes, I am."

Before reclaiming his seat on the couch, Clay poked the fire to coax more heat from the glowing logs.

"I love watching the sailboats, but on days like today I'm very glad I'm inside by a fire rather than on a cold, wet fiberglass deck," he said.

"Me, too. I had a boyfriend who owned a sailboat. I know what cold days on a boat are like."

"Oh, you had a boyfriend?" Clay said in a tone suggesting it was surprising that Sheryl had had a boyfriend. He didn't know why he had said anything. He didn't want to hear more about Sheryl's past love life. Odd, that he knew so little about this woman's life outside of the office. Though he wanted to know more, something inside him didn't want to hear anything about her past boyfriends, or present boyfriends, for that matter. Was that jealousy he was beginning to feel?

She gave him a dirty look and said, "Yes, I had a boyfriend. He was very handsome. Very rich."

"You're using past tense, so you and this guy are no longer . . ."

"I broke up with him a little over a year ago. Remember when I took a couple of personal days off from work?" Clay nodded that he remembered. "Well, that was the time. I was very upset. Turns out he was more in love with himself, his job, and his toys than in love with me."

"I see," said Clay not knowing what else to say. He could see pain in her eyes. The memory must still sting, he thought.

She looked out across the lake and took a long drink from her glass.

"Sorry I asked. I just realized that I don't know much about your personal life. I'm actually very interested in knowing more about you, Sheryl. If that's okay, of course."

She turned to face him as he stood next to the fireplace. She looked at him for what seemed an eternity. Clay felt he was being X-rayed and analyzed by her. Then, just like that, the pain and sorrow vanished from her face. The warmest, sweetest smile Clay had ever seen replaced it. "Well then, Mr. Austin, what would you like to know?"

She sat down on the couch and resumed her curled position. He sat next to her, his thigh just touching one of her knees.

"Tell me about your picnics at the lighthouse."

After a bite of celery from her Bloody Mary, Sheryl spoke. "My father's sister lived in Reef Bay. She and her husband had a couple kids within a few years of my age. For several years running, I'd stay with them for a week during the summer."

"How old were you?"

"If I remember correctly I spent summers there between the ages of nine and twelve."

"Why not later?"

"Oh, when I hit thirteen I thought I was much too 'grown-up' for Reef Bay. Boring. Besides I had friends in Everett that were more important to my life than relatives. Sad but true. That's how kids are."

"Do your aunt and uncle still live there?"

"No, they moved to Oregon when I was fourteen."

"Tell me about the picnics. What do you remember?"

Sheryl relived the childhood memories with an incredible sparkle in her eyes. "I always had a great time there. Back then there were picnic tables and a few firepits in the open area next to the residence. Us kids would run around and play games while my aunt and uncle sat together under a blanket reading their books. We'd play horseshoes, toss a frisbee back and forth, and, oh, my favorite game was pirates."

"Pirates?"

"Sure. It was a game we invented—just hide and seek. Two of us would be pirates with stick swords, and one would be the runaway island resident. We'd take turns being the runaway. It was magical, running through the cedars and brush looking for a hiding place from the pirates. It was also a little scary, too, because sometimes I'd run through the thick brush and right to the edge of the cliff. Good thing that fence was there. Without the physical barrier, I'm sure one of us would have run right off the cliff. That was part of the thrill, I guess—when you dart from behind the thick bush, and suddenly there is nothing in front of your but sky, ocean and a crumbling fence. The pretend danger was behind you. The real danger was in front."

"Did you ever go inside the lighthouse?"

"No, never. It was Coast Guard property, and we weren't allowed in. There was a white chain fence that separated the residence and lighthouse from the picnic area. Signs were posted, so you knew not to get close. Occasionally the Coast Guard guys would come out and share stories with us about the lighthouse. I think they did it just so my aunt would offer them some of our picnic lunch.

But, I remember laying in the grass looking up at the lighthouse and wishing I could be up there. I wanted to know what it was like to be that high and be able to see that far out to sea. Hey, did you climb it when you were there?"

Only in his nightmares, he wanted to say. "No, didn't have time. I just did a quick walkthrough of the house and corridor connecting the house to the lighthouse. Actually, I sat in my uncle's chair and fell asleep for about fifteen minutes."

"You have to climb the lighthouse, Clay! No way I'm going to let you own that lighthouse and not climb to the top. And take me with you, of course." There were times when Sheryl's face looked like a little girl thrilled by the gift of a double-dip ice cream cone. This was one of those times.

Truth was, Clay wasn't all that eager to scale the darn lighthouse. Nothing good ever happened to him in that lighthouse—at least not in his nightmares. What if real life was no different?

"Sure, we'll climb it someday soon. I promise. You can show me around town." Clay liked the idea of spending the day with Sheryl while she showed him Reef Bay, but he didn't have a clue when that would be.

"Great. I'm excited," she said.

A thought came to him. Since they had been talking about the lighthouse and everyone that was connected because of it, he should share his new painting with Sheryl.

"You know what? I have something to show you. Dr. Shildstein gave it to me on Friday."

"What is it?"

"It's a painting, but I don't want to say anymore. It'll spoil the surprise. Want to see it?"

"Sure," she said, looking around the walls of the living room expecting to see something there.

"It's not down here. It's upstairs."

"Upstairs? In your bedroom?"

"Yes, that's where I decided to hang it."

"I see. So, you want me to go up to your bedroom to see a painting?"

"Sure, why not?"

She just looked at him. The gleeful child was gone.

"What's wrong?" Clay asked, noticing her change of mood.

"Nothing. Show me the painting if you want, she said coolly. She drained the last of her Bloody Mary and stood up. "I've never been upstairs here before. This is what, the second or third time I've been over here, and this is the first time you've offered to show me upstairs."

"I'm sorry. I just didn't think it was appropriate before. Heck, you're welcome to see any part of the house you want."

"So, what makes today different?" Sheryl didn't understand why she was acting so defensive, so bitchy.

"I don't know, Sheryl. We've been sharing stuff about each other. I didn't think you'd feel threatened by an invitation to see a painting in another room of the house."

The fire in the fireplace popped loudly as a piece of burnt log fell away from the others and fell off the grate.

"Not just any room, Clay, it's your bedroom. And not just any painting, a painting given to you by a woman."

Clay was dumbfounded. How could she get so upset about seeing a painting in his bedroom?

"If it'll make a difference, I'll bring it downstairs, or we can forget the entire thing." This whole conversation was beginning to remind Clay of why he never got married.

"Never mind. Show me the painting. It must be something special for you to make such a big deal out of it," she hissed.

Clay forced a brave smile. "I think you're going to like it."

He headed up the stairs. Sheryl slowly followed, still greatly disturbed and not grasping why.

At the head of the stairs, Clay paused as Sheryl climbed the last few steps. He walked into the master bedroom and stood by the foot of the bed. Sheryl waited in the doorway as if held back by an invisible force field.

"Come on; you can't see it well from there. Come stand next to me."

△ △ △

She walked forward slowly; her eyes glued on him while her sock feet shuffled across the hardwood floor. This was it. A moment of truth. Was Clay luring her into this bedroom for seduction? It would break her heart. It would mean he was just like every other man she had known. Even worse, it would mean she had been wrong about Clay. It would mean that she hadn't heard the Spirit correctly either.

Over the past few weeks, she had sensed a battle raging inside him. She didn't know the source yet. He hadn't shared with her his sessions with Dr. Shildstein. But when she had prayed the other night, the voice had answered so clearly, "protect him." Plus, she couldn't ignore the electricity she felt when they touched. Up until this moment, she had been confident that the Spirit was bringing her and Clay closer. She didn't know why. But now, what if she wasn't hearing the Spirt? What if it was all a lie? Had her discernment failed her?

"There it is." He gestured to the painting of lighthouse and balloon hanging above the headboard.

Nothing could have prepared her for what happened next.

She turned her head slowly to follow the direction of Clay's outstretched arm. The lighthouse painting filled her eyes. It was perfectly lit by the late afternoon light flooding the room from the westward-facing windows. Sheryl felt herself drawn into the painting. Her sense of being with Clay in the bedroom, in this house, disappeared. She was in the painting now. Not *in* the painting exactly. She *experienced* it as if she was a soaring seagull looking down on the balloon and the lighthouse.

In a flash, her mind took her from the downward point of view of the soaring seagull, to being on the ground looking up. Suddenly she was re-living the times as a child when she would lay in the grass of the picnic area and look up at the lighthouse watching the seagulls gliding high above in the salty wind currents.

In another flash, her point of view switched like the changing of a TV channel. She was soaring above the balloon again. The sensation of flying in the painting was so real. Was she dreaming? Was she hallucinating? She felt herself gliding on the wind, sharing the sky with the balloon. She flew closer. Who were the people in the balloon's basket? Just two. A man and a woman. They were looking out to sea, their faces hidden from view. She backed away and studied the balloon. It was magnificent. The white was a pearl white that almost sparkled. She recognized the bold strokes of purple as a cross. It made her heart sing with joy. She was soaring effortlessly with this beautiful air vessel far above the majestic lighthouse high above the churning sea.

"What do you think?" Clay asked. His words came to Sheryl out of the distance like a voice in a cave. They snapped her back out of the painting like a recoiling elastic rope that had been stretched to its limit. She couldn't speak. The sensation, the dream, the vision, whatever it was had been so vibrant and real. She had never experienced anything quite like it.

"Are you okay?'

"Um, yea, I guess it just took me by surprise," Sheryl was struggling to process what had just occurred.

"You look like you've seen a ghost."

She felt weak and sat down on the foot of the bed, not confident that her legs would continue to hold her.

"Uh-oh, I must have made the Bloody Mary too strong. Do you want a glass of water or something?"

She looked up at him and smiled. "No. I'm fine. And so was the Bloody Mary." She tapped her hand on the bed. "Sit with me for a few minutes."

△ △ △

He sat down on the bed facing her, watching as Sheryl's face returned to normal. The anger, or whatever it was, had disappeared. Her womanly beauty with the excited little-girl eyes had returned. He was drawn to her again. He wanted to take her into his arms and hold her close, but he didn't dare. Instead, he just sat there and looked.

"Clay," she set her hand on his and gripped it gently but firmly. Clay could feel a warm energy in her touch. "God is at work here. I feel it, but I don't think I can explain it yet."

"What do you mean? He's at work in this room?" Clay questioned.

"Not just in this room. In your life. My life. Our life. And in that painting." She pointed to the art behind her without looking at it, afraid that she'd be drawn back into it.

"But isn't God supposed to be here? I mean isn't He everywhere? I heard that somewhere." Clay asked.

"That's right He is, but, oh dear, I'm struggling to make sense." She stood up and nervously started pacing around the bedroom. "Listen, all I can tell you right now is this." She was talking while pacing back and forth, too deep in concentration to look at Clay. "I told you about my gift of Discernment. It is strong, Clay, very strong. It's never been wrong either."

"You've never been wrong about discerning between good and evil?" Clay wanted to make sure he was following Sheryl.

"Right. When I pray, God helps me see the difference. Helps me see the truth about people. About relationships." She paused, took a deep breath and slowly exhaled to build up strength and courage for what she realized she had to say next. "Do you trust me, Clay?"

"Trust you? Sure."

"I don't mean trust me to take care of something in the office. I mean do you trust that I have your best interests at heart? Do you trust that I'd never do anything to hurt you?"

The line of questioning was making Clay a little uncomfortable. He hadn't thought this deeply about her.

"Now that you mention it, I guess I do trust you that way."

"You'd better. Because I believe I have to reveal some things to you right now that you might think are crazy." Her voice was starting to crack. Her lips quivered, and her eyes began to moisten with tears.

Seeing the emotion well up in Sheryl made Clay more uneasy. What on earth was happening?

△ △ △

She was terrified to continue. Everything was at stake. How was he going to react to what she was about to say? He'd think she was crazy. He'd say she was over-reaching their professional relationship. He'd treat her differently at work. He'd never go to church with her again. She'd be shunned. Rejected. Just like before whenever she reached out to help someone. And yet she couldn't ignore God's answer to her prayer, "protect him." She couldn't ignore the sensation of the painting. She couldn't ignore how God put together on one stage her, Clay, his uncle, that lighthouse and even Dr. Shildstein. But, what if all this was just a coincidence, nothing more? What if her gift of discernment was wrong now, right at the time when the stakes were highest?

"Get behind me, Satan!" She screamed into the room, tears streaming down a scared, determined face.

Clay jumped up instinctively, on full alert as if Sheryl had just seen a stranger enter the bedroom. He walked toward Sheryl, his arms open to bring her into him and comfort her. She held up her hand to stop his advance.

Through sobs and tears, she continued softly, "I'm okay. I'm okay. Please sit down and listen."

He did as he was told, retaking his place at the foot of the bed.

A renewed strength and courage filled her, even as tears continued to flow. From deep inside, her favorite scripture verse filled her head. *I can do all things through God who strengthens me. I can do all things through God who strengthens me. I can do all things through God who strengthens me.*

"Today, you asked me what I saw when I looked at you with my gift of Discernment. Well, I'm going to tell you now."

"First, let me say this. I am very fond of you." She was looking directly at him now, back in control. "I have always admired you. I love working for you. But, what I'm talking about is very different. Very new. And it scares me to death." She wiped tears from her eyes and continued. "God has told me that he wants me to be with you, to be close to you, to . . . to . . . to protect you."

"I don't know exactly what that means, Clay. I'm . . . I'm . . . Ohhh!" She stomped her foot in a simultaneous attempt to force the words out and trample the fear that was holding them back. "I'm attracted to you Clay, and you'd better respect that or I'll leave, I'll resign, I'll never want to see you again!" She stood there, fresh tears flowing down her reddened cheeks, her shoulders shaking slightly with spasms of sobs.

Clay rose and took her into his arms gently. She rested her head onto his chest, feeling the wool cloth of his sports coat against her cheek. Slowly, very slowly, she unfolded her arms from in front of her and brought them around Clay. She held him lightly, fearing to express too much with the movement of a hand or the strength of the embrace.

"Say something, Clay," Sheryl pleaded.

$$\triangle \ \triangle \ \triangle$$

His mind was both numb and swirling with thoughts all at the same time. Clay was really uncomfortable now. He was unaccustomed to people showing this level of vulnerability in his presence, and he certainly seldom ever ventured into these dark waters of expressing himself. On the other hand, was Sheryl saying that she liked him? He had to admit he was developing those feelings for her. Did she say 'protect him'?

He was very conscious of how wonderful this woman felt in his arms. The sensation was way more than just physical or sexual. He felt a connection, a glue as if some force was holding them together. It was fantastic, but could he tell Sheryl? *Should* he tell? He had to say something. *Time to put some words together, Clay, and they better be good.*

He kissed her forehead lightly. Then spoke, "I like you, too, Sheryl. A lot. You've been on my mind lately in ways that have surprised me and made me happy. I can't explain it, really. Just one day I started seeing you as more than my assistant."

"When did that happen?" she whispered, her face still pressed to his chest.

"I don't know for sure, but sometime in the past couple of weeks."

She leaned back to look up and into his face. He looked down into the most lovely mascara-smeared eyes he'd ever seen.

"Me, too. I started to see you differently about two weeks ago. I felt an attraction unlike I've experienced before with any other man. And then Friday night before the Yukon dinner I prayed. I sat in my car in the restaurant parking lot and prayed about what I was supposed to do. I'm not supposed to be attracted to my boss. I was confused. Then God answered me, Clay. Clear as a bell. He said, 'protect him'". Sheryl pulled away from Clay to wipe the tears that continued to flow down her cheeks.

"What does that mean, 'protect me?'" Clay asked, a bit miffed that her attraction to him might be nothing more than some motherly instinct.

"I don't know for sure." She sat down on the bed and Clay joined her, draping one arm loosely around her shoulders to stay connected. "When I'm with you, Clay, I see in you a lot of internal turmoil and pain. Most of the time it's pretty deep, but in the past few weeks the turmoil has come to the surface; like when you freaked out and fainted in your office, or when you couldn't make yourself a cup of coffee in the office kitchen."

Clay interrupted, "So God wants you to nurse me?" He said bitterly.

"Oh, not at all. What I see happening in you is a battle. A battle between what God wants for you, and what Satan wants for you. You think I'm crazy, don't you?"

"I get it; I'm this walking talking good versus evil showdown? Is that what you're saying?"

"Yes, you and everyone else by the way. Myself included. It just so happens that God has made your battle very visible to me, and he has brought us together so the three of us can fight the devil and prevail."

"Uh, you lost me. The three of us?"

"You, me, and God," she answered.

"Oh."

"Like or not, mister, God is here. Right now. In this room. He's been a busy little bee with us today, believe me," a smile returned to her face. "And that painting." She twisted around to look at it, so Clay removed his arm from her shoulders. "That painting is a signal from God. It has power."

"What does it say?"

"Oh, that's for you to figure out. All I know is that it is no coincidence that this painting is hanging in your house right now. Do you believe that?"

"Yes. It can't be explained otherwise. I do feel more peaceful when I look at it."

"Exactly. Did you have another piece hanging there? I ask because most people have some art or photographs on the wall above their bed."

"Yea, one of my favorite pieces—an old sailing ship," Clay said.

She thought for a moment, "Where is it now?"

"In the bathroom. Want to see it?"

"I do."

Clay led her into the master bathroom, flicked on the light. "There it is. I think it looks fantastic there, don't you?"

She studied the painting intensely. She didn't sense any evil in it. On the contrary, there was something majestic and powerful about the ship fighting its way through the storm. And, she had to admit, the art looked perfect in his bathroom.

"I love it! You're right. It belongs here."

A little voice in Clay's head said, *and so do you, beautiful Sheryl. So do you.*

"Since we're up here in the master suite of the Austin residence, I have one more request."

"What's that?"

"It's kinda silly. You don't have to if you don't want to."

"Just ask," he said.

"Well, you see the ladies at the office have a bet about how large your closet must be. You always dress so well, and we never see you in the same outfit twice." Sheryl was embarrassed for asking.

"Oh, so you and the women of the office are talking about me behind my back?" Clay said pretending to be bothered.

"I don't talk about you. I have heard the other girls talk, but honestly, I don't enter the conversation, but I am interested. What do you say? You showed me the painting. I sat on your bed. Don't you think we can take the relationship a step further and show me your closet?" She was giggling now and clearly having a good time. It was as if suddenly the effects of the Bloody Mary had lifted the sullenness from around her.

"The closet is right this way. I've hidden the skeletons." Clay led Sheryl out of the bathroom and into the adjoining walk-in closet—a room the size of a bedroom.

"Oh, my. You do have a lot of clothes. And everything is organized so neatly. My closet is a crowded mess; it's just too small for my stuff."

"On a serious note, Sheryl, you do realize that you can't tell anyone that you've seen my closet or bathroom? And you certainly can't say you've been in the bedroom!" Clay suddenly got worried about gossip.

She turned and looked up at him. "Of course not. I have my reputation to guard, you know." She pushed him playfully with one hand and walked out of the closet back to the bedroom to look at the lighthouse painting.

He followed her. "Let's see how the race is coming along. Should be coming to an end about now. We can look at it from the roof. We were supposed to be watching the race, remember?"

"Your fault. You mentioned the painting."

He led her to the spiral steel staircase that led up from the master suite to the rooftop seating area. Outside the air was cool, but the rain had ceased.

They walked to the steel rail at the edge of the roof and looked out over the lake. The view was sensational, even for such a gray, dreary day. To their left, the towering office buildings of Seattle loomed. In front of them, Lake Union was host to at least fifty sailboats of all sizes jockeying for position. About half the boats had changed direction at the windward buoy and were heading north again up the lake. Crews on deck scurried about busily launching the large, colorful spinnakers used when the wind is behind the boat. Up the lake about a dozen of the leaders were running fast with the colorful chutes billowing out in front of them, pulling the yachts through the water.

"Um, my feet are wet." They looked down at Sheryl's socked and now soaked feet on the wet wood decking of the roof.

"Uh-oh, let's get you back inside. We've seen the race."

Back inside, Sheryl took off her socks. "Give them to me I'll toss them into the dryer." He walked to the compact laundry room off the master suite and tossed the socks into the dryer.

"Gee, if I'd known you were such a good maid, I would have brought my laundry for you," Sheryl joked.

"Remember, you don't do coffee, and I don't do laundry." They both laughed.

"Can we talk about the painting some more?" Sheryl asked.

"Absolutely." They strolled back into the bedroom. This time Sheryl didn't sit on the bed but remained standing, looking at it closely.

"Why did Dr. Shildstein give this to you? I don't understand. Did you tell her that you had inherited a lighthouse?"

"That's the really strange thing about it. I never told her about the inheritance."

"Are you sure?"

"Positive. I never even mentioned Uncle Charley to her. We always focused on other stuff, like my hallucinations and fainting."

"Why did she give you a painting, Clay? Had you given her a gift?"

"No gifts. I only write a check after each session. I don't know why she gave it to me. Her office is filled with paintings and photographs of hot air balloons. I noticed this one during my first session. It caught my attention. You know, each time I'm there I notice that the paintings have been moved around the room. Last week a new photograph of a balloon in Sedona was on a wall. She never said why she gave the painting to me. I didn't even open it until yesterday."

"Open it? You mean she gave it to you wrapped?"

"Yea, like a gift. It was wrapped in beautiful purple paper."

"Is she Christian?"

"How would I know? I guess not, considering her last name is Shildstein, but I really don't know."

"Does she ever mention God?"

"Nope. She said something similar to what you just told me, though."

"What?" Sheryl's eyes left the painting and looked at Clay.

"She told me that I was under attack, but I'd be okay. That's eerily similar to what you told me a few minutes ago—something about sensing a battle of good and evil inside me. You two ought to have lunch sometime." Clay said facetiously.

"Is she married?" Just like that, Sheryl's tone cooled.

Clay thought for a moment before responding. "I'm pretty certain she is. I can't recall seeing a ring—haven't really looked for one—but I remember she said once that her husband had tickets to the theater for them that night."

"So, she's sharing personal information with you?" The tone was still cool. The question sounded about as harmless as a prosecutor's cross-examination.

"Not really. That was the only time. I actually don't know much about her."

"Have you mentioned me to her?"

"No. There hasn't been a reason to, so far. You haven't threatened me with a lawnmower yet." Clay wasn't letting on that he could see Sheryl's thinly concealed jealously. It was a good sign. *She likes me. Sheryl really likes me!*

Sheryl stepped closer to the painting, straining to see the artist's signature. "Who's the artist?"

"Don't know," Clay replied. "The signature is a single letter. Looks like a 'G.'"

"It does look like a 'G,' doesn't it?"

"Doubt it's Garth Brooks," Clay joked.

Sheryl laughed. "Doubt it. When is your next appointment with this doctor?" Sheryl asked, avoiding the use of her name.

"Next Friday, at 4 o'clock."

"Are you going to ask her about the painting?"

"Better believe I am."

The dryer's buzzer sounded. Clay left to fetch Sheryl's socks.

△ △ △

Standing there alone in Clay's bedroom, she looked around the handsomely decorated room. He had good taste. In furniture, in clothes, in cars, in food. She wasn't sure about women. In fact, she realized that she didn't know anything about Clay's love life. A shot of panic raced through her. What if he was seeing someone else? Today, she had admitted her feelings for him. He had done the same, but he hadn't said that his feelings were exclusively for her. She couldn't stand the thought of another woman standing in this room. She couldn't let that happen to her again.

Clay returned with the dry socks and handed them to her.

"Here you go, princess. Do you prefer that I iron them first?" He was grinning warmly.

"Thank you. I should leave; it's getting late, and you probably have plans for tonight." She headed out the door toward the stairs, socks in hand.

Confused by the mood swing, Clay followed her. "You don't have to go, Sheryl. I don't have any plans."

She continued downstairs, then sat on the couch and started to put on her socks and boots.

He stood by her. "What's wrong?"

"Nothing."

"I know you well enough to tell when you're upset. You're upset. What did I do?"

"Nothing." She pulled on the last boot.

"Please stay and tell me what's going on. Would you like another drink?"

She sat there. Arms crossed tightly, saying nothing, just staring out the large glass doors. Rain had started to fall, and the light of day was fading quickly.

Affectionately, he placed a single hand on her shoulder. "If you have to leave, okay, but I'd love it if you stayed."

Time passed. "I'm cold." Was all she could say.

"Then, I shall put more wood on the fire, but on one condition."

"What's that?" She asked quietly, still looking out the window as if searching for answers in the gloom.

"Take off your boots again so you'll be comfortable."

She looked up at him and slowly started to pull off her boots, reminding Clay of a pouting child. He poked the fire and added two logs to the embers. He was thrilled that she was going to stay longer, even though the mood swings were giving him whiplash.

"I think a snack is in order," he declared.

"Sounds good. What do you have?"

He opened the refrigerator door and took inventory. "Cheese, salami, crackers, olives... oh, you're in luck. I bought some pâté yesterday just in case."

"You thought of everything."

He didn't know how to take that remark. Was that a compliment, or something else?

"I have to admit; I was excited about being with you today. I had a lot of fun planning the brunch and this snack. I wanted everything to be right for you." Clay was talking with his back to Sheryl while preparing the snack. He turned around to place the cheese platter on the center counter. Sheryl was standing there looking at him.

"Oh, you snuck up on me."

"Were you really excited about being with me today?" She asked.

"Yes, I was excited. Nervous, too."

She walked around the counter and stood close to him. "I have to know before this goes any further. Are you seeing anyone else right now?"

Clay saw fear deep in her eyes. She was scared. She was vulnerable. She was pushing the limits of what she could bear. He placed a hand on each shoulder. Intuitively he sensed he shouldn't do more.

"No, I'm not seeing anyone. I haven't had a date in over three months. Gave up on the dating scene I guess."

After studying him carefully, the fear melted away. The confident Sheryl returned. "That's good to know, mister. What are we drinking with this feast?"

Clay opened a bottle of Texas Tempranillo from his wine rack. They carried the wine, wine glasses, and food plates to the coffee table by the couch and sat down.

"I guess this is dinner," Clay said. "It's already 5 o'clock."

"I'm not complaining," she said while stuffing a piece of French bread and pâté into her mouth.

After a period of small talk in between bites of food, Clay spoke. "This has been an amazing day. Thank you." He tilted his wine glass in Sheryl's direction as if toasting her. She smiled and nodded. "It also creates a situation for us," he said. "Can we talk about it?"

"By situation, you mean, how do we have a personal relationship and work together?"

"Yes. What we have at work is fantastic. We're an unbeatable team."

"We are that. What's more important to you, our work relationship or our personal relationship?"

The question made him pause. He wasn't used to having to make this type of choice. He almost always selected his interests and the agency over everything else.

"I want both. Can't I have both?"

"If God wants us to work together and *be* together, everything will be okay, but we have to trust Him."

Clay sipped his wine, deep in thought. How was he supposed to trust God? He didn't know God. How could he trust something he didn't understand? His mind tried to form a plan for he and Sheryl. How could they develop their relationship and spend more time together without others at the office finding out? Could he treat her as his employee one minute and his lover the next? Just the thought of conducting her annual performance review seemed a lot more complicated under these new circumstances. It could get messy.

A loud pop startled him. Then another pop sound followed as gaseous bubbles expanded to bursting inside the damp logs on the roaring fire.

"What's more important to you?" Clay thought he was clever to turn the question on Sheryl.

"I don't believe office romances are a good idea." Clay's heart sank. Was she changing her mind now? "I definitely don't think a couple should work together when one is the manager of the other. It's too difficult for them to approach business objectively, and it causes jealousy within the office—accusations of preferential treatment and such. But God has definitely brought us together at this point in time. I don't pretend to know why, or where this is going to lead, Clay. I just know that I'm going to pray a lot about us, and I'm going to trust God."

"This could be seen by Phil Manicotti as poor judgment on my part," Clay stated. "Heck, there might even be a formal policy against it." The thought just occurred to him that very soon he'd be operating under an entirely new set of employment policies.

"There probably is," Sheryl said in a matter of fact tone and slipped another slice of salami into her mouth.

He was fretting now. How was he going to keep Sheryl by his side day and night? He couldn't imagine working with a different assistant. He couldn't ignore his attraction for her either. He needed a plan. The fact that Sheryl wasn't particularly worried, gave him some comfort. If she wasn't worried, why should he be? After all, didn't she always have things under control at the office? She always knew how to put out the fire before anyone else. He relaxed a little. Maybe he could just trust Sheryl.

△ △ △

Sheryl could almost see the wheels turning in Clay's head. *Yeah, he's trying to figure it out. He's trying to plan it; to control the situation and outcome.* She knew that he didn't have a relationship with God yet. No way he could simply decide to trust God tonight. That was going to take some time.

"Well?" She asked.

"Well, what?"

"What did you decide?"

"I want to make this work. I don't have the answers, but I'm trusting you to guide us through the rough spots."

Sheryl smiled. That's a start. That's an excellent start. *Thank you, Lord.* "Then, it's settled. Tomorrow we start."

"To tomorrow; to us." Clay tipped his wine glass in a toasting gesture. Sheryl reciprocated, lightly kissing his glass with hers.

"To God. To Us," she replied.

Chapter 53

lay pulled the M5 into his private parking space at Austin-Davis Monday morning. He felt unusually refreshed and energized after the enjoyable weekend and one of the most restful nights of sleep that he could remember.

A tinge of nerves settled on him like a slight chill as he rode the elevator up to his fifth-floor office. This was Day One. This was the first day after the day that he and Sheryl had declared an affection for each other. On this day their relationship was on a different level. And that was the source of Clay's nervousness. He hadn't operated at *this* level before. The few relationships he had been in were with women outside the office and outside the industry. He was navigating new terrain.

As he stepped from the elevator door, he saw a group of three strangers sitting in the waiting area. For a moment he panicked. Was there a client meeting today he had forgotten about? Just then, Sheryl and Alicia walked briskly into the reception area to greet the due diligence team from Pitt-Needham who were there to begin the audit.

While Sheryl greeted and shook hands with the three accountants, she managed to direct a quick glance at Clay. Her eyes sparkled. He smiled back. The nervousness was replaced by a sense of peace.

He walked through the office and stopped by George's suite. Through the glass wall, Clay could see that George wasn't at his desk. In his usual fashion, his partner was drinking morning coffee and checking email while sitting in one of the leather tufted chairs of the conversation pit, as George referred to the two sofas and two chairs arranged facing each other at the end of his office.

Clay opened the door. "Good morning. How was your weekend?" Clay asked.

"Hey, partner, good morning. Come on in. We had a pretty good weekend. Oh, Alicia tells me the Pitt-Needham people are here. Right on time."

"Yep, I passed them in the reception area. And so the process starts."

"And so it starts. Any seller's remorse over the weekend?" George asked.

"Some, but it passed. The reaction of the Yukon team at dinner proved to me that clients see the potential benefits. It also revealed a potential downside that I hadn't thought about—we hadn't thought about."

"Oh, what's that?" George signaled for Clay to have a seat.

"At dinner, Barry Weitzel made it very clear to me that Yukon was concerned that after the acquisition Pitt-Needham might dump them in favor of pitching a larger airline. You know, there are going to be times when we'll have to decide on whether or not to resign a piece of business in order to take on something else.

Wasn't much of an issue before, but now that we're a part of a larger agency, the conflicts will be more frequent."

"You're right. And I'm glad the company has a smart guy like you to figure it out. Your nickname will be Soloman." George said with a confident smile that said, *not my problem.*

"Who's Soloman?"

"You haven't heard the saying 'the wisdom of Solomon'"?

"Nope."

"Solomon was one of the most famous and revered kings of Israel in the Old Testament. He was one of the most God-fearing kings, and as a result, God blessed him with much success, wealth and wisdom. Google 'Solomon and baby' some time to see just how smart this guy was. While you're at it, if you ever want some great tips about romance, check our Solomon's Song of Songs in the Bible." George winked at Clay.

Oh great, did George suspect something between Clay and Sheryl? How could he so soon? Maybe he should confide this news to his friend and partner. *No, not now.*

"I didn't know you read the Bible, George."

"Oh, since Melissa got sick I've been leaning on the Lord pretty heavy. Frankly, selling the company was an answer to our prayers. I'll be able to slow down next year and spend more time with her."

"Which means you better be choosing a successor, George, so you can start mentoring the person to replace you a year or so from now."

"You're right. I'd like to be able to promote from within, rather than have someone come from Dallas or wherever." George said, referring to the possibility that his replacement could come from anywhere in the Pitt-Needham empire. "I'll give it some thought and talk with you some more about it next month when the deal closes."

"Sounds good. I have succession issues to deal with, too, regarding account supervision. With my broader responsibilities, I won't be able to spend as much time on some accounts as now. Some clients won't care. Others are going to insist that I'm still involved. Going to be a little tricky for both of us. Can you ask Alicia to book a series of meetings next week for you and I to figure things out?"

"Great idea. Will do." George paused cautiously before bringing up the next topic. "Oh, Clay . . . what about Sheryl?"

Caught off guard by the question, Clay stammered a response, "What about her?"

"Well, she's invaluable to this office. She's invaluable to you, too. Have you given thought to her role after the deal closes?"

"I have. I'm thinking about promoting her to a role in Operations over the four shops. That's another personnel issue that needs to be worked out." Clay had difficulty thinking about Sheryl as a "personnel issue."

"I like that idea. By the way, have you noticed how well Alicia and her work together? I was super impressed with what they did last week around the announcement."

"I couldn't agree more. Hey, we should give each of them a gift for the job they did. How about gift certificates to the spa?"

"I'll take care of it," George said with a smile. He loved to show appreciation to employees for a job well done. "And I'd like to figure out how Sheryl can mentor Alicia this year. Those two can do darn near anything."

"Well, you and I have often talked about implementing a formal mentoring program at the office. Let's add that to our discussions next week." Clay said.

"Perfect." George's cell buzzed. "Oh, I gotta take this."

Clay nodded at his partner, walked out the door and headed to his suite at the opposite side of the building. On the way, he passed Suzette's old office, somewhat amused to see it occupied now with the due diligence people from Pitt-Needham who were busy getting organized there. Gerald from accounting was with them.

Clay continued to his suite. His heart rate increased as he saw Sheryl sitting at her desk. *Day One*, he thought. *Day One*.

"Good morning, Sheryl. I see you have the accountants set up. Thank you."

"Good morning, Clay."

Her smile made his knees weak.

"When you're ready, come on in and let's go over the week's schedule," he said, already looking forward to sitting with her in his office.

"Okay," she replied, still smiling.

Compared to the past two weeks, Sheryl and Clay agreed that this week was going to be more normal. Busy, but normal. Clay wanted one-on-ones scheduled with each of his account supervisors. There were six account team meetings that he needed to participate in; two client presentations; two conference calls had been set up with Phil Manicotti; numerous plan reviews, a conference call with George and Reuben, and finally his appointment on Friday with Dr. Shildstein.

With calendars synced, Sheryl said, "There's one more important appointment that's not on your calendar yet."

"Haven't you over-booked me enough?" Clay looked at her pleading for mercy.

"Six o'clock on Friday." She looked up at the door to make sure no one could hear what she was about to say. Then she said in a matter of fact tone, "You're having dinner with me at my place." She was smiling, but there was a touch of uncertainty and nervousness in her eyes.

"Hmm. Six o'clock Friday? Clay looked at the calendar on his notebook pretending to calculate how he was going to squeeze in the date. "Wonderful. I can't wait." Their eyes locked. Day One was working out pretty well so far.

Chapter 54

The week had been a blur. It was already Thursday afternoon, and Clay was exhausted. On top of everything else, the accountants from Pitt-Needham had been more of a distraction than he had counted on. As he learned on Monday, the team from Dallas weren't all accountants. One was an attorney.

Twice every day, Gerald or George would come to him with news of what the "Pitt Crew," as George called them, were questioning, or information they were requesting for analysis. They were being thorough; very thorough. The Pitt Crew had already gone through three years of financials with a fine-toothed comb. Every media contract and client agreement had to be produced for their review. Next week they were going to interview a random selection of clients and vendors. Clay didn't like that idea. From what he had observed, the members of the Pitt Crew had no personality or warmth whatsoever. They reminded him of the IRS agents he dealt with five years ago when he was audited. He didn't like the idea of his clients being questioned by cold-hearted strangers as if they were on the witness stand in court.

The Pitt Crew's attorney had been particularly interested in Suzette's partner agreement and letter of termination. That didn't surprise Clay, but the amount of time and focus devoted to it was disconcerting. For that, he connected her with his attorney, Reuben.

If a deal killer had surfaced during the week, Clay hadn't heard about it. His first call with Phil Manicotti on Tuesday went very well. No hint of trouble. Now, he was about to get on the phone with him again. It was late Thursday afternoon. Clay was treating himself to a fresh macchiato and a few moments of contemplation while staring out the window at the traffic in the canal. Contemplation wasn't the right word for it. If Clay was honest with himself, in moments like this he wasn't contemplating anything. He wasn't conjuring up some great strategy for this or that. He wasn't weighing the pros and cons of some important decision. He certainly wasn't praying to some higher power for guidance or forgiveness. Not at all. He wasn't doing any of that. Clay was in his "Empty Box."

He had read somewhere that men were prone to have periods when their conscious minds shut off. The processing of thought at the conscious level simply stopped. In those periods, men would busy themselves with mindless tasks, or nothing at all. It was so unlike the women Clay had known whose minds were never at rest. In fact, for most women, their brains worked overtime drawing connections between seemingly totally unrelated events, people, and emotions.

And so here he stood, coffee in hand, thinking about nothing except the fact that he was thinking about nothing. He didn't want to analyze why he went to his Empty Box. Why ruin it? What mattered was that it was quiet there. Peaceful. Safe.

Outside through Clay's expansive windows, one couldn't tell that Seattle's Winter was turning to Spring It looked the same. Gray wind-blown drizzle filled the air and made pedestrians on the street below hurry to limit their exposure to the cold and wet. Oh sure, a brave tree or two along the bike path might be showing off a few blossoms, but Clay wasn't fooled. It was still cold and miserable outside.

He needed a sun break. Pleasant thoughts of warm sand on a sunny island beach filled his head, officially ending his Empty Box time. Yes, he needed a vacation, but when was that going to happen? After the deal closes, he was going to be busier than ever shuttling between the four offices and Dallas.

That's right! He was expected in Dallas for the Pitt-Needham annual Board meeting. Visions of the warm beach vanished, replaced by chilling thoughts of meeting the other Board members for the first time.

With his Empty Box time at an end, he sat down and put his brain back into gear. The desk phone buzzed, and he answered. It was Sheryl advising him that Phil Manicotti was on the line. *Right on time.*

"Good afternoon, Phil. How has the week been treating you?" It was a thinly-veiled attempt to subtly find out if the due-diligence had hit a snag or not.

"Good afternoon. The week has been exceptional, Clay," Phil responded.

Phil was one of those very positive people that always seemed energized and cheerful. Clay wasn't sure if this characteristic was an act or a genuine expression of a positive outlook on life.

"You should know, Clay, that we're receiving some very positive feedback about our deal with Austin-Davis. Analysts like it. The clients I've spoken to see it as a great fit. We're really excited. The due diligence is progressing nicely, too. By-the-way, our questions about Suzette have been resolved satisfactorily. Your attorney, Reuben, was very helpful."

The other thing Clay had learned about Phil was that he talked fast and to the point. His conversations were a rapid-fire staccato style that shared concise facts and little else.

"That's all good to hear, Phil. So then, are we on schedule to conclude the due diligence by end of next week?" Clay asked.

"I think so unless the team uncovers something. They are grateful for your hospitality. Your people are leaving a good impression on them."

Clay didn't have a chance to respond to the compliment. Phil continued to talk.

"As you know, the annual meeting is April twenty-fourth here in Dallas. We want you and George to attend the annual meeting. It'll be at the Fairmont Hotel. We're going to hold our regular Board meeting the day before on the twenty-third in our office. You should plan to be available for the Board meeting, Clay. We'll invite you in right after the official vote to approve your membership. The vote is just a technicality. Your nomination was part of the Board's approval to acquire Austin-Davis."

"Looking forward to it," Clay hoped his voice sounded sincere.

"You'll love the other board members. I know they're looking forward to meeting you and having your expertise available to them. Our investor relations department is coordinating the annual meeting. I'll ask them to contact your assistant so the reservations can be made. That's Sheryl, right?"

"Yes, Sheryl is her name."

"Great. I don't want to get too far ahead of ourselves here, the deal hasn't been closed, but I think it's safe to tentatively schedule your initial visit to the offices in Portland, San Francisco, and Boise. If you agree, I think both of us should visit each office together. You okay with that?"

"Makes sense as long as I play the lead in the meetings," Clay said. He didn't want to come off as Phil's lap dog in these visits.

"Totally agree. The scheduling is going to be a little tricky, so can I have my assistant, Roberta, coordinate with Sheryl. Roberta will be able to loop in the other offices. My preference is that we spend a day in each office beginning the day after the annual meeting. I need to be in London on the fifth of May, so I want to do this tour with you and get back to Dallas."

"Okay, I'll block out my calendar and let Sheryl know to expect calls from Roberta and investor relations very soon."

"Perfect. While we're scheduling things, let's get a date on our calendars for closing the deal. Is that okay with you?"

"Sure." Clay was forcing his tone to sound like closing the deal was just another day at the office. In reality, the thought of signing the final document caused his stomach to flip.

"Let's tentatively set the date for April 20 I think I can convince my attorneys to get it done by then. Where would you like to sign the papers? Seattle or Dallas?"

Clay thought for a few seconds. "Phil, I think it's best if we sign the papers here in Seattle. I want to introduce you in person to our team here—give you a chance to speak to the group, join us for happy hour."

"You got it. I couldn't agree more."

"Okay. I'll ask Sheryl to set that up with Roberta for April 20."

"Great. Okay, I gotta let you go. Let's touch base again on Tuesday, same time," Phil said, before hanging up, not waiting to hear Clay's goodbye.

Clay hung up, deep in thought. He was troubled but didn't know why exactly. He glanced up to see Sheryl standing in the doorway.

"Is there anything that needs to be taken care of? I figured there might be."

Clay signaled for Sheryl to come in. "You figured right."

He proceeded to brief Sheryl on the conversation with Phil and what arrangements needed to be made. As he spoke, Sheryl grinned.

"What's the smile about?" he asked.

"I'm very happy for you, that's all."

"Thanks, I guess."

Chapter 55

or the next three hours, he immersed himself in the campaign strategy for TenState Trucking. The presentation to TenState's management team was set for the following week. It felt good to forget about deals and Board meetings for a few hours, so he could get back to what he really loved—marketing. He had to admit it—he was darn good at this stuff. Manicotti was fortunate to have him. *Heck, maybe one day I'll be head of Pitt-Needham.*

After recording a few last comments and suggestions in the TenState folder of the team's collaboration software platform, Clay turned off his computer, cleared his desktop of paper and headed out the door. He was the last one to leave the office.

Clay stopped for Chinese takeout before heading home. The garlic-laced aroma of the food quickly filled the car's cabin, making Clay's mouth water. He was famished.

At home, Clay flipped on the TV to watch the news while he wolfed down his meal. By 9:30 he was finished with dinner and reading his mail. There were the usual bills and advertising flyers, except for one letter. This was from Glenn Bartlett in Reef Bay. Inside the crisp white envelope was a copy of the counter-signed real estate management paperwork, a short letter, and what looked like a repair bill.

Dear Mr. Austin:

Please find herein a copy of the real estate management agreement for 3100 Deception Point Drive.

I am informing you that on April 2, I inspected the property after a windstorm. The residence suffered some roof damage which I had repaired by Seaview Roofing the next day to prevent water damage to the premises. While at the property I inspected the inside of the residence and ran the Ford pickup to maintain a charge in the battery.

The repair bill from Seaview Roofing in the amount of $459.76 is enclosed. This amount has been paid from the maintenance fund you provided, leaving a balance of $4,540.24 in the account.

Regards,
Glenn Bartlett, Esq.
Attorney at Law
Bartlett & Associates, LLP

It was comforting to Clay that Bartlett was doing his job, but the letter was a reminder that he had to decide what on earth to do with the place. He made a mental note to broach the subject with Bartlett. Maybe he should sell it.

Clay turned off the TV, tossed the takeout cartons in the garbage compactor and headed upstairs to bed.

Before climbing into bed he looked at the painting hanging above the headboard as if to find answers there for what he should do with the property. The painting still attracted him in some mysterious way. Once he started looking at it, it was difficult to turn away. The feeling was particularly strong tonight for some reason. Clay wanted to examine the painting closer. He got onto the bed on his knees, facing the painting. His eyes were level with the painting now.

The piece was remarkable. The unusual perspective. The richness of color. The detail was astonishing—almost like a photograph. Every brick in the lighthouse had been painstakingly brushed into place on the canvas. The residence was equally detailed. The structure's white clapboard siding looked slightly weathered. The shingle roof appeared as though each had been individually painted. Wait a minute! What's this? Clay looked closer at the roof. One small area looked different from the rest. The shingles from that small section weren't as weathered. They looked newer. Clay couldn't remember seeing that patch on the roof before. How could he have missed it? The difference between the old shingles and new shingles was very noticeable. He should have seen it before, but he hadn't. Then, Clay remembered Bartlett's letter. *Whiskey Tango Foxtrot!* What an amazing coincidence! The day he receives the bill for roof repair he notices a repaired roof in the painting for the first time. That was spooky.

He slipped under the covers and settled his head into the pillow. Still thinking about the roof in the painting he decided it was just a silly coincidence. Realistically, the roof of the residence probably has been patched many times over the years, considering its exposures to the winter storms that lash the Washington coast. It's not surprising that the artist painted it that way. Furthermore, Clay rationalized it wasn't really that unusual that he hadn't seen the patch before. The balloon and lighthouse were visually stronger and larger in the painting. Invariably his eyes were drawn there, not to the residence.

The painting was full of surprises, all right. Clay drifted off to sleep.

Chapter 56

n his dream, Clay was preparing for a morning on the lake in his kayak. Many of his neighbors had already launched their boats and were paddling away from the dock. He struggled to pull the craft to the dock's edge, but it was unusually heavy. He wasn't sure how to get into the unstable little boat without tipping over into the cold lake. He couldn't remember how he had gotten into the kayak before.

He called out to his neighbors for assistance, but they continued to paddle away. Eventually, he managed to squeeze into the kayak and push off from the dock's edge. As the sleek boat drifted out into the lake Clay realized he had left the paddle on the dock. The wind moved him farther away from the dock out into the lake. He began to panic. Again, he called for help, but his voice was carried away by the wind. The other kayakers paddled away, unaware of Clay's predicament. He had no control; no way to power himself back to the dock.

The sensation of movement intensified. He and his sea kayak were beginning to move faster, but it wasn't the wind. No, it was current. That couldn't be. He was on a lake. There were no currents on the lake ordinarily so why was he being swept along as if on a fast-flowing river? He was powerless to do anything. Waves began to rock his boat from side to side and splash over its pointed bow. The situation was deteriorating rapidly. He was in the middle of the lake now, battered by the waves and pulled along by the current toward the ship canal. Up ahead in the canal he could see massive barges being jockeyed into position by sea-going tugs. He was going to be crushed against the rusty steel hulls or drawn into the churning propellers. Closer and closer the current carried him. The steel hulls loomed above. The relentless current increased in velocity and pulled him past the barges, deeper down the canal. He looked to the bank of the canal and could just see the top of his office building. Could anyone see him? Was there anyone in the office able to help?

The current was moving him even faster now. Spray flew off the bow, biting into his eyes, making it difficult to see. Through blurred vision, he saw another shape dead ahead. He wiped the water from his eyes. The object came into focus. He was on a collision course with a huge blue yacht. Its spotless blue hull shimmered with reflections in the morning sun. This was one of the largest yachts Clay had ever seen in the canal. He didn't recognize it from his photo collection of famous yachts. The ship's name and home port were unreadable on the stern. The distance was closing rapidly between Clay's little craft and the massive yacht. In a few minutes, he was going to crash. He was helpless to do anything about it.

Perched on the deck high above Clay's little kayak he could see a helicopter. A man and a woman were getting into it. He didn't recognize the man, but he knew the woman. It was Sheryl. She was wearing a purple bikini and carrying a bouquet of helium party balloons. Clay screamed for help, waving his arms frantically. Sheryl turned from the helicopter and looked down at Clay. She tossed her head back and laughed, then stepped up into the helicopter with her balloons. Clay's heart sank. The situation was hopeless. No one was going to help him—not even Sheryl cared that he was about to crash and drown. The kayak's speed doubled, then doubled again. Something more than just current was now hurling the narrow little fiberglass hull at high speed toward the stern of the super-yacht. Clay could see the churning prop wash from the ship's twin propellers. He knew that once he collided with the ship, the kayak would shatter; his body would be sucked under by the powerful turbulence and chopped to bits in the swirling bronze blades.

He jabbed both hands hard into the water on both sides of the kayak in a desperate attempt to slow his progress or to change direction just enough to avoid the inevitable crash. Nothing happened. He screamed again, but no sound came out of his mouth. It would be all over in a few seconds. He looked up as the blue hull towered above him, blocking out the sky. The yacht's crew in their matching sweaters, stood in a neat line on the aft deck, pointing down at him and laughing.

Chapter 57

S tanding in the shower, Clay tried to erase the kayak nightmare from his memory. He hoped the hot water and soap would wash away the sense of helplessness and inevitable doom he felt. Even the painting of the majestic sailing ship that he could see from the shower failed to inspire him like it usually did. Instead of seeing the strength of the vessel overcoming the storm, he saw a ship struggling against the odds and slowly losing its way.

He toweled off and looked in the mirror. Clay didn't recognize the person looking back through the slightly steamed glass. His face was haggard; dark swollen circles appeared below his eyes. An older exhausted face stared back at him. But, it was the change in his eyes that shocked him the most.

Did his eyes always look the way they did this morning? He couldn't remember. Granted he seldom spent much time examining his eyes, or the details of his face for that matter. Usually, he just checked to make sure he hadn't missed a spot of beard after shaving. Regardless, he didn't recognize the eyes that stared back at him today. While his face looked much older, the eyes looked eerily younger somehow. Clay wasn't sure how that could be so. The eyes he was seeing now in his face were the eyes of a boy, not a man. The eyes looked back pleading, pleading like a dog's expression after being beaten. *Please don't hit me again.* These weren't confident, energetic eyes. Just the opposite. They were half-dead. And scared. Very, very scared.

Clay shaved quickly, trying hard to avoid looking directly into his eyes in the mirror's reflection. Then he walked slowly into his closet to dress. He stood in the middle of the closet and looked around at the neatly arranged clothes on the racks and shelves. He usually had an immediate impulse for what to wear on any given day. Not today. Everything he considered wearing, didn't seem right. The sensation was of standing in a stranger's closet looking at clothes that didn't belong to him. He'd never experienced this feeling before. A wave of despair rippled through his body like a mild electric shock.

So, this must be what depression is like. Maybe he should just go back to bed rather than dressing for work. He could call in sick. Heck, he hadn't taken a sick day in over a year.

He wandered back to the bedroom. The bed beckoned him. It looked so warm and cozy. He stepped closer to it. *Good idea, I could stay home. Sleep all day.* That sounded wonderful to him. He stepped next to the bed. All he had to do now was lean forward, crawl under the covers and close his eyes.

But that meant going back to sleep—and sleep is where the nightmares lived. Last night's scene shot through his mind, of Sheryl laughing at him while getting into the helicopter with another man. No, he couldn't risk another dream like that. Funny, the part in the dream that upset him the most wasn't the idea that he was going to crash and die a terrible death. No, it was the sharp pain he felt the moment Sheryl looked down at his helpless struggle in the small kayak, laughed, and then flew away with someone else. Sheryl's scene and the final scene of the yacht crew standing at the rail high above him pointing down and laughing kept flashing through his mind repeatedly as if stuck in some mental loop of horror.

He couldn't risk falling asleep and having another nightmare like that. The gray morning light was beginning to fill the bedroom, reminding him that a new day was starting, and he had work to do.

He returned to the closet. Clay remembered that he didn't have any client meetings today, but he did have a date. So, he selected a chocolate brown wool sports coat and gray slacks. Deciding he needed some color, he put on a pale yellow button-down dress shirt. The look was completed by a yellow and brown paisley pocket square. Before leaving the closet, he examined his collection of shoes, deciding on a pair of tobacco-colored stitched cap-toe oxfords that he had ordered from Italy but hadn't worn yet.

He inspected himself in front of the full-length mirror in his closet. He felt better. Funny how dressing well elevated his spirt and confidence.

Clay skipped breakfast. He wasn't very hungry; besides it was Friday, which meant that the office would have bagels and fruit in the kitchen for everyone. Outside, the temperature was hovering just above freezing. He put on the long wool coat from the coat closet and headed out the door to his car.

Chapter 58

t was 4 o'clock, and Clay was catching up on email in his office while enjoying the first macchiato of the day with a few strawberries left over from breakfast.

George and Sheryl strolled into his office together.

"What's up?" Clay asked.

"Just a quick status report on our friends down the hall from Pitt-Needham," George replied. "They told Sheryl a few moments ago that they were done. They're heading back to Dallas tonight."

"Really? I thought they were going to be here into next week."

Sheryl spoke this time. "That was the plan, but they told me that what work remained could be done from Dallas."

"Any idea about how the due diligence went? I mean I haven't heard anything troubling from Phil. On the contrary, as you know, he asked to set a tentative closing date for April 20."

"You know as much as we do I guess. I'll say one thing for the Pitt Crew; they are tight-lipped. Not once did they say anything about how their work was progressing," George said.

"I think it's safe to assume that if a deal breaker had surfaced, we'd know it by now." Clay reasoned.

"I agree," said George.

"But neither of you should be surprised if they bring up some issues at closing to reduce the final price," Sheryl added.

"They won't dare. They know they'd have to deal with you if they tried any last-minute funny stuff," Clay said facetiously.

"Anyway, Alicia tells me all the arrangements for the 20th are well underway. She and Sheryl are doing their usual bang-up job. Reuben will host us at his office for signing the papers. Then we'll have lunch at the Columbia Tower Club. There will be a company-wide meeting and party here at four o'clock," George said.

Clay realized he was looking at Sheryl rather than George while he spoke. He could tell that she noticed his stare but pretended to study the notepad computer in her hands. A very subtle smile creased her lips.

"Do I need to say good-bye to the Pitt Crew?" Clay asked.

"No need. I thanked them for you. Besides, I think they've already packed up and headed to the airport," Sheryl said.

"Well then, I'm going to leave. I promised Melissa that I'd be home early tonight. Any exciting plans for the weekend?" George said, looking first at Sheryl and then at Clay. Clay could swear there was a suspecting, playful tone in his voice. Was George directing the question to them as a couple, or to them individually?

Sheryl stammered her reply first, "Um, uh, nothing too exciting. Having an old friend over for dinner tonight."

Clever, Clay thought. In the moment he couldn't think of anything to say other than, "Nothing unusual for me. I might catch a movie."

George left, leaving Sheryl and Clay alone in the office.

"Old friend?" Clay asked with a grin.

"Well, I have known you for at least five years, and you are older than me." Sheryl was having a good time teasing Clay.

"I am older than you?" He realized he didn't know Sheryl's age. "How old are you?" He felt odd asking the question.

"I don't believe you're permitted to ask an employee that question, Mr. Austin," Sheryl said with a faked seriousness in her voice. The change was so sudden it took Clay off guard. Then after a short pause, she continued, "But if you're really nice tonight I might tell you."

There was *that look* again in her eyes—a strong feminine confidence on the surface with the hint of a fearful little girl underneath. In a flash, her eyes opened a story like the prologue to an epic novel. They gave a glimpse of the beautiful mystery that awaited those patient and loving enough to gain Sheryl's trust. It was all he could do to resist getting up out of his chair and wrapping his arms around her.

"Then I will be especially nice," he said. "What can I bring? Oh, what's your address? What part of town do you live in anyway?" He was embarrassed that he knew so little about her. That had to change.

"You can bring wine if you like. I live on Alki. I'll text you the address," she said.

"Cool, I haven't been over to Alki since last summer. Listen, I won't leave my appointment with Dr. Shildstein until six, and it'll take me at least forty-five minutes in traffic to get to your place."

"No problem. Speaking of timing. I need to leave a little early today to get dinner ready for my old friend."

"Of course. Take off whenever you want," he said, looking at his watch. "I need to leave in a few minutes, too. This old friend has an appointment with a shrink."

She left his office. Clay cleared his desk by refiling papers to folders in his desk drawer. He swung his chair around to look out the window for a moment of contemplation while finishing his macchiato. It was still somewhat light outside, now that daylight savings time had started. The late afternoon sun hadn't completely surrendered to the dusk of the coming night. It was encouraging to

Clay that sunset for the next few months would be occurring a few minutes later than the day before it. Longer days lifted his spirits. And he really felt as though his spirit could use a little lifting.

Chapter 59

After greeting Dr. Shildstein in her bungalow office, he quickly scanned the walls. Yep, all the art had been rotated according to what must be a secret formula. The Sedona piece that hung behind her chair last week was now on a wall by the front door, having been replaced by a striking watercolor of a hot air balloon festival over a stone chateau and vineyard fields; France he guessed.

"You've re-arranged the art again I see," Clay said.

"Oh yes, every Monday morning."

"Doctor, I don't know how to thank you for the painting you gave me last week. It is amazing in so many ways. Do you know who the artist is?"

She smiled broadly. "I saw that the painting attracted you more than the others on your first visit. I made a note of it in my journal. Unfortunately, I don't know anything about the artist. It was just one of many pieces offered for sale at an art fair by an old gentleman. You see, Clay, all the paintings here," she swept her arm in a broad arc, "Will be given to patients. Every patient, sooner or later during their treatment, will be attracted to one of the pieces over the others. There's always a deep connection between what the patient sees in the painting and what they've been dealing with in their sessions."

"That's pretty weird, Doctor. Are you telling me that every patient connects with a painting?"

She smiled broadly again. "Yes, that's how it works. I tell my husband I'm not sure if the patient picks the painting, or the painting picks the patient."

She sat in her chair and motioned for Clay take his place on the couch.

"How was your week, Clay? Did you do your homework?"

"I don't know where to begin, Laura, it has been a crazy week." He paused. "Frankly, it all started with the painting."

"Oh, how so?"

"Did I ever mention my Uncle Charley to you?"

While shaking her head side to side she flipped through her journal notes. "No, you haven't. You've talked about your stepfather, your mother. Nobody else from your family has come up."

"I didn't think so either." Clay's voice began to crack as emotion swelled up inside him. "Doctor, my Uncle Charley died recently and left me his property . . . a lighthouse. . . the exact same lighthouse in the painting you gave me last Friday."

Clay thought the Doctor's reaction to this shocking coincidence was odd. She wasn't particularly surprised. Her eyes grew large but then shut. She was very still for a few seconds before the brown eyes opened again. The Doctor had always looked at him warmly, but at this moment her eyes took on something additional. It was as if in an instant she had transformed from a warm professional into a wise, compassionate spirit that saw deep into his soul. Oddly, he was equally comforted and discomforted by the transformation.

"Tell me about your uncle," she asked in a calm voice.

Clay told her about his Uncle and Aunt Gragg: The wonderful summers of new adventures and experiences; the freedom of being away from Vic's oppression; losing touch with his uncle in the past decade; and the funeral.

"Sounds like your aunt and uncle loved you very much. Didn't they have children of their own?"

"No, they didn't. I never knew why."

"Your uncle was like a father to you, wasn't he?"

"Yes, for a few weeks a year between ages of ten and fourteen, I was with a man who treated me like a son." Clay's emotions were still bubbling inside him, nearly bringing tears to his eyes.

"How did you feel when you learned about the lighthouse inheritance?"

Clay thought for a few seconds before answering. "Shock. Guilt. Mostly guilt, I guess. Guilt from not keeping in touch with him."

"Why didn't you stay in communication with your uncle?"

"I don't know. I got busy with my career. He never reached out to me either."

"He thought about you enough to include you in his Will, didn't he?"

"Yeah, maybe he didn't have anyone else to give it to."

"He could have left it to a charity, the county, or a church even. But, he left it to you. Even though he hadn't spoken with you in ten years, he bequeathed this beautiful lighthouse to you. Can you see the unconditional love he had for you, Clay?"

Clay lost his fight against the tears. They filled his eyes and began to run down his cheeks in long streams.

"Can you see how the dreams are about your deep-seated fear of not being good enough?"

Clay shook his head, not able to make the connection.

"In the recurring dream, you're not able to fix the light in time to save the boat. You mentioned how frustrated you felt in the dream that the tools weren't right for the job and you couldn't reach some of the parts."

Clay nodded.

"This dream was your subconscious revealing fears of not being good enough."

"Makes sense, but doctor, it doesn't explain why I've been having nightmares about a lighthouse, and now I own one!" Clay's voice was raised. He was frustrated that he didn't know what was going on inside his head; that he couldn't control the confusing thoughts that battled there.

"Ah, that is a marvelous mystery, Clay. There is a lot of symbolism involved in a lighthouse. Most of which don't apply to your situation. One does fit, however. A lighthouse emits a beacon of light that others navigate by, right?"

"Right."

"A lighthouse is often seen, in the spiritual sense, as the guiding light of God. Are you following me?"

"Yes, to a point. If the lighthouse is God, why did the boat sink and the lawnmowers attack me while I was in it?"

"Ah, good question. First of all, in your dreams, the light isn't shining is it? The *light* is the symbol of God, not the *lighthouse*. Besides, the dreams aren't about God. Your dreams are about you, Clay. Dreams always have something to do with what your mind is dealing with."

Clay looked puzzled.

"Maybe this will help. I usually don't quote scripture in my sessions, but I'm going to make an exception." She removed a Bible from a small stack of books on the floor by her chair. She thumbed back and forth through the pages. "There are many references to lamps and light in the Bible. Two, in particular, come to mind if I can find them for you now." More page turning. "Ah, here's one that I was thinking about. This is from Psalms chapter 119 verse 105: 'By your words, I can see where I'm going; they throw a beam of light on my dark path.'"

She turned more pages. Clay saw that she appeared to be referring to an index of some sort in the back of the thick book before turning to a specific page. "There's one more good one . . . ah, here it is. Jesus is using a parable to make a point to his disciples: 'Nor do they light a lamp and put it under a basket, but on a lampstand, and it gives light to all who are in the house.' This is from Matthew chapter 5, verse 15 if you want to look it up later. I'll write it down for you."

She tore a page from a small yellow note pad, jotted down the verse locations, and placed it on the coffee table in front of him. He picked it up and placed it into his shirt pocket. Clay had never looked up anything in the Bible before. He wasn't sure he knew how. It didn't matter much because he didn't even own a Bible. He made a mental note to ask Sheryl to show him.

"But, Laura, none of this explains why I was dreaming about lighthouses and now own one. For that matter, is there a passage in the Bible to explain why you bought the painting, or why I was attracted to it? The coincidences are freaking me out."

"Let me just say this, Clay; the entire Bible is about this. Not the specific painting of course. The entire Bible is about how God touches us and encourages us to have a relationship with Him. The Bible is filled with one story after the other about the lengths that God goes to get our attention and bring us to Him. I am not going to try to explain the lighthouse and the painting, except that I see God's handiwork all over it. I don't believe in coincidences of this nature."

"So then, God is responsible for my nightmares?" Clay asked.

"Ah, good question. As a psychiatrist, I can tell you that dreams arise out of our sub-conscious. They can reveal deep-seated fears, or simply reflect what are mind is occupied with currently."

"I understand that, but believe me, I hadn't been thinking about lighthouses when the dreams started."

"No, but your self-perception of not being good enough was triggered by the offer to purchase your company and catapult you into a bigger role at a larger company. Reality was threatening your sense of who you are." She paused to let that sink in and could see that Clay was still struggling to grasp the meaning of her words. "Clay, you're in marketing, think about the rich imagery in your dream. Climbing stairs in the darkness, the missing tool, knowing how to fix the light, but not being able to do so in time to save the boat that was dependent on you for guidance."

"Okay, now that's beginning to make sense to me, except how does God fit in?"

"As your doctor, not your pastor, I'll say that the dreams are exposing deep-seated fears around believing you're not good enough to win the approval and love of others. This will be a central focus of our work together in future sessions, Clay."

"Then God isn't responsible for my dreams."

Wearing a compassionate smile, she replied, "That's up to you to decide, Clay. Let me leave you with this truth. In the Bible, God spoke through dreams to many of the most important characters—even to Joseph. In this room, you and I will unlock the psychological mystery. I encourage you to seek more about the spiritual mystery on your own. Do you have someone you can talk to about God?"

Thoughts of Sheryl flooded his mind. "Yes, I do. In fact, I'm having dinner with her tonight."

"What's her name? Is this a friend or more than a friend?"

The question took Clay totally by surprise. He didn't know how to answer. What was Sheryl? A friend? A girlfriend?

"Her name is Sheryl, but to be honest, I'm not sure how to classify her. We've known each other a long time, but just recently admitted to each other that we cared for one another."

"Sheryl?" The doctor was searching her memory. The name was very familiar. "Don't you have an admin named Sheryl? She has called and set appointments for you."

"Yes, that's the one."

"I suppose you two have talked about the risks of office romance." The doctor was sounding motherly now.

"We have. This is all very sudden, Laura. It was just last Sunday after church that we had the conversation. I'm seeing her tonight, and we'll talk some more."

"You went to church with her? Is Sheryl a Christian?"

"Yes."

The doctor paused before speaking again. "Well then, back to our subject, do you feel comfortable talking to her about God's existence?"

"Definitely."

Smiling broadly, "That's wonderful, Clay. Talk to her. I'd like you to consider that it's no coincidence you and Sheryl are exploring a deeper relationship with each other at this exact point in time. It's no more of a coincidence than the painting and the inheritance. Or, the sale of your business, by the way."

Clay was trying to make sense out of what the doctor was saying. It was as if he'd just been dealt a hand of cards but didn't know what game he was playing.

The doctor switched subjects. "In the time remaining today please share with me what you wrote in your journal this week."

Clay opened his journal and immediately felt guilty for not having followed the doctor's instructions more closely. There was only one entry for the week. One entry. She was probably going to reprimand him for slacking off; for not writing something every day about his "not good enough feelings." But, what if he hadn't had any of those thoughts during the week? That would explain why he hadn't written more wouldn't it? His spirit lifted slightly. He had an excuse.

He proceeded to recite to Dr. Shildstein what he had written about the dream in which the lawnmower army attacked him at the lighthouse. He included details of feelings of despair in the aftermath of the nightmare. As he spoke, she wrote furiously in her journal. He watched her carefully, expecting a concealed snicker to leak out at any time. Instead, she stopped writing and spoke directly at him.

"Was this the same lighthouse as in the other dreams?"

"Yes, exactly the same"

"Before we talk about the dream, read me your other entries."

Busted! Now the doctor was going to be disappointed in him. He prepared for the scolding and lecture to follow. But, instead of a lecture, he received another question from the doctor.

"Was the dream and the morning after the only time during the past week when you had the sensation or thoughts of not being good enough for a task or for someone's approval?" Her question was without an overtone of accusation. But he could tell she didn't believe he had only experienced one episode.

"Not that I remember," he replied.

"What about just now when I asked you to read from the journal? What thoughts went through your mind?"

"Well . . . I . . . uh . . . thought you'd get upset with me because . . . I . . . didn't do the assignment correctly?"

"Anything else?" She probed.

He thought. "For a minute I felt guilty for not doing the assignment correctly."

"Good. You already have one more thing to add to your journal for today."

"Huh?"

"You experienced a 'not good enough' episode a second after I asked you to read from your journal."

"I guess I did."

"Absolutely. Clay you've been telling yourself that for so long you don't even notice it. The little voice inside telling you that you're not good enough has been running the show—it has been controlling what you think and how you respond to people and events. The tricky thing is your conscious mind doesn't hear it. That's why you have a difficult time noticing it. The little voice that is controlling you lives in depths of your subconscious mind."

"Okay, but if I don't know it's there how am I supposed to deal with it?"

"Practice. Like anything you have to practice to learn how to recognize the voice; how to recognize a reaction you have to a person or event." She smiled and continued. "In other words, be vigilant. Keep writing in your journal. And I'm serious about recording your thoughts about what just occurred for you in this office."

"I got it. I see the purpose."

"Is seeing a purpose, a goal, or plan, important to you, Clay?"

"Definitely. I like to know that what I'm doing is accomplishing something. I call it 'moving the needle,' as in moving the needle on a gauge."

"What if you don't know the plan?'

"You mean, what if there isn't a plan?"

"No. A plan exists, but you're not aware of it."

"Then I don't know what to do," he replied.

"You don't know what to do. Why is knowing what to do important to you?" The doctor inquired.

"If I don't know the plan I might not do the right thing."

Nodding as if Clay's statement was the most rational thing she had ever heard in this office, she said, "You might get it wrong."

"Exactly." Clay was beginning to believe the doctor was seeing his side of things more clearly at last.

"What would happen if you got it wrong because you didn't know the plan?"

"We're dealing with hypotheticals here, doctor. The implications of me doing something wrong can vary."

"Granted, but in any hypothetical situation we can think of, how would you feel if you did something incorrectly?"

Clay really had to think. In a way, this line of questioning was annoying him. Seemed like a game of circular logic cooked up by a group of shrinks who had had too much to drink. "I'd feel bad about screwing up, I guess."

"What else?"

Geez, he hated it when she said, 'What else?' Always with the follow-on questions. "I wouldn't want to be blamed for doing something incorrectly, just because I didn't know the plan or the rules."

"Okay, you'd feel bad, and you'd be afraid of getting blamed. There's something else, Clay. Close your eyes and image a situation where someone, let's say your friend Sheryl, was telling you how you had screwed up for something you did or didn't do. It was something she expected of you, but you weren't aware of it. Here's a person you care for very much that is blaming you for an error. How are you feeling about it? What are you telling yourself? Keep your eyes closed. Be in that moment."

It wasn't difficult for Clay to imagine this scenario, especially after the emotional roller coast he and Sheryl had shared on Sunday. "I'd be perturbed, maybe even angry that I was getting blamed for not knowing the plan." He kept his eyes shut sorting through the thoughts that shot through his mind like wild rockets from an out-of-control firework show. Just as a shape to a thought formed into something recognizable it dissolved into darkness. Then he heard it; *if you were good enough, you would have known the plan.* His eyes shot open. "I heard it!"

"Heard what?"

"The 'not good enough' voice. It told me if I was good enough I would have known what to do."

"Very good, Clay. You learn fast. Remember this little exercise. Please continue to write in your journal this coming week. Be vigilant for that little voice, or other little voices telling you who you are. Our time is about up for today. Anything else you want to say?"

"Doctor, I can't meet next Friday. That's the date when the sale of my business is supposed to be finalized."

"That was fast! Didn't you just sign the letter of intent?"

"The due-diligence has progressed very swiftly. My partner and I are pleased. But, an appointment with you on Friday is not going to be possible. I like our progress, though. I'll ask Sheryl to set something as soon as possible after this week."

"I agree we're just beginning to crack open the door, Clay." She stood to signal the end of the session.

Clay rose, too. "Laura, I really don't know how to thank you for the awesome painting. It seems every time I look at it, I see something I hadn't noticed before."

"I'm very pleased that you like it. It was one of my favorites, too. Keep our conversation in mind today. Talk with Sheryl about it if you feel comfortable trusting her. Clay, you are part of a marvelous plan—the lighthouse, your uncle, the painting, selling the business, and Sheryl—are all coalescing at this time. You don't know what the plan is. You may never know. But this is for certain, and I want you to hear me very clearly." She paused and looked deeply into Clay's eyes. "You'll never experience the miracle of this plan if you let the lie of 'not good enough' drive your life." She shook his hand and led him to the door.

Chapter 60

Sitting in his car before vacating the parking space on Dr. Shildstein's street, Clay switched gears in his head. Gone, for now, was the introspective session with his doctor. He slipped into task mode gear as easily as shifting from first to second in his car. That was both a gift and a curse for Clay and other men—the ability to have a singular focus—unlike most women who, like expert jugglers, were able to keep many plates in the air at one time.

The task at hand was how to get to Sheryl's house on time. It was 5:05. He looked at the address Sheryl had texted him earlier in the day. After keying the address into the BMW's nav system he saw his route and estimated arrival time of 5:52. Her address in the Alki district of Seattle was southwest of Clay's current location. After checking his phone to find a wine shop along the route, he texted Sheryl. "Leaving doctor's office now. See you soon."

He eased the powerful sedan out of the parking space and headed to his date with Sheryl.

After having to wait at what seemed to be a hundred stoplights along the way, and a slow-moving line at the wine shop, Clay was now on the West Seattle Bridge heading west. The bridge crossed the Duwamish Waterway and cut across Harbor Island, an area of land devoted to marine repair and docks for loading and unloading massive container ships.

Up ahead Clay had a decision to make. He could take the longer and more scenic Alki Avenue route, or the shorter and boring Admiral Way route that was already highlighted on his screen. He tapped Alki Avenue to change routes. He'd still arrive before six. This route would be very much slower on a summer Friday night when people flock to the area for its miles of beaches and jaw-dropping views. Tonight, in cold drizzle, traffic was moderate and moving at a consistent speed.

Like a belt holding back a fat man's protruding belly, the avenue wraps around a point of land that juts into Elliot Bay. Where Clay was currently driving the street was named Harbor Avenue. To his left, an unbroken string of condos had been cut into the tall cliff, their expansive windows pointing to one of many postcard views along this route. From here the residents had an unobstructed view across the bay to the skyscrapers, Space Needle, and sports coliseums of downtown Seattle as they glistened like a magical crystal city of some sci-fi fantasy.

Soon the road took a turn to the left and headed westward around the point of land called Duwamish Head. The street's name changed to Alki Avenue. The view changed, too. To the north, now on Clay's right, was a large portion of Puget Sound. The grass park by the water's edge ended, replaced by a sandy beach and concrete breakwater. To his left, the string of condos continued. One after the other, they reminded Clay of a necklace of irregular glass beads he had seen at an art fair.

Checking the GPS, he noted that he still had a few miles yet to drive in the fading light. With his arrival only moments way, Clay began to get nervous. How should he greet her? With a hug? A handshake? A light kiss on the cheek? What was he going to talk about? God? The weather? The odds of the Seattle Mariners making it to the World Series? Maybe this dinner wasn't such a good idea.

Then, out of the blue, he had an epiphany. All he needed to do was ask questions about her. After all, he didn't know that much about the woman, except he had become attracted to her. Just ask questions; that was a great plan. He relaxed and exhaled a deep breath in relief.

To Clay's left, the tall cliffs had fallen away to flat land. Multi-story condos had been replaced by one- or two-story homes and retail businesses that looked across the avenue and beach to the broad expanse of water. It looked very much like any laid-back beach community.

The car's nav system altered him that his destination was ahead on the left in 900 feet. Although all of his attention was focused on trying to find street numbers on the homes and condos that lined the left side of the street, something white caught his eye on the right. He slammed on the brakes, fortunate that no cars were behind him.

There, on his right, at the water's edge, stood the Alki Point Lighthouse.

This is ridiculous? Are lighthouses going to follow me for the rest of my life, or what?

As lighthouses went, this one wasn't very grand. Built in 1913, it stood just thirty-seven feet above sea level, yet provided a critical navigation aid at the southernmost entrance to Elliot Bay.

Headlights reflected in Clay's rearview mirror. He couldn't sit in the middle of the street any longer. Though shaken by the lighthouse discovery, he resumed his forward progress in search of Sheryl's home.

"You have arrived at your destination." The nav system announced the end his journey. He parked on the street opposite a two-story condo. He had found the building. What was the apartment number? He checked the address information Sheryl had provided. "#2". Okay. He was set. Just walk across the street. Find the door with a number two on it, ring the bell, smile and say, hi. *Piece of cake.*

Clay reached for the wine and flowers in the passenger seat before opening the door to leave but thought he'd better check his hair in the mirror first. A quick look in the mirror told him every hair was exactly where it was supposed to be. It was 5:59. Time to go.

Panic set in. What if after tonight Sheryl learned just enough about Clay that she decided she didn't like him after all? That was a real possibility he figured.

Needing to calm down, he permitted himself to ease back in his seat. *Relax and breathe deeply. Breathe in. Breathe out. Breathe in. Breathe out.* To his right was nothing but water and the jagged Olympic Mountains on the horizon. To his left across the street, an elderly man was unloading tools from the back of an SUV. Before shutting the tailgate, he reached into the vehicle again and removed a push broom. With toolbox in one hand and the broom in the other, the old man limped toward the building next to Sheryl's.

Breathe in. Breathe out. Clay couldn't calm himself. A feeling of dread wrapped around him like a cold, slimy python wanting to crush him to death before swallowing him whole. It was six o'clock. Time to leave the car and greet Sheryl, but he wasn't ready. What on earth was going on with him? *Breathe in. Breathe out.*

The broom. The old man was carrying a push broom—no doubt to assist in clean up following the project he was working on. Clay knew all about push brooms. Vic taught him one hot summer day when they were alone in the dusty garage together. Yeah, Clay knew about push brooms.

Why was he thinking about *that* right now? He shook his head, trying to fling the terrible memory from his mind. *Enough!* He opened the car door, grabbed the flowers and wine from the passenger seat, and left the car.

Chapter 61

A t 6:02 Clay pushed the doorbell button mounted next to a door with a very stylish metal "2". This was it. *Showtime.*

Clay waited. The door didn't open. After an appropriate wait, he pushed the button again. He couldn't hear if the doorbell was sounding inside the condo or not. He waited some more. He checked his watch. Dinner was tonight, wasn't it? It was at six o'clock, wasn't it? Maybe Sheryl changed her mind. Maybe she got invited on a date with someone else that she liked more than Clay. *Maybe the guy on the yacht with the helicopter.* He knocked on the door three times.

The door swung open almost immediately. "You're late," she said through a large smile. She stepped out of the way so Clay could enter. "Please come in. I was beginning to wonder what on earth you were doing sitting out there in your car."

"You could see me?"

"Of course." Clay walked into the main living area of her condo. One entire wall consisted of windows. The view was breathtaking, even from the relatively low second story. From where Clay stood all he could see was water and the majestic Olympic Mountains to the west. Of course, she could see him seated in his car. Her condo overlooked the street.

"I . . . I . . . had to collect my thoughts for a minute or two that's all."

"Well I hope you share those thoughts with me later," she said with a twinkle in her eye.

"Not much to share, but I'll try." The man's broom was definitely not going to be a topic of discussion this evening.

"Here are some flowers for the chef and a wine I've been wanting to try." He handed her the carefully wrapped Calla Lilies and bottle of 2014 Kelley Fox Pinot Noir from Oregon.

Sheryl beamed at the flowers. "Lilies! How did you know I like lilies?"

"I Googled it," Clay said facetiously.

"Why don't you make us a cocktail at the bar while I put these lovely flowers in a vase. I'll have a vodka on the rocks with a twist of lime please."

In a corner of the room was a small portable bar stocked with a few bottles of premium liquor brands. By the time he made the cocktails Sheryl had finished placing the lilies in a vase with fresh water on the kitchen counter.

"Shall we have a seat? Dinner will be ready in about thirty minutes." She motioned for Clay to have a seat on the large couch that faced the windows.

He sat down, and she sat next to him. Not touching, but close.

"Here's to Friday night dinner," Clay said, presenting his glass as a toast to her. It was a lame toast, but he just didn't know what to say. He was feeling awkward.

"To dinner and discovery," she replied, clinking his glass and sipping the cold, clear vodka.

"Discovery?"

"Sure. Tonight we'll start to discover who we are for each other."

"Sounds like the introduction to a self-help workshop, not a dinner date," Clay said lightly.

Giggling, Sheryl responded, "I guess it did sound that way. I wanted to say something meaningful about tonight, and I didn't do a good job of it. I'm kinda nervous, actually."

"Nervous? You could have fooled me. You look cool as a cucumber. I'm the one that's nervous. I couldn't even create a good toast a minute ago. Heck, I was perfectly fine until I turned down your street," Clay said.

"So, are you saying I make you nervous?" Sheryl said playfully.

"No, I can't explain the reason, except," Clay struggled to figure out the source of his nervousness, "You never told me you live by a lighthouse."

"No reason to tell you. You've never expressed any interest in where I live. Besides, what does that have to do with you being nervous right now?"

"I don't know. Maybe I'm being super-sensitive to lighthouses now that I own one." Did he dare tell her more? What would Sheryl think about his lighthouse nightmares?

"You're nervous. I'm nervous. I guess we'll just be nervous together," Sheryl concluded.

"Here's to nerves," Clay raised his glass one more time.

"To nerves," Sheryl clinked his glass with hers.

"Well, I'm glad the confessionary period of the evening is over," Clay said.

"Could be more confessions to come. You never know," she teased. Clay's heart twitched. At this moment looking into her eyes, he didn't care what happened tonight, or what was to be revealed. He was happy to be sitting here with this amazing woman. More than happy, he was beginning to feel he belonged here next to her. A peacefulness grew from within, and the nervousness began to fade away.

"What is it? You're looking at me strangely," Sheryl asked.

"I am? Oh, sorry, I'm just really glad to be here, Sheryl. And, just a few seconds ago I noticed that I was relaxed. The nerves are gone. Good scotch I guess." Clay looked at his mostly empty glass.

Sheryl's face lit up with joy. "I'm glad you're relaxed, but it's not because of the scotch." Then as if flipping the channels on a TV she changed the topic. "How was your appointment with Dr. Shildstein? Or don't you want to share it with me?"

"I don't mind at all. In fact, your name came up."

"Oh? By you, or by her?" There was that jealous tone in her voice again, Clay thought.

"By me. She asked if I had anyone I could talk to about God. I said you."

Clay proceeded to brief Sheryl on parts of his session with the psychiatrist. He noticed that as he spoke about the doctor's explanation for the lighthouse painting, the expression on Sheryl's face softened. Whatever jealously-based suspicion that Sheryl had was gone; replaced by delight in the miracle of it all.

"Where did the conversation about God come in?" Sheryl asked.

"The lighthouse imagery. She quoted some scripture about light." He retrieved the yellow note from his shirt pocket. "Psalm 119 verse 105 and Matthew 5 verse 15."

He handed the note to her. She immediately walked over to a bookshelf and removed a Bible. Sitting back down on the couch she thumbed rapidly through the pages while holding the book on her thigh so both of them could see the passages. Clay couldn't help but notice that she was sitting closer to him now, shoulders and thighs touching ever so slightly. For the first time, his nose detected the faintest hint of perfume. The scent was very pleasing, but what he appreciated even more than the scent was the subtleness of its application. He disliked being around women who believed they had to saturate themselves in perfume to the extent that after a date his clothes reeked of the stuff. Not Sheryl. The scent was teasingly light, mysterious, sensuous, and far in the background. It had the right effect. He felt the urge to move even closer but didn't budge.

Sheryl read the two passages aloud although Clay struggled to pay attention to the words. His mind was still processing the strong allure of her perfume and closeness.

"So, she gave you a lighthouse painting and suggested these passages about emitting the light of God. A perfect conversation for an art dealer or pastor, but not a psychiatrist. There's something about the lighthouse or lighthouses that you haven't told me yet," Sheryl surmised while studying his face.

Clay had always valued Sheryl's instincts at the office. She had a sense about people that he lacked. But now these instincts were focused like a laser on him, making him a little uncomfortable. Right then, gazing out the window, Clay knew he wouldn't be able to conceal anything from her. He looked away from her out the window as if to find courage and answers.

A crack in the clouds just above the jagged mountains to the west permitted a slice of orange-tinted sunlight to escape and treat the bleakness of the early evening to a sliver of golden sunset.

"Well, you have to promise not to think I'm crazy," Clay said.

"I already know you're crazy and that's why I'm cooking a lovely dinner for you tonight in my home. You can tell me anything."

For some reason, he decided to trust her. "I've been having nightmares," he said.

A buzzer sounded from the kitchen.

Chapter 62

"Let me check the roast," Sheryl said, walking into the kitchen.

"Is there anything I can do to help?" Clay asked, relieved that he had a respite from having to reveal his nightmares to her.

"You can open the wine," she replied.

While Sheryl looked in the oven, Clay opened the bottle of Pinot Noir that he had brought and poured a taste into one of the wine glasses from the table. After swirling the wine around the glass and sniffing the vapors emitted from the luscious red wine he took a sip. Nodding his head in approval he proceeded to pour a full serving into each of their glasses.

"Something smells wonderful. What are you preparing, Sheryl?"

"Prime rib and baked potatoes. For appetizers, I'm trying something different." She held out for his inspection a cookie sheet filled with rock salt and a dozen oysters on the half shell.

"That looks like Oysters Rockefeller," said Clay.

"It is. Never fixed them before so I hope they turn out okay."

"I love Oysters Rockefeller! What a treat. I never fixed them myself though."

Sheryl removed the roast from the oven and placed the pan on the stove. She covered the meat in aluminum foil to rest. Then she placed the cookie sheet with oysters into the oven, closed the oven door and increased the temperature to 425 degrees. From the refrigerator, she removed a bowl of tossed salad and placed it on the table.

"The oysters will be ready in about eight minutes," she said and walked over to Clay to accept the glass of wine he was holding for her.

She took her glass, swirled the wine, breathed in the released vapor, and took a sip. Her eyes sparkled in response. "Excellent choice of wine, Mr. Austin, but don't think for a moment that you're going to avoid telling me about your nightmares."

"Of course not. I'm just waiting for the right time."

"You have seven minutes before I have to remove the oysters from the oven. Start talking, mister," she smiled and stepped closer to him.

At this particular moment, he didn't want to talk. He desperately wanted to embrace her, hold her close to him. The magnetic feeling was almost overpowering. She was standing so close. He fought to clear his head enough to speak. It didn't help that she kept studying his face with those amazing eyes of hers. Was she teasing him by standing so close? Or was she inviting his advances?

"Quit stalling," she whispered softly. "Tell me about the nightmare. There will be no food until you talk. We have ways to make you talk," Sheryl said in a terrible imitation of a German accent repeating the famous line from the 1970s TV series, *Hogan's Heroes*.

"There are two nightmares. One is recurring. The other I've had just once. They both involve a lighthouse that is almost identical to the Point Deception lighthouse."

For the second time today, Clay recalled the details of his nightmares. The oven timer buzzed just as he finished his summary of the lawnmower army dream.

"Those dreams are terrifying. I get shivers just thinking about them," she said, wrapping her arms around herself as if for protection from the imagery in her head. The oven buzzer sounded again. "Can I trust you with a knife to carve the roast?"

"Are you asking me if I'm sane enough to handle a knife without slicing both of us to pieces?" Clay said.

"That's the question of the moment," she said with a twinkle in her eyes. "It's common knowledge that anyone who is being sieged in a lighthouse by an army of lawnmowers cannot be trusted with knives," she playfully said over her shoulder while heading to the kitchen.

Clay wasn't sure how to take Sheryl's humorous attitude about his dreams. Sharing the dreams with her hadn't been easy. He wasn't used to being vulnerable, and now she seemed to be treating his dreams like they were cartoons, rather than expressions of a deep-seated psychological wound. He resolved to be more guarded with her.

"The oysters look fabulous. Why don't we have them with the main course rather than as an appetizer?" She said.

"Sounds good to me. I'm starving," he said, grateful that he didn't have to talk about his nightmares with her any longer.

He carved the prime rib roast while Sheryl removed the oysters and rock salt to a shallow serving dish. She handed him a serving platter for the beef and turned off the kitchen light. They carried the beef and oysters to the dining table that occupied one end of the room. She dimmed the light in the modern chandelier that hung above the table and motioned Clay to be seated across from her. Instead, he stepped behind her, pulled back her chair from the table and positioned it so she could easily be seated.

"Thank you, sir. Are you always so gentlemanly?"

"Yep. Unless I'm too busy running from attacking lawn mowers." Clay winced. Why did he say that? The remark would open the door for her to ask more questions about the dreams and his session with Dr. Shildstein. After Sheryl's lighthearted reaction to his nightmares moments ago he didn't want to go there again. He took his seat across the table from her.

"Let's pray," she said reaching both hands across the table, gesturing that he should do the same and hold her hands. "Heavenly Father, we're so grateful for the blessings of this day. Thank you, Lord, for this evening of companionship, understanding, and discovery. Give each of us the courage to share, and the wisdom not to judge. We're also grateful for the food you've provided. May it nourish our bodies and make us strong. In Jesus' name, we pray. Amen."

The prayer was over, so Clay relaxed his grip on Sheryl's hands and started to pull them back. However, she continued to hold both of his hands firmly. The action caught him by surprise. He returned the grip and looked at her. The warmth and affection from her eyes were so strong it made Clay's heart ache. He had the feeling that once again Sheryl was looking with compassion deep into his soul. She didn't say a word. She just held his hands firmly until the subtle grin on her face grew into a radiant smile. After a final squeeze she released his hands.

Whatever dark doubts about Sheryl that had entered his heart before sitting down had vanished.

"Help yourself to the oysters," she said.

With a serving spoon, he transferred one of the oysters in its shell to his plate. She did the same.

They both put an oyster into their mouths at the same time and slowly chewed.

"Fabulous. Best I've ever tasted," Clay said, his mouth still partially filled.

"Yum!" Exclaimed Sheryl. "I did good."

Sheryl passed the platters of meat and baked potatoes. Then she followed with the salad bowl. Clay refilled their wine glasses, and the two ate hungrily for a few minutes without speaking further.

"May I ask you a question?" Sheryl said, breaking the silence.

"Sure," he said as if he had a choice.

"Will you tell me more about your sessions with the psychiatrist? You've never said anything about what Dr. Shildstein had to say about your dreams or the time you fainted in your office a few weeks ago."

"That's two questions, not one," Clay said with a slight grin.

"I'm serious, Clay. Look, I care for you a great deal." Her voice started to tremble slightly. "Why won't you open up and let me know what's going on inside you? Don't you know that whatever you can tell to your doctor, you can tell me?"

"I guess I don't know that I . . ."

Before he could say another word, Sheryl interrupted. "This was a bad idea, Clay. It's not going to work out. You should leave." She no longer looked at him.

Her gaze was directed past him to the window and the darkness beyond. Tears filled her eyes.

One part of Clay wanted to stand up and leave; to escape the questions and the pressure to reveal his fears. But, the other part of Clay wanted to stay, to bare his soul to this woman. He was torn. Silence filled the room. Tears began to streak down Sheryl's eyes as she continued to look into the dark night.

"I'm sorry. I'll tell you about the sessions."

"You don't have to."

"I should tell you. No reason why not. It's just that I'm not used to sharing this kind of stuff with others."

"You share it with her!" Sheryl spat out the words.

"Well, it's her job to ask questions and listen. I pay her."

"Oh, so is that what makes the difference, Clay? If you don't pay for it, it's not worth anything? What do you pay her, Clay? Two hundred dollars an hour? Three hundred dollars? Maybe I should charge you for this dinner and use of my condo for an evening. Five Hundred dollars sounds about right. If you pay me $500 will you think I'm valuable enough to talk to?" The tears were flowing freely now. With each sentence, she became more and more distressed and emotional.

Although her words bit hard into his heart, he began to think defensively to her outburst. She was blowing this whole thing way out of proportion. He just wanted to shout back at her and tell her to chill out. Can't they just eat their dinner and talk about the weather or something?

He took another swallow of wine and collected his thoughts. He was in unfamiliar waters and had no idea of how to navigate out of the danger.

"Sheryl, I'm very sorry. Here's the difference. With Dr. Shildstein, I don't care what she thinks about me, as long as she doesn't commit me to an asylum or something. With you, though, I care deeply about what you think of me."

She looked at him, wet tears still running down her face. "So, do you just want to have a superficial relationship, Clay? Just want to tell me things that make you look good? Well, no thanks. I've had one of those. If we're going to be together, it'll be because we are both vulnerable and humble with each other. That means we talk about our warts, our inner fears, and joys." She took a drink of wine in between sniffles.

He had a choice to make. Hold or fold.

The words came from out of the blue. "Sheryl, listen carefully. There isn't another person in this world I'd rather share my innermost thoughts with than you. I mean that. But, I need a lot of help communicating this type of stuff. It doesn't come easy to me at all. Heck, most of the time I'm not sure of my own feelings. I'm willing to try with you. Will you help me?"

They looked at each other over the table. She said nothing. Clay stood up and walked around the table and stood next to her.

"Stand up a moment please," he said tenderly.

She stood and faced him. He leaned down and gently kissed her lips, still salty with tears. Then he held her closely in his arms and whispered, "I'm sorry. Can I tell you more about my shrink sessions?"

She pulled her head back from his chest and looked at him. "Our dinner is getting cold."

"While we eat I'll tell you all about what she said."

Sheryl went to the bathroom for a tissue. Clay stood by the table and waited. A slight flash caught his attention through the window. At first, he thought it was reflected headlights from a passing car on the street below. There were no cars. A few seconds later there was another flash like the turning on and off of a powerful light. Lightning? Not likely. On the third flash, he knew what he was seeing. The Alki lighthouse was operating. At this angle from the lighthouse and being onshore, not in the bay, all he could see was a small portion of the bright light as the reflector rotated.

The irony of the moment didn't escape him. Over the next few minutes, he'd be sharing the meaning behind his lighthouse nightmares while outside over his shoulder a Coast Guard lighthouse helped mammoth container ships find their way through the dark waters of Elliott Bay.

Chapter 63

n between bites of the fabulous dinner, Clay told Sheryl what the doctor had said about his recurring lighthouse nightmare. Sheryl listened and said little in reaction to Dr. Shildstein's analysis that his nightmare was being triggered by how his success at work conflicted with his self-perception of not being good enough.

Clay paused just long enough to take a final bite of salad and pour the remaining wine into their glasses.

"I have ice cream and hot fudge topping for dessert. Let me clear the dishes and then I'd love to hear more."

"Sounds good to me. Is coffee on the menu this evening?" He asked.

"No coffee, sorry, but I have tea."

Clay remembered that Sheryl didn't drink coffee. It made sense that she didn't have coffee or a coffee maker in the house. "Tea will be fine," he said.

Outside, rain began to lash against the large windows.

"Will it ever stop raining? Would you mind starting a fire? It's just gas. The switch is on the wall to the left of the mantle."

He lit the gas log fireplace at the opposite end of the room. They settled into two modern armchairs that faced the flames to eat their hot fudge sundaes.

"I'm really surprised about your perception of not being good enough, Clay. My goodness, look at what you've accomplished in your life. And, you're always so confident and strong. Actually, that's one of the things that attracted me to you— your strength and confidence without ego."

"I don't understand it completely yet. Dr. Shildstein thinks I entered a perfect storm that was an emotional tipping point. Makes sense when you think about all that's going on. The financial hole the agency was in, the layoffs, Suzette's firing, the offer from Pitt-Needham. All these things crashed on me at the same time. I've been challenged like never before. My brain started to freak out, I guess."

"Makes sense. Your circuits overloaded. Is that what caused you to faint in the office?"

"Yes, pretty much."

"But, you didn't just faint. You screamed like some monster was attacking you. Then you passed out," she said.

"Yep, well, you'd scream too if a lawnmower was trying to chew you to pieces."

"A lawnmower! You saw a lawnmower? In your office just like in your dreams? What's with all these hostile lawnmowers, Clay?"

He stared into the fire. "Let me tell you about Vic."

At midnight Clay finished telling Sheryl about Vic and the lawnmower incident, and about Vic and the stacks of wood.

Throughout his recalling of childhood memories, Sheryl had sat motionless and silent in her chair, legs pulled up close to her chest, eyes alternating between Clay and the gas-lit flames of the fireplace. Now she reached out her left hand to him. He took it.

Clay held her hand but couldn't bring himself to look at Sheryl, so certain he was that he'd see disgust and disapproval there.

"Thank you for that gift, Clay. Look at me please." She tugged his hand gently. Slowly he turned to look at her. "Thank you for sharing about your sessions with Shildstein and especially about your step-father." Instead of disapproval in her eyes, Clay saw moist eyes and deep compassion. She was holding his hand so firmly it almost hurt.

"Do you think I'm going crazy?" Clay asked seriously.

"No, but a battle is being waged inside you, Clay. Satan is telling you lies that you're not good enough for what's ahead. He's sending you nightmares and hallucinations to shake your confidence."

"Oh, great. You think the devil is in my head now. That makes me feel better," he said sarcastically. "I thought my nightmares were just because of an emotional scar from childhood, not some evil guy with horns and a pitch fork."

"Who do you think is responsible for that emotional scar, Clay?"

"Huh?"

"The emotional scar you're referring to is nothing more than a story you're telling yourself about the painful episodes with Vic."

"You're losing me."

"The terrible experience with the lawnmower happened. Deep inside, you made Vic's anger at you mean that you weren't good enough to be loved by him. Your mind made up that story, but I believe that the story—the lie—is the work of Satan. That is how he pulls us away from God. He uses deception and lies to darken our hearts, to undermine our sense of who we are—to build a wall between us and the love of God."

"You and Dr. Shildstein think alike," said Clay.

"I don't know about that, but it sounds like she's either a Christian or is familiar enough with Christianity to quote from the Bible. You know, Clay, it is very unusual for a psychiatrist to refer to God during treatment. It's no coincidence that out of all the shrinks in Seattle, you found her."

"Yeah, I guess so. The evidence keeps growing that I'm going through a pretty weird phase in my life."

"Do you consider me a part of that weirdness?" Sheryl asked seriously.

He grinned, "Oh, you are right smack in the middle of all the weirdness."
They smiled at each other in the silence.

Suddenly a deep horn sounded from off in the distance. Just a brief one-second blast followed by silence.

"What was that?" Clay asked.

"That's the foghorn at the lighthouse. It must be getting foggy outside."

"How long does it last? It's after midnight."

Laughing, Sheryl said, "You have a lot to learn about lighthouses. Many are also equipped with foghorns. As soon as visibility falls below a certain level, the horn starts sounding. It'll run until the fog lifts."

The horn sounded again as if to punctuate Sheryl's statement.

"How do you sleep?"

"You get used to it. And it doesn't sound all that often."

"Speaking of sleep, it's getting late. I should go but let me help you clean up the kitchen first."

"Oh, you don't need to do that. There's not much to do. Tell me, can I count on you for church Sunday?"

His first impulse was to make up an excuse for not being able to go, but something made him change his mind.

"Sure, if we can have brunch at my place afterward?"

"That's a deal."

"I have . . . we have . . . a big week ahead, Sheryl. By this time next week, we'll both be employees of Pitt-Needham." He stood up from his chair, and she did the same.

"How do you want to celebrate?" She asked.

"I hadn't thought about it, to be honest. Let's cross that bridge when we get to it."

"Before I forget, your travel itinerary is almost complete for the Board meeting and visits to the offices in Boise, Portland, and San Francisco."

"Thanks. One of my first conversations with Phil will be about your new position. If you're still interested, that is."

"I'm very interested, Clay, but let me first check Pitt's employment rules about couples working together."

He paused for a moment. Sheryl had said "couples." It was going to take a while for him to adjust to the fact that he was part of a "couple" now. "Oh, right. I guess after Friday we both need to read the new rule book."

Clay's pause didn't escape Sheryl. She stepped close and wrapped her arms around his waist. "How do you feel about being a 'couple,' Mr. Austin?" She asked, looking him squarely in the eyes.

"I like."

Charles Besondy

They kissed standing by the fireplace as the fog horn continued its sporadic, lonely song, and the light flashed its signal in the darkness to all who could see it.

Chapter 64

Ten days later Clay was standing at the elegant check-in desk of the Fairmont Hotel in Dallas. It was 1:30 in the afternoon. The Pitt-Needham Board meeting was scheduled to start at 3:00 at the company's office. Clay calculated he had just enough time to check in, catch up on his messages and walk the three blocks to the agency's headquarters in the Arts District at 2001 Ross Avenue.

While waiting for the front desk clerk to process his check-in, Clay couldn't help but compare this clerk and hotel to the hotel in Reef Bay—his last hotel stay. The woman clerk was impeccably dressed in starched blouse, dark blue blazer, and gray slacks. Each time she looked at Clay, it was with a courteous smile that seemed to genuinely welcome him. Indeed, the check-in was so expertly and personally handled Clay felt he had just been warmly welcomed into a friend's home, not coldly processed like a side of beef.

"Here's your key, Mr. Austin. Our concierge desk is to the right if you need anything during your stay with us. Do you need assistance with your luggage?"

"No thank you, Juanita." Clay said after noting her name badge. He took the card key and pulled his suitcase toward the bank of elevators. He stepped inside one of the cars. No one joined him, so he punched the 15th floor button. Touching the hotel elevator's button reminded him of the little elevator in his building back in Seattle that had the colorful "AD" logo on it. The button's label had just been changed from ADB to AD a few weeks earlier after Suzette's departure. Would they be changing it again? How soon before they removed the "A" and erased Clay Austin from company history altogether, he wondered.

In his room, he quickly unpacked, found the guest iron and touched up his suits and shirts to remove a few wrinkles.

While changing clothes, he began to think about the Board meeting. The more he thought about it, the more nervous he became. He had already reviewed the agenda distributed by Phil's assistant. He noted that the first item on the agenda was a formal vote on acceptance of Clay Austin as a new member of the Board of Directors. Clay wouldn't be allowed into the meeting until the vote was taken and his position on the Board approved, just as Phil had explained to him. Great, he'd have to sit in the hallway like a fraternity pledge waiting to be summoned into the room after the vote. But, what if the vote failed to approve him? That was a possibility. What if just enough Board members had their doubts about Clay's ability to contribute? What if he was blackballed? How humiliating would that be?

He'd have to leave the office and walk back to the hotel a rejected man. A man not good enough for an international marketing agency.

Clay focused on dressing to push the negative thoughts out of his mind. He slipped on his gray Armani suit, white shirt with French cuffs and an expensive silk tie he had purchased specifically for the occasion. Its colors and distinctive pattern made a subtle statement Clay thought was important. It was creative and unusual, but not so unusual that it drew attention. Clay chose a simple white pocket square so as not to compete with the tie. He examined himself in the full-length mirror.

"At least I *look* like I know something," he said to himself out loud. It was 2:30. Clay slipped his phone into the suit coat pocket, picked up his leather portfolio case and left the room.

In preparing Clay for this trip, Sheryl had provided him a map of downtown Dallas, with blue marker ink showing him the route to take from the Fairmont to the Trammel Crow Center where Pitt-Needham occupied the 35th, 36th, and 37th floors.

It was a beautiful, sunny afternoon for a walk. Clay left the hotel entrance and turned right on Akard Street. In half a block he crossed Akard and walked up Ross Street. With each step, Clay's anxiety rose. He couldn't help but think that he was walking into a situation that was going to disappoint him, or worse, utterly destroy him. He fought the negative thoughts and worked hard to replace them with confidence. After all, just last week Pitt-Needham had given he and George each very large checks. The lunch with Phil at the Columbia Tower Club last Friday, following the close of the acquisition, was encouraging as the three planned the future for the four offices now under Clay's command. The future was bright and filled with potential. No reason whatsoever to feel nervous or inferior. Good thoughts covered up the bad thoughts. He quickened his pace, now eager to get to the meeting.

Clay crossed St. Paul street and saw his destination tower above him a block ahead. The shadow of the 50-story skyscraper fell across the sidewalk in front of him, snuffing out the warm sunlight he had been enjoying. In the shade, the temperature dropped noticeably a few degrees, but Clay thought the air was still comfortable by Seattle's standards.

He was almost to Harwood Street and his destination when to the left the irritating whine of a 2-cycle engine started. Clay flinched from the unexpected sound. In the same instant, he was engulfed in a cloud of dust, leaves, and debris. He first reacted by holding up his portfolio to protect his face. Then, just as rapidly as it had started, the noise and dust stopped. Angrily, Clay looked to his left to see the source. A landscape worker with leaf blower strapped to his back stared at Clay with his mouth wide open. The worker had turned on his blower from behind a line of trees and hadn't noticed it was pointing at the sidewalk and right at Clay.

"Watch what you're doing!" Clay yelled at the man.

The worker said something in Spanish that Clay couldn't understand so Clay continued walking again, brushing the dust from his suit and hair, trying to not make any smears of dirt on his crisp white shirt.

He felt dirty and gritty as he pushed through the large rotating door at 2001 Ross Street. Worse yet, what little confidence he had restored during his walk had been blown away. He pictured himself walking into the Board meeting and being greeted by judgmental stares while the members took note of the leaves in his hair and the dirt on his shirt.

It was ten minutes before three o'clock. Time was short, but he couldn't go to Pitt's office without first checking his appearance after being engulfed in the dust. He looked around the huge lobby until he found a sign pointing toward the men's room.

He entered the restroom grateful that no one else was there to witness what he had to do. He set his portfolio on the counter while inspecting himself carefully in the large mirror. He looked okay but felt dirty. Not wanting to risk splashing water on his clothes, he grabbed a paper towel from the dispenser, wetted it and carefully wiped his face and neck. He could still feel grit under his collar, so he loosened the tie, undid the top button of his shirt and with a fresh damp paper towel wiped his neck under the collar. Next, he removed his jacket and shook it sharply like a rug to remove the dust. He noted that a barely noticeable cloud of dust appeared after he shook the expensive Armani suit coat.

With his hands, he brushed his pants. Using the damp towel from his neck, he removed the thin layer of dust that coated his Italian lace-ups.

Clay slipped on the suit coat, re-buttoned his shirt collar, adjusted the tie, and ran a comb through his hair several times to remove any possible debris.

He felt less dirty and decided after a final inspection in the mirror that his appearance was acceptable. He picked up the brown leather portfolio from the counter and walked out toward the elevators.

Chapter 65

"Good afternoon, Mr. Austin. Welcome to Pitt-Needham," the pleasant male receptionist said to Clay. "Please have a seat. I'll let Mr. Manicotti's assistant know that you've arrived."

Clay sat on a long, burgundy leather couch and was about to reach for his phone to check messages when a tall woman with long red hair walked up to him. "Mr. Austin, hello, I'm Roberta Morano, Phil's assistant. Please follow me."

Roberta directed him to a brightly colored office suite consisting of a spacious sitting area and desk. Double doors led into an executive office adjacent to the room where Clay stood. "Please have a seat, Mr. Austin. I'll take you to the Board room shortly," she said with a slight Italian accent. "Can I get you water, coffee, or a soda?"

"No thank you." He sat down in a stylish leather chair and took notice of the office suite. Roberta went to her desk and stood behind the elevated platform that held her computer keyboard and two massive monitors. There was no chair.

The entire office suite looked like it had been transported directly from an Italian museum of modern art. The furniture, carpet, light fixtures, and colors combined to give the space a decidedly international appearance. Instead of art masterpieces on the walls, Manicotti's decorator had commissioned numerous impressionist cityscapes—one for each of the 20 cities around the world in which Pitt-Needham had an office. Clay noticed that the decorator was going to have to adjust the arrangement of paintings to make room for the newest city in Pitt's footprint, Seattle.

He looked at his watch. It was a quarter past three. How long did a membership vote take, he wondered? If they took a long time was that a good thing, or a bad thing? He started thinking about all the courtroom dramas he had read or seen in which the defense attorney and the accused waited nervously for the return of the jury and the reading of their verdict.

His phone vibrated signaling a text had arrived.

It was from Sheryl, "Excited for you."

He typed his reply, "Thnx." He didn't know what else to say.

"George arriving DFW tonight. At hotel around 8." Sheryl reminded Clay that George would join him at the Annual Meeting on Tuesday.

"Got it," he replied.

"You okay?" She typed.

"Sure. Waiting for the vote. Everyone very nice." *Right, everything is great except for being engulfed in a cloud of dust by a leaf blower.*

"Great. Call me later."

"K"

He was about to check his email when Roberta walked from behind her desk toward him. "I can show you to the Boardroom now, Mr. Austin."

Showtime. He wasn't ready. He desperately wanted to check his appearance one more time in a mirror. What if he still had dust on his shirt or a twig on his Armani coat? He put on a brave smile and followed her down the hall to double doors of mahogany. A bronze plate on the door said, "Boardroom."

Clay's heart pounded in his chest. He felt as though he was being carried forward toward the massive doors by some invisible force that he had no power to resist. Roberta's right hand reached for the heavy bronze handle to open the door for Clay. He felt the force pushing him forward. Roberta smiled as she swung open the ten-foot tall door for Clay. He didn't feel his feet walking. Instead, there was a sensation of being swept forward on a moving walkway. He was at the door opening now. A few more steps and he'd be inside. In a flash, his kayak nightmare came to mind. It was the same terrible feeling of being carried toward his doom. The imagery of the dream and the sensation of having no control swirled through Clay's mind. His vision narrowed like going into a tunnel. For a split second, he thought he was going to faint. *Please, God. Not here. Not now.*

From somewhere in the distance Clay became aware of a dull noise. As his mind slowly regained its focus, he saw Phil Manicotti standing in front of him clapping. He looked around the large room. The ten other Board members were also standing, hands clapping. They were applauding him. The Board of Directors of Pitt-Needham, the 12th largest marketing agency in the world, were applauding him, their newest member.

Chapter 66

"Welcome, Clay," Phil said as the applause died down. "Please take a seat next to Tad Singh so we can continue with the agenda. There will be adequate time for you to get to know the other Board members at dinner."

Clay walked to his seat at the huge table. Tad Singh greeted him by shaking his hand firmly and motioned for Clay to have a chair next to him. Clay recalled from his research of the Board members that Tad was Founder and Chairman of Gotta, India's largest Internet service. He had engineering degrees from Indian Institute of Technology and Massachusetts Institute of Technology, plus an MBA from Stanford. Clay didn't think he'd bond with Singh by talking about Oregon Duck football.

After everyone was seated, Phil referred to the printed agenda in front of him. "I'm pleased to report that all of the topics on the shareholder ballot have been approved by shareholders. We shouldn't have any surprises in the annual meeting tomorrow. For the record that means that PWC has been approved as auditor, the number of Board members has been increased from eleven to twelve seats; and the executive compensation plan was also approved. This brings us to the topic of the Pitt-Needham growth strategy. As you know, in our last meeting we appointed Eldwin Lum, of our Singapore office to head the strategic growth committee. Eldwin's report was in your information deck, and he will present the highlights to us today."

The room lights dimmed slightly. Eldwin Lum stepped to the front of the room and just to the side of a massive LCD monitor that displayed the first slide of his report. As he began the presentation, Clay recalled that before Lum was appointed Director of Pitt's Asia Pacific operations two years ago, he had an impressive track record of building cohesive brands by acquiring businesses, stripping them down to their core, and reassembling the different businesses together into something greater than the sum of their parts. He was called the "Puzzle Master" for good reason. He came from a wealthy family that had made its fortune in finance and shipping in South East Asia.

"In conclusion, over the next twenty years, the growth opportunity for Pitt-Needham lies in two regions, Asia Pacific and Africa, as represented by the map." Then Eldwin Lum used a red laser pen to point to specific countries on the map. "Our presence in these areas is weak at the present time. McCann and Grey are particularly strong."

The slide changed to the same map with different countries highlighted in color. "These countries, however, represent the fastest growth in three key economic factors: average disposable income, mobile communications, and population growth. BBDO is the only one of our competitors so far to show much of an interest in these areas. The competition for acquiring existing agencies hasn't driven up prices as in other countries, but I don't expect this situation to last much longer. Bargains exist for now. In your packet, I included a list of six agencies. These are small shops with strong reputations in their respective countries and relatively good talent."

The slide on the monitor changed again. "My recommendation to the Board is that we approach the six firms. Our objective is to acquire three of the six, which I believe can be acquired for roughly three times earnings, or 10 million dollars." Lum returned the light level in the room to normal, turned off the monitor and sat down in his chair.

"Thank you, Eldwin. Good work. Let's discuss this openly before voting on your proposal. Who has questions for Eldwin?"

Clay noted that everyone in the room had questions for the Asia Pacific director. Many were very insightful questions that Clay never would have thought to ask. Once again, he felt that he was out of his league in this group of people.

He recognized as the newest member of the Board that everyone would be keen to hear his insight, especially since his agency had just been acquired. Had the Board gone through the same analysis and approval process for Austin-Davis? Of course, it had. Clay couldn't help but reflect on the fact that Pitt bought Austin-Davis for $21 million and was now considering purchasing three shops for half that amount. He wondered what other agencies in Seattle or Portland were on the shopping list before they decided on his company.

Clay pushed those questions from his mind. What he needed now was a really intelligent question to ask about Lum's proposal that would impress the other Board members.

He didn't have long to think because Cathy Denaghey, who sat directly across the table from Clay, directed a question at him.

"Clay, would this expansion that Eldwin is proposing give you an advantage for pitching Nike or Alaska Airlines?"

Great question. Clay didn't have a great answer. He should have had an answer. Heck, he should have been thinking about how Lum's proposal would impact the four shops under his control now. He had read the report on the plane to Dallas, but he didn't think about it from the perspective of attracting new business. It was a rookie mistake. Now he was on the spot and had to recover.

"Alaska Air hasn't shown any interest west of Hawaii and certainly not Africa. I believe Yukon Air, which the Seattle office has handled for several years, could be enthusiastic about all of our capabilities in Asia Pacific." He was careful not to reveal specific expansion plans. Even here, Clay felt he needed to honor client confidentiality.

"What about Nike?" She asked again.

"Honestly, I don't know. Austin-Davis was too small to be taken seriously by Nike, so we were never able to get a conversation going. We didn't have them on our target list. Their agency, WK, has offices in Delhi, Shanghai, and Tokyo, as Eldwin certainly knows. My guess is if we're stronger in Asia Pacific and Africa it certainly doesn't hurt us if the account ever goes out for review."

While Clay spoke, he intentionally looked at each of the Directors. This enabled him to gauge body language and ascertain how his response was being received. Unfortunately, he wasn't seeing any response. Not a good sign. No one was nodding their head in agreement. Several were making notes. Nobody looked him in the eyes. Clay sensed he'd better come up with a more positive answer to her question.

"This week I'm visiting each of the offices in my region. New business is at the top of my agenda. I want to know what accounts are currently being chased, and how the four offices can combine forces as needed for a major pitch. I'm a believer in having specific strategies for landing big whales like Nike." Clay scanned the room. Some heads were nodding.

Phil spoke up, "Clay and I are visiting Boise, Portland, Seattle and San Francisco after the Annual Meeting. And, I should remind the Board of why we acquired Clay's agency and included him on the Board. He knows how to be profitable with smaller accounts. None of our offices are very adept at making money with accounts that bill less than $5 million. Austin-Davis was very profitable, at least until this year." Phil looked at Clay and winked.

In response, Clay grinned and nodded his head as if to signal to the others in the room that he and Phil had just revealed a closely held secret. It was an act. Before now he hadn't known why his agency had been acquired. Both he and George had wondered, but at no time during the negotiations did they ask the simple question, "Why?" Furthermore, he now understood why he was sitting here in this room. He had specific expertise Pitt-Needham wanted on the Board. Clay concluded the international agency had a growth strategy that involved small-to-medium sized accounts. He was definitely going to talk to Phil more about this.

Phil's remarks appeared to have appeased Denaghey because she didn't ask Clay any more questions, but Clay could tell by the way she was scribbling in her notebook that she was irritated. He made a mental note to learn more about Cathy Denaghey.

Lum added to Phil's comment, "Clay, as we narrow down the list of acquisition candidates I'm hoping I can ask you to help me evaluate them. Your perspective will be valuable."

Clay could see that Lum was sincere. "Whatever I can do to help. I look forward to working with you, Eldwin."

"If there are no further questions for Eldwin, I propose that we vote on the proposal to proceed with the acquisition process as outlined," Phil said, eager to keep the meeting moving.

"I second," said a voice from the far end of the table. It was Larry Bloom, the Chief Financial Officer.

"All in favor raise your hand," directed Phil.

All hands rose.

"All not in favor raise your hands," said Phil.

"Let the Secretary record in the minutes that the proposal to proceed with Strategic Growth Plan 2B has been approved unanimously," said Phil.

"Before we adjourn, I remind you that the Annual Shareholder meeting begins at ten in the morning at the Fairmont where many of you are staying. As usual, those of you on the executive committee are expected to arrive no later than nine o'clock."

After a brief pause, Phil closed the meeting. "Unless there is any further business to be brought before the Board I move that the Board adjourn."

"I second," said Bloom. Apparently, it was his accustomed role in these meetings to second Phil's motions.

"We're adjourned. Thank you, everyone. Reception and dinner will be in the dining room on the 36th floor. Please take the elevator to thirty-six. Roberta will meet you there and lead everyone to the dining room."

He made it! He had completed his first Board meeting. As Clay gathered his belongings, preparing to leave the table, he surmised that his performance was adequate, but in need of improvement. He would be much better prepared next time. On the positive side, he felt good that both Eldwin and Phil had voiced confidence in him. He better understood why he was on the Board and how he could contribute. It was silly of him to think he couldn't perform at this level. He stood up from his chair just as Tad Singh did the same next to him.

In a clipped Indian accent Tad said, "Clay, I agree with Phil that your expertise with small accounts is a much-needed addition to the agency. We handle large international brands very well, but those are limited in number, and the competition is fierce. If we are to succeed in emerging markets, we must succeed with small accounts and grow as they grow," Tad said.

"It does require a different mindset and process. It helps to have a start-up mentality. I've even toyed with using a term like 'agile marketing' to convey the concept."

"I see. Well, perhaps we can discuss this further with Lum at dinner." Tad picked up his phone and notepad from the table. He motioned that Clay should do the same, so they could make their way to the elevator.

As Tad glanced at Clay's portfolio still on the table, Clay noticed a change in his expression. It happened so fast Clay almost missed it. There was a look of surprise, followed by revulsion. Then it was gone. The expression seemed totally out of context considering the nature of the conversation they had been having. Tad headed to the door without saying another word.

Puzzled by what he had noticed, Clay prepared to leave the room. He checked that his phone was still in his coat pocket, picked up his notes and started to place them into his leather portfolio. Then he saw it. A small dried leaf was lodged in the portfolio's strap. That must have been what Tad saw. Who else saw it? It was so obvious. Why hadn't he seen it before now?

Clay immediately figured out how the leaf became attached to his expensive leather portfolio. The crinkled, brown leaf was a remnant from the debris that showered Clay during his walk to the office. He recalled instinctively holding up the portfolio to protect his face.

It was just a small leaf, but Clay was horrified to think what Tad must have thought. And what about the others? They're probably whispering about him right now in the elevator—the hick from Seattle. His whole personae of valuable Board member in a tailored Armani suit had been destroyed by a single dead leaf.

Embarrassed, Clay quickly brushed the leaf from the portfolio and watched it fall to the spotless, polished hardwood floor at his feet. Shaken, he opened the portfolio and placed his notes inside. He stood by the table; the last person in the room. Through the ceiling-to-floor windows, Clay stared across the Dallas skyline to the sun low in the blue sky far to the west.

Chapter 67

lay left the Board Room, turned right in the hallway and walked to the elevators in the main reception. The reception area was vacant. Everyone had left. He punched the elevator's Down button and waited. After several long minutes an elevator door slid open. He stepped inside, pushed the 36 button, and tried to collect his thoughts. Seconds later the elevator door opened again. He stepped out into a hallway on the 36th floor. No one was there to greet him. Where was Roberta? He had no idea where the dining room was. Should he turn left, or right? He thought he heard a group conversation from his left down the hall. He ambled in the direction of the sound.

Soon the walls of the hallway gave way to a large open office, easily four times as large as Austin-Davis. Some people were still at desks, others preparing to leave for the evening. To his left was a glass-walled conference room. Many people were standing in it talking and laughing. This was the noise Clay had heard, but these people weren't Board members. He saw a cake on the conference table. These were employees celebrating an occasion with a cake at the end of the workday. A young man with tattooed arms, black t-shirt, black tight jeans and red Keds noticed Clay. He stepped out of the conference room.

"Can I help you, bro?" The young man was working on his hipness, Clay noted.

"Yes, where's the dining room?"

"Do you mean the kitchen?" Keds Boy said.

"I don't think so. There's supposed to be a dining room on this floor. The Board members are there now." Clay was beginning to feel out of place.

Keds Boy took a step back into the conference room. Clay could see him asking others about the dining room. Several heads turned and looked at Clay like he was an alien. Keds Boy stuck his head outside of the conference room as if it was too dangerous to venture closer to the alien.

"There's a dining room at the other side of the office. Just go back to the elevators and keep walking."

"Ok, thanks," Clay replied, but Keds Boy never heard him. He was already back inside waiting to be served his piece of cake.

Clay reached the bank of elevators where several employees waited. They gave him a cautious smile as he walked by. Part of Clay wanted to leave. Just get on the down elevator, go back to the hotel, check out and head for the airport to grab the next flight back to Seattle. Instead, he kept walking in the direction of the dining room.

With each step, the sensation of smallness he had experienced in Seattle began to overtake him. With each step, he felt like he was either shrinking or the office was growing larger. He couldn't do it. He couldn't walk into the dining room knowing that everyone by now was enjoying a cocktail and talking about the "the dumb leaf who blew in from Seattle."

He passed a door with a sign, "Men." He stepped inside the restroom to regroup. Clay first inspected his appearance and looked closely at the portfolio. Not a hair was out of place. No dirt or debris was visible. No renegade leaves peeked out from the white pocket square. The mirror told him he looked great, but inside he felt like a fraud. Actually, right now he felt worse than a fraud, he felt like a total fool.

Returning to the hotel seemed like the best option. He could give Phil his resignation in the morning.

Clay's phone vibrated in his coat pocket. There were several text messages. The newest message was from a number he didn't recognize. "Where are you, Mr. Austin?" Clay concluded it must be from Roberta. How should he respond? How about, "Why didn't you wait for me?" Or, "Why do you care?" Or, "I'm not feeling well. Going back to hotel." That response had his vote, but he hesitated to type it. Instead, he checked his other messages.

One from George. Three were from Sheryl.

"Landed DFW. Call me when you can." George's text said.

Sheryl's three texts in the past hour said, "How's it going?" "So proud of my international executive." "I can do all this through Him who gives me strength. - Philippians 4:13" The last message was sent five minutes ago.

Clay grinned while still looking at his phone. Whenever he was struggling Sheryl showed up out of the blue with an encouraging smile, a text message, or quote from scripture. Right now he desperately wanted to hear her voice. Before he could talk himself out of it, he tapped the Call button.

After three rings Sheryl answered. "Hi, how's it going in Dallas?"

"Hi," Clay realized he didn't know how to express what he was feeling. "Ok, I guess. Meeting is over. Going to dinner now."

"What do you mean, 'I guess'"?

"I don't know, Sheryl, I'm not sure I'm cut out for this. I'm small potatoes compared to these people."

"If they thought you were small potatoes they wouldn't have voted you to the Board of Directors."

"After today, they'll probably re-think their vote."

"What happened?" Sheryl asked.

"Long story. Look I just called to hear your voice. Thanks for the messages. I needed them."

Sheryl was getting more concerned. "Are you okay?"

"Not really. Like I said, I'm out of my league here," said Clay.

"Remember what we've talked about, Clay. God has a plan, and He never gives you anything you can't handle. If you have faith in Him, he'll give you all the strength you need. You know the story of David and Goliath don't you?"

"Boy kills giant with slingshot."

"It's a lot more than that. David's total faith in the Lord empowered him to conquer a mighty enemy warrior—a giant of a man everyone else was afraid to fight. By the way, David went on to become one of the most famous and powerful kings in the Holy land. Even though he was a flawed human being, he loved and trusted the Lord, and the Lord loved him back."

"So, I don't need a slingshot?"

Laughing, Sheryl replied, "I seriously doubt you are on a battlefield, Clay. The only person fighting you is yourself right now. Ask God for strength and wisdom and then get out of the way. Remember, you are where you are because God put you there. Reach out to Him."

"Makes sense. Thank you."

"Thank God, not me. Now, don't you have a dinner to attend?"

"Yes. I'll call you later after dinner."

"I'd like that. Bye-bye."

"Bye."

Clay tapped the phone icon to end the call. "Okay, Lord. Let's go to dinner," he said out loud.

Clay picked up his portfolio from the counter and left the restroom without feeling a need to first check his appearance in the mirror.

Chapter 68

"**O**h, there you are! We were getting worried that you had abandoned us," Roberta said with a concerned smile.

Clay had been continuing down the hall when Roberta appeared from a room and walked toward him.

"Sorry, I had to make a call. Took a little longer than expected." It wasn't a complete lie.

"My apologies, Mr. Austin. I didn't realize until a few minutes ago that you hadn't been in either of the two groups I had led to the dining room from the elevator."

"No problem, Roberta."

She stopped by another mahogany double door and opened it for Clay. He stepped inside. The eleven other Board members were standing in small groups of two or three enjoying cocktails. A few heads turned as Clay entered. Phil looked up from his conversation with Cathy and nodded to Clay with a welcoming gesture. Cathy didn't look his way. Instead, Clay noticed that right after Phil nodded to Clay, she took a subtle step to her left to position herself between Phil and Clay. The sly move blocked Clay from Phil's view.

The room was not unlike a small banquet room in a hotel, except that three of the walls were covered with art. Each of the acrylics, watercolors, or ink etchings depicted a product or logo of a Pitt-Needham client around the world. The fourth wall was all window. Its view was to the east. Far, far beyond the buildings of downtown Dallas Clay could see the flat line of a horizon in the fading light. Not a mountain in sight, not even a hill. Just mile after mile of flat suburbs, freeways, and fields for as far as the eye could see. For a Seattleite used to seeing mountains at every point of the compass, the vastness of the Texas plains was a little discomforting.

A bar and bartender were located against one wall. A buffet table with two servers was positioned along another wall. Clay walked up to the bar, ordered a vodka tonic and, with drink in hand, turned to find a conversation to join, but first he needed to deposit his portfolio somewhere, so he had a free hand. Clay made a mental note not to bring the darn thing again.

Three round tables covered with white tablecloths and four elegant dish settings were in the center of the room. Clay noticed that most of the chairs already contained personal items the Board members had placed there to reserve a seat. Clay found one empty chair and placed his portfolio on it. He wondered who he'd be sitting next to and decided it didn't matter.

For the next fifteen minutes, Clay managed to engage in two different conversations and shake hands with four of the Board members he hadn't met yet. The lights in the room were dimmed and returned to normal several times, the signal for dinner to start.

Slowly the Board members formed a line at the buffet table. Clay thought it unusual for an elite group of executives like this to be served a buffet dinner. He changed his mind when he got closer and could see what was being served. The gleaming serving bins held steamed lobster tails, sashimi, several kinds of rice, grilled vegetables and portabello mushrooms. At the end of the table, one of the servers was carving a juicy rib roast and racks of lamb.

Clay took his full plate to the table and sat down in between two people he hadn't met yet. On his left was Geoffrey Cohen, from Scotia bank. On his right was Larry Bloom, Pitt's CFO.

During dinner, Clay gained an appreciation for the challenges of running an international company. Geoffrey and Larry chatted about exchange rates and the impact of a strong dollar.

At one point, Larry said to Clay with a strong Texas accent, "How do you like your dinner? I suppose you're accustomed to great seafood in Seattle."

"This is excellent, Larry. I must confess I was a little taken aback by the buffet table when I first saw it."

Larry smiled. "Ah, let me tell you about our little buffet here. Geoffrey, you've been a Board member for two years. I bet you haven't heard the story behind our famous Pitt-Needham buffet."

Geoffrey shook his head.

Larry took a sip of his wine, signaled for the waiter to refill his glass, and began the story as if he was about to tell a tale of adventure to two young children before bed time.

"Like other agencies, we frequently wined and dined prospective clients. It was our tradition after giving a pitch to a prospective client; we'd take them to lunch at a first-rate restaurant. Well, one day Phil, who was head of this office at the time, gave a fabulous pitch to Ballard Chemical. Everything went well. They liked our strategy and creative a lot. Phil and his team took the Ballard people to lunch at Chez Noir. As luck would have it, two executives from McCann were having lunch there, too. These guys noticed our team and recognized the marketing VP from Ballard. They concluded that Ballard Chemical was looking at making a change of agencies. We suspect that they called their office from the restaurant to report what they had learned. Well, before the day was over a Board member of McCann called a Harvard school buddy of his on the Board at Ballard Chemical. The next day we got a call from Ballard's VP of Marketing. He was instructed by his CEO to review several agencies, and McCann was to be one of the finalists."

"Two months later after a shootout, the account went to McCann. The fix had been in from the start."

"From that day forward Phil made it a rule that entertaining prospective clients would be done inside these walls where competitors couldn't snoop."

"As the money guy, I'm happy to tell you that using caterers saves us a lot of money, too. We decided to have our Board dinners here as well. Privacy and frugality are important, you know. We're eating steamed Maine lobster for the cost of a small steak in some fancy restaurant. Know this; the Board has never had to reprimand management for spending foolishly. Keep that in mind, Clay. Watch the pennies." Point made, Larry ended his story by placing a large bite of lobster into his mouth.

Clay returned his attention to his own meal. *So, the $20 million the Board approved for Austin-Davis was in their view, "a good deal." They got lobster for the price of a small steak. Maybe we should have negotiated harder for more money.*

The remainder of the dinner was pleasant. After the dinner dishes had been cleared, Clay was surprised to see that everyone stood and walked to different tables. This was so people could converse with a different set of fellow Board members while they enjoyed their coffee and dessert.

As a result, Clay was able to get to know better over half of the Board. He was impressed with everyone he met, except for Cathy Denaghey. She avoided his table. He made a mental note to learn more about Ms. Denaghey.

Chapter 69

The Pitt-Needham Annual Meeting the day following the Board Meeting was impressive and inspiring. The acquisition of Austin-Clay was highlighted as one of four major strategic moves the agency had taken in the past twelve months. The company announced that it had met its profitability objectives, its share price was up twelve percent for the year, and the dividend was increased by five percent. In terms of total billings, Pitt-Needham had advanced from 12th largest agency to 10th largest agency on the planet.

Following the meeting, Phil and Clay boarded a fractional private jet and headed for Boise, the first stop in their road show where Clay would be formally introduced as their new boss. After Boise, the two visited San Francisco, Portland and finally Seattle on Friday.

During the all-hands meeting in Seattle, it was made official; the company name would change on Monday. Austin-Davis would be replaced by Pitt-Needham.

The button on the elevator would have to be changed one more time.

A few minutes after five o'clock Clay walked Phil to the limo waiting to take him back to the airport.

"Great job this week, Clay. I think every office is really excited about the new vision you presented. Is there anything you need from me to get started?" Phil asked.

"Actually, yes. I need a really strong ops person."

"Oh, have anyone in mind?"

"Yes, my assistant, Sheryl. I'd like to promote her to Regional Operations Manager reporting to me. This way I can be effective implementing operational improvements and new business," Clay said.

After a short pause, "Okay, let's try it. Just know that the other Regional VP's don't have this type of person on their staff. Let's position this as a trial role. Set it up with clear objectives. I want to know within a year whether the extra overhead is worth it or not. Got it?"

"Yes," answered Clay.

"I'll ask Holiday in HR to contact you Monday to work it all out." Phil started to step into the limo, but turned and said, "Smart man to promote Sheryl. Roberta tells me she's the real thing." With that, he ducked into the back seat of the limo and was gone.

Clay went back upstairs to his office. Although he was physically exhausted from the week, he noticed a little spring in his step. Life was good.

Sitting behind his desk he looked around the room and began to realize that he should probably think about giving up this office and selecting something smaller. After all, he wouldn't be here that often. That idea didn't appeal to him. He liked the office, the large windows, even the hideous "king's chair" at the head of the conference table.

There was a knock. Sheryl stepped into the room and closed the door behind her.

With a mischievous smile on her face, she walked directly to him, leaned over and kissed him.

"I missed you, and you were marvelous in the company meeting. I wanted to kiss you then," Sheryl said.

A little flustered by the affection, Clay managed some humor, "Is kissing me in my office your idea of concealing our relationship? What if someone walks in?"

"I'm not exactly sitting in your lap, am I?. Besides the door is closed. Didn't you like the kiss?" Sheryl said, pretending to be hurt.

"The kiss was very nice. Especially nice coming from Pitt-Needham's newest Regional Operations Manager," Clay said, smiling.

"Really? It's approved?" Sheryl leaned over and hugged him tightly. "We need to celebrate all the blessings from this week."

"We certainly do. Can I interest you in dinner at my place Saturday night?"

"I think my calendar is clear," Sheryl said playfully.

"Wonderful. Please bring a salad. And a swim suit."

"A swim suit?"

"Yes, just in case we are inclined to have our after-dinner coffee in the hot tub on my deck."

"Hmm, I'll have to consider that invitation carefully, Mr. Austin." She said with a wink.

"Is seven o'clock okay?" Clay asked.

"Perfect," she replied and left the room.

Clay thought to himself that the relationship with Sheryl was progressing quickly. He didn't know where tomorrow's dinner and hot tub would lead. From the first, he realized he wasn't scheming a seduction like he usually did on dates. This was different. He really liked being with her. He felt a longing to be closer to her. And, if he saw her body in a swimming suit, it was a nice bonus.

He asked Sheryl to call a ride to take him to his house. All he wanted to do tonight was go home, shower and fall into bed.

Chapter 70

aturday morning greeted Clay with a cloudless sky and a hint of warmness in the air. The morning was glorious. Too glorious to spend it grocery shopping. He could buy the groceries for tonight's dinner with Sheryl this afternoon. What he wanted to do now was have a little fun and enjoy this amazing day before the weather could change.

Seeing his neighbors glide by in their kayaks gave Clay an idea. He hadn't been out on the lake in his kayak since last Fall. After a quick bowl of granola and cup of coffee, Clay changed into a swimsuit, sandals, an Under Armor tee shirt and heavy oiled wool sweater. He added a cap to shade his eyes.

Outside, he walked along the narrow deck to the place where the sleek boat hung from the roof eaves. He lifted the boat off the hooks and placed it on the deck at his feet. A long paddle was mounted on hooks screwed into the side of the house. He removed the paddle and reviewed in his head the steps necessary to launch a kayak.

Getting in and out of a sea kayak was not easy. The craft were notoriously easy to tip over, and Clay had no interest in spending time in the frigid water of Lake Union. The procedure Clay had used in the past was to place the long paddle perpendicular across the top of the kayak and the house deck. By holding onto the paddle and boat, the bracing technique permitted Clay to carefully slither into the tight cockpit.

The only problem was the deck of his houseboat was at least a foot higher than the deck of his kayak. The unevenness meant the paddle was at a steep angle. The solution was less than ideal. Clay could barely hold the boat stable long enough to board, but it was the only option he had.

With the kayak in the water and bow pointed to the center of the lake, Clay braced the boat the best he could with the paddle. He slowly and carefully moved from sitting on the house deck to sitting in the kayak. It rocked and tipped precariously. He wasn't completely settled into the cockpit, so his weight wasn't well distributed when the wake of passing tugboat made the kayak rock. The motion caught Clay by surprise. His grip on the paddle and house deck slipped. Instinctively he reached out to grab the deck, but his sudden weight shift pitched the kayak hard to its side.

Clay's head hit the side of the deck hard just before the kayak flipped completely. Trapped in the tiny cockpit, Clay hung motionless upside down in the cold lake.

Chapter 71

t was the most amazing place Clay had ever seen. The colors were so vivid he thought he could reach out and gather them like grapes on a vine. But, when he tried, his hands came back empty. These multi-dimensional walls of color were on his left and right. Straight ahead was just pure white light. He had never seen light like this. It was brilliant but didn't hurt his eyes. On the contrary, he couldn't take his eyes off it.

A figure in the distance appeared to be moving toward him out of the light. It wasn't walking; the figure wasn't gliding either. Clay realized the figure wasn't moving at all. It was he that was somehow getting closer although Clay had no sensation of moving. He drew closer to the figure as if someone was operating the zoom on a camera lens that brought Clay to where the figure stood. Its shape resembled a man. The details of its features would come in and out of focus, but the voice was crystal clear.

"Hello, Clay," the figure said.

"Hello. Who are you and where am I?"

"You had an accident, Clay."

Images of him flipping in a kayak flashed through his mind.

"My kayak flipped. Oh, my God, did I drown?"

"Yes, you drowned." The simple, factual statement was delivered with love and compassion.

"Am I . . . am I, in heaven?" Clay was struggling to make sense of it but didn't feel any anxiety; only peacefulness.

"No. Heaven is up ahead," the figure said.

"Who are you?"

"You don't know me yet, but I love you and want you to love me."

Clay didn't know how to respond to that statement.

The figure continued, "Clay, our time together now is very short. I have a plan for you. A very, very important plan. Will you follow that plan?"

"Wait a minute, you're asking me to follow some unknown plan, but I don't even know who you are."

"I am."

"Who?"

"Who do you think I am, Clay?"

"God?"

"Yes, Clay. You are not seeing me completely at this moment, because you have only just begun to know me. You resist still. Why do you close your heart to me?

"I don't know," was all he could think to say. At the moment, Clay couldn't think of any reason why he wouldn't want to be connected to the incredible love that was washing over him like waves of warm energy. On the contrary, he wanted to embrace the figure.

For a moment the figure's face became clear. Clay could see a loving smile and the kindest eyes he had ever seen.

"My son, look for what sits heavy on your heart for it is what separates us. Look for anything that is not love."

"I don't know how to do that," said Clay.

"I know you don't my son, which is why I sent to you my special child, Sheryl."

A sudden sadness filled Clay. "But, I won't see Sheryl again. I drowned." He started to cry, "I love her."

"Grieve not, for I have a plan for you, Clay. Will you follow the plan?"

"What is this plan?"

"I'm not revealing it to you now."

"You're asking me to commit to a plan I don't know anything about?"

"Yes. All you have to do is love me with all your heart and trust in me."

"What if I can't do it, the plan I mean."

"Clay, trust me. You can do it."

"Will I see you again?"

"Oh, yes, Clay. And you can talk to me whenever you want. I'm always with you if you believe in me. You have wonderful work to do, Clay. Are you ready?"

"Yes."

"You have chosen wisely, my son, I'm pleased." The figure reached out to Clay. In His hand was a single lit candle. "Carry this light for me, Clay."

Clay accepted the candle. Not at all sure what to do with it. The figure with its surrounding bright light withdrew into the distance.

"No, wait, don't go! I want to talk more. I have so many questions," Clay screamed.

△ △ △

The ambulance was preparing to leave the parking lot at Clay's houseboat but was in no particular rush. There was no one to save. The victim hadn't been responsive to CPR efforts of a neighbor who pulled him from the water, nor the EMS team who showed up minutes later.

The paramedic noticed the body in the gurney twitched slightly, and the vital signs monitor began to report a weak heartbeat.

"Holy cow, this guy isn't dead!" Through his shoulder mic, he talked to the ambulance driver. "Step on it Brady, get us to the hospital. This guy isn't dead."

With lights and siren blaring, the ambulance raced toward the University of Washington Medical Center with their nearly dead patient.

Chapter 72

O n the way to Clay's house, Sheryl called him to ask what he was serving. She wanted to bring an appropriate wine. She knew he'd already have the perfect wine on the table, but she wanted to bring something besides the salad he had asked her to prepare.

The phone rang five times and went to voicemail.

"Hi, on my way. I want to bring wine. Should I buy white or red? I'll be at the store in about ten minutes. Call me. Bye."

She continued the journey to Clay's houseboat. At a market along the way, she stopped to buy the wine. Clay hadn't returned her call. She parked and called him again. No answer. This was odd. She couldn't remember ever calling Clay and not getting a callback or text within a few minutes.

She didn't have time to wait for his reply. She went into the market and purchased a bottle of red and a bottle of white.

Sheryl parked in the guest space outside the gate leading to Clay's dock. She checked her makeup in the mirror. She was nervous, but a good nervous that was combined with the thrilling anticipation of being with Clay. The salad container and her purse rested on the passenger seat. Inside the large purse was a bikini. It was the thought of being nearly naked with Clay in the hot tub that caused her the most anxiety.

While planning what to wear tonight, she had put a lot of thought into which swimming suit to wear. She removed five bikinis and two one-piece suits from her dresser and tried on each one. Several were too sexy and would send the wrong message she thought. Two others were too boring. She didn't want to convey that idea either. She settled on a cute green bikini with blue polka-dots. Not too boring. Not too suggestive. After all, Sheryl had no intentions of letting the evening go too far.

She regretted her lack of tan. She regretted more that this morning her bathroom scales reported she was two whole pounds over her target weight. No more desserts after tonight she vowed.

Her watch said it was two minutes after seven. Clay wasn't at the gate to let her in. He was usually standing there waiting when she arrived. Sheryl dialed Clay's number again. Five rings later the call went to his voicemail greeting. Something wasn't right.

An elderly woman with a small dog on a leash walked past her toward the gate. She swiped a magnetic card across the keycard reader and opened the gate to the dock. She was obviously one of Clay's neighbors.

Sheryl quickly got out of her car. "Excuse me."

The woman stopped and turned to look at Sheryl before walking through the gate. She studied the younger woman standing by the car but didn't say anything.

"I'm a guest of Clay Austin; his house is at the end of the dock on the left. He's supposed to let me in at seven. Do you mind if I follow you?"

The woman didn't say a word. Instead, she turned and walked slowly to Sheryl. The woman looked at the attractive blonde standing in front of her. "Are you a friend of Clay's?" The woman asked.

"Yes, my name is Sheryl. We work together at his company, Austin-Davis," she replied, realizing she was going to have to start saying, Pitt-Needham.

"Oh, my dear," the woman said sadly. "I'm so sorry. Clay drowned this morning."

Sheryl felt the blood drain from her head. Gripping the car door to steady herself, she knew this wasn't some cruel joke. It explained the unanswered phone calls and why he didn't greet her at the gate.

"Drowned?" Was all Sheryl could say.

The woman reached out a hand and rested it on Sheryl's.

"He flipped trying to get into his kayak this morning. I guess he got caught underneath and couldn't get out. We live next door. My husband was outside watering our hanging flower baskets and saw it happen. He noticed Clay flip without surfacing and yelled at me to call 911. Then my husband rushed over, jumped into the lake and tried to get Clay out."

The woman was sobbing now as she recalled the morning's emotional event. Sheryl was shaking. Tears streamed down her face. "It took Harry several attempts to pull Clay out of the Kayak. After calling 911, I rounded up several other neighbors to help. They managed to pull Clay and Harry out of the water and onto Clay's deck. Mr. Robinson started CPR on Clay, but he didn't respond. EMS arrived and continued CPR. I heard one of the paramedics say that there weren't any vital signs. They took him to the ambulance but didn't seem in much of a rush. Clay was such a nice young man." The woman reached into her jacket pocket for a tissue.

In shock, Sheryl tried to process the terrible news. The man she was beginning to fall in love with was dead. The irony bit hard. Less than two hours earlier she was selecting which swimming suit to wear with Clay in the hot tub, while he lay lifeless in the morgue, his lungs filled with water.

"I'm sorry for our loss, dear," said the woman before turning away and shuffling slowly through the gate, closing it behind her. The clank of the shutting gate signaled the abrupt end to a chapter in Sheryl's life.

Not able to be still she walked around and around the parking lot crying uncontrollably. After about fifteen minutes, she got into her car. *Now what?* She looked at the salad bowl in the seat next to her. She broke down again thinking about the romantic dinner that wasn't to be.

Sheryl, the woman, sat in her sports car devastated and confused. But Sheryl the executive assistant, began to take control. She had questions. Where did they take Clay? What hospital? She grabbed her smartphone. A quick search told her the closest hospital was the University of Washington Medical Center. She punched the number.

"Medical Center, how can I direct your call?" said the operator.

"Yes, I hope you can help me. A friend of mine drowned earlier today and may have been taken to this hospital. How do I verify that?"

"I'll connect you with the morgue."

The phone rang four times before someone answered. "Morgue, Cho speaking," answered a female with heavy Asian accent who sounded in a rush.

"Ms. Cho, a friend of mine, drowned this morning in Lake Union and may have been brought to your hospital."

"Name?"

"Austin, Clay Austin."

"No deceased here with that name."

"Are you sure?"

"Yes. No deceased processed in past eighteen hours."

"Is there another hospital where he could have been taken?"

"Yes, but EMS would have delivered to closest hospital."

"Thank you for your help." Sheryl disconnected the call. *Now what, Lord?* She was about to search for the phone numbers of the other nearby hospitals when she remembered what she had told Clay multiple times in the past few weeks. "The Lord has a plan for you, Clay." She didn't believe the plan included drowning in Lake Union. Her fingers tapped the number for the University hospital again.

"Medical Center, how can I direct your call?"

"Hello, please connect me with the room of Mr. Clay Austin. He was admitted earlier today." Sheryl was playing a strong hunch. She prayed while the operator searched the admittance list on her computer screen.

"Mr. Austin is in Intensive Care. I can connect you with the nurse's station."

Chapter 73

Sheryl stood by the bed and looked down at the sleeping Clay. He looked more like the victim of an auto accident than a drowning. A nasty bruise and area of abraded skin marked his forehead. A brace had been applied around his neck. Tubes fed oxygen into his nostrils. A drip IV led from the saline solution bag hanging on a stand to the needle taped to a vein on his left hand.

She held his hand and cried. The tears were from relief that Clay was still alive and from the sorrow of seeing this man lay there helplessly.

A nurse entered the room and gave Sheryl a weary smile. She checked the oxygen and IV connections, looked at the vital signs monitor, and made a few notes in her tablet computer. "Hello, I'm Angie. I've been the nurse on duty since Mr. Austin was brought in. I'm going off duty now. Gregory has the next shift and will be in to check on him."

"How is he, Angie?"

"He's a very lucky man. EMS estimated that he was underwater for at least five minutes. He was unresponsive to CPR. He had no pulse when they put him into the ambulance. But, miraculously, his breathing and heart started again. He hasn't gained consciousness yet, but his vital signs are much improved." Angie finished her professional summary without answering the primary question.

"When will he wake up and will he be okay?" Sheryl asked quickly, seeing that the tired nurse was eager to leave.

"We never know in cases like this. Dr. Osagi will be in shortly. He can explain what to expect. Good night." The nurse left.

Sheryl positioned a recliner chair, so it faced the bed. She sat down, wrapped a blanket around herself for warmth, closed her eyes, and prayed.

Around midnight, Dr. Osagi entered the room and greeted Sheryl. The doctor was short, thin and very young. Sheryl wondered just how long this man had been out of medical school. He smiled broadly at Sheryl. "Good evening, I'm Dr. Osagi. Are you Mr. Austin's wife?"

"No, a close friend," Sheryl responded. "Clay isn't married and doesn't have any family in the area."

"I see." The doctor looked at the vital signs monitor and the patient record in his tablet computer. He proceeded to give Sheryl a nearly-identical summary of the situation that nurse Angie had delivered three hours earlier. Perhaps they were reading from the same script.

"When will he regain consciousness, and will he be okay?" Asked Sheryl.

The doctor spoke for about five minutes without giving Sheryl a definitive answer. There were a lot of "unknowns," a number of "variables," and so on. In a nutshell, Clay could wake up within minutes or never. He could be fine or suffer from severe brain damage, rendering him unable to communicate. The injury to his neck wasn't severe—a mild whiplash. The doctor wasn't sure what caused the whiplash or bruise on his head. Whatever, a blow to the head must have knocked out Clay and prevented him from rescuing himself.

Doctor Osagi made a note in his tablet computer, said goodbye, and left.

Sheryl felt light headed. She braced herself by holding on to one of the bed's guardrails. Her stomach growled. No wonder she was dizzy; she hadn't eaten a thing since breakfast. She thought about the large bowl of salad in her car probably turning brown by now. She decided to find a cup of tea and a snack in the hospital cafeteria. There wasn't anything she could do for Clay at the moment.

Sheryl walked to the nurse's station, got directions to the cafeteria and headed to the elevator. Life and death were being played out in every room in the ward. The accident victims, the seriously ill suffering their latest relapse—valiant medical teams doing their best to reduce suffering and extend life.

She walked past the room next to Clay's. A woman with dark hair and gaunt face lay motionless on the bed. A middle-aged man, maybe ten years older than Clay, sat next to the woman. Head in his hands, he appeared to be in deep prayer. Life. Death.

The cafeteria was closed at this hour, but a line of dispensing machines and beverage makers provided Sheryl with what little refreshment she wanted. As she sipped her tea and chewed a nutrition bar, she couldn't help but wonder what Clay had planned to prepare for their dinner. Would he ever cook a meal for her again?

A man shuffled slowly into the cafeteria. He didn't make eye contact with Sheryl even though they were the only two in the room. The man looked exhausted. The eyes were red, hair disheveled. A shirttail hung out from below a sweater. He walked to the single-cup coffee maker and prepared something to drink. With cup in hand, he turned around and then reacted with a start to see Sheryl sitting at a table nearby.

"Oh, sorry, I didn't see you," the man said.

"That's okay. I'm half asleep myself," Sheryl said. She heard a soft voice, "Comfort him." She motioned to one of the chairs at her table. "Why don't you join me?"

The man hesitated. "Well, okay, I'm afraid I won't be much company," he said.

"I'm Sheryl."

I'm Thomas." They shook hands. Sheryl noticed his grip was weak.

"My friend nearly died today in a kayak accident. He's still unconscious," Sheryl volunteered.

"Oh, you must be in the room next to my wife's. My goodness, the staff has been talking all day about how your friend was declared dead but came back to life in the ambulance. How is he, may I ask?"

"He's still unconscious. We won't know much until he wakes," she said. *If he wakes*, she thought. "Is your wife ill?" Sheryl asked, not sure how to broach the question.

"Yes, she's been ill for a long time. Cancer. Been in hospice at our home but collapsed Friday. The doctor said she's dying and won't be going back home. I tell them they're wrong. She will go home. The Lord is bringing her home." Thomas' trembling lips betrayed his brave words of faith.

"Amen," said Sheryl.

Thomas, looked at her closely. "Are you a Christian, Sheryl?"

"Yes, I am."

"We may be the only two Christians in this entire hospital. Seattle has become such a godless place. Where do you worship?"

"Pathway Church" Sheryl answered. "What about you?"

"I'm Pastor at Seattle Beacon Bible Church," he replied.

"What's your wife's name?"

"Rhonda. And what is your friend's name?"

"Clay. Why don't we two Christians pray together right now," Sheryl suggested.

Through a thin smile and grateful eyes, Thomas said, "Great idea. I'd like that."

The two took turns praying for each other, for Clay, for Rhonda. When they opened their eyes after saying Amen, both had fresh tears in their eyes.

"Thank you, Sheryl. I feel a little better having someone to talk to. So many people from the church want to be here, but they aren't allowed in ICU. God bless you."

"God bless you, Pastor. Perhaps we will see each other again."

"God willing, we shall," Thomas said over his shoulder as he walked back to the elevators.

Chapter 74

S he had a fitful sleep in the recliner next to Clay's bed. She woke every few hours when a nurse would turn on the room lights and check Clay. At about 4:30 she woke to loud crying and a shuffling of feet.

The sounds were coming from the room next door. A man was crying. Through the glass wall that separated Clay's room from the ICU corridor, Sheryl could see staff walking quickly in and out of the room. After a few minutes, a bed with a sheet-covered body was wheeled out of the room and down the hall. A man she recognized as Thomas from the cafeteria tried to follow, but a nurse and doctor gently took his arms, turned him around and walked him the other direction out of Sheryl's view. The woman with black hair, Rhonda, must have passed away. Another soul leaving this world for a life in the hereafter, Sheryl thought. She was determined that her Clay was not going to die before he let Christ into his heart.

She firmly griped Clay's hand. "You are not dying, mister. God has plans for you." *And me too,* she realized, *whatever it might be.*

△ △ △

Clay's eyes didn't open until around 5 o'clock Sunday afternoon. It took some time for his surroundings to come into focus. Squinting in the harsh overhead light he could see that he was in a bed, but not his bed. He was in a room, but not one he recognized. He noticed the IV tube leading to his hand; he felt the oxygen tubes in his nostrils. Okay then. He was in a hospital room. Where was the loving figure in the incredibly comforting light?

The details of the room slowly became more defined. His head throbbed, and something around his neck was preventing him from moving his head freely. There was someone in a chair next to him. He tried to turn and look, but the neck brace prevented it. His throat was parched, and his tongue felt swollen. He desperately wanted a drink of water.

He tried to speak, "Waaatgr." A barely audible, gravely croak left his mouth.

He heard a voice he recognized. "Clay!" Sheryl shot up from a reclining chair next to his bed and hugged him.

With his free arm, he weakly reached out and caressed her back. "Waaatgr," again he tried to request a sip of water.

"What? Sheryl asked.

"Waaatgr," he whispered weakly.

"One minute." He saw Sheryl press a nurse call button hanging on a rail of the bed.

"I can't understand you. What are you saying?"

Clay didn't have enough strength to say it again. He closed his eyes to rest.

He heard Sheryl talking to someone excitedly. "He's awake! He tried to say something, but I couldn't understand him."

Clay heard a new voice he didn't recognize. "Clay, can you hear me?"

He opened his eyes and saw a nurse standing by the bed. He didn't think he could get another word out of his mouth. He tried to nod his head. That was difficult considering the neck brace. He managed to make an affirmative grunt.

With his available hand, he pretended he was holding a glass and tipping it to his mouth.

"Do you want something to drink?" asked the nurse.

Clay signaled yes by giving her a thumbs-up sign.

"I'll be right back."

The nurse returned with a doctor. She held a glass of water with a straw for Clay to drink.

"Take a few small sips. You can have more later."

Clay did as he was told but was tempted to grab the glass from her and chug the entire contents. He had never been so thirsty in all his life.

Chapter 75

Clay was released from the hospital on Wednesday morning. All tests were normal. The neck brace had been removed. A small bandage remained on his forehead. As the nurse pushed him in a wheelchair to the curb and Sheryl's waiting car, he felt great. His mind was clear. He had so much he wanted to tell Sheryl about his vision and the mysterious figure. If only he wasn't slurring his words so badly.

The doctor had told Clay and Sheryl that the slurred speech was the result of the lack of oxygen to the brain. The effect was like people who suffered from a stroke. In Clay's case, he was physically fine, but his speech was slightly impaired. He was told that with speech therapy he could reduce the slurring by fifty percent or more, but in all likelihood, some impairment would be with him the remainder of his life.

With Clay safely strapped into the passenger seat, Sheryl pulled away from the hospital and headed for Clay's house less than three miles away.

Inside his house, Clay was greeted by dozens of flower bouquets from well-wishers. His kitchen and living room looked like a flower shop before Valentine's Day.

Two days ago, on Monday, still not speaking clearly, Clay had written instructions to Sheryl telling where he kept a key hidden outside in the wood rack, and what the codes were for the gate and his alarm system. She was able to bring him some clothes to wear for his release and store all the flowers that had been accumulating at the hospital and office.

"Welcome home, Clay. Can I get you anything?"

"Sshhowwwr."

"You want a shower? Well, that you'll have to do by yourself, mister. I'll fix us something to eat."

Clay went upstairs slowly. He was still weak from his ordeal. By the top of the stairs he was out of breath. He walked directly to the bathroom, stripped and took a long hot shower. It was good to be home. It was especially good to be alive.

A hot breakfast of eggs, bagels, bacon, juice, and coffee was on the table when he came downstairs twenty minutes later.

"Melllssgd," said Clay.

"I used the last of your eggs, bacon, and juice," Sheryl replied, and judging by her expression, Clay figured she was not entirely sure of what he had just said to her.

While they ate, Sheryl briefed Clay on the messages he'd received since word had gotten out about the accident. She had already responded to each one on Clay's behalf. She then updated Clay on business matters as if nothing unusual had happened. He admired Sheryl for being so business-like. She had so far avoided the elephant in the room.

While in the shower Clay had had an epiphany of sorts. Maybe it was more a dose of truth than an epiphany, but while he was enjoying the hot water on his back, the stark reality of his situation became crystal clear. His livelihood and career depended entirely on his ability to communicate. To be precise, it depended on his ability to verbally persuade and inspire.

In his current state, he couldn't persuade and inspire anyone—not as long as every word out of his mouth sounded like it was coming from a slobbering drunk. Oh sure, speech therapy would help, but how long would that take? Besides, the doctor told him he'd never regain his normal speech again.

The bottom line was this: Clay Austin was finished as a marketing executive.

Sheryl continued to talk, filling the silence, but being careful not to ask questions that would require Clay to speak. The situation was becoming awkward.

Clay held up a hand. "Nnminut." He stood, walked to a kitchen drawer to retrieve a notepad and pen. He motioned for her to follow him into the living room where they took a seat next to each other on the couch.

He wrote on the lined yellow paper and handed it to her to read, "I think I saw God."

"You think you saw God? When? Where?" Sheryl asked seriously.

Clay wrote some more before passing the pad to Sheryl. "When I was unconscious. Before I woke up in hospital."

"Clay, you weren't just unconscious. You were clinically dead for up to fifteen minutes. Do you get that? You drowned. You died. You came back to life." Her voice was trembling.

He wrote more on the tablet. "I get it. While I was dead or unconscious, I think I saw God."

"Tell me . . . uh . . . write more about what you saw."

For the next hour, Clay gave to Sheryl a series of written snippets covering what he saw and heard in his vision. He'd write a few sentences and hand the notepad to her. She'd read and ask questions or hand the notepad back to him with encouragement to continue writing.

"Clay, what you had is known as a 'near death experience,' or NDE. There are thousands of reported NDEs, too many to disregard. I believe that you didn't see Jesus clearly because you haven't let him into your heart yet. You don't know him yet," Sheryl said.

Clay wrote quickly on the pad. "That's what the figure said, too. I didn't know him yet."

"You said Jesus gave you a candle?"

Clay wrote, "Handed candle to me before he withdrew into the distance."

"Did he say anything then?"

Clay wrote, "Carry this light for me."

Sheryl thought for a moment. "It's no coincidence you and I were talking about the light of God just the other day. He loves you so much He saved your life and only asked that you carry his light." Tears of joy formed in Sheryl's eyes.

Clay was getting tired. His hand ached from so much writing. He slowly stood and shuffled to the kitchen to fix a fresh cup of coffee for himself, tea for her.

While the coffee brewed, he started to read the cards attached to the vases of flowers on the kitchen counter. The first he read was from Phil. "Wishing you a rapid recovery. Call me as soon as you're able.—Phil."

Call as soon as able. Well, that might be a very, very long time, Phil. The card reminded Clay of the other topic he needed to discuss with Sheryl.

He brought the steaming cups to the couch.

"You look tired. Want to take a nap?" Sheryl asked.

He looked at Sheryl. She looked tired, too. This amazing woman had been by his side nearly every minute while he was in the hospital. Circles were under her eyes. She hadn't slept well.

He wrote on the yellow pad, "Yes, but later. Need to talk about work."

"Clay, work can wait. Everything is under control, and . . ." Clay held up his hand to stop her from speaking.

He wrote, "I can't work if I can't talk."

"Don't be silly. With therapy, you'll be fine."

He wrote, "Will never speak good enough again."

Sheryl looked like she wanted to argue with him, but didn't. "What will you do?

He wrote, "Don't know. Need time to think."

Clay noticed a change in Sheryl's expression. She became distant and quiet as if hit by a heavy thought.

He wrote, "What's wrong?"

"Nothing."

He grunted and waved the yellow pad in front of her again as if to repeat what he had just asked her.

"What about us?" She asked the question looking at the floor.

He gently tilted her head up with one hand and looked into her eyes. "Nedu," he said. Irritated at what came out of his mouth he repeated more slowly.

"Neeyou." Fully frustrated now, he grabbed the pen and notepad. "I need you!" He wrote in large letters half a page high.

"Well, why didn't you say so?" she said with a twisted grin. Clay grunted, pretending to be aggravated at the joke. They laughed together and kissed.

After several minutes of silence, he wrote, "I'm tired."

"A nap sounds like a good idea. Go upstairs and rest."

He wrote, "Take nap with me."

"Mr. Austin, shame on you. Is this some trick to get me into bed with you?" She was enjoying teasing him. Part of her would like nothing more than falling asleep in his arms, but she wasn't going to create a situation for temptation to grow.

He shook his head as if pleading innocence.

"What I am going to do is take a nap in your guest room. You should know that I'll be spending the night here to make sure you are okay. No arguments. My overnight bag is already in the guest room."

Clay could see Sheryl had the situation firmly in control. He couldn't argue with the logic, even if he could talk.

Clay headed to his bedroom, Sheryl to the guest room just down the hall from the kitchen.

Clay removed his clothes, pulled back the covers and started to fall into bed. The lighthouse painting caught his eye. It seemed like forever since he'd really looked at it. He hadn't been home much. The painting soothed him today in ways he couldn't understand. He studied it. The couple in the balloon's basket were easier to see. More details were visible. The girl had blond hair. Clay swore it had been black before, but maybe he just hadn't paid attention.

He fell into a deep, peaceful sleep.

Chapter 76

lay woke to the sound of a voice downstairs. It startled him at first until he recognized the voice as Sheryl's. She was talking on the phone. The sun was low in the sky—about to disappear behind Queen Anne hill across the lake. The digital clock on his dresser read 5:22. He had slept almost five hours; considerably longer than his usual twenty-minute "power naps," as he liked to call them.

Clay wondered if he could talk clearly. Perhaps a little extra rest had restored his speech. He said a test. "Maa aim kay stin." His attempt to say "my name is Clay Austin," told him his situation was unchanged.

He lay there and took stock of his situation as if he was assessing a client's business situation before recommending a marketing strategy. First, if he couldn't talk clearly, he couldn't be effective in his new position at Pitt-Needham. He could probably negotiate a medical leave period of a few months during which he could take speech therapy and do other tasks at the company that didn't require speaking. Second, he didn't have to work. He had more than enough money in the bank after selling Austin-Davis to support himself for the rest of his life. Three, if he left Pitt early—within 12 months—it would cost him one million dollars per terms of the purchase agreement. Four, he could also sell the lighthouse property for additional money. Money wasn't an issue, thankfully. What was the issue? That brought him to point five. He didn't know what to do with his life if he couldn't be a marketer. Marketing was all he knew. It was the only thing he excelled at. And this is where Clay got stuck. He didn't have an answer.

A shadow fell over Lake Union and Clay's house as the sun dipped behind Queen Anne hill. In the dimming light, despair and depression overtook him. Who would he be if he wasn't Clay Austin, the marketer? He'd be a nobody, that's who he'd be. What good was money if he wasn't somebody? What good was ten million dollars in the bank if he wasn't flying around the country in jets, talking to teams, making things happen? His entire sense of self-had been defined by his work. Now he couldn't do the work. His purpose in life and his identity had been taken from him by a freak accident.

His life had been cruelly ripped out of his hands. That's what he got for starting to believe Sheryl's story about God's plan for him. What a bunch of crap! To think he was beginning to believe her. On top of the pity and anger, he felt betrayed. That's what he got for letting his guard down and letting someone get too close.

Quiet sobs soon grew into spasms of uncontrollable crying. Somewhere within the self-pity of the moment, anger emerged. Like a volcano beginning to erupt, anger spewed from him. He smashed his fist again and again into the mattress while his body shook in tearful convulsions.

△ △ △

From downstairs Sheryl heard a noise that sounded like crying. She walked softly upstairs, not knowing whether to help or give Clay his privacy. Through the open door to his bedroom, she watched as Clay writhed under the covers, pounding his fists into the mattress. At that moment, standing in his doorway, her heart ached for Clay. This man she cared for deeply was in agony. She'd never seen him like this. He was violently grunting and twisting in bed like an animal trying to free itself from a hunter's snare.

She wanted to step forward and soothe him, but his violence frightened her. Sheryl stepped to the side out of view and prayed for guidance.

△ △ △

Clay threw off the covers and leaped out of bed. He paced angrily around and around the room in his underwear. The tears had stopped, but the bitter anger remained. The lighthouse painting above his bed was barely visible in the growing darkness of the room. Clay walked directly to the painting, removed it from the wall, and slid it under the bed. Nothing had gone well for him since the shrink gave him that silly thing. He never wanted to see it again.

Dr. Shildstein, the shrink, was another person in his life misleading him. He resolved right then that he was done with his therapy. What a crock! All this b.s. about his childhood.

A soft touch to his shoulder made him jump and twirl around.

Sheryl stood there looking frightened. "What's wrong, Clay?"

For a second the sight of her soothed him, but the feeling was quickly overtaken by anger. Jeez, the woman knows he can't talk, and there she stands asking her stupid questions. He just wanted to be alone.

"Leevmeaknn," Clay muttered bitterly.

"I'm sorry. I can't understand. Do you have paper to write on?"

He was in no mood to find any paper. He signaled for Sheryl to follow him downstairs, not caring that he was still in his underwear.

Downstairs he walked straight to the guest room, picked up her overnight bag from the floor and returned to the kitchen where Sheryl waited.

He thrust the bag at her. "Go," he said, the single syllable word was spoken without a slur.

Sheryl reacted as if Clay had just hit her in the stomach.

"What?" She asked in shock, not certain she understood his intention.

"Go. Lev." He repeated.

Slowly she took her bag from him as painful sobs shook her body.

He opened the front door. "Go."

Sheryl walked out into the darkness. The door slammed behind her.

Chapter 77

lay stood in his underwear alone in the middle of the living room. Flowers from dozens of people covered every horizontal surface. To Clay, the flowers didn't represent love and sympathy. They were a cruel reminder that his career was over. Yellow daffodils and pink tulips stood in their vases mocking hm. *You couldn't do it. You couldn't do it.*

He felt dizzy and sat down in his chair next to the unlit fireplace. A childhood memory filled his head. Ten-year-old Clay was on his knees in the hot sun, a pair of lawn trimming shears in his hands. Slowly he cut the tall uneven grass that the mower couldn't reach around a flower bed that encircled his house. Inch by inch he crept. Clip . . . clip . . . clip. Blisters formed earlier in the day by the shears had now broken. The open blisters stung as the metal handle of the shears rubbed against the raw flesh.

Little Clay didn't care that the beds of dirt he was trimming around were filled with beautiful flowers and shrubs planted by his mother. A sensational rainbow of colors from annuals and perennials bloomed just a few feet from his head, but all he saw was the endless line of shabby green grass that had to be trimmed.

Clip . . . clip . . . clip. Clay was lost in thought, but his hands continued to squeeze the handles of the shears again and again. Clip . . . clip . . . clip. Crawl forward. Clip . . . clip . . . clip. A shadow fell over Clay from behind. He smelled the smoke from Vic's cigarette.

"Are you going to take all day? You should have been done an hour ago," Vic said sternly. He grabbed the shears from Clay's blistered hands and demonstrated just how fast the trimming should be done. "If you were working instead of being so lazy you'd be done by now. You still have half the house to trim. Get moving. Finish in thirty minutes or else you can forget about playing this afternoon. You'll be grounded."

Vic stormed back into the garage. Clay had been trimming for over an hour. He had thirty minutes to finish, but over half the flower beds remained untrimmed. Clay could see he wasn't going to make it. His anger at Vic's unfairness burned at Clay hotter than the noonday sun.

The painful memory evaporated from Clay's head. He knew what he had to do next. He went through the room and removed the flowers from their vases. He walked to the back door, opened it and stepped outside onto the deck. His kayak lay on its side on the deck at his feet, and he almost tripped on it in the darkness. Was the darn thing trying to drown him again? He resolved to sell the boat as soon as possible.

But now he had another job to do. He threw the armful of flowers into the dark lake; returning to the house, he gathered up another armful of bouquets and threw them into the lake as well.

Not a single flower remained inside the house. Only empty vases and two teddy bears remained. He drained the water from the vases, placed vases and teddy bears in a large garbage bag and set the bag by the front door so he could take it to the trash bin in the morning. It was done.

Back to normal at last. Clay poured a glass of wine, picked up his notebook computer, and sat down again in his chair. He consumed half the wine in his glass while considering his options. He was still angry. It was time to take control of the situation.

He drafted an email to Reuben, his business attorney. It was short and direct.
Reuben,
Due to the accident I am unable to perform my duties at Pitt-Needham. I have a severe speech impediment. I wish to resign effective immediately. I know this will trigger the $1 million penalty, but I don't care. Perhaps there are medical exclusions that can be considered. Please negotiate the best deal you can and safeguard the other terms of the final payout. I want the resignation completed within a week. Keep this confidential. I'll tell George.
Regards, Clay
He re-read the email twice before clicking Send.

Next, he forwarded Reuben's email to George. His resignation shouldn't impact George's deal with Pitt-Needham, but he wanted his longtime friend and partner to be among the first to know.

Who else? What about Sheryl? Yes, she should know. His office will need to be cleared out. Clay felt a twinge of guilt for how he abruptly kicked her out of his house. He drank the last of his wine. Then, he coolly forwarded Reuben's email to Sheryl.

In a way, it felt good to be in control again. During the last few weeks, he had felt as though he was being carried along by a current not of his choosing. It had become uncomfortable. But, now he was back in the driver's seat—clear voice or not. *Funny how almost dying brings life into focus*, he thought on the way to refill his wine glass.

Clay removed a container of leftover stew from the freezer and placed it in the microwave to thaw. He retook his seat in the living room and began to scan his business email Inbox. Why? He didn't need to worry about this stuff anymore. He had quit. Clay switched to his personal email account, quickly scanned the subject lines. Nothing of interest until he saw one from Bartlett in Reef Bay marked "Urgent."

The attorney's letter informed him that another attorney representing a group of investors had made a serious inquiry about the lighthouse property. They had made an offer of $1.5 million, which Bartlett felt was a low-ball number. He had some information that he wanted to share about the investors but wanted to do so on the phone. Would Clay please call at his earliest convenience.

Clay thought about the lighthouse and his Uncle Charley while eating his stew at the kitchen counter. Selling the property made a lot of sense right now. He didn't need the distraction. Besides he had no business owning a lighthouse. It was a good time to wrap up his affairs in Reef Bay.

Time for a road trip. He rinsed his dishes and went upstairs to pack. He was leaving for Reef Bay in the morning.

PART TWO,
THE BOAT.

Chapter 78

Pastor Thomas Benton sat in his Toyota sedan in the hospital parking garage, trying to make sense of his loss. Rhonda, the love of his life for twenty-two years, had passed an hour ago. Now all that was left were a few of her belongings on the passenger seat next to him—the clothes and simple jewelry she was wearing on Friday when a sudden spasm of pain made her faint and collapse in the kitchen while fixing lunch.

He backed out of the space and slowly wound his way down through the floors to the exit at street level. The sun had not yet brought light to the new day as Thomas drove through the University district, past the football stadium, northward to his home in the Hawthorne Hills neighborhood.

Thomas was exhausted from the ordeal of the past eighteen hours. He hadn't slept in the hospital, so desperate was he to be there if Rhonda regained consciousness. He wanted to say good-bye. He wanted to say one last time that he loved her, but God took her from him. She had never woken up after fainting in the kitchen.

During Rhonda's hospice, he had tried to prepare himself for the end. They had had long talks about their love, their life, and the church they built together. They talked openly about their inability to have children. Rhonda had carried a deep guilt for many years, but through prayer, counseling, and Thomas' love, the guilt had eventually passed. The guilt was replaced with a fervent passion for the church. She had put her heart and soul into it—as much, if not more, than Thomas.

Thomas may have been "the voice" of Beacon Bible Church, but Rhonda was "the heart." Her gracious smile and faith uplifted every member, every committee even during the most challenging times. When it was the darkest, the light of her character gave people hope and energy.

As Rhonda's illness had worsened, preventing her from being as active in the church, Thomas noticed a change in the church—not so much in the membership, but in the staff and volunteers. There was noticeably more friction. The atmosphere in the offices had turned cool and business-like as if it was some government agency. Rhonda was a spark of love that fed the staff and somehow kept them connected to their mission. Without it, they floundered.

And that fact had caused a big question to overtake Thomas' thoughts while he sat next to her in the hospital. Was he strong enough to fill the void in the church left by Rhonda? Could he be "the voice" and "the heart"? Is that what God was asking of him? Or was God telling him something else entirely different?

Thomas pulled into his driveway, clicked the garage door control clipped to the sun visor, and waited. The door slowly rose. He had been deep in thought about the past during the drive home. But, when the garage door slowly revealed Rhonda's yellow Honda CR-V, the reality of today hit him line a ton of bricks. Rhonda was gone. She wasn't coming home. He was alone.

Through tears now pouring from his eyes, he could barely see well enough to drive his car into the garage without scraping its sides.

Inside the house, everything was just the way he had left it around noon last Friday. Dirty dishes in the sink, two place settings on the kitchen table, glasses with water. He started to move the dishes from sink to the dishwasher but stopped before finishing. Instead, he began to put the clean dishes from the table back into the cupboard but stopped before finishing so he could clean the counters with a dishcloth.

Thomas realized in his exhaustion and shock he was nervously bouncing from one task to another not completing anything. He regained some focus and managed to finish the kitchen cleanup. Now came the bigger test, the action he had been avoiding. The walk through the cold, empty house.

From the kitchen, he went down the hall to his study trying very hard not to notice the framed photos that lined the walls of the hallway. He stood in the middle of the room. Notes and reference materials for Sunday's sermon were strewn across his desk right where he had left them Friday when he heard Rhonda cry out before collapsing to the floor. Pictures of he and Rhonda where everywhere—at church events, on their sailboat, in Israel, and on a mission to Mexico.

This room—the entire house—was like a time machine stuck on Friday at 12:09, the time Rhonda's body hit the cold kitchen floor. Twenty-two years of marriage and life together had come to a sudden halt. Why, was all he could ask. *Why, Lord, why?*

Seeing his sermon notes on the desk reminded him of his responsibilities. He had shut off his cell phone on the way to the hospital after calling his secretary to tell her about Rhonda's emergency. He turned it back on. It buzzed with numerous alerts. He had twenty voicemails, 221 new email messages, and forty-six text messages. Thomas didn't have the strength to deal with the messages. He didn't want to talk to anyone right now. He was exhausted, mentally and physically.

He managed one text to his secretary, Betty.

"Rhonda passed this morning at 4:50. Please tell staff. I am home now. Must rest. Will call you later. Get substitute for Sunday sermon."

Thomas turned the phone off. He walked wearily into the bedroom to sleep, but the sight of the queen-sized bed with flowered comforter made him hesitate. He couldn't get into that bed right now. It was *their* bed. Thomas left the master bedroom, walked into the guest room down the hall, left his clothes on the floor and was asleep a minute after his head touched the pillow.

Chapter 79

The month of May was a blur for Thomas. First, there was the funeral. The staff had insisted on relieving Thomas of the details. After a brief consultation with him, they planned the entire service. He simply had to show up.

As a pastor, Thomas had attended hundreds of funerals and delivered the sermon at scores of others, including several local dignitaries. Rhonda's service was uplifting beyond anything he had experienced. Two thousand people attended, nearly the entire congregation. The outpouring of love for his wife warmed his heart and made it ache at the same time.

After the funeral, Thomas took another week off from his duties to organize his house. The agonizing work involved deciding which of Rhonda's possessions to keep and which ones to donate. It was a sad and lonely job. He certainly didn't want to remove her memory from the house, but he couldn't have it appear as though she still lived there and was going to walk through the door any minute.

He broke down in tears at least once every day while packing her things. A favorite dress, a special perfume, the sweater she only wore on the boat—each item was more than a thing; it was part of her.

And with each item that he put in a box, he fought the guilt. A voice kept saying *you're trying to erase her memory too soon*. That idea was nonsense, of course, but it still ate at him, slowly taking a bite with each thing he placed into a box.

The guilt was lessened when he focused on how appreciative the needy recipients would be of her donated clothes and personal items. One Wednesday, he stuffed ten boxes of Rhonda's clothes, shoes, books, and inexpensive jewelry into her little Honda SUV, and drove it the church. He walked into the church office and made his way directly to the staff member responsible for the church's programs for feeding and clothing the needy.

"Henry, excuse me. I have a special donation I'd like you to handle."

"Certainly, Thomas. What can I do to help?" Henry replied.

Thomas handed Henry the keys to Rhonda's Honda and an envelope containing its title. "This is Rhonda's car. I'm donating it to the church. It is filled with her clothes. Your program can have those items, too. I know Rhonda will appreciate that her belongings will help others."

"Of course, Thomas, I'll take care of it. Do you want a receipt now or later?"

"Later is fine. Put it in my mailbox. I'll be back in the office on Monday."

"Ok. Is there anything else I can do for you?"

"Well, I could use a ride back home."

"No problem, I'll take you right now. My next meeting isn't for an hour," Henry said.

Back at home, Thomas sat in the living room. The house was eerily quiet. If Rhonda was here, he would hear her baking one of her sinfully delicious pies while talking on the phone, giving encouragement to some committee member. But, she wasn't here. God had chosen to take her from him.

He looked at the fireplace mantle. On it was a plain-looking container that could have been mistaken for a flower vase. But this container didn't hold flowers. It held ashes; Rhonda's ashes.

He had another decision to make; another loving task to attend to for his blessed wife— what should he do with her ashes?

For some reason, they had never decided where she wanted her ashes spread. It really wasn't that important to her, and she often told Thomas he was silly to be concerned about it.

"They are just ashes, Thomas. That's all. I don't care what you do with them. I'll be in heaven." She would tell him.

Thomas could be more sentimental than his wife, and this was one of those times. He wanted to spread her ashes someplace special. Some place that was special to both of them.

Behind the urn on the wall, above the fireplace mantle, was a large photo of Thomas and Rhonda on their sailboat taken by a friend. It was one of their favorite photos of the two of them. Thomas was seated, steering wheel in his left hand, his right arm holding Rhonda close. Both were looking ahead, their eyes filled with joy and anticipation; hair blown freely by the breeze. Rhonda told him they looked like they saw God's plan ahead and were sailing joyfully in that direction. She was right. That's exactly what they looked like.

He studied Rhonda in the picture more closely. She wasn't wearing makeup, never did on the boat. She had this natural beauty that didn't require much makeup even when they were dressing for a formal charity dinner. Her long black hair streamed behind her in the wind. She wore a heavy wool sailing sweater—the same one he had just packed in the donation boxes this morning.

Guilt stabbed at his heart hard as he thought about the sweater he had just given away. He started to cry, but the tears wouldn't come. Instead, he thought of what to do with her ashes. The idea was right there in front of him. He would take her ashes out into Puget Sound, and spread them over the waves.

Thomas managed a smile. She'd like that idea. They had wonderful times together on the sailboat. It didn't matter if they went out for an afternoon sail or took off for a week's cruise in the San Juan islands. They dearly loved being on the water together.

That was it. Before he returned to work next, he'd say goodbye to Rhonda's ashes and watch the waves carry her away.

Thomas had four more days before he was scheduled to return to work following his bereavement leave. He checked the NOAA weather forecast. A front was due to arrive on Saturday. His best bet for decent weather was going to be tomorrow or Friday. He settled on Friday.

Chapter 80

Thomas arrived at the boat's slip on Lake Washington before 9:30 in the morning. A wealthy member of his church let him dock the boat for free at his waterfront house in the exclusive Laurelhurst section of Seattle. The home was less than five miles from Thomas' modest house, but about $7 million apart in value.

He stepped aboard and immediately went below deck into the cabin to secure the urn containing Rhonda's ashes. He settled on a railed shelf behind the settee containing a row of books. There the urn would be securely held even if rough water conditions tossed the boat severely.

He started the little diesel engine and let it warm up while he removed the sail covers. The Islander 36 was built in 1984 and purchased at a dealer by Rhonda's father. He lovingly cared for the boat for many years until he passed. The boat was bequeathed to Rhonda in his Will along with instructions that she and Thomas were never to sell the boat for as long as it could float.

Fortunately, with the money he also left Rhona and the fact that they could dock the boat for free, they were able to maintain the 36-foot boat all these years on a pastor's salary.

Thomas untied the dock lines and pushed off. He powered south past Husky Stadium and turned west into the canal that connected Lake Washington with Lake Union and eventually the Ballard Locks that would lead him to the deep salt water of Puget Sound.

Thomas sipped coffee from his insulated mug as he enjoyed the calm ride through the canal. It gave him time to reflect on the boat. Rhonda's father had named the vessel, *Harriet's Chariot*, after Rhonda's mother, Harriet. Her parents were avid sailors, often spending weeks cruising from little harbor to little harbor up and down Puget Sound and all the way into Canadian waters.

The sailboat had been rigged at some expense for single-handed sailing to make it easier for Rhonda's parents to use the boat safely as they aged. The main and jib sails were roller furling, so sail area could be increased or decreased by turning a winch in the safety of the cockpit. A self-steering vane was mounted to the stern and, when under sail, would keep the boat on course without having to be steered.

It was a sturdy, comfortable boat that berthed six, had an enclosed head with shower, and a roomy main cabin with galley. By now, Thomas knew every nut, bolt, screw, and fuse on the vessel. He loved to be at the wheel and feel the boat leap forward when the wind filled its sails.

No sailing was possible for another hour or so until he cleared the locks, however. He kept the sails furled and continued to slowly power past the north end of Lake Union and into the ship canal. He marveled at the office buildings that had been constructed along the canal in the past ten years. He noticed some workers at one of the buildings were removing a sign. One half of the sign was tied to a small crane. The other half remained on the building. It said, Davis. Because of the twisted angle of the first half of the sign as it was carefully lowered he couldn't read what it said. Not that he'd recognize the company name anyway unless it was owned by someone from his church.

The locks weren't crowded on this weekday; certainly not like weekends when gleaming pleasure craft and rusty workboats were herded together into the locks like cattle into a trailer headed for auction. A warning horn sounded as the huge steel doors swung closed behind *Harriet's Chariot* and five other vessels. Water began to leave the compartment, slowly lowering the boats about twenty feet. After ten minutes a second set of huge steel doors in front of Thomas opened, releasing *Harriet's Chariot* and five other vessels into the salt water of Shilshole Bay.

Thomas powered through the bay, past the navigation buoys into Puget Sound. A nice northerly breeze greeted him, so he steered the bow directly into the wind and quickly unfurled the mainsail. Then he angled the boat into a reach so the wind coming more from the side of the boat would help unroll the jib from its roller furling system. Once both sails were fully extended, he adjusted the main sheet and jib sheet until the telltales on the sails were streaming in parallel telling him his trim was good. He turned off the engine. The Islander 36 leaned over into its starboard tack and headed on a northwest course at four knots.

Thomas sat relaxed in the cockpit on the port side, his right hand gripped the wheel, eyes scanning the water ahead and occasionally checking the trim of his sails. No rain fell from the cloudy sky. The breeze was steady. The bow sliced through the small waves effortlessly. It was nearly perfect. If only Rhonda were next to him.

He recalled the last time Rhonda had been on board their boat was New Year's day. They had gone out for a short sail on Lake Washington to celebrate the new year. The day had been crystal clear and cold. Snow-covered Mount Rainer stood tall to the south as if keeping watch over the region. To the east, the Cascade mountains boasted a dusting of snow.

Though they didn't speak of it, both knew that this would likely be her last trip on the boat. The cancer was spreading quickly. Her strength declined every week. So, they made the most of the short sail, sipping hot buttered rum and munching on leftover prime rib from the previous night's New Year's Eve dinner. After an hour, Rhonda became too cold and went below out of the breeze. Thomas offered to return to the dock, but like the trooper she was, Rhonda refused to cut the day short on her account. Instead, she huddled in a blanket on one of the berths and read. Feeling the effect of her weakness, warm rum, and gentle rocking motion of the boat, she soon fell asleep. From time to time Thomas would stand in the cockpit and look through the companionway to check on her. Lately, he had dreaded whenever she went to sleep, fearing that this would be the time she never woke up.

Now four months later, here they were on *Harriet's Chariot* again, he driving the boat while she rested below deck, but this time Rhonda wasn't curled up in a blanket.

Chapter 81

The wind speed indicator told Thomas that the northerly breeze was increasing. The Islander 36 responded by heeling a few more degrees on its port side and slicing through the water at five and a half knots. Thomas continued to steer a northwest course to Port Madison at the north end of Bainbridge Island. He would be elated with the sailing conditions if it wasn't for the task ahead of him.

Now that he was out on the water to spread Rhonda's ashes he had another decision to make. Where? Did the actual spot make any difference? Of course not, wherever he sprinkled her remains the tiny particles would soon be engulfed by the sea and swept away or dissolved in the salty waves. Still, he had a decision to make. Where would he open the urn and release the ashes?

Their most memorable times were the cruising vacations spent in the San Juan Islands, over fifty miles north of his current location—much too far for a day sail. Maybe he should wait to spread her ashes until he had time to take the boat north into the islands. Thomas wrestled with the decision that took on more and more significance the longer he thought about it.

And wasn't that typical? He had always had a difficult time making decisions. Choices seemed to paralyze him. He would get wrapped up in weighing the pros and cons of every option, so afraid was he of making a wrong decision and getting criticized for it. Being a pastor only intensified the fear of criticism. He would even catch himself worrying that God would criticize him in Heaven for the stupid decisions he had made during his life.

It took Rhonda to help him out of the weeds when important decisions had to be made. Thomas marveled at how she had become so skilled at leading him through a decision-making process. He never felt like she was imposing her will on him. Just a gently nudge this way or that. She always had the perfect question to ask Thomas that would sweep away his confusion and point the way to the best decision.

Most . . . no, all . . . of the critical decisions in their lives and in the church were aided by Rhonda. He couldn't have made them by himself.

The wind speed increased slightly. The boat carrying maximum sail area was a little overpowered, but Thomas was too deep in thought to notice.

What was he going to do without her? Would he be able to make important decisions alone? That was doubtful considering here he was having difficulty with a simple enough decision as to where in Puget Sound to spread her ashes. Decisions in his life were one thing, but what about the Beacon Bible Church?

The thought hit Thomas hard. Could he continue to lead his church without Rhonda? He didn't have confidence in his ability to make important decisions without her. He had already seen the decline in staff morale and performance during her time away from the day-to-day operations.

Face it, Thomas, old boy, you're nothing without her.

A gust of wind hit the sails. The boat heeled violently to the port side. Water boiled over the stainless-steel toe rail that rimmed the deck. Thomas could have touched the water, so far over was the boat tilted. The urgent situation brought Thomas out of his trance.

The Islander 36 was carrying too much sail for the strength of the wind now blowing in from the north. With each gust, the boat heeled too far over until wind spilled from the angled sails. Then with less pressure on the sails the boat began to right itself and turn into the wind. Each time that happened boat speed fell and the boat's course zig-zagged. Thomas turned the wheel slightly to starboard to keep the bow into the wind. The sails started flapping wildly. He kept the boat headed into the wind just long enough to minimize pressure on the sails, so he could reduce the size of the jib. With one hand on the wheel and the other pulling the jib furling line he was able within a few seconds to reduce the jib area by thirty percent. *Harriet's Chariot* rewarded him by resuming its ideal heel angle and sped along its course at four and half knots.

With the sails nicely trimmed once again, and the boat under control, Thomas relaxed behind the wheel. His thoughts returned to Rhonda and the church. He seriously wondered if he could manage the church without her. Like fruit on the vine would it continue to grow, or slowly wither and rot?

One of his favorite passages of scripture came to mind and reminded him that the church is about a relationship with Jesus, not a relationship with Thomas. Or with Rhonda for that matter.

"⁵I am the vine; you are the branches. If you remain in me and I in you, you will bear much fruit; apart from me you can do nothing. ⁶If you do not remain in me, you are like a branch that is thrown away and withers . . ." John 15: 5-6, NIV

Thomas decided it was the perfect time to have a little talk with Jesus. "Jesus, I am troubled. Deeply troubled. I feel lost without Rhonda. I feel weak without her. I doubt my ability to lead the church you so graciously gave me to shepherd. Lord, I don't think I can do it without Rhonda."

He paused. The only sound he heard was the wind and the waves against the fiberglass hull. Not that he was expecting an audible voice to answer back, but whenever he prayed and talked with Jesus, the voice of the Spirit would be clear in response. He was hearing nothing now. Perhaps his question wasn't clear enough.

"Lord, I'm asking for direction. Please ease my grief and give me the strength and guidance I need to lead this church."

Still no reply. Thomas caught himself thinking of different ways to make his questions clearer in hopes the added clarity would solicit a response. That was a ridiculous notion. Another passage came to mind.

"In the same way, the Spirit helps us in our weakness. We do not know what we ought to pray for, but the Spirit himself intercedes for us through wordless groans." Romans 8:26, NIV

"Jesus, see how lost I am. I can't even pray in a manner the Spirit will respond to. You know what's in my heart, please let me hear your words," Thomas said a little more emphatically.

Silence.

Harriet's Chariot continued its northwest course into Port Madison, a bay formed by the northern end of Bainbridge Island and a portion of the Kitsap Peninsula that juts eastward into Puget Sound. The strong wind was now partially blocked by a point of land to the north of Thomas' position. The boat's speed declined as the wind speed fell, but Thomas didn't care. He was much too troubled right now to care about sailing. A decision would be necessary, however. The bay was only about two miles long. Soon, very soon, he'd need to change course or risk grounding his boat on a shoal.

Beside when to change course, another decision still had to be made. Where was he going to spread Rhonda's ashes? That was the purpose of this entire trip and even after several hours he still couldn't decide on where the perfect place would be to open the urn and let her ashes fall into the sea.

It was as if his mind had shut down. He couldn't process ideas or thoughts in his usual fashion. Even worse, he began to feel alone. Very, very alone. Tears erupted from his eyes. His Rhonda was not by his side and neither was his God. At his time of deepest need, where was God? Another passage came to his mind.

"God, my God, why have you forsaken me?" Matthew 27:46 (NIV)

The last words of Jesus on the cross, so often misunderstood, seemed to express exactly how Thomas was feeling at this moment. God had first taken Rhonda from him and now was turning his back on Thomas' desperate prayers.

Out loud Thomas shouted, "Lord, what I have done to deserve this? I have always been your faithful servant. I have built a church for You. I have brought hundreds of people to know you for the first time. Our missions relieve suffering. Why don't you hear me now. Why can't you ease my pain?"

Thomas wiped tears from his eyes just in time to notice the Indianola pier less than 100 yards directly in front of him. He'd been so blinded by his grief and doubt he hadn't noticed just how close he was getting to shore. If he didn't change course fast he'd crash into the pier.

He stood, released the jib sheet and spun the wheel at the same time. The boat's bow began to move to the left. He eased the main sheet too, ducking to permit the boom to cross over. He heard a cheer from over his shoulder. He looked back. There, standing on the end of the pier, several people were applauding his maneuver. If they only knew how close he had come to ramming *Harriet's Chariot* into the barnacle-covered pilings right beneath their feet.

The light wind was now filling the sails from the rear quarter of the boat. The Islander 36 settled into a comfortable reach on a heading that would take Thomas back to Shilshole Bay and the Ballard Locks.

But, what about Rhonda's ashes? It was time to decide. He looked around at the shoreline of the bay. It was a beautiful spot. He and Rhonda had sailed through here countless times while cruising the inlets of the Kitsap Peninsula and western shore of Bainbridge Island. Magnificent homes tucked into towering trees lined the shoreline. Why not here? Why not put her ashes here? It was picturesque, relatively calm, and better yet, the bay could be seen from the other side of Puget Sound. Whenever he wanted, he could drive to a bluff north of Seattle and look westward to the bay where he had placed her ashes.

That settled it. This was the place. Thomas locked the steering wheel to hold the course while he fetched Rhonda's ashes from the bookshelf below.

The breeze was still light across the bay, but he could see some white caps further out in the sound indicating that the wind was going to be a lot stronger as soon as he left the protection of the bay. He didn't have long.

Thomas sat in the cockpit with the urn held tightly in his shaking hands. Memories flowed through his mind. How is it possible that such a beautiful, loving soul, so full of life, ends as a small pile of ashes? He had comforted so many people who had lost loved ones, but he was struggling to come to grips with his own loss. After all, how could one explain that all the loving moments of the past twenty-two years end up as forty-eight ounces of ash?

"You took her from me too soon, Lord! We built a church for you. We had so many plans. You took her too soon. Why? Why? Why?"

Thomas slowly opened the urn. He stepped to the starboard side of the boat to be downwind. He wanted the ashes to be gloriously spread into the sea, not all over the deck. He couldn't stand the idea of having to hose down the hull to remove his wife's remains.

"Good bye, my love," was all Thomas could manage to say as he tipped the urn and watched as the freshening breeze carried her ashes into the air and sea.

Thomas replaced the empty urn in the bookshelf below deck. When he came back to the cockpit he felt as empty as the urn. His passion for preaching the gospel was gone. His confidence in leading people to a relationship with Christ had been blown away. How could he preach and inspire when God had turned away from him in his time of need? Wasn't this a clear sign that God didn't want

Thomas to lead a church anymore? With Rhonda gone, God knew he couldn't handle it. He wasn't good enough by himself to honor the Lord with his labor.

The wind increased. *Harriet's Chariot* surged forward leaving a boiling wake behind as the hull speed reached six knots. It was exhilarating sailing, except Thomas wasn't experiencing any of that thrill. Instead a darkness gradually began to fill his heart.

He reached Shilshole Bay an hour later. By the time he had furled both sails and turned on the diesel engine in preparation for entering the locks, the decision had been made.

He was leaving the church. Tomorrow he'd submit his resignation as Pastor of the Beacon Bible Church.

Chapter 82

While Thomas steered the sloop the last seven miles back to its dock on Lake Washington he contemplated the implications of his decision. He would be without a job. That meant no salary. The minuscule royalties he received for his two popular books couldn't support him. Rhonda's life insurance would help, but a lot of that was going to be eaten up by medical bills their health insurance didn't cover.

Thomas estimated he could just scrape together enough each month to cover the mortgage payment, but that was it. Nothing else for living expenses. He would have to find other employment or sell the house, that was clear enough. But that raised a big question. What does a pastor do after leaving the church? Being a pastor was all he knew how to do. Oh sure, he could work for a religious charity. Any number of them would be eager to have Thomas on staff, but could he do the work? He figured any job in a non-profit organization would require inspiring, leading, and organizing—the characteristics that Rhonda was strong in, not him. Besides, if God is indeed forsaking him, what business is it of Thomas' to continue to do the Lord's work in any capacity? After all, didn't God give Thomas a pink slip today? Didn't Thomas just get fired by the Almighty?

The Spirit hadn't spoken words of comfort to Thomas today, even when he cried out for help. Instead, there was silence. Instead of encouragement and direction, Thomas was given a powerful sense of worthlessness. Why?

Had Thomas become too proud? Too proud of his role at Beacon Bible Church? Had he looked at the church buildings, staff, and congregation as his rather than God's?

Was that why God took Rhonda away, to make Thomas see how weak and useless he was without her? Is that what was going on here?

So, was it Thomas' fault that Rhonda died?

With the weight of this crushing thought heavy on his heart, he gently nudged the hull of *Harriet's Chariot's* against her dock. He secured the dock lines and sprayed the deck with a hose to remove salt water residue.

What about his wife's urn on the shelf below in the cabin? He decided to leave it behind. He couldn't bear to look at it again; at least not for a very long time. After locking the companionway, Thomas checked that dock lines and fenders were tied securely before turning his back on the sloop and walking slowly, head down, shoulders stooped, up the pathway past the stately waterfront home and to his car parked on the tree-lined street.

Chapter 83

On June 28 Thomas stood in his living room, sipping a mug of coffee while watching through the window as the realtor placed a "For Sale" sign in the front lawn.

That's done, he thought to himself. Another item to check off from the list. He sauntered back to his office and studied the long list of to-dos written on the white board. He picked up a red marker from the tray and made a neat check mark next to the eighth item, "List house for sale".

1. Resign from church
2. Receive Rhonda's life insurance benefits
3. Cancel Rhonda's cell phone
4. Pay off hospital
5. Rent storage room
6. Prepare house to sell
7. Reserve moorage in Friday Harbor
8. List house for sale
9. Pay off doctor Warner
10. Pay off doctor Smith
11. Pay off credit cards
12. Pay off Toyota
13. Have meeting with financial planner
14. Close all utilities accounts
15. Pack boat

He was making rapid progress toward closing a chapter of his life. People had always told him that making life changes was difficult. Not really. When you didn't have many viable options, the choices became easier. Kris Kristofferson said it best in his song, *Me and Bobby McGee.*

And that's what Thomas reminded himself as he listened to the song each day stream from his phone's music library through his ear buds and deep into his brain.

He had nothing else to lose. God had taken his Rhonda away.

So, he had made his list on the white board, and began the process of unraveling his life as if pulling on a loose end of yarn hanging from an intricately woven sweater until the beautiful patterns of the sweater were converted to a pile of twisted string.

He sat in his desk chair and studied the list on the wall in front of him. How easily he left the church surprised him. Once he had made up his mind on the boat after spreading Rhonda's ashes, he never wavered. Oh sure, the executive staff at Beacon Bible Church tried to convince him that he shouldn't make such a significant decision during a period of intense grief. The church Board advised him that he was still in shock. He should simply take more time off; a sabbatical perhaps was the right answer.

But not a single person had come to him and said the words that might have made a difference: *We need you, Pastor Benton.* The staff and Board didn't express any concern that the church could survive the loss of its "voice" and its "heart" in the same month. Thomas could take their reaction only one way. The executive staff and Board were relieved to see Thomas resign. They doubted Thomas' ability to lead effectively in Rhonda's absence. They were eager for new leadership.

They had pleaded with him to stay, but Thomas didn't or couldn't recognize any sincerity in their words. He held fast to his decision. At the end of the day, a little over three weeks ago, it was settled. The church accepted Thomas' resignation, an interim Senior Pastor was named, a search committee was assigned to recruit a replacement. Thomas would deliver one final sermon and say goodbye to the 2,300 members of the church that he and Rhonda founded twelve years ago in the living room of their apartment.

True, Thomas had shed a few public and private tears over the past twenty-one days since his resignation. There was a flood of heart-warming cards, emails and phone messages wishing him well and thanking him for his contribution to the church. He knew the prayer group had included him in their prayers, too. He hoped God would listen to *them*. The Lord didn't appear to be interested in *his* prayers.

Chapter 84

S andra, his realtor and a long-time member of Beacon Bible Church, had warned Thomas that with the July 4th holiday approaching, the number of inquiries and showings for his house would be light. She estimated that in today's market the home would sell in about fifty-eight days. She had been right about the light traffic. Between June 28 and July 5 only three couples toured the Benton home. Yet on July 6, Sandra called excitedly to announce she had received an offer.

Three days later, after the usual negotiations, he signed the offer. Sandra was amazed at how quickly the home had sold and that they were able to get ninety-eight percent of their original asking price.

"God was certainly on your side, Thomas," Sandra said, smiling. "In less than a week a motivated buyer able to pay cash agreed to buy your home. With prices so high, cash deals are rare in this neighborhood. I still can't believe it. Praise God!"

Thomas thought about Sandra's statement. He didn't feel like celebrating. Sure, he'd praise God. Selling the house quickly was one more clear sign that God wanted him away from his pastoral duties as soon as possible. Wasn't it another indication that God had lost faith in Thomas? But, was that even possible? Could God ever "give up" on one of his children? Thomas didn't think so, but lately he felt like God had taken a hiatus from guiding Thomas Benton.

With the church work done and house sold, Thomas busied himself by liquidating most of his and Rhonda's belongings. He was downsizing to the extreme. The basic furniture and kitchen ware were placed in storage. Someday he might need the stuff. He packed his treasured library into boxes and they too went into storage. He permitted himself to keep ten books. After all, anything else he wanted to read could be obtained on his Kindle.

When he wasn't clearing out the house, he was preparing *Harriet's Chariot*. It would be his new home for . . . for how long? Thomas didn't know the answer. Perhaps until his money ran out, or God decided to speak to him again and give him a mission to accomplish.

The slip in Friday Harbor had been arranged several weeks ago and checked off on his white board. He felt fortunate to have secured long-term moorage in this popular harbor on San Juan Island. Another signal from God telling him to leave. He had selected Friday Harbor for his next residence because the charming town had daily ferry and float plane services, which gave him easy access to the mainland, if and when he wanted it. It was also a very charming town. The harbor was in the heart of one of the finest cruising areas in the world, the archipelago known as the San Juan Islands on the border between the U.S. and Canada.

For *Harriet's Chariot* to be a suitable vessel for living aboard, several important additions had to be made including a heating system for the cabin, and a water heater that didn't require running the engine. Once both had been installed by his favorite yacht supply company on Portage Bay, all that remained was packing the boat with clothes, food, bedding, computer, a small TV, and books.

At 9:35 in the morning of July 19, Thomas left the title company after signing the closing documents for his house. He drove directly to *Harriet's Chariot's* dock in Laurelhurst. Bernie Swartz, the homeowner who had so graciously let Thomas dock his boat there for years rent free, greeted him as Thomas walked down the path in the back yard toward the lake.

"This is it? You're really leaving us?" Bernie asked.

"No place else to go," said Thomas with a smile.

"It'll be strange looking out the window and not seeing *Harriet's Chariot* at the dock," Bernie said.

"There's a simple solution; buy a boat," chuckled Thomas, knowing full well that Bernie could afford to buy five boats like *Harriet's Chariot*.

"That's what Margaret is telling me. Of course, all she really wants is a big cabin cruiser we can take to the Husky games," Bernie shook his head, "Pretty expensive ride to a football game, if you ask me." Margaret, a graduate of the University of Washington, was fanatical about her team. Bernie, who graduated from UCLA, only cared when his team was playing the Huskies, but each year he didn't flinch when his wife donated generously to her alma matter and secured season tickets.

From where the two men stood in the back yard of the stately Swartz home they could look to the southwest and see the football stadium a mile or so away on the shores of Lake Washington. It was a pleasant ritual for Husky alumni who owned boats and season tickets to take their boats to the games rather than drive. The "sailgating" parties were legendary.

Thomas set down the box that he had been carrying in order to remove car keys from his pocket. "Here, before I forget. You'll need these." Thomas handed the keys to Bernie.

"No problem, Margaret and I will bring the car to you next weekend. We have the logistics all figured out. I'll call you to confirm the day and which ferry we'll be on."

"Much appreciated, my friend. I will want to have some wheels on the island. I won't be happy sitting in the boat every day," Thomas said. He shook Bernie's hand and hugged him firmly before picking up the box once again. He wanted to ask about Beacon Bible Church, but was afraid that Bernie would tell him all was well at the church. *In other words, Thomas, ol' boy, you aren't missed.*

"I gotta run. Need to put some miles under the keel today if I expect to reach Friday Harbor at a reasonable time tomorrow. Give my love to Margaret and the twins."

"I will. Hey, let me help you push off."

The two men walked in silence onto the dock. Thomas got on board *Harriet's Chariot*, put the box below in the cabin and turned on the engine. Bernie untied the dock lines. At Thomas' signal he pushed the bow away from the dock, tossing the lines onto the boat. Thomas moved the gear lever to forward. The sleek craft slowly pulled away from the dock that had been its home for a decade, never to return.

Chapter 85

A little before seven in the evening, Thomas steered *Harriet's Chariot* into the narrow entrance to Point Hudson Marina in Port Townsend. He had made good time under power and taking advantage of the ebb tide to push him northward.

He topped off his tank at the fuel dock, paid for a night's moorage, and steered his boat carefully into its assigned slip.

After stretching his legs with a short walk ashore to buy a bottle of wine, he returned to fix dinner aboard and plan tomorrow's itinerary. Not in the mood for preparing a meal, he cut up a few vegetables for salad and heated a can of beef stew. It had been a very long time since he had prepared a meal on his boat. It would take a little time to get used to the cramped galley compared to the spacious kitchen in his house. But, like everything else in his new life. He'd adjust.

After a day in the fresh air, Thomas was starving. He wolfed down all of the stew and salad while consuming two plastic cups of wine. For dessert he eyed the bag of donuts, but settled for a Snickers bar instead.

Rhonda wouldn't have approved, but if Rhonda had been there she would have fixed an amazing dinner, not something out of can that happened to look like beef stew.

After cleaning the dishes, Thomas unfurled a nautical chart on the settee table and reached behind him for the tide tables book. Friday Harbor lay north of his current position about forty miles. A course of 340 degrees north by northwest would take him across the Strait of Juan de Fuca, and through San Juan Channel. From the channel it was only another five miles to Friday Harbor.

The trip would take about seven hours not considering the tide, but the tide was going to be a factor tomorrow.

The next ebb was due at 7:22 tomorrow morning. That would give him a nice push leaving Port Townsend, but within two hours as he neared the middle of the Strait on his northward course the ebb current heading to the sea from the northern parts of the Sound would actually be against him, slowing his progress considerably. The bigger concern was San Juan Channel, a narrow passage between Lopez and San Juan Islands that he had to pass through. At its strongest ebb the water rushes through the channel at over three knots. At full speed under power, *Harriet's Chariot* could move at six knots. Thomas was faced with the real prospect of traveling the final five miles of his journey tomorrow in two hours rather than one.

He plotted his course allowing for the westward pull of the ebb tide and the strength of the current against his boat's hull. Satisfied with his navigation and departure time, Thomas poured another glass of wine, lit a cigar and relaxed in the cockpit.

Thomas gazed into the starlit night as a light breeze whistled through the rigging of a hundred boats in the harbor, making a lonely tune.

It was time to have another little talk with God. "Here I am, Lord. Happy now? You pushed me out my church. You drew me out of Seattle. All I know is that I'm heading to Friday Harbor tomorrow. I don't have a clue what I'm to do after that. It'd be nice to know. Is it too much to ask for an explanation of why you have taken everything from me that I love?"

He sipped his red wine and took a long drag on the Macanudo cigar. He wasn't accustomed to consuming much alcohol or smoking, and his head was feeling a little dizzy.

"That's right. You took away everything I love." He patted the fiberglass deck with his free hand, "You took everything but this boat, Lord. What's with that? I mean I'm grateful, don't get me wrong, but everything I cherish is gone except *Harriet's Chariot*. Am I supposed to be some modern-day, Noah?" Thomas laughed and continued to talk out loud to himself, not caring at this point whether anyone could hear him or not. "Excuse me for pointing this out, Lord, by my boat won't hold many animals. If your plan is to send me off and gather two of everything, like Noah, I'm going to need a bigger boat."

Thomas laughed again and tried to take another draw from his cigar. It was no longer lit. He carefully stepped down the four steps of the companionway leading into the main cabin to fetch a light. He kept matches and a propane lighter in a moisture-proof box on the bookshelf. He reached for the box—but stopped. Leaning against the plastic box on the shelf was a Bible he always kept on board. Next to the Bible was Rhonda's urn. The irony of the moment was so intense it took Thomas' breath away. Here he was, having a monologue with God about all that had been taken from Thomas' life, when he innocently reached for a lighter and there's the empty urn that once held Rhonda's ashes. He looked down at the cigar still held in his mouth at the cold ashes on the tip.

"Ashes to ashes, isn't that right, God?" He angrily opened the container, struck a match and held it to the cigar until the cold ashes on the end glowed red. He returned to the cockpit and the remainder of his wine.

After a fitful sleep, Thomas walked to the marina's paid showers and tried to enjoy a hot shower before the meter's time ran out, requiring more quarters, which he didn't have. He wanted to linger in the hot water mostly because his head ached badly. Three glasses of wine were too much. He managed to finish the shower in time, redressed, and strolled back to the boat eager for a cup of coffee and several Tylenol.

While cleaning up the galley he listened to the forecast on the weather radio. It was going to be a good day for sailing, but another front was due to arrive in the evening. According to his calculation, 9:30 was the right time to leave so he wouldn't be fighting the strongest ebb current while navigating San Juan channel.

At 9:34 Thomas left Hudson Marina, looked at the compass, and steered *Harriet's Chariot* on its heading toward San Juan Channel.

Because visibility and weather were good, the next leg of the journey across the Strait of Juan de Fuca could be relaxing. He needed to check his course from time to time making sure his adjustment for the current could accurately lead him to his destination. Other than that he could relax and even read. After an hour of powering the wind picked up out of the southeast. Thomas decided to cut the engine and sail on a reach. The Islander 36 responded well to the full set of sails that Thomas unfurled. Soon the boat was racing along at six knots. The sailing lifted Thomas' spirits. He set the self-steering vane and let the boat steer herself.

He attended to a few chores down below before returning to the cockpit with a snack of smoked oysters, cheese, crackers and a beer. Although relaxed, he periodically scanned the water around him looking for floating debris that could damage the hull, or a vessel approaching on a collision course. From a storage compartment in the cockpit he retrieved a safety harness and tether. Putting it on he scolded himself for not doing so before leaving the marina. The tether and harness would prevent him from falling overboard.

About a mile south of the entrance to San Juan Channel, Thomas retracted the self-steering vane, furled the sails, and turned on the engine. He pushed the throttle to ninety percent power to force his way against the current. His navigation had been good. He was entering the channel after it had reached maximum ebb. The current's strength would slowly diminish over the next few hours. Right now, however, the current was still between two and three knots on the bow. Thomas stood at the wheel and steered his sloop into the channel.

The sky was turning dark with heavy clouds and the wind shifted direction. The strong weather front that was forecast for this evening was coming fast. Would he make it to the harbor before the summer storm arrived? He didn't relish the idea of sailing the next few miles through this narrow waterway in a storm. Nor did he look forward to entering a tight harbor in the dark, with gusts of wind and rain making steering difficult. But, he was powerless to do anything about his situation. The boat was traveling as fast as it could against the current. Thomas gripped the wheel and kept an eye on his instruments. The barometer was falling, wind speed from the northwest was freshening. Visibility was still good although the dark clouds were prematurely bringing darkness to the day. All he could do was continue on his course. He could do nothing about the storm or the current.

Another sailboat was heading out of the channel. It had the current at its stern pushing him along. The situation reminded Thomas of a sermon he gave this time last year. It was about how faith was like stepping into a river's current. You didn't know where the river would take you, but if you didn't fight it, the journey would be filled with joy and peace. So, here was Thomas chugging against the current while the other guy in his 40-foot sloop sped by effortlessly in the opposite direction with the current.

In the summer dusk at 8:45 Thomas nestled *Harriet's Chariot* into her new home-slip at the marina in Friday Harbor just as lightning flashed across the sky and strong gusts of wind lashed the harbor with sheets of cold rain.

Chapter 86

or the next two weeks, Thomas settled into his new routine. He would start each morning at 6:30 with a brisk two-mile walk, during which he'd pray. Back at the boat he'd enjoy a cup of coffee while sitting in the cockpit writing in his journal.

He devoted an hour each morning to boat maintenance. There was always something on the boat that needed cleaning, repair, or preventative maintenance.

He got into the habit of taking a late-morning stroll, tall mug of coffee in his hand, along the guest docks at the marina. Every day new boats would come and go, giving him opportunities to meet people and engage in small talk. For the most part, the boats that came and went this time of year were families on vacation. A few were seasoned boaters. Others he could tell didn't get out on the water much and probably were just renting their boat for a week or so. Thomas turned it into a game to see if he could guess how experienced the family was with boating just by observing the boat's equipment, and how the people related to their boat. As soon as he had them classified as "rookie", "serious boater", or "blue water" he'd greet them and start a conversation. Within a few minutes he'd know for sure where they ranked on his scale. So far, he was right ninety percent of the time.

The category of boater didn't matter much to Thomas. He managed to have good conversations with most of them. There were a few loners, "hobbits", Thomas liked to call them, that made it clear Thomas' friendly intrusion into their floating life wasn't welcome. Most folks, however, enjoyed the opportunity to shake hands and swap stories, especially once they found out that Thomas lived aboard his boat here in paradise, in Friday Harbor. People who don't live aboard a boat invariably have a romantic notion about living aboard. It brings out the yearnings for the gypsy life that hides just below the surface in some people.

Many of the boaters he talked to admitted that they occasionally dreamed of just selling everything, getting on a boat and leaving their worries behind. Thomas could relate.

On August fourth, during his morning stroll down the guest dock, Thomas noticed a large sailboat approaching with obvious intentions of docking. One person stood on the foredeck with a mooring line in hand; another person stood on the stern with a second mooring line at ready. Thomas quickened his pace to reach the end of the dock in time to help the crew secure the craft to the dock, a common courtesy among boaters.

The helmsman expertly guided the large sloop closer to the dock and Thomas signaled to the crew member on the foredeck to toss him the bow line, which he did. Thomas caught the heavy braided line and quickly made a hitch around a mooring cleat on the dock. Thomas stepped to where he could receive the stern line tossed by the crewmember standing on the rear of the boat. Thomas looped the stern line around another dock cleat, but didn't tie it off. Instead he held the loose end and watched as the helmsman, with the wheel hard over, brought the stern of the boat closer to the dock until it was perfectly parallel and only three feet away. Thomas watched as the tall, portly man behind the wheel put the engine in neutral, and spun the large wheel to bring the rudder straight. Thomas pulled on the stern line. This slowly brought the stern close enough to the dock for the crew members to jump off the boat onto the dock.

One man, about Thomas' age, smiled and took his stern line, the other man, a little older, unhitched the bow line at the dock. Together the two men pulled hard on the nylon docklines until the heavy vessel's protective fenders that lined the hull were snug against the dock. They each expertly retied the mooring lines at the dock cleats with a double hitch.

The vessel's deck was four feet higher than the dock. The tall helmsman towered over Thomas as he looked down and thanked him for assisting with docking.

"We appreciate the help," said the man in a deep voice with a slight accent that Thomas couldn't identify.

"No problem. Where you in from?" Asked Thomas.

"We left Victoria early this morning. Stayed there three days after our crossing from Maui." He said it like crossing the Pacific Ocean in a sailboat was the same as coming back from the grocery store down the street. "What about you?"

"I live aboard. This is my home." Thomas gestured with his hand sweeping around the marina.

The helmsman took a quick look around the harbor and marina. "Nice spot. So, you know these waters pretty well?"

"My wife and I used to cruise the islands every year. Yes, I'd say I'm very familiar with the area," Thomas said.

"We want to do a bit of exploring. We'll be here another couple weeks before heading back to San Francisco. Say, why don't you join us for happy hour and dinner tonight? You can give us some tips."

"That would be wonderful. I'd enjoy it. What time?"

"Five o'clock. My name is Otto." He reached a large, suntanned hand down to shake Thomas' hand.

Thomas reached up to shake. His own hand felt small and weak in the grip of this large man. "I'm Thomas Benton. Dinner sounds good. See you back here at five." Thomas turned and walked away. He had gone about twenty feet when he heard Otto's voice booming from behind.

"And bring your wife, too."

Thomas stopped. He was too far away to shout an explanation that everyone on the dock could hear. Instead he just waved signaling that he'd heard the man. Then he continued up the dock and back to *Harriet's Chariot.*

This wasn't the first time since he'd relocated to Friday Harbor that a stranger had assumed he was married. After all, he still wore his gold wedding band. So, why was he feeling so low? As he stepped aboard his sloop in the permanent mooring area of the marina he sensed depression descend upon him like a damp cloud. He hadn't felt like this in many days. This morning, on the contrary, he had been in very good spirits. What had happened to change his mood?

On his chore list today was cleaning the boat's head and floor—not his favorite chore by far, but just as necessary as all the others on his list. He retrieved the cleaning supplies from one of the storage lockers beneath a seat in the cockpit and proceeded to clean the toilet, sink, and walls of the little compartment that was his bathroom on the boat. Then, with a little broom, he swept the cabin's floor and went over the floor with a damp cloth. George Strait tunes kept Thomas company as he wiped and scrubbed. In a half hour his daily boat chores were done, but it was laundry day, too. He always did laundry in the middle of the week when the marina's laundromat was less crowded.

Sitting in the laundromat while his clothes were in the washer, Thomas had difficulty concentrating on the book he had been reading on his Kindle. The depressed feeling from earlier hadn't left him. Something was eating at him. What was it?

He retraced his steps from the morning. When did this odd feeling first strike? He was fine until . . . until he shook Otto's hand! Okay, now he was getting somewhere. He had pinpointed the moment but hadn't identified why his mood changed after the hand shake.

While he tossed his wet clothes into the dryer Thomas was deep in thought about Otto's handshake. Otto had been friendly, gregarious even. Standing tall on the deck of his yacht, he had an air of confidence that was immediately obvious. Thomas recalled the man's words, "We stopped in Victoria after our crossing from Maui." It was said so nonchalantly; like it was no big deal that he had just sailed a boat 2,300 miles over open ocean. Thomas calculated that the total miles of the cruises he had taken in his life wouldn't come close to what Otto had accomplished in just one voyage. There was another fact, too. Thomas had never been in a small sailboat on the open sea. The closest he had come to bluewater sailing was the year he crewed on a friend's boat in the annual Swiftsure Yacht Race, but the 140-mile race course only took the racers about fourteen miles offshore to a buoy, which they rounded before returning eastward to the start-finish line in the Strait near Victoria, B.C.

Thomas admitted he was a little envious of Otto's sailing accomplishments. Maybe envy was responsible for the weird feeling possessing him now. No, there was something else. Other laundry-doers came and went, but Thomas didn't notice. In his perplexed state of mind he saw little. What was it about shaking the strong, tanned hand, rough with callouses from days spent steering and handling lines? Thomas' mind went around and around just like his clothes in the dryer.

Slowly he began to unpack his emotional reaction to the handshake, but he didn't get to the bottom of it until he started folding his dried clothes. Coming into contact with this strong, confident man reminded Thomas of just how weak and inadequate he was. That's what was eating him all right. Thomas believed he couldn't lead the church, or his life, without Rhonda. He had depended on her, and when she died he was lost. He didn't have the courage to take the reins at Beacon Bible Church by himself. He was a weak, scared, inadequate man without a reason for living.

Yeah, that's what was bugging him. Otto's strong, confident handshake was such a contrast to Thomas' inadequate little life.

Chapter 87

The laughter was contagious. The four men seated at the galley table aboard Otto's yacht were recalling their most embarrassing moments while sailing. Some of the stories had to do with events on board a boat, others on shore in some dark bar in a faraway harbor.

Despite Thomas' self-pity earlier in the day, he was in good spirits now partially because of the contagious bonhomie of the three men, and partially because of the wine. They had just finished their third bottle and Otto was uncorking a fourth.

Two hours earlier, the three men had warmly welcomed Thomas aboard the Little Harbor 54, named *Ocean Angel.* Of course, Thomas had to first explain why he arrived at the boat without his wife, whom Otto had made a point to invite.

Tonight's dinner was going to be the closest thing to a party that Thomas had attended since Rhonda's passing. He missed her presence by his side immensely. Worse yet, he wasn't used to having to carry his own weight in a group conversation. He suddenly realized just how dependent he had been on his wife to keep a conversation going during social gatherings. It was different now. He couldn't just sit with a drink in his hand and smile while she chatted and made friends with everyone. He had to talk. He had to be personable. He had to forge relationships with these three strangers.

Together they consumed the first bottle of wine while conversing in the large cockpit and waiting for the pizzas to be delivered from the gourmet pizza restaurant in town just a few blocks from the marina. For Thomas' benefit they each told their story.

The three men of *Ocean Angel* couldn't have been more different. Otto Vikander, 49, was a large, burly man of Scandinavian descent. He had run a boutique venture capital firm in San Francisco until late last year when he stepped down as managing partner due to "health reasons," which was all Otto would say about it. He certainly looked healthy to Thomas. The man was built like a quarterback. He stood about six-foot-three and Thomas guessed he weighed in at around 225 pounds. Otto's physique and deep, booming voice betrayed his gentle, intelligent eyes.

Otto had owned *Ocean Angel* for over five years, and in that time had taken her as far south from San Francisco as Cabo San Lucas on the southern tip of the Baja peninsula to follow migrating Gray whales. Not to show a preference for any species of whale, the following year he steered the large sloop westward to Hawaii to arrive during the Humpback whale migration. Including his most recent trip, he had sailed to Hawaii and back twice.

Thomas admired the man. He was wealthy, confident, smart and accomplished, but did he have Jesus in his life? At no point in the conversation had Otto given a clue as to his religious leanings. That was the pastor thinking again— looking for souls to save. Thomas pushed the thought from his mind. He had his own soul to worry about now. Besides, God didn't want him in the soul-saving business anymore, did He?

Matt Kani, 52, was the jokester of the crew. The black man with a strong South African accent had the fastest wit Thomas had ever known. It didn't surprise Thomas to learn that when Matt traveled, which was often, he sought out comedy clubs on open mic nights. This gave him the opportunity to perfect his improvisational style of comedy.

Beside comedy and sailing, Matt knew his way around the business table. He was the oldest son of one of the wealthiest businessmen in South Africa. He had finance and business degrees from the London Business School and Stanford. Rather than follow in his father's footsteps at the family's minerals conglomerate, he convinced his father to invest in a rental car business he wanted to start. He sold the company six years later, securing an excellent return for his father and providing himself enough money to buy another company without outside funding. Matt became a serial entrepreneur. He had made a lot of money on his own, but it was nothing compared to what he inherited when his father was killed in an auto accident. Matt was much too polite to mention specifics of his financial situation, but he did let slip that he didn't have to work anymore. It was a full-time job just managing his investments.

He had some real estate holdings in San Jose, California, and three years ago while in the city on business he stepped into a local comedy club for open mic night. As fate would have it, Otto was there with business associates, and was so taken by the South African's show that he invited Matt to his table. Soon the two discovered their mutual love of investing and sailing. Since that night the two had invested together and sailed together.

The youngest man of the three was slender, with long hair and full beard. He looked like a guitar player in a rock band, and that's exactly what he was. Jerry Levine, 38, was born in Israel, moved to New York City with his parents, attended Juilliard, dropped out, and left home "to find his muse."

After drifting back and forth across the country for a year he met a struggling band in Portland that had just lost its lead guitarist. He stood in for a night and the rest is history. Jerry Levine became the lead guitarist and song writer for DelivrUs, a band that during the next seven years sold over 32 million albums and performed to sold-out arenas around the world. Three years ago, the band broke up, and Jerry devoted his time to writing and producing.

One day he was speaking to a friend about his current project, a rock opera that he envisioned on Broadway. He was looking for a financial partner in the project. His friend happened to play tennis with a wealthy investor named Matt Kani. An introduction was made.

A year later *Against The Wall* opened on Broadway to rave reviews. The show was still running to sold-out audiences, and the two men were in negotiations with a large media company to produce a movie version. In addition, DelivrUs was talking about touring again, but Jerry was too exhausted to consider the grind of a tour.

Matt convinced Jerry to take some time off and join he and Otto on board *Ocean Angel* for the "Maui Wowee Adventure," as they referred to it.

After the three had told their stories, it was Thomas' turn. He had nervously looked up at the dock in hopes of spotting the approaching pizza delivery person that would provide a convenient excuse for not telling his life's story. With no rescue in sight, Thomas had no choice but to start talking.

In normal circumstances, among normal people, telling his story wouldn't have been that difficult, but these weren't "normal" people relaxing with him around the cockpit of a 54-foot yacht. Each of these men were wildly successful and wealthy. Thomas knew his story was going to sound pathetically small and insignificant compared to these giants of business and the arts.

While Thomas spoke about his decision to attend seminary and his calling to start a church in Seattle, he watched the other men carefully. He was looking for early clues that they were getting bored, but Otto, Matt and Jerry sat attentively, listening to Thomas and sipping their wine. Their polite interest encouraged Thomas to continue.

"We had humble beginnings, like most churches. Just half a dozen people would crowd into the small living room of our one-bedroom apartment on Sundays to study scripture together. Those friends invited other friends and within a few months we had outgrown our apartment. We started having church in a movie theater that rented us space Sunday mornings, but we had to clear out of the space before noon when the first matinees would start. It's funny to think back on those days. Rhonda and I were always the last to leave. On the Sundays when blockbuster movies were running at the theater, we'd walk out the door carrying our boxes of materials and be face to face with a line of people waiting to buy tickets for the next *Star Wars* or whatever was playing. Three times as many people would see the first Sunday showing of a film than heard us talk about the Word.

"Anyway, one thing led to another and we built the church over ten years to what it is today."

Otto spoke, "Did you say the church had 2,300 members?"

"Yes, that's correct. A nice size. Large enough to have the resources to make a difference for a lot of people around the world and in Seattle, but not too big."

"That's an interesting number, Thomas. You know, we just sailed 2,300 miles from Maui. Your church has 2,300 members. That's quite a coincidence, don't you think?"

Thomas watched as the three men thoughtfully nodded their heads in agreement.

Then Jerry changed the subject. "How long was your wife sick before she passed?"

"Thirteen months. After six months of surgery and chemo the doctors were cautiously optimistic. She had a couple of good months. Her hair grew back after chemo and we thought she had beat it, but in January the doctors said the cancer had spread to her lymph glands. The prognosis was downgraded to terminal. She entered hospice care at our home in April. She collapsed at home and died at the hospital on April 28." Thomas took a long drink from his wine glass and stared out across the harbor with moist vacant eyes.

He felt a hand on his shoulder, then another, and another. Matt, Jerry and Otto each placed a hand on his shoulder. Jerry spoke softly, "Thomas, we're going to pray for you. Oh God, come to Thomas' assistance. Please take the consuming anguish he feels right now; take it from him and hold him in Your arms. Heal his broken heart and bind up his wounds. Amen."

Otto and Matt said together, "Amen."

Each man removed his hand and resumed sitting. Thomas looked at them. Six compassionate eyes looked back. The laying on of hands had happened so suddenly. He recognized the prayer as a personalized version of Psalm 147:3. He felt some relief after the prayer, and what surprised him the most was the prayer had been led by Jerry, a Jew.

"Thank you, very much. That was an unexpected gift," said Thomas. "And much needed I might add."

"You're welcome, Thomas," Matt said.

"Jerry, that was a wonderful prayer. You adapted the Psalm passage perfectly. Please don't take this wrong, but I'm a little surprised you know scripture so well," Thomas said.

"You mean because I'm Jewish?"

"Frankly, yes."

"I love aspects of Judaism and Christianity. I was born and raised a Jew, but when I joined DelivrUs they had been experimenting with a musical fusion that blended Christian rock with Country-Western and Swing. It was amazing music.

Easy to listen to. Easy to dance to. The lyrics told stories of love, faith and healing that were a joy to sing.

"The other band members were Christians. The more I got into their music the more drawn I was to Jesus. Before I knew it I was studying the Bible and writing music for the band. One day in Omaha while on tour, the drummer, Barry, baptized me in the swimming pool of the motel we were staying at. The album we recorded that year, *Water Wings*, went platinum. I wrote ten of the twelve songs on it. The Spirit was certainly at work in me. Praise God."

"I'd love to hear the album. I'll download it tomorrow," Thomas said.

It was Matt's turn to speak. "What we haven't told you, brother, is that each of us have suffered deep personal losses and found comfort in God. My wife divorced me and took our children to London. Otto lost his father and mother in a tragic ballooning accident in Santa Fe."

"Yeah, I was supposed to be in the balloon with them that day but had to go to a clinic to stop my nose from bleeding," Otto said. "I never have bloody noses, but that day I did. After the doctor packed my nose with gauze and stopped the bleeding he told me to rest. I said I had a ride in a hot air balloon scheduled for the afternoon and he insisted I not go. So, I didn't. The bloody nose saved my life.

"After losing my parents like that I was lost and bitter for quite some time. I even took on some guilt for not dying with them. Grief counseling helped a little. Eventually I reached out to Jesus for answers and comfort. What I received two years later was a heart attack. I sold out to my partners and semi-retired. I'd be totally retired if these two bozos wouldn't keep bringing me into fascinating deals."

"Don't blame us. Talk to God about it if you have a problem," Jerry said with a grin.

A voice coming from the dock interrupted the conversation. "You guys order a couple of pizzas?" The four men looked down from their position in the cockpit. A teenage boy holding an insulated pizza carrier stood there looking up. It was dinner time.

Chapter 88

Once the pizzas were in the teak-lined cabin, the mood and conversation changed from somber to jovial. Thomas began to relax and joined in on the good-natured dialogue that bounced from politics to sports to movies.

He marveled at the size and beauty of the yacht's interior. The yacht was eighteen feet longer and nearly three feet broader than *Harriet's Chariot*. From his place at the galley table Thomas could see the navigation station to the right of the companionway. Digital displays from navigation, radar, weather, and communications instruments lined the middle shelf. The control panel containing dozens of buttons and switches was to the left of the main instrument cluster. Several nautical charts were spread out on the polished desktop. The setup was much more advanced than Thomas' vessel. He relied on his charts, depth sounder and compass primarily, although he did install a simple GPS system a few years ago.

Otto noticed Thomas studying the navigation desk.

"Like my toys?" he asked.

"Pretty impressive setup, Otto," Thomas said.

"I do so much offshore sailing, I feel more comfortable having good instruments and some redundancy. Besides, I hate fog."

Matt spoke up, "Yeah, his navigation isn't that great. He needs all the help he can get."

The men laughed.

Jerry added, "Some time ask Otto to tell you about getting lost in the Sea of Cortez." More laughter.

Otto just grinned and shook his head in response to the good-natured ribbing.

The men finished their pizzas and salad. It was agreed the fourth bottle of wine would be best enjoyed with cigars in the cockpit. One by one they climbed up the four teak steps into the center cockpit of *Ocean Angel*.

Thomas felt compelled to ask about their voyages together. There was something about being aboard a real blue-water yacht that brought out the wanderlust in Thomas. Since having to sell his Seattle home, he had simply viewed his boat as a roof over his head. In reality, it was well-equipped for cruising the inland waterways of Puget Sound. Maybe even offshore.

With the fourth bottle gone, Otto began to ask Thomas questions about the best places to see in the San Juan Islands. They wanted to spend some time cruising the islands before heading back to San Francisco.

Thomas did his best to give them an overview of the best anchorages of each island. After a few minutes Otto just held up his hands to stop Thomas. "Wow, I can't remember all that. Tell you what. Why don't you be our tour guide? Can you get away for a week?"

"I live aboard and don't have a job, Otto. I'm always as free as you can get. What do you have in mind?"

"Just show us around the islands. You can join us on board, we have a spare bunk."

The idea of sailing with these men thrilled Thomas. "I have another idea. Since arriving here I haven't sailed my boat. Why don't we take both boats and cruise together? Each of you can take turns crewing with me, if you like."

Otto, Jerry and Matt looked at each other. Jerry said, "I move that we take a vote. All in favor of *Ocean Angel* joining *Harriet's Chariot* for a bit of gunkholing around the islands, say 'aye'."

"Aye" all three said in unison.

"Okay, it's settled. When do we leave?" Otto asked.

"Ten o'clock tomorrow," Thomas said, surprising himself with the certainty of his answer. "Let's meet for breakfast at eight at the Bay Café. We can plan our first day. I'll bring a chart."

Chapter 89

During breakfast they planned a loose itinerary for the week. They agreed to sail for four to six hours each day and anchor in a different bay or harbor each night. Otto wanted to return to Friday Harbor on August 11 so *Ocean Angel's* crew could spend a few days preparing her for the return voyage to San Francisco on the fourteenth.

Matt suggested *Ocean Angel's* crew take turns riding with Thomas aboard *Harriet's Chariot*. He volunteered to join Thomas today.

Ninety minutes later the two yachts powered out of Friday Harbor and turned northwest before unfurling their sails in the light breeze.

By mid-afternoon both sloops were securely anchored in Roche Harbor located at the north end of San Juan Island. Thomas had towed his inflatable tender behind *Harriet's Chariot* from Friday Harbor, and now used it to transport the four men ashore for supplies and to stretch their legs.

Walking by the hotel restaurant they studied the posted menu. It looked appealing, so the men decided to have an early dinner ashore before returning to their boats. During a dinner of fresh crab, scallops and warm sourdough bread, the conversation turned to offshore sailing. As the men talked about their adventures together on the open sea Thomas became more and more envious. He smiled and politely asked questions, but behind the smiling façade he was becoming uncomfortable. These men had accomplished so much. In comparison, what had he done besides start a church—a church God didn't want him to lead anymore.

After dinner the men walked back to the dinghy. Thomas started the little outboard motor and steered the inflatable boat out into the harbor as the sun began to set.

Jerry insisted that Thomas join them aboard *Ocean Angel* for a nightcap and cigar. Thomas tried to decline, but the other three insisted that he join them.

Once they were all situated in the cockpit with cigars and port, Jerry directed the conversation to Thomas' church, as if he could sense Thomas' growing discomfort.

"Thomas, I have to say I admire your faith and determination for starting a church. I don't think I could do it," Jerry said.

"Me either," Otto concurred.

Matt simply shook his head in agreement.

Jerry continued, "How did you do it? Man, from zero to over 2,000 members. That's really something."

"I've frequently asked myself that question. Why does one church grow and another doesn't? If they are all serving God, why aren't all churches successful? That's the main question," Thomas said.

Matt spoke, "Yeah, exactly. Why does God permit some churches to fail? Or why does he allow a church that is only loosely oriented to the Bible become a mega church?"

Thomas puffed on his cigar thoughtfully. "The answer has more to do with mankind's free will than it does with God's Will. Any church, after all, consists of people; people with free will. They have the free will to make decisions that follow the Word, or not. They have the free will to hear and follow the Spirit, or not. Sure, God has a plan for each of us, but we can screw it up if we're not connected to Him."

"I can certainly look back on my life and see the times when I made the wrong decision. In every case it was during a time that I wasn't that connected to God," Otto said.

"And Satan sure likes to mess with our churches, doesn't he?" Jerry said. "My goodness look at what happened in Tennessee last month. A very successful church there is now on the verge of collapse because the lead pastor was weak and became tempted."

A shiver ran through Thomas. Did Jerry suspect that Thomas left Beacon Bible Church because of some scandal? Was Jerry fishing for more information?

"Unfortunately, the church is not immune to sin. We were blessed, however. Our church had its ups and downs, but never suffered a scandal. I resigned because I didn't think I could lead effectively without Rhonda by my side. To tell you the truth, I think God wanted me to step down."

"Really? You think that way?" Matt asked.

"That's what I believe, but who knows. I thought I used to know what God's plan was for Rhonda and me, but I was wrong. Very, very wrong."

"I don't think we ever know God's plan. Not really. All we can see is maybe one step ahead. Only God knows all the steps in our life journey," Otto responded.

Thomas was becoming melancholy again. All he wanted right now was to be alone. "Well, gents, I think I will call it a night. Let's plan on pulling up anchor no later than 8:30 so we can get an early start heading to Prevost Harbor on Stuart Island." Thomas tossed his cigar in the water and moved to the stern to step down into his dinghy.

Before Thomas started the outboard, Jerry said, "Hey, I'll crew with you tomorrow."

"Okay, I'll come over and pick you up in the morning." Thomas started the outboard, untied the dinghy from *Ocean Angel* and drove off.

△ △ △

The three men sat down in the cockpit and looked at each other. "We need a strategy," Otto said.

"Indeed, we do," Jerry said.

"Yep," Matt agreed. "Let's pray for guidance about why God has put Thomas in our path. It's clear the man is hurting and lost, but what are we supposed to do about it, if anything?" After praying and meditating the three discussed what they individually heard from the Spirit.

Otto was first to share, "I kept hearing 'past behind', 'past behind'."

Matt said, "Trust. I heard 'trust' very clearly, but I don't know if the word was meant for me or if I'm supposed to help Thomas with trust."

Finally, Jerry had shared, "'Let go'. That's what I heard, 'let go', and I saw water when my eyes were closed."

Otto summarized, "Here's what we know. Thomas lost his wife over three months ago. He left his job thinking he couldn't handle it without her. From what I can see he is still grieving and has completely lost his confidence. I haven't mentioned this, but I knew the man was deeply troubled as soon as I shook his hand for the first time. It was one of the wimpiest handshakes I've ever experienced from a man."

"I fear he's losing his connection with God," Matt said.

"Me, too. He's under attack and losing strength," added Jerry.

"Are we in agreement that God wants us to help Thomas?" Otto asked.

They all nodded.

"Okay then. Thomas is our next project. Time is short, we only have until the fourteenth when we head back to San Francisco," Otto said.

△ △ △

Thomas secured the dinghy to *Harriet's Chariot* and climbed aboard. The cabin of the Islander 36 seemed cramped and plain after the time he had spent aboard the larger, better equipped yacht. Although he was still a little buzzed from the evening's alcohol consumption, Thomas settled into his usual nighttime routine when cruising.

He flipped the switch on the control panel to turn on the masthead light that would signal to other boats in the night that he was at anchor. He checked that all other switches were in their proper position. Then he turned on the weather radio while spreading a chart on the desktop.

It was his routine while cruising to always know what the weather would be during the night and the coming day before going to sleep. He also liked to plan the next day's trip by studying the chart, paying particular attention to any shoals to avoid. When his course and destination were settled he'd check the tide and current tables that would impact the journey the following day.

The NOAA weather radio report told him to expect normal August conditions for the next twenty-four hours. Winds would be light and variable, barometric pressure steady. Looking at the chart he refreshed his memory of the best course to take to Prevost Harbor. After referencing the *Tide and Current* book he felt well-enough informed for tomorrow that he could sleep without worry.

Replacing the *Tide and Current* book on the shelf next to his Bible and Rhonda's urn, reminded Thomas that he hadn't read the Bible or prayed today. He had let the excitement about sailing with *Ocean Angel* interrupt his daily routine.

Now, standing alone in his boat, reading or praying wasn't of interest. He couldn't shake the feeling of being less of man than the three he just left aboard Ocean Angel. He was without anyone to love him, without a job, without a purpose. He was a pathetic little man with a pathetic little bank account sailing nowhere in a small boat with an empty urn that used to contain his wife.

Thomas angrily turned off the cabin lights and shuffled forward to his berth.

Chapter 90

The next morning, after breakfast, Thomas ran the dinghy over to *Ocean Angel* to pick up Jerry, who was waiting for him with a guitar case in hand.

"Morning, Jerry," Thomas said as Jerry stepped carefully into the dinghy with the guitar.

"Good morning to you, Captain Thomas. Sleep well?"

"So-so. I never sleep soundly when I'm at anchor, even when tied to an anchor buoy. I've dragged anchor at night a few times."

"I hear ya. Done that myself."

Otto's booming voice from above Jerry and Thomas called out, "Hey, Thomas, which way you taking us today?" Otto stood on the deck high above the dinghy holding a chart in his hand. He'd obviously been studying his own chart.

Speaking over the sound of the idling outboard, Thomas replied, "The more scenic route is eastward through Spieden Channel. It's a little longer, but a lot more interesting. We'll turn northward at the Green Point Light on the southern end of Spieden Island.

"Understood. See you in Prevost." Otto gave a quick salute and disappeared from view as he readied his boat for departure.

At *Harriet's Chariot*, Jerry stowed his guitar below before walking to the foredeck to wait for Thomas' signal to untie the line securing them to the anchor buoy.

Thomas turned on the engine, checked his gauges and signaled to Jerry to untie the anchor line.

Within minutes both vessels were powering slowly through the calm waters of Roche Harbor toward Spieden Channel.

The "light and variable" wind that Thomas had heard the night before on his NOAA radio greeted the two sailboats in the channel. The southerly breeze was barely strong enough to fill their sails on a starboard reach as they headed eastward. At the Green Point Lighthouse on the southern tip of Spieden Island both vessels changed course to the north. The breeze freshened somewhat and they were able to make way on a broad reach at three knots toward their destination to the northwest.

Onboard *Harriet's Chariot*, Jerry and Thomas relaxed in the cockpit, sipping coffee, and watching the rugged shoreline slowly go by on the port side.

"This is sensational sailing, Thomas. What a paradise. You're very blessed to be able to just take off whenever you want," Jerry said.

"Yeah, it doesn't get any better than this," Thomas said.

"I was looking at the chart last night. There must be hundreds of places around here to drop the hook for the night or tie up at a marina."

"That is true. Although this time of year every little bay and harbor will be full of boats by mid-afternoon."

"What impresses me is you don't need to sail long distances each day to reach a new destination. A half-day sailing in any direction opens up a new world of possibilities for exploring and meeting new people."

Thomas nodded in agreement. "You're right. And, I'm really glad you guys came along and got me off my duff. I need to be enjoying all this before the weather changes. Believe me, sailing in an open boat is not so enjoyable November through April."

Both men sat in silence for a while. The only sound was the breeze through the rigging and the water moving past the hull. The light fog of the morning was nearly gone, and the sun began to warm the air.

"Jerry, take the wheel for me. I'm starving. I'll fix a snack for us," Thomas said.

Jerry took his turn at the wheel and Thomas went below.

Moments later Thomas carefully stepped up through the companionway carrying a plastic plate loaded with pastries, assorted nuts and sliced cheese. He set the plate on one of the bench seats in the cockpit, disappeared below one more time, and emerged with two mugs of steaming coffee.

Admiring the odd combination of food on the plate next to him, Jerry said, "Very creative."

Thomas laughed, "Yeah, isn't it? No different than the finest brunch buffet at some fancy European hotel. We have a policy on *Harriet's Chariot* of treating our guests well." Thomas took a large bite from a jelly donut.

Jerry selected a slice of cheese and a few nuts, which he ate while seated behind the wheel. With the calm seas and light breeze the sailing continued to be easy. Though the boat was only making 2-3 knots, the weather conditions were perfect for what Jerry had decided must be done.

Thomas was perfectly comfortable letting Jerry steer his boat. After all, the man had a lot of experience on a large yacht that had made long voyages across the open sea. Jerry probably knew more about boats than Thomas even. He pushed a slice of cheese into his mouth and decided it didn't pair well with the jelly donut he had just consumed.

"Rhonda would fix the most wonderful snacks and meals when we cruised together," he said. "I was always amazed at how innovative she could be in the galley. It took me having to start cooking for myself to realize that she hadn't been improvising all those snacks and meals; she had planned them well in advance.

That's why we always had whatever she needed in the icebox or food locker. She had planned the meals and bought the food we needed."

He put a handful of nuts in his mouth, chewed and washed them down with coffee. "Since she passed I've been kinda lost in the galley, but I manage. I haven't poisoned myself yet, and on the good side, I've lost ten pounds. Not being a good cook has been beneficial to my waistline." Thomas patted his stomach.

"Jerry, it seems every time I turn around I experience another way to miss my wife. It still feels like a big part of me is missing. I just don't feel whole without her," Thomas said. "I know the Bible says I am whole and complete in Christ, but I don't feel His presence as strongly anymore."

"Thomas, how about some music? I brought my guitar. Mind if I play on this beautiful morning?"

"Yes, please do. Great idea!"

A few moments later Jerry was back in the cockpit with a well-worn Martin guitar. "The humidity on a boat is really hard on a guitar, but I can't be separated from one for more than a day. So, I dedicated *Rehab* here to be my boat guitar. Every few months I take her to my guitar repair shop in San Francisco and they do their best to put her back into shape."

"*Rehab*? Interesting name for a guitar. Are you referring to the woman named Rehab in the book of Joshua, or are you making reference to personal rehabilitation of some sort?"

"A little of both," Jerry said and began to play.

For the next hour Jerry played the guitar and sang, while Thomas listened and steered *Harriet's Chariot* northward. As waves of music emitted from the sloop, seagulls danced in the wind above them. A colony of sea lions warming themselves on a grouping of rocks raised their heads, and like a lazy audience sitting on the grass at some city park concert, watched the sloop slowly go by.

For the most part, Jerry was playing his own music this morning. He rarely did that, preferring instead to play songs from other musicians, but this morning was different. He wasn't playing for himself to pass the time. He was on a mission.

△ △ △

Thomas thought Jerry had a wonderful tenor voice—soulful, a touch of gravel—like a good blues singer. It wasn't the clean, clear voice of a lead singer in a church choir. Not at all. Jerry's singing had a rough edge. The tone and emotion of his singing seemed to come simultaneously from the heart and deep in the gut.

Thomas was also amazed at Jerry's guitar playing skills. He had known a lot of guitar players who played in the church band every Sunday. All of them had been accomplished players, but none were in Jerry's league. He was more than gifted. He was blessed.

But it was the lyrics that moved Thomas the most. Each song, each verse seemed to be written just for him. It was uncanny. He was accustomed to being uplifted by the worship music at his church. Beacon Bible Church was known for its excellent contemporary Christian music. The music each Sunday gave him joy and peace. It melted away whatever concerns were on his mind and heart at the time. Today was different. He was experiencing something much deeper. The chords and words of Jerry's music were touching Thomas in a thousand places. Like the hands of a massage therapist seeking out the knotted muscles that pinch the nerves and cause the pain, Jerry's music was finding the hurt in Thomas and somehow making it fade away.

Jerry stopped to take a drink of his coffee, now cold.

"I'm speechless, Jerry. Were those your songs?" Thomas asked.

"Yeah, haven't played them in some time. They're dear old friends I like to visit now and then. But, like visiting old friends, they also bring up some pain."

"I could tell. One song in particular was about losing someone you love," Thomas said.

"Uh-huh. I wrote that after my son was killed by a drunk driver."

The words ripped through Thomas' peacefulness like a jagged knife.

"We had just given Reggie a new bike for his twelfth birthday. He was so excited as he rode down the street for his first ride. He never came back, Thomas. An hour after Reggie rode away a policeman knocked on our door. A drunk driver had swerved into the bike lane and hit him. They told us Reggie probably died instantly considering how far his body had flown after being hit."

"My wife never recovered. Something snapped inside. I had to place her in a private mental hospital. She's still there." Jerry strummed the guitar strings absent-mindedly.

"Jerry, I'm so sorry. I can't imagine the pain and suffering you must have gone through," Thomas said.

"My faith was tested. I'm still tested whenever I visit my wife. She doesn't recognize me. Just stares out the window. My wife and son were taken from me that day."

After a few moments of silence, Thomas said, "I can't believe that we all have lost loved ones. Otto lost his parents, you lost your son and wife, I lost my wife. Matt's wife divorced him, but she and the children are still alive, aren't they?"

"Yes, they're alive in London, but they might as well be dead to Matt. His Ex re-married and managed to turn the children against him," Jerry said.

"He didn't mention any of that yesterday when we sailed together."

"Not surprised. He's still trying to forgive and forget. He'll probably open up later."

"The three of you are very close," Thomas said.

"We are brothers in so many ways."

Jerry started playing another song. This one was much more upbeat. It was about friendships. It was a country swing tune that made Thomas want to dance in the cockpit of the boat.

When it was over Thomas applauded. "That was great, Jerry. One of yours?"

"Yep. Wrote that one night when I had the midnight watch on our first cruise. I was all alone in the cockpit, *Ocean Angel* was moving along very nicely at about seven knots. Not much for me to do, so I just started playing some chords and jotting lyrics down on a notepad using a red light flashlight so the glare wouldn't affect my night vision. I finished the song just as the eastern sky started to get a little lighter with the new day."

"Awesome."

"Yeah, God wrote the song, I just held the guitar."

"Amen. Tell me more about the guitar," Thomas said.

"*Rehab?* Oh, she's seen and lived a lot. I bought her from a country studio musician named Burt Dwellings. He had owned it for ten years, and after hearing DelivrUs play one night in Denver, he insisted on giving it to me. Of course, he didn't call it Rehab. Can't remember the name now. You see, he had advanced arthritis in his hands. Couldn't play anymore. He wanted his guitar to have a good home. It's a Martin. When he handed it to me I felt energy flow through it up my arms. I swear!"

Thomas was watching with fascination as Jerry told the story and picked at the guitar strings. While Jerry talked it seemed the guitar was talking, too.

"What about the name?"

"Of course you know the story of Rehab, the prostitute in Jericho that hid the Israeli spies and proclaimed her admiration for the God of the Israelis. Her new-found faith saved her and her family from destruction by the hands of the Israeli army that surrounded the city. Well, I was like Rehab. I was a Jew who fell in love with Jesus, and in return Jesus spared my life."

"Spared your life?"

"When I met DelivrUs I was on drugs. Big time. Smack, coke, pot, speed, you name it. I thought I was living the rock 'n roll dream, but it was really a nightmare of addiction. The band went into intervention mode for me. They prayed daily. They gave me tough love, but supported me. They also gave me an ultimatum. Get clean or leave the band. In between tours I checked into a Christian rehab center in Phoenix. It was there that I got the revelation to name the guitar *Rehab*. She has played sweetly for me ever since. I've been drug-free ever since then, too. You've noticed that I drink, but not to excess. That's a real bonus, because Otto, Matt and I like our wine," Jerry stopped talking and started singing a country western tune about whiskey for men and beer for their horses.

The song made Thomas laugh. "And with that, I think we both deserve a beer. Take the wheel, Jerry." Thomas ducked below to grab two cans of beer from the cooler.

When Thomas returned with beer and a bag of corn chips, Jerry asked, "How much longer to Prevost Harbor?"

"About two hours at this speed. That's John's Pass up ahead and to port. Thomas looked ahead, squinting in the bright sunlight. "Looks like *Ocean Angel* will get there about thirty minutes before us, if we continue sailing. The wind is starting to die."

Jerry checked the location of the other boat ahead. He returned *Rehab* to her case in the cabin.

"Thomas, did you and Rhonda spend much time up here?"

"You mean at Prevost?"

"Yeah."

"I think we came here twice. It's pretty far north. You know, the Canadian border is only five to six miles ahead. From Prevost it would take us three days to get back to Seattle. We usually took just a week of vacation, so that wouldn't give us any time to just relax at anchor somewhere. Three days here, three days back. Too much for a week. On several occasions we took a longer vacation and that's when we ventured up here."

"I take it your wife liked to sail."

"She loved it. Grew up sailing. This boat was her father's. He left it to her when he passed. We certainly couldn't have afforded something like this on a pastor's salary."

Jerry said nothing. Instead he sat pensively sipping his beer.

Ignoring Jerry's contemplation, Thomas continued to talk about Rhonda— their good times on the boat; their inability to have children; how they grew the church together; the outpouring of love when she passed; how helpless he felt in her absence.

Jerry just listened. Thomas kept talking. He was on a roll now. With each sentence the self-pity grew and the sense of worth declined.

"Yeah, I think about all she did for us and for the church every time I look at her urn."

Jerry turned his head sharply to look at Thomas. "Her urn?"

"Right, I still have the urn that used to contain her ashes. It's down on the shelf next to my Bible."

"It's empty?"

"Correct. I spread her ashes in Port Madison a couple months ago before moving up here," Thomas said.

"I see," Jerry said, closing his eyes. He prayed hard and prayed silently. If Thomas was continuing to talk Jerry never heard him, so concentrated was he in prayer.

Jerry opened his eyes. "Thomas, I'd like to see the urn. Do you mind bringing it up here?"

Surprised by the request, Thomas replied, "Sure. I'll get it. Watch the wheel again."

Thomas returned to the cockpit and reverently handed the ceramic urn to Jerry. It was a simple, inexpensive urn, but Jerry handled it like it was a priceless vase from the Ming Dynasty. For the moment anyway, he wanted to show the object some respect.

"What do you think when you look at this urn, Thomas?"

"I think of how beautiful she was and how much I miss her."

Jerry nodded slowly, all the while looking at the urn in his hands. "What do you miss most about her?"

"Everything! I'm just not myself without her."

"It's normal to feel that a part of you is missing. What strikes me about what you've said to me today is that you feel less of a person, less of man without her."

"That's true. I admit it. I couldn't run the church without her."

"Said who?"

Thomas stopped to think. "Well, no one had to say it. I figured it out for myself. Rhonda was the heart of the church. Without her I couldn't hold it together and keep it beating."

"You told yourself that?"

"I looked at the facts and deducted it, sure."

"Then, if this urn was a mirror, when you looked at it, what would you see?"

"A guy who was dependent on his wife. A guy who wasn't much good without his wife." Thomas' eyes were getting moist.

"To be clear, nobody told you that. The church Board didn't say that to you, did they?"

"No, but they didn't beg for me to stay either. Oh sure, they wanted me to take more time off, but they weren't begging me to stay. I think they were relieved that I was leaving."

"Think so, huh?"

"I can read people pretty well, Jerry. I know what they were thinking," Thomas said, with a touch of defiance in his voice.

"That may be, but Thomas, I think you suck at reading yourself."

"Huh?"

"And to make matters worse, you've forgotten who you are in Christ."

Thomas stared at Jerry. He was becoming irritated with this guy. "Don't forget you're speaking to a Christian pastor. I darn well know who I am in Christ!"

Jerry leaned closer to Thomas, "If you remember who you are in Christ why are you letting the death of Rhonda force you from the church that God gave you to shepherd? Why are you running away—sailing away—from God's plan?"

Thomas started to speak but stopped. He stared at Jerry. Jerry looked back with determined compassion in his eyes. Neither man noticed that the wind had completely died and the boat's sails hung limp from the rigging. The ebbing current stopped the boat's progress and began to carry it backward slowly.

Thomas drained the remaining beer from its can. "Okay, look, I know you're just trying to help. I've prayed long and hard about all this and I think God did want me to leave Beacon Bible Church. I don't know why. I don't know what He has in store for me next, but I am trusting Him."

"That's good, but do you really think God wants you to believe you are weak and small in the absence of your wife? Goodness, Thomas! Who gives you strength and skills? Not Rhonda. It's God! Sure, he used her to give you confidence and guidance, but she was just a marvelous vessel, a channel, for God's love directed at you." Jerry paused, took a deep breath and continued. "Maybe, just maybe, God's plan includes you standing on your own two feet without a worldly crutch. Maybe He wants you to depend on Him totally, not another person, even your blessed wife."

Jerry gripped his hands together, so Thomas wouldn't see them trembling. He didn't know where the words he just said had come from. He was worried that these tough words would enrage Thomas, or send him into deeper despair. Maybe even like the death of Reggie sent his wife into a chasm of despair never to return.

"Oh great, so now you're saying Rhonda had to die to teach me a lesson? That makes me feel better," Thomas said with biting bitterness in his voice.

"You and I both know that God doesn't work like that. Don't be ridiculous and don't grasp at another thing to add to your pity party either. Neither you or anyone else knows why Rhonda had to die now. It's a waste of time to even ask 'why'. The question you need to ask yourself right now, right this minute is: are you going to reach to God every day for strength, or are you going to reach for an empty urn?" Jerry picked up the urn from the seat next to him where he had placed it earlier.

Thomas looked at Jerry, then at the urn, then his eyes returned to Jerry. He bowed his head, resting it on his arms as they held the steering wheel. His body began to tremble. The sound of deep painful sobs bounced off the hard fiberglass deck and into the still warm air.

Jerry let Thomas cry in peace. He prayed that he had said the right words, that he had been tough enough and loving enough, but he knew today's job wasn't done. The toughest part was next.

After a minute or two, Thomas raised his head, removed a large red handkerchief from his pants pocket, wiped his eyes and blew his nose. He was panting slightly as if out of breath. Then he looked at Jerry with eyes bloodshot from crying, "Did you ever consider being a pastor or a shrink? You'd be good at it."

Jerry grinned slightly, "Nah, no money in it," he said with a wink. "Besides my gift is music, remember? That's how I introduce tens of thousands of people to Jesus."

"Thank you for being tough with me this morning. I see that in my grief I was pretending to listen to God, but actually I was turning away." He glanced up at the sky. "Forgive me Lord, for forsaking You."

Jerry held up the urn. "Thomas, this urn once held Rhonda's remains. Those ashes are gone, but Satan has occupied it. Satan is using this urn to turn you against yourself and God. Because each time you look at this urn you convince yourself that you're nothing without Rhonda, that you're not good enough to lead a growing, vibrant church. That's Satan's lie. Do you believe God or Satan's lie?"

"I believe and trust in Jesus, my savior."

"Good. Then Thomas, take this urn from my hands and toss it into the sea." Jerry pointed to the smooth, wave-less water that surrounded the hull for as far as he could see.

Thomas took the urn from Jerry's hand and looked hard at it. With disgust he shouted, "Satan, get behind me." He threw the urn hard to the rear of the boat. It splashed twenty yards away. The two men watched as it slowly filled with water and sank below the surface.

Jerry faced Thomas, placed both hands on his shoulders and looked him in the eyes. "Good work, brother. Now you're ready to accept what God is preparing you for, whatever that is." He quoted scripture.

"As you do not know the path of the wind, or how the body is formed in a mother's womb, so you cannot understand the work of God, the Maker of all things". —Ecclesiastes 11:5

"Amen," Thomas said.

"Amen. And speaking of the path of the wind, we are totally becalmed," Jerry said.

"You're right. I didn't even notice until just now. In fact, we've drifted back almost to John's Pass. I'll fire up the engine. Can you see *Ocean Angel*?"

Jerry strained his eyes looking into the distance. "I think I see them up ahead. They've turned toward the harbor under power."

The two men worked to quickly furl the jib and mainsail as the Islander 36's diesel pushed the bow forward at six knots.

Chapter 91

Otto guided *Ocean Angel* slowly into the harbor. The chart was on the seat next to him, and he carefully watched the depth sounder. Prevost Harbor on Stuart Island was guarded by a smaller island, Satellite Island. It made an ideal anchorage protected from wind and current. He slowed the boat to a crawl and steered it toward a small cove on Satellite Island that was removed from the marina area across the harbor. Matt readied the anchor and at Otto's signal released the heavy hook and chain into the cove. The anchor struck bottom thirty feet later. Otto reversed the engine, pulling the anchor backwards along the bottom until its flanges dug deep into the muddy bottom. Matt let out more anchor line as scope in case the wind picked up, but not too much to permit *Ocean Angel* to swing too close to shore.

Within an hour *Harriet's Chariot* was tied to *Ocean Angel* and all four men gathered onboard the larger yacht for happy hour.

The men agreed that cigars were in order and soon they were relaxing in the spacious cockpit enjoying drinks and cigars while studying the quiet, pristine beauty of Prevost Harbor. They felt a million miles away from everything. An eagle soared above them and landed in a tall tree on Satellite Island.

Everyone was in high spirits after the enjoyable day of sailing. Thomas was feeling especially good following the emotional release of the urn a few hours earlier.

"I know you three have been to some amazing cruising areas—Baja, Hawaii— but this is hard to beat," Thomas said, sweeping his cigar-holding hand to point at the natural splendor in front of them.

Matt responded, "You got that right. This is pretty special. It's so darn peaceful. I feel like talking in a whisper, so I don't disturb anything."

Everyone chuckled at Matt's observation, but agreed they too felt the same way.

"Maybe they should have named this place Library Harbor," Jerry said. That comment brought out more laughter.

"Hey, who wants to explore in the dinghy?" Thomas asked.

"Great idea. I'll go," Otto said.

"Me too," Matt said.

"You guys go. I'll get things organized for dinner. We're grilling steaks, right, Otto?"

"Yep. Steaks, corn and baked potatoes. Good idea to put the spuds in the oven now," Otto said.

With that decided, Matt, Otto and Thomas stepped aboard *Harriet's Chariot*, down the short ladder and into the dinghy. Thomas started the outboard and they slowly moved away from the two anchored boats.

"It's so calm, let's go all the way around Satellite Island," Thomas suggested.

"You're driving," Otto said.

For the next ninety minutes the three men explored the little coves and rocky outcroppings of the shoreline. They ventured south then turned northeast through a narrow passage that opened to miles and miles of water known as Boundary Pass, the dividing line between the U.S. and Canada. Hugging the shoreline of the little island they turned northwest, eventually coming to the main entrance to Prevost Harbor that their respective boats had entered earlier in the day before anchoring.

Thomas steered the inflatable dinghy over to the Stuart Island shoreline where numerous small docks extended into the harbor. As the day was coming to an end, the small docks were lined with boats tied up for the night. Several more boats were anchored out. Thomas knew that come October, this place would be like a ghost town.

Back at the two boats, Otto lit charcoal for the small grill that was clamped to the stern railing of *Ocean Angel*. The aroma of baked potatoes wafted upward from the galley. Before long, the conversation turned to the destination of day number three in their adventure. Leaning over charts spread out on the galley table, the three men listened attentively as Thomas pointed to his recommended destinations for the remainder of their week. Each day was planned so they'd sail about six hours and either anchor or dock for the night. He alternated between remote coves and popular marinas, allowing them opportunity to buy fuel, groceries, ice, and take showers. By the seventh day of their adventure they'd arrive back at Friday Harbor.

With the remainder of the voyage settled, the charts were removed, and the table set for dinner. Otto attended to the steaks and corn on the grille.

After dinner they cleaned the galley and dishes before returning to the cockpit for a nightcap. The night was clear without clouds or fog. Displayed high above them was a thick blanket of sparkling stars. Being far away from the glare of city lights, the heavens were clearly visible in all their glory. The men sat looking up to the sky without talking for the longest time.

"This is one of my favorite experiences while sailing," Matt declared, breaking the silence.

"What? Drinking Drambuie after dinner?" Otto chuckled.

"No. The stars. God puts on quite a show when you're far out to sea. The dark ocean and dark sky meld into one seamless black canvas. There's a billion stars displayed above you. If you're lucky the wake of the hull is glowing with bioluminescence. It's hard not to get closer to God during the night watch."

"Jerry sang a song for me today that he had written on watch one night. It was amazing," Thomas added.

"We're frequently serenaded at night by this guy," Otto said, pointing to Jerry. "The soothing music, the motion of the boat, puts me right to sleep."

"Jerry, remember your guitar is still on my boat," Thomas said.

"Oh, that's right. I'll get it." Jerry left the cockpit to fetch his guitar.

When he returned the guitar case Matt said, "While you have it in your hand might as well play something."

"Please do," Thomas said.

Jerry removed the guitar from its case. After tuning a few strings, he began to play. He took requests from the other three men at first. After three or four requested songs he switched to his own music. One song flowed into another as if he was in concert. Thomas noticed the Jerry didn't seem to be playing for them anymore. He was oblivious to their presence. His eyes, when they weren't shut, were looking into the dark sky as if saying to God, "Let me Worship you with the gift you gave me, Lord."

Jerry played for over an hour before taking a break. As he set the guitar down carefully on the seat, the sound of applause could be heard in the distance. Thomas stood and looked out into the harbor. About thirty feet from where the two boats were anchored he could just see the outline of five or six dinghies containing people. Evidently the sound of Jerry's music had carried across the harbor, and people wanted to move closer to hear better. One by one, while Jerry had been playing, they quietly moved their dinghies closer to *Ocean Angel*.

A voice from one of the small boats in the darkness called out, "Please play some more DelivrUs songs."

Jerry took a drink from his glass of liquor, slipped the guitar strap over his head and walked to the stern of the boat to play an encore just like he had done hundreds of times before in concert halls and arenas around the world.

"What would you like to hear?" he shouted into the darkness.

"*Because I Believe.*" "*Loving You.*" "*Mountain High.*" Different voices shouted back DelivrUs song requests from the darkness.

And so Jerry played and played. After each song the applause grew more enthusiastic. Other clapping could be heard coming from the shoreline of Satellite Island a mere fifty yards from where the two boats were anchored.

After playing six songs for the audience in the harbor. Jerry said, "Thank you, folks. Good night and God bless." He returned to the cockpit and sat down. Otto handed him another drink.

"That was truly amazing," Thomas said.

"Yeah, but not that unusual," Otto said. "Whenever Jerry picks up a guitar a crowd starts to gather. We're lucky that it is dark, and the people out there can't see that the person who is playing DelivrUs songs so well is the guy that wrote the songs, Jerry Levine. When folks know it's The Jerry Levine, it can get a little crazy."

The men could hear the outboards start in the distance as the nighttime audience drove their dinghies back to their boats.

Thomas thought about Jerry's remarks earlier in the day about how his music brought thousands and thousands of people closer to Jesus. He had just witnessed the power of Jerry Levine's Divine gift. A small ember of envy tried to ignite in Thomas. He recognized it and pushed it away. *My words have brought thousands closer to Jesus. I have gifts, too. No reason to carry the sin of envy in my heart.*

"Well, gents, it's been quite a day. I am pleasantly exhausted and heading to bed," Jerry said.

The others agreed.

"Thomas, if it's okay I'll crew with you tomorrow," Otto said.

"Okay. I'm looking forward to it. Let's plan to leave by 9:30," Thomas said.

"Right. Let's start breakfast at 8:15," Otto said.

Before Jerry could go below deck, Thomas embraced him. "Thank you for today, Jerry."

Jerry gave a tired smile, "Don't thank me, thank Him," pointing up to the stars.

Chapter 92

The next morning the two sloops left Prevost Harbor with *Harriet's Chariot* leading the way. They were soon greeted by a brisk breeze from the north. Sails were unfurled and both boats settled into a close reach on a fifteen-mile course up Boundary Pass to Sucia Island.

Otto and Thomas settled into the cockpit, enjoying the sailing conditions and the mugs of hot coffee in their hands. The morning was cool and cloudy. Thomas had heard on the NOAA weather radio the night before that a weak front was due to arrive later in the day. Indeed, the barometer in his cabin indicated a change in weather.

But for now, all was well. *Ocean Angel*, with a longer waterline and more sail area, was steadily pulling ahead of *Harriet's Chariot*. She'd arrive at their destination first if the wind held.

Thomas noticed that Otto was studying *Ocean Angel*.

"You probably don't get much of an opportunity to see your boat from a distance under sail," Thomas commented.

"You're right about that. I am admiring her. I'm reminded that when I return home I need to have the sails re-cut, or replaced. They're losing shape."

Thomas studied his sails. "What do you think about mine?"

Otto studied the mainsail and jib carefully. "For cruising they're in pretty good shape. I wouldn't go off shore with them, however. How old are the sails?"

"Gosh, I don't know. Could be more than ten years old. I've had the boat that long. Don't know if the sails were new when Rhonda's father died."

"Well, you're due for new sails. They won't hold up in a blow. I'm surprised the shape is still pretty good."

Thomas thought about his limited financial resources. Did he have a reason to spend that kind of money on new sails? That posed the basic question, what good is a sailboat without good sails?

For the next two hours the two men talked about sailing and sailboat equipment. Thomas was fascinated by Otto's retelling of his offshore adventures. He couldn't imagine sailing for days and days without sight of land. Even now, in order for him to get his bearings he simply needed to look to his right and see Waldron Island, to his left across Boundary Pass was Saturna Island, up ahead was little Skipjack Island, which marked the point they would alter course slightly more to the east. But what if there were no islands, no landmarks, no buoys? Just mile after mile of open ocean.

"Did you ever get lost or go badly off course?" Thomas asked.

"Oh, sure, but I wasn't lost for long. As the guys were only too happy to mention, I got lost in the Sea of Cortez once at night. Got disoriented. Read my instruments wrong. To be honest, I can't tell you how I did it, but we ended up at the wrong little island near La Paz," Otto said. "After that I learned to check my calculations with the other guys. All three of us on *Ocean Angel* are good navigators now. We check each other, and we use redundant systems. Heck, Matt is even learning to use a sextant. If our electronics fail us, we can get by. Of course, if the electronics go out and we can't see the sun or stars then we're screwed."

"That's when the instrument of prayer comes in handy," Thomas said with a wink.

"Yes, and that's when your hotline to God better be in good shape," Otto said.

"Hey, want to take a short cut and sneak up on *Ocean Angel*?"

"Sure. My boat doesn't like this light air. It's built for stronger winds. What do you have in mind?" Otto was looking at the islands and water around them. His boat with Matt and Jerry were ahead about a mile and further to port of he and Thomas' position.

"I know this morning we talked about a course outside of Skipjack Island. That's it ahead. But in these conditions we can safely cut the corner and go between Skipjack and Waldron Islands. There are rocks, but we can see them clearly enough."

"Let's do it. Those guys are too far out to change course now."

Thomas pointed the bow on a course between Waldron Island on the right and Skipjack Island on the left. Otto adjusted the sails. *Ocean Angel's* longer course would take her to the left of Skipjack. The race was on.

"Otto, how did you name your boat? *Ocean Angel* is a fantastic name?"

"Yeah, the name fits doesn't it? If I ever get another boat I'll name it *Ocean Angel II*. Actually, the three of us brainstormed ideas on the phone one night after I had announced that I was getting a new boat. I think at the time Matt was in New York, Jerry was in St. Louis. We started sharing ideas for names. Within about ten minutes I think it was Jerry who suggested *Sea Spirit*. I loved it. Then Matt said, '*Ocean Angel*'. Almost in unison we all said, 'that's it!'"

"That's cool all three of you collaborated on the name," Thomas said.

"Uh-huh. Even though I own the boat, they treat it like owners, too. That attitude started with working together to name the boat."

Thomas nodded his head. "To be honest, I've never liked the name *Harriet's Chariot*. It's cute and clever, but Harriet was Rhonda's mother, and while I loved my mother-in-law, I really don't want a boat named after her."

Otto chuckled, "I understand. Why haven't you changed the name?"

"I didn't even consider it when Rhonda was alive. Now that's she's gone I guess I could change the name. Isn't it supposed to be bad luck?"

"Oh, if you want to believe in superstition, it's best not to rename it. I prefer to believe that God has blessed me with a boat and I want to honor Him with its name and how I use it."

"I like that viewpoint," Thomas said.

"I figured you might," Otto winked. "But, you'd be surprised at how many boat owners will not change the name of a boat because they believe disaster will shortly follow."

"Otto, do you mind taking the helm for a bit? I'm thirsty. How about a beer?"

"A splendid idea," Otto said.

Thomas returned to the cockpit and glanced to see the position of *Ocean Angel*. "Pretty soon, if they're paying attention, they'll notice we're taking the inside course."

"Trust me, they'll notice. They're probably looking at the chart right now, reviewing this morning's discussion, and concluding that we're trying to out-smart them," Otto said. "They won't panic or change course. They'll look at the chart and figure out what's happening. Matt and Jerry are both scary smart. Put them together on a problem and the combined brain power cuts through the issue like a laser."

"The Holy Spirit is strong in Jerry. I experienced it firsthand yesterday on the way to Prevost."

"Isn't it amazing! He shared with us about the urn. Good work, Thomas," Otto said.

Wanting to change the subject, Thomas said, "Back to the boat name. Do you really think I should change it?"

"Okay, let's look at the pros and cons. First let's list the reasons for changing the name. You believe the current name is kinda hokey, right?"

"Right."

"And it's named after a mother-in-law, right?"

"Right."

"And it reminds you of a past life with your wife. Not that that's a bad memory, it's just that you're working really hard to release the grief and move on."

"Yes. That's true."

"Okay. There are three strong reasons for changing the name. Now why shouldn't you rename it?"

"Bad luck, which I don't believe in," Thomas said.

"What else?"

"The cost of repainting the stern, and the hassle of changing the name on the registration, insurance, etcetera," Thomas said.

"What else?"

Charles Besondy

"I don't know a good name."

"In my opinion, the pros outweigh the cons. The new name will come to you. You can use the prayer method, the cabernet sauvignon method, or the combination," Otto said with a grin.

"Will a prayer-and-beer method work equally well?"

"I don't know. Never tried," Otto said, scratching his chin.

"Let's do it. Want to help me rename this boat?" Thomas asked.

"I'd be honored, sir," Otto said, sipping his beer. "Permit me to lead us in prayer."

"Heavenly Father, years ago you blessed Thomas and Rhonda with this sailboat. A boat which gave them much enjoyment, rest, and time together during the busy season of their lives when they built a thriving church for You. Now, Lord, we ask for your guidance. What is your plan for this magnificent sloop and for Thomas, its owner. We ask that you let the right name be known to us today. Let the name inspire man and honor You. In these things we pray in Jesus' name, Amen."

"Amen. Thank you, Otto. Nicely done. I suggest we think in silence, then share our ideas."

"Okay."

The two men sat in the cockpit. Otto continued to steer the boat as it slowly made way on its northeast course. The light breeze was barely enough to keep the sails full and pulling the sloop forward.

After a few minutes, Otto spoke, "'Answered Prayer'. That's what I heard first. Then, I thought of, 'Here on Earth'; saw that name on a boat somewhere. Always liked it," Otto said.

"Wow, those are really good. I had trouble thinking of anything besides 'Sea Spirit' the name you almost gave to your boat."

"So, we have Answered Prayer, Here on Earth, Sea Spirt. Let's be silent again and hear what the Spirit says."

A few minutes passed. Otto had several ideas, but held them in reserve. He knew it was imperative that Thomas create the name.

"Excuse me a minute, I need my Bible." Thomas dropped through the companionway into the cabin and returned seconds later with his Bible in hand. He proceeded to thumb through the pages, stop and read. He smiled and looked off into the distance without saying a word.

Otto watched his sailing partner. He could tell by Thomas' reaction that the Spirit had whispered, and Thomas had heard.

"Justified," Thomas said. "I'll rename her, Justified. During silence I kept hearing 'Romans 8: 33, Romans 8:33." So here's the passage verses 28-30 and 33.

"[28] And we know that in all things God works for the good of those who love him, who have been called according to his purpose. [29] For those God foreknew he also predestined to be conformed to the image of his Son, that he might be the firstborn among many brothers and sisters. [30] And those he predestined, he also called; those he called, he also justified; those he justified, he also glorified. . . [33] Who will bring a charge against God's elect? God is the one who justifies" - Romans 8: 28-30,33.

"Great name, Thomas. How does that speak to you?" Otto asked.

"It touches me on several levels. It reminds me that God has had a marvelous plan for me and my only job is to listen and be obedient. I need to have faith that I am supposed to grow as a result of what I've gone through during the past eighteen months. I am to grow taller, not shrink in the face of adversity."

He took another drink of his beer before continuing, "The other thing that resonates with me is this: I've been carrying around a lot of guilt. I've been telling myself that without Rhonda I'm not good enough to be a pastor. Effectively I was assigning all the credit for my success to Rhonda, rather than to Jesus. I knew this lack of faith was a huge sin, so I was feeling guilt, a lot of guilt. The more guilt I felt the more I wanted to give up and walk away from the church."

"Excuse me, Thomas. Check my course. I see rocks and seaweed ahead to starboard."

Thomas stood up and looked ahead. He climbed out the cockpit and walked carefully to the foredeck to get a better view.

Returning to the cockpit Thomas said, "You're good. Aim a little more to port. Stay at least fifty yards from the rocks. There's plenty of water underneath us. Be mindful of the effect of current through here, though. At our low speed we could be pushed or pulled one way or the other."

"Please continue. What else about *Justified* resonates with you?"

"As I was saying I carried a lot of guilt. Because of it I told myself I had another reason why I couldn't lead a church anymore. Well, the passage reminded me that I shouldn't be against myself because God is for me. I can't feel guilty about sinning because Jesus died for all my sins. I've been cleansed by the blood of Christ. And I've been justified."

"Just think, every time you think about the boat, you'll be reminded of who you are in Christ, not of your mother-in-law," Otto tried to keep a straight face, but laughed. Thomas joined him in laughter. The two men sat in the cockpit giggling like school kids.

Just as Thomas had predicted the courses of the two boats intersected an hour later east of Skipjack Island. The wind increased, and the clouds got heavier in the sky. With the stronger wind, both sloops gained speed nicely, but the larger *Ocean*

Angel steadily pulled away. If the wind held they'd be in Echo Bay in about two hours.

Chapter 93

Both boats were anchored together in Echo Bay. The men decided to take a short hike ashore to stretch their legs before the weather worsened. Before the men climbed into Thomas' tender, he baited a crab trap, carefully lowered it to the bottom forty feet below, and tied the line to a cleat on *Harriet's Chariot*.

"Worth a try. If we don't catch anything for dinner, maybe we'll catch something for a crab omelet tomorrow morning," Thomas said.

For the next few hours the men walked the hiking trails of Sucia Island then returned to the tender just as rain began to fall.

They went back to the boats. No crab had ventured into the crab pot yet, so it was agreed that dinner would be spaghetti, garlic bread and salad.

For the next three days the pleasant ritual was repeated. Sailing to a new destination. Sharing stories about each other's lives, feasting, and reverently praying multiple times each day.

Finally, at three o'clock on August 11, seven days after leaving Friday Harbor, the two boats returned. *Ocean Angel* found a suitable slip on the guest dock. *Harriet's Chariot* returned to her permanent moorage dock.

The next day Thomas busied himself cleaning his boat thoroughly and inquiring at the marina about who they knew that painted names on boats. He called the artist and made the arrangements for the work to be done later in the week. That night he hosted Otto, Matt and Jerry for happy hour on his boat then insisted on treating them to dinner ashore.

It was agreed that they'd have an early dinner together one last time on August 13. *Ocean Angel* would depart early on August 14 for the voyage west out the Strait of Juan de Fuca and then south to San Francisco.

At seven in the morning, with a mug of coffee in one hand, Thomas waived good-bye to Otto, Matt and Jerry as *Ocean Angel* carried them away. Sadness swelled in his chest. "God please protect them on their journey," he whispered.

He had told them at dinner the night before that they were the best friends he had ever had. He thanked them profusely for their prayers and love during their time together. They thanked him for the wonderful seven-day journey and for the privilege of seeing the Spirit work in him. They had exchanged phone numbers and addresses.

With *Ocean Angel* out of sight, Thomas turned and walked slowly back to his boat. Would he ever see these men again? Would he ever have an opportunity to help someone the way these three helped him find who he was in Christ?

Chapter 94

O n the seventeenth of August, an artist named Linda arrived to paint the new name on Thomas' Islander 36. After Thomas selected one of the font styles she had suggested, he helped Linda secure his dinghy to the stern to give her a steady place to sit while working. Then he busied himself with chores on board while Linda began the work of removing the old name and applying the new name.

Four hours later, Linda called up to him from her seat in the dinghy. "Thomas, it's done. Please look."

He stepped onto the dock and walked to where he could see the full stern clearly. There it was in dark maroon paint, "*Justified*."

"I love it! Great job, Linda, except you misspelled it."

A look of horror crossed Linda's face and she whipped her head around to study the name she had just painted. She checked the spelling. She looked back at him with a questioning look only to see Thomas grinning broadly back at her.

"Just kidding. It's perfect," Thomas said, now feeling a little guilty for scaring the artist so badly.

After Linda had packed her materials and left, Thomas stood on the dock and admired the stern of his boat. A strange sensation overcame him. He felt he was looking at a different boat, one that was built just for him. He gave praise, "Lord, I am again humbled by the blessing of this boat. Thank you for this vessel. May it continue to give me shelter. May it carry me on the course you have designed for me. May it become a tool for bringing your light to others. Amen."

The next day after breakfast, he researched the churches on San Juan Island and made a list. Today, he'd visit churches and inquire about work. It was time he got back to being a pastor. He reasoned there had to be at least one church on the island that needed his experience.

He decided to visit the churches in town that he could reach by walking, then use his car to drive to churches in the few other little communities on the island.

Thomas wasn't prepared for the reaction he received. He had expected to be greeted with open arms by the clergy of these churches. He believed they'd be eager to have his experience on staff. He naively believed that he'd have a job offer within one day.

What happened was just the opposite. Every pastor he met was coolly cordial towards him. Each church was struggling to survive on the sparsely populated island. They couldn't relate to Thomas' experience. Indeed, more than one pastor had suggested to Thomas that his "big city" experience was worth nothing here.

Each person he spoke to made it clear there were no openings on staff, but of course he was welcomed to come to service each Sunday and become a member.

Tired and depressed after a long day of rejection and disappointment, Thomas walked slowly down the dock to *Justified* as dusk's shadow fell over the harbor.

After dinner he prayed and thought deeply about what he was going to do. Sooner or later he was going to need steady income. The tourist season would be over in another month at which point even the local restaurants and shops would be reducing staff for the slow winter months ahead. True, his expenses were low, but besides earning some cash, he needed to do something useful with his time. The thought of spending twenty-four hours a day inside the small cabin of his boat during the long, gloomy winter months did not appeal to him.

At some point while sitting at the table in his cabin, the reality of his situation hit home. He couldn't live like this much longer. Maybe the very best thing he should do was return to Seattle and start applying for jobs at churches there. He knew that Beacon Bible had already hired a new senior pastor, so he couldn't return to his own church in that capacity. Or, what about Tacoma, or Bellingham, or Edmonds, or any other town in Washington State for that matter. Maybe he should prepare a resume and start job hunting. Contact a few of the recruiters he knew that specialize in finding pastors for churches.

He was beginning to feel better. A plan was coming together. Heck, within a few months he'd be on staff at a church somewhere, fully recharged and ready to take on whatever challenges God had in store for him.

Thomas prepared for bed then settled into his bunk to read a book he'd picked up at the town library, *A World of My Own* by Robin Knox-Johnson. It was the story of the first man to single-handedly sail non-stop around the world.

The real-life adventure of the brave master-sailor gripped Thomas. When reading in bed he usually fell asleep within half an hour, but not with this book. It lit up his imagination. He continued to read well past midnight before turning off the light and closing his eyes. Outside, a summer storm brought wind and rain to Friday Harbor. Thomas laid in his bunk and felt the wind tug at *Justified's* rigging. The rain fell hard on the fiberglass deck just a few feet above his head. He imagined that he was at sea en route to some faraway exotic land. He drifted off into a peaceful sleep.

Chapter 95

O ver the next three days Thomas worked diligently on his resume and
building a list of churches to contact. He began a new ritual. Each morning
after breakfast he'd walk uptown nearly a mile to the small city library
where he'd research and work until eleven. Then he'd walk back to the dock,
stopping along the way to treat himself to a latte from the espresso shop. Back at
his boat he'd fix lunch and read the Bible. In the afternoon he'd tend to his chores
and relax in the cockpit with Knox-Johnson's book. Without realizing it his mind
began to be filled with thoughts of sailing adventures.

On August 21 he left the library, purchased his usual coffee, but instead of
returning to *Justified* he found himself walking to the local sail maker. For some
reason this morning the poor condition of his sails were heavy on his mind. He
might as well inquire about the cost.

"Good morning," Thomas said, as he opened the door into the sailmaker's
office.

A man in his mid-thirties looked up. He was deeply tanned and sported a full
beard. He looked like a sailmaker. "Good morning, can I help you?"

"Could you give me a ballpark idea of what it'd cost to replace a mainsail and
jib on my Islander 36. Both are roller furling."

"Do you want to replace, or recut?"

"Not sure. The sails are over ten years old."

"I'd have to look at them, but for ten-year-old roller furling sails I think
you're best off to buy new. There have been a lot of advances in roller furling sail
design and materials in the past ten years."

"I can imagine," Thomas said.

"What kind of sailing are you looking to do with these sails? Cruising or
offshore?"

Simple question, but Thomas hesitated to answer. What *was* his intention
anyway, and why the heck was he standing here pricing new sails when in a few
months he'd be on staff at a new church somewhere—a church that could be
hundreds of miles from any salt water? Suddenly he felt foolish talking to this
man. He needed to escape this conversation.

Thomas flinched and reached for the phone in his jacket. He looked at it.
"Excuse me, I have to take this." Thomas put the phone to his ear, "Hello." He
walked out of the sail maker's office as if to talk in private, but he kept walking.
He replaced the phone in his pocket. There had been no caller, but pretending was
the only way Thomas could exit the awkward situation he had put himself into.

What was that all about, Thomas? He felt like a schoolboy who had just tried to flirt with a girl and failed miserably. Why on earth was he even considering new sails? That should be the furthest thing from his mind right now. He was going to find a new church to lead, right? Right?

He hadn't ventured down the guest dock since August 14 when *Ocean Angel* left. He headed that way now.

The dock was full. Every slip was occupied with all sorts of craft. He played his game again, guessing the renters, the weekenders, the serious cruisers, and the offshore veterans. There were several vessels that fit the latter category. He imagined their bows plowing through the swells offshore, the sails full and well-trimmed. He pictured himself standing in the cockpit, in control, the wheel firmly in his grip driving the boat to some exotic harbor.

It wasn't that long ago that he gripped the pulpit the same way during his sermons. He drove not a boat, but a church. His words were the wind that moved the church forward. Would he ever be in that position again? Was he capable of being in that position again? Doubt began to creep back into his heart.

Standing at the end of the guest dock looking across the harbor, he sensed that he was at some crossroad. He was being pulled in two different directions.

Back aboard *Justified* he was preparing lunch when his phone buzzed, this time for real. "Hello, this is Thomas Benton."

"Hi, Mr. Benton, this is Harold Benedict, with Benedict Associates, I'm returning your call."

Thomas remembered that Benedict was one of the recruiters he had called earlier in the week. "Yes, of course Mr. Benedict, how are you today and thanks for returning my message," Thomas said while turning off the flame under his pan of soup. "I am looking for a senior pastor position, hopefully in western Washington, and wondered what opportunities were like out there."

"You said senior pastor, correct?"

"Yes, I was founder and senior pastor of Beacon Bible Church in Seattle until I resigned in May."

"I see. May I ask why you resigned?"

Thomas was prepared for the question. "My wife passed. She and I had built the church together. It didn't feel right to continue without her." Which was a true statement as far as it went.

"I'm sorry for your loss. How large was Seattle Beacon Bible?"

"2,300 members, up fifteen percent from the previous year." Again, Thomas was prepared. Churches want to hire new pastors that they believe will grow the membership base.

"Impressive. Well, I'd have to see your resume of course, but I can tell you that there are very few positions in western Washington open for senior pastors right now. If you said you were looking for an Internet Pastor position in a church, I know five churches desperately looking for pastors who can expand a church on the Web, but it sounds to me you're looking to be the head pastor."

"That's correct," said Thomas.

"Send me your resume, Mr. Benton, I'll keep it on file. You said western Washington. What about further east?"

"My preference is the Puget Sound area. I enjoy getting out on my boat from time to time." Thomas didn't feel it necessary to say he was *always* on his boat these days.

"I see. Well, send your resume and I'll be in touch."

"I'll email it to you today. Thanks for your call," Thomas said.

Benedict clicked off. Thomas poured hot soup from the pan into a bowl and placed it on the table next to his sandwich and iced tea.

The call was depressing. He didn't want to consider that positions weren't open. He had naively believed that within a matter of a few weeks he'd be interviewing at multiple churches and have his pick of the offers. This could be a longer process than expected.

He ate his lunch slowly and read more from Knox-Johnson's book while salt-laced air and noonday sunlight flowed seductively into the cabin.

Chapter 96

The next morning Thomas placed 224 envelopes with his resume into the mail at his mailbox rental store. Two hundred were addressed to leaders and elders of churches that he had been researching at the library. Another twenty-four were sent to recruiters specializing in religious organizations and not-for-profits. The same morning, he had also posted his resume on Web job boards that serviced church and not-for-profit employers.

Now he just had to wait. If he was on the mainland he could also network by having coffee with church leaders, but he was here. The mail, email and his phone would have to suffice.

He returned to *Justified* from his morning at the library and mailbox rental store. Not ready for lunch, he sat in the cockpit soaking up the warm sunlight and reading copies of yachting magazines that he had purchased.

One issue was devoted to expert reviews of the latest in boat instrumentation for navigation, radar and communications. Thomas imagined that he was selecting new equipment for *Justified* and read the reviews carefully. He remembered the impressive array of instrumentation on *Ocean Angel.* With those instruments and new sails, he could go anywhere. His mind wandered further. What if he just gave up the idea of finding a new church? What if he took off on a sailing adventure? He could always give sermons and save souls in every harbor he came to. Maybe he could be Pastor Thomas Benton, the Boaters' Chaplain. The idea appealed to him. Why be stuck in one location? Why wait for people to come to him, he'd go to the people. After all, boaters need God too.

The idea caught fire in Thomas. Two hours after he had dropped 224 resumes in the mail he was getting excited about a completely different plan.

With the magazines in hand he hopped off the boat and briskly walked back to town.

His destination was a marine repair and supply company. He showed the article he had been reading to a salesman who pointed out a display of instruments on the show floor. They engaged in a lengthy conversation about instrumentation.

"I assume, based on the models you're considering, that you want some serious gear for offshore navigation," the salesman said.

There was the question again. Offshore or not offshore. "I'm going to be doing some offshore for the first time. God is my pilot, but I want to help Him out a little with good instruments," Thomas said with a grin.

"Good radar and a better prayer always worked for me," the salesman said.

"What are we talking about cost-wise for the VHF radio, GPS chart plotter, and radar? I want a nicely integrated system. In fact, include an estimate for new depth sounder and log impeller. Include installation and training. A cost estimate is good for now. Don't worry about being exact."

The salesman's eyes sparkled at the growing possibility that he would make a sizable sale on this day. "Give me a few minutes to run the numbers."

Thomas continued to browse the store while waiting for the salesman. He felt like a kid in a candy store. It was funny, but only a few days ago he was worried about his money running out and now he was seriously considering spending a lot.

"Sir, the equipment you're looking at, including installation and tax, will be around $5,000. Pretty reasonable considering you're protecting your life and boat."

Five thousand was a lot of money for Thomas. Plus, he needed new sails and who knows what else. He should have thanked the salesman, turned, and walked away. Instead he asked another question.

"Do you have everything in stock? How soon can it be installed?"

"No, we'll need to order most of it, but we can get it within a few days from the distributor. As for installation, I'll need to check with the shop, but usually once I put the order in and parts arrive they can jump on it."

"If I buy today, I want a guarantee that installation and training will be done before the end of August."

"Shouldn't be a problem."

Thomas took a deep breath. Before he could change his mind he said, "Okay, write it up." It felt strangely good to make a decision to blow $5,000 on a collection of wires, lights and circuit boards. In his mind he pictured the equipment impressively arranged around the nav station on *Justified*.

"Excellent! Please have a seat at my desk while I do the paperwork."

Both men sat at a hopelessly cluttered desk.

"Gosh, I've been rude. I'm Roger." Roger reached his hand across the desk to shake.

"I'm Thomas Benton, nice to meet you." Thomas shook Roger's hand. Evidently it took a $5,000 sale to earn a handshake here.

"Thomas, do you have an account with us?"

"I don't think so. I've only purchased a few maintenance supplies here. I live aboard."

"Let me look to see." Roger tapped on the computer keyboard that was on the desk fighting for room in a losing battle with the paper piles.

"Ah, here you are. Thomas Benton. You live on *Harriet's Chariot* in slip H-34. Is that correct?"

"Yes, except the boat's name is *Justified*. I changed it recently," Thomas explained.

"Okay, I'll make a note of it. I see it's an Islander 36. Yes, you've purchased some supplies from us and paid with credit card. Is that how you want to pay now?"

"Yes."

Roger updated the record in the computer. "Hmm, Thomas, did you know you have a credit on your account with us?"

"A credit, no. Did I overpay for teak oil or something?"

"Actually, Thomas, you have a $5,000 credit dating from August 13."

"What? That's impossible. I haven't added any money to my account. I didn't even know I had an account," Thomas exclaimed.

"Yes sir, it's right here in our notes. On August 13 a Matt Kani made a $5,000 deposit to your account.

Stunned, Thomas sat motionless in his chair.

Chapter 97

t was the last week of August. Thomas noticed on his stroll down the guest dock that most of the boaters here were getting ready to return home. Vacation season was over even though the weather in September and early October was almost always spectacular up here.

His phone buzzed in his pocket. "Hello, this is Thomas Benton."

"Hey, Thomas, good morning this is Otto, Otto Vikander."

Totally surprised, Thomas answered, "My goodness, Otto. Great to hear your voice. Where are you?"

"San Francisco. We got in a few hours ago. Just wanted to let you know we arrived safely. I didn't get lost once," he laughed.

"How was the trip down?" Thomas asked.

"Can't complain. Took two days longer than expected. Ran into bad fog off the Oregon coast, but we got through it. How are things in Friday Harbor?"

"I've been busy, but first let me ask, is Matt there? I want to thank him."

"Matt? Yeah, he's still here although he's busy flirting with the women on the boat next to us. Hey, Matt, Thomas wants to talk to you." There was a pause while Matt walked to where Otto was holding out his phone.

"Hey, brother, what's new?" Matt said.

"Matt, I don't know why you gave me $5,000, and I don't have the words to express my gratitude. I'm still in shock."

"Oh, you found out about the money already. Good. I hope it will come in handy. I just felt like it was the best way I could help you and repay you for the magical week we had in the San Juans."

"Repay me? I should repay you guys. You're the ones that intervened to set me straight. And listen, because of your gift, Matt, I bought equipment for *Justified* and am planning on going offshore for the first time."

"Marvelous, Thomas! That's great news. Where are you going to go?"

"I haven't gotten that figured out yet. I want to leave soon though before the weather turns ugly."

"Definitely. Don't go out in bad weather. We want to see you again. Hey, you could come to San Francisco," Matt said.

"I'll take that into consideration, Matt. Look, if there's anything I can do for you just ask, okay?" Thomas said.

"I will definitely do that."

"Is Jerry around? I'd like to say hi to him, too."

"Nah, he had to rush and catch a flight to join DelivrUs in a studio session somewhere. He's always finding ways of getting out of helping with the serious boat cleaning after a voyage. I'll give you back to Otto. Take care, brother, and let us know what your plans are."

"Bless you, Matt," Thomas said.

Otto got back on the phone. "Hey, what's all this talk about you coming to San Francisco?"

"It's a possibility. I'm getting *Justified* ready to sail offshore. So, I might just plan a trip where I hip hop down the coast and knock on your door."

"We'd love to see you here. Do your research on the trip, though. And, realize this, Thomas, if you get here in the next month, you can forget about sailing home for months. The weather will be terrible. Just plan on trucking your boat back," Otto suggested.

"Or keep sailing south," Thomas said with a laugh.

"Well there's that option, too. Don't tell me you've given up on finding a new church."

"Not really. I've been talking to people and sending out resumes. I guess I'm just letting God take me to the right place. In the meantime, I'll do a little sailing," Thomas said.

"Okay, listen, I have to let you go. My battery is almost dead. I've been on the phone all morning. Keep in touch my friend."

"I will. God bless, Otto." Thomas clicked off the phone. He had been walking down the guest dock while talking on the phone. Now he stood at the end, looking across the smooth water to the entrance of the harbor. Was he really planning on leaving this beautiful protected harbor for the open sea? Was he crazy? Was he listening to his ego or to the Holy Spirit? At this very moment, he wasn't sure which.

Chapter 98

O n August 25, Thomas was reading his Bible in the cabin when he heard voices outside and a knock on the hull.

"Hello, Mr. Benton?"

Thomas stuck his head out the companionway to see three men with tools and a cart filled with boxes.

"Good morning. You're right on time. Ready to start work?" Thomas asked.

"Yes sir. Before we start can I confirm with you what we're installing?"

The foreman from the marine supply store came aboard and reviewed with Thomas the long list of electronics that they were to install. Thomas showed him the navigation station. They agreed on where the new instruments would be mounted after the old electronics had been removed.

"If everything is correct, please sign here." The foreman handed the clipboard and pen to Thomas who immediately signed it. He was excited. This was like Christmas.

For the remainder of that day and half the following the men worked installing and testing the new gear. Finally, after all the boxes and dust from drilling were removed from the cabin, the foreman handed to Thomas a thick stack of user manuals.

"Happy reading," the foreman said.

"I have my work cut out for me. I think Tonya from your shop is coming down on Thursday to train me on all this."

"Good idea. Tonya's great. A real geek, but an exceptional teacher," the foreman said before climbing up the companionway for the last time and disappearing up the dock with his crew.

Thomas admired the sophisticated electronics. He went up to the cockpit and inspected the instrument displays that had been installed outside on the port side of the companionway. He couldn't wait to learn how to use the gear and go out for a test sail.

The new roller furling sails he had ordered from the local sailmaker would be delivered in two weeks. After that he could shove off. Where to sail to was the next big question, but he'd figure it out. The important thing to Thomas right now was that he was taking action. He was preparing *Justified* to take him wherever God wanted him to go. He was on a mission.

Thomas went below, opened a can of beer and sat on the settee admiring his new electronics and thumbing through the user manuals. He reached into a drawer to get a highlighter when he noticed the sheets of stamps he had recently purchased. That reminded him of the 224 resumes that had been mailed. What if he got an inquiry? What if someone wanted to hire him right away? That would postpone his offshore adventure. Part of Thomas didn't want an offer to come. At least not now.

Chapter 99

Four hectic weeks later, on September 23, Thomas used a fresh ebb tide to push *Justified* out through San Juan Channel and into the Strait of Juan de Fuca. His new sails were filled with a brisk breeze and the current helped push him along at seven knots. It was a good sign for the start of his voyage to San Francisco.

In the past four weeks he had studied hard, practiced navigating with his instruments in fog and nighttime, and packed *Justified* with fuel, food, water and emergency equipment.

His Plan A was to sail westward from Neah Bay, at the entrance to the Strait of Juan de Fuca, for about 150 miles, then turn on a southerly course parallel to the coast all the way to San Francisco Bay. He calculated the trip would take eight to ten days, but that was totally dependent on the wind. And the weather.

He was pushing his luck to leave this late in September. Beginning in October one storm after another roared downward from the Aleutian Islands and made this part of the Pacific treacherous for small craft. But Thomas believed he was following God's plan, and he prayed that God would give him fair winds all the way through the Golden Gate Bridge.

Late that night, Thomas sat nervously in the cabin of *Justified*. The boat was tied securely to its dock in the Neah Bay marina. This was to be the last night of security for the next ten days. After tonight, Thomas would only be allowed to sleep a few hours at a time, for even though he had self-steering he had to be vigilant because of the busy shipping lanes that he would be passing through.

Was he prepared? Would he ever reach San Francisco, or would he flounder and end up crushed on some desolate rocky shoreline? He prayed and then fell into a restless sleep.

By seven o'clock the next morning on September 24, Thomas had piloted *Justified* out of Neah Bay. By eleven, Cape Flattery was rapidly passing by on the port side. Thomas adjusted course and sails. They were moving along smoothly through the ocean swells. Thomas' spirits were high, but he was still very much on edge. As the rocky cliffs of Cape Flattery grew smaller and smaller behind him he knew he was finally sailing offshore, but each hour under sail he was moving further and further away from the security of a port.

The first issue he had to contend with was seasickness. He wasn't used to the up and down motion caused by the five-foot ocean swells. Chamomile tea and Bonine took away the worst of the symptoms.

For the next twenty-four hours he'd be sailing through shipping channels and areas in which fishing boats operated. He'd have to be on watch during this period. His self-steering wind vane relieved him from being at the wheel constantly, but it was up to Thomas to keep his eye on the horizon and on the radar display that he turned on once each hour.

Justified sailed westward on a close reach at 5.5 knots. They were making good progress toward the turning point marked on his chart plotter. Conditions were excellent. Thomas' upset stomach from earlier had eased. He decided to fix a simple hot dinner to eat now, and coffee and snacks for the long night ahead.

Sailing at night had always been a pleasant experience for Thomas. It was a time to reflect on the miracle of life and the grace of the Almighty. For the most part, navigating at night in Puget Sound was easy. Lights on shore were almost always visible and there were adequate navigation lights to follow. But in the open ocean it was a very different experience.

In this, his first night at sea, clouds hid the stars and moon. The only light he could see from where he sat in the cockpit came from the orange glow of his instrument panel and the white light far above on top of the mast. Otherwise, the darkness was total. The sound of wind and invisible waves were all around him.

The sensation of sitting in a tiny boat floating on a very large dark ocean was humbling and unsettling, but he adjusted to it after a few hours on watch. He talked to God, he talked to himself. He smoked a cigar, drank coffee and ate chocolate. He had to stay awake on watch until sunrise. Then he could sleep for a few hours. He was already looking forward to noon when he would gybe, pointing *Justified*'s bow south for the long downwind run to San Francisco.

During the night he wondered about the 224 resumes he had mailed a month earlier. He hadn't received any response prior to his departure. Tomorrow he could check his email via the satellite weather and internet service he subscribed to for the voyage. If a church reached out to him via email he'd be able to respond. And tell them what exactly? *Thanks for your interest in my resume I can't talk to you for ten days. I'm sailing on a mission.* Okay, but was that a lie? What was his mission? Bring God to rich boaters in San Francisco? *Get serious. That's not exactly on par with digging wells in Nairobi so villagers can have drinking water, is it?*

The question of why he was out there started to bother Thomas. Was he really following the Holy Spirit? The change in his life was unlike anything he had ever experienced. Five months ago, he was happily married and the leader of a vibrant church. Tonight, he was all alone in the dark in a 36-foot boat, 100 miles off the Washington coast. Was he where God wanted him to be? That was the question of the night, and while he wrestled with the answer to that question he had no trouble staying awake.

At daybreak, Thomas read his position on the chart plotter and checked the radar for vessels approaching on a collision course. Happy with his position and absence of encroaching traffic he collapsed into his bunk for a few hours of sleep.

Chapter 100

At exactly 12:03 p.m. on September 25, Thomas re-furled the mainsail, turned the wheel to the left and let out the jib sheet. *Justified* was now headed on a due-south course with a 22-knot wind from behind. Even with just the jib flying, she was speeding forward at 6.5 knots. The knotometer jumped to as high as 8 knots when she caught the waves just right and started to surf.

"Yeah, baby!" Thomas thrust his two arms into the air and shouted in excitement as if he had just scored the winning touchdown. At this pace, he'd be sailing beneath Golden Gate Bridge in less than six days.

So far, the weather forecast he had last received on his satellite weather system while in Neah Bay had been accurate. That forecast told him ideal sailing conditions along the Washington coast were expected to hold until the 28th, at which time the first winter storm was due to crawl down from the north. He wasn't worried because his speed and course would put him several hundred miles or so ahead of the storm.

On September 26 a change in the boat's motion at noon woke Thomas from a nap. He was dog-tired from yesterday's adrenalin rush and stress. He looked out the companionway. Dense fog greeted him. The seas were nearly calm except for the swell. A light, inconsistent breeze wasn't enough to keep *Justified's* sail full. The fog was totally unexpected.

Thomas turned on the radar screen to see if there were any vessels in the area to be concerned with. He was greeted by two blips on the color display. One about 50 miles away; the other only 20 miles away.

Thomas sighed and started heating water on the stove for coffee. He needed to be awake and alert while watching the courses of the two other vessels. If *Justified* collided with a tanker in the fog, *Justified* would lose.

He got dressed, put on his coat and safety harness, filled his insulated mug with hot coffee, climbed up the companionway, and sat in the cockpit. He couldn't see more than ten feet from the boat, so he listened carefully for any sounds that could tip him off that another vessel was in the vicinity.

Drifting in the fog was unsettling. It made him restless. After an hour he couldn't take it any longer and turned the radar on again.

The radar display confirmed that neither vessel was on a collision course with *Justified*. With no imminent danger, Thomas could relax. The next question was how long would this weather pattern hold? He knew he could spend days becalmed and make little more than a few miles progress each day. Did this unexpected fog mean the weather pattern had changed?

He went below to check the satellite weather forecast on his laptop. He was hoping that the system would tell him the fog would move on by late afternoon and be replaced by clear skies and a 20-mph breeze from the north. Instead what he saw made his heart race and stomach tighten.

He was in an area that would remain calm and foggy for the next 24 hours. But by the 27th a storm would be on him. He could expect miserable conditions with winds gusting to 45 mph, swells of fifteen to twenty feet, rain, and temperatures in the upper forties. The storm front had formed faster than expected in the Gulf of Alaska and the jet stream was pushing it right into Thomas' part of the ocean ahead of schedule. For Thomas, rather than be hundreds of miles to the south and out of harm's way, as was his original plan, he was going to be engulfed by the storm front thanks to this fog and zero wind.

He tried to calculate how long he'd be in storm conditions once they arrived. With luck, the storm wouldn't push too far south, and he'd sail out of it after a few hundred miles when he was off the Oregon coast. Unfortunately, this storm wasn't the only one he had to contend with now. The weather off Northern California was changing, too. The window of opportunity available for reaching San Francisco was slamming shut. *Justified* was going to be spit out of one storm right into the path of another, but the California storm would be worse because the strong winds and waves would be from the south and on his bow.

Staring at the forecasts and weather maps in front of him on the laptop, Thomas rubbed his weary eyes and tried to think of options. If he did nothing now, he would be in storm conditions for the next five days or however long it took him to reach San Francisco. It wasn't an appealing thought to battle wind and high seas without rest for several days only to be greeted with a second storm as he tried to navigate the dangerous waters approaching San Francisco. *Justified* might be able to take the pounding, but he would be beyond exhaustion after days without rest.

In the end there was only one option. Cut the trip short and head for the nearest harbor. San Francisco would have to wait. Because of being becalmed in the fog he had made little progress on his course to the south. He was still off the Washington coast. He could look for a safe port in Washington, or further down the coast in Oregon, if necessary. The wise choice was to get into port as soon as possible.

He studied the chart and his research notes. Other boaters had mentioned in their cruising journals that there was one excellent port for small boats on the Washington coast that didn't involve a dangerous bar crossing. Though the entrance to the bay was tight and guarded by reefs, it was well marked and could be navigated in most conditions. He tapped the plotter screen and the instrument gave him a course to inside the nearest harbor. Just two days after leaving Neah Bay he was returning to the coast with his tail tucked between his legs.

Dejectedly he furled the useless jib, turned on the diesel engine and pointed *Justified* through the dense fog on an east by northeast compass heading to Reef Bay.

Chapter 101

Around midnight *Justified* was still 100 miles offshore when a breeze from the northwest pushed the fog away. Thomas unfurled only twenty percent of the jib, not wanting to be caught with a larger sail area if the wind picked up suddenly. He cut the engine and reset the self-steering vane. He was making three knots along his course to the coastline. The sailing was slow and easy. It gave Thomas time to prepare himself and his boat for tomorrow.

The first gust hit the sloop at eleven in the morning on September 27 as it sailed along some fifty miles offshore. Thomas was prepared for it. All loose gear below was secured. He had forced himself to eat a hearty breakfast because he didn't know when he would be able to cook again, and he needed energy. He had hot coffee and hot chocolate waiting in thermos bottles. He had also prayed hard that God would give him and his boat the strength to endure this test.

With the wind came driving rain and low clouds. This cut visibility, so each hour he'd check radar for vessels approaching. He got into a routine of spending thirty minutes in the cockpit and sixty minutes below in the cabin. The violent motion of the boat made being below a miserable experience, but he had to rest and warm himself. There was little he could do outside anyway.

By five o'clock in the near darkness the storm intensified. The seas grew steeper, the wind was steady at 45 mph with occasional higher gusts. Waves with breaking tops towered above the boat. The only thing propelling *Justified* now was a tiny bit of exposed jib. He was driving now, hands firmly on the wheel. In high breaking seas there was a risk of getting broadside to a large wave and being knocked over, or worse yet, digging the bow into a steep breaking wave that dumps tons of water on top of the boat. This was new territory for Thomas. He had never sailed in conditions like this. The howling wind had been bad enough in the dim light of the stormy day, but now it was getting dark. The waves were coming at him from the rear port quarter and made steering extremely difficult. It seemed to Thomas that each wave had as its sole mission to knock *Justified* from its course. It was if an endless line of angry devils took turns smashing against the hull to push it off course and away from Reef Bay.

He was rapidly approaching the coastline. Fatigue was taking its toll from being in the strong wind and wrestling the wheel to keep *Justified* under control in the waves. With each mile closer to the shore, Thomas grew more tense. If his navigation was off by as much as 200 yards he and his lovely yacht would be crushed to pieces against the jagged rocks. He didn't dwell on it, but in the back of his mind was the thought that these next few hours could be the last hours of his life.

That made him want to double-check his course and position. The chart plotter display in the cockpit revealed he was right on course. Although his plotter and radar were doing a masterful job of guiding him to safety, he didn't like to rely on them 100 percent. Not when it was a matter of life and death. He reset the self-steering so he could go below briefly.

In the cabin, with one hand holding himself steady against the roller coaster motion of the boat, he unrolled a paper chart on the desk. He had previously drawn the same course on the chart as the electronic chart plotter had given him. Now he studied the navigation aids that would guide him to safety.

Based on the calculations and notations on his chart, in a few hours he should be able to see the beacon from the lighthouse on the south shore of the entrance to Reef Bay. Seeing the beacon during the night would enable him to take a bearing and check it against the chart plotter's position.

According to the charts, the Point Jeopardy lighthouse beacon was visible to thirty miles. But that was in clear conditions. In these nasty conditions he was going to be lucky if he saw the light five miles out.

Two buoys marked the entrance to Reef Bay. The chart told him the buoys were unlit. The radar would be able to see them in advance, but at night his eyes wouldn't see the dark steel objects until he was practically close enough to touch them.

What he was attempting was lunacy, but he had no choice. God willing, he'd live to see the sun rise.

PART THREE,
THE LIGHT.

Chapter 102

t was going to take some time to adjust. Not being able to speak clearly was a real drag. Several times this morning Clay had reached for his phone to make a call and had to stop himself. No one would be able to understand him. He wanted to talk with George. He wanted to call Bartlett in Reef Bay. He wanted to call his cleaning service. He wanted to apologize to Sheryl for kicking her out of his house yesterday. Instead he sent emails to everyone; everyone except Sheryl, that is. He told himself that he needed more time to think about what to say to her. He resolved to send her a message from Reef Bay.

Clay packed a bag with clothes for several days. He didn't know how long he'd be at the lighthouse. Hopefully he would be down there just long enough to negotiate and sign the papers to sell the property. Reef Bay wasn't his kind of place. The less time spent there the better.

In the mirror he didn't like what he saw—a dark bruise on his forehead, a bandage over the skin that had been scraped by the rough dock, and the silly neck brace. He removed the brace and slowly moved his head in small circles to test the pain level. The neck was tender and stiff but he could bear the discomfort. He tossed the brace on the countertop. A screwed-up voice was enough of a handicap. He didn't need his head to be restricted, too. Besides, the neck brace would attract attention and questions, which Clay couldn't answer in a way that anyone could understand.

He definitely needed to settle his business in Reef Bay quickly and get back to Seattle to start speech therapy.

The drive from Seattle on May 3 was uneventful except for the non-stop thoughts that ricocheted around inside his mind. To say he had mixed feelings about his sudden decision to resign from Pitt-Needham and to push Sheryl away was an understatement. One minute he was feeling free and light, as if a huge burden had been lifted off his shoulders. The next minute he was bitter and filled with guilt.

He was still reflecting on the whipsaw nature of this life as he parked outside the law offices of Glenn Bartlett's in Reef Bay. Before leaving the car, he removed a yellow writing pad and marker pen from his computer bag. In large letters he wrote on the paper, "I am Clay Austin. Here to see Glenn."

In his email to the attorney he explained about his accident and inability to speak clearly, but he didn't know if the receptionist had gotten the word or not. He was going to have to carry pen and paper with him wherever he went; at least until he was finished with speech therapy.

Clay walked into the small office and was greeted by Betty, the same assistant he had met in his first visit to the office.

"Good afternoon, Mr. Austin. We've been expecting you. We're so sorry to hear about your accident, but very, very grateful that you are okay. I have fresh coffee if you'd like some," Betty said.

Clay nodded and winced. His neck was sore. Betty handed him a cup of coffee and smiled. Before Clay could sit down, Glenn opened the door of his office and entered the reception area with his hand outstretched to shake Clay's hand.

"Hello, Mr. Austin. Please come in."

Once seated in the office, the attorney continued to speak, "In your email you mentioned that you had a kayak accident, hit your head, and as a result you can't speak clearly. Is that correct."

Clay nodded again.

"Gosh, well, I'll do my best to communicate in a way that won't require long answers," Bartlett said.

Clay held up is yellow pad and pen for Bartlett to see.

"Ah, of course, you can write responses. Excellent. Shall we begin?"

Clay nodded gingerly.

The attorney pushed a folder across the polished desk to Clay. "Inside the folder is a formal offer to purchase your real estate at 3100 Deception Point Drive for $1.2 million. As I mentioned in my email to you, the offer is by a group of investors, two of whom have been trying to get their hands on that property for years. One of the investors happens to be the mayor of Reef Bay. Name is Roger Bildgewood."

Clay had been scanning the offer document, but his head jerked up, causing a shot of pain in his neck, when he heard the attorney mention the mayor. Clay scribbled a note on his pad and showed it to Bartlett.

"Met mayor at funeral," read Clay's note.

"Yes, he was there all right. I feel it's my duty to give you some background on our mayor and his relationship with your uncle. What you do with the information is up to you, of course. In the end, the property is yours and the decision to sell, and to whom to sell, is yours."

Clay gestured for Bartlett to continue.

"It's no secret that Mayor Bildgewood and his investors want to build a resort on the property. It goes back years to just after your uncle acquired the place. They tried to convince Charley to sell. He wasn't interested. After Bildgewood was elected Mayor things got nasty. He worked behind the scenes first with the tax appraiser in an attempt to raise the property taxes so high Charley couldn't afford to keep the place. I helped your uncle fight that one. Then they tried to buy a piece of adjacent land so they could deny Charley's easement for the road that leads to the property. We fought that one, too."

"The mayor and his cronies are powerful people here, Mr. Austin, but they've never been strong enough to totally control the City Council. The Council has narrowly voted to support your uncle in several key instances."

"You see, four of the seven council members belonged to your Uncle's church, where he was very active and very loved. They always voted for the right thing, even when it was extremely uncomfortable politically for them to do so. That only made Bildgewood angrier and more determined to get your uncle off that land.

"I can't prove it, but Charley suspected that Bildgewood hired some local no-gooder to follow him some nights on the road driving back to the point and scare him."

Clay recalled his nighttime experience with a truck and animal screams after leaving the Surf View Bistro. Could there be a connection? After all, he had just met the Mayor that day at the funeral. They knew he was in town.

"Anyway, Mr. Austin, those are the people who have extended the offer. In the folder you'll also see the latest tax appraisal of $2,250,000, and two comparable sales of ocean-view property. The mayor's offer is over a million less than the appraised value. I must say, this group is either assuming you want to dump the place as fast as possible, or else they have something else up their sleeve. I just don't see how they can make a serious offer for that little."

Clay noticed a news clipping in the folder. The article from the *Reef Bay Journal* included a picture of the Point Deception lighthouse and a lengthy article. He held it up, indicating he wanted Bartlett to explain.

"Ah, the article talks about a group of citizens here in town who are pushing the State of Washington to classify all decommissioned lighthouses on the Washington coast as historical monuments, so the structures have to be maintained and cannot be destroyed. They call themselves the 'Friends of the Lighthouse'.

"From what I can tell, the group is interested in saving all old lighthouses, not just the one on your property. If the State passes a law like this, it could require you to make extensive improvements to the structure and never remove it. That of course would limit your options with the property and impact its value."

Clay held up the offer document in one hand, the press clipping in the right hand. He wiggled both in front of Bartlett.

"Yes, I know what you're thinking. Odd coincidence that this committee has started its campaign right about the time you get a low-ball offer for the place."

"Uh-huh," Clay said, grateful he could at least say that clearly.

"Which is why Betty, my assistant, has asked her sister, Meredith, to volunteer on the committee and report to us what she learns."

Clay gave a thumb up signal and smiled. Bartlett might be a small-town attorney, but he thought and acted like a big-city attorney.

"The offer is good for another forty-eight hours. What would you like me to do?"

Clay wrote on his pad. "I need time to think."

"Certainly. Are you staying in town for the next two days?"

Clay wrote, "Yes. At lighthouse."

"We assumed that you would stay there. You'll find everything is in order and Betty even put a few things in the refrigerator for you."

Clay wrote, "Thnx. Very kind."

"Shall we communicate by text and email?"

"Uh-huh." Clay stood, gathered the files together and walked out of the office. He said bye to Betty on the way out, but it sounded like 'baah'.

Chapter 103

lay drove slowly down the last stretch of gravel leading to the covered carport at 3100 Point Deception Drive. Nothing had changed since the last time he was here. Correction, nothing had changed with the property. Everything had changed for Clay.

He parked next to the pickup, removed his suitcase and computer bag from the car and walked to the front door. He made a mental note to drive the pickup and check out the tool shed while he was here.

He shut the front door behind him and stood in the living room. He owned the place, but it sure didn't feel like his. After placing his suitcase in the bedroom, he went to the refrigerator and opened it. Just as Bartlett had said it contained a few items: beer, orange juice, milk, bread, and lunch meat. The freezer contained a few frozen dinners. Clay was pretty certain he wasn't going to eat one of those, but he removed a can of beer before shutting the door.

He fetched Bartlett's file folder from the bedroom and sat at the kitchen table to read all the documents carefully. From the table he could look out a window across the expanse of grass and to the gray ocean beyond. It was cold in the house. Though it was the beginning of May, the outside temperature wasn't much above sixty degrees and the dampness made it feel even cooler. Clay got up from the table to find a thermostat that controlled the furnace, but after a search of every wall he concluded that the residence didn't have a furnace. The only source of heat was a square iron stove in the living room. If he didn't want to freeze while staying here he would have to build a fire in the stove. That meant he needed to find a supply of wood somewhere.

Clay hadn't recalled seeing a stack of wood anywhere outside, but he hadn't been to the back side of the house yet. He stepped into the corridor leading to the lighthouse and walked out the door that led to the rear of the property. Sure enough, under the overhanging eaves of the corridor was a large stack of wood. Next to the stack was a large stump with a rusted axe sticking in it.

One more reason not to keep this place. No way am I going to build a fire and stack wood every time I'm here.

He cut some kindling with the axe and carried an armload of wood into the house. Within thirty minutes of lighting the wood in the stove the house was warming up. As it turned out, the stove and a ceiling fan in the living room were very effective at heating the small house. It just required keeping the fire burning. He didn't want to think about how much wood had to be stacked each year to supply the stove. It didn't matter. This would be someone else's problem soon enough.

Back now at the kitchen table he read the newspaper clipping, the offer and other documents. Bartlett had been correct. The offer was way below a reasonable estimate of market value. It didn't make sense. He could understand if the initial offer was $250,000 below market value, but not a price that was half of the market value. It was an odd way to start a serious negotiation, unless the mayor's group knew something Clay didn't.

He scanned the news article again. If the state legislature passed a law protecting all decommissioned lighthouses, as the Friends of the Lighthouse group was proposing, anyone who owned one had to maintain its appearance and couldn't destroy it. There might even be restrictions on what could be done with the property. If that was the case, the buyers couldn't develop this land either, so why would they want it?

Clay rubbed his sore neck while trying to think. A sentence in the news article caught his attention, ". . . to preserve the historical heritage of lighthouses in the state by whatever means the legislature deems necessary." That was pretty strong language. Any means necessary could mean applying strict covenants covering lighthouse ownership, or the state purchasing the property and handing it over to the Parks department.

Clay swallowed the last of his beer. He reached for his phone and sent a text to Bartlett.

"Do the buyers have connections in State government?" He tapped Send.

While waiting for a response Clay fixed a simple sandwich, grateful the Betty had been so thoughtful. He turned on the hot water in the kitchen sink. Yep, she had turned on the hot water heater, too.

With sandwich in hand he walked outside to look at the tool shed. One of the keys in his set unlocked the door. He opened it and felt around inside the door for a light switch, found it, and turned it on. The fluorescent light overhead revealed a clean, neatly organized shed that doubled as a workshop. A sturdy workbench ran the entire length of one wall. Tools of all kinds were mounted on pegboards and shelves above the bench. Clay grinned as he saw along the back-wall a familiar sight—a rock saw, grinder and polisher were positioned in a row. Mounted on the third wall were various yard tools.

Something on the floor was under a tarp. He lifted a corner of the tarp to see what it was. A shiny green riding lawnmower! It looked brand new. It couldn't have been used more than a few times. Uncle Charley must have bought it so he could still mow the lawn in his advancing age.

But there was something else under the tarp, too. Clay pulled the canvas back further. When he saw what was there he didn't know whether to laugh at the irony, or run as fast as he could out of the shed.

Two old Briggs & Stratton lawn mowers sat there looking up at him.

Clay felt a little foolish in how quickly he re-covered the lawnmowers with the tarp, as if to prevent the machines from seeing him. He turned, shut off the light and left the shed, relocking it behind him. He halfway expected to hear the mowers angrily trying to escape the shed as he walked away.

This, the south side of the house, was protected from the prevailing northerly winds. It felt warmer on this side out of the wind. An area of tilled soil told Clay that his uncle probably grew vegetables back here. He strolled along the gravel path that paralleled the house, corridor, and lighthouse.

Now, standing next to the lighthouse, he looked up at the impressive structure that rose more than a hundred feet above him into the gray sky.

It was uncanny how alike this lighthouse was to the one in his nightmares (and Dr. Shildstein's painting). The similarities were numerous—the shape, the height, the color, the small windows that dotted the sides. As if to verify that he was standing next to a real lighthouse and not in a dream, he placed his left hand on the wall. The damp coolness and texture of the masonry assured him he wasn't in a dream. But for verification, he placed his right hand on the wall, too. *It's okay, this is real.* Then he looked up the rounded wall of chipped white paint toward the sky. His stiff neck protested, but he held his head in that position for a long time, just looking up. The experience reminded him of the time as a kid when he was in the Redwood forest of northern California. He had hugged a massive sequoia tree with his short arms and looked up as it towered above him.

He recalled the sensation he felt while hugging that tree and placing his tender cheek on the rough bark. He felt united with the tree, as if the tree was welcoming him to its world. Clay had loved tall trees ever since.

Oddly enough he was having the same sensation now. Standing here with hands raised against the towering lighthouse walls he felt connected to it, a part of it.

His neck was really hurting now. To relieve the pain, he tilted his head forward. Then, recalling his experience with the tree, Clay rested his forehead against the lighthouse wall, hands still planted on the wall above his head.

At this moment, with his forehead and hands resting on the cold wall of the lighthouse, Clay felt completely overwhelmed with emotion. Thoughts and images flowed through his head at a rapid pace as if he was now plugged into a channel of streaming media. Images of his aunt and uncle walking with him on the golf course, his mother baking a birthday cake, George, his partner, giving him a high-five, Sheryl tenderly kissing his lips, and Dr. Shildstein handing him a painting.

The visions were a parade of people who loved Clay. He started to weep. The visions continued. Some were new, others repeated. On and on they flashed through his mind, but eventually began to fade. Clay thought the visions might be over and was about to detach himself from the wall when a much stronger vision flooded his brain.

He was no longer standing beside a lighthouse. He was on a path with brilliant colors on both sides. Not flowers, just glorious, shimmering colors of light that pulsed and swirled hypnotically. Up ahead, on the path was an intense light and out of that light a figure flowed toward Clay.

He recognized this as the same vision he had had after his drowning accident. He wasn't apprehensive about the approaching figure this time. In his vision he stood on the path, welcoming its advance.

The figure stood before him now. Its features weren't discernible, except for the eyes. Could eyes be any more loving and compassionate than these? Clay felt they were looking right through him and into his heart.

"Hello, Clay. I'm pleased that you are here."

"Jesus, is that you?"

"Yes. Your heart reached out to me. I am here."

"I'm confused. My life has turned upside down."

"Clay, what did I ask you when we met before?"

Clay had to think. He recalled talking to Jesus in his near-death experience, but he had forgotten the specific words.

"You don't remember do you?" Jesus said in a tone that was completely factual yet without any blame whatsoever.

"No, Jesus, I'm sorry."

"I gave you a light and asked you to carry it for me."

"Oh, I remember now. I completely forgot. I'm sorry, you see I lost my ability to speak because of the accident and I've been dealing with my job, my . . . wait a minute . . . I'm talking to you perfectly okay right now."

"That's right, Clay. When you speak from the heart I hear you. And I know everything that has happened and everything that will happen. But, I see a darkness that has settled into your heart. The darkness blocks the light, but the light dissolves the darkness."

Clay was pondering the meaning of that statement when Jesus continued.

"You are very special to me, Clay. I have loved you from the beginning."

"The beginning of what?" Clay asked.

"From the beginning." Jesus paused before continuing. "Listen, carry this light for me," Jesus said, handing Clay a lit candle that appeared in Jesus' hands like magic.

"What am I supposed to do with it, Jesus?"

"It's not what you'll *do* with the light, it's what you'll *be* with the light."

"I don't understand."

"You don't need to understand. Just accept this light. And never forget that I am with you always."

The vision ended as suddenly as it had started. Clay slowly removed his forehead and hands from the damp walls of the lighthouse. He looked at his surroundings. He was back at 3100 Deception Point Drive all right. He felt a little chilled and headed to the warmth of the house.

The thought occurred to him that in his vision, or dream, or whatever it was, he had been talking normally to Jesus. Could he talk normally now?

He spoke, "Da litshowse is al." Nope. Clay's speech impediment was still present. Clay was upset with himself for not having the presence of mind in the vision to have asked Jesus to heal his voice.

Clay laughed. *Right, I expect myself to be thinking rationally and clearly while hugging a lighthouse and seeing Jesus in front of me? I suppose I could pray about it later. People pray about things like this. I'll give it a try.*

Chapter 104

After fetching a beer from the refrigerator, Clay sat down at the kitchen table where the documents he had been reviewing earlier were still spread out. He tried to study them again, but realized he wasn't interested anymore.

Something was happening here. Something was happening to him, and he couldn't explain it. All he knew was that in the past week he had almost died, Jesus came to him in a vision, he lost his voice, got angry, pushed Sheryl away, resigned from his job, drove here to sell the lighthouse, and Jesus paid him another visit. Not a normal week by any measure.

And now, staring down at the papers in front of him, he realized that his feelings about this property had shifted 180 degrees in the past half hour. He looked out the window across the grass field, past the fence guarding the cliff's edge, to the ocean in the distance. A sense of peace filled him. It felt like a tightly wound spring had been removed from inside his gut.

He noticed another sensation, too. His neck was no longer sore and stiff. That was a relief. Had Jesus healed his neck? If his neck, why not the voice, too? Where was the logic in that? Clay needed his voice a lot more than he needed a pain-free neck.

God, I don't understand your priorities, but I am grateful for removing the pain. Could you work on restoring my voice next?

Clay didn't think that was a very good prayer. Praying was something he needed to learn more about.

But for now, out of all the uncertainty and weirdness of his life, one thing was exceptionally clear. He wasn't selling this lighthouse to Mayor Bildgewood, or to anyone else for that matter.

He picked up his phone and wrote a text message to Bartlett.

"Refuse offer. Not selling. Continue research into Friends of the Lighthouse," Clay tapped. He wanted to know what this group was up to, and who was pulling the strings in the background.

Clay wandered through the small house. Heat from the stove made the four rooms cozy. The place had charm but looked old and worn. That could be fixed with paint, furniture, art, a new floor perhaps. He could ask his decorator in Seattle to take a look. For some reason Sheryl's condo entered his mind. Its décor had really appealed to Clay. The thought of Sheryl reminded him that he had a letter to write.

He headed for the bedroom to get his notebook computer but stopped short. It wouldn't do any good to write the letter on the notebook. The house didn't have

WiFi. He couldn't send the email once written. WiFi was another thing to be installed if he was going to be spending any time here at all.

Clay sat down in the easy chair with his phone in hand.

Though the small keypad on his phone made typing slow, he kept at it for the next two hours and two more beers. He'd write a paragraph, delete it, and start over. It was the hardest thing he had ever written.

At last he was done. He read it one final time before sending. He couldn't believe it had taken him so long to write so few words.

"*Dear Sheryl, I have been a real ass. There are no excuses for my behavior when I forced you out of the house yesterday evening.*

I woke up from my nap angry at everything and everyone, including you. I was expressing anger, but inside I was scared. Without my work, Sheryl, I'm nobody. I don't have an identity. I don't know how to live or relate to others outside the context of my work. So, when I realized that I couldn't do my job without being able to speak clearly, I panicked. I lashed out at the world, at God, at you.

Yesterday I believed that losing my ability to speak put an end to all my dreams, all my plans. Maybe so. More likely it put it an end to a chapter of my life and forced me to turn the page to the next chapter.

I can only imagine how much my actions must have hurt. I wouldn't blame you if you never forgave me for what I did. But I beg you to understand at least. It wasn't the real Clay who pushed you out into the cold night. It was someone else.

The real Clay adores you. The real Clay is falling in love with you.

I'm writing this from the lighthouse in Reef Bay. I received an offer to sell it but decided a few hours ago to keep the place. I'm going to fix it up and spend time here. But, the big news is this. Jesus paid me another visit this afternoon. Told me to carry his light for Him, just like in the other vision I told you about.

Pretty interesting that Jesus asked me to carry his light when I'm literally standing at the foot of a lighthouse, don't you think?

But, back to you and me. If you can find a way in your heart to forgive me, I swear to never hurt you again. I miss you very much. It's weird, but as I walk around the house I keep imagining you here with me. Your absence makes the place seem empty, even though you've never been inside the house. In my mind you should be here with me.

I'm sorry.

Clay"

He hesitated multiple times before finally tapping the Send button. He wondered if he would ever see Sheryl again.

Chapter 105

lay was hungry, weak, and exhausted. He needed to take better care of himself. After all, he had been clinically dead less than a week ago.

He walked back to the kitchen and opened the freezer. A few frozen dinners greeted him. He shuddered. That's not what he wanted, but he was too tired to go out for groceries or a restaurant. So, he took out a package of mushroom ravioli, read the instructions for how to prepare it. There was a bag of pre-cut salad makings in the vegetable drawer and a small bottle of Italian dressing.

Thirty minutes later his dinner was ready to eat. He sat at the table and ate. The ravioli was surprisingly good. He ate the entire box and his salad. He cleared the table and looked for the dishwasher. There wasn't one.

Add that to the list. Dishwasher and WiFi were necessities in Clay's household.

On a bookshelf in the living room was a box humidor. Clay lifted the lid to find six cigars. He smiled. Seeing the cigars reminded him of the time at his uncle's cabin when little Clay stole a cigar and some matches. He hid them by a tree in the forest beyond sight of the cabin. Each day while playing outside in the woods, he'd light the cigar and take a few puffs before carefully extinguishing it and reburying the cigar and matches in the ground at the base of a pine tree. He never got caught, or at least his aunt and uncle never let on that they knew he was sneaking a smoke in the woods.

Clay also remembered the time in Medford when his mother had caught him smoking. She didn't punish him, but Vic sure did. Vic made him sit down in the living room and smoke a cigarette with him the way he smoked, deeply inhaling every drag from the unfiltered cigarette. Little Clay was dizzy after two puffs, and very ill after six.

"If you're going to smoke, smoke like a man," Vic said as little Clay raced to the bathroom to vomit.

Clay selected one of the cigars, clipped its tip with the clipper tool, lit it, and walked out into the night.

The darkness was total. He stepped back into the house and checked for a switch that might turn on lights outdoors. One switch ignited several flood lights that illuminated the grass field. Clay went back outside and walked through the field toward the fence that guarded the cliff.

He was enjoying the taste of the cigar and the feeling of the damp, salty wind on his face.

I just might do this every night, Uncle Charley.

Clay reached the fence. It was spooky to stand here, with nothing but darkness visible beyond, hearing waves crashing into rocks far below. Without the fence. One false step and he'd be dead. If that happened would Jesus come to save him again? The second time in one week. Clay laughed in the dark.

To his left, on the southern side of the entrance to Reef Bay, a light flashed. Ah, that must be the same light he saw weeks ago from the Surf View Bistro. What was the name? Point something. *Jeopardy. That's it, the Point Jeopardy light house.* Clay thought it was highly unusual to have two lighthouses within a few miles of each other. Granted his wasn't operational. He made a mental note to learn more about his lighthouse.

Clay grew very weary and made his way back to the house.

Back inside, he checked out the bedroom. It occurred to him that the sheets probably hadn't been changed since Uncle Charley's death. Clay was not going to sleep in his uncle's sheets.

Peeling back the bed covers revealed no sheets. Someone had removed them. Clay found a linen closet in the bathroom that contained several sets of neatly folded sheets and towels. Glenn and Betty had really been taking care of the place.

He made the bed and was pleasantly surprised to see a high-quality foam mattress. It was almost like Clay's. He got ready for bed, added another two logs to the stove to keep the fire going longer, and crawled into bed.

When he turned off the light the last thing he remembered before falling asleep was the sound of the breeze coming off the sea.

Chapter 106

On Friday after breakfast Clay took another stroll around the property. He had to turn up the collar on his jacket against the brisk breeze. He walked around the front of the house along a gravel pathway that encircled the residence and lighthouse. When he reached the lighthouse he noticed something lying in the un-mowed grass close to the lighthouse wall.

It was a tall wooden ladder of the type Clay had seen frequently used in the orchards around Medford when he was a kid. He picked up the ladder to take it around to the tool shed, although he thought it would be too long to fit inside.

Picking up the ladder, he noticed the fifth wooden rung from the top of the ladder was broken in two. He didn't think much about it at first until he recalled the conversation with Mayor Bildgewood at his uncle's memorial service.

"The poor man was up a ladder re-caulking a window when he fell and hit his head. Why someone his age was twenty feet up a ladder in the first place is beyond me."

Clay was holding the ladder that his uncle fell from. He imagined the old man losing his balance and falling to the hard gravel path. What made him fall? Clay looked up and saw the first of the lowest of several small windows at different levels on this side. That was the only window reachable by a ladder. That was the window his uncle was probably re-caulking when the accident happened. Clay hoped his uncle didn't suffer. How long did he lay on the ground before he was found?

Clay lifted the heavy ladder and began to carry it around the lighthouse to the tool shed. As he walked he kept looking at the broken step. Could that be the cause of the fall? He stopped walking and looked more closely at the rung. He imagined it snapping and his uncle's foot falling through, causing him to lose balance and fall to his death. Why did the rung break? The sturdy ladder was in good shape. All the rungs were very solid with no sign of wear or rot. What he did notice though was intriguing. Whereas the break was jagged from the front of the rung, it was a clean break from the inside third of the wooden step. Clay had broken and cut enough wood in his life to know that when a board is broken it leaves a jagged edge, unless it has been cut.

He pushed the two broken pieces back together. No doubt about it. The inside one-third of the step had been cut. All it took was the weight of a grown man on the cut wood to make it snap.

Clay returned the ladder to where it had fallen. He had the unsettling feeling that he was standing in the middle of a crime scene. Someone had wanted his uncle dead.

He hurried back to the house. His hands were shaking as he typed a message to Bartlett.

"Can you come to lighthouse? Something important to show you."

The attorney arrived an hour later and knocked on the door. Clay met him, shook hands and immediately motioned to follow him outside. The two men walked along the path to the ladder. Clay picked it up and showed the broken step to Bartlett. He traced with his finger the straight line of the saw cut and motioned back and forth with his free hand mimicking the act of sawing.

At first the attorney didn't know what Clay was getting at, but then the lights came on.

"This is probably the ladder your uncle was on when he fell. The postman who found him said he was lying on the path and the ladder had fallen over next to him; like he had lost his balance and pulled the ladder back on top of him."

Clay nodded and pointed again at the broken step.

"It looks like this step broke and that's why Charley lost his balance."

Clay nodded and pointed again at the straight cut line.

"It appears the step had been cut. What are you trying to say?"

"Purpux, ill," Clay sputtered.

Bartlett shook his head indicating he couldn't understand. He opened the portfolio case he had been carrying and offered Clay a pen. Clay immediately grabbed the pen and scribbled on the top sheet of paper, "Step cut on purpose. uncle was killed."

"Who would want Charley dead. Everyone loved him. Maybe he accidentally cut it while working on another project," the attorney reasoned.

Clay scribbled again, "Doubtful. I want the police to investigate."

Chapter 107

By noon it seemed every cop in Reef Bay was on the scene. Small town police departments don't get to investigate many potential homicide scenes, so everyone on duty and off duty wanted in on the action.

By three in the afternoon a yellow "Crime Scene" tape marked off the area where the ladder was found. The ladder itself was strapped to the top of one of their SUVs and hauled off to be examined.

Bartlett and Clay sat in the living room after the police had gone.

"With all the excitement this morning I forgot to mention that the buyers increased their offer by $200,000."

Clay wrote on his yellow pad, "No. Don't want to sell."

"I understand. I will convey the message to them loud and clear that no means no."

Already Clay was writing something else. He handed the pad to his attorney.

Bartlett read it aloud, "Be careful; I think the mayor may have something to do with the ladder." He looked at Clay. "You must be kidding. What makes you think that?" He handed the pad back to Clay who wrote rapidly before passing the pad back to Bartlett.

"Who has wanted this property badly for years?"

Bartlett answered after reading the note, "Yes, the mayor has tried every trick to get the land. And it's no secret he and your uncle did not get along, but murder?"

"It's possible," Clay wrote. "Are the Chief of Police and Mayor close?"

"No, they are not. Most people expect Chief Smith to run against the Mayor in the coming election."

Clay wrote, "That is good."

"Listen, I got to get back to the office unless you need anything more from me," Bartlett said.

"Dnx. Bah," Clay said, shaking Bartlett's hand.

The day was almost over and Clay hadn't even checked his email. He sat in the La-Z-Boy recliner and looked at email on his phone.

Reuben, his attorney in Seattle, reported progress with the resignation agreement. George expressed his sorrow at Clay's decision and prayed for his health. Other messages from people at the agency expressed similar sentiments. Then he saw the email from Sheryl. His heart raced as the message displayed on the small screen in his hand.

"Clay, you are right. You are an ass. If you ever do that to me again I will drown you in the lake myself, and I'll hide the body so God can't even find it.

Yes, you hurt me terribly. I have spent the past day crying, praying and eating ice cream. Any weight I've gained is your fault, mister.

And by-the-way, your resignation has turned the world upside down around here. Everyone was coming to me shocked for an explanation; even George. What was I to tell them? Oh, he's just lost his mind, no problem. Oh, Satan just took over his heart and soul no big deal.

And you quit without any consideration for what that means for my job. I was your assistant. I was to be the new Regional Operations Director reporting to you. Well, you don't work there anymore so my job is in total limbo, thanks to you. That was a very selfish, self-centered move, mister.

You stay right where you are because Saturday I'm driving down there. Right after I kiss you I'm going to slap you. And you deserve both.

Beginning-to-Love-You-Too, Sheryl"

Clay re-read Sheryl's note. All-in-all, it was positive he thought. She was going to come down here and kick his butt, then they'd make up and decide what to do with their lives. It should be a fascinating weekend.

He replied to Sheryl, asking what time he should expect her. After that he made brief replies to all the other emails he had received. Then on the phone he searched for the Reef Bay Library. He saw the address and was surprised to see that on Fridays and Saturdays the library was open from noon until eight. He jumped out his chair, grabbed the keys to the pickup, and headed out the door.

Driving the Ford F-150 truck was very different from his BMW M5, but he liked it. He found a country music station on the radio and drove to town.

At the library he showed a note to the elderly librarian at the counter that read, "I want to apply for a library card." The librarian smiled and handed Clay a short form to complete, as if she was accustomed to dealing with people who couldn't speak.

After returning the completed form to the librarian, he wrote another note for her to see. "Where can I find non-fiction about lighthouses?"

She looked at his application form before answering, "Well, Mr. Austin, there will be books on lighthouses in the travel section, in architecture, and in our marine section, which we're particularly proud of."

"Dnx," Clay sputtered and walked off to explore the aisles of books.

Twenty minutes later he returned with two books he had found about the structure and maintenance of lighthouses. The librarian checked him out and gave him his temporary library card plus a photo copied calendar of library events for May and June. He scanned it. For a small town, this library was extremely active.

Every day multiple events were scheduled. This would be a good place to hang out and meet the locals. Of course, with his speaking handicap that might have to wait.

"Excuse me, Mr. Austin. Are you new to town?"

Clay nodded.

"I noticed that your address is 3100 Deception Point Drive. That's Charley Gragg's lighthouse isn't it?"

Clay nodded and wrote on his pad. "Yes. Mine now. Charley was my uncle."

The librarian read the note, looked at Clay and smiled. "Well, dear. We're sorry for your loss. Your uncle was such a dear man. He loved to read books to the children here every Saturday morning."

Clay smiled, eager to take his books and leave.

"Will you be living on the property, Mr. Austin, or have other plans for it? Gosh, it's none of my business of course. It's just that that lighthouse means a lot to this town. Most of us would hate to see anything happen to it." The librarian was clearing fishing for information. Clay didn't doubt for a second that whatever he told her would be known around town before sunrise the next day.

Clay wrote on his pad, "Not selling. Live there part-time. Remodel."

She read the note and her face beamed. "Oh, that's such good news, Mr. Austin. Perhaps you'd be interested in joining our group, Friends of the Lighthouse. She handed him a flyer from a different stack on counter. We meet here on Monday nights at 5:30."

Clay was liking this library more and more. It was probably the central hub of information flow in the town. He wrote, "Interesting. I'll keep it in mind. What's your name?"

"Gladys Jones."

He shook her hand warmly and left the library.

On the way home, he stopped at a drive-in for a burger and shake. He felt like he was in high school again, sitting in a car at a drive-in on Friday night.

He looked around at the other cars parked in the stalls. Most cars contained a boy and a girl sitting close in the front seat. Yep, this was like high school all right. Clay sitting alone and everyone else on a date. He was always on his way to work to stock shelves at the grocery store. He worked nearly every Friday and Saturday night, and all-day Sunday. The job restricted his social life. Not that he would have had one anyway. Vic only permitted him to drive to work and back. Besides none of the girls he was interested in were interested in him. Through three years of high school he had a grand total of one date. One. And that was to the Senior Prom.

It had been a fun date. He vaguely remembered the girl's face and pretty pink dress. Clay wished he could remember the girl's name though. He saw her once or twice after that until he found out that she was seeing an older boy in a local community college. She told Clay that she was breaking it off with the guy, but Clay knew that was a lie. Besides, she was one year younger than Clay and he'd be off to college in a few months. Though he couldn't remember the girl's name, he did recall that whenever he was with her he had very mixed emotions. Being with her was a reminder that he couldn't have the "A" girls to whom he was attracted. He had to settle for the "B" and "C" girls that were interested in him. Every time he was with this girl, he was reminded that he wasn't good enough to have what he wanted. And so, he stopped calling her. And that was that. *Geez, what was her name?*

After finishing his meal, Clay drove back to the lighthouse and settled in for the night to read his lighthouse books.

Chapter 108

A t 11:30 Saturday morning Clay heard the crunching sound of car tires on the gravel road inside his gate. It was Sheryl's white roadster. She was right on time. Clay's heart was pounding through his chest. He was elated that she was here, and he was scared to death that he'd blow it again.

He watched through the small window in the front door as Sheryl parked behind the pickup. She didn't get out the car for the longest time. Time stood still. The car door didn't open. Should he go out to meet her? Was she expecting him to come out? Was this some kind of test? That could be it. Sheryl could be testing to see just how desperately he wanted her here. Just as he reached for the door knob, the door of the Mazda opened, and she stepped out of the car. With purse in hand she walked slowly toward the house, head down.

He opened the front door and went out to greet her. Their eyes met. Dark, swollen semi-circles of skin hung below her reddened eyes. He was overtaken by guilt. He had caused this. He had deeply wounded this smart, beautiful woman. Her sad appearance shocked him. They both hesitated, looking at each other. Then slowly they came into each other's arms. Second by second their embrace grew stronger. Sheryl buried her head in his chest, not yet looking at him directly.

After what seemed an eternity, Clay gently lifted her head up and kissed her lips; lightly at first and then with more intensity as she responded. Sheryl stepped back from the hungry kisses, looked directly into Clay's eyes and before he knew it slapped him across the cheek.

The slap stung. The look of determination in Sheryl's eyes told him everything he needed to know. She wasn't going to put up with any more crap from him. He had one more chance.

Clay stood there rubbing his cheek as Sheryl walked past him through the open front door.

He followed her inside. She was already touring the place, giving each of the four rooms a cursory inspection. He just let her look and then followed her into the kitchen.

"Cute. Has potential, you know," she said.

"Uh-huh," grunted Clay.

She looked at him, "Is your speech any better?"

He shook his head.

"You mean you can't argue with me?" She stepped closer.

He pointed to his yellow tablet sitting on the counter.

"Ah, yes, you can write." She took another step closer.

He nodded.

The suddenness of her embrace took Clay by surprise. She stepped into his arms and began kissing him passionately. They stood in the kitchen kissing and embracing without saying a word.

Then she stepped back, releasing his embrace. "Aren't you going to offer the lady a drink?"

Clay opened the refrigerator to reveal two beers. He pointed to the cans and shrugged his shoulders.

"Beer is all you have? Okay I'll drink a beer, but in the future, you better have a better liquor and wine selection when I'm here."

Clay playfully saluted and removed the two beers, pouring one into a glass for her.

For the next four hours the two sat on the couch and communicated as if nothing had happened between them. She talked, he wrote notes, they laughed frequently even though the challenges were significant that each faced in their lives.

They decided that Clay should spend the summer here remodeling the house and identifying what maintenance was necessary on the lighthouse. At the least, this place would be an ideal weekend retreat for them. Whenever she could on weekends during the summer, Sheryl would come down and visit.

The subject of Clay's speech therapy was more difficult to resolve. In all likelihood the closest specialist was in Seattle. Would Clay need to make weekly trips there for the appointment? Sheryl offered to research options for him.

With $10 million dollars in the bank and income from the office building that he and George owned, Clay had little to worry about financially. With care and prudence, he was set for life. With Sheryl it was a different matter. She didn't have much of a cushion to fall back on if she lost her job at the agency.

Clay assured her that, if necessary, she wouldn't have much difficulty finding another job. "Three, four months max," was what his note said in response to a question about how long it would take to find a new job in Seattle. Clay thought the possibility of her being let go was remote.

He thought about calming her concerns by promising to support her during a period of unemployment but decided against it. Sheryl wouldn't react well to suggestions of being a "kept woman."

Clay did the best he could to communicate about his second visit from Jesus. She sat riveted to her place on the couch while he wrote note after note and passed it to her. In turn she asked many questions requiring just short answers. Both of them grew weary.

They fell asleep on the couch and didn't wake until seven o'clock.

"What's for dinner, Clay?" she asked tiredly.

"Frzn ers," was his response. In his sleepy state he had forgotten that he couldn't talk clearly.

She handed him his notepad. He declined to accept it, leading her instead by the hand into the kitchen where he proudly opened the freezer door to reveal a single TV dinner. Sheryl removed the box. "Crispy fried chicken, green beans and mashed potatoes," Sheryl read the box in mock horror.

Clay rubbed his stomach, "Yumm," he murmured with a grin.

"You serve me beer and now you want me to eat a TV dinner? What's happening to you? I got news for you, mister. You're taking me out to a very nice dinner, and tomorrow after church we're going grocery shopping for you."

Clay blinked. Before he knew it, his Sunday had been planned for him.

"Why don't I try to get a reservation at Surf View Bistro?" Sheryl asked.

Clay gave a thumbs-up signal.

Sheryl brought a small overnight bag in from the car. She caught him looking at the bag.

"I noticed there is only one bedroom, so I will be staying in a motel tonight. I'll check in after dinner."

Clay protested, trying to indicate with pantomime that he would sleep on the couch.

"No, I think it's best that I sleep elsewhere tonight, but you really should consider adding a second bedroom in the remodel plans. I mean, that is if you want me to stay here with you from time to time."

Clay smiled and kissed her forehead.

She retreated to the bathroom to change for dinner. Clay did the same in the bedroom. Within fifteen minutes they were on their way to the bistro in separate cars.

Chapter 109

B y arrangement, they met the next morning at the Reef Bay Bible Church for the 9:30 a.m. service. Clay hadn't been back since Uncle Charley's service. It brought up memories of Billy's banjo performance and the wonderful people who paid their respects to his uncle.

The sermon was from the book of John. For twenty-five minutes the pastor spoke about a single verse.

"But if a man walk in the night, he stumbleth, because there is no light in him." John 11:10.

When the verse displayed on the screen behind the pastor, Clay could feel goosebumps on the back of his neck, and Sheryl nudged him with her elbow. It was just yesterday that Jesus paid a visit and handed a lit candle to him with instructions to "carry this light for me." Now here he sat listening to a sermon about light and darkness. Clay listened to every word from the pastor as if his life depended on it.

He was fascinated about the different meanings that the passage could have. He was beginning to learn that the Bible was seldom literal, and by design it encourages one to explore meaning, and in the journey of exploration find that one meaning that touches the heart. It was as if the Bible was stating that two plus two can be four, but a few of us need to see the sum as six, for one to hear what God wishes us to hear.

That was a refreshing perspective to Clay who was used to people talking about the Bible in absolute, black and white terms.

After the service there was a social in the room next door, the same room in which refreshments had been served at his uncle's memorial service. Clay wasn't eager to socialize. How could he without talking? Sheryl insisted they go and led him into the room.

It became uncomfortably obvious to Clay that he and Sheryl were receiving second looks from most of the people in attendance. This was a small church in a small town and new faces were unusual. Clay didn't have time to ponder his uncomfortable feeling, Sheryl was leading him by the hand right toward the pastor, who was standing with a paper cup of lemonade in the center of the room.

The pastor was a portly man in his early seventies. He wore a dark suit, white shirt, and tie—a contrast to the jeans and casual shirt uniform of the pastor at Sheryl's church in Seattle. As they waited for an opportunity to introduce themselves, Clay studied the man. He was warm and friendly to everyone. The smile on his face seldom faded while talking. Though his eyes sparkled with delight at being with "his flock," Clay could see lines of fatigue around the pastor's eyes.

Within a few minutes the pastor saw Clay and Sheryl standing patiently, waiting their turn to speak with him. He politely ended his conversation with a young family and walked over to greet the new faces in the room.

"Hello, I'm Jon Oberlin. Welcome to our little church. This is your first time here isn't it?" While talking his eyes moved back and forth from Sheryl to Clay as if trying to register their faces in his memory.

Sheryl spoke, "Not really. I attended here occasionally about twenty years ago when visiting relatives. I think you had just come on board as Pastor around that time."

"Oh, goodness yes, the Lord brought me here twenty-two years ago."

"I'm Sheryl and this is Clay. He had an accident recently and can't speak clearly."

"Oh, I'm sorry to hear that, Clay." The pastor studied Clay's face. "Excuse me, Clay, but you look familiar. Haven't I seen you before? Haven't you been here before?"

Clay nodded and motioned for Sheryl to do the talking.

"He attended his uncle's memorial service here last month," Sheryl said.

"That's it! You were at Charley Gragg's service. You sat in Charley's seat. I remember now. Oh, we miss Charley so much around here, but we know he's in a better place now. Oh my goodness, you're his nephew, uh, great-nephew." Pastor Oberlin placed a large hand on Clay's shoulder. "He spoke of you often and always with a lot of love. You were the son he never had."

Clay's eyes began to moisten. All he could do was nod and smile sadly.

"What brings you two to Reef Bay?" Pastor Oberlin asked.

"Clay inherited the old Deception Point lighthouse from his uncle. He's here making plans to remodel and live here part time," Sheryl said.

"Wonderful. Wonderful. You know, every year on Easter your uncle would let the church have the children's Easter Egg hunt on his property."

"What a great idea!" Sheryl squeezed Clay's hand and looked at him. "I'm sure Clay wants to continue the tradition, don't you, Clay?"

Clay nodded in agreement and tried to smile. The thought of dozens of hyper kids scampering around the property didn't appeal to him that much.

"Clay, I'm sorry for your loss of speech. The Lord moves in mysterious ways sometimes. There is someone here you must meet." The pastor scanned the room. "Ah, see the gentleman in the gray sweater by the window? That's Dr. Taberman. Before he retired and moved here he was a speech language pathologist. He's a modest man, but he was one of the top specialists in his field. I encourage you to go introduce yourselves before he leaves. And, I pray that I'll see both of you here often."

"Thank you, Pastor, we'll be back" said Sheryl.

Five minutes into the conversation with Doctor Taberman and Clay was already getting annoyed. The doctor seemed very much more interested in Sheryl than he, his potential patient with a debilitating speech impediment. Granted, Clay couldn't answer any of the doctor's questions, but he wasn't asking questions about Clay's condition anymore. Instead he was learning all he could about the beautiful and charming Sheryl Landing.

But just before Clay was going to jerk Sheryl's hand to bring her back on point, she coyly turned the conversation back to Clay and his condition. The doctor asked Clay to attempt pronouncing a few words, after which he nodded his head and agreed to see Clay twice a week for the next two months. He made it clear that he was making an exception—he was retired after all—and he only accepted cash. No insurance, which was okay, because Clay wasn't going to have insurance much longer.

The beautiful and charming Sheryl thanked the doctor, giggled, and led Clay away toward the refreshment table.

"What's wrong, Clay, never seen a woman flirt with an older man to get what she wants? I knew in the first thirty seconds that he wasn't going to take you as a patient if we just asked. He is a lonely old man who thinks he's forty."

Clay fumbled for his writing pad. "Oh, don't worry, you can thank me later," she smiled and poured both some lemonade. Thanking her wasn't what he wanted to write.

A burly man in his fifties stepped up to introduce himself. "Hello, you must be new to the church. My name is Aaron Bender. Welcome."

"Hi, Aaron, nice of you to introduce yourself. I'm Sheryl and this is Clay. He's having difficulty talking right now so please excuse his silence." Sheryl was getting good at this.

"Oh, sure, no problem. A lot of spring colds and laryngitis going around. What brings you to our little church?"

"Clay is the new owner of the Point Deception lighthouse, and I came down from Seattle to see him," Sheryl said.

"No kidding. You bought Charley's lighthouse? I didn't know it was for sale," Aaron said.

"It wasn't sold. Clay inherited it. Charley was Clay's great uncle."

"I'll be darned. Well, you certainly have a fine piece of land out there on the point, Clay. What are your plans, if I may ask?"

Clay nodded to Sheryl giving her permission to go further.

"We're going to remodel the residence. Modernize it, expand it, but keep the same exterior character of course," Sheryl said.

Clay hadn't recalled agreeing to an expansion. He really needed to get his voice back soon, so he could take back control of his life.

"Great idea. Listen, if you want a bid on the construction I'd love to work on that lovely place. Here's my card." He wisely handed one card to Clay and another to Sheryl.

The card read, "Aaron's Custom Homes. Design. Build. Remodel."

Clay smiled and nodded, thinking this was going to be the end of the conversation. Sheryl had other ideas.

"Aaron, we'd like to see some of your projects. If we decided to work together how quickly could you start?"

"All my projects are displayed on the website in the portfolio section. I'm finishing up one project in a few weeks. I had another ready to start, but the customer had problems getting loan approval. So the short answer is, I can start in about two weeks."

"Excellent. We'll be in touch. Clay will communicate by email, if that's okay."

"Sure is. Pleasure to meet you two."

The builder walked away.

"See what happens when you come to church, Clay? You meet the nicest people. And you make it easier for God to place the right people in your path. Thank you, Lord."

Clay nodded. He had to admit that meeting a speech therapist and a contractor on the same day in the same room was amazing.

"Clay, this is a clear sign from God that you belong at this church. You must promise me that you'll attend regularly even if I'm not here. Agree?"

He nodded. He had to admit this church felt like the right place to be.

They left the church and drove in Clay's car to the grocery store where Sheryl helped Clay select his food for the week. Not that he needed help. Grocery shopping had never been a problem for Clay, unlike many bachelors he knew. But, he realized that Sheryl was being Sheryl right now. She was taking care of things, looking out for Clay, making stuff happen. While she picked out vegetables and chatted away, he tried to convince himself that he appreciated what she was doing, but deep down inside, resentment was beginning to smolder.

He could select his own lettuce. He wasn't completely helpless. He and his note pad had been navigating through life just fine without her taking over.

On the way back to the church to pick up Sheryl's car before returning to the lighthouse, Sheryl continued to chatter merrily about the remodel. Clay nodded or grunted from time to time in response, but he wasn't really listening. He had checked out of the conversation. He found himself looking forward to the time after lunch when Sheryl would return to Seattle and give him some peace and quiet.

Chapter 110

They were washing dishes together after lunch when Sheryl said, "Be sure to include a dishwasher in the remodel list, Clay." It was a perfectly normal and reasonable thing to suggest under the circumstances, but Clay snapped.

Ever since her arrival yesterday she'd been giving orders, taking control over his life like he wasn't capable of doing anything himself. Was he so stupid that he couldn't see that the absence of a dishwasher was a huge pain?

He threw the dish towel hard onto the counter and fetched his note pad from the kitchen table.

He angrily wrote, "It already is," and thrust the pad in her face to read.

Seeing his anger Sheryl said, "Wow, what's with you? I simply reminded you to put a dishwasher on the list. You've been acting distant ever since we left church. What's wrong?"

Clay was angry and totally frustrated that he couldn't talk. Not that he knew how to answer her question. He was very upset and not quite sure why. He retreated to the living room, tossed another log into the stove, and sat in the La-Z-Boy chair to think and calm down.

Sheryl followed him a few moments later. She curled up on the couch and looked at him.

"Do you want me to leave?" she asked, dejectedly.

He stared straight ahead, avoiding her eyes.

She stood up, retrieved her coat and purse before stepping to the front door. "If I leave now, like this, you won't ever see me again." She opened the door and slowly walked out without closing the door behind her.

One part of Clay was saying, *Good riddance, girl, now I can have my life back.* The other part of Clay was saying, *Hey, you schmuck, are your crazy, why are you chasing away the best thing that ever happened to you!*

He reached her just as she was opening the car door. He slipped his body between her and the car to take her into his arms. She protested and tried to push away, but he lovingly held her tight while kissing the top of her head. "Nah go. Stah," he pleaded with her to stay but his voice sounded like a baby trying to talk.

Mascara was streaking her cheeks in trickles of tears. She stopped pushing him away, but neither did she return the embrace. She stood arms to her side, sniffling.

Back inside the house on the couch they sat facing each other. The note pad was in Clay's hand ready to reveal whatever thoughts and responses Clay needed

Sheryl to know, but his mind was a blank. After urging her to come back inside the house he didn't have a clue what to do or write next.

"Why are you so angry?" Sheryl said, breaking the silence.

He wrote, "Don't know."

"Well, look at it. You're going to get to the bottom of this right now, or else I'm leaving."

Oh, great she was putting the burden on him, as if he was to blame for all of this. She's the one who walked in here and took over as if he couldn't handle anything. He glared back at her and started to write, "You're controlling, micro-managing."

"Where? Where am I controlling you?"

"Dishwasher," he wrote.

"Dishwasher. Are you kidding? All I did was remind you to add a dishwasher to the shopping list. That's all. How's that controlling?"

"I already knew," he wrote.

"How was I to know you had already discovered the missing dishwasher. You never told me. If you don't tell me things, how am I supposed to know?"

Clay shrugged.

"There's more bugging you than a silly dishwasher. What is it?"

Clay gazed out the living room window across the grass field, hoping that the answer would parade by on a big sign or something.

"You started to get cold and distant after our conversation with Doctor Taberman. Are you still upset that I flirted a little with the old man to get him to agree to treat you?"

Clay had to think about that one. No, he wasn't annoyed by her flirting. It was innocent and necessary to get the old man's attention. But, he was bothered by it regardless. Why? He wrote a few words, scratched them out, and started over.

"You didn't think I could," he wrote.

"I didn't think you could do what, convince the doctor to treat you?"

Clay nodded.

"Clay, the odds were against you being successful with him. He is retired, remember? He probably would have referred you to someone back in Seattle, Tacoma, or Olympia. I saw him warm up to me immediately and I used that to our advantage. What's important is that you're going to receive excellent treatment right here in Reef Bay." She paused. "Wouldn't you have done the same for me if the situation was reversed?"

Clay nodded. He was losing this point in the match.

"Okay, I used my womanly charms to persuade the doctor to treat you. I reminded you to put a dishwasher on the purchase list. How is that controlling?"

The conversation went back and forth for another hour. Clay would raise a point and Sheryl would systematically dismantle the point. Each time he tried to illustrate how she was micro-managing the situation and taking control of his life unnecessarily, she would deflect the blame and show him how incorrect was his view. She kept telling him to look deeper into why her actions today drove him to anger.

Ever so slowly he began to see that she was making sense, but that meant he had to admit he was in the wrong. He wasn't ready for that.

After a period of silence Sheryl said, "You know, I have to leave soon. I have a request."

"Wha?" murmured Clay, disappointed that the protective silence had been broken.

"I want to see the top of the lighthouse, and I want you to see what's making you angry."

"I'm angry because you are controlling," he wrote.

"No you're not! What have we been talking about for an hour and a half?" She stood up. "Unless you think it's 'controlling' to request a look from the top of the lighthouse, let's go. When we come back down you tell me what triggered your anger."

Chapter 111

The steel stairway wound its way up the inside wall of the lighthouse like a giant black snake. As Clay and Sheryl climbed the dimly-lit stairs he couldn't stop thinking about how similar the real lighthouse was to the one in his nightmare. It was uncanny—the same steel stairs and landings, the same little windows at each landing, the sound of the wind outside as it brushed against the outside walls.

Up and up they climbed until the stairs ended and they stepped into the lamp room. At least they didn't have to climb a ladder through a trap door in the floor like in his dream.

"Wow! What a view," Sheryl exclaimed as she pressed close to the thick glass windows.

Clay agreed, the view was spectacular. The blue-gray ocean spread out to the horizon. Far off shore he saw a freighter heading north. To his right was the rugged coastline as far as he could see. To his left, south, he clearly saw the Point Jeopardy lighthouse. That lighthouse and the point it was on were lower in elevation, so Clay looked down on the white structure and its surrounding grounds a mile or so away.

He looked down to the bay's entrance. Turbulent water on both sides of a channel indicated rocks just below the surface. More than likely it was the rocky entrance that gave the place its name, Reef Bay. The rusting hulk of a small fishing boat was aground on the northern shore leading into the bay. A narrow entrance, reefs on both sides and a ship wreck—it was a forbidding entrance to a lovely, calm harbor.

Sheryl hugged him. "Isn't it beautiful up here? Gosh, I feel like a bird, or riding in a balloon." She looked up at him. He was lost in thought and gazing out the windows, not toward the ocean, but looking down at the grass field below.

"What do you see?" she asked, still holding him close.

"Grass needs mowing," he wrote on his note pad.

"Is that a bad thing?"

"Reminds me of Vic and mower," he wrote.

"Clay, isn't it interesting that while you're looking for the answer to your anger with me you see a beautiful green field and think of Vic?"

"So?" He wrote.

"We've talked about this; Dr. Shildstein talked to you about it, too. On that day you told yourself you weren't good enough to mow the lawn and earn Vic's love. Right?"

Clay nodded.

"That's exactly what happened today. Because you couldn't talk, you couldn't get the appointment with the speech therapist, you couldn't interact with the builder, and you couldn't ask the butcher for a better cut of meat. These events triggered the 'not good enough' in you. You told yourself that because of your temporary lack of speech, you weren't good enough for my love."

Clay slowly shook his head while continuing to gaze out the window at the field. He wasn't really disagreeing with Sheryl. It was just a lot to process at the moment.

"The dishwasher was the last straw for you. You probably thought, 'how dare Sheryl think me so incompetent that I wouldn't have noticed the need for a dishwasher'." She turned his head to look at her. "Clay, you are good enough for my love, and while we're standing in this tall beautiful lighthouse let me remind you that God loves you, too. In fact, you don't have to do anything to earn His love. It's here all around you. Just let it inside. Let the light of God's love into your heart, Clay."

She hugged him. "Let's go downstairs, I'm getting cold up here."

Back in the house Sheryl stood next to the wood stove to warm herself. Clay was on the couch, again deep in thought.

"I have to go soon. Tell me what you're thinking."

He wrote, scratched it out, wrote something else, tore up the sheet of paper and started again. "I see the impact of not good enough," was scribbled on the paper.

She sat down on the couch close to him and read the note in his hands.

"I'm glad it's beginning to make sense. Can you see that it was a flareup of not good enough that made you force me out of your house last Wednesday?"

Clay frowned. He didn't like thinking about that ugly moment but had to agree that his outburst had been triggered by a sense of *not good enough* to be an exceptional marketer once the ability to speak had been taken away.

"Yes, I can see that," he wrote.

"I didn't make you angry then or now. You made yourself angry by being triggered by memories of a childhood wound." She paused. "Is there something you'd like to say to me, before I go?"

"I love you," he wrote.

"I love you, too, and wouldn't it be healing for you to apologize for your behavior today?"

He wrote, "Why?"

"For one reason you hurt me, for another reason we've spent this precious time together debating when we have so much else to talk about."

"I didn't mean to," he wrote

"I know you didn't mean to, but an apology is still the right thing to do now."

An apology meant he had done something wrong. Vic always made him apologize for stuff. To apologize meant Clay accepted that he had made a mistake. He was owning the fact that his actions messed up their day. Was he man enough to admit his screw up—especially to someone from whom he desperately wanted acceptance and love? An apology was a tall order.

One more glance at Sheryl and he picked up his pen to write.

He waved goodbye from the driveway as she drove her white roadster up the gravel road toward the gate.

What a day it has been. He was suddenly very tired. He poured a glass of wine from the bottle left over from lunch and settled into his chair to read. His phone buzzed. Sheryl had sent him a text while buying gas outside of town.

"Thank you for a wonderful weekend. I'll remember it forever, especially our time in the lighthouse. Thank you for being humble, apologizing, and seeing the cause of the issue today. This week remember the 'not good enough' is caused by the 'not God enough'."

Was Sheryl an angel, or simply the most amazing woman he had ever known? Either way, his life wasn't going to be the same from here on out.

Chapter 112

Over the next four months Clay settled into his new life in Reef Bay, although his life was anything but "settled."

The remodel was nearing completion. His speech therapy was making progress slowly. Every Sunday he went to church and miraculously met people there that were important to know, like the Chief of Police.

The investigation into his uncle's death was proceeding at a snail's pace, but Chief Smith had assured him on multiple occasions that it was making progress. That's all he would share. He was running for mayor in the November election against Bilgewood. Clay had contributed generously to his campaign.

Nearly every weekend Sheryl drove down from Seattle, and after checking into the La Quinta Inn, worked with Clay doing whatever they could to help the builder's crew. Saturday dinner at the Surf View Bistro became part of their routine.

As their love grew over the summer months, Clay and Sheryl began to talk about a future together. But there were so many unanswered questions. What was Clay going to do? Where was he going to live most of the time, Seattle or Reef Bay? If they got married, would she continue to work? Where would they live? And, the biggest question of all—if they got married, would they have children?

One Friday night in early September Sheryl arrived at 3100 Deception Point Drive after a difficult drive from Seattle. This was supposed to be a very special weekend. The remodel was complete, and they were going to celebrate. Unfortunately, the situation at the agency had deteriorated in the past few weeks. Today at four o'clock Sheryl and ten other employees were let go. Their second largest account, Yukon Air, had fired the agency. The situation weighed heavily on her mind during the drive.

She drove up to the gate, punched in the key code and the lovely new steel entry gates responded by swinging open, as if mechanical arms were opening to greet her. She was thrilled. She had helped select the gates a month earlier. They had been installed that week, and Clay had texted her the key code.

She drove through the gate and watched in the rear-view mirror as the two large gates slowly closed behind her. No more getting out of the car in the rain to unlock and lock the gate. Seconds later the house came into view at the end of the gravel road. She stopped the car and just stared. The sight was so beautiful it made her heart jump. Clay had turned on every light inside the house and opened the shades so warm light poured out from all the windows. Framed against the September dusk, the house and lighthouse looked like a postcard.

The simple remodel idea that Clay had originally envisioned gradually was discarded once she and Clay started working with the builder on the plans. It took some urging, but Clay had finally agreed to expand the house significantly. She won the debate with three points. First, they might not be able to expand in the future if new legislation was passed prohibiting it, thanks to the efforts of Friends of the Lighthouse. Second, wouldn't it be nice to have extra rooms for friends to come visit. And third, what if they had children.

So, here she was, sitting in her car looking at a charming two-story house containing three bedrooms, three bathrooms, gourmet kitchen, central heat, media room and the best dishwasher money could buy.

Aaron, the builder, had designed the exterior to maintain all of the character of the original house. It looked the same, a two-story version of the original.

As Sheryl continued to drive down the driveway toward the house she reflected on the miracle that the completed house represented. God's hands were all over the place. How else could anyone explain the events of the past four months—the perfect builder with an available crew, approval of the building permit in record time, good weather, and no progress on the legislative front by Friends of the Lighthouse that could impede the construction, though some on the committee were outraged by the expansion plan. The biggest miracle of all was the speed by which the construction had been accomplished.

Sheryl, Clay and Aaron had been racing against the clock. The "Lighthouse Heritage Bill" as it was called, was taking shape at the state capitol in Olympia, thanks to pressure by the Friends of the Lighthouse group, but the bill had not progressed to a vote yet. Many members of the state legislature were busy with reelection campaigns leading up to the November election, and saw the bill as nothing more than a distraction. Passage of the bill wouldn't influence enough votes to matter, therefore lots of lip service was extended to the ideals of the bill, but very little action. All that could change after November, however.

The other issue encouraging rapid construction was the time of the year. Beginning in October, one Pacific storm after another would buffet the coast and continue for seven long months. The driving rain and wind wouldn't stop construction, but it could certainly slow it down. So, at one point ten workers swarmed over the project. As it turned out, Aaron was an inspired architect and marvelous project manager. The entire project came together without a hitch.

Sheryl parked next to Clay's BMW under the expanded carport roof. From the small trunk she removed her overnight bag. Now that the guest room was finished she had her own room. No more La Quinta for her. One more item remained in the trunk. She decided to leave it there until later.

She walked to the front door, now a stylish double door of hand-carved wood. The door swung open before she could ring the bell.

"Orry, musik on, didn hear car," said Clay before embracing her tightly. Music from the latest DelivrUs album was playing in the background.

After pouring her a glass of wine they toured the home together. It had been two weeks since her last visit because the situation at the office was so crazy. The amount of work that had been done on the house in those two weeks was astonishing.

There wasn't a stray ladder or tool in sight. The workers had cleaned up and left for the last time only three hours earlier.

The home was simply gorgeous. Two bedrooms, a bathroom, media room and small office were upstairs. Downstairs was the open living room and gourmet kitchen, a dining area, the master suite and another office. The steel stove had been moved to the shed, so it could provide heat there when Clay was working in the shop. Central heating had been installed in the house, but a beach stone fireplace provided the ambience of an open fire.

They sat at the new dining table for the first time and shared the meal that Clay had prepared. Steamed crab, shrimp-stuffed mushrooms and a tossed salad. He paired the succulent crab with champagne, which seemed appropriate to celebrate the occasion.

"You eem troubled." Clay was speaking much better after the months of therapy. Some sentences he could say perfectly, others were slurred, but his progress was noticeable.

"I was laid off today."

"What!"

"Yukon Air fired us. George got a call from Deborah Wright at Yukon. She had heard that Pitt-Needham was pitching Coastal Airlines. We didn't know anything about it. Deborah was very irate and fired us on the spot.

"Turns out, the LA office was invited to pitch the account a month ago and they accepted the invitation rather than discuss it with us first. Now they are one of the three finalists. And I'm out of a job. George was nearly crying when he fired us. Very tough on him. He told me in confidence that someone on the Pitt-Needham board was working behind the scenes to make the pitch possible for LA."

"Who?"

"He said Cathy Denaghey had some connections at Coastal Airlines and pulled the strings. Did you meet her when you were in Dallas?"

"Yeah, a snake," said Clay, recalling Denaghey's catty questions during the Board meeting.

There would be no celebration on this night. Clay spent the remainder of the evening consoling Sheryl. At nine o'clock, exhausted and a little drunk from too much champagne, she walked upstairs to her room.

Clay cleaned up the kitchen and settled into his reading chair by the fireplace.

Chapter 113

Saturday, they shopped for towels and miscellaneous household items. That night they had dinner at Surf View Bistro, as usual. Sheryl was in better spirits during dinner and talked about updating her resume.

Sunday, they drove to church in the truck. They felt at home at Reef Bay Bible Church now that they'd been attending for four months. They were on a first-name basis with many of the members. Pastor Oberlin appeared more tired than usual today although his voice was full of energy. It was a momentous day for him at this church.

The Pastor announced to a shocked audience that for health reasons he was retiring. He would step down within sixty days. The elders would start interviewing candidates, including the current assistant pastor.

He also mentioned with reverent glee that today was Baptism day at the church. It would be the 45th Baptism that he had conducted while pastor of the church these past twenty-two years. A portable pool had been erected outside and any who wished to be Baptized were welcome to the water immediately following today's service.

Clay didn't notice, but Sheryl was watching him closely out of the corner of her eye.

In church, Clay always sat in his uncle's favorite seat. It always seemed to be open and waiting for him as if a Reserved sign was on it. Sheryl sat next to him on the right. Over time she got to know Trisha and her mother, Molly, very well because they always sat in the same row. Trisha, who never saw a stranger she didn't like, had made a point to tell Sheryl that she had given Clay some cookies when he was here for Uncle Charley's funeral.

A verse appeared on the small video screen behind the pulpit.

"Repent and be baptized, every one of you, in the name of Jesus Christ for the forgiveness of your sins. And you will receive the gift of the Holy Spirit. — Acts 2:38

Pastor Oberlin delivered an inspired sermon about Baptism, what it means and its importance to Christians. It was all very fascinating to Clay, who was hearing this for the first time. The idea that Baptism was about letting the Holy Spirit into your heart, about being renewed, about being "born again" as a new person—this was heady talk. Regardless, ever since the two visits by Jesus he was taking all of this biblical stuff seriously.

It occurred to him while the Pastor spoke that he probably couldn't "carry the light" like Jesus asked him to do without the Holy Spirit being in him, without being "washed of sin", which he had plenty of. In fact, maybe if the Holy Spirit was in him he'd actually understand what "carry the light" actually meant and what he was supposed to do.

And just like that he made the decision. He was going to be Baptized today.

The sermon ended and the small band began to play as the members shuffled out of the church. Clay and Sheryl followed the crowd as they walked to the flat lawn behind the sanctuary where a portable pool had been erected. Clay didn't know if all these people were getting Baptized, or were just here to watch.

Pastor Oberlin was helped up a few steps to the pool's edge and someone else who was already in the pool assisted him as he stepped down into the chilly water. He might be sick, but nobody was going to stop him from performing his last Baptism at the church.

Three people stepped forward wearing gym shorts or swimming suit. They were prepared. One by one they were escorted into the water, Pastor Oberlin greeted each one, and asked them to repeat after him.

"I believe that Jesus is the Christ."

An Hispanic woman in her twenties repeated, "I believe that Jesus is the Christ."

"The son of the living God."

"The son of the living God," she said

"And I accept Him as my Lord and Savior."

She repeated, "And I accept Him as my Lord and Savior."

Pastor Oberlin said, "Isabella, I now baptize you in the name of the Father, the Son, and the Holy Spirit, for the forgiveness of your sins, and the gift of the Holy Spirit." He waited for Isabella to plug her nose and then gently lowered her back so her face was completely submerged by the water. After a few seconds the assistant and Oberlin raised her to a standing position again. She was smiling broadly as everyone watching applauded.

After Isabella left the pool to receive a large towel, Benjamin, a strapping teen, came forward. The process was repeated.

Third was Hank, a tough-looking man in his late fifties whose heavily-lined face made him look much older. When the man walked away from the pool with his towel wrapped around him, he looked ten years younger.

Pastor Oberlin shouted, "Anyone else want to come to Jesus today?"

Clay raised his hand. There were cheers from the audience. He looked at Sheryl, who gave him one of her classic "I knew you would" looks. He walked to the pool steps, took off his shoes and socks and jacket. Then he climbed the stairs and back down into the pool.

"This is a pleasant surprise, Clay," said Pastor Oberlin.

"I know, for me too," Clay responded.

"Do you know I Baptized your uncle in this same spot about eighteen years ago?"

"That's cool. Wish he here to widness this."

"I bet he is here, Clay. You're speaking more clearly these days. Praise the Lord. Are you ready?"

"Yes, sir"

"Repeat after me, I believe that Jesus is the Christ."

"I beleeve Jesus is the Christ."

"The son of the living God."

"Theson of the living God."

"And I accept Him as my Lord and Savior."

Clay repeated with some difficulty, "And I . . . aksept Him my Lord and . . . Savor."

Pastor Oberlin said, "Clay, I now baptize you in the name of the Father, the Son, and the Holy Spirit, for the forgiveness of your sins, and the gift of the Holy Spirit."

They guided him backward. The cool water covered his face. It seemed like he was under for a long time before strong hands lifted him up. He took a breath of air and heard the applause.

Sheryl greeted him at the foot of the stairs with a big kiss and a dry towel.

As he dried off people stopped by to congratulate him. A man of about sixty-five with a square jaw and short cropped hair slapped him on the back. "Guess you decided at the last minute to take the plunge, right son?"

"I certainly did-did-did," Clay said, his teeth beginning to chatter.

"Good man. You listened to your heart. My name is Raymond Bailey, Coast Guard Retired."

"Peesed to meet you, sir, I'm Clay and this is Sheryl."

"I've been meaning to talk to you, Clay. I know you own the Deception Point Lighthouse now. When I was in the Coast Guard it was one of the lighthouses under my command. I've actually spent a few nights in the residence up there."

"Wow, that's amazing. You know more about it than I do."

"I probably do. I've even worked on the light. It has always been a little temperamental. About five years before I retired, I oversaw its decommissioning when the automated Point Jeopardy light came on line. I'd sneak up to the property every now and then after your uncle bought it. We'd play cards and drink bourbon. Your uncle was a wonderful man and a lousy card player," he laughed.

"Would you mind . . . visting us soon? I have so many . . . questens about the histry of the light and the . . . mechix of the light itself."

Noticing Raymond learn closer to Clay to hear his slurred speech better, Sheryl said, "Raymond, Clay had an accident in April and is still recovering his speech. He has made wonderful progress."

"No worries, son. My hearing isn't what it used to be either. Here's my card, Clay. Just give me a call anytime. Now, you better get out of those wet clothes. Nice to meet you, Sheryl." He turned and left.

They walked quickly to the truck. Considering his wet clothes, he was glad he had decided to take the truck to church today rather than the BMW.

"I'm proud of you, mister. Why didn't you tell me you were thinking of being Baptized?"

"Last minute. Not until . . . Pastr . . . Obrlin asked if anyone else wanted to come to Jesus."

"It's no coincidence that Mr. Bailey introduced himself minutes after you were Baptized. I remember seeing him at church, but he never stepped forward until now," Sheryl said.

Chapter 114

Clay removed his wet clothes and took a hot shower while Sheryl prepared a lunch of home-made clam chowder, French rolls and an artichoke with garlic butter.

After lunch, they strolled hand-in-hand around the property while formulating a job search plan for Sheryl. The couple sat for a long time gazing out to sea from a wooden bench just inside the fence that guarded the cliff edge.

After returning to the house, Sheryl heated some tea and Clay built a fire in the new fireplace. Both of them had gotten chilled during their time outside. They sipped tea and snuggled together on the new couch, admiring their surroundings. The residence had been converted from a mere cabin to a fabulous home that they had designed together with Aaron, the builder.

"The walls need some art," Clay commented.

"Oh, I almost forgot!" Sheryl got up and raced outside. A few minutes later she returned with a large rectangular object wrapped in a blanket. "I took the liberty of fetching this from your house. It belongs here I think." She removed the blanket to reveal the lighthouse painting that Dr. Shildstein had given him.

"Wow, I had forgotten about it. You're . . . absluutely right. It belongs here. Where shall we hang it?"

They looked around the room.

"Above the fireplace," Sheryl said and held it there for Clay to see.

"Yep, above the fireplace." Clay took the painting and held it in place, so Sheryl could stand back and see it.

Clay fetched his tool bag from the corridor building. Minutes later the painting hung above the fireplace. The painting and room appeared to have been designed for each other, so well did the frame and colors coordinate.

"Perfect." Clay said. "Which reminds me, I owe the . . . doctr a call to tell her what's going on. I sorta went dark on her ever since the Pitt deal and my . . . axident."

Clay and Sheryl stood in front of the fireplace admiring the painting. It looked different somehow than the last time he saw it. He was seeing more details. The painting was amazing. Every time he studied it after a period had passed, little details would appear that he hadn't noticed before. It was as if a ghost artist was continually working on it.

Today Clay was noticing an object mostly concealed in the tall grass at the foot of the lighthouse. He couldn't tell what it was, but he didn't recall seeing it there before. And what was that leaning against the house? Clay stepped closer, his face just a foot away from the painting's surface. It looked like a broom. A broom was leaning against the house.

"What is it?" Sheryl asked.

"Oh, nothing, it's just that every so often I see details in the painting I hadn't noticed before. Today, for example, there's something in the grass and a . . . brum. Never saw them before."

Sheryl looked closely. "Oh, I remember seeing it, but I thought it was a rake or shovel, not a broom."

Shaking his head in disbelief, Clay said, "Looks like a . . . brum to me. Whatever, this is a cool painting and I'm glad you . . . brot it. It belongs here. Just like you do." He kissed her.

They sat down again on the couch. Sheryl rested her head on Clay's shoulder. Within minutes both had drifted off to sleep as the glow of the fireplace filled the room with warm light.

△ △ △

The sun felt warm on Clay's back as he placed the tall ladder against the lighthouse. It was a good day for painting. He stuck a brush handle first into the back pocket of his jeans. In one hand he held a can of white paint. He used his other hand to grip the ladder as he climbed.

The area that needed painting was going to be difficult to reach with this ladder, but he had to try anyway. He was now standing on the third ladder rung from the top. A tiny label on the ladder warned, "Do Not Stand Beyond this Point." He stretched out as far as he could but couldn't reach the area. He took another careful step up the wooden ladder. He was a good twenty feet above ground and grateful the wind wasn't blowing today. Almost high enough to reach the spot. He dared to take another step. He was now on the second rung from the top. He didn't feel secure at all and knew he was taking a risk, but the area he was trying to paint was the only area requiring paint. Somehow it had been missed.

Carefully so as not to disturb his balance, Clay reached around and removed the brush from his back pocket. Slowly he dipped the brush into the paint and reached as high as he could to the unpainted masonry surface. He applied the paint with smooth even strokes, re-dipped the brush in the can, and repeated.

After about ten minutes of work the section was completely painted. Clay was glad he had finished and started to carefully take steps down the ladder.

442

"Do it over!" an angry voice shouted from below startling Clay. His heart jumped. "Do it over!" the voice demanded. For fear of losing his balance Clay didn't dare turn his head and look down.

Clay didn't see why he should paint the section again anyway. He looked up at the area. The area he had just painted was gray and chipped. What happened to the paint?

He stepped higher to repaint the section. After re-applying the white paint, he started his descent of the ladder again.

"Do it over. Can't you do anything right?" The voice was even more demanding and angry than before.

Clay looked up to the section above the ladder. Instead of freshly applied white paint, gray and chipped stone seemed to mock him. Why wasn't the paint sticking? He felt terrible that he couldn't do such a simple thing as paint a few square feet of wall.

"Do it over," screamed the voice from below.

Clay was confused. Why was the man yelling at him? Couldn't he see that Clay was trying the best he could? Something must be wrong with the paint. Why was the man so angry? Clay climbed higher to paint the section one more time.

"Can't you do anything right?" was ringing in his ears. He stretched to reach the gray area with the brush, but now he couldn't reach it. He was standing on the second to last rung of the ladder—just like before. But now he couldn't reach the spot. He was shorter.

"Do it over!" the voice demanded.

Clay took another step up. Now he was precariously standing on the top rung of the ladder, but he still couldn't reach the area with his brush. He pressed into the wall to steady himself. His right arm stretched as far as he could reach above him, but it wasn't enough.

"Don't take all day. Do it over." The voice spit out the words.

Standing on his tip-toes on the last rung of the ladder, twenty feet above ground, his brush was just able to reach the bottom of the gray section now. White paint dripped down from the bristles to the handle and over Clay's fingers. It was getting difficult to hold the brush.

"Do it over!"

Why can't he understand what's happening up here? Why doesn't he help? Why is he so upset with me?

"I'm trying. I'm really trying." Clay cried out.

The brush slipped in his wet hand. He moved to catch it, but the sudden motion threw him off balance. The ladder began to wobble. Standing on the top rung Clay had nothing to grip to steady himself. He dropped the can of paint to free his other hand, but it was too late. The ladder jerked to the right. Clay dropped like a rock.

$$\triangle \ \triangle \ \triangle$$

When he opened his eyes, Sheryl was looking into his face with concern. "Wake up, Clay, you're having a bad dream." She stroked his hair and face to sooth him. Reality replaced the dream. He was still on the couch with Sheryl in their living room. The fire still casting its merry glow into the new room.

"Tell me about it," Sheryl said.

Through words and sentences that sometimes slurred together, he did his best to recall the details of the nightmare for her.

"Who was on the ground telling you to 'do it over'"?

"Don't know. Never saw him."

"It was a man's voice, though?"

"Yeah . . . definly man's voice—an angry voice. Sounded a lot like Vic."

"Vic? That's interesting. You haven't had any dreams about him or lawn mowers lately have you?"

"No. Haven't had any nightmares since I've been here."

"In the dream the voice kept saying 'do it over'. You've told me about the wood stacking and lawn mowing episodes. Was there a painting episode, as well?"

"No painting."

"Nothing involving a brush?"

"No." Clay looked across the room into the fire, then up to the balloon painting hanging above the mantle. He recalled earlier noticing a broom resting against the side of the house in the painting. He hadn't seen it there before today. Just a few thin strokes of paint illustrating a broom. In the perspective of the painting the broom was minuscule, barely detectable, which is why he had missed it until today. A broom. Not just any broom either, but a push broom.

"What are you thinking?" Sheryl asked.

"I think . . . brum . . . trig . . . triggard . . . my nightmare."

"How so?"

"Be . . . besids the wood and lawn mooowing , there's one other eps . . . eps . . . . episode with Vic that sticks in my memory like an infected sore. It invols sweeping the garage."

Clay gazed straight ahead, as if in a trance while he recalled the event for Sheryl.

"It was the first year being with Vic after Mom remarried. One day he told me to sw . . . sw . . . sweeeep the garage. I was seven, maybe eight years old. Had never swept a floor. Never used a push br . . . brum. He just orders me to sweeeep the gaage. So, I grab the broom and start sw . . . sweeping. It was a double-car gaage, and it took me a long time. When he came to inspect the job he got really upset. He pointed to all the dirt I had missed."

"And he told you to 'do it over,'" Sheryl interjected.

"Exactly. So, I sw . . . sweeept the garage again. He inspected it one more time and got even angrier with me. He said I had missed a lot of dirt, that I was a sp . . . spoiled kid who didn't know to do a job right. I mean, I looked at the concrete floor where he was pointing, and I didn't see any dirt that I had misssssed. But he insisted I do it over. I must have sweeeept that garage over and over five times that day, but he was never satfied."

"Didn't he show you how?"

"Oh, probably. I remember he wouldn't let me puuull the broom across the floor, only puuuush it," Clay said.

"He got angry with you, even though you were trying hard?"

"Yep. Fur . . . Fureeous. Same as with moooowing the lawn and stacking wood. He was really good at getting angry; not so good at pat . . . patiently working with me until I learned how," said Clay.

"What did Doctor Shildstein say about all this?"

"I never told her about the garage-sweeping inci . . . inci . . . incident, but she said as a small child I couldn't understand why he was so angry with me. I made his anger mean I wasn't guh . . . guh . . . good enough for his love."

"Makes sense."

"Yeah, when I think about it now, I get really angry with him." Clay stood up and started pacing the floor while he spoke. "I mean, would it have been too much to ask for him to be a little pa . . . patient?" His voice grew louder and angrier with each step. "Or, here's a booold concept. Why couldn't he just work with me? Make a game out of it. I don't know, make it a little fuuuun. But he didn't have to be such a jerk."

"Clay are you aware that you are shouting now?" Sheryl asked calmly although she was alarmed. The last time she had seen him act this way was just before he kicked her out of his home after returning from the hospital.

"Maybe it's about time I ex . . . expr . . . expressed some outrage. That jerrrk screeeewed me up. Made me think my entire life that I wasn't guh . . . guh . . . good enough for big things like love and business success." He walked into the kitchen. "Want some wine?"

"Sounds good, please," she responded.

Clay returned to the couch with a bottle of Chilean Carménère and two glasses. He sat on the couch and poured each of them some wine.

"Clay, did Vic ever tell you he didn't love you?"

"No. Never said he loved me either," Clay said angrily.

"I've never heard you say a kind thing about Vic. Was he that bad?"

"I grew to ha . . . hate the guuuy. I didn't want to even be in the same room with him for long. He never beat me or anything. I'll give him credit for that much," Clay said.

"He must have done something nice for you over the years. What about on your birthday or Christmas?"

Clay sipped wine and thought about Sheryl's question.

"He sur . . . prised me twice when he acted like a normal, cool dad. One Saturday he draaaagged me to the hardwaaare store. While buying some stuff he noticed the frame of a go-cart hanging on the wall. He bought it. We took it home. I don't think I understooood what was going on at first. For the rem . . . rem . . . remainder of the day and into the night he worked on the go-cart. He remooved an engine from one of the old lawn mowers and mounted it on the go-cart. Then he rigged up a hand throttle. There weren't any foot controls. Left hand worked the throttle lever, the right hand pulled a lever that moved a steel rod against a rear tire—that was the brake. There was a dirt alley next to our how . . . how . . . house and I was permitted to run the cart back and forth on the alley only. That was pretty cool. I loved it."

"That's amazing. He went to a lot of work to give you something he knew you'd like."

"True."

"You said there was a second time."

"Yeah, the second time I was in my senior year of hiiiigh school. For some reason he and my mom had decided that I should have a different car than what I had been driving. All I know is I drea . . . dreaded having to go car shopping with him. We went to a used car lot and I walked in one direction and he walked in another. After a while he shouted at me to come to him. When I got there he was standing with the car salesman next to a red Miata sports car. He said, 'Let's go for a ride'. "Next thing I knew I was the owner of a red sports car convertible."

"You see, Vic wasn't so bad. He could have stuck you with a boring sedan on that day, but he bought you something really cool."

"I guess you're right, but technically I bought the car. It was my money."

"Whatever. That's not important. What's important is he knew how important driving a cool car is to a teenager. He permitted you to have that experience."

Clay nodded in agreement.

Sheryl got up from the couch and walked across the room to be by the warm fireplace. She turned to look at him still sitting on the couch. "Want to know what I think?"

"Sure," Clay said.

"Your resentment and hate for Vic is eating you up. It's boiling under the surface. Don't you think there's a reason you're having these nightmares?"

"Prob . . . probably so, but why all these nightmares in the past few months?" Clay responded.

"You're having nightmares about not being good enough and about Vic because the Spirit is bringing these things to the surface so you can deal with it. Do you think God wants you to feel hate for Vic or anyone? Did God create you to be not good enough?"

"You're telling me my nightmares are messages from the Holy Spirit? Can't he just send an email or suuumthing?" Clay said.

Sheryl grinned and sat down beside him again. "The Bible has many instances of God and angels speaking to people through their dreams. Joseph received a message that way easing his mind about Mary's pregnancy. Later, after Jesus was born, an angel came to him in a dream with a warning to flee to Egypt with Mary and baby Jesus."

"Seriously, are you telling me every dream is a message from God?"

"No, only those dreams with a message that is supported by Scripture. That's how you know it's a message from God and not Satan," Sheryl explained.

"How do you explain blood thirsty lawn mooowers, then? Where is that in the Bible?"

"Don't get so literal. The message in your dream wasn't about a lawnmower. It was about the deep wound that needs to heal. Look, before the nightmares and anxiety hallucinations that led you to Dr. Shildstein, you weren't even aware of the severity of that wound, were you? You weren't aware of how a belief that you weren't good enough for love and acceptance had been running your life."

"True," Clay said.

"It's safe to assume that without the dreams you wouldn't be aware of how much the wound was limiting your potential and joy."

"Also true, but what am I sup . . . sup . . . supposed to do about it? Wait until the dreams stop? I thought I was done with them until today's featured event. Geez, after today I'll think twice before climbing any ladder," Clay said.

"No, you aren't supposed to wait." She poured more wine into their glasses. "You're supposed to forgive."

"Forgive? Who, Vic?"

"Yes, forgive Vic. The hate and resentment you hold in your heart is preventing God's love from filling it completely. You accepted Christ today when you were submerged in that pool, but as long as you permit the darkness of hate and resentment to be present, God's light can't fill your heart and heal you."

Clay stared at Sheryl defiantly. He didn't want to forgive Vic. Not ever. Yet he couldn't argue with her reasoning either. He was stuck. He wanted to let go while at the same time he wanted to maintain his grip on the hate. "I can't forget what he did."

"Forgiveness is not about forgetting. Forgiveness is about releasing. Forgiveness is so important Jesus included it in his instructions to the disciples when they asked him how they should pray."

"How so?"

Sheryl reached for her smart phone and tapped the Bible app. "In the book of Mathew, Chapter 6, Jesus gives his disciples a pattern, or template, to follow when praying to God. We now call it 'The Lord's Prayer.' I'll read it to you beginning with verse nine:

"This, then, is how you should pray:

"'*Our Father in heaven,*
hallowed be your name,
your kingdom come,
your will be done,
on earth as it is in heaven.
Give us today our daily bread.
And forgive us our debts,
as we also have forgiven our debtors.
And lead us not into temptation,
but deliver us from the evil one.'

"Jesus instructed his followers when praying to always forgive someone for something they had done. This was so important that in verses 14 and 15 immediately following, Jesus explained:

'*For if you forgive other people when they sin against you, your heavenly Father will*
also forgive you. But if you do not forgive others their sins, your Father will not forgive
your sins.'

"When you forgive, you're opening your heart for God to fully bless you with his light, and fully forgive you for your sins."

Clay didn't speak. Sheryl was silent, letting the man she loved process what he had just heard from her.

"I've hated him so long, seems weird and hypo . . . hypocr . . . hypocritical to forgive him now," Clay said.

"God isn't going to think it's hypocritical if you forgive from your heart. Do this. Pretend Vic is seated over there in the chair. Forgive him for what he did."

Clay gazed at the chair. Seeing Vic there was the last thing he wanted to visualize, but he trusted Sheryl. Soon he envisioned Vic sitting in the chair smoking a pipe. Clay tried to speak and couldn't. What he really wanted to do was walk over to Vic and hit him in the face, not forgive him. But, at that very moment he saw the impact his hate was having on him. He wanted to strike out instead of forgiving. Clearly that wasn't healthy. After taking a long drink of wine he started talking in slow, measured sentences.

"Vic, I for . . . forgive you for being imp . . . impatient and angry with me. I for . . . forgive you for deeply wooounding me. I know you weren't trying to hurt me but were only trying to teach me as best you could. It's not your fa . . . fault you didn't know how to love and nurture a young boy. You probably were raised the same way and didn't know any different. I see that you just did what you knew how to do. I made your actions mean that I wasn't good enough for your love and acc . . . acc . . . acceptance, which I desssperately wanted. Vic, I forgive you."

Clay looked away from the chair and to Sheryl who sat next to him, tears streaming down her face. She hugged him tightly.

Maybe it was his imagination, but he did feel lighter, as if a weight had been lifted from his shoulders.

"You know what?" He asked Sheryl.

"What?"

"Forgiveness makes me hungry. Let's fix dinner," he said without a single slur or stammer.

Chapter 115

ix days later in the afternoon, the security app on Clay's phone alerted him that someone was at the front gate. It was probably Raymond here on Clay's invitation to tell him everything he knew about the Point Deception Lighthouse. He tapped the video camera icon. Sure enough, Clay's phone showed a video feed of the square-jawed head of Raymond Bailey leaning out of the driver's window and squinting into the security camera.

Clay spoke into the phone; the app carried his voice to the speaker next to the gate's keypad. "Good afternoon, Raymond. I'll open the gate for you." He tapped the Open button in the app. A minute later he heard the crunch of truck tires on the gravel driveway and stepped outside to meet the retired Coast Guard officer.

Looking around at the new structures, Raymond said, "Goodness, I hardly recognize the place. I heard Aaron was doing some work for you, but I had no idea the extent."

Chuckling, Clay replied, "Yeah, what started as a simple upgrade of the original cabin turned into a full-scale remodel. Come on in. I'll give you a tour."

After the walk-through of the residence the two men settled into chairs in the living room. Raymond started talking as soon as they were seated.

"Let me start with the history of the place, Clay. After that we should climb up to the lantern room so I can explain the workings of the light." He didn't wait for agreement from Clay. He proceeded to give a fascinating and concise briefing as if he was delivering a verbal report to his commanding officer.

"The original lighthouse was built in 1858. It was the last of ten or so lighthouses built along the Oregon and Washington coast between 1848 and 1858. You see, the U.S. had just taken over this territory from Britain in 1846 as part of The Oregon Treaty. Maritime trade was growing rapidly, and ships were being lost at a frightful rate. Congress passed a bill to fund the construction of the navigational lights. This was the last built, because Reef Bay was the smallest port and the lowest priority compared to other places."

"I had no idea this place was that old," Clay said.

"Indeed, it is. Well, at least some of it is that old. You see, the original lighthouse structure was built out of wood; just fifty feet high. It burned to the ground in 1872. It was rebuilt in 1874 using stone and brick. The height was extended to 117 feet, which is very unusual."

"Why? Aren't lighthouses supposed to be tall?"

"Not necessarily. It depends on how far out to sea the beacon needs to be seen by ships, and how high above the sea level the light needs to be in order for its

beacon to be seen at that distance, considering the curvature of the earth."
Raymond used his hands to illustrate the concept for Clay.

"Interesting. Reminds me of my high-school geometry class."

"Exactly. The Lighthouse Board had received complaints from mariners that
the light couldn't be seen more than fifteen miles off shore. The main shipping
lanes, at the time, were twice that distance. The engineers did the math and rebuilt the light to be visible 30 miles away. A record at the time. The lens, as I
recall, is nearly 300 feet above sea level because of the high bluff on which the 117-
foot tower was constructed."

He continued the history lesson for Clay. "In 1939 the Coast Guard was given
responsibility for all lighthouses in the country. Your light performed admirably
until 1946 when a strong earthquake centered less than fifty miles to the
northwest caused severe damage to the tower, although thankfully the tower
didn't collapse and destroy the lens. By 1947 engineers successfully had reinforced
the structure. It still stands today having withstood additional earthquakes and of
course the hellacious storms that slam the coast with regularity."

"How did my Uncle Charley get a hold of the place?"

"In 1998 we brought the Point Jeopardy light on line. That's the light you've
probably noticed on the other side of the bay's entrance. It's the newest and most
modern of all the lighthouses along the coast. Jeopardy was my last assignment
before retiring."

"Why build a new lighthouse rather than modernize this one?" Clay asked.

"Cost. Modernizing this place, considering the age of the tower and the
residence, was prohibitive. The other factor was the beacon didn't need to extend
thirty miles out to sea anymore—twenty miles was sufficient now that ships have
radar and other navigational aids available to them."

"What about my uncle?" Clay was eager to direct the conversation back to his
original question.

"The Coast Guard ceded the property to the town of Reef Bay in 2000. After
heated debate on the city council they decided to put the property up for sale
rather than pay to maintain the place. Our current Mayor Bildgewood was on the
Council at the time leading the argument to sell the property."

"I've met the Mayor. Wasn't impressed."

"Neither am I, but he has developed a power base of sorts in the community.
The thing is, he pushed the city to sell the property because secretly he and a few
others had plans to develop it. Build condos or something."

"Where does my uncle enter the picture?"

"I'm getting there. Bildgewood's plan was uncovered at the last minute
during a very contentious Council meeting. The city attorney said the bylaws
prevented any Council member from directly profiting from a vote or Council

decision. The vote passed, but Bildgewood was prohibited from bidding on the property. He was really steamed at the attorney and the other Council members." Raymond paused to clear his throat. "My throat's dry. Got anything to drink around here that's fit for an old man?"

"Oh, sorry, I'm forgetting my manners. What would you like? Beer? Wine? Something stronger?" Clay offered.

"Beer is perfect."

Clay fetched two bottles of beer from the kitchen. After taking a long drink Raymond continued the story of the Point Deception Lighthouse.

"After the vote the Council authorized the City Manager to advertise the lighthouse for sale. Maybe a month later your uncle drives into town and buys the place. Made a big splash in the newspaper. Hey, I bet you could go through the newspaper's archive and find all the articles written about the sale and the council debates."

"Good idea," Clay said.

"Yep, Charley settles in and starts maintaining the place. A lot of work for a guy his age, but he loved it. Took his time. Did a little work on the place every day."

"Were you two close?"

"We became good friends, yes. He mentioned you fondly many times, by the way."

A pang of guilt gripped Clay. "He was very dear to me. I really regret not keeping in touch with him. Gosh I didn't even know he was here, just a few hours drive from me in Seattle."

"He didn't want to bother you, Clay. Besides, your uncle was a very private man. He really liked living up here all alone. In fact, he was sort of a hermit the first six months or so—was seldom seen around town. Then one day he shows up at church, that's where I met him. After that he got very involved with the church. He even volunteered at the city library reading to the children once a week. He attended city council meetings, too. That's where the feud between he and Bildgewood started."

"Oh? What was the feud about?" Clay's memory flashed back to finding his uncle's ladder with a sawed rung. Maybe his theory about the mayor being involved in his uncle's death had merit.

"There were several public disagreements over the years, Clay. The two never saw eye-to-eye on anything. When Bildgewood ran for mayor the first time, your uncle actively worked on his opponent's campaign. Bildgewood was, and still is, a pro-growth guy. If he had it his way, Reef Bay would become a little Las Vegas or something. Your uncle was very much in favor of slow growth that maintained the character of the town. Heck, he was certainly doing his part by maintaining the lighthouse and not building a big condo or something next to the lighthouse."

"That's very interesting. Are you aware that the honorable mayor and some partners tried to buy this place from me?" Clay asked.

"No sir."

"They made several low-ball offers and I refused each one."

"Well, watch your back, Clay. Bildgewood holds grudges." Raymond drank the remainder of his beer. A stunned look crossed his face. "Wait a minute. This talk reminds me—there was a big news story in the paper a while back about a police investigation here. I can't believe I haven't asked you about it."

"Yep. I found evidence that suggests Uncle Charley's deadly fall wasn't an accident."

"What have the police told you?"

"Nothing so far. I've been too busy with the remodel, but I need to check on their progress. I have a bad feeling about it."

"Pray about it, Clay. Ask the Holy Spirit to help you find and see the truth," Raymond suggested.

"Good advice. I'm still learning about prayer. Sheryl's helping me with it."

"And you're wise to listen. I could tell the minute I met Sheryl last Sunday that the Spirt is strong in her. You two got plans for the future?"

"We've discussed getting married, yes. She just lost her job, so we're working out how that impacts things."

"Well, take some advice from this old man. God put that woman in your life for a reason. If your gut is telling you to marry her, that's the Spirit's voice urging you to do so. You've been baptized. The Sprit is in you. Listen for it always."

"Good advice, Raymond, I will. Say, what else can you tell me about this place?"

"You know the history already. First built in 1858. Rebuilt after a fire in 1874. Rebuilt again in 1947 following the earthquake of '46. Decommissioned in 1998 and sold to your uncle in 2000," said Raymond.

"She takes a lickin' and keeps on tickin'," Clay said repeating a famous old advertising theme for Timex watches.

"Yes, in a way I think God is very determined that this lighthouse remain standing. For what purpose I certainly don't know. But, each time it was damaged or destroyed it rose again. And lately, when it could have been sold to Bildgewood who would have demolished it to clear the ground for some ugly condos, your uncle shows up from nowhere to buy it. Now you have it and are lovingly looking after the place. Gives me goose bumps to think about it, but I think God wants this place to stand. We just don't know why yet."

"I can't wait to tell Sheryl about the history of the place. You know she used to have picnics up here as a kid."

"No kidding! I remember when the Coast Guard owned the place, we'd open the grounds to the public on weekends. On more than one occasion my crew and I would be here working during the weekend. We'd talk to the families. Sometimes they'd share their picnic lunches with us. We'd answer questions about the lighthouse."

"What years would that be, Raymond?"

"Gosh, let me think. I was assigned to Waterways Management in '83. I was stationed here in Reef Bay between 1993 and 1998."

Clay did a calculation in his head. "There's a strong possibility that Sheryl was in one of the families your crew spoke to. She would have been ten in 1993. Wow, I can't wait to tell her."

"God works in mysterious ways. I wouldn't be surprised if the fried chicken I ate back then was handed to me by little Sheryl standing right out there in that grassy field."

Both men looked out the living room windows lost in thought.

Clay broke the silence. "What about the light, Raymond? Does it still work?"

"Ah, the light. Let's you and I hike up to the top of the tower and I'll tell you all about it."

The two men made the trek up the narrow steel stairs. Clay was glad that the older Raymond paused on every other landing to rest so he too, could catch his breath. Huffing and puffing they made it to the lantern room.

"Darn. Getting old," Raymond said, gasping for air. "Used to climb these stairs carrying a twenty-pound tool box without breaking a sweat."

"When was last time you were up here?"

"In an official capacity it was February 18, 1998. That's when we decommissioned the light. Your uncle and I came up here once or twice after he bought the place, but the older we got, the tower seemed to grow higher and higher, so we stopped making the climb," Raymond chuckled.

Raymond put his hand on the lens, "Your lighthouse is equipped with a relatively modern, electric light. It generates 150,000 candlepower and can be seen twenty miles to sea. The lens is actually plastic, not glass. The different panels and angles you see in the lens are based on catadioptric technology developed by a Frenchman named Fresnel. Look closely and you can see a system of reflectors with the prism and lens. The purpose of the lens of course is to concentrate and magnify a small amount of light, making it an intense beam that projects for miles."

"Does it work?"

"No. See that switch there? Well, as part of the decommissioning process we destroyed the switch so the light couldn't be turned on. Also, I think in the months after decommissioning and before your uncle moved here, vandals got in and messed with the light. It doesn't rotate properly, and the wiring seems to be a mess."

"Can it be fixed?"

"Oh, sure. The only tricky part is the switch. The part isn't available anymore. I have to ask why you want to bother? Legally you can't ever turn it on. It could cause a disaster."

"I understand. Tell me, did my uncle want the light to be operational?"

"Yes he did, Clay. He didn't like the idea of owning a lighthouse that didn't work. It bothered him somehow. We talked about fixing it, but never got around to it."

Clay thought back to his visions of Jesus asking him to carry a light for him.

"I can't explain why, but something, maybe the Holy Spirit, is telling me to fix the light. Would you help me fix it?" Clay asked. "I don't know anything about electrical stuff, but I'd like to learn."

Raymond looked at the younger man. "I'm pleased you asked. I feel the same way as your uncle. Seems a shame to own a lighthouse and know that the light doesn't work. The light is there just waiting for us to step up and make the connection."

"And I want you to charge me for your time, Raymond."

"I wouldn't think of taking your money, but you can buy me dinner from time to time. After we fix it, however, you can never turn it on without Coast Guard approval. Promise me you won't get excited some night and flip the switch." Raymond said.

"I promise. Speaking of dinner, if you're free tonight have dinner with me here. Sheryl went back to Seattle this morning. I was going to grill some steaks."

"You drive a hard bargain. I accept."

Over the next several weeks of September Raymond and Clay got together on Wednesdays and Saturdays to work on the light for a few hours before relaxing over drinks and a meal. During their time together the two grew close. Clay appreciated how the elder man patiently taught him about the workings of the light. For Raymond, Clay was the son he once had but lost.

After four work sessions the light was fixed except for the switch. Raymond approached an electrician in town and commissioned him to build a switch. The electrician asked for two weeks' time and one hundred dollars. Raymond agreed.

With only the switch remaining to be done, Clay and Raymond were celebrating the completion of their light repair by sitting together on the cliff-side bench overlooking the setting sun, sipping 14-year-old single-malt scotch and smoking cigars.

"Can I ask a direct question?" Raymond said.

"Sure."

"When are you going to start being a man and ask Sheryl to marry you?"

Chapter 116

It's going to get nasty tonight," Billy McMaster, their usual waiter at the Surf View Bistro, said. Sheryl and Clay looked up from their menus.

"It is? I thought the storm wasn't due until tomorrow night," Clay said.

"Nope. Latest forecast has it arriving tonight. Barometer is falling fast."

"What's good tonight, Billy?" Sheryl asked, more interested in appeasing her appetite than just another storm front.

"I'm supposed to push the cod, but the scallops are particularly nice," Billy said.

"Then I'll have the scallops."

"Me, too," Clay said. "And a bottle of your Cloudy Bay Sauvignon Blanc."

"Yes, Mr. Austin. Right away." Billy hurried off to place their order and bring the wine.

"Any response to the resumes you sent out?" Clay asked. Sheryl had been out of work for less than a month and had only put resumes in the mail two weeks ago.

"None. I'm getting nervous."

"It's still early. I wouldn't worry. Don't you have several meetings coming up with the people George and I referred you to?"

"Yes, next week and the week after."

"Something will shake loose. Stay confident and pray of course."

"I am. It certainly helps to have your support, Clay. I'd go crazy if I didn't have you to talk to about this stuff."

"That's what I'm here for, to listen."

"It's more than that and you know it," Sheryl said.

Billy brought the wine and ice bucket. After Clay approved the label, Billy opened the New Zealand wine and poured a sample in Clay's glass. Clay swirled the wine, inhaled the vapors, took a sip, and smiled. "Ah, this is very nice, Billy."

Billy poured two glasses and left to fetch a basket of bread.

"I've been meaning to ask you something. You've been kinda nervous and on edge all day today. What's wrong?" Sheryl asked.

"Me? Nervous?"

"Well something is bothering you. Is it because I've been here longer? It has been a week. The longest we've been together under one roof."

"We spent years under the same roof at the agency," Clay said.

"That's different. It wasn't twenty-four hours a day. I can go home tomorrow if you want, or even tonight."

He held her hand on the table. She wasn't kidding around. He could tell she really thought he wanted her to leave. "To be honest, this week has been wonderful. I've loved having you in the house. It just felt natural. I wish we could be together longer. I hate it when you have to drive back to Seattle."

"Really? She asked, carefully dabbing a single tear with the corner of her napkin so as not to smear her makeup.

"Yes, really."

"Well, why have you been edgy then? Gosh, everything is going so well—the house, Mr. Bailey's help, your speech therapy."

Clay took a long drink of wine and looked out the window to the dark night. He could barely see the trees beginning to dance in the wind as the storm approached.

"I've been nervous because of what I'm going say next." He held her hand tightly. This was it. "Sheryl, I can't imagine living my life without you. Will . . . will you marry me?"

Every head in the crowded bistro turned suddenly as Sheryl's shriek of joy split the air. She threw her arms around him and kissed his mouth hard.

"Yes, I'll marry you Mr. Austin."

An embarrassed Billy was standing to the side holding their dinner plates. Clay noticed him.

"It's okay, Billy, you can serve us. It's a big night. Sheryl has agreed to marry me."

Over dinner the couple excitedly discussed the next steps. They agreed on a March wedding six months away. She'd sell her condo on Alki Beach. They'd keep the Lake Union house and split time between Seattle and Reef Bay. They figured the best course of action for Sheryl over the next six months would be to look for part-time work. After that, both of them would think of something they could do separately or together, such as consulting, that didn't require always being in Seattle.

Clay paid the bill and helped Sheryl with her coat. They raced through the driving rain to the car. They were both soaked, but happy about tonight's momentous occasion.

Sheryl's job worries had vanished for the time-being. Her mind was already planning the wedding.

A few minutes before ten, they drove down the final hundred yards of the driveway toward the house. The headlights of Clay's BMW shined across the house and lighthouse. The ladder he had been using earlier in the day was still resting against the lighthouse. He needed to put it away or set it on the ground so the strong wind wouldn't knock it over, or worse yet, send it hurtling through the air like a wooden missile.

On their way from the carport to the front door Clay said, "I forgot to put the ladder away. I better go get it."

"Okay." Sheryl unlocked the front door and went inside.

Clay walked as fast as he could down the dark gravel path. He should have asked Sheryl to turn on the flood lights. It was pitch black except for the light coming from the house windows. The gusts made walking difficult. It was as if a giant hand was pushing him back. The rain was being driven horizontally into his body and stung his face. He was going to be completely soaked by the time he got inside the house.

He reached the ladder and tried to take it down so he could carry it around to the protected side of the lighthouse. The wind caught the ladder and almost ripped it from his hands. He managed with difficulty to hold it low and horizontal to the ground. He walked to the edge of the lighthouse. Some twenty feet separated the wall of the lighthouse and the cliff. It was terrifying to be out there in the dark. He could sense the closeness of the lighthouse wall just two feet to his left. But on right was nothing but dark, the shrieking wind and sheets of lashing rain. He kept walking, eager to get to the other side and out of the wind. A gust hit the long ladder and it slammed hard against the lighthouse wall. Another ten feet and he'd be out of the wind. Clay squinted ahead into the darkness.

Something wasn't right. He was looking south. He should be seeing the flashes from the Point Jeopardy light. But, there was nothing but darkness. Clay finally got to the protected side of the tower. He placed the ladder on the ground and looked again to the south. Still no blinking lights. He thought maybe a tree was blocking his view, so he walked back toward the cliff into the wind and rain. He counted his steps away from the wall. Even though a sturdy fence guarded the cliff he didn't want to get too close when he could hardly see his hand in front of his face. Ten, eleven, twelve, thirteen, fourteen, fifteen. He stopped. He was small paces from the wall. The fence must be close. He wasn't going to venture any further.

There was no light to the south. The Point Jeopardy lighthouse was dark. He decided to race back into the house and call the Coast Guard in case their monitoring systems hadn't told them the light was out.

He turned to make his way back to the safety of the tower wall but stopped. Had he seen something below outside the bay's entrance? He turned back around and shielded his eyes from the driving rain. He had seen something all right. In the distance he saw the red and green bow light of a boat. There was also a white light, possibly a mast light. In the darkness that was all he could see. What on earth was a boat doing out at night in this storm? What if they didn't have radar? How could they navigate the narrow entrance to the bay safely without Point Jeopardy for reference?

He raced back toward the tower, tripping and falling twice in the darkness before reaching the wall. He stayed on the south side of the buildings this time out of the wind. Soon the glow from the house windows was giving him just enough light to see. He raced around to the front door and rushed inside dripping wet. Sheryl walked in from the kitchen holding a glass of wine.

Soaking wet he raced past her through the kitchen and just before he disappeared again out the back door he yelled, "Call the Coast Guard and tell them the Point Jeopardy light is not working." Before she could say a word he was gone out the door. He flipped on the corridor light, grabbed the canvas tool bag and a flashlight, swung open the heavy door to the lighthouse and stepped inside the tower.

This was lunacy, but it was the only thing he could think of to do. If the boat wasn't approaching the bay entrance correctly it would crash on the reef. Survival for those aboard in the storm conditions was doubtful. His plan was simple but filled with risk. If he got to the top of the tower and saw that the boat was approaching the entrance wrong Clay was going to turn on his light. He and Bailey had fixed the circuit problems. Everything had tested out, but they hadn't turned on the light. It was illegal to do so without a special permit. But, that's exactly what he was prepared to do. If he got to the top in time, and if he remembered Bailey's instructions, he was going to let the light of Point Deception shine just long enough to help the boat.

But there was huge risk for the boat, too. If the captain saw the light and thought it was Point Jeopardy he'd steer much to the north and end of crashing in the rocks on north side of the entrance. Clay was betting that the captain had read his chart and knew the difference between the signals of Point Deception and Point Jeopardy.

By morning Clay was either going to be a hero or a murderer.

He raced up the steel stairs. He wanted to run, but knew he had a long way to go and must reserve his strength. Up and up he climbed while the sound of the wind outside the walls intensified and howled. He could hear the sheets of rain lash the tower like a firehose.

He reached the fifth landing breathing hard. He wanted to rest just a minute to catch his breath, but something kept pushing him on.

By the ninth landing, approximately 100 feet above ground, Clay thought he was going to pass out. His lungs struggled to suck in enough air, his heart pounded inside his chest. He pushed on.

He was close to the top. His legs wobbled, threatening to buckle underneath him. He was dizzy too. Then a wave of nausea overtook him. He vomited his dinner over the staircase rail and down into the darkness. With the bitter taste of bile still in his throat he climbed the final stairs until at last he was standing in the lantern room.

Breathing hard, his legs shaking, Clay looked through the thick glass windows toward the sea. Even in the darkness Clay could tell the little boat was not where it should be. It was coming in too far to the south. That told Clay the little boat was having difficulty navigating.

He dragged the canvas tool bag next to the large lens housing. The beam of his flashlight found the plate that covered the hard-wired circuits. To get the light to work, he had to basically hot wire it, as if hot wiring a car to steal. Bailey had shown him the corroded switch that made the hot wiring necessary. The switch was irreplaceable, but Bailey knew an electrician who could build one for them. That hadn't happened yet.

Clay fell to his knees and frantically tried to unscrew the plate that would reveal a confusing mess of wires and circuits, two of which he needed to bridge with a piece of wire to make the light turn on and the reflector rotate.

He removed the plate and placed it with the screws in the tool bag. He shined his flashlight beam into the light housing. How could such a simple light have so many wires?

He studied the circuits. He saw the wires that led to the back of the switch. They hung loose and away from the switch where Bailey had left them. Next, with of a piece of spare wire from his tool bag he bridged the two wires and twisted the ends. One last thing to do. He crawled to the wall and with great difficulty managed to stand up. With his legs trembling uncontrollably, Clay reached for the lever on the master switch mounted to the wall. He flipped it to on. There was a whirring sound as the light began to warm and brighten. He had done it!

Now, would the captain be smart enough to follow this beacon properly? With light reflecting off the glass window Clay couldn't see a thing, so he carefully walked down the stairs to the 9th landing where he could look out the little window to the southwest.

He was seeing the bow lights of the little boat differently now. Both the red and green lights were equally visible, meaning the bow was pointing to the north in Clay's direction. The boat must have changed course suddenly away from the southern reef. But it wasn't until Clay saw the red bow light slowly disappear that he knew the captain had changed course again and was heading eastward following the deep channel into the protection of Reef Bay.

The little boat was going to be all right. Clay climbed unsteadily up the last few stairs to the lantern room. He flipped off the master switch. The Deception Point light went dark. He couldn't risk that his light would be mistaken for Point Jeopardy. He prayed that other boats weren't out there in the night trying to find their way to safety in Reef Bay.

Legs weakening, he leaned against the wall and slowly slid down until he was seated on the cold steel floor of the lantern room. His mind kept comparing the reality of tonight with the lighthouse nightmares that used to haunt him. In the nightmares he couldn't figure out how to fix the light in time to save the boat. But tonight, he made the connection that turned on the light in time. What was the difference? Raymond Bailey was the difference. Without Raymond's knowledge, there was no way Clay could have known the hot-wiring technique required to make the light work tonight. Clay reflected on the day in church when Raymond introduced himself to Clay, who was still dripping wet from his Baptism. The one man who knew the most about the Point Deception lighthouse attended the same church as Clay and Sheryl. It was a "God thing" as Sheryl fondly called this type of incident in life.

It was a "God thing." How else could he explain the choreographed events: Clay inheriting the lighthouse and moving here; going to the same church as Raymond, a lighthouse expert; after dinner tonight seeing the ladder that needed storing away from the gale; noticing the boat approaching the harbor entrance without benefit of the Point Jeopardy light; Clay being able to turn on the light just in time; and—perhaps the most "God thing" about the night—the boat's captain deciding at the last minute to follow the light that literally saved his life.

No, tonight's fortunate turn of events wasn't just because of Raymond. What about Clay's role? He had seen the potential disaster unfolding. He had acted and climbed all the way up here. He had hotwired the switch to turn on the light. He had saved the boat. Tonight, when it counted in real life, not in some nightmare, he had been *good enough*.

His nightmares always ended with Clay sitting on the floor crying, utterly defeated, filled with shame and guilt. Tonight, though shaking with exhaustion, he felt completely different.

He was elated, relieved, as if a heavy weight had been removed from his shoulders.

You finally did it, Clay, you were good enough tonight.

But, why tonight? Why on earth did it take the challenge of a near-disaster for Clay to feel good enough about himself?

Of all things to remember at this moment while sitting on the cold floor of a small dark room 117 feet above ground, Clay recalled his Film as Literature class in college. In the course he was introduced to the Auteur Theory in which the director is seen as the driving creative force for a movie, not the writer of the screenplay, nor the actors.

And there was the answer. God was directing this play. God was directing Clay and Raymond and the captain of the boat. God put them together on this wind-swept stage. For what purpose, Clay wasn't sure. Was it just to save the people on the boat? Or, was each of the actors in this play to have an epiphany that would change their lives?

Clay wondered again why tonight, so eerily like his nightmares, had ended in elation rather than despair. What was different? He felt the lighthouse tremble in the wind. It was standing strong against the gale, as it had ever since it was first built. Through the shadows of the dark lantern room Clay saw the truth.

He had let God into his heart. That was the difference. Since his baptism his life had begun to shift. He had been talking to God more, trusting that God would guide him, listening for the Spirit's loving direction.

With God who strengthens me I can do anything. Clay couldn't remember the Bible verse exactly, but he remembered the point. And with that point he had his epiphany.

The cacophony of noise from the wind and rain was deafening and downright frightening. The storm intensified outside as if to protest Clay's revelation. Over the noise he thought he heard a shout echo from below. It must be Sheryl. She had to be worried about him. He gathered all his strength, picked up the tool bag and slowly walked down the stairs to his fiancée waiting anxiously 117 feet below.

Unnoticed by Clay in his descent down the dark staircase, the Point Jeopardy light on the other side of the bay's entrance flickered and came back to life, once again beaming its powerful beacon out to sea.

Charles Besondy

PART FOUR,
THE SPIRIT.

Chapter 117

This was tense sailing. *Justified* was moving fast in the dark toward the narrow entrance to an unfamiliar harbor now only five miles ahead. Thomas repeatedly checked his course. The compass and plotter told him he was right where he was supposed to be, but why wasn't he seeing the light from the lighthouse? He checked the paper chart and plotter again. Both indicated a Point Jeopardy lighthouse on the southern bluff above the harbor entrance. It had a white light that flashed two short and one long. Where was it? Certainly, he was close enough by now to see its beacon.

At ten o'clock, he decided the safe thing to do was power the rest of the way. He started the engine. He thought he heard a "pop" sound from inside the cabin, but over the noise of the diesel and wind he couldn't be sure. With the diesel engine running, he furled the jib completely, then disengaged the self-steering.

He stood behind the wheel and peered hard ahead into the darkness. Still no light blinked from the bluff. The waves were getting rougher and the wind was picking up the closer he got to shore. Occasionally he throttled back and listened carefully for the sound of surf, but he couldn't hear anything but wind. The orange glow of his compass told him he was still pointed in the right direction but had no way of knowing if the current was carrying him one way or the other. He tapped the plotter screen to wake it up. Nothing happened. He tapped harder. Just a dark screen. He jumped into the cabin and flipped the on-off switch. Nothing. In fact, all of the lights of his new instruments were dark.

He was two miles away from the unlit entrance to Reef Bay. None of the $5,000 of electronics were working. He remembered the "pop" sound. A fuse probably blew, but he didn't have time to find a new fuse and replace it. Did he even have spare fuses for the new equipment?

Thomas rushed back up to the cockpit. His old depth sounder, compass and paper chart were all he had for navigation. He really needed that lighthouse beacon *now*. If the wind and current slowly pushed *Justified* toward the southern side of the bay's entrance, there was supposed to be a rocky reef submerged just three feet below the surface of the waves.

Even though he was frightened and exhausted, Thomas experienced a moment of extreme clarity in the pitch dark. The reason he was in this situation was his silly ego—trying to be like Otto. The reason he was risking his life in icy waters was an attempt to prove himself good enough to be a man. And to think he used as an excuse for this adventure that God wanted him to bring the Word to boaters around the world. This wasn't the Holy Spirit's doing. It was Satan's lies.

He recited a passage from the book of James that he had used many times in his sermons over the years, "Humble yourselves before the Lord, and he will lift you up."

"Lord, please forgive me for my foolishness. Please forgive me for my weakness. All I really want to do is serve you. I know that with you I am strong enough to lead a church. If it is your will that I survive this situation I will forget this offshore nonsense and find a church to shepherd. But, if it is your Will that I perish tonight. So be it. Bring me home. Amen."

After clearing tears from his eyes, Thomas checked his course and depth sounder. Not good. He only had twenty feet of water beneath him. According to the chart, if he was on course he should have sixty feet of water under the keel. He throttled back, not sure whether to turn left or right. The wind and waves kept pushing him forward and to the right. He frantically studied the chart. Based on the depth and wind he figured he was probably off course to the right, which meant he was heading toward the reef. But he wasn't totally certain. In his confused state the boat might even be on the north side of the harbor entrance, which was equally shallow.

Just then a flash from above caught his attention. It came from the north. At first he thought it was lightning, but the initial flash was immediately followed by another, then two shorter flashes. The flash repeated two longs, two shorts; there was a pause then two longs and two shorts again. That was a light from a lighthouse all right, but it was the wrong darn light. Where was he? Could it be that he was approaching the wrong bay?

He looked again at the chart. Sure enough, the chart showed a lighthouse on the northern bluff above the harbor entrance with the words "Decommissioned" written next to it.

"It may be decommissioned, but I'm sure as Jesus going to follow it!" Thomas spun the wheel hard to the left and watched with relief as the depth sounder readings began to increase: 22, 25, 30, 32, 45, 60. Within minutes he was back in the main channel, glancing at the chart, he estimated what his compass heading needed to be to travel between the entrance buoys. He spun the wheel hard to the right, settled on a compass bearing and straitened the wheel. In this narrow entrance, *Justified* was being tossed around in confused seas like a cork.

Within a few minutes he heard the buoy bells as they rocked in the waves. It was sweet music to his ears. Moments later *Justified* slipped past a green buoy with the white number "7" on it bouncing up and down in the waves only ten yards away to port.

Twenty minutes later at 11 o'clock, Thomas reduced the throttle as the hull of Justified sliced through the smooth, protected waters of the bay. The warm lights of the marina made long welcoming reflections towards him in the still water, as if pointing a path for Thomas to steer. He had made it to safety.

Thomas said out loud, "They say 'any port in a storm,' well Reef Bay you're the *only* port in my storm. Praise God."

Chapter 118

The sound of boat engines woke Thomas at 6:30 Sunday morning. He had fallen asleep still wearing his foul-weather gear. He felt damp, chilled and utterly exhausted from the previous day's experience.

He wandered up the dock as daylight tried to cut through the thick clouds that raced across the sky overhead. It was peaceful here, but Thomas guessed the storm was still raging outside the protective bluffs. He found what he was looking for, a pay shower. After using up three dollars of quarters he felt warm and clean. There was a café overlooking the marina and Thomas ambled toward it.

Thinking he might get served faster, he sat at the counter. He was weak from hunger and wasn't in the mood to wait. He had just finished his first cup of coffee when his order was placed in front of him by an elderly waitress that looked like she had worked as a waitress her entire life.

He bowed his head and prayed before eating. He had much to be grateful for, and much to pray about. He opened his eyes and attacked his eggs, sausage, hash browns and stack of pancakes on the side.

"Are you always that hungry after prayer?" Asked a square-jawed man in his late sixties sitting next to him.

"No, I'm particularly hungry this morning. Had a very long day yesterday. Name is Thomas Benton. I sailed in last night from Friday Harbor."

"Thomas, I'm Raymond Bailey, nice to meet you. Did you say you sailed in last night? You were out in this storm?"

"Uh-huh," Thomas mumbled with his mouth full.

"Goodness, you're lucky to be alive. What size boat?"

"Islander 36, a sloop," Thomas said.

Bailey's eyes grew wide with disbelief. "Forgive my questions, Thomas. You see, I was supposed to go fishing today, but none of the charter boys will go out in these conditions. If the pros won't go out in this stuff I gotta wonder what you were doing out there."

"I was on my way to San Francisco when the storm arrived early and caught me. There's another storm off Northern California so I was screwed. I made a run for the nearest port. Here I am."

"Where's your crew?"

"You're looking at them."

"You got here in a bad storm single handed. I salute your sailing skills. I'm retired Coast Guard and spent many years saving the asses of boaters less fortunate than you," Bailey said.

"My pilot was watching out for me last night." Thomas raised his eyes. "Praise the Lord."

"Say, after the experience you've had I bet you'd welcome the chance to worship in church today."

"I would indeed. Is there one within walking distance?"

"No, but I'm headed to the Reef Bay Bible Church for the 9:30 service. I'll drive you there and bring you back here after."

"That's very brotherly of you. When do we need to leave?"

"I had planned to leave about ten after nine. Meet me in the restaurant parking lot."

"Sounds wonderful. Thank you."

Thomas finished his breakfast and stopped by the marina office on the way back to *Justified*. He paid for two days moorage and inquired about longer term availability and rates. Back at the boat he thought he'd better let Otto know that he wouldn't be coming to San Francisco anytime soon, at least not by boat. Plus, Otto would probably be very worried about him once he learned the weather forecast.

He sent a text, "Won't make it to SFC. Caught in storm. Holed up in Reef Bay, WA. God saved me last night."

The restaurant parking lot was cut into a steep slope above the marina restaurant. He could feel a strong breeze now that he was a few hundred feet above the harbor's edge. From the vantage point of the parking lot Thomas could see the calm bay and rows of docks below were mostly surrounded by land that climbed steeply from the water's edge to 1,000 feet or more. Looking further up the slope, the trees on the ridge, long ago bent over from decades of winter gales, were swaying wildly. The storm was still raging outside the protective barrier of land. Thomas silently thanked God again that he wasn't out on the open ocean battling the wind and waves.

Raymond, standing by his truck, waved to Thomas as he walked into the restaurant parking lot at 9:10.

"Right on time. Ready to go?" Raymond asked.

"I certainly am. Thank you again for the offer," Thomas said, climbing into the immaculate Chevy pickup. The only odor inside the ten-year old vehicle was Raymond's aftershave.

"Don't mention it." Raymond drove out of the parking lot and followed the narrow two-lane road as it wound up the hillside to the highway.

"Have you lived in Reef Bay long, Raymond?" Thomas asked.

"Just since I retired. I was actually stationed here for a while."

"You said Coast Guard, right?"

"Yep. Served my country by helping to keep the Washington coast safe." Raymond glanced at Thomas and winked. "I did an outstanding job, too. Do you realize that while I was in the Coast Guard not a single enemy dared attack the Washington coast?" He chuckled.

Thomas laughed with him. "I appreciate your service, Raymond, whatever you did."

"Thanks, but I was honored to serve. Learned a lot about life and leadership in those years. I spent the first five years at different stations as part of lifeboat crews. Then they promoted me to Petty Officer on a cutter. After a year of that the Coast Guard in its wisdom, assigned me to Waterways Management."

"What's Waterways Management?"

"It's the arm of the Coast Guard responsible for maintaining the navigational aids on waterways. You know, ATON, LORAN, buoys, lighthouses, markers. I bet you didn't know that there are 38 lighthouses in Oregon and Washington. My crew was responsible for 21 lighthouses in Washington."

At the word "lighthouse," Thomas' head snapped to the left to look at Raymond. "Lighthouses? You maintained lighthouses?"

"We certainly did. Maintenance and conversion. What we liked most was converting old lighthouses to automated systems."

"Well, one of your lighthouses nearly killed me last night, Raymond. The Point Jeopardy was out," Thomas said.

Raymond looked hard at Thomas for a second before returning his eyes to the road. "That doesn't surprise me. That lighthouse has been a nuisance ever since it was built. Command wanted us to use a different system. We pushed back because we thought there'd be incompatibilities between it and our master control system. They insisted. I'm glad your radar and plotter brought you in safely."

"That's just it, Raymond. All my electronics went out when I was about two miles away. Blew a fuse I think. I thought I was screwed, especially when the depth sounder read only twenty feet under the keel when I was expecting sixty feet," Thomas explained.

"How on earth did you navigate in without a beacon or instruments?"

"Oh, there was a beacon all right, but not the Point Jeopardy light. The light I saw came from the north side of the bay's entrance," Thomas said.

"The North side? Are you sure? There's no light to the north. At least . . . not an operational one."

"All I know is the chart said the Point Deception lighthouse was decommissioned, or something, but Raymond, I swear that light came on when I was heading toward the reef. If it wasn't for that light appearing at that exact moment—not before, not later—you would have read about me in the morning paper today, instead of taking me to church."

"I'll mark it down as a miracle, I guess, except . . ." Raymond let the sentence trail off.

"I'm certainly considering it a miracle of grace. I've been a little rough on God lately. He just smiled anyway, wrapped His loving arms around me, and led me safely out of the storm," said Thomas.

"Amen to that. And here we are." Raymond pulled into the church's lot and parked.

Before Thomas could open the truck door, Raymond placed a firm hand on his left shoulder.

"Something tells me your day of miracles isn't over. Who knows what words God will have for you inside those doors," Raymond said.

Thomas looked at Raymond. "After the past twelve hours, Raymond, nothing God does will surprise me."

Worship had started by the time the two men entered the sanctuary. They found seats in the back of the church and began to sing along with the congregation.

Thomas sang loud and strong, his arms open and eyes looking up.

For the third and last song, a young man entered the small stage carrying a banjo. He stepped to the microphone, adjusted it, and closed his eyes for two seconds in calming prayer. Then his hands began to strum the instrument.

Thomas wasn't prepared for the soulful melody that flowed unexpectedly from that banjo. An instrument usually associated with knee slapping folk tunes was now delivering a rendition of *Amazing Grace* as moving as any guitar, piano, or Scottish bag pipes.

His voice melded with the banjo's tone,

Amazing grace! how sweet the sound,
  That saved a wretch; like me!
I once was lost, but now am found,
  Was blind, but now I see.

When the young man finished the worship song, the misty-eyed congregation applauded enthusiastically. Thomas bowed his head, closed his eyes, and began praying fervently.

Pastor Oberlin stepped to the front and began his message. His voice sounded strong, as if standing in front of his flock somehow gave him strength.

Thomas didn't hear any of the words to the sermon. While the sounds in the room were muffled to his ears and the sights were blurred to his eyes, the connection he felt to God was crystal clear at this moment. This sensation was in stark contrast to the past few months when he had felt so disconnected and distant from his Lord and Savior.

"Thomas, are you okay?" Raymond gently nudged Thomas in the arm. People were leaving the sanctuary. The service was over.

The room came back into focus for Thomas. "Uh, oh, I'm okay, Raymond. Actually, I'm more than okay. I'm great."

"Well then, if you're feeling up to it there's someone here you absolutely must meet."

"I'd love to."

The two men walked into the social room where at least a third of those who had been present at the service today remained to linger in conversation while enjoying refreshments.

As they waited in the refreshment line, Thomas felt a tug on his jacket. He looked down and into the eyes of a little girl.

"Hi, mister. Be sure to take a brownie. My mommy and I made them," the girl said in a proud voice.

"Trisha, don't bother the nice man," her mother said, standing next to her. She looked at Thomas. "Sorry about that. I don't know what got into her."

"Not a problem at all," he said to the mother. Then, looking down to Trisha, he said, "And it just so happens that brownies are my absolute most favorite cookie in the entire world." He bent down to be a little closer to Trisha and lowered his voice, "I'm going to take two brownies, but don't tell." Trisha grinned from ear to ear.

Straightening up again, Thomas smiled and introduced himself. "I'm Thomas Benton, a guest of Raymond Bailey."

"I'm Molly Clements and this is Trisha." She extended her hand and Thomas shook it.

To Thomas her hand felt soft and warm, but strong. It reminded him of his wife's hand.

"Are you a friend of Raymond?" Molly asked.

"I'd like to be. You see, we just met at breakfast today at the marina restaurant. He was nice enough to invite me to church."

"What brings you to Reef Bay, Thomas?"

Thomas noticed that while Molly talked to him her eyes never left his. Ordinarily that kind of focus from a stranger would make him uncomfortable, but not from her. "That's a very long story. I came here last night on my boat to escape the storm. So, I'm holed up here for a while I guess."

Thomas noticed a change in Molly's eyes like a painful memory had been released.

"I'm certainly glad you are safe and sound with us, Thomas. The entrance to our little bay can be very treacherous."

"Yes, indeed it can. God was watching over me last night. Praise the Lord," Thomas said.

"Praise the Lord. There's probably a reason the Lord wants you here," Molly said warmly.

"The thought has occurred to me more than once since last night, Molly. I've been praying that the Spirit will guide me."

"I will pray for you, too," Molly said.

"I appreciate that. Very kind of you."

While talking they had slowly moved through the line to the refreshment table. Thomas placed two brownies on a paper plate and showed the plate to Trisha who grinned and giggled gleefully. He poured a cup of coffee and stepped out of the line. Turning back to Molly he said, "Very nice to meet you Molly and Trisha. Perhaps we'll meet again."

"I'd like that," Molly said with a nervous smile.

Raymond stepped over to Thomas' side as they walked to the center of the room.

"I see you had a nice conversation with Molly."

"Yes, she was very nice, and her daughter is adorable," said Thomas. "Where's her husband?"

"She's a widow. Thomas, by any chance when you were fighting the storm last night did you see the hulk of a fishing boat on the rocks at the northern entrance to the harbor?"

"I did."

"Well, that boat belonged to her husband, Jake. He and three other crew members perished on it about five years ago when little Trisha was only three."

"That's terrible."

"It was tragic. According to the reports the vessel lost steering as it was returning to port in a storm very much like the one you experienced. She's doing a fine job of raising that child by herself, but everyone is praying she'll find a good man to be a loving husband and father." Raymond took a sip of coffee and scanned the room with his eyes. "But, my friend, there is someone here you must meet before he leaves."

"Sure. Lead on."

Raymond led them over to where a man and a woman were standing in conversation with Pastor Oberlin.

"Good morning, Clay, Sheryl. Powerful sermon as usual, Jon. I want to introduce you to a new friend of mine and a special guest." He gestured to Thomas with a large smile. "This is Thomas Benton, who arrived last night and has something in common with Clay," Raymond said with a twinkle in his eye.

Thomas firmly shook hands with Jon and Clay. When he reached for Sheryl's hand their eyes locked. For an instant he saw reflected in her face the same inquisitive look he knew was on his. "My goodness, but you look familiar, Sheryl. Do I know you?"

"I was about to say the same thing," Sheryl said. "Where are you from, Thomas?"

"Well, most recently Friday Harbor on San Juan Island. Before that I lived in Seattle."

Sheryl studied him. "Seattle. I'm from Seattle, too. Do you go to Pathway Church?"

"No, Sheryl. In Seattle I went to Beacon Bible Church. Actually, I was the head pastor there until May," Thomas said.

"I've seen you before somewhere. I think I've even talked to you before. Your voice and face are so familiar," Sheryl said. "Thomas, didn't you and I meet at the cafeteria of the University Hospital in late April?"

"That's it! We surely did. I was there for my wife and you were there visiting a friend, I believe."

"Yes, and this is the friend, Clay. He's a bit more than a friend now." She elbowed Clay playfully.

"I remember we prayed together in that empty cafeteria. Your last words to me were, 'Perhaps we'll see each other again,'" Thomas said.

"Then you replied, 'God willing, we shall'. Well, here we are. This is so amazing. What brings you to Reef Bay?"

"A storm actually. I was sailing to San Francisco when the storm caught me. Reef Bay was the nearest port," Thomas said.

"Now this is where you come in, Clay," interjected Raymond. "Oh, Pastor, you'll want to hear this, too. You see, my friend Thomas here had a very unusual and very blessed encounter with a certain lighthouse beacon last night."

Thomas summarized for the four people standing with him the series of events involving his approach to the harbor entrance. As Thomas spoke, Raymond, like a detective looking for facial reactions during an interrogation, watched Clay closely.

"I don't how it happened, but the lighthouse on the northern bluff above the harbor entrance started shining at the perfect time. I would have crashed on the reef. I wouldn't be here with you fine folks this morning if it wasn't for that light coming on when it did. Praise the Lord."

Clay and Sheryl glanced at each other and then stared at Thomas with mouths open. The color drained from both of their faces.

Raymond spoke, "Clay, have you been playing with your lighthouse again?"

"That was you in the little boat last night?" Clay asked, voice quivering.

"Yep. Don't tell me you were in the lighthouse."

"I was. We had just come back from dinner and I noticed that Point Jeopardy wasn't working. Then I saw your lights and noticed you were on a bad course," Clay said.

"Clay, how on earth did you turn on the light? There wasn't a switch," Raymond asked.

"I don't know. I just figured if the switch wasn't working I could hot-wire it. Never hot-wired anything in my life, but I had to try something. I figured it was the boat's only chance," Clay said.

"God bless you, Clay." Thomas stepped forward and embraced Clay tightly. "You saved my life."

"Truly, friends," Pastor Oberlin said, who had been spellbound by the conversation. "Both of these brothers in Christ heard the Holy Spirit last night. They not only heard; they followed, and a life was saved. What a joyous occasion this is."

"Thomas, did I hear you correctly a few minutes ago? Didn't you say that you had been the head Pastor at Beacon Bible Church in Seattle?" Sheryl asked.

"That's correct. My wife and I founded the church, but after she died in April I felt like I couldn't carry on there without her. So, I resigned," Thomas said.

Sheryl, Clay, Jon and Raymond exchanged glances. Jon said, "Have you found a new church to lead?"

"No, Jon. Not yet. Though just a few weeks ago, I sent out two hundred resumes," Thomas said.

Jon draped his slender arm over Thomas' shoulder. "Let's walk across the room so I can introduce you to some of our Elders. It just so happens they are searching for someone to replace me when I retire in a few weeks."

Chapter 119

The townspeople of Reef Bay in later years would look back on the months of October and November of that year as the time when God smiled on the town and swept evil from their midst.

On the third Sunday in October, in a moving ceremony, Jon Oberlin gave his last sermon as senior pastor of Reef Bay Bible Church. The sanctuary was packed with church members eager to hear their beloved pastor deliver his final sermon and make the announcement of who the Elders had selected to be the new senior pastor.

The sermon's title had been promoted in the church newsletter and across a large banner hanging from the eaves of the church, "Be the Light".

A frail Jon Oberlin walked to the podium as the band finished its third song of worship.

"Good morning, it is nice to see so many of you here today. Based on the size of the audience perhaps I should have delivered my final sermon more frequently if that's what it takes to bring more of you to the Word of God," he said with a warm smile, eyes scanning the standing-room only crowd.

Low laughter rippled through the audience.

"I must confess something to you. Until Wednesday I had no idea what I was going to say to you this morning. For the first time in my life, I was at a loss for words." He paused to let the gentle laughter from the audience die down before continuing.

"I mean, what could I say to you fine people that I haven't already said? What scripture could I quote? I started writing at least a dozen different sermons only to discard each and every one.

"Then, Wednesday night I was having dinner with Clay Austin and his fiancée, Sheryl Landing, at his beautiful home at the Point Deception lighthouse. Clay shared with me how in a vision Jesus came to him at that lighthouse. Jesus handed Clay a lit candle and said, 'Carry this light for me.'"

Clay had given permission to mention his vision. Regardless, he felt very uneasy as hundreds of eyes looked his way. Sheryl squeezed his hand to steady him.

The pastor walked to a table holding a single lit candle in a vase. He picked it up and held the vase out at arm's length toward the audience. "'Carry this light for me,' Jesus told him. 'Carry this light for me.'"

"When Clay recalled his vision and the miraculous event that was to follow, a passage from Matthew chapter five came to me. At that point I knew what this sermon, my last sermon, had to be." He returned the candle to the table.

On the video screen behind the pastor, scripture was displayed next to the photo of a burning candle:

"You are the light of the world. A town built on a hill cannot be hidden. Neither do people light a lamp and put it under a bowl. Instead they put it on its stand, and it gives light to everyone in the house." Matthew 5:14-15

"My friends," the Pastor continued, "These words appear in what we call The Sermon on the Mount. Jesus gave his followers—and us—direction for how to live in a way that pleases God. The Sermon on the Mount literally consists of words we can and should live by. Jesus is using the metaphor of a light on a stand to represent the glow of the Spirit that is in each of us who believe.

"Here's another way to put it: You're on earth to be light, bringing out the God-colors in the world. God is not a secret to be kept. If He made us light-bearers, do you think he wants us to hide under a blanket? On the contrary, God is putting each and every one of his children on a hilltop to shine and be seen.

"Why does Jesus want us to be seen? Hear me carefully. Jesus isn't telling us to preen and parade around like peacocks attracting attention." The audience laughed as Pastor Oberlin strutted around the stage imitating a proud peacock.

"Not at all. Let's look at verse sixteen." A new verse appeared on the screen. *"In the same way, let your light shine before others, that they may see your good deeds and glorify your Father in heaven." Matthew 5:16.*

"He's telling us to keep an open house, be generous with our lives. By opening up to others, you'll prompt people to open up with God, this generous Father in heaven."

For the remainder of the sermon Pastor Oberlin gave six examples of how members of the church have "shined" and made a lasting impact on others.

"In order to shine with the Spirit's light we must first invite the Spirit inside us and humble ourselves in obedience to it. This brings me to the seventh and final example." A breathtaking photo of the Point Deception lighthouse appeared on the screen. Taken at dusk, the photographer had captured the instant when the powerful lamp beamed its light out to sea.

"Just three weeks ago on September 27 Clay and Sheryl were returning home from a very special dinner at which Clay had proposed to Sheryl, and she had accepted. Upon arriving home, Clay went outside to stow away some equipment, so it wouldn't blow away in the wind. If you recall that night, the first bad storm of the season arrived. While he was outside in the gale he noticed that there wasn't a light coming from the Point Jeopardy lighthouse. And, at the same time, he saw the bow lights of a small boat attempting to navigate the entrance to our harbor.

He recognized the boat's course was too far south on its approach. It was heading toward the reef and to certain disaster." He paused for dramatic effect before continuing.

"What could Clay do? Watch the disaster unfold? Call the Coast Guard? Well, what he did was nothing short of a miracle. He raced to the top of his lighthouse, all 117 feet of it. The switch was missing so he had to hotwire the light in order to turn on a light that had been dark for twenty years.

"Many of you in this room own boats and recognize the risk Clay was taking. If his beacon was mistaken for Point Jeopardy it would completely confuse the boat's captain and lead him to doom."

"But God was with Clay and the boat's captain that night. Clay trusted the Lord to guide him. He literally turned on his light. And, at the same time the captain of the small boat decided to trust the light he saw, a light coming inexplicably from a decommissioned lighthouse on the north side of the harbor's entrance."

"The little boat made it safely into the harbor that night. A precious life was saved. But there's much more to the miracle, my friends." The Pastor walked slowly to the other side of the low stage while never losing eye contact with his flock. This was his final sermon, and he was delivering it with every ounce of energy and faith his weakened body could muster.

"Why was the little boat out in that storm at night? The boat had been on a voyage from San Juan Island to San Francisco when the storm overtook it. The captain changed course and headed to the safety of Reef Bay. All was well until his navigational instruments failed him. No instruments. No Point Jeopardy beacon. Terrifying winds and waves threatened to overcome him and his vessel. He was lost. He could hear surf crashing ahead of him in the darkness. It appeared to the captain that God had abandoned him at his greatest time of need.

"But the man at the wheel of that sloop fell to his knees and prayed to God to forgive him for his sins. He surrendered himself to God's Will.

"And that's when he saw the light, the light of Point Deception that Clay had so bravely turned on. He trusted the light was Point Deception even though his chart said the light was decommissioned. In that moment he leaned into his faith and was saved. Praise the Lord." Thomas Oberlin stood, looking skyward, arms outstretched. Several people in the spell-bound audience applauded and said "Amen."

"But, the miracle of our Savior wasn't over." Pastor Oberlin paused again. His eyes scanned the room. He was clearly enjoying the suspense and drama being created in the room by his delivery.

"You see, I haven't told you the full story of the captain and his sloop. Four months before he miraculously found safety in our protected harbor, he had lost his wife to cancer. In his grief he left a prominent job in Seattle and sold everything he owned except the sailboat. He was momentarily adrift in life.

"But, if we are faithful, God will put us back on the right path, won't He? God had a plan for the captain—a plan that included our community, our church.

"Did I mention that the boat's captain had quit his job? Yes, he had resigned as the head pastor of Beacon Bible Church in Seattle. A church he and his beloved wife had founded and grew to over 2,500 members. He was a pastor in search of a flock. We were a flock in search of a senior pastor.

"My friends I will now end my final sermon as your head pastor by introducing you to your new Head Pastor, and one very blessed boat captain, Thomas Benton."

Chapter 120

I n the social following the Sunday service, Chief Smith walked over to Clay and whispered into his ear, "I have some news to share with you. Let's step outside."

The two men ventured outside where they could talk privately.

"We've made an arrest in connection with the investigation of your uncle's accident," Chief Smith said.

"Really? Who?"

"A drifter named Enrique Rodriguez. We have evidence that proves he tampered with the ladder to weaken it."

"But why? Did he know my uncle?"

"No, he did not. Late last night he confessed that he was paid $500 to saw the ladder's rung. He claims he was told by the person who hired him that it was a just a prank."

"Do you know who hired him?" Clay was watching the Chief of Police closely.

"We have a pretty good idea. Rodriguez was very cooperative as part of his plea deal. I fully expect we'll be making an arrest very soon. Keep all of this to yourself, of course. I shouldn't be telling you, but Charley was your uncle, and I appreciate the support you've given my campaign for mayor," Chief Smith said.

Clay shook hands with the Chief. "Thank you for the information, Chief. Sounds like I don't have long to wait for all this to play out."

The Chief winked at Clay, turned, and headed to his cruiser in the parking lot.

Two days later Clay was in the kitchen making drinks for their happy hour when his phone buzzed.

It was his Reef Bay attorney, Glenn Bartlett. "Clay, sorry to bother you but I have news you want to know."

"Hi, Glenn. No problem. What's up?"

"As you asked, I've been in touch with my sources at the courthouse and in the police department. Another arrest has been made in connection with your uncle's murder. Are you sitting down?"

"No, I'm standing with a hand-crafted margarita in my hand. Wait, let me put my phone on speaker so Sheryl can hear this, too. Okay, tell me what's going on."

"The not-so-honorable Mayor Bildgewood was arrested a few hours ago and charged with first degree murder of Charley Gragg. It'll be all over the front page of the morning paper. You'll probably get a call from a reporter at any minute asking to make a comment or statement. My advice is to not say anything."

"Thank you, Glenn. Good work. I'm not surprised by this, are you?"

"I don't know what to think. Bildgewood is a greedy, vengeful man, but I never expected him to have someone killed."

Sheryl spoke up, "He wanted this property so desperately he was willing to kill for it. That's really sad. And sick."

"You're right, Sheryl," Bartlett said. "I've seen the plans he had for the property. He was going to tear everything down, including the lighthouse, and build luxury condo units."

"He wanted to destroy the lighthouse, too?" Clay asked.

"Correct. Just think, if he had bought the place instead of your uncle, you wouldn't be in Reef Bay today," Bartlett said.

"Or if you had sold it to him after you inherited the property, you and the light wouldn't have saved Pastor Benton that night in the storm," Sheryl added.

"Listen, I'll let you two get back to your margaritas. Congratulations again on your engagement, by the way. When's the big day?"

"Some time in March. We haven't picked a day yet," Sheryl said. "You'll receive an invitation of course."

"Wouldn't miss it for the world. Clay, I'll keep you updated on what I hear from inside."

"Sounds good. Bye, Glenn." Clay ended the call.

"Bildgewood wanted the lighthouse destroyed. God wanted it to stand. God won." Clay summarized before sitting down at the table with Sheryl.

The arrest of Mayor Bildgewood overnight became the biggest scandal to ever hit the coastal town of Reef Bay. Released on bail, the Mayor quickly called a press conference and denied all the charges, claiming it was a desperate political act by Chief Smith to compromise the Mayor in the final weeks before the November election. The Mayor also announced that he was instructing the City Council to vote on firing the Chief of Police for misconduct.

The Chief of Police held his own press conference together with the prosecuting attorney. They revealed the charges and the events leading up to the Mayor's arrest. Twelve hours before the mayor was arrested at his home, the police had arrested Gary Grogan, his assistant. Grogan was the man Enrique Rodriguez described as the person who had hired him for "the prank." It didn't take long under interrogation for Grogan to reveal who had instructed him to "get rid of that old man Gragg."

The story dominated the front page of the local newspaper in the weeks leading up to the election. It didn't surprise anyone that Chief Smith won the November election in a landslide.

Bildgewood's trial was slated for January 12. The two-week trial concluded with a conviction on charges of first-degree murder. Clay and Sheryl were in the courtroom when the jury's verdict was read and the former Mayor was led away in shackles to spend the rest of his life behind bars.

One early evening in February Clay was opening a bottle of wine for their happy hour and dinner when his phone buzzed. Caller ID told Clay that Glenn Bartlett was calling him.

"Good evening, Glenn. What's up?"

"Excuse the hour, I hope I'm not disturbing your dinner," Bartlett said.

"No, we're just starting happy hour."

Bartlett laughed, "It seems every time I call you two are drinking."

"Well, every time you call it's happy hour. Try calling at different times of the day and see what happens. What's up this time?"

"Good news. The state legislature has declined to bring the Friends of the Lighthouse bill to the floor for a vote. The newly elected Speaker of the House said in a letter that the bill was unnecessary and redundant."

"So, no threat of new legislation that would impact us?"

"No guarantee they won't try again, but for now your options are wide open. I expect this ruling will increase the value of the property significantly should you ever decide to sell."

"No plans for selling the place. But, tell me this, Glenn. Why was the Bildgewood behind the Friends of the Lighthouse movement if it would actually restrict what he could do with property if he ever got his hands on it?"

"I think it was all a charade. He knew the bill would never pass, but it made him look good in the eyes of the public. I also think he was betting that the threat of a restrictive bill would spook you into selling," Bartlett said.

"Well, all I can say is Reef Bay is a better place now that he is behind bars."

"And the Deception Lighthouse still stands tall," Bartlett said.

"It certainly does. Which reminds, me. Did you know that the Council approved a new logo for the city? It features the lighthouse with a beam of light. Pretty cool."

"That's pretty cool, all right."

Chapter 121

ooking out the living room window at the March sky above the large tent being assembled on the grass, Sheryl frowned. "You promised me it wouldn't rain today. Those clouds don't look good."

Clay smiled and held his fiancée close to his side. "The forecast is for rain to start tonight. Just clouds during the day with a few sun breaks."

"You'd better be right, mister."

Two cars moved slowly down the gravel road toward the house.

"Mom is here. Looks like Karen's car behind her. They're right on time. You know what that means."

"Yep, I'm leaving. I'll check on the caterers before I go to Raymond's house," Clay said with a smile.

Clay greeted Florence, his future mother in law, with a hug and said hi to Karen and Michelle, two of Sheryl's best friends. He placed a small suitcase and garment bag into the BMW and then walked over to where the caterers were preparing for the event.

"Going to finish on time, Lucy?" Clay asked the catering supervisor.

"Right on schedule, Mr. Austin. Things fall into place quickly once the tent goes up. We'll be ready when the first guests arrive at eleven o'clock."

"Good, and you received my special instructions for the sound system, right? We have a very special musician coming to play for everyone today," Clay said.

"Yes, everything is in order."

"Good to hear. I have to leave now. I won't return until eleven. If you need anything just ring the doorbell. Sheryl is inside."

"Yes, sir. Don't worry. Everything will be perfect."

"Thank you." Clay walked away from the caterer but before he reached his car he turned around to inspect the site. A white tent large enough to hold fifty people now stood on the manicured lawn about fifty feet from the house and lighthouse. The tent was positioned on the lawn so its one opening faced the lighthouse. Inside the tent, tables were being placed by the catering staff. A red carpet led from the house to the tent's door.

With more than a few butterflies in his stomach he drove away to Raymond's house.

Raymond greeted him at the door with a firm shake and a hug. "Ready for the big day?"

"I think so, Raymond. Looks like it's really going to happen."

"Well, you can put your things in the guest room and change when you're ready. Can I get you anything?" Raymond asked.

"I could use a cold beer, actually."

"I know what you mean. I think I drank at least three before my wedding," Raymond grinned and went to the kitchen. He returned with two bottles of beer. "I might as well join you." They clicked the bottles together and drank. "Everything in order?"

"Yes. The caterer is on schedule. I received a text from Pastor Benton. He said that Otto, Jerry and Matt are in town. He's ready, too. Sheryl's mom and her bridesmaids arrived at the house just before I left."

"We need to be back there at eleven, correct?"

"Yes. Ceremony is at 11:30. Reception at noon. Oh, before I forget, let me give you the ring. And, thanks again for being my best man."

"It's an honor, Clay. You and Sheryl are dear friends and, well, so is the Point Deception lighthouse." He clicked his bottle again against Clay's.

An hour later Clay stood in Raymond's living room. He had shaved and changed into a brand new suit that he and Sheryl had selected during a trip to Seattle to close on the sale of her condo.

Raymond entered the living room wearing his Service Dress Uniform for the Coast Guard.

"Look at you. And it still fits after all these years," Clay said.

"To be honest I had a tailor loosen it up a bit," Raymond said with a grin.

"Well, you cut a handsome figure in that uniform, Raymond. I'm so happy you agreed to wear it on my wedding day."

"Under the circumstances, I think the uniform is what I should be wearing. It gives me goose bumps to think that I used to work on the silly light and had no idea that years later I'd be the best man at a wedding there."

Clay looked at his watch. "Time to go. Guess we're taking two cars. I'll see you there. Got the ring?"

Raymond patted his coat pocket. "Right here."

"See you in a few minutes, my friend."

Clay drove back to 3100 Point Deception Drive and parked. Guests were already arriving and being led to a parking area at the upper end of the property. He knew he wasn't allowed into the house where Sheryl and her wedding entourage were huddled, so he walked to the tent to mingle.

Two men were enjoying a drink at the bar with Thomas as he sipped on a club soda.

"Good morning, Thomas. Good day for a wedding isn't it?" Clay said cheerfully.

"It is. It is. Hey, here are two of the three guys I told you about. "Clay, meet Otto and Matt," Thomas said.

"What a pleasure to meet you guys," Clay said, shaking their hands. "I've heard so much about you from Thomas you seem like family. We're so pleased you accepted the invitation to come all the way from San Francisco."

Matt spoke, "We wouldn't miss it for the world. We wanted to meet the guy who saved Thomas' life. And see the light, too."

Otto chimed in, "God's fingerprints are all over this place and each of us. How can we not be here considering all that has occurred? We encouraged Thomas to sail offshore, which he does. A storm brings him here. You save him with your light. He finds out about the opening at the Reef Bay church and gets the job. Now he's marrying off the guy that saved him, in the lighthouse no less. It's a beautiful and blessed story."

Thomas added, "Oh, it gets even better. Sheryl and I met back in April at the hospital when Rhonda was dying. Clay had had a boating accident and was in the room next to hers. Sheryl and I met in the hospital cafeteria and prayed together. Now, nearly a year later, here I am marrying her to the guy who saved my life. I mean, if God isn't behind all of this, who is?"

"Amen," Clay said. "But, where's the famous Jerry Levine?"

"He's in the tent setting up," Otto said. "Believe me it's a good thing you didn't announce that he'd be playing here today. You'd have a real crowd control problem on your hands. He has to be really careful. His popularity can really get in the way sometimes. That's one of the reasons he likes sailing with us. It's hard for crowds to find him in the middle of the ocean."

"I am very honored that he agreed to perform. It's funny, but I started listening to DelivrUs just in the past few months. The band at church played one of their tunes, then I heard another on the radio. I like the music a lot and bought a few of their albums. I was floored when Thomas told me he knew Jerry and that he had inquired if he could play at my wedding.

"It was a tough decision. It came down to deciding between a local DJ and a world-famous recording artist." Clay winked. "Sheryl convinced me to go with Jerry."

"How are we doing on time, Clay?" Thomas asked. "You don't want to keep Sheryl waiting."

Looking at his watch, Clay said. "Uh-oh, gotta go! Come on Thomas, hope you're wearing comfortable shoes."

Clay and Thomas caught up with Raymond, who was standing tall by the front door to the house. In his uniform it looked like he was standing guard.

"Is it safe to enter?" Clay asked.

"Yes, we are permitted to pass directly through the house to the lighthouse," Raymond responded.

The three men walked through the house and out the back door into the corridor building that was now brightly lit.

"Well, men, this is where we find out who's in better shape," Clay said. He turned and started up the winding staircase.

After a few pauses on landings to catch their breath the three men reached the lantern room that had been decorated with flowers and rose petals on the floor. Below, they could hear female voices as Sheryl and her two bridesmaids began their trek up the stairs.

The day was mostly cloudy but beams of sun broke through in places. Clay looked down to the scene below—the tent, people milling around, the vast sea. It was quite a spectacle.

There was movement from the corner of his eye. Then he heard it. A hum, like the sound of a thousand angry bees. His heart jumped. *Oh, God no. Not today. Not another hallucination!*

Outside the thick windows a drone buzzed around the lighthouse and hovered in place. The wedding photographer was using a drone to capture photos and video. No killer bees. Clay felt his heartbeat slow.

He heard Sheryl's voice and he turned from the window. The most beautiful woman he had ever seen was standing in the lantern room looking at him. His heart leapt again, but this time out of love, not fear.

She and her two bridesmaids didn't want to arrive at the top huffing and puffing so they had paused on the previous landing for several minutes to catch their breath. The three stood there looking like they had taken an elevator up 117 feet, rather than climb the stairs.

The couple took their place in the small room facing out to sea. Raymond was next to Clay. Karen and Michelle stood next to Sheryl. Thomas stood with his back to the sea, facing the couple.

The ceremony and vows were over in ten minutes. Thomas declared them "man and wife" and they kissed while the drone buzzed noisily outside the windows, capturing the moment on video.

It was done. Congratulations and hugs were exchanged.

"Before we go, there's one more thing you need to do, Clay," Raymond said.

"What's that?"

Raymond retrieved a letter from his pocket. "This letter from Coast Guard command in Seattle officially gives the Point Deception Lighthouse permission to turn on its light for no more than five minutes not before 11:30 and not after twelve hundred hours on March 21, 2018." Raymond smiled and replaced the letter in his pocket. "I still know a few people," he said. "So, Clay, when you're ready, flip the switch. I've already turned on the master."

"Come on Sheryl, we're doing this together." She placed his hand on his. He reached to the new hand-made switch and flipped the lever. There was a whirring sound and then the light began to flash. The wedding party stood behind the light and watched the reflection in the windows.

"Oh, Lord, we light this beacon to honor you and this marriage, which you made possible. And though its beam will last but five minutes, your light will show through Clay and Sheryl for as long as they shall live. Amen."

After five minutes the switch was turned to the off position, the drone flew away, and the wedding party made its way down the stairs to the guests waiting below.

They emerged from the house and walked across the red carpet while the guests applauded. Everyone made their way into the tent where lunch was being served.

Otto, Jerry and Matt sat with Thomas at his table and were introduced to Thomas' guests, Molly and Trish, both of whom could not believe they were sitting at the same table as Jerry Levine.

Many people from Reef Bay Church were there, as were twenty or so people from Seattle, including Clay's former partner, George Davis, who was also celebrating his retirement from Pitt-Needham this month.

After the usual speeches and toasts, Raymond announced that music and dancing was next. "Please welcome a special guest, and friend of Pastor Benton, Mr. Jerry Levine."

A loud applause greeted Jerry as we stepped onto the riser, slipped the guitar strap over his head and adjusted the microphone's height.

"Hello Reef Bay. Thank you for inviting me."

He played and sang. People danced and those that knew the songs, sang along.

Before his fifth song, Jerry announced, "I want to bring a special guest on stage to play this next song with me. I believe most of you know Bobby McMaster."

Those in the audience from Reef Bay Church cheered enthusiastically as Bobby stepped shyly to the stage carrying his banjo.

Jerry continued, "This next song is on our second album. I wrote it one night when I was on the Greek Island of Rhodes taking a few days off from our European tour. After touring many ancient ruins during the day, I relaxed on the veranda overlooking a bay. I felt an urge to read my Bible. Randomly I opened it to a page. It was the Song of Solomon in Psalms. I was so moved and inspired by the passages that I stayed up all night writing this song. It's a waltz, so I invite the bride and groom to have their dance. It's called *Pure Love*."

Half the audience cheered wildly when they heard the name of the tune, easily one of the band's most beloved songs.

Sheryl and Clay left their table and walked hand in hand to the small dance floor. They stood in the middle of the floor looking lovingly at each other as they waited for the music to start.

Jerry said, "Mr. and Mrs. Austin, this song is for you."

For the next four minutes the familiar chords and lyrics of *Pure Love* played as Clay and Sheryl swirled around and around the small dance floor. A few couples joined them after Clay urged others to dance, too.

Jerry's lyrics re-told the Biblical story of two impassioned lovers who remained pure until their wedding day. The heat of their intense passion was second to their desire to honor each other by remaining celibate until after the wedding.

The song's intensity grew toward a crescendo. The interplay between guitar and banjo was masterfully performed. Through the first two-thirds of the song the two instruments exchanged brief solos, as if speaking to each other. In the final third, both instruments harmonized together, at time playing the same notes at the same time, to emphasize the beauty of the marital union.

When the song ended, Jerry and Bobby received a long, standing ovation. Jerry smiled graciously. Bobby blushed. Clay and Sheryl, with misty eyes, walked up to the riser to shake hands with the two musicians.

The guests began to leave an hour later, and by three o'clock all the cars were gone except for the catering truck. The crew was hurriedly taking down the tent and packing their truck so as to be done and gone before dark.

The newlyweds relaxed inside their house. Clay selected a 2012 Oregon Pinot Noir from the humidity- and temperature-controlled wine closet that Aaron had installed for them off the dining room. "I've been saving this for a special occasion. Of course, when I bought it six years ago I had no idea that I'd be opening it on my wedding day. That's another cool thing about cellaring wine for special occasions, I never know in advance what the special occasion is going to be. But, I buy the wine with full expectation that there *will* be special occasions in my future worthy of an expensive bottle of wine."

"I've never thought about it that way, but you're right. Does that make you an optimist?" Sheryl wondered.

Sitting on the couch close to her he replied, "I guess so, but more than an optimist it makes me a Christian. I trust that God during my life will bless me with many special occasions and special people worth celebrating," Clay said.

"Oh, I like that point of view." Sheryl kissed him.

Clay held up his glass of wine and clinked it gently against Sheryl's. "We drink this wine in praise of Jesus, our Savior, for making this marriage possible."

"Amen," Sheryl said. She sipped the wine. "Yum. Good choice, mister. I better be careful, or I might drink too much and let you take advantage of me," she said with a twinkle in her eyes.

"We wouldn't want that to happen, now would we?" Clay leaned over and kissed her tenderly up and down her neck.

"Mr. Austin, are you trying to seduce me?" Her eyes were closed in pleasure.

Still kissing her neck and ears he whispered, "Indeed, Mrs. Austin, I am seducing you." He stopped caressing her neck and looked at her seriously. "You know it occurs to me that we have no idea if we can sleep together or not. We might not be compatible. I mean, you might like lots of covers and I don't. Or you might like a soft mattress and I prefer a firm one."

Sheryl teased Clay's ears with her tongue.

"Or, or, you might . . . snore . . . and I don't. Or . . . you like to . . . watch . . . TV in bed." Sheryl's tongue and lips were hungrily exploring his neck.

Groaning, he was unable to concentrate. "And what if . . ."

Sheryl placed her fingers on his lips. "Shh. You talk too much. Take me to our wedding bed, mister. And don't forget the wine."

Chapter 122

Nine years later.

Sheryl had just finished placing the breakfast dishes into the dishwasher when she heard the sound of a lawnmower. The sound surprised her. It was different. Rough and loud, the sound had a mean tone to it.

As she closed the door to the dishwasher her first thought about the sound was of the evil, terrifying lawnmowers of Clay's nightmares—those angry mechanical monsters that shook Clay to his core.

But, she wasn't dreaming, and the sound was real. She knew the green riding mower that Clay used to cut the grass field had a refined, well-muffled exhaust tone. That isn't what she was hearing now.

As she walked to the kitchen window her mind tried to decide if she should be simply curious, or frightened. When she reached the window would she see a perfectly normal explanation for the strange sound, or something macabre?

She hesitated before slowly pushing the curtains aside to give herself a better view.

△ △ △

Thirty minutes earlier, Clay and little Charley, their eight-year-old, had cleared the breakfast table and stood side by side in the spacious kitchen.

"We men have important work to do outside, sweetheart," Clay declared.

"Okay, I'll finish in here. Remember, the Bentons are coming over for dinner tonight. I'll need help later," Sheryl said.

Clay and Charley left the kitchen and made their way together to the toolshed.

Charley didn't know it yet, but today was the day he would learn how to mow a lawn.

Clay unlocked the toolshed door, but before opening said, "You know what? Before we go inside, walk with me to the front side of the house."

The two walked around the house and Clay led them into the grass field. He knelt on one knee. Charley mimicked his father and did the same thing.

Clay ran his hand through the green grass that stood over six inches high. "Feel the grass like I am."

Charley moved his hand back and forth through the grass.

"Do you feel any water on the grass?" Clay asked.

"A little," Charley said.

"Right. It's a little damp, but not as much as if it had rained, right?"

Charley thought a minute and inspected his hand. "Right."

"The grass is dry enough to mow. It should be cut today because it's supposed to rain tomorrow, and we're having company tonight. We want the yard to look nice for Pastor Benton and his family, don't we?"

Charley nodded in agreement.

"Well, son, I could really use your help. How would you like to help me mow the lawn today?"

"Really? Can I drive the mower?" Charley said excitedly.

"Not today. I want you to learn to use a different mower first. You see, anyone can ride a mower, but it takes skill to operate a regular power mower. I think you're big enough now to handle a mower. What do you say?"

"Sure." Charley replied with pride that his father thought him big enough for the job.

"Okay, I'll race you to the shed." And Clay took off running with Charley right behind him.

Clay muscled one of the old reel lawn mowers out of the shed. He had planned this day for several weeks and had secretly worked on the mower, so it was operational.

Charley was eager to get started. "How do I start it, daddy?"

"I'm glad you're eager, but I want you to understand the machine before you start to use it. You see, any time you work with a machine it's important to understand how it works so you can operate it without hurting yourself. Machines can be very dangerous, especially lawnmowers." He pointed at the rows of blades on the reel-type mower. "These blades can cut off a hand or a foot in a second. Understand?"

Charley nodded.

Clay proceeded to explain the operation of the mower—the throttle, the clutch, the pull cord, and the carburetor choke.

"All right, let's start the mower and move it over to the grass. Remember, what I told you. When it starts it is very loud. Don't be surprised."

Together they moved the mower at slow speed around the house to the edge of the grass field. When they arrived, Clay reached down to the engine and turned it off.

"Ok, I'm going to show you how to mow the lawn—you walk next to me and watch. Then we'll operate the mower together. Finally, after you've got the hang of it, you can do it alone."

"Okay." Charley was fidgeting with excitement.

Clay fired up the engine, pointed it to the far side of the field and engaged the blades, the mower jumped forward, spitting grass cuttings behind it. At the end of the row clay disengaged the blades, spun the mower around in the opposite direction and stopped. Above the roar of the engine he yelled, "See where the wheel is. I'm overlapping a little with the row I just cut."

Charley nodded.

"All right, your turn. I'll keep one hand on it, too."

Little Charley reached up to grasp the handles and engaged the clutch. The mower shot forward and twisted back and forth as Charley tried to control it. With his one Clay kept the mower from going totally out of control, but let Charley wrestle with it all the way back to the starting point near the house.

"Get ready to turn it, son."

Charley didn't turn fast enough or sharp enough. The machine started to go in the wrong direction and he panicked. The little boy didn't know what to do. The mower was heading diagonally across the field with Charley and Clay hanging onto it.

Before the mower went ten feet further. Clay reached over to disengage the drive clutch to stop the forward motion. He decreased the throttle all the way to idle.

Charley looked up at Clay with trepidation, knowing that he had done wrong. For an instant Clay didn't know where he was, or who he was. Who was this little boy in a red t-shirt and jeans looking up at him? Images of Vic screaming at him sped through his mind. He had the sensation of shrinking, shrinking down into the earth. Out of the shrinking sensation anger began to swell inside his gut. The anger was coming fast.

And then the anger vanished, just like that. He shook his head to clear it. Little Charley was still looking up at him apprehensively.

"Ok, son, what did you just learn?"

"I don't know. I couldn't turn in time."

"That's right. Changing direction is the most difficult part. It takes practice. You'll get the hang of it before we're done today. What else did you learn?"

Charley shrugged.

"What did I do when the mower got out of control?"

"Oh, you reduced the throttle and stopped the wheels from turning," Charley said.

"That's right. Just stop. The mower is very powerful, but you have the controls."

Clay put his hand on Charley's shoulder. "Let's look at the row you mowed."

They walked the length of the row. Clay's first row was straight. The wheel marks from Charley's row were irregular. In many places tall grass stood where he had veered too far from the other row. At the end of the row Clay said, "Look all along the wheel mark here. Is it straight?"

"No"

"No it isn't straight at all, but for a first time it's very good. Better than I did at your age."

"Really?"

"Oh, my first rows were terrible. But I learned how to correct the mistake. Want to know?"

"Yeah."

Clay showed him how to line up the mower with a larger overlap to the previous row. Together they directed the mower up the row.

Back and forth father and son directed the lawnmower. Sometimes they'd have to recut the row, other times it was nearly perfect. After seven rows, Clay removed his hand and let Charley take total control. Three rows later, Clay stepped up to the mower and turned it off.

"How do you think you're doing?" Clay asked his son.

"Okay, I guess."

"Let's take a look." They stood inspecting Charley's latest rows. "Did you have the hiccups?"

"No."

"Are you sure? Looks like you had hiccups while steering the mower," Clay said with a playful grin. The two looked down at the irregular wheel track in the grass.

"See, right here," Clay pointed to the ground. "Hiccup." He pretended to have the hiccups while steering a lawnmower. "Hiccup."

Charley giggled at the site of Clay walking down the row, steering an imaginary lawnmower and jerking it every time he said, "Hiccup."

"Doggone it, you did a really good job except for the hiccups." He ruffled his son's blond hair with his hand. "I better cure you of the hiccups so you can mow straight today."

"How?"

"Clay reached down with both hands and started tickling Charley under the arms. The boy squirmed, giggled and tried to escape by falling to the ground. It didn't work. His father went down to the ground with him and soon the two were laughing and wrestling around together on the grass.

From her kitchen window Sheryl had watched the scene with her husband and son unfold on the grassy field. He hadn't told her that this was going to be the day—the day of the lawn mowing lesson. A big test; not for little Charley, but for Clay.

So, she prayed while watching the two try to tame the wild lawnmower. "Father, may the light of your love fill Clay at this moment. Give him patience, kindness and love. Don't let his past live in the now. Keep the enemy away. Let Clay be the loving father that Vic didn't know how to be. Let the chain be broken. Amen."

Sheryl sobbed with total joy as she witnessed Clay and Charley laugh and frolic in the green grass beneath the lighthouse. She was happier than she had ever been. This special moment made her reflect on her troubled past and what might have been different if her parents had loved her the way Clay was loving Charley right now.

ABOUT THE AUTHOR

For information about Charles Besondy and his upcoming works, please visit CharlesBesondy.com.

Charles Besondy

Made in the USA
San Bernardino, CA
22 January 2019